SILVER MAGE

C M Debell

The Long Dream Book One

For Laurie, who loves dragons.

CONTENTS

PROLOGUE

AT THE END of the world, an old man stood alone. The night was silent around him, shrouding him in its heavy darkness. The black peaks that had once been the perches of dragons stood empty and mournful, and the welcome he had once felt in this place was gone. The birthplace of life on Andeira now stood as a herald of her end. The sadness of it brought tears stinging to his eyes, but he brushed them away. There was no place now for that grief. Too many others were crowding in on him—for a friend lost, for the war that was coming, for everything he loved that was slipping away.

For the fault that was his, for the pride that had led him to keep it to himself.

And yet I hoard my secrets still, even now when the world is collapsing around me.

His hands clenched tight in the folds of his white robes, the robes of his rank: the eldest, the speaker of a generation. *I keep them because it is my duty,* he told himself fiercely, but the reassurance was empty, worthless, for the secret he kept had brought them to this.

'Duty?' murmured a deep voice from the darkness. 'What a burden that must be, Lorrimer.'

Cold fear slivered down his spine as he turned. 'I was not sure you would come.'

A wry smile tugged at his enemy's mouth. 'Then why are you here?'

Lorrimer held the man's gaze, straining to see past the shutters that kept out the world. There was nothing to be read there, not anymore. He shrugged. 'Hope, perhaps. Fear, mostly.'

'Fear?' Aarkan quirked an eyebrow. 'You fear me?'

Lorrimer shook his head. 'What you are becoming, not what you are.'

A soft laugh answered him as Aarkan moved closer. Lorrimer looked at the man who had brought his people to this edge of ruin and felt a shaft of bitter grief for everything he had been. Tall and dark, black hair brushing his

1

shoulders, Aarkan returned his gaze. His skin was coloured a deep tan by the sun, his hard, handsome features sculpted from granite. Features so achingly familiar yet changed beyond all recognition.

A smile twitched that face to wry amusement as Aarkan permitted his silent scrutiny. Arms crossed over his chest, back resting lightly against the rock of the ledge, he was utterly composed.

Why should he not be? Lorrimer thought bitterly. *He has within him now more power than any mortal creature.*

'What am I becoming, Old One?' Aarkan asked then, gently mocking.

Lorrimer closed his eyes. He wondered where Srenegar was and knew the great dragon would be near. These two could no longer hold themselves apart for long. They had looked into the heart of creation, just as he once had. They had seen the power it held, and they had opened the way to the river of bright power that would carry them on its soaring, glorious tide to the centre of all things. He forced himself to confront it, opening his eyes to find Aarkan's dark gaze on his. 'Something other than you were born to be.'

'Something greater.'

'No.'

The denial was instinctive. It was utterly wrong, this thing they had done. Men were the children of Tesserion, of the maker of life, charged to stand guard over her creation, not to remake it. To preserve the world as she had made it.

Long ago, when Andeira was young, Tesserion had given her first gift to the new world she had made. She gave the dragons, riders of the winds, children of flame. Wild and free, they had roamed the empty world, wielding the elemental magic that was their birth-gift, but the world was still unfinished, and their magic incomplete. Tesserion had another gift to give, another race to birth. Humanity followed after and brought about the dawning of the Second Age. To men, Tesserion entrusted the other half of the magic that was Andeira, the elemental power that brought forth life, sustained it, and carried it home in death.

The magic that divided the races brought them together and bound them tight. The union of their elemental powers of Earth, Air, Water and Fire, brought forth the final element—the Spirit of Tesserion breathing life into a half-made world.

That union, the Joining, defined existence. It paired humans and dragons together, enriching their shared lives, melding their magics and meshing their thoughts. It was a partnership that served the needs of both races, that tempered their vulnerabilities and their strengths, and it had made the world whole at last.

But for Aarkan and Srenegar, having looked into that darkly beautiful place at the heart of creation, it could no longer be enough.

Lorrimer drew in a breath, steadying himself. 'Give up this folly,' he pleaded. 'Do not challenge the council. Return –'

'To what I was? Is that why you came? Did they send you to reason with me, to beg?' Aarkan shook his head, his smile almost kind. 'You cannot stop me, Lorrimer. Nor should you try, for this is my right. And I do it not for me, but for us all.'

'Your right? None of us has that right, Aarkan. You trespass where you do not belong, and if you choose not to see that others cannot be so blind. This union you seek is wrong, worse than wrong. To join one soul with another is to take creation into your own hands, and that was never the province of any save the Maker herself. Such a thing as you will become was never meant to walk Andeira's fair lands. It takes neither courage nor strength to resist you. If we want to live, we have no choice.'

He saw anger then, for the first time, a wildness seeping into his enemy's eyes. Aarkan took two fierce steps towards him before control pushed back the shadows of madness—the madness that would consume him and tear him apart before it destroyed him utterly. Breathing hard, hands clenched, he recovered himself. And Lorrimer knew real fear then.

'I do not bring death to my world,' Aarkan told him, his voice rough-edged with anger. 'Why should I wish to destroy? What would be left for me to –'

'For you to rule?'

Met by silence, the quiet words seemed to echo around them for an age. Then Aarkan threw his head back and laughed. 'Does not the Maker rule her creation, old man? Should I not do the same with mine?'

Lorrimer felt something break inside him at that. The last thread of hope, perhaps, or the final ending of a friendship that had spanned four centuries. He turned away, gazing once more at the world he loved. 'I have come to warn you.'

Aarkan laughed again. 'How noble. What is your warning, Old One? That the council will refuse me? That my own people have turned against me?' It was said mildly but there was sudden fire in his eyes. And somewhere out in the vastness of the night a dragon was stirring. 'That it must be war?'

Lorrimer shook his head. 'What need have you of such warnings? No, I have come to show you your future.'

'My future?' Aarkan scoffed. 'What can you show me, old man, that I have not already seen?'

'You see only what you choose. Not what is, not what will be.'

Aarkan took a step back, and Lorrimer felt the shifting strands of his magic begin to grow. 'Do I?' he asked silkily, and as he spoke the landscape around them began to change. The sun rose, though dawn was many hours away, and its pure golden light shone down on a new world. A world that Lorrimer knew, and yet was not his. 'I will show you what I have seen, Lorrimer, what *you* have seen.' And the far-flung web of his magic settled all around them.

Lorrimer saw the Maker's world brought to glorious bloom under a golden sun, even the smallest blade of grass, the lowliest creature, full to overflowing with Tesserion's grace. The sky itself seemed to shimmer in a heat-haze of swirling magic, and even the breeze that plucked at his cloak whispered with life.

But his eyes saw more clearly than Aarkan's. Beneath the heady, frantic pulsing of life lay the start of the decay, and he knew this vision for what it was—the last flowering of Andeira before her decline. Before the sheer power of the magic Aarkan would unleash burnt her to a husk.

It would pass in a heartbeat, this one moment of pure perfection, the instant in time that Aarkan's vision held steady by force. It would pass and leave behind it a dead, decaying world, empty of the life that filled it now. But even he could not help but glory in it.

'You see what I will do?' Aarkan asked, his voice unsteady with rapture. 'Do you not see?'

And Lorrimer did see. He saw to the very heart of it, to the ambition that had twisted his enemy's soul. No longer content with partnership, no longer content to be constrained by the limits of mortality, Aarkan and Srenegar believed themselves poised on the edge of something infinitely greater.

Lorrimer ached to his bones at the tragedy of it, for he had once stood where Aarkan did now, and he too had dared to dream this dream. The man before him was no longer truly a man, and his dragon had no kinship now with others of his kind. No longer two souls, not yet one, the individuals they had been were crumbling away. In their place was something *other*, something that merged the patterns of their minds as one. Where two races had brought to each other one half of the elemental whole, they sought instead to make just one, born of the two, that would *be* the elemental whole.

Oh, he knew their dream. He knew it well. Aarkan believed he could rise to the greatness of Tesserion herself, creator of life, and that her creation would be his to control. But he was wrong, and they would all suffer for it. There would be no glorious flowering of Andeira, there would be no ecstatic triumph over their mortal natures. Instead there would be a war that would bring an end to his world, as those two became one and that one knew neither who nor what it was, only the hunger for power.

'I see,' Lorrimer replied, tearing his gaze from the treacherous vision lest it snare him too, as it had almost done, so many years ago. 'But do you?'

As Aarkan turned to him, catching the sorrow in his voice, Lorrimer urged gently, 'Look closer, my friend. Look further. At the heart of life there is only death.'

Silence fell, so cold and deep it seemed to freeze them both. Then rage rose in a sudden wave, sweeping aside that beautiful, dying world. The blackness of night crashed down, hiding the light of the burning sun, and the dragon hidden in the black mists below screamed in fury.

'Even you would deny this?' Aarkan demanded, as the darkness closed in on him. 'Even you, who has seen what I have seen?'

'Even I,' Lorrimer replied sadly. *Is that not what I have done, all these years?* 'You do not know what you have done.'

He expected to die then. He had seen his death in Aarkan's eyes when he had dared deny his dream. But it did not come, and he would never know why. He wanted to believe that even then, at the brink of his descent into the creature he would become, there remained enough of Aarkan in the man before him that he could not murder one who had been a friend. But as Lorrimer looked one last time into his face, he saw nothing there that he recognised, only dark anger and darker purpose, and the black dragon that raised itself up behind him.

The thundering of great wings fanned the air into eddies, snatching at Aarkan's cloak so it whipped around him like living shadow. Then they were gone, leaving him there, old and alone at the ending of the age.

PART ONE
Amadorn

ONE

Caledan

New Age, 2024

Three thousand years later…

KINSERIS WATCHED HIS prisoners approach from the shadows by the window of his study. The night was sweltering, no whisper of sea breeze easing the oppressive heat in the complex. He could see the sheen of sweat on the Ancai's face as he hustled the bedraggled couple across the darkened courtyard, one hand on the woman's elbow. Her husband kept pace with them, his head bowed in weary submission, and Kinseris ruthlessly suppressed a surge of sympathy. Such feelings endangered them all.

There would be no justice here tonight. As the Vela Frankesh, the head of this chapter of the Kas'Talani priesthood, justice was his responsibility, his sacred duty. *Sacred duty.* The words coiled like nausea through his gut, a mockery of everything he once thought he had believed in. Where was the justice in condemning a man and his pregnant wife to death for protesting the corruption and mismanagement of their regional overseer? Where was the justice in enforcing his Order's foot at the throat of the peoples of Caledan? And yet, at the crux, he found his courage deserting him.

Kinseris felt his hand shake as he turned from the window. Everything felt wrong tonight, and for a moment he considered abandoning the couple to their fate. It was a foolhardy risk he was taking, beset as he was by his high priest's spies and his own haunting doubts. And for what? To save the lives of a peasant farmer and his wife who had not the wits to keep their discontented tongues still until his Order's representatives had left their village?

But if their lives would serve no good purpose, neither would their deaths. And that, perhaps, was why he waited here when he should be purging his

9

household of every man who knew his secrets and praying to the Maker that he could deflect his superiors' imminent suspicions.

For an instant he saw Darred's face, his friend's forced smile barely covering fraught nerves as he had mounted his horse and ridden out through the chapter house gates to answer the unexpected summons from Vasa, the high priest of the Order. The summons to return to the capital Kas'Tella had come almost two months ago, shattering their belief that, if not forgiven, the friends had at least been forgotten as they languished in exile in the sail-hand's dive that was Frankesh port. The more time that passed without word from Darred, the more nervous Kinseris became.

He curled his hand into a fist, grinding it into the wall. Why only Darred? That was the question that gnawed at him. For his own transgression against the Holy Will, Vasa would never stop seeking ways to destroy him. Did he hope to divide them, split their loyalty, and play one against the other? Did Vasa summon Darred now to lure him with promises of promotion, of power—all the things his friend desired and his low birth denied him?

Darred's role in their guilt was of association, incidental at most. Forgivable? Unlikely, given who he was. Kinseris at least was Safarsee—the ruling priestly class—and had once been groomed for high honours. Darred's value was slight in the eyes of his brotherhood, raised to rank for his undeniable strength but consigned to serving the needs of his Safarsee masters. Yes, if Vasa wanted to move against him, Darred was the weapon he would use. And for the first time Kinseris regretted his insistence that his friend should not involve himself in his minor treasons. He regretted even more that he could not be certain that Darred would maintain his silence if he had no share in guilty secrets to bind his tongue.

And yet, he reflected, as the Ancai's firm footsteps stopped outside the door, he had not compelled Darred's lack of participation in what he did here. The Islander lacked the compassion that drove Kinseris's efforts to spare his people from the harsher injustices of his Order's rule. He could only hope that the bond of friendship, already stressed by this ignominious exile, was strong enough to survive their high priest's blandishments.

Kinseris turned as the door opened, admitting the Ancai and his charges.

He nodded once to his captain, and the big man bowed and retired, but not before the priest had seen the worry lines creased into his brow. The Ancai too sensed the increase in danger that accompanied this night's work.

Pushing those thoughts firmly from his mind, Kinseris walked to his desk, seating himself in the ceremonial chair. Everything in his office, from the elaborate ebony desk to the rich tapestries and the bone effigies on their five altars, was designed to humble and impress any who crossed its threshold. Kinseris might stand low in his order's favour, but in his presence in this room no outsider would ever know it.

He laid his hands on the desk and faced the terrified couple. 'Do you understand the crime of which you have been accused?'

The man's head jerked up and just as quickly turned away. He shook his head. His dirty face was pinched with fright, one arm wrapped around the wilting body of his young wife whose pallor threatened collapse. He tried vainly to comfort her as she began to cry, and Kinseris felt his heart lurch in sympathy. They were young and the woman was pregnant, but there was little enough he could do for them.

They had been brought here under guard two days ago, and the acolyte who accompanied the party had already attested to their treason. Kinseris had almost laughed at the suggestion that these two presented a threat to the government and privately agreed with much of what the man had said. But it was a Kas'Tellian priest who had ordered their arrest, and in such cases judgement was passed before the accused even made it to the courtroom— which was why they were here in his private offices. He could not offer them justice, but he was not entirely powerless.

The woman was sobbing. 'Mercy, my lord. What wrong have we done?'

Kinseris regarded them in silence. He had a role to play and more than just their lives depended on how well he carried it off. At last he said, 'You were heard criticising the overseer of your region. As that man is a full priest, your comments reflect directly on your loyalty to your ruler.' He let that sink in. 'However, I struggle to believe anyone would have been so foolish.'

The man looked up. Kinseris realised with a sinking heart that he was going to argue.

'My lord, he would not allow the men of the village to begin the harvest until after the rains came. The crops were spoiled. Our people will starve.'

'Are you admitting your treason?'

'No, my lord. We meant no disrespect to the high priest, we just –'

'Enough!' Kinseris closed his eyes, pinching the bridge of his nose to forestall the threatened headache. Refusal even now to distance themselves from their remarks meant there was nothing he could do for them. If they did not have the sense to recognise the lifeline he was throwing them, he could not risk sending them from his land. He hardened himself to that decision, shamed by the relief that followed in its wake, when the woman stopped her pathetic snivelling and gazed at him in impassioned appeal.

For an instant, as those dark-lashed brown eyes locked on his, his world was rocked to its core by uncanny recognition. Kinseris blinked, shaking off the cobwebs of memory, trying hard to maintain his composure. This woman was not Shakumi. Her features were blunter, her skin rough and weathered in a way Shakumi's would never be. But her eyes—bright jewels in her peasant's face—hurled him back into memories far too recent not to sting him to grief. Aware his purpose could be unstrung by emotion, he tried to bury the guilt Shakumi's memory woke in him, but the glimmer of understanding in the woman's eyes told him his loss of composure had not passed unnoticed.

'What is it you require of us, my lord?' she asked.

Kinseris steadied himself. 'The penalty for treason is death. As your accuser is beyond reproach, I cannot simply overturn that verdict.'

The woman paled, her husband holding her as she staggered.

'My lord, have mercy! My wife is with child. Let her live, I beg you.'

'I have not finished,' Kinseris barked, holding the man's gaze as he subsided into terrified silence. 'I may, at my discretion, commute the sentence of death to one of exile—if you agree to my terms.'

He watched them carefully. The relief on their faces turned swiftly to confusion, then suspicion. It did not surprise him that it was the woman who spoke first.

'My lord, to leave these lands without permission is almost as great a crime as treason. We do not have merchant credentials, and we will never get permission from Kas'Tella. You offer us nothing but death.'

Braver too, to speak to him like that. 'Mercantile rights I can grant you,' he lied airily. 'But your passage must be one way. Will you accept exile?'

Kinseris watched with impatience as some wordless communication passed between them. If they would just say the word, he could save them, before good sense prevailed, and he abandoned them to their fate. One word, and he could bind them by their consent, and it would be done.

The woman made a helpless gesture. 'We accept exile, my lord.'

Power fizzled for a brief moment, then died and was gone. They never noticed the spell that settled gently into them and would ensure they never risked a return to their homeland. Only he was aware of its presence, or its passing, though for a short instant it had seemed to brighten the room. The bedraggled pair had not changed, though he searched their faces as he always did. What he looked for he did not know, nor why he expected to find it.

These were simple folk, with the angular features, dusky skin, and dark hair characteristic of the region. They would not pass unnoticed in Amadorn, but neither would their presence provoke question. Recent decades had seen many Caledani granted the right to engage in foreign trade, a practice that had been rigidly controlled since the earliest days of Kas'Talani rule, but which Vasa, for reasons of his own, had chosen to relax.

No one could deny that trade with Amadorn had brought the empire great wealth, but it had also brought curious foreigners, given to meddling where they were not wanted, and the priesthood's tolerance flew in the face of all known precedents. It was yet another of Kas'Tella's recent eccentricities that Kinseris could not fathom, and what he could not understand he distrusted. Vasa's motives were seldom simple or straightforward, and they were always intended to benefit only one thing—the position of the high priest.

'You will stay in the town tonight,' Kinseris instructed his newest recruits to the merchant trade. 'In the morning my men will escort you to the docks and find you passage on a northbound ship. The captain will see you safely to the Illeneas Archipelago. You may remain there or travel on to Amadorn as you please. There is only one thing you must remember, and remember it well. Should you ever speak of this bargain, there *will* be a reckoning for the crimes from which you have been spared today.'

They would wonder why he was doing it, but he could not tell them. He could not explain that a woman's eyes, reminding him for the briefest moment of someone he had loved, had spurred him to abandon good sense and risk subverting the course of an execution at such an uncertain time.

He did not look at them as he stood and walked around the desk. He opened the door and spoke quietly to the Ancai, who nodded and entered the room. Kinseris slipped out behind him and walked swiftly away. He trusted the Ancai to get them safely aboard a ship or, if things went wrong, to ensure they did not live to repeat their tale. He could not feel guilty. It was the price they would have paid but for his intervention.

Kinseris stopped at the door of his apartments, leaning his head against the door as a wave of dizziness washed over him. When it passed, he entered the room, securing the wards behind him. Only then did he feel safe, as safe as he could be within these walls. But that did not stop his hands shaking.

This could not go on, he knew that. With these two today—three if he counted the unborn child—that made eighty-three men, women, and children he had sent across the sea in the last two years. Not many, perhaps, but more than could be safely concealed. Yet time and again he threw caution to the winds. That he could not bear to see innocent people executed for voicing their resentment with the system that oppressed them had become meaningless in its repetition. In this heart he knew he did it because he was afraid. Afraid of what his Order had become and the corruption at its heart. The tenets of his faith could no longer support him, and he drew back from them day by day, waiting and hoping for a chance to one day redeem his people and his land.

Needing air, Kinseris stumbled to the window, his fingers fumbling over the catch as he yanked it loose and hurled the shutters open. He took a deep breath, drinking in the smells gusting in from the desert hinterlands mixed with the salty tang of the sea. It was a wild and beautiful land, this northern backwater, but he missed the sights and smells of Kas'Tella the more sharply for it. Here, in the wide-open spaces he was stifled, because here he was hemmed in and constrained, his slightest order scrutinised by his superiors, no matter how far from him they were—which made his present activities sheer madness.

Abruptly he stiffened. Almost hidden by the shadows of the garden wall, he saw a shape twitch in the darkness. Too big for a *meneta*—the great desert lizards that sometimes ventured into the town—it moved stealthily in the direction the Ancai must soon take to lead his charges to Frankesh town and a safe berth for the night. There should have been no guards in the inner complex that night, nor any other, as every man in the garrison knew their Vela's desire for privacy. Until tonight he would not have thought they would dare to cross him.

Kinseris cursed, resisting the urge to kick something. He doubted the man had been sent to spy on him. More likely he just wanted a night in the town, to drink himself senseless in the taverns and maybe buy a few hours of female companionship, and for that the swiftest route—and the one least likely to attract the attention of his officers—cut straight through the Vela's courtyard. Tonight that decision would cost him his life, for he would see something he was never meant to, and Kinseris could take no chances.

With Darred's departure he had noticed a lessening of deference in the manner of many on his staff. Those who had not come with him from the capital, whose lives had begun and would end here in Frankesh, had already started to dismiss him in their minds, assuming that Darred's return would see a new Vela, a new head of the Chapter, installed in his place. Until Darred returned to confirm or deny that rumour, his threats would have little effect. And he could not afford to wait on the chance that Vasa's summons was not directed against him. Matters were precarious enough, and the two so recently saved from death could not now be risked, not with his conjury still fresh on them for any trained eye to see.

I have no choice.

He tightened the warding spells around the inner courtyard, sealing the hapless witness within its confines. When the Ancai returned the following morning, he need only bribe the gravedigger to bury one empty coffin.

TWO

Amadorn

New Age, 2032

AARIN WAS SEVEN when his mother left. He still remembered that night, how the storm howled through the hills and the rain plastered his hair to his face as he hid by the window and listened to his parents fight. He heard his mother's voice, low and angry, as she thrust clothes into a bag. When she started to pack his things, Ecyas grabbed her arm and swung her around.

'I will not let you raise our son in your ways, Sedaine. He stays with me.'

'He belongs with his mother,' she shot back, shaking herself free. 'I will not let you rob him of his birthright.'

Ecyas's face darkened. 'Do you really think I will let you take my son and make him a puppet for your false cause?'

'It is your cause that is false,' she spat. 'You who would condemn him to forever seeking a future in the past. Why can you not see this way is best, for all of us?'

There was in her voice then a tremor of a plea, though what it was she could not quite bring herself to ask Aarin never discovered, for their words made no sense to a child. But the realisation that his mother was leaving was like a blow to his chest. He ran from his hiding place, flinging himself into her skirts. He clung to her, begging her not to leave, and heard her triumphant cry as she turned once more to his father.

'See, Ecyas. It is me he loves, not you. You cannot think to keep him from his mother.'

'He is a child, Sedaine,' his father replied. 'He does not understand, but he will.'

Aarin felt a heavy hand on his shoulder, pulling him away. He whimpered, not wanting to let go of his mother but unable to disobey his stern father.

'Come away, Aarin,' Ecyas said gently. 'Your mother is leaving but you will see her again. Come away.'

Reluctantly he moved to his father's side, huge grey eyes focused all the time on his mother's face. She seemed to falter, a sheen of tears brightening her gaze, then she turned from them both and continued her frenzied packing. Without a word Ecyas scooped Aarin up in his strong arms and carried him from the room out into the rain.

The water soaked them in seconds, running under their clothes and streaking rivulets down their faces. Ecyas did not say a word, but Aarin could feel his chest heaving and knew his father was weeping, the rain mingling with his tears to splash on his son's head. They remained there by the door, engulfed by the wild fury of the elements, and Aarin knew his home would never be the same.

Aarin was seven when the world he knew broke apart. He remembered that night, how the storm howled through the hills and the rain plastered his hair to his face as he watched his mother walk away into the night. She paused as she passed them, her long dark hair hanging flat against her back and her delicate features thrown into stark relief by the haunting light. That was how he recalled her best, standing there in the rain, with the heavens thundering their anger to match her own. Then she was gone, swallowed by the storm, and his frantic cries went unanswered.

It was several years before Aarin learned the extent of his mother's betrayal, and still more before he understood just how deep that betrayal went. His father rarely spoke of her, and no one else would speak her name in his hearing, though as he grew older he realised they spoke often of Sedaine among themselves.

At seven he was not party to the heated debates in the taverns, the anxious, snatched meetings that followed her departure, nor the seismic shock that jolted his small community. He was too young to recognise the frisson of hope that drove some to leave as she had done. Or the angry denial of others, like his father, that irrevocably divided his land. And even when at last he heard what she had done—breaking forever from their beliefs and proclaiming a new way, a new order—it would still be years before he understood just how much she had hurt them.

But even before she left, Aarin's home was fading. Luen had once been a large, prosperous settlement. Legend recalled it as a centre of learning, a haven for scholars and mages who sought to escape the chaos of the years that followed the Severing. If so, that learning was long gone, buried by the onslaught of ignorance that followed—the Lost Years.

The Luen of the New Age was still a haven for those with the spark of magic, but they were few, and the once-great city was now just a collection of old dwellings and older ruins. Those who lived there kept to themselves, practising their dying craft and passing on their traditions with little hope for the future—until Sedaine left, and in leaving sowed the seed that shattered a way of life that had endured for centuries.

Aarin's was a lonely childhood, spent mostly with his father. His home was in part of what had once been a grand building but was now just three small rooms with a narrow, walled garden and a backhouse. The walls of the main living area were covered in fading murals of dragons on the wing, and there was one—a great silver dragon that curled protectively over the hearth—that Aarin came to love. Sometimes, as the fire flickered on cold nights and his father told him tales of ancient times, the silver dragon seemed almost to come alive. But when he was older Aarin knew it was only a trick of the dancing flames. The dragons were gone. From his earliest childhood that knowledge had filled him with a great sadness, as if there was an empty place inside him and he had lost something he had never known.

Ecyas withdrew into himself after his wife left, afflicted by bouts of illness that kept him in bed for weeks at a time. Aarin's memories of those years were of long hours of learning by his father's bedside, practising the basic theories of his art, and more hours spent listening to tales of ancient glory.

Closeted with his father, he became almost a stranger to the other children. Where once he had spent many happy hours in their company, he found now not friendship but distrust. Born to an outsider, he became an outsider. The slight lilt to his speech, learned from his northern mother, became a target for their teasing, just as his reclusive father earned the ridicule of their parents. The children repeated overheard snatches of conversation they were too young to understand and transferred the scorn of their elders for the father onto the son.

It grew worse on the rare occasions he joined their lessons, when his natural ability meant he had already mastered many of the basic skills they were still struggling to learn. Instead of respect or liking, it brought him only more suffering, as their jealousy drove them to cruelties only children can inflict.

After his first encounter with the true power of the magic, the teasing stopped. But it was fear, not respect, that brought his reprieve.

Aarin had been out with the other children, learning the feel of the currents of the earth in the months before the spring renewal. His teacher's voice had droned on, while his feet slowly turned to blocks of ice and his fingers began to ache from the cold. It was a lesson he had heard many times, repeated over and over to the children by their elders, to prepare them for the ignorance they would encounter in the outside world if they chose to leave the safety of their land.

'You must remember this,' the teacher told the circle of fidgeting children. 'For so many will not understand. They have seen only the magicians and their illusions. They believe this is magic. But it is not. Magic does not exist only in a few, a thing to be imposed on the world. It *is* the world and gives life to everything in it. These currents of the earth that you feel are a mystery to most, but to master them you must only be able to see and feel that which exists all around you...'

Aarin stifled a yawn. The few lessons his father permitted him to attend always began like this, a reiteration of the nature of the magic.

'... and in the long-forgotten years, ages past, when the currents ran free and pure through all Andeira, there was no limit to what we could achieve, bound in partnership with the dragons. No limit save for the one we imposed upon ourselves, never to transgress into the realm of the Maker, the creator of life. But now there are limits, and you must learn to act within them. When the dragons left, they took with them the knowledge and mastery of the Lost Elements, and they left us only with the memory of those times.'

The teacher turned from his less-than-attentive audience and pointed to the fire, barely big enough to stave off the worst of the winter's chill. 'There you see Fire, the only manifestation of Andeira's core now left to us. Yet though we can see it we can no longer work our will upon it. To stoke this fire we must feed it, not with magic, but with the food it needs to burn.'

Aarin never knew why he chose that day to speak up and disagree, for the teacher was right. But his father, in making the same point to his son, had always finished by encouraging the boy to look closer. Ecyas accepted no self-imposed limits. He refused to believe, as the others did, that with the passing of the dragons certain avenues had closed forever to mankind. Yes, the Lost Elements were indeed lost to them, but that did not mean that there were not ways of using what they had to compensate for that which they lacked.

The teacher had asked him to demonstrate, his amusement barely masked behind scholarly tolerance, and suddenly the class had come to life. Whispers ran through the children behind him. Someone prodded him forward, evoking a jeer from the rest, and his certainty deserted him. He tried to do what he had done many times before, but tormented by the jibes of his fellows, his usual dexterity failed him. Hemmed in by their surreptitious needling, the simple trick he had mastered in secret would not show itself to his audience.

That night he fretted over his failure as he knelt by another fire. Shamed and angry, Aarin set himself to building up the blaze, attacking his task as though he fought his tormentors. The flames of the fire leapt higher as he added more wood, and his eyes were drawn to the strange dance. A dry branch crackled, throwing up a burst of sparks that fluttered in the warm draft. Aarin watched as they spiralled upwards and were carried away by the smoke.

In his eyes the fire took on a life of its own, twining itself around his magic. This was the secret he had tried to show them, the trick he had discovered months ago—that it was possible to coax more life from spent logs if he bolstered them with earth energy of his own. He did this now, pouring himself into his craft to prove it could be done. And before he realised what was happening, the elemental force within the flames drew strength from his reckless weaving. Recognising a talent ages old, Fire strove to meet him.

A tide of power engulfed the boy, tearing at his defences as it sought to reach an ability long lost to mankind. Something in him rose in answer to that primal contact, something basic and undeniable. Somewhere in the back of his mind, Aarin was aware of his father hurrying towards him, but he was locked in a struggle he could not comprehend. He knew only that he could not turn his eyes from the Fire.

He did not remember falling, or his father crying his name and the hands that held him and rocked him. He did not remember the days that followed, only the grey haze that sucked him deep within himself, and the burning that came from somewhere inside and soaked his sheets with sweat. The nightmares that scoured his mind made him twist and turn in his sleep, crying out in fear, but he did not see how his pleas wracked his father's heart.

When eventually Aarin returned to himself he saw his father sitting by his side. His eyes were red, his face lined and haggard. Ecyas cried aloud when he saw his son's eyes open, gathering the boy into a tight embrace that almost strangled the air from his lungs.

'I'm so sorry,' his father told him, stroking back his damp hair. 'I thought I had lost you. I'm sorry.'

Aarin loved his father so much in that moment. He did not want to let him go, but to hold him forever. Then suddenly he realised that Ecyas was weeping, as he had not done since the day his mother left, and he was filled with shame for causing his father such pain.

That was a hard lesson. It taught him many things. A harder lesson followed, when he rose from his sickbed and went back out into the world and recognised the coldness of the people around him for what it was.

He never again made the mistake of speaking to others of the things his father taught him. The first time he had realised that the dragons lived only in Ecyas, his heart had broken. He had run home, tears falling in an anger that hurt him to the core, demanding to know why he had been lied to. It had taken Ecyas several hours of patient argument to make his eight-year-old son understand what so many grown men did not: that it was easier to deny the existence of what was lost than admit the failings that meant it could never be reclaimed.

'But you must never forget, Aarin,' Ecyas had told him. 'Never forget that they are real.'

His father's sickness came on him more frequently in the years that followed. He would spend days shut in his room, or sitting silent in his chair before the fire, and Aarin had to care for himself. When he was able, Ecyas continued his son's training, but he was more cautious now and Aarin grew impatient. In Water and its uses he was far ahead of others his own age, and in the workings of the element of Air, as they knew it, he made rapid progress. But his father was wary now of Earth, forever fearing the call of elemental Fire burning in its depths. Aarin wearied of his constant warnings, undeterred by an experience he could barely remember. All that was left to him of that dark passage of dreams was the burning of his skin to the touch and his father's face when he woke.

Then one evening as his father sat by the fire, he called Aarin to him. One hand tangled in his son's dark hair, he began to speak once more of the dragons, spinning the legends of the First Age that had so delighted Aarin when he was younger. It was almost as if he had forgotten that his son had grown.

Then, when he had been silent for some time, his story hanging half-told, Aarin quietly pulled away to return to his chores. Ecyas looked up and caught his hand.

'I know you think you are ready, my son,' he said, and Aarin realised he had not been lost in memory, just deep thought. 'You are patient with me, but I see the fire in your eyes and know you long to learn, as I did. You must understand that it is not through any failing on your part that I hesitate. Knowledge is a burden, Aarin, and you are so young yet. I do not want to take your childhood from you.'

Aarin began to speak but his father cut him short, gripping him now with such urgency that he could feel the bruising pressure of his fingers.

'I do not want to,' Ecyas told him, 'but now I have no choice. I do not have long left in this world, I can feel it, and I fear to leave your talent unschooled. No hush,' he said gently when Aarin started to protest. 'It will be as it will be and neither you nor I can change it. I must teach you what I know of the old ways. There is too much strength in you to be safe without guidance. It will be dangerous, but if you truly believe you are ready, we must begin your training in the greater patterns.'

The elation Aarin felt at those words was beyond anything he could have imagined, pushing aside even the wrenching fear of moments ago. But he composed his face, knowing his father would accept only his considered reply and not the boyish impatience he felt. He said gravely that he was ready.

Ecyas smiled, proud of his control, then the smile fled. 'What I am about to show you will not be taught to the others. There are few now with the skill to control such a construct, and what they cannot do the people here treat with suspicion. Sit, and follow what I do.'

Aarin folded to the floor and closed his eyes, willing his heart to cease hammering against his chest. He sent a wash of icy calm over the turmoil of his emotions and wiped them from his mind, feeling his father do the same. Then, poised in readiness, he watched the subtle spellcasting unfold before him.

In later years, Aarin tried many times to explain that 'seeing' of the magic, for it was not a visible force. Rather, the presence of magic was so potent, so vital, that it touched all the senses to some awareness of it. Almost as a blind man cannot see the table before him but senses a change in the feel of the space, a mage could feel the path of any magic he engaged, and follow the workings of another if they were close and powerful. Just so did Aarin now watch his father's magic come alive.

First Ecyas drew the flows of elemental power into himself, careful to do so always as he had taught his son, in a measured and cautious manner. Then he cast outwards with his senses, threading his way through the coils of power that danced within his grasp. All this Aarin knew well, the balancing of the power drawn from the world with that which resided in the user, and the careful blending that would follow to create a pattern of intent.

The patterns his father made were like none he had seen. He could work one element with another, or one alone, always in tiny amounts, but the swift melding he now witnessed was something he had not imagined possible.

Ecyas did not look at him, intent upon his work. What he did now was no simple spell, no purpose-driven construct, but a demonstration of possibilities. He let none of the magic escape to act upon the individual patterns as he showed his son how to use his power to manipulate the world around him. He flung his web far, taking it to the very edges of the Lost Elements yet steering clear of the precipice beyond. He showed Aarin the shadowy presence of those they lacked as they touched the edges of his pattern, that undefined emptiness that was somehow full and bountiful, and just out of reach.

He sensed his son's desire to plunge into the glowing magic and gently restrained him. Only when Aarin's reckless urge subsided did he allow him to tag onto the signature of his awareness and follow him step by step through each strand of the pattern. None of the power did he allow to touch his son, nor would he permit Aarin to reach out with any of his own. He let him see and feel the workings of the elements that remained in all their possibilities but kept him well apart from the dangerous weight of their living presence. That would come later.

THREE

DAY AFTER DAY, Aarin continued to learn, yet always he followed his father's lead, never allowed to stray into the threads of power Ecyas wove around them. He tried to be patient. He listened as his father warned him again of the dangers of coming too close to the limits of his perception, but he longed to reach out for himself and grasp the twisting web.

Each time it was different, and as Aarin's understanding grew, Ecyas began to explain how he believed the linking of the races had worked. The Joining of humans and dragons. His words woke a fascination in the boy for the unspoken promise that what had been severed could one day be healed. Years later, Aarin wondered whether his father had known the effect his subtle teachings would have, for it was only then that he recognised the extent of the frustrated desire Ecyas had harboured. Only then did he understand the reason behind his desperate last rush to see his son prepared for the future.

Then one day, as he waited for his father to return, the itch to experiment on his own drove Aarin to forget his father's warnings. Excited and nervous, he settled himself on the hearth and opened himself to the trance. At once the tingling of waiting energies enlivened his senses, filling him with the rapture of unending possibilities, and all his trepidation disappeared.

As Aarin wove his web, letting the elements flow from him and around him, he felt his confidence soar. All caution disappeared as he revelled in his newfound skill. Why his father had tried to keep this from him he could not understand. It was so simple, so beautiful, and wholly his as he had made it. Then he saw it was not truly his, not in the way he had been taught. Something alien hovered at the edges of his construct. Something that had been absent from his father's magic was pressing in on his, and a half-recalled thread of memory awoke in him as it called. For an instant he hesitated, then his childish curiosity asserted itself and he focused his mind on the anomaly, trying to draw it out of the shadows.

There! He could see it, the faint coiling threads of flame that were elemental Fire. They licked at his spell, dancing through it like red serpents. He sat entranced, unable to lift his eyes from the tracings of their presence, marvelling at the way the half-seen threads matched themselves to the design he had made, almost as if the magic sought to take on a life of its own.

Then he heard voices outside and Ecyas's heavy tread on the path. Aarin turned to the door as it opened, smiling joyfully at his father.

'Look!' he cried, holding his arms wide to encompass all he had made.

Ecyas stood frozen to the spot, watching his son sit within the swirling threads of magic.

'I can see it, father,' Aarin told him. 'I can see the Fire. It is there, and there. Look how it moves. Can you see it?'

'Fire,' Ecyas breathed, stepping into the room at last, his fear swamped by a sudden rush of longing. 'What is it like?'

Aarin smiled, one finger tracing the path of the thickest strand. 'It moves like Water, but it feels like Earth and is as light as Air.' He looked up to meet his father's eyes and Ecyas's heart turned over as he saw the wisdom of the man his son would become gazing back at him.

'I cannot see the Fire itself,' Aarin told him solemnly, 'only its reflection as it crosses the path of that which is part of me, but I feel almost as though I could touch it if I tried.'

'No,' Ecyas warned sharply. 'You must not try.'

But Aarin was no longer listening. He had caught another flash of red flame and for an instant it had seemed like it was there in truth. Heedless of his father's cries, he flung himself after it, hunting its elusive passage as it once again vanished from his sight. He went deeper and deeper into his own construct, his consciousness ranging far outside the confines of his body. When it appeared again, he followed it almost to the edges of its possibility. He was too close to a world that was not his own, but he barely noticed, seeing only the burning imprint of the fire.

Ecyas could not see the passage of elemental Fire, he could only see the boy losing his way amidst the maze. Aarin's eyes glazed, and all around him the threads of his pattern trembled as he followed something that should not have been there.

Gripped by awful panic, Ecyas threw himself into the circle of power, treading unstable pathways in a desperate rush to claw back his son. In the shadows of the edge he finally found him, poised to pass from his body into the void, and there was no time left for thought. The father acted without care for himself to save his child, latching onto the boy's presence and snatching the impulse to follow to himself. Though he did not have his son's sight, he was still a mage, and the channels existed within him too. Aarin's intent carried him beyond his own abilities and into the darkness, and if Ecyas's consciousness shielded the boy from the contact, he could not also shield himself.

Ecyas rushed to meet the Fire as it rushed to meet him. For an instant it flooded him, and he felt the searing heat course through his body, then it rebounded against the barrier of his humanity and tossed him aside.

He spiralled deeper and deeper into the darkness and there was nothing to cling to. There was nothing he knew that could erase the pain of that rejection, and he drifted away. There was comfort in that nothingness, a comfort that stole away all the griefs of his life, and he welcomed the approach of death.

Then into the shadows he heard it, a small voice calling him back.

He turned away, blocking his son's voice from his mind, but Aarin would not give up. Ecyas felt an intent questing towards him, following where he went, and knew that the boy would hurl himself after it without thought for the danger. Ecyas could not allow Aarin to throw his life away for a man already lost. He was dying, he had known it for months, and it no longer mattered what became of him. It was Aarin who had to live.

So Ecyas answered that faint call, clawing his way back to the body that confined him, and turned his back on the endless dark. He heard his son's wordless cry of relief, but the magic that gently guided him home was not the weaving of a child. It was the subtle, strong touch of a man grown into his art and the knowledge of its treacherous ways.

As the pain that greeted his return forced his consciousness to flee, he wished that the price he had paid for unveiling that skill had not been so bitter.

In his desperation to save his father, Aarin felt his consciousness hurtle ever closer to the void. There was no time now for caution. The thread of Ecyas's life grew fainter with each heartbeat and he threw himself after it. Yet no matter how he tried to anchor that wayward soul, the distance between them grew ever greater.

Smothering a howl of despair, Aarin paused in his flight. Ecyas paid no heed to his blind attempts to gain a hold of his mind. He was running away from him, seeking his fate, and he would not be coerced. Aarin's desperation turned to sorrow, and his grief that his father could so easily abandon him permeated every strand of his magic. He cried out his anguish, and somewhere, far away, he felt the wetness of tears on his cheeks. And then, only then, did he sense a hesitation in Ecyas's purpose. He called again, appealing to a father's love, and felt a sensation of regret brush over him, as though in calling Ecyas back he had stolen from him something precious. But he clung tenaciously to that answering voice. Inch by inch he clawed his way back, bending the magic to his purpose and unravelling the construct behind him. Then, finally, he opened his eyes to find himself back in his body and Ecyas sprawled unmoving by his feet.

For a moment Aarin could not move. Then he pushed himself to his feet and ran to the door. Brannick, his father's friend, still stood at the end of the path. At the sight of Aarin's terrified, tear-stained face, he ran towards him. The boy stood aside to let him pass, unable to put words to his need, but as soon as Brannick crossed the threshold he felt the resonance of spent power jangle against his nerves. He recognised the feel of magic gone horribly wrong even before he caught sight of Ecyas's limp body on the hearth.

'What have you done?' Brannick cried, falling to his knees beside his friend. 'Speak, boy!'

'I did not mean to,' Aarin wailed. 'I thought only to do as he taught me. Then the Fire...'

'Fire again?' Brannick breathed, horrified. 'What will it take to stop you

28

meddling in such things? Did the last time teach you nothing? You cannot go where the ancients did. It is no longer possible. Do you not know what it cost your father to bring you back to us the last time?'

Aarin shrunk from his anger, letting go of his father's hand. 'I'm sorry,' he whispered. 'I did not mean–'

'No, you did not,' Brannick conceded, his tone softening. 'But you have done so all the same.' He stood slowly, Ecyas supported in his arms like a child. 'I will do what I can for him, Aarin,' he promised. 'Though I do not know that I can help.'

Aarin watched him walk away and could hold back his grief no longer. Curling up on himself, he hugged his knees to his chest and muffled his heartbreak in his shirt. His father was dying. Brannick's eyes had told him so, and he knew it was his fault. The tears fell in a torrent of misery and they did not stop until sleep finally claimed him.

It was deep in the night when Ecyas came back to himself and he found Brannick at his side. His old friend was asleep, head pillowed on his arms on the edge of the narrow bed. The room was cold, the shutters opened wide to the winter air, and a gentle breeze stirred his greying hair. Ecyas would have let him sleep, but fear for Aarin overrode concern for his friend. He reached out a hand, wasted by long sickness, and shook Brannick's shoulder.

His friend came awake instantly. 'Ecyas. I was beginning to fear we had lost you. How do you feel?'

'Where is my son?'

Brannick straightened. 'Sleeping. He's fine. It is you I am worried about.'

Ecyas shook his head sadly. 'Do not worry for me, my friend. It has been too late for that for many months. Please, let me see my son.'

'Later,' Brannick urged. 'He took no hurt from his misadventure.' His mouth twisted into a grimace. 'It is only you he has hurt.'

Ecyas sank back with a sigh. 'Do not blame Aarin. Do not let him blame himself. I know what guilt can do to a man. He does not deserve that.'

He paused, his breath was coming in shuddering sighs. 'There is so much I have to teach him still, so much he needs to know. You have not always agreed with me, but you have been a true friend. Promise me you will watch over him, that you will teach him what I cannot. Promise me.'

Brannick was silent so long that, his face so grim, that Ecyas feared he would refuse.

'He must know this is not of his doing,' he pleaded. 'I am dying. I have known it for a long time. It is not Aarin who did this to me. If I had not interfered, if I had stopped to think...' His voice trailed away as he closed his eyes in painful recollection. 'He was in no danger. I see that now. The Fire would not have hurt him.'

Brannick shook his head in disbelief. 'Has three years faded your memory so much? His foolish actions then nearly killed him.'

'Perhaps,' Ecyas replied. 'Or perhaps not. Nothing I did to ease him in those days made any difference. He came back to us on his own. Changed, though he did not know it. But now I think I understand more clearly. It is almost as though the Fire has claimed him for its own, that *they* have claimed him from me, and I must let him go. There is no room left for me in his future.'

Brannick started to protest but Ecyas silenced him. 'I know my time has come and I am not afraid. I will return to my Maker and She will guard my long sleep.' His gaze turned inward, his eyes taking on a dreamy look. 'Then I will see all the wonders of the old world and find my peace at last. I... I dreamed once that I would be the one. But it was never meant to be me.' He gripped his friend's hand. 'You must teach him, for I would not have him so unprepared for what he must do.'

'Ecyas,' Brannick began, shaking his head. 'You cannot believe...'

'I am sure,' the dying man said firmly. 'Promise me, please.'

Brannick sighed. The shadows of approaching death were crowding into the room, and he gave a promise he did not know he could keep to give Ecyas the peace he craved.

Ecyas grasped his hand in silent thanks. 'I need to see my son.'

Brannick nodded and silently left the room. He found Aarin curled where he had left him, his head resting on one pale arm, his face streaked with tears. Gently he picked up the sleeping boy and carried him to his father's bed.

Ecyas lifted one hand and curled his fingers through his son's hair. His eyes filled with tears. Aarin stirred in his sleep, snuggling deeper into the warm embrace as Brannick gently tucked the blanket around them both.

'You are a good friend,' Ecyas told him softly. 'Thank you.'

Brannick could not speak. He knew that he would never see his friend alive again, but his throat was dry and all the words he wanted to say would not come. So he left them there, father and son, and went to wait in the room beyond for the first cruel sounds of grief that would tell him a boy had been left fatherless.

When the pale light of morning woke Aarin from his restless sleep he found himself in his father's room, curled by his side. The events of the evening before seemed no more than a bad dream. Here he was, safe in his father's arms. Nothing could hurt him.

He rolled over, stretching cramped muscles, and saw Ecyas awake, his grey eyes watching him. Aarin smiled in greeting, but moments later the smile slipped from his face. Something was wrong, his father's gaze unfocused and staring.

'Father,' he whispered, unnerved by his stillness. As his hand pressed against Ecyas's shoulder he let out a shuddering cry. The skin beneath his hand was too cool, and he knew his father was dead. A pressure settled in his chest. He did not realise he was shouting until the door burst open and Brannick rushed in and pulled him away, hushing him gently. Tears came then, a great storm that left him breathless and hurting. When the storm passed, he was cold inside, and there was nothing that could ease the ache of that emptiness.

Brannick took his father's body to the cliffs looking out over the sea and there built a pyre to burn him. Aarin stood apart from him, staring at the waves crashing onto the rocks below, silent tears rolling down his cheeks. He looked back only when Brannick finished his work, then he moved to his father's side to say his last farewell. He reached out, taking one cold, lifeless hand in his, and inside he was pleading with Ecyas to wake, to open his eyes and look at him. To forgive him. But the outer shell was empty of the spirit that had once burned with life, and there was no final absolution, only the coldness of death and the loneliness of lost years.

Aarin made a promise that day, standing there in the cold winter wind. He promised to enter the place that had claimed his father, enter the nothingness and find instead its promise fulfilled. He would find the dragons, and he would bring them out of the shadows and into the light of Andeira's sun. Because that was what Ecyas had wanted him to do, and it was the only thing he knew that could absolve him of his part in his father's death.

Brannick walked to his side, placing a heavy hand on his shoulder as Aarin gently released his grip on his father's hand. Then he knelt beside the pyre to start the blaze.

'Aarin, you must stand back now.'

Aarin shook his head and Brannick sighed. Sparks leapt onto the tinder of the funeral pyre and tongues of red flame began to dance around the base. Brannick stood, the heat of the fire on his face, and took Aarin's arm to pull him away.

The boy shook him off. Sparks were flying in the wind, singeing Brannick's hair and clothes. He brushed them away, his pleas becoming more urgent. The smoke clogged his lungs and closed his throat, and he coughed, stumbling away, calling out to Aarin. But Aarin ignored him and Brannick saw that the smoke and flames did not touch him, swirling around and above him as though he had some shield about him that protected him from their fury.

As he stood frozen, staring at the sight, Aarin turned to him, a sad smile on his face. 'It's all right,' he promised. 'It knows me.'

Then he turned back to his father and stepped inside the circle of the fire, Brannick's cry of alarm echoing in his ears. The flames leapt up all around him, engulfing him in a barrage of heat, and though the fire in his blood burned him from the inside out, his flesh was untouched. Orange turned to blue as the fire licked across the surface of his skin and rippled on his clothes, caressing him with its touch. The roar of the flames was a primal language that whispered to him, and he knew the fire would not hurt him.

Aarin climbed the pyre to stand in the swirling smoke by his father's side as blue fire ran up and down his arms. Then he knelt and touched his fingertips to his father's body, and the flames leapt between them wherever he touched. In an instant Ecyas was consumed by bright flame, and Aarin lost sight of his father's face in the fury of the blaze. He stayed where he was, his hands resting on Ecyas's breast, and murmured the words that commended his spirit to Tesserion, the Mother of all.

Then the smoke became too thick to see and the heat made him weary. He lay down amid the flames and remembered nothing more.

Brannick stood on the cliffs watching the blaze, grieving for the father and the son, angry at the senseless waste of it. When the fire had died down, he forced himself to approach the pyre. There among the ashes he saw Aarin. Asleep, blackened with soot from head to foot, but whole and alive when he should have been dead.

Shaken to his core, Brannick could only stand there and stare, wondering at the child who could control elemental Fire—the child sleeping peacefully on the charred ground where any other living thing would have been burnt alive—and did not have the courage to understand. Instead he carefully lifted the boy and carried him back to his empty home, and never said a word to anyone about what he had witnessed on the cliff tops that winter day.

FOUR

Caledan

New Age, 2040

KINSERIS STOOD BY the window of his study, watching the sunset turn the grounds of the chapter house a deep red. He leant his shoulder against the stone wall and rested his head in the crook of his upraised arm, giving in for a moment to the exhaustion that dragged at him.

The view from this window never changed. The same stone courtyard with its dusting of desert sands, the same shadowed archway that led to the compound beyond. Yet he was feeling the passing of time keenly these last weeks, Darred's surprise return reminding him of how quickly two years of exile had become eighteen. Reminding him forcibly of the last time his friend had returned unexpectedly after the summons to Kas'Tella, and how his news had turned their world upside down. And now Darred was back again, returned, however briefly, from the assignment Vasa had given him, and was once again in Kas'Tella. And once more Kinseris was left waiting and gnawing his fingernails in worry.

Not three weeks ago Darred had returned from Amadorn, disembarking from one of Vasa's own ships in Frankesh port, returned after sixteen long years. It should have been a joyful occasion, two friends reunited, but Darred had been reserved, and he had not lingered long before beginning his journey to Kas'Tella. In his time in Frankesh they had spoken little, and then formality had prevailed where before they would have spent the night drinking and sharing stories of their time apart. And that, Kinseris, admitted, was the real reason for his growing disquiet.

Sixteen years was a long time—it had changed them both. But he could not believe it was that simple. Memories of their long-ago parting flitted through his mind. He remembered the unease he had felt even then, though he had smothered it as best he could, thinking it unworthy of either of them. When Darred had returned from that unexpected summons to Kas'Tella, triumphant and preening, it had been to find Kinseris sick with fear, made to wait two months to discover the cause of Vasa's sudden interest in their affairs. The awful certainty that his treachery had been discovered had been hard to shake, and his reaction to Darred's appointment had been unguarded. He had let his disbelief show when it would have been better kept hidden, for it had caused an ugly row.

It had been late and they had both been weary, Darred from a long ride and Kinseris from hours spent on the magistrate's bench, resolving petty disputes and awarding fines. As he always did, Darred had brought wine— had seemed, in fact, more than a little drunk already—but he had been cagey about his long absence. In the end Kinseris could take no more, and Darred's amusement at his squirming unease had been conquered by his own desire to boast, and so they had come to the crux of the matter with very different emotions.

'He has made me his emissary to Amadorn,' Darred had told him that night. 'I am to take ship for the northern continent.'

Kinseris set his glass down before he dropped it. 'He's done what?'

'Made me his emissary,' Darred repeated, his smile slipping. 'To Amadorn. Why do you look like that?'

Kinseris raked a hand through his hair, staring at his friend in consternation. Permitting a degree of trade was one thing, opening diplomatic relations quite another. And when it happened—*if* it happened— he could not believe that Darred would be the appointed emissary. He had been publicly disgraced, they both had. 'Why?'

'Why not?' Darred had demanded. 'Why should it surprise you that this honour has gone to me? Am I not as fit for it as a mainlander, is that what you think?'

'You know it isn't. Have I ever thought that way? I am surprised, and a little afraid. Almost two years we have languished here, all but forgotten. Why now does he remember us?'

Darred's eyes flashed dangerously. 'He remembers me. Not us. Me.'

The fierce pride in his voice made Kinseris wince. How many nights had they sat together, drinking and talking, giving voice to thoughts that should not be spoken, angry at the injustices of their ruler? But Darred's anger went deeper still. He knew the southern islander harboured a great bitterness towards the Order that had raised him from his humble beginnings then left him to rot in a backwater no different to the one he had left behind. As he had looked into Darred's strained face that night, Kinseris had seen all his dammed-up resentment for a life lived in obscurity, denied the respect of rank enjoyed by his brothers in more privileged postings. For a boy born into the relentless poverty of the southern ports, Darred had risen far. Yet he had gained no satisfaction from his success, only a festering anger at what he had not achieved.

As an emissary to Amadorn, Darred had at last been handed a way to expunge the shame of his birth, and Kinseris had no doubt his friend would wring from it every advantage he could. In a land where the colour of his skin marked his low status for all to see, he had had to fight for every step. Now he would go to a place where he would no longer stand out, where he could rise higher and faster than he had ever dreamed. Which way would he turn then? Would he revert to his oath and serve his Order well, or would he use this promotion to maul that same Order, to savage it and revenge himself upon it? How far he might take his revenge on those who had thought to use him—for revenge it could easily become—Kinseris had not liked to guess.

'When do you leave?' he had asked, keeping his concern from his voice. The young couple he had spared from his Order's justice the night before last had been waiting to take ship for the Illeneas Archipelago, where Darred would also be bound on his way north. The vessel due to carry them on the first leg of their journey was to leave for the island port with the morning tide and he had disliked the possibility that Darred would also be on it. A few moments of contact would reveal his hand in their exile, and he had feared to place Darred in the position of abetting their escape when he was so newly come into his rank. He had not feared betrayal, not then. His friend's hatred of his Order went too deep, but time and power might yet heal that breach. One day, he might remember them, and his thoughts would return to

Frankesh. One day, loyalty to the Order might dictate that he close that escape route. If that happened their friendship would be brushed aside.

Darred had never pretended to understand his compassion for those who fell foul of Kas'Talani tyranny. His complaints of injustice did not encompass the downtrodden masses of the empire, only the slight to himself. Whatever treasonous feelings they shared arose from very different sources. Did they even share those feelings still?

That night, Darred had recovered his composure quickly. His orders would arrive within the week, he told Kinseris as he looked for a chair. 'Forgive my harsh words. It has been a long ride and I am more tired than I realised.'

'There's nothing to forgive,' Kinseris had assured him, sitting in his turn and forcing a smile to his face. In a week his exiles would be safely away. 'We must celebrate your good fortune, for I suspect it will be many years before we meet again. I fear I am destined to remain here until Vasa forgives my misdeeds. Or remembers them,' he added darkly. 'He has grown more erratic every year since Seledar disappeared.'

Darred gave him an odd look and seemed about to speak, then covered the impulse with a smile and raised his glass. 'A weak memory to our revered leader,' he proposed and Kinseris grinned and drank.

And just like that, Darred's anger had faded. They had been younger then, their friendship as yet undamaged by the seeds of mistrust. Kinseris felt a rush of regret for those easy days. The man who had returned from Amadorn three weeks ago was utterly changed. It seemed to Kinseris that Darred had chosen his path, his loyalty. No longer given to raging against his lot, his displays of emotions carefully measured, there had been a subtlety to his manner that Kinseris did not recognise. And he wondered.

As they had worked their way through bottle after bottle of the vinegary local wine that night sixteen years ago, Darred had become increasingly erratic. Kinseris had put it down to nerves and excitement over the impending voyage, but there had been something else. Many times his friend had begun to speak only to stop himself, leaving Kinseris with the impression that the words he uttered were not quite those he had intended. He had not pressed, his curiosity dampened by drink, and over the years had forgotten the half-warnings, the careful phrasing, thinking it only the ever-present necessity of coded talk that made his friend speak so strangely.

But now, through the veils of memory, he realised there had indeed been something Darred had wished to speak of. Something that had disturbed him. And Kinseris wished he had forced this thing from his friend. For whatever it was, it was a part of him now. There were doubts no longer. Perhaps, if he had pressed, he would still have a friend, not this man who hovered somewhere between enemy and friend, and who would be whichever suited him best as the occasion demanded, a creature of the Order.

The sound of footsteps interrupted his thoughts and he started in guilty surprise. Darred lounged against the doorframe, a bottle of cheap spirits swinging from one hand. Kinseris looked into his delighted face, dark hair smoothed back and narrow beard freshly trimmed, and could not help smiling at this glimpse of the friend he had known.

'You were quick,' he said, covering his surprise well. 'We did not expect you for another week at least.'

'Well, there's a welcome,' Darred laughed, catching him in a one-armed embrace and walking them into the room. 'These are good times, my friend, and I have decided we must celebrate.'

'Celebrate?' Kinseris asked suspiciously, remembering the coldness of their reunion a month ago. 'You have news?'

'Such news. And all good.'

'That I guessed. I take it that he has not revoked your posting to Amadorn. Tell me, does our *conquest* go well?' He could not quite keep the sneer from his voice and saw a ripple of annoyance cross Darred's face. It was quickly smoothed away.

'It goes well,' Darred replied carelessly as he drew a tumbler towards him and poured a generous slug of the liquor. He pushed it towards Kinseris. 'If it did not, I would not stand before you now.'

That at least was truth. Vasa had always been unforgiving of failure. And betrayal? Well did Kinseris remember how his high priest dealt with that. It would only be worse now. The thought brought that fear to his lips and it tumbled out before he could stop it.

'He said nothing...' He paused, his throat dry. 'Nothing of...'

'You?' Darred finished, quirking an eyebrow. Then his face broke into a smile. 'Ah, Kinseris, so jumpy still? I take it you continue in your folly?'

Kinseris schooled his rigid features to relax. He would not play this game. 'I act as I see fit,' he replied coldly. 'I sought only reassurance from one I consider a friend.'

'These are dangerous times,' Darred answered. 'Who is a friend anymore? Ah, do not fret so. Do you not trust me?'

'Of course.'

But he did not, not anymore. Darred's appointment to Amadorn all those years ago had driven a wedge between them. Kinseris had to be careful now, with his words and his actions, especially as he had so much more to lose. He had not sat idle for sixteen years, and the webs of his intrigues far surpassed his earlier, tentative forays. The man who stood before him, sipping his drink with a smile, dark eyes watching him so closely, was no longer his brother, bound to him by shared disgrace and fated to live out the rest of his days in obscurity just as he was. He had risen high, and Darred would keep his secrets now only if it suited him.

'You doubt me?' Darred asked quietly, and there was a challenge in the question. 'You think after all these years I have forgotten our friendship?'

'I do not think that,' Kinseris replied carefully. 'But I wonder what that friendship might cost you now. I would not blame you if you were to cast me off, for loyalty to our Order makes great demands on us, and you have far further to fall now than you ever had before.'

Darred snorted. 'Ever the diplomat. I think you know me better than that.' He raised his glass, the liquid sloshing over the sides. 'Darred's loyalty is to himself,' he proclaimed with a dry humour. 'At the present time I find that serving Vasa suits me well, but in the future, who can say?'

Kinseris recognised that there was both truth and falsehood in those words and wondered what Darred was really saying. He had sidestepped Kinseris's concerns, avoided a promise to guard his secrets—all but admitted that he would betray him if it proved useful—and instead had said what? That he might betray Vasa also if he judged such an act to be in his interests? Kinseris suppressed a shudder. Such a man was far more dangerous than one whose loyalties were firmly set.

He forced himself to smile as he raised his own glass. 'Then I wish you good fortune and hope that your plans and mine never come into conflict.'

Darred's answering smile mocked his subterfuge. 'To both our intrigues,' he offered instead. 'And may they one day come together.'

Kinseris choked, looking into those dark, laughing eyes. 'Indeed,' he managed, his throat burning as the raw liquor scorched a passage to his belly. But before he could react, Darred's next comment shattered the last of his composure.

'She asked after you,' he said softly, reaching for the bottle to refill his glass. 'She came to my chambers as I was leaving and asked to be remembered to you.'

Kinseris froze, fearing another trap and unable to stop himself falling headlong into it. 'Shakumi? She came to you? Did anyone see?'

Darred's eyes flashed with sudden anger. 'Of course no one saw! I am not so incompetent as to let another spy on my private rooms.' He sighed. 'I promised myself I would say nothing to you, that I would not let the memory of her provoke you to another foolish act. You have risked ruin once for a chance to look on that pretty face. Vasa will not be so forgiving again.'

Kinseris laughed bitterly. 'It seems I have wronged him. I had believed my sojourn in this cursed corner of the empire was an act of punishment, not forgiveness.'

'You should count yourself fortunate, my friend,' Darred murmured, his voice taking on a warning edge. 'Vasa has done worse since, much worse. Kas'Tella is a hive of suspicion. Most I saw there would speak no more to me than a swift greeting, and those who did each whispered different tales of treachery and warned me from the rest. You are lucky indeed to find yourself here and forgotten. Seek a meeting with the whore now and he would kill you in a heartbeat.'

Kinseris's face reddened even as he recognised phrasing chosen deliberately to inflame. 'Shakumi is no whore.'

Darred shot him a look dripping with scorn. 'A beautiful whore is still a whore. And worse than that she is Vasa's whore, and the mother of the squealing brats he drowns in his courtyard fountain.' He saw his friend's face pale and carried on, remorseless. 'Six children at least she has borne him, all but one of them sons and all of them dead, and every one of them has left her changed. You would not recognise the pretty child you knew if you saw her now. Perhaps if not for the first, he might have let them live.'

Kinseris's face went slack with shock.

'The first,' Darred repeated. 'Your daughter.'

Kinseris turned, staggered, catching himself on the table.

'Mine? But we never...'

His affair with Shakumi had been one of stolen glances and impossible fantasies. They had snatched brief meetings but a handful of times before they had been discovered, and in those moments they had done little more than gaze into each other's eyes and whisper foolish promises. It was not possible that a child she had been carrying could have been his, as Darred knew perfectly well. And in the end he had chosen the priesthood over her, submitting to Vasa's violent rage in exchange for his life. He had left her in Kas'Tella and accepted his exile to this far-flung port, so paralysed by fear and relief that he had left her to Vasa's revenge.

But he had not known she was with child, and if he had, what would he have done? He remembered the man he had been almost twenty years ago, full of passion and consumed by jealously that she belonged to another. Had he known she was carrying Vasa's child, even knowing she could not have excused herself from attending the high priest's needs, might that not have steeled his resolve to abandon her? The thought shamed him. But even now, knowing the consequences, he could not be sure which way he would have chosen. Would he have risked his life to save a child not his own, and the lives of the ones who followed, equally innocent and equally strangers to his blood? Yet the child's death angered him for the senseless, selfish waste of revenge.

'You know that, and she knows it,' Darred said. 'But Vasa had only your word and clearly he was not disposed to believe you.' He shrugged, but for one unguarded instant Kinseris could see the lingering resentment in his eyes.

'So, you see, my friend, that you are not the only one who has suffered for your foolishness. Shakumi has lost far more than you, and I...'

He stopped, brushing away the thought as of no consequence. But Kinseris knew he would never be allowed to forget that Darred believed his own period of exile had been a punishment for their friendship, no matter how far and or how high he rose.

Yet Darred bore a share of the guilt, if guilt there was. Eighteen years ago, already bitter and resentful, he had encouraged Kinseris's infatuation with Vasa's concubine, even helped arrange their clandestine meetings. It had been his small rebellion against the authority that bound him to servitude where he wished to rule, and Kinseris had never questioned his motives.

Was he so different? Were not his actions here to protect the common folk merely an expression of his own pathetic rebellion against the man who had taken his career from him? His stubborn refusal to let the injustices of his Order take their hard, miserable lives—what did he do it for, if not revenge? The day would come when the secret would come out and he would be recalled to Kas'Tella to face his master's deadly rage. Not simply whipped until the bones of his ribs stood out through the bloody, torn flesh of his back, this time Kinseris would pay with his life. His fragile network of spies would be irrevocably compromised, the rebel network would falter and fail, and Shrogar's people would be destroyed by Vasa's armies under the remorseless command of Fader Wedh. There would be no redemption, no restoration, and Vasa would have won.

Suddenly the room was too small, too suffocating for the two of them. Carefully, deliberately, Kinseris lifted his glass and drained the last of the liquor. Then he returned the glass to the desk and walked out without another word, leaving Darred to his celebrations. A friendship had ended, and the world had just become a little more dangerous.

FIVE

Amadorn
New Age, 2047

IT WAS FOUR years since Aarin had left Luen behind him, four years since he had turned his back on his father's people. And in those years, he had rarely given a thought to the place he had once called home. But for all the relief he had felt when he had climbed onto the merchant's cart and ridden out of the coastal hills, he discovered in his travels that there were still some things he missed about his homeland.

There was little left of the old devotion in the cities or their people. The country folk remembered best, reliant on the land and all it could give them. There they honoured Tesserion the Maker and blessed Andeira for her bounty. It was there, in the villages and the rolling hills of the southlands, that Aarin felt most at home. He wandered the plains of Situra, working the harvests in the autumn and the lambings in spring, keeping summer and winter for himself, until the day came when he could no longer deny the heat of the fire in his blood. Soon he would leave to brave the mountains of the North. For only there, in the cold wastes of those grey peaks, could he hope to find some sign of the dragons.

When that day finally came, in early summer, he knew he was ready. He slipped out of the barn in the grey light of dawn and it was only as he reached the end of the village that he paused to look back at the place that had been his home every spring since he had left Luen. He had collected the money owed to him the night before. The old farmer had been gruff in his farewells, expressing the hope of seeing him next season, but something in the man's eyes told Aarin he knew he would not be seeing his farmhand again, and was sorry for it.

He had the food and clothes the farmer's wife had pressed on him as he left their cosy cottage. They had taken him in four years previously, little more than a boy, and they had welcomed him back every year with something akin to love for a little-seen son. He would miss them, and the kindness they had shown him, and promised himself he would return one day and repay that kindness if he could.

But, for now, he turned his face to the road. It was time to be gone.

This leave-taking was different to the last. Driven now by longing rather than fear, he could look back on his past flight through wiser eyes. His last years in Luen had been haunted by dreams that grew ugly and twisted, full of a foreboding he could not explain. And gradually that sense of dread had entered his waking life, as though a presence stood always at his shoulder, threatening him. In the end, hounded by irrational fear, he had run. The wool merchant passing through that day had been neither amiable nor fair, and had demanded hard work even for so short a passage, but he had been leaving at once and Aarin could wait no longer. He had just enough time to throw his few possessions in a bag and spend one last moment in front of the silver dragon before the man's harsh voice called him out to the street.

Running out, he had bumped into Brannick. His father's friend had gazed at him with sadness but also relief. He had not tried to stop him leaving— had said little, in fact—though Aarin sensed he wished to say more. He had not waited to find out, still hurt by Brannick's coldness after Ecyas's death. Instead Aarin had muttered a farewell and hastened to the merchant's cart where the man was shouting to his boy to tie down the bales. Brannick watched them leave. He did not wave, nor did he move, until a bend in the road put him out of sight. That memory had haunted Aarin ever since.

The wool merchant had taken a route that skirted the edges of the wildlands heading south. Few travelled any further across that bleak landscape than necessary, journeying to Luen but rarely. For a while Aarin had intended to head to the nearest town in Situra, but as their road peeled off from the boundary of his land he had parted company with the carts, gripped by a sudden urge to see his mother again.

As the train of carts disappeared into the dust, Aarin stood staring at the empty landscape. He had never travelled this far south, never been to Redstone, but he knew where the old manor stood from the tavern talk.

Nearly eight years had passed since Sedaine had disappeared into the storm, and he had heard the rumours. Now and then someone would return from Redstone full of tales of the wisdom and prosperity of the new community there. They all spoke of the way she disregarded the ancient lore, calling instead for her followers to claim their place as the true children of Andeira. The dragons were dead and gone, she told them, and they did not deserve a place in the earth's order.

Everything he believed in cried out against that. But she was his mother, and he had to see her, just once, before he embarked on his journey.

Many of those who returned to spread these rumours eventually left again, and it would cause heated talk among the men in the taverns. Some angrily rejected his mother's pronouncements, others equally passionately embraced them. And each time a few more would make the journey south.

Now Aarin was making that journey himself. When at last the manor came into sight he stopped, throwing down his bag amidst the heather and sitting on a rock to stare at the settlement. The size of it staggered him. Expecting only a rundown building like those of his home, he had been unprepared for the great sprawl that circled the walls of Redstone. He did not think so many of his people had left Luen.

Aarin had sat silently, watching the comings and goings until the sky began to redden with the onset of dusk. Only then had he gathered himself and begun the trek down the muddy road to the gates. And there he had stopped, frozen in shock to see his mother walking towards him, a slight, black-garbed man at her side. The sight of her brought memories crowding back. Her dark hair, glowing red with the last rays of the setting sun, hung glossy and long below her shoulders. She was dressed in finely made leather leggings and tunic that suited her much better than the long skirts he remembered. But she was a stranger to him, unknown and strangely threatening. Unprepared, Aarin had backed into the shadows of the gatehouse and she had passed without seeing him. She stopped just outside the gates and he had heard the words she exchanged with her companion.

'There are things I must attend to elsewhere,' the man had told her, his voice brisk. 'I will return in the autumn.'

His mother murmured something in response, and he heard the man break in harshly. 'It was just as well I was here, Sedaine, and that I could bring you word. Now there can be no misunderstanding over where your duty lies.'

'There never was,' she replied. 'I know my duty, Councillor Darred.'

'Ah, but do you, my dear?' the man had asked softly. 'Don't think that I am unaware of how difficult this must be.' He paused, and Aarin heard the clatter of hooves as a horse was mounted. Then Darred spoke again. 'Remember, Sedaine. All bargains ride on this. Should he come here, you know what you must do. Lose the boy and lose everything.'

'I understand, my lord,' he heard her answer. 'And if you find him first?'

Aarin heard dry laughter. 'Fear not, my lady. I shall still need you. Who else will be able to earn his trust?'

Without waiting for a reply, the man urged his horse into a canter and disappeared into the gathering dusk. Aarin stayed where he was, afraid to breathe in case she heard him. They had mentioned no name, but he had not needed one. He *knew*. Fear kept him pressed into the shadows until long after she had returned to the manor.

So, he had forsaken Redstone without even crossing the threshold and struck out once more to join the track that would take him far from that place. And now, as he faced yet another lonely road, he struggled to force those memories away. It was inevitable, he supposed, that now he was finally embarking on his journey his thoughts would turn to that almost-meeting, for then, as now, he was all alone with a strange country before him.

Settling his bag more comfortably on his shoulder, Aarin shook off all thoughts of his past and prepared to embrace his future. Though he had hesitated and avoided this moment for years, he had spent many hours planning for this day. He would follow the main highway through Situra to Forthtown, the gateway to the northern kingdoms and the first safe crossing of the Istelan west of the Vale. He would not take the Vale's dark road unless he had to, for although he hungered to taste the forces that swirled within its isolated depths, there were warnings of the old forest that he would be foolish to disregard. From Forthtown he would strike north, entering the rolling foothills of the Grey Mountains at midsummer, with several months of good weather before him. He had thought little of what he would do when he reached the peaks, or how he would know what to look for. But there was nowhere else in all of Amadorn with such majestic mountains, and he knew in his heart that if the dragons were to be found anywhere, it would be in those dizzying, grey heights.

As it was, Aarin did not reach Lothane until late in the season, the road from Forthtown far longer and harder than he had imagined. As the warm days began to wane, he took work with the last of the westward caravans and crossed the low passes into Elvelen, uncomfortable at the thought of wintering in his mother's homeland.

That winter was harsh, with fierce frosts and frequent snowstorms, and the border towns were far from welcoming. His slight Lothani lilt marked him as a potential enemy to those veterans of cross-border rivalry, and he was forced to scratch a living where he could, his coin disappearing almost as soon as he earned it. Come spring he was gratefully away, seeking passage to Lothane with the same merchant who had employed him in the autumn. This time he wasted no time in seeking the high passes, welcoming the isolation of the snow-capped peaks after the crowded confines of the last few months.

Aarin spent midsummer in the Kamarai pass, alone but for a small fire, reflecting on the year that had just gone and looking ahead to the next with trepidation.

'Tesserion guide me,' he whispered aloud. 'Show me where to look.'

The words sounded unnaturally loud in the night, and he realised that in the weeks since he had parted with the caravans, he had had no cause to use his voice. For a moment he was tempted to abandon his search for a time and head down from the mountains to the people of the valleys, but only for a moment. It took only the unconscious act of feeding more energy to the spluttering fire to remind him of the reason he had chosen this path. The magic that was all around him, in the ground beneath his feet and the currents of the air, was the spur that forced him to continue. He could never cease his search, for it was all that sustained his lonely heart.

Needing to connect with the magic that drove him, Aarin reached out. He felt the chill of the night crisp against his skin and welcomed the touch of the elements. But he would not give in to them, not with the fire that blazed before him and the rock of the mountains at his feet. He was older now, and wiser, and he recognised the danger his father had warned him of—the pull of the emptiness at the edges of his perception that would snare him and carry him away, as it had done to his father. The contact he sought instead was guarded and knowing, and the magic responded to his perfect control to cradle and protect him and soothe away the loneliness.

As he felt the natural world rise up to meet him, Aarin allowed his consciousness to meld with the deep thrum of the earth. Connection with the elements always brought him peace. His father had taught him to think of them as the building blocks of all magic. Fire, Earth, Water, and Air. Each gave rise to a variety of forces a mage learned to control and manipulate into an intricate web of energies. But it was not as it had been. When the link with the dragons had ended, so too had humanity's access to full elemental mastery. The magic that remained to them was incomplete, and some things had been irrevocably lost.

Both races commanded different aspects of the earth's forces. In keeping with their given nature, the great dragons had natural mastery of the element of Fire. It was inseparable from their very beings. They lived and breathed fire, a race birthed in the white-hot crucible of the earth's core and brought to sentient life sheltered in its fiery embrace. And when this most ancient race had taken its place in a world still in its infancy, they had soared through the empty sky on huge wings, their scales tempered to steely perfection through the scalding passage of their creation. For theirs also had been mastery of the winds and the silent stone. They had made their homes in the vast rock caverns and steep, blackened escarpments of the ancient world, and there they had remained until the coming of man.

In the beginning, Ecyas had told him, all of mankind was born able to touch the magic of Andeira. Their lives had been the catalyst that changed the face of the world, altering the landscape of creation forever. Humanity had drawn energies from the very soil of the earth. The air they breathed had changed its makeup, their needs had spun trees and plants, created great oceans and rivers and trickling mountain streams. Their turbulent, passionate natures encompassed the constant growth in all living things. Harnessing the resources of the earth had been their gift, and the element of Water, so essential for the life that evolved with their coming, was the fundamental aspect that was solely theirs to command.

But the nature of their creation yet sat uneasily with the world of the dragons. New, green life could not flourish in the barren landscape of the dragons' haunts. The tidal oceans that flooded the low places were an anathema to those creatures of Fire, and fear had ruled the minds of men until the races had come together and put aside their individual interests. Through the ecstasy of the Joining, both human and dragon had gained a new understanding of the world they shared. Aligning their gifts, they had brought harmony to a divided earth, forging it anew in its unity. The purified elements had granted access to the realm of Spirit, the finishing gloss of perfection. Legend spoke of the moment of Joining as the day Andeira glowed with golden light as the freely given gift of trust between the races set the final seal on a creation thousands of years in the making.

But something had gone wrong. The link had ended, and the dragons had vanished. The Joining had been severed and the elemental harmony that sustained Andeira had been shattered. Why and how no one living now knew, and only those like Aarin, gifted with the perception to hear Andeira's lament, could understand just how much it was hurting them all.

The dragons had to be found. Over the centuries many had searched, but as time moved on, fewer had departed on the long journey. Now no one was left who remembered the last. Ecyas's youthful dreams of the search had been delayed then crushed completely by Sedaine's arrival and her departure. Only Aarin would not give up, not even when all hope had been abandoned by his people. Because of his father. Because of Ecyas's dreams and his stories and the burning in his blood from the long-ago touch of Fire. But most of all, because he had made a promise to his father the day his body burned, and he could not, would not, let that go.

SIX

RENEWED CONVICTION SUSTAINED Aarin through to late autumn when the early snows forced him down from the mountains. He had scoured every cave, every hidden place around the pass of Kamarai, and found nothing besides evidence of long-abandoned human habitation. That the dragons had once abided in such places he had no doubt, but the suspicion was creeping up on him that these ancient peaks were still too young to remember the first ages of the world.

At last, bitter with disappointment, he surrendered his search for the winter and retreated to the valleys. He returned to Lothane to find a nation in turmoil, rumours flying of the death of the prince and the madness of the king. The kingdom was falling into chaos, and he was in Kamarai town just three days before he saw just how deep it had sunk.

The armourer he visited to purchase a new dagger shrugged regretfully at his request. 'The Eagles were through here a week ago, lad, I'm sorry. Took all my stock and I'm still waiting for a delivery of materials. Can't promise you anything in under a fortnight unless you can find me some steel. Clean wiped me out and left only worthless royal chits to pay for the goods.'

'Royal chits?' Aarin asked in surprise. 'The king has hired mercenaries?'

'Most of the northern clans. Though whether it is the king who hired them I couldn't say. Like I said, worthless. Who should I present them to for payment?'

Aarin nodded sympathetically and muttered his thanks.

'You could try Jeran over in Besuna, if you're in real need,' the armourer called as he left. 'The mercenaries were heading east to Rhiannas and likely passed it by. It's not far, perhaps a day's walk south.'

'Thank you, I will,' Aarin replied, fingering the broken shards of his hunting knife. He felt lost without the little weapon, more so since realising the troubled state of the kingdom.

He found the road to Besuna with little difficulty and followed the dirt track through the hills. The village turned out to be little more than a collection of dwellings, an inn, and the armourer's shack, but it was soon apparent that the mercenaries had not passed it by. The houses were shuttered and the knot of people in the street vanished inside at his approach.

His head heavily bandaged, the old armourer gestured sadly in answer to Aarin's query. A sweep of the small workroom revealed the thoroughness with which the mercenaries had carried out their search. Tables were upturned, tools strewn on the floor, and when Aarin turned to take his leave the bruise on the old man's head took on an uglier significance.

'Did they do that?'

Jeran nodded, his eyes flat. 'Took our food too,' he said as he leant down stiffly to right a fallen bench. Aarin took hold of the other end and helped him set it upright, assisting the old man as he sat shakily down. 'They threatened the widow who runs the inn, took everything she had. I don't understand it.'

'They're mercenaries,' Aarin replied through his simmering outrage. 'What do they care about other folks?'

'They have never troubled us before, but this time...' Jeran's lined face crumpled as he surveyed the ruin of his workshop. 'We did not think. We welcomed them. They are usually good for business. They come here to have the dents in their blades hammered out, and drink ale by the barrel.'

'And this is how they repaid you. Why?'

The old man sighed. 'I do not know, lad. There have been troubles. Everyone has heard it. But not here. Their leader told me I must give them my weapons, by order of the crown. I told him they are not for us, but to sell, and there have been no raids in these parts for many years.'

Aarin left the armourer slowly setting his workshop to rights, and took the southern road out of the village, eager to put some distance between himself and this evidence of the looming unrest. It was a few miles out of Besuna that he came upon the mercenary. The man was lying by the side of the road, only his boots visible through the thick screen of bushes. Signs of a struggle marked the stretch of road, spent arrows lying in the mud, and here and there what appeared to be blood stains spattered the ground. Aarin approached the prone man cautiously, his broken knife in his hand, but as he pushed aside the branches his fear dissolved into anger. Dressed in a padded tunic over leather leggings, he wore the faded badge of an eagle on his left shoulder that identified him as one of the mercenaries who had raided Besuna. The right side of the tunic was soaked with blood and the dark face was patterned with bruises.

Aarin wavered, half tempted to leave him where he lay, but he found he could not. He knelt, placing his fingers on the exposed throat and felt for a pulse. It was there, faint but steady, and he turned his attention to the red stain leaking through the tunic.

The man did not stir as he lifted the garment. The wound curled in a vicious slash along the mercenary's ribs from under his right shoulder round onto his chest. It was nasty, and had bled heavily, and Aarin sat back on his heels, wondering what he should do. He could not leave the man where he was to bleed to death, but neither could he carry him, and they were several miles from the nearest town. And even if they were not, he knew the clansman would find no help there. He remembered the desolation on the face of the old armourer and guessed that the inhabitants of Besuna were more likely to assist the man's passage into death than try to save his life.

The only shelter close to hand was the small thicket where the mercenary lay that bordered a grove of trees. In the trees they would have some protection from the elements and be out of sight of the road. If there were bandits around, or local townsfolk out for revenge, it would not be safe for him to be caught out in the open in the company of this clansman.

The mercenary showed no sign of waking as Aarin took his broken knife to the blood-stained fabric and wrapped a makeshift bandage round the injury. He had no experience of treating injuries. He knew only that he had to stop the bleeding and that movement would certainly aggravate it.

He looked at the sky. The sun was already beginning to dip behind the western horizon and there was only another hour of daylight left. The man before him stirred and groaned, a slight tremor running through his long frame. Aarin felt the coolness of his skin and knew he would need a fire to keep him warm. He sighed, glancing again at the unconscious face. The mercenary had no claim to his aid and might even be a danger to him, but he would surely die without care and warmth. The most prudent course would be to leave him and continue in the hope of finding somewhere more sheltered before stopping for the night, but that would mean abandoning an injured man to die alone in the cold of the autumn dark.

Angry with himself, Aarin shifted his position and placed an arm under the mercenary's good shoulder. The man was taller and heavier and a dead weight besides, and Aarin managed to do no more than raise his upper body to rest against his chest. Gritting his teeth, he heaved again, but his grip slipped and the man fell heavily to the ground, crying out in sudden pain. His eyes opened, glazed and unfocused, and stared into Aarin's, his mouth forming words that never came. Then his eyes rolled back as he passed out again. There was no help for it. Shaking him mercilessly, Aarin was rewarded by a flickering of eyelids and a muffled groan. A moment later the brown eyes snapped open, alert and wary.

A strong hand grasped his forearm. 'Who...?' The word came out on a ragged breath as the mercenary struggled to push himself onto his elbows. 'Stay back...'

'It's all right,' Aarin soothed. 'I'm a friend.'

'Don't... know... you,' the man breathed, his arms collapsing under him.

Aarin saw resignation cross the man's face as he slumped back. As his eyes slipped closed, the mage ground his teeth in frustration. 'I need you to help me. You're hurt. I need you to get up. I have to get you somewhere safe.'

He did not know whether his words had been understood, but when he reached out cautiously to place his arms under the man's shoulders, he felt muscles tense in an effort to help. Staggering under the weight, he managed to haul them both to their feet, the mercenary hanging at his side. Placing the limp arm firmly round his neck, Aarin took a step forward. For a moment it seemed like the injured man would collapse, but then his legs started to work, dragging his feet slowly over the uneven ground.

They made slow progress, with Aarin supporting most of the clansman's weight, stopping every few steps to readjust his grip.

'Help me, damn you,' he muttered, and to his surprise the weight on his shoulders eased a little. Then the mercenary stumbled and almost fell, dragging them both to their knees.

Aarin heard a string of curses spoken in a harsh tongue, as the man braced his good arm on the ground and staggered back to his feet. Aarin caught him as he swayed and let the momentum carry them to the edge of the trees.

The grove was tiny, the trees strung in groups around a muddy clearing. Aarin laid the mercenary down and saw he was once more unconscious. His wounded side was bleeding again.

It was Aarin's turn to curse. If he could not stop the bleeding, all his efforts so far would come to nothing. With no other option, he found himself tearing strips from his own spare shirt. Peeling away the sodden bandage, he tied the fresh one more tightly around the injury. Then he took off his cloak and tucked it around the mercenary's shoulders.

Having done as much as he could, Aarin turned his attentions to building a fire. With the dusk had come a bitter wind, and they would both need the warmth a fire would provide. The autumn had been wet, and most of the dead wood was damp and rotten, but Aarin coaxed the moisture from the branches and placed the tinder-dry wood in a growing pile in the centre of the small clearing.

With the magic singing in his blood, he allowed his attention to wander outside himself, feeling the currents on the air that spoke of the coming frosts, the distant rainstorms, the cruel snows of midwinter. He forgot the mercenary as he worked, losing himself in the whispers of the wind, and the senses that should have been alert missed the small sounds of the man waking behind him. It was only when he laid down the last log and began to think of lighting the fire that he heard a rustle of movement, but before he could turn a heavy weight pushed him flat, then a hand grabbed his hair and forced his head up. Aarin felt cold steel at his neck and a deep voice growled in his ear, 'Don't move, or I'll slit your throat.'

He did not breathe, cursing himself for a fool.

'Who are you?' the man demanded. 'Where is my company?'

When he did not reply, the pressure at his throat eased a fraction.

'Aarin,' he gasped. 'And I don't know where your companions are. You were alone when I found you.'

Silence greeted this statement, but when he tried to twist around, the hand in his hair forced his head back down.

'I said don't move!'

Aarin spat out a mouthful of dirt. 'I am not your enemy. You were hurt. You needed help.'

'I don't need your help,' the mercenary retorted, but he released his rough hold and the weight was lifted from Aarin's back.

Aarin rolled over and scrambled backwards. 'Then leave,' he said, rubbing his throat. 'If you can,' he added, looking into the fierce, dark face. The man still held the knife, but his eyes were glazed, and one arm was wrapped protectively around his injured side.

'You shouldn't be moving,' he pointed out, but he kept his distance. He was not a complete fool.

'I'm fine,' the soldier growled, but his hand was red from fresh bleeding.

Aarin sighed, groping behind him for his pack. He pulled out the remains of his spare shirt and threw it at the mercenary who looked at him in confusion. 'Go on, take it. You've reopened that slash and I wouldn't like you to bleed to death after all the effort I've gone to.'

The man reached out to take the shirt and pressed it to his side. 'Thank you,' he muttered, the words barely audible. 'Why are you helping me?'

'I honestly have no idea,' Aarin retorted. 'After what your people did to the villagers. Take what you need and go if that's what you want.'

He turned his back and after a time he heard the mercenary riffling through his pack. Moments later, the man appeared beside him, perched awkwardly on his heels. He held out a bundle of soft fabric.

'I'm Kallis. And I'm sorry for hurting you.' He gestured with the cloth and Aarin raised his hand to his neck. The knife had sliced a shallow cut across the skin and his fingers came away sticky with blood. He had not even felt it. Grateful, he took the cloth and dabbed it to the wound.

'What about you?' he asked, looking pointedly at the makeshift bandage Kallis had fashioned from his shirt. 'You should let me look at that.'

'I can care for myself,' came the immediate response, but when Aarin gave him a disbelieving look he thought he saw a faint smile curve the corners of the mercenary's mouth. 'Most of the time.'

He sat back with a grunt of pain. The shirt around his midriff was slowing turning red. Aarin watched with growing concern, and when he saw the mercenary's eyes flicker, he reached out to steady him. Kallis's shoulders tensed at his touch then just as quickly relaxed as he sank all the way back.

'Stubborn fool,' Aarin whispered as he knelt beside him and peeled back the bandage. A hand grabbed his wrist.

'I heard that,' Kallis murmured. 'Need to stop the bleeding... stitch it. Press down hard... will not... hurt me.'

'I doubt that,' Aarin replied wryly as Kallis's hand fell away. He did as he was told and felt the mercenary flinch in pain, then go limp. Grateful that the man was unconscious, he kept pressure on the wound until the blood flow lessened and finally stopped. Then he rewrapped the bandage and lowered the mercenary's shirt. He could not attempt to close the wound in such poor light and was thankful for it. It was not a task he relished and he would need the mercenary's instruction. The treatment of injuries was not something he was familiar with.

In the half-light he studied his find, seeing him properly for the first time. His skin was dusky, not a natural tan as Aarin had first assumed, and his close-cropped hair was dark and coarse. Not northern, perhaps not even Amadorian.

Aarin knew little of the mercenary clans to which Kallis belonged, but he had believed them a close-knit society, distrustful of outsiders. And there was something unfamiliar in the way Kallis spoke, a slight thickening of the vowels that marked him as a foreigner almost as clearly as his dark skin.

But whatever else the man was, he was also badly hurt. The wound was bad and Aarin was no healer. He realised that there was a very real possibility that Kallis would die before he had the chance to find out any more about him.

It was late the next afternoon when the mercenary woke again. Aarin had his back to him and heard the gasp of pain as he rediscovered the damage to his body. He turned to find Kallis curled on his side, his fingers pressed so tight against the wound that his knuckles were white.

Aarin crossed swiftly to him and tried to prise his hands away, fearful that he would cause himself more hurt. Kallis's eyes snapped open and Aarin watched as fear turned to confusion then recognition.

'You,' he breathed. 'I'd hoped you were just a bad dream.' Then, 'You didn't stitch it.'

'Too dark. And I will need your help.'

Kallis's head sank back. 'Perfect,' he muttered. 'Just my luck to be found by a green boy who's never done more than bandage a cut finger.'

Aarin felt a growing irritation. 'Unfortunate indeed. You could still be lying in that ditch enjoying your own company. I can take you back if you wish.'

The mercenary grimaced as Aarin tugged on the bandage harder than necessary. The lines around his eyes tightened. Satisfied, Aarin finished unwinding the length of soiled cloth with more care.

'Give me a moment,' Kallis muttered, then sucked in a breath as the pain flared again. 'I may have deserved that. You'll need to boil some water.'

'Already done.'

Kallis sighed. 'Remarkably keen to stick things in me, aren't you?'

'Just trying to save your life.' As Aarin straightened to fetch the water, Kallis's hand on his arm detained him.

'You have. And for that I thank you. Not many would have stopped, and fewer still would help me as you have. You hold a blood-debt of mine and I will not forget it.'

A glib response dried on Aarin's lips. Caught wrong-footed by the sudden shift, he nevertheless recognised that something of importance had just passed between them.

Kallis released his arm and lay back. 'Now give me back my belt.'

It took Aarin a moment to register his words, then he remembered the belt he had removed the night before. He returned to the fire and found it discarded near his pack. Kallis nodded his thanks as Aarin handed it to him and began to rifle through the small pouches. Items fell onto his chest—a whetstone, fire strikers, scraps of leather, coarse thread, a silver coin and three coppers. Aarin watched in fascination, picking up a small wooden carving of a woman. Kallis glanced at him and when his eyes settled on the carving he reached out and snatched it from Aarin's hands.

The mage shrugged and picked up a small bag. Feeling Kallis's eyes on him he shook it, expecting at any moment to have it to taken from him. The bag was heavy and solid but its contents made no sound. He turned it over and shook it again. Fine white powder streamed out, covering his hands and leggings. He glared at Kallis who watched him with a lop-sided grin.

'Chalk. Here.' He held up cloth-wrapped bundle. 'Now get the water.'

Grinding his teeth, Aarin did as he was instructed, setting the skin of boiled water securely between two stones. Then he unwrapped the bundle and blanched as he saw what it contained. Silk thread was wrapped around a needle the length of his index finger.

Kallis caught sight of his white face. 'I know it looks ugly, but it's sharp as a scorned woman. Are you up to this? I'd not relish the task all to myself.'

Aarin nodded. The thought of that needle pulled through his flesh evoked a sudden rush of sympathy. 'Just tell me what to do.'

SEVEN

AS AARIN FINISHED the last stitch he set the needle down carefully and stumbled away. He got only a few steps before he was hunched over and retching. Kallis had endured the ordeal in grim silence, the only visible sign of his pain in his laboured breathing and the tightening around his eyes.

'The first time I had to do what you just did, I emptied my guts, same as you.'

Aarin nodded, grateful for the words he did not believe. He looked from the bloody rags to the crude stitches that marked the mercenary's side and swallowed past a fresh surge of nausea. Moving unsteadily back to Kallis, he began to collect up the soiled bandages, intending to bury them, when he felt a hand brush against his sleeve.

'Besuna. You were there?'

Aarin nodded. 'I arrived after you had done your *work*.'

Kallis winced. 'I am not proud of what we did, but we had our orders.'

'Orders?' Aarin scoffed, the anger helping him forget the queasiness. 'You were ordered to steal from widows and beat old men senseless? Who would give such orders, and what kind of men would carry them out?'

'For what it's worth, I never laid a hand on the old man,' Kallis told him hoarsely. 'But neither did I stop it, and if that makes me guilty in your eyes, so be it. But the old fool should have known better than to offer defiance to Girion in a rage. None of us relished what we had to do, but we had orders to strip the border towns of weapons and for the most part we accomplished that without bloodshed.'

'And that makes it all right?' Aarin demanded. 'What threat are those villagers to the king in Rhiannas?'

'Oh, you are priceless,' Kallis replied, as he attempted to raise himself on his elbows. 'The villagers are no threat to anyone. But these people have suffered at the hands of one side or the other for a hundred years and more—

long enough to know it is far easier to comply when the king's troops come through. Well, they should have. They may have had peace for a generation, but the old squabbles are rising to the surface and they will feel it first.'

'What are you talking about?'

Kallis shook his head in disbelief. 'The crown prince of Lothane is dead. Murder some say. He succumbed to a sickness that not even the king's most experienced physicians could cure. Do you know what that means?'

'You tell me.'

'It means the kingdom is without an heir,' Kallis explained, a grimace flashing across his face. 'And Lothane's enemies will soon be lining up to take full advantage. The king has cousins in Elvelen, and they will not sit quietly while he grieves for his only son. An heir must be named, and soon, before every distant relation comes out of the woodwork to make their claim. If that happens, when that happens,' he corrected himself, 'this country will sink into civil war so fast and deep that it will be years before order is restored. Who do you think will suffer then? The lords in their grand city mansions, or the villagers in these forsaken borderlands? The rivalry between Lothane and Elvelen has always been decided here, far away from the courts of kings.'

Aarin shrugged as Kallis lay back, exhausted by his outburst. 'If you seek to convince me you care about the safety of these people then you can save yourself the effort. Since when have the clans cared about the people caught up in the squabbles between rulers? If not for these wars you would be no more than lawless bandits.'

'I did not say we cared about the squabbles of rulers, or the wellbeing of these people. Nor do I,' Kallis retorted, his voice strained. 'I am merely attempting to explain to an ignorant boy who should know better why things are the way they are.'

'Why?' Aarin demanded. 'If I am so ignorant, why bother enlighten me?'

'Because you saved my life!' The words were almost a shout, and he curled around his wounded side. 'Tesserion find me a fool, I want you to understand that the man you saved is not as undeserving of your trouble as you seem to think!'

Aarin was at his side in an instant. 'We do not have to speak of this now.

If I have judged you harshly there will time for you to prove me wrong when you have recovered.'

'I do not need to be coddled,' Kallis growled, pushing his hands away. 'I have marched three days over the mountains hurt far worse than this.'

Aarin moved away. 'Very well. Since you have no need of me you may as well be on your way.'

'Now who's the fool? Sit down, boy, and listen. I will explain this just one more time.'

Anxious now that the mercenary would do himself more harm, Aarin sat, drawing his knees up to his chest and watching Kallis sullenly.

The mercenary nodded, relaxing taut muscles with visible relief. 'The people of the borderlands must be disarmed for their own protection as well as the king's. That way they have no weapons to be taken by the enemy, and it also ensures that they are not foolish enough to fight, for then they will all be slaughtered. It has happened before. I do not pretend that the king cares more for the second than he does for the first, but his actions serve them just as well.' He gave Aarin a hard look. 'Do not make the mistake of thinking that I enjoy this duty, but when my captain undertakes a contract, it is not for me to question him, nor to forget that in doing so he puts money in my pocket at little risk to myself or my brothers. Do you understand?'

When Aarin nodded, he lay back. 'Now leave me alone. I need to sleep.'

Kallis slept for almost two days, and Aarin understood that this was a man who had dealt often with injury and submitted willingly to the demands of his body. They spoke little, for even when the mercenary was awake, he was irritable and sullen. Aarin suspected that pain and unaccustomed dependence on a stranger lay at the heart of it, but that did not stop him fuming each time he found himself on the receiving end of Kallis's temper.

Yet despite this, he found himself drawn to the man. He admired his self-sufficiency, his worldly knowledge, and was intrigued by the unknown he embodied. Through the early days of Kallis's convalescence, Aarin refrained from the questions he dearly wanted to ask. On the third night he got his opportunity as they sat together round the small fire.

'The night I found you, what happened?'

Kallis stopped playing with his knife. 'Why?' The tone was flat.

Aarin ignored the warning. 'I would like to know who I saved you from.'

He left unspoken his real question, but Kallis's eyes narrowed as though he sensed it nonetheless. 'Outlaws, bandits,' he said dismissively. 'The land around here is crawling with them. They ambushed us just as we reached the bend in the road. Besuna's handful of old men and farm boys could not have covered the distance so fast, nor are they such fools.'

'And outlaws are?' Aarin asked, mortified that his thoughts had been so transparent. 'I saw none of their dead, only you.'

'They outnumbered us. And they would have carried off their dead. As would we.'

'Yet they left you.'

A flash of anger crossed the mercenary's face. 'We do not leave our own behind,' he replied sharply. 'They must have thought me taken, or they themselves were hard pressed. There was no sign of any others?'

Aarin heard the weight behind the casual question and felt a stirring of sympathy. 'Of a fight, yes. But no others. You were alone.'

Kallis nodded, lapsing into silence. Aarin turned away, feeling awkward.

'Ten years I was with them,' the mercenary muttered darkly after a time. 'Ten years, and they left me behind.'

Aarin looked up, surprised. 'You were all but hidden. Perhaps they simply could not find you.'

Kallis shot him a dark look and did not reply. He was silent so long that Aarin gave up on the conversation.

'They broke their oath when they left me.'

'What?'

Haunted dark eyes met his as Kallis said, 'From the moment I was sworn into their brotherhood, each and every member of the Clan had a duty to me, and I to them. They should never have allowed one of their own to fall into the hands of an enemy.'

'I am an enemy?'

'Don't be pedantic, boy,' Kallis warned. 'You know what I mean. As a last resort, if the wound had been mortal and they were too hard pressed to carry me with them, they should have slit my throat. Either way, we should not be having this conversation. Ten years,' he said again, and this time he made no attempt to hide his rancour. 'Ten years and still they could not do me that honour.'

Aarin stared at him. 'You're upset they didn't kill you?'

Kallis looked away, but not before Aarin saw the confused anger on his face, and he understood that the mercenary was not so much angry that his clan had failed to kill him, but that in the end they had not been his clan at all.

'Ten years is a long time,' he agreed, keeping his voice neutral. 'If you were not always of the clans, what were you before?'

'Before?' Kallis shrugged. 'Before I was nothing. My parents were little more than beggars in this land, scratching out a living where they could. That life was never for me, so I set out to make my own, and a hard time I had of it. It isn't easy making your way in Amadorn with a face like this. You're none too fond of my countrymen.'

'Your countrymen?'

Kallis gave him a strange look. 'I'm Caledani, boy. Perhaps you have heard of it?'

'I know where Caledan is,' Aarin muttered. 'I just didn't realise it was possible for an outsider to join the clans.'

Kallis grunted. 'It's not impossible.'

By now Aarin had learned to respect that tone and did not press him for answers.

'I think I am entitled to a question,' Kallis said into the awkward pause. 'Since you now know about me, where are you from? You speak like a northerner, but you don't look like one, and you've certainly displayed your ignorance of these parts.'

Aarin ignored the jibe, recognising the distraction for what it was. And Kallis was right. The Northern peoples were mostly tall and fair. His own hair was not dark enough to be called black as his mother's had been—the legacy of her Farnorian mother—but the rich brown locks held a hint of the red that had been hers in certain lights. He had inherited her fine, chiselled features, though his eyes, shifting grey like an autumn sky, were the image of his father's. Like his father he had not grown tall, yet he lacked the broadness of shoulder that had made Ecyas seem so big when he was a child. His speech he had inherited from his mother, who was northern to her core, but the land of her birth would always remain a stranger to his blood.

'East of Situra,' Aarin replied vaguely, and could see Kallis working it out. East of Situra there was only the wilds.

'You're a long way from home,' he said after a while. 'Now I understand why you know so little about the affairs of the kingdom. I didn't think your folk mixed much with others.'

Aarin gave a shrug. 'I have been gone a long time. It's not my home any longer.'

'Quarrelled with your father, did you?' Kallis asked good-naturedly. 'What did he do? Disapprove of the girl you took a liking to?'

'My father is dead.'

Kallis grimaced. 'I'm sorry.' He shrugged. 'Mine too. Your mother?'

Aarin looked away. It had been years since he had last seen his mother and where her path had taken her since that day he could not guess. When he turned back to the fire, Kallis was watching him curiously.

'I had heard,' he said casually, 'that your people could not survive long outside your lands, that there is some sort of magic there that sustains your lives yet destroys all others.'

Aarin dismissed this with an impatient shake of his head. 'That is just superstition.'

'Superstitions often hold a grain of truth. I went to your wildlands once, years ago. We were in the service of a Naveen lordling who believed it would be quicker to cross that wilderness than circling around and fording the Istelan at Carter's Ferry as any sane person would do. I'll grant that on a map it looks like a shortcut, but we chased our tails there for three weeks. Some even claimed the land itself was trying to trick us.'

Struck by a sudden fondness for the unpredictable landscape of his home, Aarin grinned. 'It can be confusing.'

'Confusing?' Kallis's eyebrows climbed skyward. 'We are accustomed to travelling through unfamiliar territory. The Eagles do not get lost. So, there really is no magic there?'

'I didn't say that,' Aarin said slowly, carefully. 'And it is true that those not of my... my people... find it hard to live there, but that is only because they do not understand the land the way we do.'

Kallis levered himself up on his elbow. 'And what way is that?' he asked curiously. 'Are you also magicians?'

Aarin drew in a sharp breath. 'The magicians are charlatans. What they do is not magic.'

Kallis gave him a doubtful look. 'Now you are playing with me. I have witnessed their magic with my own eyes. I have seen them create a whole army of soldiers. They –'

'Did they fight?' Aarin interrupted. 'Did you fight them?'

'We did not. Only a fool would have engaged so many. We retreated that day, but...'

Aarin grinned. 'You should have attacked. Those soldiers were not real, and they could not have hurt you. They were an illusion, as are all things the magicians create, illusions spun from the belief of those who see them.'

Kallis's face twisted in sudden anger. 'Are you trying to get me killed?'

Aarin shook his head, holding out his hand. On his palm lay a twig. 'What do you see?'

'What?'

'What do you see? In my hand?'

Kallis shook his head in frustration. 'A stick. What –?'

'Now what do you see?'

Kallis looked again, then jerked back. 'Put that down,' he said sharply. 'I did not mean to mock you.'

Aarin held out the knife hilt first. 'Take it then.'

The mercenary gave him a long, measured look then reached out and grasped the little dagger between his thumb and forefinger. A moment later he dropped it with a yelp of surprise.

'Is something wrong?' Aarin asked as Kallis stared at the knife.

The mercenary did not reply. He picked up the knife again, turning it over in his hand and running his fingers down the flat of the blade. 'I don't understand. I see a dagger yet I feel a piece of wood. How is that possible?'

'Because it is a piece of wood. I cannot change the true nature of a thing and create another, just as the magicians cannot. To do that would be to bring a thing into this world that was never meant to be here. Creation is only for the Maker.'

'Leave theology out of this, boy,' Kallis replied gruffly as he continued playing with the knife. 'How is it that I can see something that is not real?'

'You see the knife because you do not believe me. Your eyes tell you it is there, and it is hard for you to disregard what you see before you. If you wish to banish the illusion, you must convince yourself that I speak the truth.' He paused, measuring the moment, then said, 'Try it.'

'What?'

'Try to cut yourself with the knife. It will not hurt you, I promise,' he added hastily as the mercenary's expression darkened.

'It had better not,' he grumbled, and sliced the blade across his open palm. The skin flushed red in its wake but there was no blood, nothing other than the slight scratch a twig would leave.

For a moment there was silence as Kallis examined his palm and the knife, then he laughed aloud and snapped the twig in two, tossing the broken halves into the fire.

'Nothing but tricks after all. To think that all these years the magicians have inspired so much fear with so little cause. Though,' he said more slowly, 'something in me is disappointed that the magic is not real.'

Aarin's head jerked up. 'It is real. It is the only real thing there is.'

Kallis rolled his eyes and nodded his head at the fire. 'That was not real.'

'I said that the magicians' power is false, not the magic. It is woven into Andeira's very being. It *is* her being. Our world survives only because of that magic, and that too is why she is dying.'

He stopped, catching sight of Kallis's disbelieving smile. The mercenary shook his head, still grinning.

'You're a strange one. The world is not dying. Look around you. The trees grow, the flowers bloom and animals graze. The sun rises and sets each day, and believe me, I would notice if it did not.'

'That is not what I mean,' Aarin insisted. 'Andeira will endure, she will always endure, but the land we know will change, and continue changing until we can no longer survive here. Thousands of years ago the world's magic— its harmony—was broken, and ever since we have faded. Each day we lose something precious and do not even realise it. We think all will be this way forever and we are wrong. From each generation to the next the world around us changes, the winters grow colder, the summers warmer, and the waters of the world rise, but it happens so slowly we never notice. We don't look, we don't listen, we...'

He broke off, embarrassed. The fire in his blood burned with a heat he had not felt in years, and he had to clasp his hands together to stop them trembling. He looked at Kallis and saw that the mercenary was watching him steadily. He mumbled something and turned away, discomforted by the intensity of his regard, but Kallis caught his arm.

'I'm listening. You have earned that much from me.' Then his eyes narrowed, and he shifted his grip on Aarin's wrist, his fingers probing the skin beneath the thin shirt. When he looked up his face was full of concern. 'There is a fever on you. Why did you say nothing?'

Aarin jerked his arm free and tugged his cuff down. 'I'm fine. I must be too close to the fire.'

'I am closer, and I am not so hot. You helped me. Let me help you.'

'No.' Aarin hugged his knees to his chest. 'It is not a fever, and not a danger to me or I would have died long since.' He forced himself to look Kallis in the eye as he said, 'The Fire burnt me long ago, to remind me that its nature is not mine to master. I should have died, but my father saved me. But I did not remember the lesson. My father is dead because once more I reached out where I should not have, and again he saved me, but he could not save himself and neither could I. My father died because I killed him.'

The words hurt, they hurt as much to say now as they had all those years ago when he had understood what he had done. Aarin could feel tears starting in his eyes and angrily brushed them away.

'Tears for your father are nothing to be ashamed of,' Kallis said gently, reading his thoughts. 'Your father sounds like a good man who loved you very much. Do you think he would have shed no tears for you had you been the one to die?'

'You don't understand,' Aarin protested in a choked voice. 'It was my fault. And my tears are for me because I can't bear it. What does that make me?'

'Human,' Kallis said simply. 'Look, boy, I cannot tell you that your guilt is misplaced. Only you know what happened that day, but you are right. I cannot pretend to understand your talk of magic and warnings. So, if you want to bludgeon yourself with your guilt, do not hide behind my ignorance to do so. Tell me.'

Aarin looked up, startled. His first thought was to refuse. He had not spoken to any but Brannick of his father's death, and those memories were painful enough. Not with any outsider had he dared talk of the magic so candidly. Yet no other person outside Luen had ever offered him such understanding, let alone invited him to speak of the desire that lay so close to his heart. It would be a relief to unburden himself, to share his hopes and the fears, and suddenly it mattered little that his listener might not share his beliefs or understand the mysteries of the world that came to him as naturally as breathing. It was enough that he would listen.

EIGHT

'DRAGONS?' KALLIS LAUGHED, shaking his head. 'I have heard some tales in my time, but that has to be the tallest. Boy, the dragons are just a myth. You're chasing dreams.'

When Aarin remained stubbornly silent, the mercenary sighed. 'Why?' he asked. 'Why would you waste your life? What makes you think they are hiding somewhere waiting to be found?'

'Because we are here. If the dragons were truly gone, this world would be dead.'

'Ah, that again. The dragons are part of this, this...' Kallis waved his arm vaguely. 'This magic harmony you were telling me about? Now you're sounding like Caledan's bloody priests.'

'Caledan's priests?' Aarin asked, feeling his heart lurch with unexpected excitement. 'What do they say?'

Kallis opened his mouth to speak then seemed to think better of it. 'It doesn't matter. They're just, well, let us just say they are not known for their devotion to the truth.'

Aarin felt a surge of frustration. He was about to insist when the mercenary turned to him, and Aarin recognised his expression as the one he wore when he prepared to hold forth on a subject he felt Aarin should understand.

'I grew up in Caledan,' Kallis told him, and Aarin noticed that when he spoke of his homeland his accent thickened. 'My parents made the journey to Amadorn when I was maybe ten summers, but until then I lived on the edges of the great Northern Desert. That is a hard place. Water's scarce, almost non-existent in the deeper desert, and the sun bakes down day after day, year after year. It is so hot in the day that the sand will scorch the skin off your feet, and the nights are so harsh that even if you survive the day, you might die of cold. Now that's a place I could imagine dragons.'

He propped himself up on one elbow, and his voice held a hint of nostalgia.

'When I was young, I used to hunt the *menetas* near my home. They are big lizards,'—he held out his arms just short of their full extent—'that live in the desert. They're fearsome creatures, vicious.' He laughed. 'Well, so they seemed to a boy. They have big claws and sharp teeth, and they are not afraid to use either. They spend most of the day sleeping in the sun, just lying there when every sensible person has found a bit of shade, and if you were quiet you could catch them unawares. Of course, that was the easy part.'

'Why did you hunt them?

Kallis shrugged. 'They are considered bad luck. My people believe they are fire spirits, because sometimes on a winter night you might find a circle of them just outside the light of a campfire, eyes glowing red from the flames. It is said to be a sign of a death coming to the tribe—that the *menetas* have come to feast on the flesh of the dead.'

Aarin shivered. 'Why are you telling me this? What has this to do with the priests?'

Kallis gave him a long, measured stare. '*Meneta* is an old Safarsee word. It means "little dragon". That is how the dragons are thought of in Caledan, when they are thought of at all, for the priests discourage any talk of those legends. The *menetas* are feared for their likeness to the old tales, not because they eat dead flesh. Many creatures do that. Aarin, you are searching for the creatures my people blame for the destruction of the ancient world.'

Aarin felt a moment of total shock that quickly gave way to anger. 'That is what your priests say? That the dragons were at fault for the Severing? That we did nothing?'

Kallis held up his hands. 'I don't know what they really believe. Few do. I have told you only what the people believe, and the legends are older than the Order. With or without the Order's suppression of the old legends, the superstitions remain. Few are disposed to think kindly of that race.'

'But it was men,' Aarin whispered, devastated. 'We broke the ancient trust. That's why they left.' That was the lesson that had been drummed into him all the years of his childhood.

'If that's true,' Kallis asked carefully. 'Why should they wish to return?'

Aarin paused. It was a possibility he had never considered. If the dragons had abandoned mankind, why indeed should they ever wish to re-enter that union? But in the end the answer was clear. 'Because if they do not, men and dragons both will perish.' He caught Kallis's disbelieving gaze and tried to explain himself. 'I know it is hard to understand, but our two races are bound to one another, even now. We need each other. We are two halves of a whole and as long as that whole remains broken, the magic that sustains this world cannot function properly.'

'And if that whole is broken forever. What then?'

'It isn't.'

Kallis sighed. 'If what you have told me is true, if this decay is taking place around us, then it seems impossible that the dragons can still exist in this world to be found by anyone. You have to accept that they might be gone forever, and if that is so all you can do is take Andeira as she is now, as the rest of us must, and live the best life you can. Do not ruin the beauty that still is by dreaming of a perfection that will never be again.'

'If you are right,' Aarin said slowly. 'Then that is all I can do. But you are wrong, and I have to keep looking.'

Kallis nodded, accepting a conviction he could not change. 'Then I wish you luck and hope you succeed. For that is all I can do.'

'How does it feel?' Aarin asked, watching Kallis practise with his sword, moving with the blade through a series of forms, testing the strength of his healing side.

The mercenary lowered the sword tip to the ground and turned to face him. 'I'm stiff, and my arm is weaker than a kitten's, but there is little tenderness. I think I can pronounce myself healed.'

Aarin laughed as Kallis flopped down to join him on the grass. 'What now?' he asked, knowing that it could not be long until they parted ways. The mercenary would wish to rejoin his company if he could. Kallis's presence was an anchor in this foreign land, but it also hindered his search. Come spring he would return to the mountains, and the mercenary would be helping rich lords indulge their squabbles with their neighbours.

The thought saddened him. He had enjoyed the unexpected friendship. He had not thought to find companionship in one so removed from his people, but Kallis's calm acceptance of all he had said that night, almost three weeks past, had won through his carefully guarded distance. He was aware of the soldier's scepticism, but he had expected nothing less, and Kallis's gentle teasing did not grate as much as he had thought it would.

Kallis rested his hands on his knees. 'My days with Girion and the Eagles are over, I think. I find myself increasingly bitter about being left behind, though I know such thoughts are foolish. It is hard to trust men who have failed you once. It makes you edgy, and it is not good to be edgy when going into battle.'

'You're forsaking the soldiering life? I can't see you as a man of leisure.'

Kallis grinned. 'One of these days I'll have enough money to retire in comfort, buy my own estate, and pay others to fight for me, but I doubt it will be soon. No, I meant only that I doubt I will be returning to that company. It is time to find another, but there is no sense in doing that until the spring.'

At Aarin's puzzled look, Kallis shook his head in exasperation. 'I keep forgetting you have been rather removed from events these last couple of years. Have you heard of the Istelan Valley?'

'Of course,' Aarin replied, affronted. The Istelan Valley extended both sides of the great river, straddling the North and South.

'Not the valley itself, the battle.' At Aarin's blank look, Kallis continued, 'Six months ago Loran of Nava met with his border lords there when their in-fighting turned into outright rebellion. The magicians brought the two sides together in the Vale to broker a peace, and they were to remain to ensure that neither side broke the truce.' Kallis stopped, a snarl of pure anger on his face. 'They did not. At the very moment Loran and his rebellious vassals met to begin the negotiations, they withdrew their people from the camp. Both sides interpreted this as a sign that they had been betrayed. There was no more talking that day.'

'What happened?'

Kallis laughed bitterly. 'What do you think happened? We fought.'

'You were there?'

The mercenary nodded. 'Almost every clan was there. The Eagles were in the pay of Lord Forthron, hired as his bodyguards for the negotiations. His own men were there too, but we were his prestige. Many other lords had done likewise, as had Loran. He must have spent every penny he had twice over to pay their fee. The Wolf Pack does not come cheap, even to a prince, but their reputation is such that fools pay. Well, it was,' he finished regretfully. 'Good as they were, even the Wolf Pack could not survive that slaughter. There were twenty of us for every one of them.'

Abruptly Kallis shoved himself to his feet and stalked a couple of paces away. 'That was a bad day, and we still bear the scars. I knew the life I was tying myself to when I chose to make my living by the sword. I knew there would be times when I would find myself face to face with a friend across bared blades, but to mercenaries it is the clan that comes first, in everything. The clan is your life, your family, and you never, *ever* forget that if you want to stay sane.' He gave a snort of laughter. 'There is not as much rivalry between the clans as people think, but the rumours are useful to keep the prices high. There are very few outsiders among our number. Most are born into the life, born and raised to hold a weapon before they can walk, and the webs of family relationships have stretched between clans for so long that there is no one who does not have a brother, a cousin, a friend, who marches under another banner.'

He turned back and Aarin saw deep regret in his eyes. 'The clans have a way of dealing with it or they would be torn apart. Blood bonds and friendship belong to everyone, but the only true loyalty is owed to the badge you wear and the men who fight beside you. If blood ties you to another clan, that tie comes second to the oath you swear to your brothers-in-arms. Break that oath and pay the ultimate price. If those you have betrayed do not take your life, you are an outcast. To one born of the clans, that is worse than death.'

'Yet you are not born of the clans,' Aarin observed. 'Nor even of this land. Why choose such a harsh code?'

The mercenary sighed. 'That is another tale altogether. Suffice it to say that I have sworn my oath and I will not walk away from it, even though by the laws of the clans I was freed the moment I was left behind. It is the only life I know.'

Aarin nodded. That was something he could understand. 'Then you will submit to another oath?'

'I will,' Kallis agreed. 'But not yet.' The anger returned to his eyes. 'We were to join the other clans for the winter, as is the custom, but it will not be the same. Honour and loyalty are rare and valuable things, but they should never be prized above the survival of a people. That day should never have happened, and if not for unquestioning obedience to an unfeeling code we would never have allowed so many of our own to come up against each other in battle. Hundreds died; the Wolf Pack was destroyed. Sutis, their captain, is dead, and there will be many seeking to fill the void left by his death.'

Kallis sighed, sitting back down. 'Perhaps I am growing tired of such rigid honour. I find that I cannot stomach that kind of fight again. This winter will see many changes, and the Eagles are likely to find themselves in the thick of it. Girion has long had his eye on Sutis's position and he will be ruthless in pursuit of it. I wish most heartily to be elsewhere until things calm down. Perhaps I will return to my company then, but I think it might be healthier to seek a less ambitious clan.'

Aarin recognised doubts that had been festering for some time and had the sense to keep quiet. He was party to these thoughts only because Kallis needed to talk, not because his advice was wanted.

'Besides,' Kallis continued after a while. 'Now that I'm able, I thought I might repay some of my debt to you.'

Aarin looked surprised. 'You have no debt to me.'

'Whether you acknowledge it or not, the obligation exists, and I will discharge it. These lands are dangerous, Aarin, and will only get more dangerous. Here.' He held out his dagger, hilt first. 'Take it. You will need it, and I will make sure you know how to use it.'

'I don't need a weapon,' the mage replied sharply. 'Nor do I wish to fight anyone.'

'What you wish will matter little to the other man. I am offering to teach you how to use it should you need to, that is all. What you do with the skills

I give you is your business, but I will sleep easier knowing you can defend yourself. After all,' he said with a crooked grin. 'You saved my life. Maybe one day this knife will save yours.'

Aarin reached out and grasped the dagger. He looked up at Kallis and nodded. 'Then I will thank you now.'

The mercenary's grin became a wide smile. 'Let's begin.'

NINE

Amadorn

New Age, 2050

THE GROWING UNREST in Rhiannas dominated the council of Lothane. Darred knew only too well what had caused it, as did the assembled lords. Tensions between Lothane's merchants and the Caledani traders had reached boiling point, and nothing short of the expulsion of the foreigners would satisfy them. And that was not a course of action that any member of the council would entertain. Too many of them had money tied up in the exotic goods sold by the Caledani, and the rest would be unwilling to give up the luxuries the foreign merchants brought to the North.

'There will be trouble soon, my lords,' Darred told them, and they nodded sombrely. The mood in the city grew more tense and angry every day, and even the lords, safe in their mansions and surrounded by guards, could not fail to sense the unrest that had gripped the populace.

'I have met with the garrison commanders and the heads of the mercenary clans currently in our pay,' Darred lied smoothly, and saw several of them wince. The cost of the hired swords on the city's coffers was devastating, and only the new taxes were keeping them afloat. 'They all know what to do. At the first sign of trouble, the ringleaders will be rounded up and taken to the cells until after the ceremony.'

One or two looked nervously at each other. He marked their faces.

'Perhaps we should delay the ratification,' one suggested, somewhat timidly. That he meant the delay to be permanent was left unsaid.

'That is your decision,' Darred replied respectfully. 'We must all think of the good of the country. But, if I may, my lords, I would advise you rather to move the ratification forward. That way Nathas will be installed as heir before his enemies have time to act.'

He paused, letting the idea sink in. There were many on the council who were still in shock at how quickly a once secure succession had unravelled into chaos. The city had been prosperous, the royal line strong. There had been two healthy children, a son and a daughter, both more than fit to rule. But the daughter had vanished and, years later, the son had died, leaving only the king's bastard son. A smooth succession had become a tangled mess of intrigue and ambition, as any with the slightest claim descended on Rhiannas, and the king had slipped away from them, mired in his private grief.

In those few brief months before King Kaefal's death, Lothane had been in turmoil, and all the long years of prosperity and peace had been torn apart. Trade had suffered, the councillors had suffered privations they were not accustomed to. And worse, their neighbours on all sides had closed in, sensing weakness and prepared to exploit it.

It had been no easy task to convince this group of unpractised regents that Nathas's claim—a distant cousin and a lord of Lothane's long-standing rival Elvelen—should be given precedence over the king's bastard son Tueren, who had taken the mantle of prince for himself on his father's death. Kaefal had lavished attention on the boy, but he had never formally claimed him, for he still had a son, and Prince Crian had grown into a well-respected young man. His death to a mystery illness at the height of his strength had come as a devastating blow and sent the king into a spiral of despair that robbed him of the strength to rule.

It was then that Darred had come, and the magicians had come with him. He had ingratiated himself into the old man's affections, gaining his trust as he played on his fears. He had manoeuvred his way to favour and power with such skill and confidence that few had questioned his right to be there. Gradually he had come to dominate this council—the vaunted Lords of the North—winning their trust as he had won their king's. Only Tueren had dared to challenge his position, but Tueren's obsession with the belief that he was destined to rule after his father had been his downfall. His arrogance had lost him what friends he had at court and Darred had not even needed to intervene to bring him down.

'In your wisdom you have decreed that the king's cousin is the rightful heir, and your decision to favour Lord Nathas has benefits we all recognise,' Darred continued. 'He is the nephew of Lord Delgar, and the friendship of the Duke of the Valan Lakes is not something to be disregarded lightly. If the current royal line in Elvelen should fail, the Duke's family stands high in the succession. A king in Lothane with a claim to the throne of Elvelen, a king moreover already acting as regent over Naveen, would be a formidable power in the North.'

They were nodding again. He almost had them. 'Such a power could challenge the might of the Golden Alliance, perhaps even open up the trading routes they have closed to us, force them to lower the taxes on the goods our merchants buy from them.' He was watching their faces closely now. One or two were sitting up straighter, listening to his words with renewed interest. How far would they go? They wanted peace, and a return to the prosperity of Kaefal's rule, but the months of turmoil had seen encroachments on their power, and even the rich had suffered at the hands of the administrators of the southern alliance. They might have weak stomachs for war, but they were not incapable of sending other men out to do the dying for them.

'Think, my lords,' he urged. 'Think of the possibilities. Under Nathas, Lothane could unite the North. Build up your power behind the Istelan and when you are ready, strike!' He banged his fist down on the council table and several of them jumped. 'The South has grown soft. Their standing armies are little more than toy soldiers parading around in fancy uniforms. They are no match for your forces.'

'What are you suggesting, Councillor?' Lord Morven asked. 'An invasion of the Golden Alliance?' He laughed, glancing around to see if any of his fellows shared his amusement. They did not.

'Oh, come now,' he scoffed. 'This is preposterous. The other kingdoms would never stand for it.'

'Wouldn't they?' Darred asked softly as he studied the old man's face. Here was the last real danger to his plans. Though they showed little sign of it now, others would be listening carefully. Morven had been a councillor under Kaefal and his father before him, and it had been a struggle for him to abandon his loyalty to the royal family and endorse Nathas's claim. 'I think you'll find they have their own troubles to deal with. Farnor's new queen has alienated too many of her allies, and without Farnor to draw them together, the coastal kingdoms are no threat. And the Golden Alliance has wielded too much influence for too long on both sides of the Istelan. Few would weep to see her humbled.'

As the old lord began to protest, Darred cut him short. 'But, as it happens, my lords, that is not what I am suggesting. Not yet. No, what I propose is merely a show of strength. Show them Lothane has bite to her steel yet. Perhaps allow a raid or two across the river. Unleash a mob on the toll stations of Forthtown and drag your feet about sending in troops to impose order. One cannot be too careful with diplomacy in these days.'

He smiled. Before long the penny-pinching Alliance administrators would be begging them to restore order in the border towns. He had not lied when he had said they had too few soldiers to handle an outbreak of violence so far from the major cities. Whittling down the alliance garrisons had been one of the more useful achievements to come out of his time in Situra. The Golden Alliance could not afford outright war. 'I think you'll find it easy to bring them around to your way of thinking.'

'Which is?' Morven demanded.

Darred felt a flash of irritation. This man was too prominent to simply disappear. Besides, he needed him to see this through. 'Recognition of Lothane's sovereignty in the North,' he answered calmly. 'Of Lothane's rightful place as a leader among nations. You will have a southern queen,' he reminded them. 'They will think it a sign of the respect you hold for them.'

Morven laughed. 'A merchant's whelp? They will not care one way or another what becomes of her. Nathas has made a poor choice.'

'Not so, my lord,' Darred corrected him, careful to keep his voice respectful. 'He has chosen wisely. Years of administrators have weakened their nobility. Birth alone no longer counts for what it should in the South, and they pride themselves on this. In a society of traders, money is what drives them, and her father is a rich man. A merchant's whelp she is not. She is the daughter of one of the richest men in Situra, perhaps in the whole of the Alliance. He has influence, and that you can use.'

He saw his words strike home. There was not one among them who had not deplored the rise of the merchant class in the South, pure-blooded nobles that they were to a man. They knew he was right, and suddenly they began to believe in the rich future he wove for them.

The girl had been a stroke of genius. Nathas had seen her once, at a ball in Situra, and been captivated, and this one of his requests Darred had been happy to grant. He had spoken only truth to the councillors when he had reminded them of the vagaries of southern society, but old ways could die hard, nevertheless. In the end her blood would count against her, and her execution would not demand a declaration of war from Situra. There would be protests, but the Alliance would not risk war, and suddenly her father's wealth would become less important than his trader roots. He was well enough connected that his complaints could not be ignored. Relations between the two would sour. But by then Sedaine would sit on the throne of Lothane, Elvelen would be humbled if not conquered, and the true power would be firmly in his hands.

While the hatreds he had stirred up boiled over into chaos, Darred would be free to resume his search for Æisoul. He was not worried by the thought of a long absence from Rhiannas. This was one wave he had no desire to ride all the way to the shore. He would return in time to pick up the pieces of the wreckage it left behind and begin building his empire.

TEN

AARIN SAT IN the smoky inn and listened to the murmur of conversation. It was bitterly cold outside, and he was content to sit and let the warmth soak into his weary bones. He had little love for Rhiannas, Lothane's capital, finding the city too caught up in politics and trade. But the early snows in the mountains had forced him to turn around and head east, and this once he was glad of the comforts of a soft bed in a warm room.

Raised voices drew his attention to the group drinking in the corner, tough men all by their scars. From their attire he guessed they were mercenaries. He had seen several clans already in the city and wondered at the rumours of unrest in the streets and the growing rivalry among the merchant factions. Lothane was the richest of the northern kingdoms, and most of its wealth came from trade with the South and the dour merchants from Caledan. If there was trouble brewing in Rhiannas, he would linger no longer than necessary. He would find a caravan heading south and offer his services to its master to pay his passage into the Golden Alliance.

The sound of laughter caught his attention and his gaze flickered to the mercenaries once more. A barmaid was at their table, serving drinks, and the men were beginning to get rowdy. The girl's smile seemed fixed, and he caught several other patrons turn to stare, their expressions hostile. Then he heard a voice he recognised call out a lewd remark after the girl's retreating back and saw Kallis's distinctive dark face among the laughing soldiers. He had not seen the mercenary since they had parted ways almost two years ago, had not, in fact, expected to see him again, and yet here he was. Before Aarin had a chance to react, an angry muttering broke out among the men around him and several got to their feet, hands on their weapons.

The mercenaries grew quiet and he saw that they too were armed. He felt a thrill of alarm that the atmosphere had grown so tense that townsmen and clansmen alike felt the need to bear arms in the taverns.

Then Kallis stood, swaying slightly from the drink, and Aarin saw with some relief that his hands were empty. 'I said the wench had a pretty arse,' he repeated, good-humouredly. 'Would any of you dispute that?'

His companions pounded their approval on the trestle table, ale slopping from their flagons, as a stout man pushed his way through the gathering throng.

'I would!' He challenged them, resting both fists flat on the table. 'And I say what goes on under this roof. That's my daughter, and I won't hear such talk from the likes of you!'

'The likes of me?' Kallis queried to the cheers of his companions, and Aarin buried his head in his hands. The mercenaries were obviously in fine fettle, and as yet their posturing was all for show.

'Caledani scum,' the landlord roared back. 'There's too many of you black-faced foreigners in our town. We don't want your custom, or your dirty hands on our women!'

Kallis swayed again, but not from drunkenness this time, reeling as though the words had been a physical blow. And instantly the mood altered. What had until now been friendly banter on the part of the mercenaries had quickly changed to real anger. Kallis's companions stopped thumping the tables and he could hear the distinctive sound of weapons being drawn.

'My countrymen,' Kallis repeated flatly, as though he was unaware of the movements behind him. 'Oh yes, you blame us for all your misfortunes. Perhaps you should look for the fault closer to home! What harm have we done you?'

Immediately Aarin sensed a subtle shift at the mercenaries' table. One or two were looking at Kallis, and there was something in their expressions that was not entirely friendly. It was clearly unwise for Kallis to identify himself with the Caledani rather than his brothers, however loosely.

The landlord turned to his patrons, his hands spread wide as if to say: *he asks what wrongs have been done to us?* The response was immediate, a barrage of insults and accusations hurled from the crowd. Kallis's face grew darker, and Aarin recognised a recklessness that came as much from too much drink as from the dilemma of divided loyalties.

'You blame our merchants for your misfortunes,' Kallis bellowed over the noise. 'Then you call in more foreigners to sort out your problems. Have you always lacked the spine to stand up for yourselves?'

He was inciting a brawl, Aarin saw with dismay. Was he insane? By the look of his companions, they were in half a mind to let him deal with it alone.

Aarin glanced around. Every face was turned to the confrontation.

'Is that not why I am here?' Kallis demanded. 'Because you invited me?'

'Not you,' the landlord retorted. 'We hired the clan lords. You we never wanted!'

'And do you think I want to be here?' Kallis shouted back. 'Do you think any of us wants to be here, in service to the magicians? At least we don't have to grovel to them like you do.'

Aarin watched the clansmen warily. If Kallis had been unwise before, he had compounded it with a far greater mistake. He remembered Kallis's words when they first met: *when my captain undertakes a contract, it is not for me to question him, nor to forget that in doing so he puts money in my pocket at little risk to myself or my brothers.*

Well he had questioned it, and publicly. Worse, he had also voiced what was likely an uncomfortable truth. Since the Istelan Valley, hatred for the magicians had settled deep in the clans. Even Aarin had seen the truth of that in the last two years. The mercenaries might still take the magicians' gold, but they would be reluctant to acknowledge it. His friend had chosen a dangerous moment to decide that his time as a mercenary was at an end, for by the look of his fellows that was precisely what he had done.

Aarin stood slowly and began scanning the tavern for his likeliest exit just as the man beside him upended his tankard, dousing Aarin's boots with cheap beer, and hurled it across the room. The missile caught one of the mercenaries across the temple, sending him sprawling to the floor, and every head turned to the table where Aarin stood. He blanched and tried to duck behind the bulk of the true culprit, who promptly seized him by the collar and pitched him over the table as a vanguard to his own charge.

Aarin grabbed at a bench to slow his fall, missed, his feet skidded out from under him as he landed on the wet floor and he slid to a stop in front of the mercenaries' table. The landlord's stream of invectives had not relented, and they were more than happy to view his undignified arrival as the opening sally in the hostilities. Aarin shouted indignantly at Kallis, whose bemused expression only deepened to see him there, then he grinned and shrugged as the man next to him overturned the table, spilling tankards, coins, and the irate innkeeper across the floor. Aarin curled his body, tucked his head between his knees, and cursed viciously as they stampeded over him in an inglorious rush to stave in each other's skulls.

He had seen bar brawls before. Frequenting the cheaper variety of tavern made them somewhat hard to avoid, but it could usually be counted on that the participants hurling themselves into the fray did so from sheer drunken exuberance rather than the kind of nerve-jangling hostility that had broken out all around him.

The next few moments were, in his opinion, highly unpleasant. He was shoved roughly aside as men behind him struggled to reach their targets, and as he dodged a flying projectile, he found himself face to face with one of Kallis's grim-faced companions. Realising that as far as the mercenaries were concerned everyone else was the enemy, he looked frantically around for a means to avoid the confrontation.

A voice called out, 'Not him!'

Aarin caught the flash of a grin from Kallis before he was once again lost from sight in the whirl of the fight. His adversary shrugged and turned aside to find another target.

Several men were already down and bleeding, but the mercenaries were not yet fighting to cause real harm. How long that was last, he did not know. The townsmen's blood was up. It was only a matter of time before someone was badly hurt.

As he edged towards the back door, Aarin saw Kallis take a nasty blow to the face, blood spurting from his nose. He staggered, and the landlord swung a chair leg at his head from behind. The mercenary went down, sprawling limply on the floor. As his opponents swarmed over him, the inn door crashed open. Framed in the entrance was a company of regular soldiers. Instantly, the melee paused as each man reassessed his situation. Then the guard captain shouted an order to arrest everyone in the inn, and a new scramble began as the brawlers tried to extricate themselves from the latest threat.

Aarin did not wait. Running to where Kallis lay, he cast a web of illusion over them both before grabbing the mercenary by the collar and dragging him through the crush of unseeing faces and out through the side door into the alley beyond. Kallis was still only semi-conscious and stumbled as he walked. Aarin slung his arm over one shoulder and hauled him bodily down the street, stopping only when the sounds of the fight faded into the night.

Kallis slipped from his grasp as he halted and fell to his knees in a loose-limbed heap on the cobbles. He gave his head a testing shake, the movement splattering blood over Aarin's already ale-soaked boots. The mage shot him a disgusted look and moved away.

'How badly are you hurt?'

'You,' Kallis growled as he shoved his way to his feet and slumped into the wall. He tipped his head back, one hand cupping his bleeding nose. 'What are you doing here?'

'Helping you, it seems,' Aarin replied tersely. 'Again.'

The mercenary grunted, spitting a mouthful of blood on the cobblestones. 'What happened?'

'The city guard arrived. They're in there now, mopping up the aftermath of your little altercation with the landlord.'

'Oh, I see,' Kallis retorted. 'You think that was my fault? Black-faced Caledani scum! What does the man expect if he throws that in my face?'

'Perhaps he was just a father protecting his daughter.' Aarin was disinclined to be understanding. His ribs were throbbing from a well-aimed fist or three and in his rush to leave he had left behind all but his meagre savings and the clothes on his back.

'Did you see me touch her?' the mercenary shot back. 'Come on, boy. That had nothing to do with his bloody daughter, even if she did have a pretty arse. Besides, I seem to recall you hurling yourself into the fray with great enthusiasm, or wasn't that you I saw in a puddle of ale on the floor?'

Aarin fixed him with a stony glare. Kallis had the grace to look sheepish as he asked, 'My company?'

'Spending the night in the cells, I imagine. Care to join them?'

'What do you think?'

Aarin glanced at him in some surprise, remembering the fierce loyalty of the mercenary clans.

Kallis appeared not to notice, his next words muffled as he prodded experimentally at his jaw. 'Never did like those places much. Cold, damp, and only rats for company. You?'

'I'm leaving,' Aarin said pointedly. 'And if you've any sense you'll do the same. I get the feeling you're not very welcome here.'

Kallis grunted again, and Aarin realised he was having trouble speaking round the swelling of his face. 'What will you do?'

Kallis shrugged. 'Leave too, I suppose. I want no part in what's happening here.'

The undercurrent of anger piqued Aarin's curiosity almost as much as the swiftness with which Kallis prepared to abandon an oath he had previously been adamant in upholding. 'What is happening? This whole town seems on edge. Those men —'

'Were spoiling for a fight. I know. There's bad feeling here, and it's not accidental.'

'What do you mean?'

'Have you not noticed? The good merchants of Rhiannas are not happy that so much of their wealth is going to line the pockets of my countrymen, and their chief councillor is busy fuelling the fires of their discontent. With the succession still in doubt, his authority here is virtually unchallenged and he is stirring up trouble for reasons I cannot fathom. Lothane profits in many ways from the Caledani merchants, and the Lords of the North most of all. Yet this man seems intent on destroying it all. The Lothani merchants might complain now, but they will find their profits suffer even more if one of their biggest markets disappears. That is why we are here,' he added, referring to his company. 'And others like us. In this time of unrest, Councillor Darred is concerned that the garrison should be bolstered by men whose only loyalty is to gold.' He spat, showing his contempt for his employer. 'He might just discover that even mercenaries have some honour.'

His anger surprised Aarin. When he had last seen Kallis he had shown little concern over the often harsh treatment of those of his countrymen who made their living in the North, past a sneering contempt for the ignorance of the Amadorians who feared men based on the colour of their skin.

As he fumbled for a response, Kallis shrugged off his anger. 'And you? Still chasing dreams?'

When Aarin nodded he laughed. 'Any luck?'

'Not much. No more than you it seems. I thought by now you would be retired somewhere and enjoying your wealth with the rest of the old-soldiering gentry.'

The mercenary grinned. 'The lords of the land have been cagey with their money of late, and little given to violent dispute. Of course, that seems to be changing. Just my luck I number among the intended victims this time.'

Aarin could not help smiling. 'Well, if you are seeking more accommodating employers, I am heading south of the Istelan and would welcome the company.'

Kallis grunted. 'The Golden Alliance? Not much work there for a soldier. The South is too peaceful for a man of my talents.'

'Then you have been away too long,' Aarin teased. 'Even the Southern kingdoms have their troubles these days. When I passed through Taslor a year ago, the country was on the brink of civil war.'

The mercenary brightened. 'I heard nothing.'

'Well, they didn't actually go to war …'

Kallis threw him a disgusted look. 'And I heard rumours of dragons dining on daisies with the Queen of Farnor.'

Aarin raised an eyebrow in polite query, though his lips were twitching.

'But it turned out the lady had merely invited her father's bellicose old councillors to sup with her on a dinner of beef and hemlock. She, declining to touch meat during her mourning, managed to survive, and I hear she has a new council more to her taste. The ladies spend their time sewing and discussing frocks. Trade, they say, is booming.'

Aarin laughed. That was not quite the tale he had heard of the Petticoat Revolution, as it was called, but the outcome was much the same. After a rash of deaths among the old men of her late father's council, Farnor's new queen had promoted her ladies-in-waiting instead, and much of the unrest in the capital had been eased by their more peaceful government.

'If the offer stands, I'll take it,' Kallis said unexpectedly. 'I think I've finally had enough of this life. Just as far as the Istelan, mind. Chasing dreams won't fill my stomach. You're heading to Forthtown?'

Aarin nodded. 'Forthtown or Sarena. I thought to find a caravan heading south and join them for a while.'

Kallis shook his head in amazement. 'Where have you been? You won't find many caravans prepared to try that route, not at this time of year with the troubles on the roads. Lothane is a bloody mess, and Naveen not much better. Besides, what's in it for a trail master to take you on?'

'I have my uses,' Aarin retorted, stung.

'Ah, I forgot. A magician, very handy.'

'Not a magician.' His response was immediate and heated, and Aarin saw a flicker of surprise cross the mercenary's face. 'Not a magician,' he repeated. 'I am nothing like them.'

Kallis raised his hands. 'I thought we established my ignorance of such matters a while back. And anyway, your kind is about as welcome as I am right now. Common men don't make distinctions between one magic and another. And here they'd as likely break your head as pass the time of day with you if they knew what you are.'

That alarmed Aarin, and Kallis grinned again.

'You have been out of things, haven't you? The magicians have run this place with an iron fist since the king died. It is them and that damned councillor who have stirred up all this trouble, and the people here are none too happy about it. Oh, they might be eager enough to wrest back some of their old trading monopolies, but the magicians have not made themselves popular with their handling of the succession and taxes gone sky high. I keep my ear to the ground, as you should do,' he added, after a moment. 'A good mercenary always knows where the fighting is going to break out.'

'A useful skill, I'm sure. And if there are no squabbles you start them yourself. I can see it must be a profitable business.'

'It was,' Kallis agreed. 'But all that changed after the Istelan.'

Aarin remembered the grim tale of the battle that had devastated the northern clans. Clearly Kallis's predictions of trouble in the wake of that slaughter had been right.

'Girion's Eagles fill the place of the Wolf Pack now,' Kallis said at last, filling the awkward silence. 'Their supremacy is accepted, and everything should be as it was, but it isn't. They can't seem to forget. Or forgive. Too many were lost, and the anger is still there. The old ways of the clans are breaking down and too many broken oaths are eroding the trust between brothers. It won't be long before the mood of this place infects them too. They might tolerate me for now, but the hatred of the Caledani merchants is all but ready to boil over. In these times my face is a stark reminder that I am not really one of them.'

Aarin grimaced. He thought Kallis had done a good job of reminding them of that all by himself, but he wasn't about to say so. At least he now understood Kallis's readiness to break his oath. Where before he had spoken of himself as one of them, now he seemed careful to keep himself apart from the clans. 'We' had become 'they' and Aarin realised that the growing hostility towards the Caledani was partly responsible. However hard Kallis tried to distance himself from the people of his birth, it would be hard to maintain that distance when they were being persecuted. If things were truly as bad as he seemed to think, Aarin wondered how far the mercenary might take his burgeoning allegiance.

'If we're leaving,' Kallis said at length, 'we should start now. The peace in this place is fragile enough and I do not want to risk being caught at the gates and taken back to my brothers. They will not be best pleased with me.'

'Are you sure you want to do this? From what you told me, not best pleased will be an understatement once they realise your intention was to desert.'

'Which is precisely why we should hurry.'

'We have no provisions,' Aarin pointed out. 'All I had was in that tavern.'

Kallis shrugged. 'Then we'll have to do without. There are villages near the city. I have some coin, though most is with Leumas. And we can hunt. You do remember how to use that knife, don't you?

Aarin's eyes flashed with irritation. 'Of course.'

'Well then, we'll be just fine.' He gestured ahead, a macabre grin on his bloody, swollen face.

Aarin nodded, and with a last backwards glance followed the mercenary through the dark streets to the city gates, hoping that they would not find them already barred and tightly guarded.

ELEVEN

NEWS OF THE clash between the mercenaries and the city's residents reached the gatehouse just after sundown, as Darred was concluding his meeting with the garrison commander. It was only a short detour to take in the inn on his return to the palace, and he was curious. It was rare for the clans to break faith with their employer—the damage it did to their reputation could make work scarce—but their hierarchy had been in chaos since the slaughter in the Istelan Valley two years ago. The mercenaries had grown unpredictable, and it would do no harm to ensure his gold was still their primary concern.

And, if he admitted it to himself, he was also on edge. Though he pretended it was merely the pressure of his plans brought so near to fruition, that was not the whole truth. His masters were stirring, growing restless in their need, and their anger battered down on him. The longer the key to their triumph remained lost, the angrier they became. Darred knew that before long, whether his plans in the North were successful or not, he would be forced to throw all his efforts into the recovery of the boy.

It was with these grim thoughts swirling in his mind that the councillor made his way down the muddy street to the inn. Scattered groups were still milling around outside, no doubt hoping for some further entertainment, and they parted for him respectfully.

Darred permitted himself a small smile for the guard who held open the door, but the moment he crossed the threshold the smile began to slip. To his trained eye, the ripple of disturbance in the elemental balance was as clear as the violence that had reduced the common room to splintered wood and shattered glass. The feeling that something important had happened was pure instinct. In a city teeming with magicians, magic was not uncommon, though the magicians usually refrained from practising their arts for the entertainment of the populace. And a tavern brawl in the poorer end of the craftsmen's quarter was not the place any sane man would expect to encounter a magician. Darred was beginning to wonder if they drank at all.

With an effort he withdrew his attention from the unseen to the clearly visible. Surveying the devastation with something close to amusement, he spoke briefly with the sergeant who pointed out the innkeeper, standing forlornly beside his wrecked bar. He looked up when Darred approached, a flash of uncertainty crossing his face as he recognised the city insignia on his black tunic.

'My lord, I did not know to expect a dignitary. I assure you my establishment does not normally... That is, most unfortunately and unexpectedly tonight –'

'I know about the brawl,' Darred interrupted. 'That's why I'm here.'

Turning away, he let his concentration wander, exploring the room for some trace of who had been there, and what they had done. The lingering resonance of spent power intrigued him. It was faint now, almost gone, and he knew that no staggering piece of spellcraft had been worked here tonight, but there was an economy to the fading pattern that spoke of a deft touch and a skilled mind.

He turned his attention back to the nervous innkeeper. 'Who was here tonight?'

The man looked confused. 'My lord?'

'In your tavern. Who was here?'

'Well, let me think. My regular customers, of course. And old Fletcher, with his apprentice, that lad of Marlin Cotton's from over west way...'

Darred sighed. 'Other than your regular customers?'

'Oh, yes, I see,' said the flustered innkeeper, who clearly did not see at all. 'Well, the mercenary company, my lord. The ones with the raven badge. A bad lot those. Not picky, if you take my meaning.'

Darred, who had begun to pace the floor, stopped abruptly, shaking his head. 'Anyone else?' He looked around him, eyes raking the room. 'I am told there was magic used here.'

'Magic?' the innkeeper said doubtfully. 'You must be mistaken, my lord. There were no magicians here.'

'Magicians,' echoed Darred with a hollow laugh. No, this was no magician's work. 'Did anything strange happen? Anything at all?'

The innkeeper trembled under the intensity of his gaze. 'Strange? No, nothing. This is a respectable establishment, my lord. I don't let just anyone in here, you understand.'

'How commendable,' Darred drawled. 'Are you sure you noticed nothing? A good innkeeper, so I'm told, prides himself on knowing everything that goes on in his establishment.' He put a slight emphasis on 'everything' and saw the man bridle.

'Now that you mention it, the guards took away all the mercenaries, and my customers too, but he wasn't with them, my lord, the ringleader. Vanished, you could say. The guard captain asked me, see, to point him out, and I know he was there when they came in. Knocked him out myself, I did. Didn't know what hit him.'

'Really?' Darred's eyebrow quirked in amusement and the innkeeper reddened. 'Maybe he simply left by the back way.' He gestured at the small wooden door that gave access to the alley behind the tavern.

The innkeeper shook his head. 'The door is barred, as you see, and has been so all night. The guards did not even bother searching the alley. I told them no one had used it all evening.'

'Well, perhaps they should have,' Darred murmured. He had crossed to the door and was running his fingers over the wooden planks and the heavy iron lock. Yes. Earth current had been used here. *Oh, very good, perfectly done.* But that was not the extent of the magic that had been performed. Another spell, a glamour most likely, had hidden whoever had escaped that way. The spent energy felt like a fine mist against his skin as the last threads of water magic faded away.

'The mercenary? He was a foreigner?'

'Yes, my lord. From the far continent.'

Darred signalled for one of his escort then dismissed the innkeeper. As the man scurried away, the guard cleared his throat. 'My lord?'

'I want you to question the mercenaries in the city cells, the Black Ravens. Find out everything you can about the one of their number who is missing.

If they seem unwilling to talk, remind them who pays their wages. I want to know everything. His name, his origins. I especially want to know if he or any of them has had contact with an easterner from the wildlands, and anything they know about him. And have someone send Lord Vianor to my chambers. You will report to me there.'

As the man turned to leave, Darred stopped him. 'Double the guard on the gates. No one is to leave the city until I tell you otherwise.'

'Are the men to look for anyone in particular?'

Darred paused, thinking it through. 'No,' he decided finally. Likely they were long gone, but if not, he did not want to show his hand too soon. There were too many places to hide in Rhiannas. 'Just seal the city. No one comes in. No one gets out. If the merchants protest, tell them to take their complaints to Lord Nathas.'

Darred looked up as the magician entered the study, his black robes fanning out behind him with each long stride. He sat back, steepling his fingers under his chin. Beside his immaculate neatness, the other man's wavy white mane and loose garb seemed positively unkempt.

'So, Vianor, I trust you have better news this time.'

'Everything is in place, Councillor,' the magician replied icily. 'Just as we discussed.'

'Excellent.' Darred bent his head once more to the reports on the desk. 'And the garrison? I trust you have solved our little dilemma.'

Vianor growled. 'You insult me, my lord. The replacements have been made. When Nathas makes his claim, there will be none of the prince's supporters free to act. He could take the city tomorrow if he wished.'

'That is good to know.' Darred cocked an ear to the doors where the sounds of a scuffle could be heard. 'I think our tame lordling grows impatient.'

The magician raised an eyebrow. 'You will see him?'

'Of course.' Darred's arm swept outwards in a lazy gesture and the doors swung open, causing the irate petitioner to make an undignified stumble into the room. The guards smirked as he straightened and his face flushed red.

'My Lord Nathas,' Darred greeted him, rising to his feet. 'Come in.'

'My lord, councillor.' Nathas bowed, flustered, his eyes darting from one to the other. 'I must apologise, I merely...'

'Nonsense. Apologise for what? We are here to serve the city's needs, your needs. Come, sit. Tell us your concerns.'

'No, thank you.' Nathas's eyes swivelled to the magician, then back to Darred, the anger that had driven him to burst in on them turning to uncertainty under his councillor's benevolent gaze. 'My residence is besieged by merchants. The city has been sealed without my knowledge, for a reason that no one has seen fit to tell me. I demand to know why they have been directed to me for answers.'

'But where else should they go?' Darred asked with every appearance of confused surprise. 'Are you not their king, but for minor formalities?'

'I –'

'The city has been sealed,' Darred continued, as though he had not noticed the interruption, 'because there has been some small trouble with one of the mercenary clans. A question of loyalty, but nothing to worry about, I assure you. It was my hope to apprehend the troublemakers before they left the city, so they could be suitably, and publicly, punished. However, I fear they may already be gone. You may order the gates reopened if you wish.'

'No, no,' Nathas assured him. 'As you see fit.'

'Well then,' Darred suggested. 'Perhaps it would be best if you informed the merchants of your decision. You may, of course, keep your reasons private. A king is not expected to share his fears with his subjects.'

Nathas turned purple, but he had been neatly trapped, and he knew it.

'Was there something else, my lord?' Darred asked, casting a delicate glance at the stack of papers on his desk.

Nathas shook his head. He got to his feet, his head beginning to bob in a bow before he remembered his status.

'Very good.' The doors swung open once more and Nathas endured his dismissal with as good a grace as he could muster.

'He fears you,' Vianor observed as the doors closed. 'He is weak.'

Darred laughed. 'Weak, yes. But angry too, did you not see? He does not like us, Vianor, nor our kind. We frighten him, and he is right to fear, isn't he? When your niece returns, he will lose not only the kingdom but his head. And with Nathas dead, his family in Elvelen will demand retribution. Lothane will go to war and Naveen will have no choice but to join them if it is to survive. While the soldiers squabble, the North will fall into your hands like an overripe plum.'

'Into the hands of the Kas'Talani, Councillor Darred,' the magician corrected him. 'Your hands.'

'Very good, Vianor. But then it is my gold that pays for it, is it not?'

'That was the bargain,' the old man admitted stiffly.

'Ah yes, the bargain,' Darred agreed as he sat. 'I have another small task for you now. A man was in the city last night, one who is important to me. It is probable that he has already left in the company of a renegade mercenary of the Raven clan. I need you set aside all your other duties to find him.'

The magician shook his head. 'Let him wait. Now is not the time for distractions.'

Darred laughed. 'You always were a fool, Vianor.'

The old man bridled. 'Then who is he?'

'Someone much more important than all of this,' Darred said casually, flicking through the pages of official documents. 'Someone who makes all of this irrelevant.'

He looked up at Vianor's shocked expression and could almost hear the frantic turning of his thoughts. Nathas was but days away from seeking ratification of his claim before the council, the goal they had worked towards for years. Those among the garrison commanders who might have contested the succession out of loyalty to Kaefal and the prince had all been safely dealt with, but there were still those in the council who, despite their avowed allegiance to their chosen heir, might yet change their position. Everything they had gained could still be lost. That Darred was prepared to split his focus at this point would tell Vianor this man was important. But would he make the connection?

Darred saw the beginnings of comprehension dawn on Vianor's face and felt a smile of his own twitching his lips. Vasa's fear of the one called Æisoul had grown over the years, fed by dire warnings whispered in his ears. In his fear he had shared his secret with too many. Even the magicians knew of the Kas'Talani's bane, though they knew nothing of his true importance, and just as Vianor thought now, so did the rest—that this man could be the lever to prise them free of the binds of their bargain and make them equal where they now were forced to serve. *If* they could reach him first.

Darred allowed himself a concerned frown, conscious of Vianor's probing gaze, and saw calculation blossom in the magician's eyes.

'You wish me to depart immediately?' the old man asked. 'How will I know this man when I find him?'

'If you remain a while longer you will have a description,' Darred replied carelessly, then paused. 'Come in,' he called, an instant before a knock sounded on the door.

As Vianor turned, the doors swung open to admit the guard sent to question the mercenaries held in the city cells.

'My lords.'

Darred waved him to a chair. 'What did you discover?'

'His name is Kallis,' the man replied. 'He's a Caledani by birth, and he has been with the Ravens for two years, near as I can tell. Previously he fought with Girion's Eagles but became separated from them when he was injured in a raid and left for dead, some six months before he took up with the Black Ravens.'

'He changed clans?'

The guard nodded. 'As you may know, my lords, such circumstances are rare but not entirely unheard of, and the Ravens' commander settled the matter with Girion at the first opportunity. Since the Eagles are also in Rhiannas, I took the liberty of corroborating the story with Girion himself. He confirmed that he released Kallis from his service once he discovered he was alive.'

'So, left for dead and yet not dead,' Darred mused, still intrigued by the unusual fact. 'Did he ever tell them what happened, or how he spent the time before he joined them?'

The guard shook his head. 'Not really, my lord. It was not in their interest

97

to ask, other than to ensure there had been no breach of his oath. Over the years he has said only that he was found by a traveller and spent some time with him before seeking acceptance in another clan.'

Darred nodded, resting his chin on steepled fingers. A Caledani like himself, yet not like him at all. That could be useful later. 'The traveller who helped this man. What do we know of him?'

'Nothing, my lord. It seems he rarely spoke of him.' The guard paused. 'There was one thing, though. It may mean nothing.'

'Go on.'

'One of the Ravens recalled something he thought strange, tonight at the tavern. At one point in the fight Kallis called out to him to let one of the townsmen be. He did.' The soldier shrugged. 'It likely means nothing.'

'I'm sure you're right.' Darred smiled as he stood, dismissing the guard. Then he turned to Vianor. 'Go to the cells and question this mercenary. You'll find he can give you the description you need to find our man.'

'And when I find him?'

'Take him to Redstone. I will meet you there.'

The answer took the old magician by surprise. 'What has Sedaine to do with this?'

'Why, did you not know? Darred replied airily. 'He is her son.'

When Vianor left, Darred drew a map of Amadorn towards him. Everything was falling into place, and sooner than he had hoped. His work for the Order he had done well, too well perhaps. Vasa had long dreamed of conquering Amadorn and he had sent Darred not as his emissary but as his vanguard. And Darred had sown the seeds of unrest from one end of the continent to the other. But he had done more than that. For his work here had been his own, not Vasa's, and he had no intention of simply handing this land to a man he despised.

But none of that was why he was really here.

Darred considered his next move, one hand idly caressing the device hidden under the folds of his tunic, gently drawing forth the power it contained. He had done Vasa's work in Amadorn only because it suited him.

And because, as fate would have it, the magicians' ambitious scheming for a northern empire had given him the opening he needed.

Vianor had resisted at first, it was true. Groomed in a magician's arts and a statesman's craft, Sedaine had already been poised to inherit the throne of Lothane, and her uncle had been reluctant to remove her from the succession. The deadlock had persisted for months, and Darred had only succeeded in bending the magicians to his will when he had offered them something they wanted almost as much—the chance to destroy their rivals in power, the mages of the eastern wilds.

They had reached a compromise, and even Darred had to admit it had many advantages, not least of which was the girl's willing cooperation. For, in the final negotiations, Darred had sworn to secure the throne of Lothane in her name, along with the other northern kingdoms. He had promised her the empire her uncle dreamed of if she would consent to help him, and she had. She had her uncle's ambition.

As Vianor so wished, she would weaken the unity of the eastern lands, divide the mages against themselves, for though they were weary and dispirited they might yet prove a threat to him. And one last thing, such a small thing: bear a child by a certain man and give that child up to him. Darred was not such a fool that he had not considered that love for the child might make her stray from her chosen course, and he had planned for such a possibility. Whether she took the boy with her, or left him in Luen, he would be safe enough until Darred came to claim him.

But his plans had gone awry, and in a way he had not foreseen. The boy had disappeared. And the rage of his true masters had been such that he could feel the vestiges of their punishment to this day.

The boy Vasa wanted dead more than anything. The boy who had unmasked himself tonight in a tavern in Rhiannas.

Darred knew he stood poised at a crossroads. It was time to decide once and for all where his loyalty lay.

But in the end, there was no choice at all. He might fear his high priest's rage, but he feared the others more. And even more than fear, it was greed that swayed him now, just as it was greed that had swayed him then. He had always been an ambitious man, and when he had glimpsed the power that lay outside the confines of the priesthood, he had given himself to it without hesitation. It had not been necessary to buy him with knowledge; it was enough just to know that knowledge existed. He had been bought from the moment he recognised a power so great it made all the achievements of his people seem no more than the dabbling of children. That was what he wanted, and he believed unquestioningly in the promise that it could be his, if only he stayed his hand from the death his high priest demanded.

TWELVE

'NO, NOT THAT ONE.' Jeta waved away the dress presented by her maid and returned to peering out of the caravan window. 'And not that one either,' she snapped, catching a glimpse of the elaborate silks Alyce was unfolding from her trunk. What was the point of such finery when she was cooped up inside all day? With an impatient gesture she indicated a plainer gown and submitted to being dressed with ill grace.

Later, clothed and groomed, her curls brushed and arranged about her face, Jeta sank back into the cushions, picking up her book and discarding it again after reading only a page. Beside her, Alyce had begun to fuss over the hem she had ripped the day before, head down as though determined to avoid her spiteful mood. Well, the girl was learning sense at last, but there was still no excuse for that sullen countenance. It was not as if Alyce had to marry the stupid man.

Every time she thought of the wedding, her resentment went up a notch. As a member of the merchant class of Situra, Jeta had believed herself free of the burden of the nobility to be married off for the sake of political alliances. But she had not counted on her father's ambition, nor his distant connection to a noble family in Elvelen. She could see now that she had underestimated both, but the speed with which the marriage had been arranged still astonished her.

What angered her more, however, was their blind faith that Nathas, a minor lord of no great standing, could somehow become king of the most powerful nation in the North.

Jeta had received the best education money could buy. She understood the politics of the nations of Amadorn well enough to know that Nathas's succession in Lothane was about as likely as a king returning to Situra. Or at least it should have been. So she knew, she just *knew*, that her parents had involved her in the kind of stupidity that got people killed. People like her.

She ran the problem round and round in her head, as she had done every day since they had left, and came once again to the same conclusion. If Nathas could not hold onto his new kingdom—and he had yet to take it—she might be forced to share whatever brutal fate his rebellious subjects dreamed up for him. And yet here she was, travelling to Rhiannas to marry the man, and there was not a damn thing she could think of to do about it.

Pushing those uncomfortable thoughts aside, Jeta snapped at Alyce to fill her empty glass. If she would soon have to endure the scorn of a nation, she would indulge herself for her last few days of freedom.

Morning ran into afternoon, the late autumn sun making the caravan stuffy and uncomfortable. Just as Jeta thought she might die of boredom, the caravan shuddered to an abrupt halt and she cursed as the glass slipped and red wine splashed on her dress. Shouts erupted outside. Leaning over to the small window, she dragged back the heavy drapes. Alric ran past shouting at her to stay inside.

'What's happening?'

'Bandits, my lady. Outlaws. Bar the door and stay inside.'

Bandits. She felt a moment of pure outrage, then the carriage heaved as something smashed into the side, and she was jolted from her feet. The shouting intensified. She could hear men running, and the unmistakable sound of bows. Frightened now as well as angry, she hastily drew back and heard a muffled sob. Alyce was hunched over in the corner, paralysed with fright.

A man screamed and Jeta jumped. She could not stay locked in here waiting for them to take her.

'Get up. Quickly, girl,' she snapped at the terrified maid. 'Help me.'

Jeta flung herself across the cramped space and began to rummage through her trunks, packing her jewels into a small leather bag. She grabbed a cloak and settled it over her shoulders.

Alyce had not moved.

Jeta shook the girl. 'Get up,' she ordered. 'Move.'

Alyce seemed not to hear. Jeta grabbed her arm and tried to haul her to her feet but the maid whimpered, cowering in fear. Giving up, Jeta slung the little bag over her shoulder and turned away. If the girl preferred to stay here, that was her choice.

She risked a glance outside. Her guards were backed against the side of the caravan. They were holding off the outlaws for now but even she could see there were too many of them. Turning her head, she saw trees no more than ten yards away and made up her mind.

'Last chance,' she called, but the girl shook her head.

Jeta moved to the doors, pushing them open cautiously and jumping to the ground. One of the outlaws gave a shout. She froze. Then Alric was behind him, driving his sword into his back and the man collapsed, a bubble of blood bursting on his lips. She averted her eyes, heart hammering in her chest.

'Go!' Alric shouted, and then she was running, pelting towards the trees, her little jewelled knife in her hand. Branches plucked at her dress. A root snared her foot, tripping her up, but she scrambled to her feet and ran on. Then a woman's scream sounded in the distance and she skidded to a halt.

Alyce! Her hand flew to her mouth. The screams came again, louder and more desperate, turning into yelps of pain. A twig snapped somewhere to her left. She spun around as whispered voices filtered through the trees. They had found her.

Jeta panicked, took a step forward, tripped and fell headlong into the arms of the man who appeared suddenly before her. He grabbed her roughly and she lashed out with her knife, feeling it score across flesh. He let go with a cry of pain and she whirled around, knife at the ready.

There was another man behind her, dark eyes watching her steadily.

'Easy, girl,' he said, 'No one's going to hurt –'

She lunged, desperate with fear, but the stranger caught her arm, turning her wrist so the knife fell from her hand. She sobbed in frustration, trying to claw at his face, but he was too strong for her, catching her other arm and holding her off with ease.

'Let me go,' she spat, but the man ignored her. Looking over her shoulder he called out a query to his friend, the one she had wounded.

I hope it hurts, she thought savagely. *I hope you bleed to death!*

'I'm fine,' the first man answered, dashing her hopes, and appeared at the other's elbow. She saw a shallow cut on his upper arm near the shoulder, but to her disappointment the bleeding was already slowing.

'Well, what do we have here?' her captor asked softly, gazing at her with interest.

'Let go,' she demanded again, as his friend knelt and picked up her knife.

'Stop frightening her, Kallis,' he said wearily. Then he smiled at her. 'We're not going to hurt you.'

'Like you didn't hurt Alyce?' she retorted. 'Like you didn't hurt the men back there?'

He looked at her quizzically, head tilted to one side. 'You're from the caravan? Let her go, Kallis,' he snapped and Jeta fell over with a thud as the man suddenly released her.

'Thieves!' she spat, rubbing her wrists, a red flush of embarrassment tinting her cheeks to find herself sprawled in the dirt at their feet. 'Murderers!'

'Got a mouth on her,' Kallis muttered. 'You'd better watch out, Aarin,' he warned as his friend crouched down beside her. 'She might cut you again with those claws of hers.'

'Ignore him,' the man told her, holding out his hand to help her to her feet. 'I'm Aarin, this is Kallis. We are not here to harm you.'

Jeta glared at him and struggled up without help. Kallis was leaning over to pick up the bag she had dropped, and she snatched it from his hands, holding it to her chest.

'I am Jeta Elorna, of Situra. You should know my father will pay well for my safe return. And Lord Nathas,' she added as an afterthought.

'Lord Nathas, eh?' Kallis chuckled. 'His mistress, are you?'

She reddened in outrage. 'I'm his wife!'

Kallis's smile turned hard. 'Nathas isn't married.'

'He will be soon! We are betrothed.'

'Well, well,' he murmured. 'So, you're the southern lady whose choice has caused such uproar. Yes, I can see he might pay well for your return, fool that he is. Oh, we don't want your valuables, girl,' he reassured her when she blanched. Then, noticing the way she held the bag protectively before her added, 'nor your honour.'

'You'd get neither!'

Kallis gave her a frank once over and Jeta saw a flicker of amusement cross his dark face as he turned to Aarin. 'Still think this was a good idea? She's an ungrateful little bitch.'

'Ungrateful!' she exploded. 'Why you –'

'That's enough!' Aarin broke in and Jeta was so surprised at his tone that her mouth snapped shut. 'What happened?' he asked more gently. 'We heard screams and we came as fast as we could. Are you hurt?' His eyes had strayed to the wine stain on her skirts.

'Only by you,' she snapped, still rubbing her wrists. 'Who do you think you are?'

Kallis laughed.

'You tripped,' Aarin protested. 'I was trying to catch you.'

Her eyes strayed to the cut on his arm then back to his face. He did not look like bandit, she realised then. Neither of them did. The older one was clearly a soldier. The younger one, Aarin, was dressed in worn leathers over a linen shirt with a thick cloak around his shoulders. The shirt was dirty but good quality, not at all like the filthy rags worn by the men who had attacked her caravan.

Before she could think of a reply, the whisper of voices came through the trees behind them. She looked around in panic, but the men were already moving. A sword had appeared in Kallis's hand and Aarin was urging her to move.

'It's not safe here,' he said with a reassuring smile. It was the smile more than anything that calmed her enough to let him lead the way into the trees. Kallis followed, his face grim.

A moment later and Jeta could clearly hear was the sound of pursuit as the outlaws called out to each other. Snatches of conversation reached her, enough for her to know they were looking for her. It was all she could do not to vomit as they joked about what they had done to Alyce. Then it was as if a cloak of silence fell around her. Save for the sound of her footsteps, she could hear nothing. The surprise made her stop short and she saw that Aarin too had stopped, an expression of controlled fury on his face.

'Are they gone?' she asked, trying to keep the tremor from her voice. One moment the voices had been following them through trees, the next they were gone.

'They're not,' Kallis said gruffly, taking her arm and forcing her to move. 'Much good that will do,' he muttered to Aarin as he passed. 'If we know where they are at least we have some hope of evading them.'

Abruptly the veil of silence lifted and the sounds of the forest returned. They pushed on, faster now, and the pursuit began to fade into the distance. When at last they halted, the only noise was the sound of her ragged breathing.

'Where now?'

Aarin exchanged a glance with Kallis then pointed skyward. 'The trees.'

She followed the direction of his arm and scowled. The trees were tall, and it would be an undignified climb. But she accepted Aarin's cupped hands to boost her upwards. She wobbled dangerously until she got her feet under her and looked down to watch Aarin swing himself up onto a neighbouring branch with ease.

He grinned at her and gestured upward, indicating she should climb further. She nodded, ignoring the dirt stains and tears on her ruined dress, and silently allowed Kallis to help her haul herself up until she was clinging to a narrow branch and hidden by the thick canopy. There was a rustle of leaves and Aarin appeared.

'Are you all right?' he asked in a whisper.

She swallowed, trying not to think of the long fall below or her perilous purchase on her sanctuary.

He smiled reassuringly. 'Sit with your back to the trunk and let your legs hang down. You will find it more comfortable, and we may have to stay here for a while.'

Jeta edged back cautiously and felt the trunk at her back. She leant against it, holding the branch with her hands, and allowed her legs to drop down. Aarin reached out a hand to steady her as she swayed, her dress twisted round her knees. She drew it up to sit in crumpled folds across her lap, her face red with embarrassment, and did not look at him.

Then she heard movement below and was overtaken by a new fear. The outlaws' voices drifted up through the leaves and she closed her eyes, praying to Tesserion that they would not be discovered. Alyce's screams still echoed in her ears, the wailing of terror that turned to cries of pain. *Please, Lady Mother, let me not suffer that fate,* she whispered, and after a time the voices receded, leaving her trembling and empty and close to tears.

THIRTEEN

THEY RETURNED TO the caravan as night fell. Even before they reached it, Jeta could see the orange glow of flames rising above the tree line and smell the burning wood. As they neared the edge of the trees, Aarin held out an arm to stop her.

'Are you sure you want to do this?'

Jeta nodded. She had to know, she had to be sure they were gone. And if the outlaws had left anything of value behind, she would need it.

When Aarin still hesitated she brushed past him, then stopped in horror as she saw what he had seen.

The burnt-out shell of the caravan lay where it had collapsed. The tapestries and curtains had been ripped off and the brocading removed before they too had been set alight. The back doors were hanging open on their hinges, and Jeta could see that the horses were gone, their harnesses lying charred and twisted around the front wheels. Bodies lay sprawled amidst the wreckage, blood and weapons littering the rutted ground.

She took a deep breath and regretted it. It was not just the caravan burning. Her stomach revolted and she vomited noisily. Footsteps sounded behind her, but she thrust her arm out desperately and no one came near.

It took her a full minute to bring her breathing under control, and a few minutes more to gather herself. But she had to do this. These men had died so she could escape, and she owed them this much. Alric most of all.

She found him as she rounded the other side of the caravan, hunched in a sitting position against one of the wheels. He looked almost as though he had dozed off except for the cut on his temple that had dripped scarlet onto the worn and faded leather of his jerkin. For a moment she allowed herself to hope he was merely asleep, but then she saw the blood on his chest was not only from his head wound. The broken shaft of an arrow protruded from his left breast, pinning him to the wood of the wheel.

Jeta walked towards the hunched figure, dropping to her knees by his side. He had known her since childhood, always dependable, always there. She had not always been kind to him. Now she found those memories returning to haunt her.

'Oh, Alric,' she whispered as she wiped blood from his face. 'I'm sorry.'

Aarin crouched at her shoulder. 'Who was he?'

'Our coachman. He has been with my family for years. He used to play with me when I was a child. Look how I have repaid him.'

Aarin shook his head. 'You didn't do this.'

'I know that,' she snapped, scrubbing the tears angrily from her face. 'We should move him. I can't leave him like this.'

'Let me,' Aarin insisted, pulling her gently away.

As she stepped back, he pulled the old man free of the wheel and lifted him in his arms, carrying his body to where her dead guards lay. Kallis was there, kneeling with his back to them. Behind him Jeta caught sight of ripped skirts, and she realised what Kallis had found. Aarin had seen it too, because he lay Alric down then stood in front of her, blocking her view.

'Come away,' he urged. 'You don't have to see this.'

She shook her head numbly. 'Is it Alyce?'

He nodded, taking her arm and trying to turn her away.

Jeta shook him off and took a tentative step forward. Kallis surged to his feet, grabbing her by the shoulders.

'Don't look,' he ordered. 'Aarin, take her away from here.'

Jeta struggled against him. 'I left her. I will see what they did to her.'

'Don't be a fool,' Kallis retorted. 'There's nothing you can do for her now, and she would not want you to see her like this.'

'How do you know what she would have wanted? She was my maid. Now let me pass!'

The mercenary let Jeta go reluctantly and she stumbled towards the dead girl. Her skirts were all but ripped away and the rusty stains on her legs told their own gruesome story. Her bodice was torn open to the waist, exposing pale breasts sheeted with blood from the wound where her throat had been cut.

As her eyes took in the horror of it, Jeta felt her knees begin to shake and fell heavily to the ground. Then she was retching again, the painful heaves burning her throat. She remembered the shouts of the outlaws as they searched for her and tried not to imagine them doing those things to Alyce. Then she did something she had not done in years. She wept.

Later, Jeta was vaguely aware of Aarin leading her away, of his voice talking gently as they walked, but she did not register the words. At some point they must have stopped because she was sitting with his cloak around her shoulders and it was dark and cold.

After a while Kallis appeared, slipping through the shadows to join them. She felt calmer now, her misery a dull ache behind the weariness, and but she dared not let herself think.

She looked up as Aarin stood. Kallis was beside him, gathering his things in grim silence. Aarin offered her his hand. 'We should leave,' he explained. 'There is a place not far from here where we will be safe. Those men might still be out close.'

It was a reminder of her danger and it was effective. Ignoring his hand, Jeta scrambled to her feet, following silently where they led. She barely noticed when they finally stopped. She was so tired she just collapsed where she stood, and the velvet dark of sleep rushed in to claim her.

Aarin jerked awake from a familiar nightmare, his heart hammering in his chest. A shaky hand wiped the wetness from his face as he opened his eyes to see Kallis striking a piece of flint along his blade to send sparks leaping into the small pile of tinder at his feet.

'Bad dream?'

Embarrassed, Aarin turned away and looked around for the girl, hoping she had not seen him wake. His eyes scanned the small campsite and found no sign of her.

'Where is she?'

Kallis grunted. 'Her highness took herself off a while ago.'

'What?' Fully awake now, Aarin looked at Kallis in consternation. 'You let her go?'

The mercenary shook his head in amusement. 'She's not gone far.' He jerked his head behind him. 'There's a stream just over there. She's gone to clean up. Took her precious bag with her. I get the feeling she doesn't trust us.'

'Do you blame her?'

A shadow crossed the mercenary's face. Whatever Jeta might think of him he was not heartless, and Aarin had seen the raw fury on his face when he had found the dead girl.

'You don't need to remind me,' Kallis growled. 'I...'

He stopped, eyes widening as Jeta appeared at the edge of the clearing. Aarin twisted round to see what Kallis was staring at, and felt his mouth drop open in astonishment.

She had washed the stains from her skirts as best she could in the icy stream, and the wet fabric clung revealingly to every curve. Her hair, freshly washed, hung long and heavy down her back, thick curls dragged almost straight by the weight. A few golden strands, glistening in the morning sun, framed a face scrubbed clean of yesterday's dirt, her cheeks glowing pink with cold. At her throat she wore a thick silver band inlaid with sapphires that set off the blue of eyes outlined in sweeping lines of kohl. But even the touch of colour applied to her lips could not disguise the creeping chill that touched her through her wet clothes.

Jeta stood still for Aarin's astonished gaze until he lowered his eyes, a red flush rising in his own face as he realised the indecency of his regard.

Kallis had no such scruples, and gave the girl a long and frank inspection, nodding to himself.

'Well, perhaps you are who you say you are,' he conceded at last. 'Though doubly foolish for displaying it so plainly. Take off your jewels, girl, before someone decides to take them from you.'

Jeta ignored him utterly. Turning to Aarin with a dignity undented by the shivers of cold, she announced, 'I have decided not to go to Rhiannas.'

Aarin blinked. 'What?'

Jeta tossed her head. 'I will not be continuing to Rhiannas. I have chosen not to go through with the marriage, so I will require an escort.'

'Is that so?' Kallis drawled. 'Well you've not much hope of finding one round here. I suggest you head to Forthtown. Plenty of fools there.'

Aarin sighed as Jeta drew herself up in outrage. Much as it amused him, he wished the mercenary would not bait the girl. They both knew there was no way they would abandon her in such dangerous country, if only she would swallow her pride and ask them civilly for what she wanted.

'I have money,' Jeta told him. 'I can pay you well.' She threw a heavy leather purse to the ground at Kallis's feet. 'There are enough jewels in there to pay my passage to Taslor, and I will double it when we arrive.'

Aarin choked back a laugh just in time when he caught sight of the expression on his friend's face. 'We don't want your money,' he said gravely. 'We –'

'But since you offer it,' Kallis interrupted, fishing the purse from the ground with a stick and flicking it into his lap. He tugged open the drawstring and whistled as he looked inside. Casting a warning glance at Aarin, he said pleasantly, 'This will do nicely.'

'Kallis...'

'Aarin,' Kallis responded in the same tone. 'Let me handle this.' He turned back to Jeta. 'You want to go to Taslor, girl? We'll get you there safe and sound, never fear. I just hope you have the means to make good your promise.'

'Of course,' Jeta answered stiffly. 'But it is "my lady".'

'Beg pardon?' the mercenary asked, mocking her tone.

Jeta scowled at him. 'You will address me as *my lady*, not *girl*. And you will treat me with the respect I am due.'

Kallis chuckled, tossing the little purse to Aarin. 'You've bought my service, girl,' he told her firmly. 'Not my servitude. I'll treat you with the respect you earn, and so far that's not much. We will take you to Taslor if that is your wish, but you will pull your own weight and do your share of the cooking and washing our clothes. If that doesn't suit you, say so now, because the first word of complaint I hear from you I'll leave you by the side of the road and lose not a moment's sleep over it. Do you understand?'

Outraged, Jeta turned to Aarin.

He shrugged. 'It was your choice to offer us payment.'

'So you say now when the money is safely in your keeping,' Jeta snapped. 'But if I have not bought your servitude neither have I sold mine. I am paying you to be my escort. I will not do your washing.'

Before Kallis could object, Aarin said quickly, 'Fair enough.' And he saw the flicker of relief that she tried to hide.

Kallis rose. 'I'm glad we all agree.' He dusted off his leathers and stretched. 'We need more wood for the fire, and water,' he told Jeta. 'One moan,' he reminded her as she began to protest.

Jeta turned on her heels and stalked away without a word. Thinking for an instant that she had chosen, in her anger, to make her way on her own, Aarin was about to call after her when Kallis stopped him.

'Let her go,' he advised. 'Collecting wood will cool her head, and if she's angry at us she's not thinking about yesterday. Besides, best we get her accustomed to it early, then maybe she'll stop this *my lady* nonsense.'

Aarin's surprise must have shown on his face, because Kallis gave him a hurt look. 'I am not completely without feeling, you know. But I am no servant and I will not be treated like one.'

'Such sensibilities,' Aarin murmured. 'And from one used to taking orders in exchange for money. Who would have thought it?'

The mercenary treated him to a look of utter disdain. 'And your pockets are just bursting with coin, I imagine. Pride is all very well, but you'll starve for it if you don't learn a little sense. She has money and we have none. She wishes a service from us, and she can pay for it. Why should we not take her money?'

Jeta returned sometime later, dumping the wood on the ground before Kallis. The mercenary twitched his feet aside to avoid the falling sticks and favoured her with a condescending smile.

'Not for me,' he explained slowly. 'For the fire.'

His smile widened as she shot him a killing look and walked away, leaving the wood in a haphazard pile where she had dropped it.

'Fair's fair,' Aarin murmured with a grin. Then he got up and retrieved his cloak and went to fetch the last of the stale bread they had purchased three days ago. Food, he realised, was going to be a problem. Their hasty flight meant that he and Kallis had few provisions, and now they had another mouth to feed, and he was suddenly grateful for Jeta's jewels.

There was some small discussion over their route, a discussion that became heated and angry before Aarin's patience snapped and he shouted at the others for silence. Kallis and Jeta glared at each other and at him. He did not even know why they were arguing. As far as he could tell they were in complete agreement. It was his plan they objected to. But Jeta had erupted with such fury to his suggestion that it would be safer to bypass the main river crossings and head through the Grymwood into the southlands that Kallis, despite his own misgivings, had felt obliged to enter the argument in his defence.

Aarin massaged his aching forehead. 'So, the Vale?'

The Grymwood Vale was their only safe route through to the South, if Jeta was right that Nathas would send his soldiers to look for her when she did not arrive. He and Kallis would not fare well if found helping her avoid her marriage, particularly Kallis. He knew enough of the mercenaries by now to know Kallis was unlikely to survive that reunion. But Lothani soldiers would be unwilling to follow them through the ancient forest, around which swirled many dark legends. If they went that way, as he had patiently explained, they would be sure to lose any pursuit once they entered the Vale.

In the end Jeta abandoned her resistance, though Aarin guessed it was more from fear of her spurned lord than trust in him.

The journey to the Grymwood would take several days, and they would have to pass through the open land of Lothane's rolling plains. Aarin had travelled through the Vale a year ago, seeking out the wild magic of the lands near his home as a balm to the bitterness of yet another fruitless year of searching. Though he knew the way, he had never travelled this country in fear of pursuit and instinctively turned to Kallis to guide them, trusting in the mercenary's skills to find the safest path to the Vale.

Kallis's chosen road was a rambling journey that clung to the sides of the shallow valleys and avoided the more open spaces of the plains. Out on those plains, rising like a molehill in the middle of a grassy lawn, was Convocation Hill, no more than a day's hard walking to the northwest of the Grymwood. And it was up those steep slopes that Kallis took them on their third day.

'There.' Kallis nudged Aarin and pointed to the left. The mage followed his gaze, peering against the darkening twilight to see what had caught the mercenary's attention. They had reached the tree-ringed summit only minutes earlier, and it was in one of the trees that they now sat, shielded from view as they searched the land behind them for any sign of pursuit.

'There,' Kallis insisted. 'At the edge of the valley. Horsemen.'

Aarin looked harder, and this time he saw a flicker of movement as the party of soldiers rounded the edge of valley.

'Twenty, perhaps thirty,' Kallis guessed. 'We don't know they are looking for us.'

'Not us. Jeta. Who else? They will have sent out searchers as soon as she did not arrive. I don't like this.'

'Nor I,' agreed the mercenary. 'Why don't we just give her back? It would save us a lot of trouble.'

Aarin grinned. 'But you would lose your gold.'

Kallis grunted. He was leaning out on the branch as far as was prudent, keen to snatch every benefit from his vantage point.

Convocation Hill was so named, Kallis had explained, because it had been used by opposing sides in Lothane's many disputes to meet and discuss their quarrels. Rising incongruously high in the centre of the gently undulating countryside of central Lothane, the hill afforded an impressive view of the land around, and both sides could assure themselves there was no ambush waiting to trap them. From the fragments of bone and rusted arrowheads littering the summit, it was clear it had also been the site of many battles. Before the unification of the country some two hundred years ago, the Lothani had been a notoriously quarrelsome people.

Aarin looked at the battle-scarred ground and wondered how many men had died on these slopes. But Kallis had insisted they come here, and he had to admit there was no better place for scouring the land. He twisted round, looking over his shoulder at the dark shadow of the Grymwood on the horizon and knew that if they could evade the soldiers they would reach the edges of the forest by nightfall tomorrow. That would be the dangerous time. He was unwilling to enter by night, already weary from a long day, and while they waited for the dawn the soldiers might come on them. He doubted it, for he guessed they would steer well clear of the Vale in their search, but it all depended on whether they could avoid the notice of the group following the rim of the sloping valley to their north.

'Will they not have the same thought?' he asked Kallis. 'From here they could search for us as easily as we do for them.'

The mercenary shook his head. 'It is growing dark already. They will be able to see nothing until morning and by then we will be well away. No, I think they will head down the valley's edge to the lowlands for the night and come this way in the morning. If we leave by the southern slope before it gets light, we could be out of these accursed plains and into the rough country before they have even reached the summit.'

Aarin accepted the logic of this argument. 'I should get back to Jeta,' he said, swinging off the branch and dropping lightly to the ground. He looked up at Kallis. 'Are you staying?'

'I'll wait until they stop for the night. If their commander has any sense, he will do as I have said, but rank does not always mean brains.'

Aarin nodded, hoping this Lothani officer was a man of sound judgement, and returned to where they had left Jeta. She was pacing the summit's clearing, her back to him, and Aarin watched as she reached the limit of her line and turned around.

As soon as she saw him the fear disappeared and the cool, composed mask fell into place. 'Are we followed?'

'Perhaps,' he replied, and saw a flicker of apprehension in her eyes. 'There's a party of soldiers a few hours distant. They may be seeking us, but we cannot be sure. Kallis says we will be safe here tonight.'

She nodded, her eyes drifting to the trees where Kallis watched.

'We cannot risk a fire,' he continued, though the truth was he was just too weary of the relentless demands on his magic that concealing a fire cost him. 'And we must be away before first light. Tomorrow we will reach the Vale.'

Jeta's eyes narrowed at the mention of the Vale. 'How long?' she asked, and he knew she was asking how long it would take them to cross.

He shrugged. 'Two days, three. Then we will be in Situra, and safe.'

'Safe?' she echoed scornfully. 'You think they will stop at Lothane's borders? That he won't continue to search for me?'

'I don't know,' Aarin replied honestly. 'It's not too late to change your mind. They will be making camp not far from here. You could go to them now, seek their protection and return to your prince.'

'Why should I do that?'

Aarin studied her curiously as she perched herself on a fallen tree, instinctively smoothing tattered skirts. The longer he knew her, the more her decision puzzled him. 'You know what you are giving up. You could be queen of Lothane, have everything you ever wished for. Why have you thrown that away for an uncertain future?'

'It was not a match of my choosing,' Jeta replied, not meeting his eye. 'It was arranged by my parents, a union of convenience meant to bring Lothane closer to the Alliance states.'

Aarin said nothing, thinking it unlikely that a merchant's daughter, however wealthy, would do much to ease the tensions between North and South, and she seemed to sense his scepticism.

'My father is an important man,' she said stiffly. 'A member of the high council. Situra, like our allies, has few old-blood nobility. The North calls us a federation of traders, and maybe we are, but then our leading merchants are our lords, and their daughters our princesses. Nathas knows this. As do the magicians,' she added bitterly.

Aarin's ears pricked up. 'The magicians? What have they to do with this?'

'Everything. It was the magicians who first carried word to my father that Nathas was seeking a bride. And it is the magicians who have controlled Lothane since the king's death. The magicians and Councillor Darred.'

Darred again. Kallis had mentioned him. Aarin felt sure he had heard the name before, but he could not find the memory. 'Who is he?'

Jeta shrugged. 'Some say he rules the Lords of the North. Certainly, he holds much of the power there. Years ago, a man by that name was a member of the high council of the Alliance. Perhaps it is him.'

'Not a magician?'

She shook her head. 'Not that I have heard, though they seem to do his bidding.' She sighed. 'Does it matter? In the end it is all the same. My parents have given me to the man the magicians—not the people—wish to sit on the throne of this wretched country. The crown prince may be dead, but the king's bastard son is very much alive, and he has made no secret of his own ambition.'

'You fear a rebellion?'

'Wouldn't you?' she challenged him. 'Why else must this Elvelen lord surround himself with clan mercenaries? I will not be the cause of that,' she said after a pause, sounding surprised at her own words. 'I will not be the reason that hundreds of people die, nor do I wish to meet my death in a civil war not even my own.'

'What war?'

Aarin turned to see Kallis behind him.

'They have gone down into the valley. Is there anything to eat?'

Aarin waved him to their packs as his own hunger made itself known and took the bread and hard cheese from the mercenary gratefully. Jeta accepted hers with distaste, but at least she had stopped complaining about it. He chewed mechanically, his thoughts elsewhere, which made the meal somewhat more bearable. His eyes were drawn inexorably in the direction of the Grymwood, and over the course of the evening he saw the same was true of the others. He sensed their worry and knew that if not for the danger of staying in Lothane, they would never have agreed to this route.

FOURTEEN

IN THE END the night and the next day played out much as Kallis had predicted. They slithered and stumbled down the southern slope in the deep darkness of early morning, making the Vale's outer reaches as the sun rose. By late afternoon they arrived at the edge of the Grymwood itself. As the sun began to dip behind the forest's canopy, long shadows reached out from the trees. Behind them was the great wasteland of the Vale and the plains beyond, and before them only the dark silence of the Grymwood.

The focus of Aarin's attention was far from the others as he met the rising tide of magic. The Grymwood was ancient beyond the memories even of his people, wild and overgrown, and few paths marked safe passage through its forbidding depths. He reckoned it would take them two days to cross the vast forest, and there was the Istelan to ford, swollen by the autumn rains. It would not be easy, and the wild magic of the eastern lands was strongest here, strong enough to touch even the untrained mind. He would do what he could to guard them from that, but the ancient forest was truly a force of nature. The unease they would feel in its dark depths was why he hoped, he believed, that no pursuit would follow them on this route.

'We should camp here for the night,' Kallis advised, eyeing the dark canopy with distrust. 'We should be safe enough.'

Aarin nodded, still caught up in the first glorious rush of recognition. He agreed to Jeta's request for a fire, despite his misgivings. He would have to shield it with wards to keep them hidden from their pursuers and felt uneasy at the thought of using his magic so close to the borders of this ancient power. Kallis insisted on taking the first watch, unwilling to leave their safety entirely in the hands of a magic he did not understand, and Aarin agreed to that as well.

He did not think he would be able to sleep, but in the end sleep came quickly, and with it came the dreams. They came as they always did now, crowding his mind with glimpses of another time, past and future, peopled with faces he knew and those he had never met. They were indistinct, untouchable, yet the clarity of his thoughts defied the ephemeral nature of the dream world. Images passed before his eyes, blurred visions of a time before the memories of mankind. A mage, ancient and terrible, magnificent in his mastery. Dragons, huge bodies of bunched muscle and shining scales that tore at his heart with longing. Appalling conflict between unseen enemies; destruction, bloodshed, death. Always death. And always life. Cities teemed with people, overflowing into the valleys and plains and taking axes to the forests. New towns sprung up, flourished and decayed, and men rode to war to lay claim to a dying land.

Then the cycle stilled, hovering for an instant over the crouched figure of a black-haired boy, his face turned in intent focus on darkened figures in the distance. Before him Aarin saw torches flickering in the night and heard the hushed murmuring of many voices. Then he was rushing past, leaving the boy in the dust, the sun rising in his wake as he flew above a vast desert. A lone figure stood on the baking sand looking up, one hand shading his eyes against the glare of the sun. He heard shouts, saw the man wave his hands, and was sure he heard his name. The vision drew closer, edges sharpened and grew crisp, and he could see the man's face, hear his voice calling out...

The dream shattered with a force that sent him reeling, torn apart by the rough hand on his shoulder shaking him awake. Still fuzzy from sleep, Aarin opened confused eyes and found himself looking into the darkened skin and brown eyes of the face from his dream.

'You?'

The world seemed to slow with the shock of recognition. He felt his body jerk rigid, then shake with running tremors. He sensed rather than heard Kallis's cry of alarm, and the hands that gripped more tightly around him. Then his conscious connection with the present snapped as his awareness poured like syrup back into the landscape of his dream.

Against a backdrop of violence and treachery, he saw a man cradling the body of a dying woman, his dark, aristocratic face streaked with blood and tears; the black-haired boy wading through the bodies of the dead, crying out to the frightened men who surrounded him. Beyond them stretched the desert wastes of a foreign land, and he felt the burning heat of a blazing sun as it shone on the structures of an alien culture. And he flinched from the blinding light reflected from the thousands and thousands of drawn swords of a vast army.

Then just as suddenly his mind cleared, and he found himself staring into Kallis's disbelieving eyes.

'What's wrong with you?' the mercenary demanded. 'Now is not the time for a fainting fit. They're almost on us.'

The words made no sense. Aarin rolled onto his side as his stomach flipped over, his senses spinning away from him. Only Kallis's hand on his shoulder kept him grounded enough to collect his scattered wits. Dismay greeted his return to the present as Kallis's words slowly filtered into his mind. He groped clumsily for his ward-spells, set every night since Rhiannas to hide their camp from prying eyes.

'They're gone,' he murmured, stunned. He looked at Kallis, still unable to comprehend what his senses were telling him. 'How are they gone?'

The mercenary frowned. 'They're not gone. They're here.'

Aarin's face screwed up in concentration. The soldiers. He could feel them now as he scrambled to reknit the fraying edges of his magic. There was another there too, one whose identity was unknown to him but who could not come within such close proximity without alerting each of them to the other. But he sensed no recognition from the other man, no answering probe of awareness. The magician who led these soldiers was as stunted as any of his kind and could not read the subtle weaves that surrounded his men. It could not have been the magician who had unravelled his spells of guard. He must have let them slip while the dreams consumed his sleep.

'Jeta?' he asked groggily.

'I'm awake,' he heard the girl answer from somewhere behind. She sounded scared but calm.

Aarin shook off Kallis's hand and staggered to his feet. 'The fire,' he said in consternation, realising its now-unshielded light was like a beacon marking their presence.

'It's too late for that,' Kallis replied. 'If they're near they'll have seen it already. Better to keep it lit and hope they think us unawares.'

Aarin did not reply, moving mechanically to gather his things as they backed away from the fire to conceal themselves under the eaves. He kept his eyes trained on the darkness outside the circle of light. He knew Kallis was right. The soldiers were out there, their presence jangling against his senses, and the magician was there also. There was a flicker of movement on the edge of his vision and he nudged Kallis. The mercenary had already seen it, his hand reaching for his sword.

A soldier inched forward, clearly reluctant to leave the safety of the darkness, and even in the dim light they could see the insignia of a black raven next to the golden badge of Rhiannas. He heard Kallis draw in a hissing breath and knew the mercenary had reached the same conclusion. These men might be searching for Jeta, but she was not their only prey.

'It's time we were gone,' Kallis whispered, but Aarin caught his arm and gestured for him to stay still. They could not move now without being seen, and illusion was the one spell he could not now risk for the magician would surely sense it. He cursed himself for letting the wards fail.

They watched in nervous silence as the soldier reached the fire, going down on one knee where they had lain only minutes before, his eyes scanning the trees. Long moments passed then he raised his hand in a signal and dark shapes slipped into the light. Aarin counted fifteen, but knew there would be more, hanging back in the darkness.

The soldiers spread out, prowling around the perimeter of their camp. One came so close that they held their breath, ducking their heads to avoid his piercing stare. At length he turned and spoke quietly with another man, who broke away and returned moments later with a cloaked figure at his heels.

Aarin felt Kallis tense as the magician finally appeared, his midnight robes blending into the blackness so that he seemed at once both there and not there. He stopped at the edge of the fire, his head turning from side to side as though he sought a fickle scent on the breeze. Finally, his gaze fixed on the shadows that concealed them.

'This would be a good time to take our leave,' Kallis hissed urgently, unsettled as much by the magician's hungry stare as he was by the presence of his clan.

But Aarin's gaze was riveted on the old man, the first of his kind he seen so close. He looked harmless enough, his white hair long and wavy and his face lined with age. But his eyes were sharp, and his gaze was fixed steadily on their hiding place.

'Aarin,' Kallis growled, and the mage could feel the disquiet pouring from him in waves.

'I know you are there,' the magician called suddenly. 'I know you are watching. Will you not come out?'

Aarin froze. Nothing moved in the uncanny silence, as though the whole world held its breath with him. Then the fire popped and spluttered and the spell was broken. The mercenaries milled about uneasily, fingers curling around the hilts of their swords as they waited for an enemy to appear.

'You cannot escape,' the magician called. 'The forest you hide in will not protect you, and you would be foolish to test its ire.'

Aarin felt Kallis's alarmed glance and shook his head. He knew now that the magician was unlikely to risk following them into the Grymwood, but the mercenaries' expressions were grimly determined. They might well be prepared to take the risk to get their hands on their oathbreaker.

'We mean you no harm,' the magician continued. 'We seek only the girl you have taken from us.'

Aarin heard a muffled squeak from Jeta. She was hidden some way behind them and unaware of the significance of the soldiers.

'She is betrothed to our future king. She belongs to us.'

Aarin heard Jeta make a noise of pure outrage, but before he or Kallis could stop her she was on her feet.

'I belong to no one,' she called defiantly, moving out of the shadows.

Her hair was snarled in tangles and her skirts stained with mud. The magician's bow was low and mocking as he surveyed her bedraggled appearance.

'My lady. Vianor, at your service.'

Aarin felt a ripple of shock. He knew the name, as anyone who spent any time in the North must. It was a name to be respected, even feared, for its bearer was a man of great renown and influence in the courts of the land. He shot a nervous glance at Jeta, but the girl was uncowed.

'You may tell Lord Nathas that he must seek a bride elsewhere. I have decided to end the betrothal.'

Aarin heard Kallis curse viciously behind him and realised that the mercenaries were taking up positions around them.

'Perhaps your own messenger went astray, lady,' Vianor suggested coldly. 'For I am sure you must have sent Nathas word of your decision.'

Aarin saw a flicker of fear cross Jeta's face, but she did not back down. 'Please relay my regrets to Lord Nathas and tell him that his roads are so infested with outlaws that they are no longer safe to travel, or my messenger would have reached you some days ago.'

Vianor inclined his head. 'We came to rescue you, my lady, but it seems you are quite content in your present company. I shall convey your regrets to Lord Nathas,' he said silkily. 'Though I think he will feel few himself when he hears his bride has been despoiled by brigands, apparently willingly.'

As Jeta launched herself at the magician, Aarin lunged to his feet and caught her by the arm. 'Don't be a fool,' he whispered angrily. 'You're making it easy for them.'

As Kallis moved to stand reluctantly beside him, he turned to the magician. Vianor stared at Aarin, his eyes raking him from head to foot. Taken aback by the intensity of his regard, Aarin let his hand fall from Jeta's arm.

'Well, we meet at last,' the old man murmured. 'Forgive me, you are the very image of your mother.'

The words were like a punch to the stomach, robbing him of thought and speech. He reacted on pure instinct, calling down a curtain of silence around them, keeping everyone else out. Somewhere in the back of his mind he felt the magic of the Grymwood stir in response.

'You know my mother?' he asked at last, his voice tight.

'Of course,' Vianor replied, bowing low. 'Allow me to greet you properly, my lord. The Lady Sedaine is my niece, which makes me family to you also, and your sworn servant.'

'My lord?' Aarin echoed, his head reeling. 'I'm nobody's lord.'

Vianor quirked an eyebrow. 'She never told you?'

'Told me what?' Aarin demanded. 'What didn't she tell me?'

Vianor did not answer at once, studying him with his head tilted to the side. At last he asked, 'Does it anger you, the way she abandoned you when you were a child?'

Aarin felt cold. 'What didn't she tell me?'

Vianor smiled. 'I see that it does. Her duties required her to leave you, just as now they require her to claim you once more. The time of Sedaine's ascendancy is at hand, and she should have her son at her side as she takes her throne.'

Aarin frowned. The conversation was moving too fast. 'What throne?'

There was a pause as the magician watched him, half-smiling. 'Lothane.'

Aarin laughed out loud. It was ridiculous. 'Lothane? How could my mother take the throne of Lothane?'

'Because she is Kaefal's own daughter,' Vianor replied, advancing on him. 'Because she is the princess who vanished twenty-five years ago, who disappeared into the wilderness and met your father, and bore him a son. You.' As he spoke his words became louder, more forceful, rising to a climax on the last word so that Aarin almost covered his ears.

'You,' the magician repeated. 'Grandson of a king, prince of a kingdom, and bound to that kingdom by blood.'

'It's not true,' Aarin whispered desperately. 'It can't be.'

'Sedaine will become queen,' Vianor insisted, closing the distance between them remorselessly. 'And you will stand beside her, for that is the place of a son, and the place of a magician. You are one of us, boy,' he said coldly at Aarin's horrified look. 'Never forget that. Born into a line older than this age of the world, and that blood will not be denied. You will serve, as others have served before you, and you will also rule. In our name.'

As he spoke, Aarin felt the haunting touch of fate brush against him, felt it take him and trap him in this magician's world. 'I will not.'

Vianor began to speak again, but he cut him dead. 'I will never become one of you, never walk your twisted path. My mother can become queen of

Amadorn for all I care, but she has no claim on me that I acknowledge, just as you have none. I suggest you leave now while you still can.'

Vianor regarded him without visible reaction. As he looked into the old face, Aarin saw something that made him reach out to his magic, drawing deep of the endless, swirling well of the Grymwood. In this place his magic would be supported and strengthened by the Vale's ancient power. If it came to a contest, there would be none.

Vianor continued to watch him, reading his thoughts. A slight mocking smile curved his lips. 'You're strong,' he allowed. 'You could stop me if you chose, but there are many more you would have to defeat, and two others to defend. Tread carefully, boy, or all your potential might end on the swords of my men.'

As he spoke, Aarin felt the magic in which he had shrouded them collapse around him, and through the broken threads of his wards the sounds of the night rushed back, reminding him of the greater peril. The mercenaries had closed in on them, surrounding them in a ring of steel. Kallis stood with Jeta at his back, holding the girl behind him with one hand. His sword was in his other hand.

Swallowing, Aarin turned back to Vianor. 'What do you want from me?'

'Nothing that is not within your power to give,' the magician assured him. 'Would you deny your birthright?'

'Yes!' Desperate to stop the magician's advance, he acted without thinking, setting a barrier of Air between them.

Vianor stopped short, and Aarin could see him feeling out the boundaries of the obstruction. He extended it, shielding not just himself but Kallis and Jeta too. The soldiers prowled around just beyond the wall he had made, and their eyes watched him, waiting for him to break. He began to sweat, the strain of maintaining his control over the volatile element awakening the fiery rush in his veins. Vianor saw, and his eyes sharpened on the weakness. Time passed, each moment dragging for an age, and still the barrier held.

'How long can you hold us all out?' Vianor asked, his manner exuding all the patience of an old and practised adversary. 'Not long, I think.'

'Long enough,' Aarin ground out, the strain beginning to tell.

The magician raised an eyebrow. 'For what? There is no one to help you. I am all you have.'

Aarin frowned.

'But I am the enemy?' Vianor answered for him. 'Oh, you are wrong. There are worse enemies than me, but I can protect you from them. If you trust me.'

Abruptly, Aarin's control snapped and the warding spell unravelled. The mercenaries surged forward. Kallis thrust Jeta back into Aarin, almost knocking him from his feet, and the mage called out desperately to Vianor.

The magician snapped out a command and the soldiers halted. Then their captain took a step forward, raising his sword. For a split second Aarin thought he meant to kill them there and then. But the mercenary turned to his men and shouted an instruction. They fell back a step, muttering. Their officer silenced them with a word, the anger in his voice cracking them into swift retreat. He turned to Kallis and moved to stand before him.

Vianor watched them with a cruel smile. 'The Ravens have a quarrel with this man that they insist upon settling. To this I have given my permission.'

Aarin's alarm deepened as he watched the sword come up to hover under his friend's chin. Kallis's face remained impassive but beads of sweat stood out on his forehead as he faced his erstwhile commander

The captain continued to stare, and the sword in his grasp did not waver. At last Kallis said, 'Leumas. I ask for the right of combat.'

The mercenaries began to thump their weapons on the ground and their captain smiled grimly. 'At least you choose to die with honour.' He spat on the ground by Kallis's feet. 'I name you oathbreaker, and accuse you of treachery, but not, I am pleased to see, of cowardice.' He took a pace backwards and raised his sword to his forehead in a salute. 'I speak now for the Clan. Kill me and you may leave here with your life, your crime answered for to the Ravens, but you will be forever an outcast to the Clans, and any other who wishes to claim the debt you owe to all our brotherhood is free to do so. Do you accept these terms?'

'I accept them,' Kallis snarled. 'And let any other who wishes to challenge me do so. I will kill them as I will kill you.'

Horrified, Aarin realised they meant to fight to the death, and his eyes frantically sought out Vianor, already beginning to walk away.

'You told me to trust you! Is this how you earn my trust?'

The magician turned. 'This is between the Ravens and their oathbreaker. Neither you nor I can interfere.'

'And is this what you came for?' Aarin demanded. 'Whatever you want from me, you will never get if you let him die.'

The ghost of a smile flittered across Vianor's mouth. 'I don't bargain with prisoners,' he replied, then nodded to the mercenary captain. 'You will not be harmed,' he told Aarin. 'Whether the same is true for the others now rests with your friend. I warn you not to interfere or the renegade will forfeit this combat and the penalty will be both their deaths.'

'Stay out of this, Aarin,' Kallis snapped. 'This is how it is done among my people.'

'But these aren't your people,' he protested. 'You don't have to do this.'

'He took the oath,' Leumas said mildly, cutting off Kallis's angry retort. 'He is one of us unless his sword can prove otherwise. He does not wish your interference, or your help. If you do not desist, my men will ensure your silence.'

The mercenary captain turned his head a fraction to meet Aarin's eyes and the fickle moonlight fell full on his face. The mage caught a glimpse of blond hair framing a face that would have been handsome if not for the scar that had almost taken his left eye and ran down to his jaw. It was a hard face, but not cruel, and he held his tall body with the deadly grace of a skilled swordsman and all the arrogance of one used to command.

A grin flashed across Leumas's face as he noticed the inspection, then he turned back to Kallis and suddenly it was as if there was nothing else in the world to these two men but each other.

The Ravens spread out around them, two of them taking Aarin's arms and pulling him back. He tried to shrug them off, turning his head to look for Jeta as he heard her cry out, and saw another restraining her. Vianor was nowhere to be seen.

Sensing his fears, the mercenary on his right leaned in and said softly, 'Our quarrel is with the oathbreaker. Should he win, you need have no fear for your life. Our honour is at stake.'

Aarin twisted his head to look at him. 'It's not my life I fear for.'

The man shrugged. 'We have no wish to hurt the girl, whatever the outcome. As for the oathbreaker, his life is in his hands now. If he kills Leumas he may go free, but I think he will not.'

Aarin was about to reply when the ring of steel drew his eyes back to the combatants. They crossed their swords twice, pacing round each other with eyes locked, then there was a shout and the fight began. Leumas danced in and out, going on the offensive with quick, darting attacks. Aarin's heart sank. He could recognise talent when he saw it, and to this man his sword was but an extension of his arm. He remembered something Kallis had said two years ago. *Most are born into the life, born and raised to hold a weapon before they can walk.* Watching Leumas now, he finally understood those words.

The blond man circled Kallis, wearing a lopsided grin that twisted his scarred face grotesquely. Kallis's own expression was of grim concentration, his sword held loose and easy in his hand, tracking Leumas's movements as a hunter tracks his prey. Suddenly he was moving, his sword flickering in and out, testing his captain's defences. Leumas answered with a lightning parry, turning Kallis's blade, and for a moment the mercenary was wide open. Then, as Aarin watched in breathless fear, he twisted to one side, slipping his blade free and whirling out of the way of Leumas's counter stroke.

They faced each other again, each measuring the other, waiting, and then Leumas feinted left, recovered the action and thrust hard into the space Kallis had left, but the mercenary had anticipated the move, pretending to follow, and dropped to his knees, slicing his blade upwards to score a narrow cut at his opponent's waist.

The captain leapt back, bringing his weapon swinging down, but Kallis had started rolling as soon as he had struck and Leumas's defensive action was a fraction too slow. Aarin heard the men shouting encouragement to their leader and began to re-evaluate the odds. The Ravens' captain had a brilliance to his style, but Kallis was far from outclassed. And he began to hope.

FIFTEEN

KALLIS PRESSED THE attack but his adversary was ready for him. Leumas's sword came up to parry the blow, and the force of the contact sent tremors down his arm. Quick as a snake, the captain twisted his wrist and slid his sword clear of the deadlock. He spun to one side, forcing Kallis to follow as he took the lead once more.

Round and round they circled, and the soldiers moved to give them room. The spectators were silent now, intent on the dance of swords. Kallis tightened his grip on his hilt, marking his opponent's stance and moves, looking for an opening. He knew that in a prolonged contest Leumas would beat him. He had watched his former captain fight many times over the years and respected both his skill and endurance. He had to finish this quickly. Their blades met and rebounded a dozen times in quick, testing blows, each taking the measure of the other. Then Kallis allowed his sword to drop a fraction, angling the blade away from his body, and the captain struck into the opening he had left. He danced away, his sword twisting in a double-handed grip to parry the strike, then Leumas as stumbled past him he struck out at his unprotected back.

His sword glanced across the leather vest, slicing a shallow cut in the skin. The edge glinted red as he met his captain's shocked gaze, and he grinned. Then he thrust forwards, using his momentum to drive his adversary back a step, then another. Leumas's face was contorted with effort as he met each blow, his sword alive in his hand as Kallis forced him to defend. The pace of his movements did not falter. As they closed again, Leumas lashed out with his foot, catching Kallis's ankle and sending him sprawling to the dirt. For a moment he lay stunned, his grip loosening on the blade. Leumas was over him in an instant, his knife in his left hand, but as he was about to strike, Kallis twisted to one side, balled his knees to his chest and kicked out. The knife spun harmlessly aside but the sword cut into his right forearm and the blood fouled his hold on his own weapon.

He surged to his feet, reeling as the pain from the slash made itself known, but Leumas's cry of triumph turned to angry surprise as, without pause, Kallis transferred the sword to his other hand and once again slipped it in low under the captain's guard, scraping another painful cut across his ribs.

They were both panting with exertion. Leumas had one arm wrapped around his chest, cradling hurt ribs, and was staring intently at his opponent. Kallis returned the look, each of them knowing that it must end soon. He had the advantage now, for he realised that Leumas had either not known or not remembered that he could fight as well with his right hand as his left. As he stepped forward again, the captain was forced to spend valuable seconds reassessing the altered dynamics of the fight. The advantage of the knife was gone, and he could not straighten without searing pain across his chest.

Kallis saw his discomfort and knew he must use it. The injury to his own arm he could ignore, for now, but the intensity of the contest was draining him. As their blades met, he saw the same exhaustion in the eyes of his captain and realised the man's concentration was faltering. Without pausing he danced closer, sending quick, sharp jabs against his opponent's guard. Then he let his foot catch a loose stone and dropped down to his knees. Leumas's strike passed over his head, and as his enemy was extended, he stabbed his blade up and deep into his chest, feeling the point exit through the flesh of his back.

The mercenary captain staggered, and Kallis yanked backwards, twisting as he did so, and the last traces of life winked out of his enemy's eyes.

Kallis felt his head droop, and for a moment he could not move. Then he ground the point of his sword into the dirt and forced himself upright as the Ravens surged around him. Leumas lay twisted in his side, his back arched in his death agony, the scarred side of his face to the ground so that only the handsome man stared sightlessly at the night sky as his men dropped to their knees by his side.

One of them moved to stand before Kallis, Leumas's sword in his hand. He held it out, hilt first, the blade lying across his open palm, and Kallis hesitated only a moment before taking it.

'His sword you have won,' the man said gruffly. 'And your honour.'

Kallis gave a helpless shrug. 'The terms were his, Lorac, and I accepted them. But I am sorry that it had to be this way.'

Lorac nodded. 'The code is life and law. Though Leumas was my cousin by blood, he was also no more to me than any other brother of my Clan. In such matters we are all equal. For his death under law no blame attaches to you.'

Kallis grimaced at the formal phrasing. 'And that which is governed by no law?'

Lorac shrugged, as if to indicate his contempt for such questions. 'For your debt to my Clan, I am bound by his words as my captain to absolve you. Do not ask me to forgive the hurt you have done me personally. The forms will be obeyed.'

Kallis accepted his words with a dip of his head, casting a final glance at Leumas's body. Then he looked at the magician, standing off in the distance, his eyes trained on Aarin.

'I wanted only my freedom,' Kallis murmured. 'I want it still.'

'Leadership of this Clan is yours to claim,' Lorac answered, understanding his intent. 'But I advise you against it. You know the law, and we have accepted this contract. We will not follow you, and you cannot kill us all.'

Kallis looked at him, a gleam of mischief in his eyes. 'But I don't want you to follow me,' he said slowly. 'That is the last thing I want.'

Lorac frowned, and Kallis did not give him time to think about it. He turned to the gathered Ravens and held the sword high in the air. 'By the right I have won in combat, I claim your allegiance,' he announced in a ringing voice, freezing the scene into stillness. He looked over the mercenaries and caught Aarin's eye, nodding his head in the direction of the Grymwood. He saw the mage follow his movement, saw him turn to Jeta, whispering in her ear. Beyond them the magician, Vianor, was advancing angrily towards him, shouting to the mercenaries to take them, but the clansmen stood rooted in confusion, unsure how to react. He held the right under their law to claim their loyalty, but that right had never before been exercised by an outcast.

'I have defeated Leumas,' he reminded them. 'This is how your leaders are made! Do you dispute this?'

'It is indeed how our leaders are made,' Lorac said heavily at his shoulder. 'But this is a risk. Do you really expect them to accept you?'

'All I want is my freedom,' Kallis repeated. 'And the freedom of my friends. You can give me that at least. Me they might question, but you could convince them.'

Lorac studied his face, seeing the grim determination there, and seemed to reach a decision. Stepping up, he took Kallis's wrist in his hand and raised it high. 'By the right of combat,' he shouted. 'Do you dispute this?'

The mercenaries hesitated, murmurs of dissent spreading through their ranks. Lorac faced them down, holding firm to his position at Kallis's side. 'Leumas is dead, killed by this man. It is his right to command you!'

Kallis saw Vianor from the corner of his eye as he reached the mercenaries. Before the magician could interfere, he raised the sword once more. 'It is my right to command you, and I do so now. Cease your assistance of this man's attempts to capture us!'

He pointed the sword at Vianor, and the mercenaries followed his gaze. He knew Aarin believed that the magician would not dare follow them into the Grymwood alone. That was why they had come this way, and he watched his former brothers carefully, trying to guess which way they would jump. He could see the calculation on their faces, their dislike of the magician warring with their wary respect. It was not just his authority he was asking them to accept, but the breach of a contract sealed under their own laws.

'Now!' Lorac urged. 'You must do this now.'

Kallis flashed him a quick grin and turned to Aarin and Jeta. They were already moving, the packs clasped against their chests. He nodded to Lorac, raising his sword in a farewell salute, and began to back away. Leumas's cousin moved aside to let him pass, standing between his brothers and their outcast, between Vianor and his prey.

The magician rounded on his soldiers in impotent fury, but Kallis could see that they had reached a decision. He knew these men. He had fought beside them for years, and he knew their contempt for the magicians, a contempt that had deepened to hatred after the Istelan Valley. Faced with such a choice, they would remember that battle, and hesitate just long enough to give them the time they needed.

But the magician was another matter. His eyes never left the old face as he retreated to safety, and Kallis sensed the moment when Vianor's desperation peaked into action. 'Now, Aarin!'

But the mage needed no warning. Even before the words had felt his mouth, Kallis felt that peculiar sensation as Aarin raised a protective barrier between them and their enemy.

'Run!' he shouted, turning away at last and sprinting to the forest. He reached Jeta, catching her as she stumbled, and dragged her bodily along. A glance over his shoulder told him Aarin was close behind, and that the defences he had erected were holding—for now. Then the mercenaries disappeared from his sight as they entered the Grymwood and the forest's shadows fell around them.

They ran until they could run no more, collapsing to their knees amid the tangled roots of the great trees. Kallis flopped onto his back, Leumas's captured sword still in his hand. He sheathed it in his empty scabbard, listening for any sounds of pursuit, but all he could hear was the sound of their laboured breathing.

He rolled onto his side and saw Aarin, hands on his knees, head bowed. Aware of Kallis's gaze, the mage kept his own eyes fixed on the ground. The mercenary frowned, remembering the half-heard snatch of greeting before Aarin had called down his silence. *We meet at last.*

Kallis propped himself up on his elbow, his gaze wandering to Jeta who was also staring at Aarin. The mage ignored them both.

Kallis broke the silence first. 'What was that about?' It was clear to him now, inexplicable as it was, that though Vianor might have been searching for Jeta, it was Aarin he had come for. And by the look on Aarin's face when Vianor had greeted him, he had been as surprised as anyone.

Aarin shot him a look that fairly begged him not to press, but Kallis was a man who liked to know what he was up against. Something had passed between the magician and the mage when they were cloaked in that ghostly quiet, something that had unsettled Aarin badly.

'Who are you?' he asked quietly, too quiet for Jeta to hear.

Aarin looked wounded. 'The same as I have always been,' he replied just as softly. Yet even he did not sound as though he believed it.

Kallis sighed. He was being asked to trust, without understanding, and that did not come easily. But Aarin had saved his life at least once, so where instinct prodded him to dig for answers, friendship held him back, and he let it go. For now.

As Aarin picked himself up, Kallis looked down at the sword at his waist. Leumas's sword. He had won it fairly, but the blond captain's presence would always reside in the length of sharpened steel. He found he did not resent the shared ownership. Leumas might never have been a friend—the hierarchy of the clans made that almost impossible—but he had been a good man and a better captain. He had kept his people apart from the power struggle that had engulfed the clans after the battle of the Istelan. That was why Kallis had chosen the Ravens for his temporary haven. And it had always been temporary. He could see that now. Ever since Aarin had found him, hurt and abandoned, the clans had ceased to be his home.

He looked up, and found he was being studied in his turn. Aarin was watching him with a concerned frown, and Kallis realised he had been gripping the hilt of his captured sword so hard that a section of the guard had driven into his palm. The trickle of blood from the cut mingled with the sluggish flow from the wound on his arm.

Aarin nodded at the injury. 'That looks painful.'

Kallis shrugged. 'Not as painful as it would be if you stitched it for me.'

Aarin grimaced and Kallis found himself grinning. His muffled laughter dispelled the tension, and relief gave way to helpless hilarity. It felt good. Later, he would grieve for Leumas and the final breaking of the bond that tied him to his old life. Right now he was just happy to be alive.

He stood. 'Come on. Let's not sit around waiting for them to find us.'

SIXTEEN

THAT FIRST DAY in the Grymwood was hard for all of them. Kallis maintained a morose silence and Aarin laboured along at his side, caught between reliving the disturbing encounter with Vianor and the constant need to shield his companions from the oppressive presence of the Vale. Their preoccupation weighed down on Jeta, and she walked between them, quiet and subdued.

The trees grew thicker, the shadows darker, as they penetrated deeper into the forest. Tangled roots and fallen trunks blocked their path every few paces and the constant delays chafed at their nerves as half-heard whispers rustled on the wind. They walked side by side when they could, eyes fixed on the path ahead, avoiding the threatening shadows among the trees.

They reached the Istelan in the late afternoon on the second day, and the fast waters churned dark and ominous.

'How will we cross?' Jeta asked as Aarin pulled a rope from his pack, purchased days before in anticipation of this moment.

He tossed an end to Kallis who caught it easily and began to tie one end around the stump of a tree and other around his waist. 'Kallis will cross first, and secure the rope on the other side, then he will come back for you and take you across. I will follow.'

Kallis wrapped the slack of the rope around his forearm and walked to the edge of the bank. He shook his shoulders in preparation for the water's chill and plunged into the swift-running river.

Aarin watched his progress uneasily. He was almost positive that this was the ford—it certainly looked to be the right place—but the waters were much higher than the last time he had been here, and he hoped the floods had not washed away too much of the bottom. But Kallis reached the other side safely, his shivers visible even at this distance, and cold fingers took several moments to knot the rope securely to a tree on the opposite bank. He shrugged the pack he had secured high on his back to the ground and plunged back into the water.

A few minutes later he was back, lips blue with the cold, and gestured for Jeta.

'The rocks are slippery,' he cautioned. 'Go slowly. Keep hold of the rope, whatever you do. I will be right behind you.'

She nodded nervously and allowed him to lead her down the bank and into the river. Again, Aarin watched their crossing, heightened senses fraying his nerves, and again he watched Kallis climb safely out at the far side, yelling at Jeta to take off her wet clothes and wrap herself in a dry blanket. The mercenary waded into the shallows at the water's edge, gesturing for Aarin to begin his crossing, and the mage untied the rope from the tree and secured it around his waist. He hesitated a moment and Kallis called out, urging him to hurry.

It is just my imagination, he told himself firmly. *This river is no more aware than any other.*

As soon as his foot entered the water, he knew that was not true. A surge of raw power shot through his body, engulfing him in a wave of recognition. To those on the other side it must have seemed as though he had lost his footing on the wet rocks and stumbled, and he could hear them calling in concern. Kallis was reeling in the rope, and the line tugged taut, urging him to move. He ordered his body to get up, but he remained stubbornly on his hands and knees with the icy river swirling around him.

The unshielded elemental presence was brutal. It pummelled him, sucking him under until he felt as if his head really had been submerged. Yet there was no malice in this contact, no intent to harm, it was mere exuberance, playfulness even, but with a plaything that was not strong enough to endure it unscathed. Just as he thought he must drown, Aarin felt the flood flow past him, the last threads of it whipping against his skin in a final farewell. He looked up to find Kallis halfway back towards him and waved him back.

Kallis stopped. 'What's wrong?'

'I slipped, I'm fine.'

Kallis shook his head, exasperated, and waited for Aarin to reach him.

Ignoring the mage's protest, he slipped one hand under his arm and did not let go until he had dragged them both out on the other side.

'You took your time,' Jeta observed with a bite, her face almost hidden in the folds of a blanket. 'How much further?'

'Not far,' he assured her through chattering teeth, turning his back on Kallis's doubtful look. 'We're almost at the outer edges of the forest now, no more than half a day. But we need daylight to find our way. If we've come the right way there should be a good campsite nearby.'

She scowled. 'If?'

Aarin winced. 'We've come the right way.'

To his great relief he was not proved wrong. They had not gone further than a few yards when the dense foliage gave way to a wide clearing. Large boulders, the first they had come across, lay scattered here and there, and in the centre the remains of an old fire had blackened the ground in a crude circle.

'Yours?' Jeta asked as she sagged against a rock, her fingers tracing a pattern on the stone's surface. 'How odd that these should be here.'

Aarin kicked at the charcoal circle with his foot. 'When we get the fire started, spread your clothes over them. They'll dry faster.'

They built the blaze big and high, and the flames reached above their heads and forced the shadows back to the far edges of the trees. The night was crisp and clear. The moon was new, stars shone in bright clusters in the sky, and as the fire crackled merrily and brought life back to their frozen limbs, they could almost forget the perils that had brought them to this place.

But once the clothes were dry, Kallis let the fire subside, feeding it only when the flames spluttered and shrank, and the shadows crept back. There was an uneasy stillness to the night, no breath of wind to rustle in the trees, nor any sound but the fire. Aarin sat up straighter, tense and watchful, but even the magic of the Grymwood seemed quiescent. Too quiet. He had never known such calm in the currents of the earth, and he wondered whether Vianor had risked the forest after all. But if the magician was near, his presence would be greeted by a cacophony of sensation, not silence. The Grymwood would not extend its welcome to one such as him.

Looking around, Aarin saw he was not the only one affected. Kallis was working a piece of wood with his knife, but his movements were distracted and jerky. Jeta sat close by his side and her face was pinched with cold and fear. Her gaze flickered from the fire to the trees as though she believed some danger lurked just beyond her sight. He put his arm round her shoulders before he realised what he was doing, and it was a mark of her distress that she did not rebuff him.

Abruptly Kallis set down his knife. 'What is this feeling I have?' he demanded. 'This feeling of waiting, of expectation. Where does it come from?'

Jeta sat up. 'I feel it too. A pressure in my head, like wearing a hat that fits too tightly.'

Waiting. That was it. The Grymwood was waiting, but for what?

'Aarin?'

He shook himself and turned to Kallis. 'I'm not sure,' he confessed. 'Two nights ago, I think we awakened the spirit of this place. It is aware of us, exploring us.'

Jeta's face went white. 'It's aware of us? You said it was safe.'

'It is,' he assured her, feeling the twitch in the air at her agitation. The Vale did not like her anger directed against him. 'There is nothing here that will hurt us.'

'Has this something to do with your fall at the river?' Kallis asked more shrewdly. 'Was the Istelan also *exploring* you?'

'In a way, yes. But I am already known here. It was more of a greeting.'

'Some greeting,' the mercenary observed, settling back down. Aarin was surprised by how quickly he allowed himself to be reassured. It was as though his lack of understanding was so complete that he had no option but to trust that Aarin would always be truthful, and right, in his assessment of their danger. Jeta, on the other hand, would have none of his evasive half-truths.

'How can this forest be aware? It's just a collection of trees.'

Aarin looked up as those trees swayed gently in the gathering breeze.

'Don't be ridiculous,' she snapped, following his gaze. 'I've never heard such nonsense.'

Kallis chuckled. 'Which is not for lack of it, I assure you. Try him. Oh, go on, Aarin,' he urged when the mage started to protest. 'We have nothing else to do, and I'll wager none of us will get much sleep tonight. You may as well keep us entertained. Convert us.'

Aarin glowered at him. Tempted to refuse out of injured pride, he realised that what Kallis was really saying was *distract us*. Even so he would have refused if Jeta had not added her voice to the mercenary's, and her thinly veiled amusement challenged him to answer.

Very well, he would do as Kallis asked, but not what he expected. He dredged up his father's wildest tales from the happy memories of his childhood, when Ecyas had woven a tapestry of invention to entertain his son.

The tale he spun for them now was a long time in the telling, a heady mix of magic and mystery from a past they had never imagined. And if they suspected that as much came from Aarin's imagination as from his knowledge, they did not care.

Jeta listened, grudgingly at first, but with growing delight as Aarin recited the creation myth as he knew it, the story of the coming of the Maker's children to Andeira, and the mysteries of the First Age that no man had ever seen because it was before the time of their birth. He told them of the magic and the Joining, the link between the races that had brought the first act of creation to an end, and revelled in far-fetched stories of the mages and their dragons. And then, though he had not meant to speak of it, he found himself drawn into the sorrow of the ending that none now remembered, and the peril facing Andeira now the link was broken.

When at last he was done, Aarin lapsed into silence, exhausted yet strangely exhilarated.

'Why did it end?'

He looked at Jeta, curled up in her cloak watching him. There was an eagerness in her eyes that she was trying hard not to show, and he counted that a small victory.

'No one knows why the dragons left,' Aarin replied, picking up his thread once more. 'All we know is that something happened to break the partnership between our races. Loss of the link was catastrophic. The legends tell of a breaking in the stuff of the earth. Lands were torn apart, cities destroyed, and the people scattered. So much knowledge was lost. You will know it as the Lost Years, though few still remember the reason for the name. We lost ourselves and the truth of what happened was lost with us. Maybe it was never recorded, we may never know.'

He sighed. 'And now no one cares. Once my people sought to restore the dragons to Andeira but even they have turned their backs on that dream. Some of us have even...' He hesitated, suddenly ashamed of his people's faithlessness. 'Some have even begun to think like the magicians and say that what we have now is all we need, and that the dragons' return is something to fear, not to hope for. My land is divided now between two factions: those in Luen who still cling to the old ways, and those in Redstone who disregard their past in their search for a future.'

'I have heard of Redstone,' Kallis observed. 'It is at the edge of the wilds, not far from here. The magicians in Rhiannas spoke of it sometimes.'

Aarin frowned. The thought made him uncomfortable.

'How do you know they are wrong?' Jeta asked. 'Perhaps they are right. I see no sign of dragons.'

He felt Kallis glance quickly in his direction and knew he was remembering a similar conversation.

'I know they are wrong in ways that are hard to explain,' he told her. 'To feel the magic is to know that it is incomplete, and that this is not how it should be. I can feel the resonance of ages past, the waning of that power, and know that it will continue to lessen. I can feel it slipping away from me. And because I can feel that which gives life, I can also feel it taking life as it fails. If the future is for humanity alone, why should Andeira's beauty be fading?'

Jeta snorted. 'It's not fading. What are you talking about?'

Aarin cocked his head. 'Isn't it? Did the Istelan always flood the southern plains in the spring? Were there not islands once off the eastern coast? Don't your farmers complain every year that the harvests are getting poorer?'

'But that's...' Jeta paused, looking at him sceptically. 'You expect me to believe there have been a few years of poor harvests because the dragons have vanished from the world?'

Aarin sighed. 'No, not really. Because it is so much deeper than that, and you wouldn't understand.'

'Right, I wouldn't understand,' she scoffed. 'So you don't even have to try to convince me.'

Aarin caught sight of Kallis's face and realised the mercenary was enjoying this a bit too much. And all of a sudden he was sick of people laughing at him for what he knew was truth.

'You want me to prove it to you, but are you prepared to believe?' he challenged her.

'That's up to you,' she retorted. 'I believe that you believe it, but that doesn't make it true.'

Kallis sat up straighter, a look of mild concern on his face. 'Aarin...'

But Aarin ignored him. He ignored the subtle warnings he sensed in the still night that told him he should leave well alone in this place. Instead, he focused his awareness inward and conjured an illusion he had practised many times before. As the glowing orb sprung into being, both Kallis and Jeta shifted away in alarm.

'It won't hurt you,' Aarin assured them, sweeping his arm through the image, making it shimmer and flicker. Then he closed his eyes, concentrating hard, and the image changed.

Rotating in the air between them was a perfect, iridescent globe. There was no discernible colour, yet to look on it was to know that it encompassed every shade of colour in creation. Delicate channels criss-crossed its surface, dividing it into segments, and in the very centre was a smaller sphere, its shimmering surface catching the light as it spun.

Jeta, her scorn forgotten for a moment, said, 'It's beautiful. What is it?'

'Our world,' murmured Aarin, 'as she is in her essence. Imagine that this is the soul of Andeira, and these,' he pointed to the channels that intersected the globe's surface, 'are the different facets that make up her personality, the very strands of her being.'

She shook her head. 'I don't understand.'

The mage smiled, his eyes alight with the magic. 'In magic, as in all things, there are five elements: Fire, Water, Earth, Air, and Spirit. Each has its own nature and fulfils a different purpose, but between them, both separately and together, they underpin our entire existence.'

Stretching out a hand, Aarin traced his finger down one of the channels, crossing the globe from top to bottom, and as his finger passed over the surface the channel began to glow a delicate, rippling blue.

'The channel of elemental Water. It is essential to all life that lives and grows on Andeira. Without Water there would be no fish, for there would be no seas or lakes or rivers. There would be no plants and trees for there would be no water to nourish them, and no birds or beasts. No people. For this reason, humanity has priority over the element of Water. It is the mainstay of our magic.'

Reaching out again, this time with both hands, Aarin traced the vertical lines on either side of the shimmering strand of water. His forehead creased with the strain. This time there was a slight delay before the channels flashed to life and they were duller than the first, more sluggish. The left did not change colour, for it had no colour, but became somehow clearer, more transparent, and yet was also brighter than it had been. The other was kaleidoscopic. A myriad of different colours swam across its surface, changing so swiftly that it was impossible to identify one from the next. It too spiralled towards the bottom of the softly glowing orb.

Aarin indicated the left-hand channel. 'This is Air.' Then the right. 'And this is Earth. These I will call shared elements, because although they are as pure as Water, humanity cannot fully access their power. Priority is divided between two races.'

'The dragons.' Kallis supplied, leaning casually on his elbows.

'The dragons,' Aarin agreed. Beads of sweat stood out on his forehead now, despite the cold. 'Air and Earth belong to both humans and dragons equally and their properties are divided to reflect this. The air we breathe, that gives life to us and all Andeira's children, is ours to wield but not to master. Only the dragons can conquer the air, and for that reason it is shared between us. But Earth…'

Aarin paused, watching the swirling stream of colours as the globe rotated. 'Earth is more complex.'

He reached out with one hand and grabbed a handful of soil from the ground. 'In simple terms, this soil, this earth, is separate from these rocks.' Aarin rapped his free hand on the stone he leant against. 'But elemental Earth encompasses both equally, and their disparate qualities are as one in its essence. However, these differences are what divides the use of the element between the two races. Just as trees draw their nourishment from the earth through their roots, so do humans grow food, graze their animals, and provide for themselves from the soil. The dragons loved and needed the stone. They are most akin to this aspect of Earth.'

He raised his hand again and let his finger run down the final line. At first nothing happened, then quite suddenly the channel started to glow with a heat they could almost feel.

'This last is Fire, and its use is lost to us since the link was destroyed and the dragons left Andeira. Although we use fire, and its warmth is essential to us, we are not like the dragons, whose very existence is defined by the flames in which they were born. And in magic, as in all things, there must be balance, and so although we are permitted fire, we cannot know its deeper mysteries, nor tap into its elemental powers, just as the dragons cannot bear the touch of water. Not until the link is restored.'

No one spoke for a moment, and Aarin felt a certain measure of satisfaction as he watched their faces, absorbed by the illusion. It was just an illusion.

'What you see now is Andeira as she is. While each element still exists in the world, and still acts within creation, it is as though a part of them sleeps. Though Water still holds its own, and Air and Earth do so partially, this has created an imbalance in nature. The fact that we have not yet been swallowed by the oceans should tell you that this process is gradual, but who can say whether that might happen, one day. Fire grows ever weaker and sleeps the deepest. If it sleeps too long the world, our world, will die.'

Aarin closed his eyes again. 'Now I will show you Andeira as she was always meant to be.'

The globe spun wildly for a moment before it settled back into steady rhythm, but it was utterly changed. The elements flooded down the channels in a torrent of radiance, bright with life and colour like oil on water.

But it was what was happening inside the globe that was the most remarkable.

As the elements reached the bottom of the orb and met, they emerged altered. Their energies combined and spiralled up the middle, pulsing through the central sphere and shooting towards the highest point. Passing through the centre they became pure gold, blindingly bright, and other channels, previously unnoticed, began to glow. Strands of light stretched out from the centre to touch each of the lines intersecting the surface, ringing them in a band of gold, and the energy streamed up towards the meeting point of the four and began to flow downwards. Soon all the channels ran with golden light, and the sphere glowed with the beauty of perfection.

'Spirit.'

Aarin was only distantly aware of the other two now. 'You thought your world was beautiful now. Look how she could be.' The longing in his voice was replaced by terrible grief. 'Look what we have lost. Until we can find the dragons and bring them back into union with our race, we will never see such beauty again. We need to find the dragons, as we need nothing else, and this is what I have sworn to do.'

Aarin's voice trembled over the last words. He swayed. The simple illusion was draining his strength more than it should have done, and suddenly he was weary beyond measure.

'Aarin, enough,' Kallis said gently, grasping his shoulder.

But Aarin could not hear him. There was a shadow on the edge of his awareness, a tumultuous force bearing down on him. The physical world dropped away as his spirit turned to face it, and at last he recognised it and knew what he had done.

A tremble ran through the ground beneath them and Kallis looked around in alarm. Another tremor rumbled under their feet, stronger than the first, and the fire leapt up, the flames dancing higher and higher. He swung back to Aarin, shaking him roughly.

'Stop it!' he yelled. 'Stop this now!'

Aarin's head came up weakly. 'I can't,' he whispered. 'Tesserion save me, Kallis. I can't stop this.'

Somehow his illusion had not been illusion at all. He had tapped into, or alerted to consciousness, the true elements themselves. And now he would pay the price.

He should have heeded the warning of the Grymwood, heeded the burning in his blood. In some subtle way the magic had changed since his confrontation with Vianor. It was waiting now, the world was waiting, and into that expectant void he had flung the false promise of deliverance. Too late he realised his mistake, and he was given no chance to back away and save himself as the magic crashed down.

SEVENTEEN

AARIN FACED THE approaching storm, his defences ripped wide open. He knew he was seeing his death, yet his eyes danced with tears for the sheer, unrivalled oneness of it as he embraced the flood that would tear him to shreds. A hurricane of sensation whipped through his mind, sending him hurtling over the edge and into the void. Just for a second, for the barest of instants, he was engulfed by a moment of purest perfection and hung suspended over a place of total calm, the eye of the storm. Surrounded by emptiness, he found himself staring into an even greater emptiness, darker than the blackest of blacks, so black it was of no colour and all colours. Darkly beautiful, soothing, and threatening, where all things meet and become one, and he knew he was never meant to look upon it.

Then the storm swept him up, ripping him with agony. It was tearing him apart, sucking the life from him, as magic he could not comprehend sought entry into his being. It sent him spiralling into a different blackness that swallowed him whole.

When he came to he was far from that place, in a room he did not recognise, with an aching gap in his memory. As the walls swam closer, he saw something he did recognise. Dragons. They curled and twisted their way around the room, their long, sinuous bodies glittering with dark scales. It took him a moment only to recognise the paintings. They were the ones from his home, the shape of each familiar to him, but the names he had given them would not come to mind. For although they were the same, they were subtly different. Where they had been friendly, now they seethed with menace.

He recoiled, tormented by their horror, and his mother appeared. She smiled, raising a cup to his lips, and bitter liquid rolled down his throat. The world swirled and the edges of his vision grew dim. Aarin's head rolled to one side, and as his eyes drifted over the paintings a huge black dragon seemed to sweep over his sight and everything went dark.

He was in his room. It was a few days after his father had died. He knew from the way his few possessions were strewn in violent disarray about the small chamber. He had been in a rage, but he was not angry now. He was empty, cold, a vessel to be filled, a coin to be spent, and he had never been as unprotected as he was in that moment. With the clarity of a dreamwalker, gifted with hindsight, he recognised the shadow that had hung over him then, the shadow of another destiny, another purpose, and knew that if he had but taken that path his whole life would have been different. And it was not his choice that had saved him, but the kindly interference of a neighbour who had chosen that moment to intrude on his grief.

He heard Maralis come in and call his name, and he felt himself trapped in a moment of indecision. The child he had been longed to ignore her, to stay silent and still until she left, but his older self would not let him. So he got to his feet and walked into the main room.

Maralis smiled when she saw him, but it was a nervous, worried smile. 'Aarin.' She gestured to the bundle under her arm. 'I've brought you some food and some clothes. Those boys of mine have no more use for them.' She looked up, stopped, and mutely handed the bundle to him. Aarin nodded his thanks, his throat too tight to utter the words, and her smile broke.

'Will you not come to live with us?' she asked, as she had asked every day since his father died. A part of him was touched, the part of him that was not dead, and he knew he should be grateful, for there were few others in Luen prepared to show him such kindness. But her two sons were older and given to taunting him about his father even before his death, and he could not bear the thought of living with their sneers. She smiled sadly each time he refused, but she was kind to him, making sure he was fed and did not lack for anything.

'I cannot,' he said at last. 'I must stay here...' His voice trailed off because he found he could not recall why. Stay here and do what? Hone the magic that had killed his father? Find some way to atone for that tragedy? 'My father...' he tried again. 'I must do this for him, for what he believed...'

'Aarin,' Maralis said gently, taking him by the shoulders and kneeling so she could look into his eyes. 'Your father was never the same after your mother left. I won't say he lost his mind, for who am I to know, but he has filled your head with nonsense. The dragons lived a long time ago, and they are never coming back. We are what we are now. You cannot change that. Neither could your father. But he was a good man and don't let anyone tell you otherwise.'

'I don't,' Aarin said with the fierce pride of a child who was a child no longer but hovered on the brink of adulthood. 'And I will prove he was right. I will prove it to all of you.'

Maralis sighed, dropping her hands and rising slowly to her feet. 'Don't waste your life by searching after the dead, Aarin,' she said sadly. 'I know you loved him, but you have to let him go, his dreams with him.'

He spun away from her, and his anger invaded even the emptiness inside him. 'You're wrong,' he shouted, and suddenly he was a child again, his grief overflowing to fill that yawning chasm. 'My father wouldn't lie to me! I won't let you say so!'

She tried to calm him but he would not listen, shouting at her that his father was right, telling her to leave him alone, until the force of his anger dissolved into a flood of tears and he fled the room.

The weeping deflected that terrible coldness, turning guilt to grief. His father, who had been everything, was gone. They would never again walk along the cliffs, drinking deep of the unbridled power of the great ocean at their shore and letting their dreams take flight in the billowing wind.

That thought took him deeper within his memories, dragging him back in time and spitting him out on those same cliffs.

'We betrayed them,' his father whispered, and Aarin recognised the beginnings of a familiar lament. 'We broke the trust and they broke us. We were scattered, lost, wandering homeless across a world changed beyond our recognition. Some of us settled here, built this great city you see now only in the faded glory of its dying days.' His hand swept out, encompassing the ruins of Luen nestled between the hills and the sea. 'For a time, we flourished, broken and despairing but determined to survive. But we were arrogant, my son. We had not learnt our lesson, and everything we sought to save has now been lost. Our libraries are the greatest in the northern world yet of truth they tell us nothing. Of histories of our city we have a hundred volumes or more, all that speak of pride in our tremulous rebirth, yet there was such anger, such bitterness in us still that we could not recognise our sin, nor set words to it. And now it is too late, for it is forgotten. A fraction of what we knew then is known now, arts long lost that are ours by right, by blood. But it is not beyond us,' he said fiercely. 'It is not beyond *you*.'

Aarin thought he would say more, but the light in his eyes faded and his shoulders sagged. His voice was once again dull as the grey winter sea. 'Every day we weaken, boy, and every day another piece of this beautiful world dies. As long as our skies remain empty of dragons, as long as the fire in our veins is dormant, Andeira will slowly fail, until the last of her children are forced to scratch out a living on barren land before they too fade from the world.'

Ecyas stared out at the stormy coast, and Aarin followed his sad gaze. 'This used to be a peaceful land,' his father murmured, and Aarin was surprised at the longing in his words. 'Before the Eastern Isle sank beneath the sea it shielded our shores from the worst of the winter storms, and in the summer the water was as flat and clear as glass. As a child I would spend my summers on the beach, swimming, fishing, or just basking in the sun.'

A soft smile touched his lips for an instant. 'It is too dangerous now. There was a great storm, before you were born, that washed away the last of the settlements and the few islanders who thought they still had one more season at least before they had to abandon their homes. I remember standing on these cliffs, watching the boats trying to reach the shore, knowing they would be splintered on the rocks, and I raged that day that we could not command the power of the elements to save them as once we could have done. None survived. The storm washed away our harbour and most of the fishing fleet, but after the Eastern Isle was gone there was no need for boats. None but the bravest or the most foolish now test the fury of the winter seas, and there are so few of us left.'

His voice cracked, his eyes seeing the past, not the present. 'So few of us left that in summer we can fish from the rocks around the bay and catch as much as we need. But our children can no longer swim in these beautiful waters, for the storm stirred up the seabed into great ridges and now dangerous currents swirl in the bay. Not even we, who claim the Water for our own, can tame them.'

Aarin watched his father mourn the lost days of his youth and the beauty of his land, and knew it was a greater loss he suffered, every day, alone in his understanding. *We betrayed them,* Ecyas had said, and there was such sadness and regret in those words that Aarin knew they were true.

He never asked his father how he knew these things, never questioned, never doubted. It was enough that his father believed them. And more than that, Aarin realised now, he had desperately wanted to believe. As his father stood on the cliffs that day, mourning the passing of the world he had known, Aarin felt himself lulled by the lilting words and sucked deep into Ecyas's vision. It was then he had first decided that he would bring that past back, that one day he would make his father's dreams real. At ten it had been a child's fantasy, born of a desire to give his father the gift he most wanted, but after Ecyas's death it became an all-consuming passion. The failures he had suffered so far notwithstanding, the conviction that it not only could but must be done had stayed with him. When, two years later, he had found himself standing on those same cliffs, gazing at his father's cold face for the last time with the savage sea at his back, he knew he could only return riding on the back of a dragon.

The dragon murals of his home swirled back, snatching him away from the cliffs as he sank deeper into memory, to times barely remembered. He was back in his home, with his mother. He was safe. Aarin felt calmness descend. Everything was all right, the rest just nightmares. Then Sedaine came running towards him, a look of alarm on her face.

'Hide,' she told him urgently, she begged him. 'Hide for me, little one. For your mother.'

He just stood there, frightened and confused. Hide? Was this a new game? They had been playing together, he remembered. She had been hiding little gifts around the house and he had been searching for them. Did she want him to hide now so she could find him?

Sedaine reached him, scooping him up in her arms and running into the bedroom. She set him roughly on the bed and suddenly he knew this was not a game. His mother was scared. Aarin started to cry, his small body shaking with sobs, and she tried desperately to quiet him as she grabbed a basket and lifted it from the floor.

'Quickly, my love, under here,' she pleaded, ushering him under the wicker carrier.

He remembered the way the light had filtered through the weave of the basket, little pinpricks in the darkness, but this time his memories had a clarity the child had not possessed. He could see his mother's legs as she paced the small room, and he knew that she was wringing her hands in the way she had when she was nervous.

Then he heard footsteps, a man but not his father. He could recognise the sound of Ecyas's footfall anywhere, even now. The footsteps stopped, and he could see a man's booted feet in the corner of his vision. Then his memory failed him. He heard voices but they were muted, mere whispers, and his older self recognised a ward, a spell to hide the sounds. Aarin could have unravelled those wards with ease, but it was the child he was inhabiting, and that child, one sense thwarted, resorted to another. He watched himself lift the edge of the basket and peer at the stranger who had entered his home and frightened his mother. The man's gaze flicked down, just for a second, and he saw the stranger's face looking back at him.

The image splintered, leaving Aarin with a fleeting sense of recognition. He was alone again in his room, in his bed. He could hear his parents just beyond his door. They were arguing. They were always arguing. He covered his head with the pillow and tried not to hear. But their voices were too loud, rising in a crescendo of anger as the tide of their argument rolled on.

'You have lied to me,' his father shouted and Aarin was too young to hear the pain beneath the anger. 'All these years you have lied to me. Why?'

'Because I had to, because you would never understand.'

Aarin recognised the tone of his mother's voice. It was the one she used when she had run out of patience. Aarin had learnt to respect that tone, to be wary of it, but his father seemed not to have heeded the lesson.

'Kaefal's daughter died,' Ecyas insisted. 'Even here we heard that news. He has named Crian his heir and —'

'I did not die! The Lords of the North will never permit my brother to take the throne ahead of me. They will hold true to the oath they swore my father. My position is and always has been secure!'

'How, if you are not there to secure it? Do you really believe Lothane will allow a mage and her lowborn eastern son to sit on the throne?'

There was silence, then Aarin felt his mother brush the hair from his face, startling him. 'Hush,' she murmured. 'You will wake him. It is too soon'.

'He must know, Sedaine,' his father replied, but his voice had changed.

'He will, but I will be the one to tell him. He is my son.'

'So he is,' the man agreed. A man who was not his father. 'I have not forgotten. It was I who made him.'

There was a rustle of cloth as his mother stood. 'That is not true!' she hissed. 'I am his mother and Ecyas his father. We made him, not you!'

There was a soft laugh. 'You know what I mean, Sedaine. Do not flaunt a mother's outrage before me, not when I have seen the strength of your ambition. It is too late to back away now.'

Again, Aarin felt that sense of recognition as the timbre of the man's voice resonated in another memory.

'Do you never tire of using people?' he heard his mother demand, and her words slid through his mind without meaning. 'Enough people have suffered, enough people have died. And more will die! That poor Elvelen lord will meet his end on the gallows, hundreds of my people will be killed! Do you really think I want to take my throne this way? You have taken my freedom, my life, do not also take my son's. You don't need him for this.'

'Don't I?' the man asked silkily. 'Perhaps it is you who feels his presence isn't needful. After all, his is the one claim that can challenge yours.'

'You dare too much, my lord,' she said dangerously. 'If I thought –'

'If you thought,' he interrupted coldly, 'you would see just how much you need him. You are no longer young, Sedaine. Time is not on your side. Let us put pretence aside and speak the truth with one another. This guilt you show is but a token thing, and you know it. Do not try my patience with empty threats. We made a bargain, and you abandoned your son to this path. Now you must let me guide him. Your part in his life ended long ago.'

Those words penetrated even Aarin's feverish haze. He heard the menace in that voice and knew he must defend his mother. She had not abandoned him, she...

He forced his eyes open.

I'm dreaming, Aarin reminded himself. *This is a dream.* For the face he saw glaring at his mother was the face of the man he had glimpsed years ago at Redstone, the same man he now realised he had seen years before, as he peeked out from under the basket they used to collect wood. He remembered his confusion as his mother had picked it up. She never went out with the other women to the fields. She hated it. Hated it because she was royal? *Was* he dreaming?

The man looked down. 'Awake at last,' he said with satisfaction.

Sedaine spun around and dropped to her knees by his side. 'Aarin,' she whispered, stroking his face. 'Do you know me?'

He looked from one to the other, taking in the tears on his mother's face and the smirk of the man at her shoulder, and realised he was not dreaming. He shook his head, delayed understanding of their words filtering through his foggy mind.

'What have you done?' he whispered, the words creaking in his dry throat. 'What bargain?'

'Oh, Aarin,' she cried, and he saw tears in her eyes. 'Not now. It is too soon.'

Her companion did not agree. 'I think he is ready, Sedaine.'

She closed her eyes as though in unbearable pain, and Aarin's bewilderment deepened. He did not know where he was, or even *when* he was, for this was no memory he knew.

'Very well, my lord Darred,' she said at last, though he had to strain to hear her, and she stood and moved from his side without looking at him.

Aarin knew he should recognise the name. He had heard it somewhere, heard it spoken in anger, and knew this man was no friend to him, but the memory that had been an open book to him only moments ago was locked away from him now.

Darred moved to his side. 'Do you remember me, Aarin? We have encountered one another before, have we not?' He bent down and leaned in close. 'I have seen you. Oh yes, I remember the inquisitive child who snatched a look at a stranger from where his mother had hidden him, and I recognise the signature of the man who worked an iron lock in a tavern in Rhiannas. And now at last the face and the magic come together. Do you remember me?'

'I remember you,' Aarin replied hoarsely, and he did. He remembered the man who had come to Luen when he was young, and he remembered the man at the gates of Redstone. He recalled his name too, from the lips of both Jeta and Kallis, a harbinger of trouble. His enemies had found him. All his life they had been there, hovering over him, dogging his steps, but he had not realised it until this moment. 'I remember you.'

'Good.' Darred stepped back. 'It saves some explanation.' He walked to the wall, leaning casually against it, and his gaze drew Aarin's remorselessly after him. 'What Vianor told you is true. Your mother is the heir to the throne of Lothane, and one day soon she will come into that inheritance.' He tilted his head, watching Aarin steadily, enjoying his confusion. 'You understand that as her son you would be the crown prince of that country –'

Aarin ground out a desperate denial, screwing all his concentration into the effort. He would not let these people involve him in their deadly game! He needed to be free.

'No?' Darred repeated curiously, and his eyebrows climbed to his hairline. He said nothing for a moment, then seemed to reach some decision, for his attention flicked back to Sedaine.

'Your son is determined,' he said wryly. 'And I have not yet told him what I want from him.'

'I know what you want from me, and you will never have it,' Aarin hissed. 'I will never be your puppet.' The memory of Vianor's assertion that he was a magician born, and would serve them, still filled him with horror.

The surprise on Darred's face deepened. He was angry though he hid it well. 'You will. You have no choice. Give him more of the drug,' he ordered Sedaine as he crossed to the door. 'I would have him more tractable when next we speak.'

'But, my lord,' his mother protested. 'The *mesiola* is potent. Too much could kill him.'

'Oh, I doubt that,' Darred replied carelessly. 'Give it to him, Sedaine. I will return later.'

The door closed, and Aarin was left alone with his mother, staring at her in horror. She took a step towards him and he drew back, edging away from her, but his limbs were barely under his control and he could not escape. She sat on the edge of the bed and reached out to him, tears flowing freely. One hand brushed his hair aside, the other held the cup of the *mesiola*. The poison that had opened his memories. And those memories chose that moment to swallow him again, and once more he was lost in the past, watching his mother carry some medicine to him as she had when he had been sick. He could not resist her touch, or her voice as she coaxed him to drink, but when the bitter taste of the concoction touched his lips, his throat closed desperately against it.

She did not look at him, and he knew that she could not because she had betrayed him.

EIGHTEEN

THE DRUG TOOK hold fast, sending Aarin spiralling back into the dreamworld. His vision dimmed from grey to black, blanketing everything in a chill darkness. Then light returned. A shaft of sunlight fell across him, dividing his sight. He looked out of two pairs of eyes as his past merged with his present. He saw two rooms, two people: the mother he had loved, sitting by the side of her sick son, and the woman who was a stranger to him, who called his enemy 'my lord'.

'Where am I?'

His voice came from far off, an echo of his thoughts. His mother smiled at him, stroking his forehead, soothing the raging heat of his fever with her cool hand. He nestled closer.

'Where you want to be, Aarin.' Sedaine's voice floated somewhere above, and he saw her standing over him, wisps of dark hair framing her hard face. 'Is this how you remember me?'

He stared at her, confused, then turned his head and looked into his mother's gentle eyes as she murmured soothing words. He felt a rush of sadness and regret pulse like crystal through the fog of the drugged haze. 'Yes,' he answered sadly. 'This is how I remember you.'

Sedaine's face never changed as she looked at her other self. 'Was I ever truly this woman?' There was no flicker of recognition in her eyes.

'Yes,' he insisted, but already the image from his memory was dimming, fading at the edges. He held on to it, clinging like a child to the way he wanted her to be. 'You loved me.'

Sedaine shrugged, even as his mother continued to care for him, raising a glass to his lips to let water cool his parched throat. 'I love my country also. I did what I had to do.'

'I am your son.'

A glimmer of emotion showed through her mask. 'You are.'

He felt her hand on his forehead again, felt the tenderness of the touch, and struggled to remember. 'Is this a dream?'

'Are you dreaming?'

He frowned. 'No.'

She smiled, a crooked smile that never reached her eyes. 'Then this isn't a dream.'

'Are you really here?'

No answer. He turned to the other, the memory of his mother. 'Are you really here?'

'Hush, Aarin,' she whispered, smiling gently. 'Of course I'm here.'

He sighed, feeling contentment like a rush lulling him towards sleep.

'Don't fool yourself, Aarin.' Sedaine watched him live out his memory. 'You can't hide in the past. You have to face this.'

Then he did remember, and the two sides of his vision joined into one. Sedaine was standing at the foot of the bed, alone. The memory of her was gone, vanished as though it had never been, and try as he might he could not bring it back.

'She's gone, Aarin. I am all there is.'

He shook his head, the drug still clouding his thoughts. 'Why? Why did you do it?'

'Why?' Once more he thought he saw something in her dark gaze, something that mirrored his memory of her, then it was gone. 'I did what I had to do,' she repeated. 'As you will.'

'That is no answer.'

'Not the answer you want. My country must come first.'

Aarin raised a hand to his face to cover his anguish. 'It is not my country. I cannot do what you ask of me.'

'I ask nothing of you,' she snapped, a flush of anger colouring her cheeks. 'I never did.'

'And you gave me nothing,' he retorted, angered in his turn.

'I gave you life.'

He looked into her shadowed face, framed by raven hair. 'But you withheld the life I should have had.'

'Should?' She looked almost amused. 'There is no *should*, Aarin. There is only what is, and what you make of it.' Her head cocked to one side. 'What will you do?'

'Not what you want.'

'Don't be too sure you know what I want, my son. You know nothing about me.'

'No,' he replied slowly. 'You made sure of that.'

She shook her head sadly. 'This serves no one. Will you waste this time?'

He frowned. 'What time is this?'

'A time for truth.'

He laughed at that. 'Then why are you here?'

He saw the angry flush colour her cheeks. 'I am here to warn you—if you will listen.'

There was something deadly serious in her tone, and he listened even as his vision began to grey and the image of her flickered. Her voice seemed to come from far away, a murmuring carried on the breeze.

'Darred lies,' she told him, and he wondered why she sounded so urgent when he felt so relaxed. 'Listen to me, Aarin,' she implored. 'Hold on a moment longer.'

'Can't,' he murmured. 'Going.'

All at once the world seemed to snap back into focus, and her face was close to his, her eyes boring into him.

'His lies are in what he does not say, not what he does. If he offers you a bargain, don't treat. It is only Darred who stands to gain.'

He nodded, eyes sliding close once more.

'Do you understand?' she asked, but her voice faded into nothing before the words were finished.

Aarin woke with a jerk. The room was empty. The vile taste of the *mesiola* was in his mouth, making him retch, and he pushed back the sheets and leaned, gagging, over the edge of the bed, forcing his body to expel what poison remained in his stomach. His head was reeling with the effects of the drug, and he could feel the creeping heaviness spreading through his limbs. He grabbed the jug and poured water down his burning throat, retching again as it hit his abused stomach. He drank more, desperate to purge the drug from his system. In large enough quantities the *mesiola* plant could induce a deep sleep for days at a time, and he had no desire to return to that world of shifting memories.

The door seemed a mile off, the hallway beyond an interminable distance. Aarin moved in a lurching stagger, unable to lift his feet clear of the floor, yet with every step his head became clearer and the grogginess receded. Reaching the door, he leaned heavily against it. The corridor outside was silent. He could hear no voices, nor any footsteps, so he opened the door a crack and peered through. When the world stopped spinning, he saw there was no one waiting beyond to keep him there. Darred must have trusted the drug to keep him unconscious. It was Sedaine, somehow, who had brought him back.

The hallway twisted ahead of him as he stepped through the doorway. The rush of cool air soothed his burning skin and he rested wearily against the wall. Eyes that were grainy and sore slid closed. When he opened them, he could no longer banish the haze at the edges of his vision.

With a sigh Aarin pushed himself off the wall, taking a shaky step forward. The corridor had become a tunnel. The walls were closing in on him at an alarming rate, the light of the window at the end shrinking to a pinpoint. Trailing a hand along the blocks of smooth stone, he forced his tired body to put one foot in front of the other. He did not know where he was going, only that it was away from that room, away from the waking visions that haunted it and the people who had put him there.

He passed doors on his right and left but ignored them all. The way out would not be through one of them. At last he reached the end of the hallway and found it branched in both directions. He could hear muffled voices from his left, the sound of a door closing and someone heading his way. He drew away instinctively. The footsteps drew closer and he reached out blindly to find a door through which he could hide. Grasping fingers closed round a heavy handle and he leant all his strength on it, feeling it turn. He heard a woman's voice call out as he fell backwards across the threshold. The heavy door slammed closed behind him, cutting off her cries. He twisted round to rest his back against it and saw the figure of a man watching him, his back to the window and his face in shadow.

'Aarin?' Kallis was crouched by his side. 'Are you all right?'

Aarin could not respond. Alarmed, Kallis tipped his head back, and whatever he saw made his mouth thin in an angry line. He left the room and returned moments later with a skin of water, holding it to Aarin's lips.

'Drink,' he ordered, as Aarin turned his head away. Water spilled from the skin onto his shirt and Kallis grabbed his chin, forcing his head back, and poured the liquid down his throat.

Aarin coughed, choking, but Kallis's grip was firm and he no choice but to drink. Almost immediately he was doubled over, retching up watery bile. Kallis held him as he was sick, and when he was done made him drink yet more. Only when it seemed like he had brought up everything he had ever eaten did Kallis set the skin aside and help him gently from the ground. Aarin let him drag him stumbling into the sleeping chamber and flopped down gratefully onto the narrow cot.

He tried to voice his thanks, but his throat was too raw. Kallis closed the shutters and soothing darkness descended. He slept.

When he awoke it was to a different kind of darkness. Thin slivers of moonlight cast eerie shadows across the unfamiliar room. He closed his eyes, falling back on his other senses, and smelt the faint tang of *mesiola* on the air and the sour taint of sickness. Ripples of cramping pain stretched out from his middle, and he uncurled contorted limbs to gain a measure of relief. When he opened his eyes again his mind was calmer, the first frayed edges of consciousness smoothed over by stubborn reflex. His sight adjusted to the gloom, and beside him he saw Kallis, asleep in a chair.

Memory returned with a force that stole his breath. He was in *Redstone*.

How did I get here? He looked at Kallis, snoring softly. The last he knew he had been in the Grymwood. The last thing he had felt was the blinding passage of the Vale's magic scorching a path through him. 'Why did you bring me to this place?' he asked aloud. 'Why here?'

'I had no choice,' Kallis replied, making him jump, and he saw that the mercenary was awake and watching him. 'We were desperate. I could not rouse you, nothing I did could reach you. I thought you were dying, and I could not help you. You needed your own people, and this was the only place I knew to find them.'

Aarin closed his eyes. Bringing him here had almost certainly saved his life, but in trying to help Kallis had unknowingly handed him to his enemies. He could not be more helpless.

'Aarin?' Kallis asked tentatively.

'These are not my people,' he murmured wearily. 'It would have been better to let me die.'

'It is never better,' Kallis snapped, his voice rising in sharp reproof. 'You are not that great a fool. And whatever your differences, these people took you in and cared for you. The lady herself tended you.'

Aarin drew in a shuddering breath. Kallis truly did not know what he had done. 'Her name is Sedaine,' he said softly. 'Do you know who she is?'

'Sedaine?' Kallis shook his head. 'I don't –'

'You should,' Aarin said with a twisted smile. 'You of all people. Haven't you always prided yourself on knowing the goings on in Lothane?'

Kallis's frown deepened. 'I don't understand. We are not in Lothane.'

'No, we are not, and neither is she. But she should be, for that is where she was born, in Rhiannas.'

'What are you saying?' Kallis demanded. 'That she is Kaefal's Sedaine? Lothane's lost princess?'

Aarin nodded.

Kallis looked stunned. 'If you are right, that would throw matters into a pretty mess,' he muttered to no one in particular. 'But what is she doing here? Why... what is it?' he demanded abruptly, catching sight of the misery on Aarin's face.

'She is my mother,' Aarin said bitterly. 'Sedaine is my mother.'

The mercenary stared at Aarin in disbelief. 'Then you,' he began. 'That would make you –'

'It makes me nothing! Nothing more than a tool.'

'Aarin. Think what you are saying! If she is who she says she is, she could claim Lothane's throne tomorrow and there is not one of the northern lords who would stand in her way. They would welcome her. Maker, they would be so welcoming it would be years before the feasting came to an end!'

'What about Nathas?'

'What about him? He's a distant cousin and a foreigner. Sedaine is the king's daughter! His claim could not stand against hers.'

'It could not,' the mage agreed, as the weariness he could not seem to shake crashed down on him. He ran his hands over his face, pushing back the tangles of hair. Sedaine's angry denouncement of Darred's plans had told him too much. 'But if her claim is to take precedence over his, it must be made before he is crowned. If it is made afterwards?' he shrugged. 'The lords will be forced to stand by their choice because that is the law. Think, Kallis. You once lectured me on this very subject. What will happen then?'

The mercenary stared at him in consternation. 'The people will flock to her,' he said slowly. 'They don't want an Elvelian king, and they already blame Nathas for the trouble the magicians have caused. There are tensions between the merchants, taxes are sky high, and the city is full of mercenaries. It would be a bloodbath. But why should she wait? If she wishes the throne, she has but to take it.'

Aarin shook his head, closing his eyes. 'No purpose at all, if Lothane is the only throne she means to claim. But I think the whole of the North is the true prize.'

Kallis sucked in a breath as understanding dawned at last. 'Nathas is hated. He would be overthrown, executed, and Elvelen's lords would never stand for it. There would be no avoiding war, but with the resources of Naveen to draw on Lothane would surely win.' He whistled. 'That is a piece of cunning, and an exercise in patience. Sedaine has been gone twenty-five years at least, too long surely for this to be her work.'

'And there you have it,' Aarin said flatly. 'This is not her work alone, far from it. You told me Darred is behind the unrest in Rhiannas. Well, this is Darred's doing, his and the magicians. She is not just Kaefal's daughter, Kallis. She is also niece to one of the most powerful men in the North, one of the most powerful magicians in the North, and this empire we stand on the brink of is really theirs. Tesserion help me, they are building themselves a dynasty and I am a part of it. Merciful Maker, I am a part of it!' He was shaking, tremors running through his exhausted frame, and he clasped his hands around his knees to keep them still.

'I can't do it,' he whispered. 'I will not be a part of this, but they will make me. They will take away everything I have, everything I want, and tie me to a life of tyranny over their new nation. I cannot do it. I won't.'

'And is that why?' Kallis asked gruffly. 'Did you take the drug to end this before it can start?'

It was only then that Aarin understood his sharp-edged reproof. Kallis thought he had deliberately poisoned himself. The realisation jolted him from his misery. Darred would be returning soon to find him gone, and he would search Redstone. He sat up, swinging his legs off the cot, dizziness making him sway. 'We must leave,' he said urgently. 'Now. They will be coming.'

'Damn it, Aarin,' Kallis burst out. 'Tell me that isn't why!'

Fighting back a surge of impatience, Aarin met Kallis's concerned gaze. 'Your fear is misplaced,' he assured him in a tight voice. 'The drug was not meant to kill me. We do not have much time. He will be coming for me soon, and I cannot let him find me here.'

The frown on Kallis's face eased slightly. 'Darred? He is here? No, wait,' he said as Aarin stood. 'We must think. We can't just run. We need a plan.'

Aarin reeled and Kallis caught him. 'Think swiftly,' he snapped. 'The longer we stay here, the deeper we are trapped.'

'I know that,' Kallis retorted. He pushed Aarin back down. 'I need to find Jeta. If revolution is the means they will use to take control of the North, then her marriage to Nathas is an aggravation that can only add weight to their schemes.' He laughed. 'And to think I should ever willingly agree to take that girl anywhere. Stay here. I will not be long, and Darred will assume the drug will ensure a few more hours of sleep at least. I will fetch Jeta, see to finding some horses. It would not be wise to leave on foot.'

Aarin gripped his arm. 'Be careful,' he warned. 'They will be watching.'

'I know,' Kallis assured him with a grin. 'Don't worry. I can be subtle when I need to be.'

NINETEEN

AARIN LAY BACK, giving in to his dragging exhaustion, but sleep would not come. The beginning of a headache throbbed in his temples. He sighed, drawing his knees up to his chest to rest his aching head.

Minutes ticked by. The door opened and someone stood in the entrance. Not Kallis. The footfalls were too light.

'What do you want?' he asked testily. Jeta was the last person he wished to see him now.

She slipped into the room, unperturbed by his rudeness. He expected a prickly retort, or at the very least a sharp rebuke to pull himself together. Instead she said simply, 'I want to help.'

He looked up, startled. 'Why?'

Taking his question as leave to stay, Jeta perched herself upon the room's only chair, and swept her skirts into a semblance of neatness. Someone had found her new clothes. Not silk this time, but good, plain linen, and if the fit was a shade too snug for comfort, the resulting curves were nothing if not pleasing to the eye. He looked away quickly before she could read that thought.

'You once asked me how I could turn my back on a kingdom,' she said. 'Now I ask you the same question, and perhaps when you have thought about it you will understand me a little better. No one likes to be used, Aarin, and I know how it feels when it is the people you love who use you.'

'No, you don't,' Aarin shot back. 'You have no idea how it feels to know your own mother has betrayed you. How could you? Just leave me alone.'

'So you can wallow in self-pity? You are no longer a child and sulking does not become you.'

Aarin snorted, turning his back on her and disdaining to reply.

'I do know how it feels,' Jeta added after a pause. 'Perhaps you think that being sold into marriage to a stranger to further your parents' ambitions is no great hardship. After all, Nathas is a rich man. He would have provided for me, given me jewels, dresses. And I must believe my parents thought he would be king one day, but he is still a stranger, unknown to me and to my father. Is he a kind man? Will he treat me well? Will I be happy? Questions my father never asked because he did not care about the answers, only his own desires. And my father's desires would have brought me to a very unpleasant fate.

'You see a girl who has been spoilt by privilege,' she continued quietly, 'who cares for nothing beyond her own needs, and maybe that is true. But my life has been narrower than yours, and I have been raised in the knowledge that it will only grow narrower still once I take a husband. All I had to make that future bearable were my dreams of a man who would love me, and whom I could love, who would give me beautiful children and long years of contentment. That dream died the day my parents sold me in marriage to a foreign lord. Do not tell me I can't understand your pain, because I know it all too well.'

Ashamed, Aarin could not think of anything to say.

Jeta stood, and walked to the door where she delivered her parting shot. 'Your mother is too old now to have another child. If they sit her on the throne the succession will be as precarious as ever, for there will be no blood heir if you refuse to play your part. Without you this whole thing could collapse.'

'Are you telling me to do this?' Aarin asked incredulously. 'For the sake of my mother?'

'I'm not telling you to do anything,' she snapped. 'I am pointing out that a clear line of succession is everything in these things. Were Sedaine a man there would be no problem, but she is a woman and she will bear no more children. So where does that leave the royal line? Ask yourself that before you assume you know everything. If the magicians truly intend to back her claim over Nathas's, and I believe they do, they must have considered this. You would be foolish to believe this a matter in which you have a choice.'

And with that she was gone, her warning ringing in his ears. He knew she was right. Darred would not let him go, and Aarin was not sure he could stop him doing exactly as he pleased. He was furious with his mother for putting him in this position. He had to know why.

Ignoring Kallis's injunction to stay where he was, Aarin made his way to his mother, his feet finding the way on instinct. He would confront her, demand to know how she could be a part of this vile scheming. He did not know what he would do then, but in that moment it did not matter. All he wanted to know was why.

He found her sitting alone in her room, awake despite the lateness of the hour. She jerked to her feet as he appeared at the door and he watched as the surprise on her face turned to nervous hope. Then she took a step towards him and the anger in him bubbled over.

'Stop,' he snapped. 'Don't come any closer.'

'Aarin...'

'No!' he shouted, angry beyond rational thought. 'No more lies. I want the truth.'

Sedaine sagged against the wall. 'And what truth is that?'

'Don't try to trick me,' he warned. 'You know what I want.'

'Ah, but the truth is a tricky thing, Aarin. It is many things to many people. Tell me, whose truth do you want? Mine, yours, Darred's?'

'I want to know why,' he said coldly. 'Why did you do this to me?'

'What have I done, Aarin?' Sedaine asked bitterly. 'I kept you safe as long as I could. I left you behind with your father though it broke my heart to do so, and I told myself you were dead. I made myself believe it so no one would ever guess the truth. Again and again I lied to my masters. I told them there was no child, no royal babe to claim the throne. Then suddenly there you are, not dead perhaps but dying, and I saved you.' Her voice lost its bitter edge and became weary with resignation. 'I cannot lie now, Aarin. What would be the point?'

'Yet you do,' he growled. 'I heard you, five years ago. You and Darred, here. I came looking for you when I left Luen. You did not see me, but I saw you. He was looking for me even then, and you... you knew how he planned to use me, and still you were helping him.'

Sedaine paled. 'You were here? You came to me?'

Aarin looked at her in disgust. 'You do not even deny it.'

'Deny what? That Darred knew of you, yes, that I admit. But what he wanted you for I never knew. My uncle's plan was always to place me on the throne of Lothane, and Darred promised it would be so. But my uncle, the magicians—my merciful masters—they never knew you existed, because I never meant you to be used as I knew they would use you. I thought to protect you, and when Darred brought word that you had vanished, Tesserion save me, I hoped you would stay vanished. For then you would be free, as I have never been.'

He stared at her, caught between anger and a need to believe her words. She laughed at the expression on his face. 'What did you think? That I hid you because I feared you might take the crown from me, and that I claim you now only because I have no choice?' She pushed herself off the wall, pouring a cup of wine from the half-empty pitcher. Her hand shook and he realised she was drunk.

'Are you ashamed of me, Aarin? Do you look at me and see only what I did not do for you, or your father? Or do you pity me, left alone and dangling from my uncle's line? Well, I don't need your pity,' she slurred. 'You have no idea what I have done for you.'

He shook his head, snatching the wine from her grasp and hurling the cup at the wall. 'I don't want to know. You had your chance to be a mother to me and you failed. It is too late to take back the past. There is only now, and you have robbed me of that too, just as you robbed me of a mother.'

'Idiot boy,' she spat. 'You think I wanted this? You think I wanted to give myself to a man I did not love and grow fat and clumsy with his child? I did not want to love you, but love you I did, even though one day I knew I must leave you. Once a year he came, and I would hide you, do you remember? And then I would tell him I still had not conceived, even when the changes to my body spoke my lie to the world.'

She laughed, stumbling backwards and onto the stool as Aarin listened in horrified fascination.

'I was a fool to think I could keep you from him. Always a fool.' She looked up, and Aarin saw tears in her eyes. 'Darred knew I had borne a son. Any one of the villagers could have told him that, but still I pretended.'

'Then why did you leave?' It was the question that had tormented him for so many years. 'Why not simply stay, forget about Lothane? Why did you abandon us?'

Pain flashed in her eyes. 'Abandon you? I could not stay in that place, even had I not already been in too deep to back out. I could not watch your people continue to stumble along in their ignorance while the rest of the world moved on and left them behind. I grew weary of your father's pious prattling. And my masters had other plans for me that called me away whether I wished it or not. I wanted my throne, Aarin. I want it still. Lothane is my country and I will not let her fall into the hands of an outlander king.'

'Your throne,' he sneered, outraged. 'What about your family? What about my father? Did you never think of him?'

Sedaine seemed oblivious to his grief. 'There was nothing between us in the end. When I did what I did, he was angry, but not surprised. I think he knew in his heart it could never work, and he sent me away.'

'You're wrong,' Aarin protested. 'My father loved you. He loved you until the day he died. He would never have made you leave!'

'No, Aarin,' Sedaine said sadly. 'He may have loved me once, but that love had started to fade long before I left. He knew I did not believe as he did. I never pretended to, but he thought he could change that, that just by loving me he could bring me round. At some point he realised that would never happen, and it was then that he changed. His love was never truly for me,' she said bitterly. 'The dragons were his only true love, the dragons and you. How could I compete with creatures out of legend?'

Her hurt was real, Aarin realised, and for a moment he allowed himself to imagine what it must have been like for her, for he was the one person who could understand the depths of Ecyas's obsession. For someone who could not share it, it would have been a lonely, frustrating existence.

Sedaine was watching him. He knew she had guessed his thoughts.

'It was the magicians who sent me to your father, boy. But it was Darred who told me to bed him. He is the strongest, he told me. Breed with the best. But there was more to it than that, more that I did not realise then. It was not just your father's strength he wanted. It was his blood. Vianor thinks to sit you on a throne to do his will, but that one wants your very life.'

Aarin shivered, feeling again that same strange touch of fate. 'Why? What am I to him?'

She shook her head and her whole body swayed. 'Don't ask me, Aarin. I am not party to his secrets. And that man has secrets within secrets.'

Once again Aarin glimpsed a future he did not, could not, accept, and felt the same compulsion to deny it now as he had then. 'Know that I will never give in to him,' he said, his voice quiet and dangerous. 'Neither to the throne nor any other scheme. I will never believe in your way. Never.'

'Oh, well said,' a new voice drawled, and Aarin spun around to see Darred watching him from the doorway. The man leaned against the wall, a mocking smile tugging at the edges of his mouth. 'I admire your conviction, boy, truly I do, and your loyalty to your foolish father is touching. But you are mine now, and you will do as I bid you.'

Incensed, Aarin took a step towards him, hands clenching in rage. 'I am not yours. And I will sit on no throne and do no one's bidding but my own. You have used my mother against me, against her will, and there is no claim on me you can make that will force me to submit to you!'

Darred laughed. 'No claim on you? Don't you understand? We made you, boy, I made you. And he who creates is the master of his creation. You are mine. And as for the throne, why, I have your mother for that. You are neither needed nor wanted for that role.'

Aarin stared at him in dumb shock. 'You created me? Who are you to claim ownership over any man, or take upon yourself the role of our Maker?'

Darred quirked an eyebrow, unmoved by his anger. 'I see Ecyas taught you a true devotion. No doubt he hoped it would force you to follow the path he had laid out for you. Did he also tell you that you are free, that your choices are your own to make?' He took a step into the room. 'He lied to you, Aarin. Your father manipulated you from the day your mother left, twisting your mind to seek only one thing. You might believe this search you make is your own choice, but he took your choices from you long ago.'

When Aarin started to protest, he cut him off. 'Ecyas used you poorly,

Aarin. He knew what he had done, what he had brought into the world. Not at first, I grant you, but he soon realised you were different, and when he found out who your mother is, he sent her away. But he never told you why, or who you really are. I will tell you, for I am responsible for your birth.'

Darred advanced another step, then another. 'I will tell you who you really are, and then I will let you make your choice, the only true choice you have ever been given. Remember that, and make no swift judgement you might regret.'

'Do not try to win me with trickery,' Aarin warned, his anger transforming into sharp readiness. There was threat laced through Darred's every movement. 'I will not listen to your lies.'

He pushed past Darred, making for the door without even a glance at Sedaine, hunched over in drunken misery behind him. The man let him pass, but as he reached the door he said softly, 'There is a prophecy, Aarin, that concerns you. One day, it promises, two ancient bloodlines will cross, the heirs of the Severing, and they shall make a child.'

There was a singsong quality in Darred's voice and Aarin halted to listen as though rooted by an invisible force. 'The centuries of enmity shall be washed away by their union, a union of love, and the strengths of each line will give to you, their son, the power to restore all that is now lost.

'Your father and your mother, Aarin,' Darred said, 'are the two sides of that ancient divide, and you are the seed of their coupling. But they did not come together through chance, or through love, and you are not the hope that the prophecy promised. You were born in a house of hate, your birth brought about through human intervention to force that prophecy to fulfilment. You are tainted with the ambition of your makers, and you belong to them, to me. That you can do what is needed of you I do not doubt, but the ways and means of that doing are not within your control. You are a man born into the wrong age, before either you or the world is ready. You are flawed, and the salvation you seek can never be yours. Go your own way if you will, and seek the return your father dreamed of, but you will only fail. I can offer you that dream—the return of the dragons to Andeira—but first you must submit yourself to us and cede to us your right to claim a part of that future. If you truly wish only to restore the magic of the world, and not power for yourself, then you will not find that too much to ask.'

Aarin felt a shiver run through him, one not induced by words alone. For a moment, as Darred had spoken of the dragons, a strange, haunting power had risen in the room, a power that was alien to him and yet chillingly familiar. He glanced at Sedaine and saw her posture had gone rigid. He turned back to Darred. 'Cede to you my place in that future? You want me to die for you, to die to fulfil this dream.'

Darred shrugged. 'Perhaps, in the end, that is all you can do. Can you not feel it in you even now, feel the prophecy that is burning you from the inside out? It is killing you, driving you to your death, and it deceives you with its fickle promise. Do not be deceived, Æisoul. Should you fail the prophecy, the dragon-fire that burns you now *will* consume you.

'And so now I offer you a choice, Æisoul, the name out of prophecy. Come with me, and I will bring you to your dream. Or leave here and continue your hopeless search. For without me to guide you it will be hopeless. If you seek a way to avoid death, you will not find it down that road.'

Into the silence that followed, Darred delivered his final warning. 'You have time to consider your choice, but there is one thing you should understand. My offer is open to you alone. If you choose not to join me, the girl will return to Rhiannas to go through with her marriage. As for the renegade, he will be returned to his brotherhood's justice.'

And then he was gone, leaving Aarin frozen in horror.

'Aarin,' Sedaine called softly, watching him through eyes red with drink and old tears. 'Your father was a good man, don't let him tell you otherwise. He was good, and kind, and strong, back then, before −'

'Before you broke him,' he said flatly, waking from his shock. 'Before you destroyed his life and broke his heart. Do not speak to me of my father. You have not the right.'

'Maybe not,' she agreed, and there was a weariness in her voice that went deeper than the lateness of the hour. 'But I can't sit back and let that man take away your memories of the father you loved. Ecyas never knew what we did, he and I, when we made you. He knew nothing of any prophecy. You are what he made you, but he did as he did from love, and the dreams he gave you are real. It is Darred who lies, Darred who manipulates.'

'How can I know what to believe?' Aarin protested. 'Each of you tells me I have been lied to. My father is dead, and I cannot ask him, and though you might be my mother you have never been that to me, and I dare not trust what you say. Darred speaks of prophecy and offers me a chance to make our magic whole again, but to do so I must die and let that magic pass to those who would reshape it for their own ends. Who am I to believe? What choice am I to make?'

'Perhaps there is no prophecy, Aarin,' Sedaine countered. 'Maybe you are only who you are, and you can do only what any of us can, if we choose. Darred cannot force you to do anything you do not wish to do.'

'Can't he? He holds my friends' lives over me and tells me he gives me a choice, only choose wrongly and they die. That is no choice at all.'

'Then you will do as you have to,' Sedaine said wearily. 'And perhaps when you are forced into doing something you despise you will judge me less harshly.'

Aarin stared. *No one likes to be used.* Jeta had said that. He was not the only one who had suffered through Darred's schemes.

'Perhaps,' he said stiffly. He could not think about that now. He could not think about anything but Darred's voice, reciting the words of a prophecy that took from him everything he had thought he had.

Sedaine did not try to stop him leaving. When he looked back, she was reaching for the flagon of wine and would not meet his eye. He tried to remember her as she had been when he was a child, but he could not banish the sight of her misery, nor summon the words to forgive her. So he left.

Kallis stalked through the darkened hallways, furious with himself for letting Aarin out of his sight. He had returned to find the room empty, and Jeta recently arrived. She had brought all the things he had told her to fetch, but when he asked after Aarin she had been unable to tell him much. They had spoken, she had left. He was gone when she returned.

When Aarin did not reappear, Kallis ordered Jeta to wait and went out to look for him. He was heading for Sedaine's quarters, unable to think of anywhere else Aarin might be. He had already checked the room where they had taken him on their arrival, but it was empty and there was no sign that Aarin had returned there. He turned a corner and almost ran into Sedaine herself.

'Where is he?' The question came from both at once and they stepped back, surprised.

It was Sedaine who broke the silence first. 'If you know you must tell me,' she implored. 'He is in danger.'

'Yes,' Kallis agreed, grabbing her by the arm and dragging her to the wall. He flung her roughly against it. 'From you, woman. Now it is your turn to tell me: what have you done with Aarin?'

Sedaine gave a tight shake of her head. 'He left me an hour ago, on his own and free. I thought he had returned to you.'

'And where were you going?' the mercenary demanded. 'To tell your magician masters?'

She laughed. It started as a low chuckle and ended in a fit that left her breathless. Kallis drew back, unnerved.

'Why tell them what they already know?' she asked, wheezing. 'Darred himself let him walk out of my chambers with the promise of freedom for a price. Perhaps he has taken it?'

'What promise?' Kallis's hand flicked out and pinned her to the wall, one hand closing around her throat. 'What did he promise? What price?'

Sedaine paled. 'Your lives spared if Aarin would join with him,' she gasped, and squirmed free as the mercenary's grip went lax. 'Your deaths and his freedom if he did not.'

Kallis stared at her as she massaged her neck. 'Aarin would not make that trade,' he said, but without much confidence. He did not believe Aarin would betray them, but he was not himself. The shock, the drug, his panic—they all gave Darred a lever with which to manipulate him.

Sedaine saw the doubt and could not let it stand. 'He would not make that choice. But I doubt he even has one. Darred will not let him simply walk away from this.'

'Darred, Darred,' Kallis muttered. 'You blame Darred and excuse yourself. Is this not all for the greater glory of Sedaine and her empire of the North? Why should I believe a word you say?'

'Because I am his mother!' she flared. 'And I do not want to see his life ruined as mine has been! I want to help, not to harm, and I was coming to offer my assistance.'

'Help from you we can do without,' Kallis retorted. 'I would rather share my bed with a scorpion.'

Anger flashed in her eyes. 'Do not mistake me for my masters and lose a chance to save yourselves. You and the girl are nothing to me, but Aarin will not leave here without you and so I must help you if I wish to help him.'

Kallis laughed grimly. 'That's one honest thing I have heard from you, at least.'

She grabbed his tunic, jerking him towards her. Up close he saw the tracks of old tears and smelt the lingering sweetness of wine on her breath.

'I would rather you went with him,' she said dangerously. 'But I will see that Aarin leaves here with or without you, and you will not be so cocky when Darred tosses you back to your oath-sworn kin.'

'Do not threaten me,' Kallis growled. 'You won't win my trust that way.'

'Trust be damned!' she exploded. 'I do not care whether you trust me, Kallis, only that you get Aarin away from here. I do not seek an alliance with you, just cooperation.'

The mercenary ripped his tunic from her grasp. 'Then talk fast. And we shall see.'

She stepped back, satisfied. 'There are wards all around this place. I must disable them before you can safely leave. And I need time to organise horses and supplies. I will send word.'

Kallis nodded. 'How long?' he called after her as she began to walk away.

'I need no more than an hour,' she replied over her shoulder. 'You had best find Aarin fast. Escape will be easier at night.'

TWENTY

AARIN ARRIVED BACK at Kallis's quarters just after dawn. He had spent the small hours wandering aimlessly through the great house until he no longer knew where he was going.

Kallis flung open the door at his first knock. 'I told you to stay here! Where have you been? Sedaine said you left her hours ago.'

'You've seen my mother?' Aarin asked, surprised, then waved away Kallis's reply. It didn't matter. None of it did. He saw Jeta over Kallis's shoulder and felt the pressure of Darred's threat deepen. 'I have been mistaken in the magicians,' he told them. 'We all have. Darred's plans extend far beyond the North, far beyond Amadorn. This just a by-play. I have been mistaken in their ambition. What is a country to them? A continent? The true prize is something much greater.'

He saw uncertainty flitter across their faces as they exchanged a weighted glance, clearly thinking him stripped of all sense. That the magicians should scheme for an empire was frightening enough, but Darred gambled for all of Andeira, and he could not let them know that the threat to their lives might be the lever that compelled his compliance.

'What are you talking about?' Kallis demanded impatiently. 'What prize?'

'The ultimate prize, the greatest of all.' He could hear the hysteria in his voice and knew he had to get a grip on it, but instead it all came tumbling out. 'My enemy seeks the dragons, even as I do. It is not a throne he wants me for, but the dragons!' He was laughing now, shaken loose from his crumbling control, tears streaming down his cheeks. 'But there is a price, of course there is a price! Generous as he is, Darred has promised me my death in exchange for this gift. There is a prophecy, you see, a straight line drawn across time, and he has manipulated that prophecy, trapped me in it, all to create an instrument he can control! Don't you see what he has done? There is nothing I can do to escape this *because it has already happened!*'

'Aarin, stop it!' Kallis barked, catching him by the shoulder and trying to shake some sense into him. 'These are words, only words. He will say anything, tell any lie, to get you to do as he wants. How do you know any of this is true?'

Aarin stepped back, feeling the mania begin to dissipate. 'I am alive,' he said simply, calmer now. 'I have been allowed to live when any other would surely have died. And I never questioned why. But I should have. Perhaps then I would not have walked so blindly into this trap.'

The fire in his veins had risen in response to Darred's words, the fire that should have killed him years ago. He could not hide from that truth, nor try to change it, he could only accept it.

'The fact you live signifies nothing,' Kallis retorted. 'It only makes it possible for Darred to set his trap.'

Aarin shrugged. 'Even if what you say is true, there are other threats he can make and there are things I would not put at risk.'

The mercenary glanced at Jeta. 'We know,' Kallis told him. 'We know Darred has threatened us, but it changes nothing. All we really know about this man is that he cannot be trusted. There is no reason to think he will keep his promise if you give him what he wants.'

Aarin nearly broke then. He had not expected it to be so hard to push them away. But he had to give them a chance to abandon him while they still could. 'You don't understand.' He jabbed his finger in Kallis's chest. 'You I have seen torn open and bleeding, but I have never seen you as close to death as you are at this moment. And you,' he whirled on Jeta. 'Your hold on life is just as frail, a sacrifice on the altar of Darred's ambition. Neither of you has a chance against this man –'

'That's enough!' Jeta snapped, and slapped him, hard. 'We understand just fine. It is our lives at stake here, as you have so eloquently reminded us. Our lives that have been caught up in this mess. But it was Darred who did the catching, not you, and I am quite capable of deciding my own future. I don't need you to do it for me. Darred might return me to Nathas, but that alone is not a death sentence. I will not let you take responsibility for my life.'

He stared at her, one hand on his face where she had slapped him. The silence stretched on until it felt ready to burst. He could not find the words to argue.

A knock at the door shattered the silence and they all turned towards the sound. Kallis had his hand on his sword. The knock came again, then the door opened and admitted a grey-haired stranger into their midst.

The man raised his bowed head as he crossed the threshold and Aarin felt his breath catch in his throat.

'Brannick?'

This was too much. On top of everything else he could not bear this now. There were tears in the old man's eyes as their gazes met, then he stepped forward and caught Aarin in a tight embrace.

'Oh, my boy,' the old man said in a trembling voice. 'You don't know how glad... how could you? I thought you dead years ago. I thought I had lost you, as I lost your father. Then I heard you were here. I had to see for myself.'

Aarin backed away, scrambling to refocus his thoughts. Jeta and Kallis were watching him curiously, but he had no attention to spare for them. 'I was travelling, searching... I'm sorry I did not return. I did not think that you... I thought...'

'That I blamed you for your father's death? Aarin, I am sorry. I promised Ecyas I would take care of you, and I failed. I let you blame yourself for what happened. But it was not so. I –'

'No,' Aarin said abruptly, running agitated fingers through his hair. He did not want to dredge up those memories, not here, not now. 'Why have you come?'

There was hurt in Brannick's eyes at his curt question, but this was too much! It was a trial for his mind to leap so fast from one thing to another and Brannick was a memory from an unhappy time.

The old man smiled sadly as if he knew this. 'When your father died, I told myself it was not because of what had happened, that he was dying anyway, but I did not believe it. No, let me finish,' Brannick said as Aarin tried to stop him following that train of thought. It coincided too closely with his own. 'I did not blame you. Ecyas made me understand it was not your fault, that you could not help who you are. But I did not truly believe it. How could I accept it when that meant accepting what you were? That you had power, yes, that I knew. No one else could have called him back from the place he had gone. But I was afraid. I promised him I would teach you, but what could I teach a pupil who was so far ahead of me he left me breathless in his wake? And so, in the end, I failed him, as I failed you. And then when you left, and the years passed without word, I thought you were dead. I thought you had died as your father had, chasing a dream long vanished from this world. Tesserion forgive me, Aarin, I started to doubt it all. Not just your father's wisdom but everything I knew about the world. For nearly a year I wrestled with myself, seeing only the futility in what we did, the hopelessness of our old folk and the ignorance of our children. Then one day I left. For a while I thought to look for you, but I had no idea where you had gone. Instead I came here. I did not mean to stay, just to try to understand. But here I remained.'

'And what have you learned?' Aarin asked with brittle anger as Brannick reopened old wounds, and at such a time. 'That my father was wrong? That he wasted his life in pursuit of something long gone?'

Brannick shook his head. 'Never that. Perhaps once I thought that way, but there is nothing here that is greater or truer than what I left behind. Only twice in my life have I met anyone with the courage to challenge the world we now live in. Your father was one. You are the other.'

When he did not reply, Brannick sighed. 'You have to trust someone, Aarin. If it cannot be me, let it be yourself.'

Aarin laughed mirthlessly. This was no innocent visit from an old friend. It was too much of a coincidence that he should appear now, with those words on his lips. 'Why are you here, Brannick? Why this sudden change of heart?' If everyone was intent on telling him where to place his trust, he would find out why.

Brannick cast a sideways glance at Kallis and Jeta. When neither seemed inclined to give them the privacy he clearly desired, he looked at Aarin in appeal.

'They stay,' he said firmly. 'This concerns them too.'

'Very well. I did not know then what I know now. Darred's role in this I never guessed, nor what that might mean for all of us.' He took a deep breath.

'And until then I did not really understand what your father taught me. It is possible, Aarin. The dragons can be returned, and you must do it.'

Aarin felt his anger grow. Those words could have come straight from Darred, and that he should enlist this man, his father's friend, to cement his trap was almost more than he could bear. There had been no closeness between them, unless the shared grief of Ecyas's death had been a closeness of sorts, and it was Ecyas's ghost, standing always between them, that had thwarted both their efforts to breach that distance. Even so, he would never have believed Brannick would betray him this way.

'I don't come from Darred,' Brannick said quietly. 'Oh, I see your thoughts plain on your face, and I do not blame you for your suspicion, but it is on another's behalf that I am here.'

'So, you come from my mother. I fail to see the difference.'

'Then you are fool! She told me everything. Aarin, your father never knew any of this,' he said urgently, unaware Ecyas needed no defence. 'He loved your mother for who he thought she was, who she truly was then. I remember when she came to us. I remember their courtship. There never was a love that burned as bright as theirs. She –'

'She left him,' Aarin finished and Brannick flinched. 'She never loved him. She was sent to him by Darred to conceive a child. Me. And whether my father knew it or not does not change the fact that my life has been ruled by others since before I was born.'

'Yes, it does,' Brannick said gently. 'It changes everything. You are what your father made you, no one else. Darred made a mistake in leaving you with him. He should have taken you from your mother at birth, for by allowing your father to keep you he allowed Ecyas to imprint his dreams in your heart. I see him in you so clearly it breaks my heart. You forget, Aarin, that I have known you since you were a child. I watched you grow, I watched you learn. Everything you have, you won by your own efforts, none of it was not handed to you by prophecy. This does not make you less.'

'You are right,' Aarin replied bitterly. 'It makes me more. It makes me dangerous. You were right to stay as far from me as you could.'

Brannick shook his head. 'I was wrong. I should have been brave enough to understand what I had seen and cherish you as your father had, but I am not the man he was and it was easier to believe that I had been mistaken.'

There was a pause, then Brannick asked, 'Do you remember the day you said farewell to your father?'

Aarin nodded. 'I could hardly forget.'

'I remember it too,' Brannick said quietly. 'I have thought long about that day. Sometimes it seems as though I have thought about little else. You walked into that fire, Aarin, and it was a part of you. I thought you would die, and I did not have the courage to follow and fetch you back. But you did not die. I saw the fire on you, and I saw you bring that fire to your father, and how it passed from you to him. And yet the fire took only him and left you unharmed. I found you asleep, safe as if you were in your own bed, and still I did not have the courage.'

Aarin felt the muscles in his chest contract painfully when Brannick began to speak of that day—a day that was seared on his memory by a passage of grief this man could not begin to comprehend—and it took him a while to marshal control enough to ask, 'For what did you not have the courage?'

The old man smiled, a sad smile that spoke of past recriminations and a bitter battle with himself. 'To recognise you for what you were, for who you are. I saw the old times in those flames. I saw the presence of something I had thought lost forever, and instead of joy I felt only fear. Such a power as I had seen—how could anyone prepare you for that?' He caught Aarin by the shoulders. 'Show me the strength I know you have in you and follow your heart, not Darred.'

Shaken, Aarin gently disengaged himself from Brannick's grip and walked to the window. He stared out at the grounds of Redstone as his heart hammered in his chest. For a moment, for one glorious moment, he had been able to believe. He recalled his dream vision of Sedaine, leaning so close, so urgent, willing him to stay with her.

His lies are in what he does not say, not what he does. If he offers you a bargain, don't treat. It is only Darred who stands to gain.

Perhaps it was possible that Brannick was right, that Kallis and Jeta were right, that Darred had lied and there was a way out of this. He turned back to his father's friend. 'If you truly wish to help me, show me a way out of this madness.'

A frown tightened Brannick's brow. 'Can you accept my help if it comes also from your mother?'

Aarin sucked in a painful breath, torn between anger at Sedaine and desperation to flee from Darred.

Suddenly Kallis was there. 'Just say the word, Aarin, and we will leave here, together, Darred or no Darred.'

Aarin nodded to Brannick. 'If that is all you can offer me.'

Brannick's eyes closed briefly, his relief plain to see. 'There are three buildings before you reach the eastern gate. The second has an entrance at the front and one at the rear. Do not use the front way. It opens into a storehouse that is still in occasional use. Go round the back and you will find a small outhouse. Supplies are hidden there. Horses will be saddled and waiting for you outside the complex itself. If you follow the path to the cliffs, there is a thicket on your right, just as the path dips down out of sight of the house.'

Kallis glanced at Jeta, who moved to the door. Aarin looked at him in surprise.

'We have already taken thought for this moment,' Kallis assured him. 'I need only arrange the details. When I say stay here, I mean it. Be ready.'

'Be careful,' Brannick warned. 'It might seem as though no one is watching, but Darred has eyes everywhere.'

Kallis nodded. 'I'll take care.'

Then they were gone, and Aarin was alone with his father's friend. He found he did not know what to say at this final parting.

'I need no words from you, Aarin,' the old man said. 'It is enough to have seen you again. I ask only one thing, that over time when you think of her, you remember your mother as she wished she could be to you. She does love you, Aarin.'

'I know.' The words sounded strange, but he could not deny them. 'If she ever...if she asks, you can tell her that I cannot forgive when there is nothing to forgive.'

Kallis led Jeta unerringly to the building Brannick had indicated, intending to leave her there while he went to check on the horses. But as they entered the windowless barn, a light flared in the darkness.

A dark-haired man walked out of the shadows. 'Kallis, Jeta, welcome. I was beginning to think you weren't going to come.'

Realisation of betrayal hit Kallis hard. He had never trusted her, but he had believed her when she said she wanted Aarin free of this man. 'Sedaine!' he growled, as the light illuminated Darred's face. 'She did this.'

'On the contrary,' Darred replied. 'I merely anticipated her rather unimaginative attempt to betray me.'

At a gesture, guards appeared through the door behind them. Kallis's hand flew to his sword.

Darred smiled. 'By all means, draw your blade. It hardly matters to me whether you die now or later.'

'What do you want from us?' Jeta demanded.

Darred shrugged. 'Nothing at all. I merely wish to separate you from Aarin.' And he ordered his men to disarm Kallis. A knife at Jeta's throat persuaded the mercenary to relinquish his blade. The guards bound his hands with rough twine, the thin strands gouging his wrists. He kept his eyes on Darred the whole time, and the man endured his attention with a thin smile.

The man holding Jeta jerked her by the shoulder and spun her round. As another grabbed her hands to tie them, Darred stopped them. He cupped a hand to her chin, tilting her face into the light. 'Such a pretty thing, you are,' he murmured. 'I think perhaps I will not waste you, my little queen who never was.'

Jeta shuddered and something in Kallis snapped. 'Don't touch her!'

He lunged forward, struggling against the guards, straining to reach Darred and throttle him. 'Hurt her and I'll gut you front to back and stake out your carcass for the crows!' He was blinded by rage, unaware of the blows to his body, remembering the girl he had not been able to save, whose body he had burnt on that senseless pyre.

Darred ignored him. 'Take him away.'

As he was dragged out screaming and cursing, Darred turned back to Jeta, and the last thing he saw as the door slammed shut was her face, white with terror

TWENTY-ONE

BE READY, KALLIS had said. Well, he was ready and had been for some time. Aarin paced the small room, counting the ten strides it took him to reach the far wall, kicking it when he reached it. Where were they? It had been over an hour since Brannick left. What had Kallis said? *I need only arrange the details.*

The sharp knock sent him running to the door. He flung it open, expecting Kallis and Jeta's return, and was shocked to see Vianor instead.

'My prince,' the magician murmured, bowing low. 'I beg leave to speak with you in private. May I come in?'

As Aarin stared, open-mouthed, Vianor walked calmly past him into the room.

'Why are you here?' he demanded. 'I have nothing to say to you.'

'You may not,' the magician replied, 'but I have something to say to you. We do not have much time.' He drew up a chair and sat, indicating that Aarin should do likewise.

Aarin ignored him. 'Why are you here?' he asked again.

'Because there are things we need to speak of, you and I,' Vianor replied. 'And a bargain we need to make.'

'It is too late for bargains,' Aarin shot back. 'It was always too late.'

Vianor's smile was grim. 'Be careful before you reject what you have not even heard. The lives of your friends may depend on it.'

Aarin stiffened. 'Careful, old man. I grow tired of threats. Say what you will, and quickly.'

'Patience, my prince,' the magician murmured, his use of the honorific only fuelling Aarin's anger. 'It is an indispensable quality in a ruler, and one you would do well to learn.' He held up his hand to silence Aarin's furious protest. 'Let us not argue over things we cannot change. By blood you are my prince, but you will never hold that title. It is something else I ask of you.'

185

Aarin made a disgusted noise. 'Everyone wants something from me today. I'm not in generous mood. Get out.'

Vianor was utterly unperturbed. 'No.'

Aarin felt a growl rise in his throat. 'Very well, if you have something to offer, I will hear it. But I need your price.'

'Ah, the price. This is a bargain. We each give something to the other. I would prefer not see it as a price.'

'And I am not interested in your preferences. A price is a price. Name your terms.'

'You are direct,' Vianor observed. 'Very well. Darred must be destroyed.'

Aarin laughed. 'That's all? You may as well ask me to stop the sun from setting!'

'Do you fear him, my prince?' the magician asked. 'He is only mortal.'

'Mortal or not, this is an impossible task you set me, and I would know why. Why do *you* wish him destroyed?'

'He is a traitor,' Vianor said simply.

Again, Aarin laughed. 'To whom? To you?'

'To everyone, I suspect, even his Order.'

Aarin froze. 'His Order?'

The magician looked faintly smug. 'So, you find there are some things you do not yet know. And on that we bargain.' He stretched out his booted feet, easing the pain of old joints. 'Darred is Kas'Talani, a priest of that Order, and he is here on their behalf.'

'Kas'Talani? From *Caledan?*'

Vianor smiled at Aarin's shock. 'Just so. The Kas'Talani believe they are the guardians of the magic of Andeira. They have built an empire on this foundation and they have long been active in Amadorn, seeking to extend their control, and *religion*'—he gave the word a bitter twist—'over this land and its people.'

'An unpleasant prospect,' Aarin conceded. 'But what has this to do with me?'

Vianor sighed. 'The Kas'Talani maintain their control over Caledan because they are by far the most powerful force in that land or this. Do you understand? For all your strength you are but a child beside Darred's power, Kas'Tella's power, and that power is jealously guarded. They fear only one thing, a man they call Æisoul, a figure out of legend they believe will destroy them.'

Aarin felt his heart skip a beat. Æisoul. It was the name Darred had used when he had called on the power of ancient prophecy. He felt cold. 'What do you know of Æisoul?'

Vianor was watching him closely. 'I know that he stands before me now, or so Darred believes. And it puzzled me at first that he should let you live. Darred is not a man to pass up renown and whoever delivers Æisoul to Kas'Tella could name his reward. Were you not Sedaine's son, I would be tempted to do so myself.'

'I'm surprised a little thing like blood should engage your scruples,' Aarin sneered. 'You seem remarkably free of them in all other respects.'

'Indeed, I surprise myself at times,' the magician agreed dryly. 'But for Darred to let you live, he must have another purpose for you, one that is not of his Order.'

Aarin dropped his gaze to avoid Vianor's piercing stare. *He knew.*

'Æisoul's existence and the destruction of the Kas'Talani are but cause and effect. It is not his purpose, is it, my prince? It is not your purpose.'

'Enough,' he said quietly. 'We both know what Darred wants me for. If you have a point to make, do it quickly. I tire of riddles.'

'Riddles within riddles,' Vianor murmured. 'And plans within plans. Has this plan succeeded? Will you be swayed by his promises and follow him to your destruction?'

'I will do what I must. What concern is it of yours?'

'Do not ask foolish questions, boy,' the magician snapped. 'You know very well that what you do will affect every land on Andeira. I make no secret of the fact that my brothers hold the dragons in no reverence, nor in any expectation of return. But if this prophecy is indeed genuine then it will be fulfilled, and if that is so then I would see the dragons returned cleanly, not in thrall to Darred's purpose.'

'What makes you think you have a choice? If the prophecy will be fulfilled, what does it matter what I do? What difference will it make?'

Vianor gave a small shrug. 'The future is constantly changing. Even as we sit here we are changing it. To say the prophecy will be fulfilled and the dragons returned is not to say how or when that will happen, or what it will mean. And so we come to the bargain.'

Aarin waited out the moment in agitated silence, willing Vianor to state his terms.

'I want your pledge as a prince of this land,' the magician obliged. 'I want your oath—sworn freely and bound into you—that you will die before you let Darred use you.'

'You are a prophet yourself, my lord,' Aarin said bitterly. 'For you have just hit upon the only certainty in this madness. Darred himself will see to that.'

'Then I have your pledge,' Vianor pressed. 'You will swear it before me now? You know that if you do you cannot remove that stricture later? It will hold you.'

Aarin stepped back. 'So far I have heard only one side of this bargain. We each give the other something, remember?'

The magician reined in his impatience with an effort. 'In exchange I will give you the means to save your friends' lives. As of an hour ago, Darred has them in his custody and will soon be returning them to Rhiannas, the girl to her marriage bed and the oathbreaker to the mercies of his former brothers. A fate that neither of them will relish, as I understand it.'

Aarin had to stop himself from leaping at the old man's throat and shaking the information from him. 'Speak,' he said curtly. 'If what you say holds true, you may have my pledge.'

'Not good enough,' Vianor stated, rising to his feet. 'I will have your pledge now, or not at all.'

'What is to stop me rescuing them without your help?'

'Only this. Darred's strength alone is no greater than yours, but it is bolstered by the power his Order possesses, and with that he will surely crush you.'

'Go on.'

'You agree to the pledge?'

'I agree to nothing yet!' Aarin snapped. 'And you will never get my agreement by threats, only truth.'

The old man inclined his head. 'Very well. You must break his connection with that power if you hope to destroy him. The connection stems from a small ornament he wears, hidden under his tunic. I know no more of it than that, except that its signature is invisible to my people. Perhaps to Æisoul it will not be so. Now, the pledge.'

Reluctantly Aarin approached the waiting magician. He rolled up his right sleeve and knelt amid a cresting tide of apprehension. Vianor took his wrist, feeling for the pulse of blood just below the skin.

'Wait!' Aarin cried, snatching his hand away, stalling for time. Everything in him screamed that this was a mad risk. 'First I would hear the words of this oath.'

Vianor's eyes narrowed but he did not argue. There was no power in duress and he would know that. 'On your very life you will swear to relinquish that life before you allow your actions to further Darred's purpose, or that of the agency he represents. You will swear to do all in your power to destroy him, to kill him if you can, to prevent him from succeeding in his goal.'

'I will not be bound to murder,' Aarin said flatly. 'The rest, yes.'

The magician considered this. 'As you will then.' He took Aarin's proffered arm, reaching again for the pulse of life. He closed his eyes, seeking out the mage's elemental core, to bind him by that with which he was already one. As he spoke the words, Aarin's soft voice repeating the phrases, Vianor wove the pledge through every strand of his being.

Aarin felt the enchantment settle in him and experienced an odd sensation of dual awareness as his consciousness was overlaid by a fragment of another man's will. Then it was done and Vianor let his hand fall, taking one staggering step back. He looked much older suddenly, every line of his face delineated sharply by the harsh light, and as Aarin climbed to his feet, also unsteady, he caught Vianor's eye and saw a twinkling of amusement.

'Perhaps you bargained I would not be able to do that,' Vianor said with a faint smile. 'I won't say that my time with Darred hasn't been educational.' He shook himself and there was a hint of discomfort on his face.

Shedding himself of my cobwebs. He will have strange dreams tonight.

The old man straightened. 'Your friends are being held in the outbuildings near the east gate. They were led to believe there would be horses and provisions waiting for them there, and assistance in leaving the grounds undetected.'

'Led to believe by whom?' Aarin demanded, massaging his wrist that still tingled with the afterburn of conjury. 'My mother?'

Vianor sighed. 'Your mother's attempt to assist your escape was ill-advised, but all of you have behaved entirely predictably. Did you not wonder why there are no guards, why you have been allowed to move freely as you plot your escape? Did you think perhaps that Darred truly offered you a choice? It never mattered what you chose to do. You cannot leave this place, any of you, unless you first disarm its defences, and Darred *is* those defences. Hence our bargain. And now I will be leaving you, and I sincerely hope we never meet again.'

'Likewise,' Aarin muttered, pausing only to grab the few possessions Jeta had collected for him before following Vianor from the room. He would worry about what he had learned later. He had to find his friends.

Vianor's directions might have been plain to someone familiar with Redstone, but Aarin had never been outside the building and knew only that he had to head east, in the direction of the sea. He did not bother with stealth. If what Vianor had told him was true, it would be pointless to try to conceal his movements. And Kallis and Jeta were running out of time.

Once outside, it was a matter of seconds to reach out with his magic and orient himself towards the ocean. Then he was running, and almost at once saw Kallis being herded along between three armed men. He ducked around a corner, pressing himself against the wall, his heart thudding painfully in his chest. Risking another look, he saw the mercenary being marched through a gate in the inner wall of the complex. Of Jeta there was no sign.

Aarin waited until Kallis and his escort had disappeared through the gate then ran silently across the empty courtyard. He knew he did not have time to delay and look for Jeta. Those men might only have been taking Kallis back to Rhiannas, but he doubted it. They looked more like executioners.

Reaching the gate, he peered round the crumbling stonework. Beyond was a garden of sorts, and beyond that there was only scrubland stretching to the far wall, a scattering of trees and overgrown weeds. And Kallis on his knees in the mud.

Aarin did not stop to think. His magic lashed out, binding the soldiers' limbs and slamming them into each other. He heard the sickening crunch of bone and a cry of pain as the three men fell backwards. One lay still and Aarin wondered distantly if he was dead. He darted forward, reaching the second man as he pushed himself groggily to his knees, blood streaming from his nose. The pommel of the dagger Kallis had given him connected with the man's skull and he collapsed without a sound.

He heard a sound behind him and then Kallis was moving, throwing himself onto his back and kicking out with his feet. A guard staggered, bent double, and Aarin hardened the air and savagely flattened the man to the ground.

He dropped to his knees beside Kallis and used the dagger to free his hands. It was all over in a matter of heartbeats and he did not allow himself to think about what he had just done. There would be time for that later.

'They're not dead,' Kallis warned.

'Where's Jeta?' Aarin asked frantically as he hauled them both to their feet. 'Why isn't she with you? She should be with you!'

Kallis wiped blood from his mouth, sagging against a tree. 'Darred took her. Aarin, I'm sorry. I tried...'

Aarin felt a burst of panic. 'Where? Where did he take her?'

Kallis shrugged. 'I don't know. He planned to send us off together, I think, then changed his mind. I don't know where he took her.'

He bent down to retrieve his sword from the unconscious soldier, but Aarin was already running. Darred had taken Jeta, and his world was suddenly rocked by the possibility of a terrible loss.

Darred poured a glass of wine and offered it to Jeta. 'A drink?'

She knocked it from his grasp, spilling a red stain across the silk carpet. Her hands were trembling.

191

Darred laughed. 'How delightfully fiery you are, my dear. I can see why Nathas had to have you.'

'Nathas doesn't have me,' she retorted coldly. 'And neither will you.' But it was empty bravado, and she knew it.

'Oh, I think I will,' he said, amused, as he put down his wine.

Jeta retreated until her back hit the wall. Her heart was pounding so hard she felt faint. She wanted to scream for help but there was no one to hear.

Darred watched her as he advanced unhurriedly across the room. 'No one is coming to save you, my dear. It's just you and me.'

'How romantic,' she sneered, and slapped him.

He caught her wrist and pinned it to the wall. She gasped at the pain and looked up into his eyes, close now and dark with desire.

Darred brushed a strand of hair from her face and leaned in close. 'Don't make this hard for yourself,' he murmured as his hand caressed her shoulder and dropped down to unlace her bodice.

Jeta turned her head away and closed her eyes. Her body might be forced to endure this desecration, but she would not.

Aarin ran. Darred had taken Jeta. Why? Where? He tripped, sprawling into the mud, and pushed himself up to run on, sending his awareness soaring out ahead of him, seeking her. He captured an image of her in his mind—the fall of blond curls across pale skin, the animated blue eyes. That teasing half-smile and sharp, stinging tongue. *There she is. Find her!*

He was running blind now, following the call he had sent out. He felt an answering probe, a shield hastily formed as Darred was alerted to his approach, and sent a whiplash of honed power through the ward, bringing it crashing down. On the other side Darred swayed, rocked by the attack, and then Aarin was on them, flinging open the door as his magic answered his unformed impulse to shatter the chains set to keep him out.

Darred whirled round to face him, controlled fury on his neat face, but Aarin's gaze went not to the priest but to Jeta. She cowered in a corner, one hand clutched at her dress to hold it together, eyes dark with fear. Rage filled him, rage such as Aarin had never known, that touched the core of his being like a spark to tinder. His vision exploded into slivers and he sliced through the bindings of sorcery that protected his adversary, scattering the threads of his magic to expose his mortal self.

But Darred was not finished. He was not even started. He drew deep from a well Aarin could not access, fashioning his answer to this challenge from an ancient and living source. And somewhere, far distant and beyond this world, Aarin heard a dragon cry out in agony. An answering cry was dragged from him, his world tilting precariously to spill him to his knees as Darred's crippling counter-spell struck him full in the chest.

At first there was no pain, just a pressure on his ribs that stopped his breath and sent sparks skittering across his vision. Then he felt the stirrings of agony deep within. Something was terribly wrong inside him, and he clamped down so hard on the burgeoning pain that the effort almost drove him under.

Time slowed almost to a stop as he dragged breath into crushed lungs. He could see Jeta's horrified face staring into his and tried to smile. A trickle of wetness ran down his chin, and the hand he raised to wipe it away came down glistening with his blood.

Darred knelt beside him, one hand taking his chin and turning his face.

'What hurts more, I wonder?' he asked, his voice clinical and cold. 'The damage inside you, or the knowledge that there is a power in this world you will never know as your own?'

Aarin forced himself to hold that expressionless gaze, trying to read the man behind it. Darred had killed him. He knew that with the sick certainty of a mage who could look inside himself and see the wreckage of his body. What he did not understand was why.

'Oh, you won't die,' Darred assured him. 'Not yet.'

With a jolt Aarin realised that the priest had kept hold of the spell he had used to cripple him. If he chose, while the spell maintained its integrity, he could use its power to reverse the damage he had done, as much or as little as he liked. Enough to save him from death but keep him enslaved by animal pain. Enough to use him to fulfil his destiny.

Darred watched the realisation dawn on Aarin's face. 'Your decision to make, Aarin. It doesn't have to be this way.'

Aarin shuddered as a sliver of pain sheered through his defences. His shoulders slipped against the wall and he slid awkwardly down to lie on his side. Blood ran into his mouth, faster now, his breath bubbling in his lungs as they filled with liquid. He looked away from Darred to Jeta. She was on her knees, the unlaced edges of her bodice clasped tightly in one hand, and she was watching them in mute terror.

Aarin blinked against the darkness. Jeta faded to a shadow as the terrifying weakness spread through him. Darred was waiting, patient as a statue, close enough to touch if he had the strength. But there was no strength left in his body, only his mind still worked. His thoughts unshackled by the pain he refused to acknowledge, Aarin was aware of every moment. He felt what it was like to die, inch by inch, the blood pooling in his lungs hindering each strangled breath. It became a struggle to focus on Darred and not to give in to macabre fascination with the process of his own death.

Death. It was something he had known would come one day, yet until this moment he had never really considered it, nor realised how much he wanted to live. Vianor's words hammered through his mind. He knew what had defeated him. He knew what he had to do. As he looked at the priest crouched above him, he could see the glint of silver where his cloak had slipped from his shoulder. He tried to raise his hand, to take the thing he wore, but his movements were growing rapidly feeble.

Darred continued to watch him, his eyes measuring the rise and fall of his chest, weighing his time, and Aarin knew he could not afford to wait much longer. Darred seemed to reach the same conclusion, for abruptly he pushed himself to his feet and Aarin felt the swirl of power begin to flow into shape. He braced himself to resist, to fight the healing, for no matter how desperately he wanted to live, it had to be on his terms, not Darred's. If he could not save himself, far better to die now than allow the helplessness of his shattered body to make him this man's tool.

But the first, dreaded rush of power, of unbearable temptation, never came. Instead there was a shout of rage and a blurry shape hurled itself at the priest, knocking him to the floor. Kallis had his hands around Darred's throat, trying to choke the life out of him, and in the violence of his attack, the device

Darred wore was torn loose and went skidding across the stones and into the shadows.

Aarin watched it fall, a flash of silver that burned across his sight. He sensed Darred's desperate groping for his magic prop, and with an immense effort he dragged himself upright and threw himself across the room towards the place it had vanished just as Kallis screamed and fell away, clutching his hands.

Darred saw him in the same instant, and their eyes met in a moment of silent understanding. The priest tensed, ready to spring past and claim his lost weapon, and Aarin did the only thing he could. Lurching to his knees, he held out a bloody hand triumphantly to let a flash of silver show.

Darred froze, his eyes riveted on the device on Aarin's bloodstained palm. It was a bluff, an act of sheer desperation, but Darred could not know that. He could not feel his own power, he could not see the illusion, because Aarin had anchored it with his life. While he lived the illusion would hold its power, and if Darred could not see the illusion he could not see the truth. His own mind betrayed him.

Their eyes locked, the contest dissolved to a battle of wills. Aarin held the power, but he was close to death, and he could see the calculation in the priest's eyes. He had not acted, *could not* act, for he did not truly possess the thing, and Darred must believe he did not have the strength, and he need only to wait for the weakness to claim him.

Aarin felt tremors fan out through his body. Time was growing short, but the illusion limited his scope to act—he could do nothing without revealing the truth.

Darred's deadly spell, his healing spell, remained half-formed and forgotten. If he could but touch it, Aarin knew he could save himself, but to do that he would have to fling the magic wide open once more and bring it under his control. It was also an effort that would take the last of his hoarded strength.

The walls of the room disappeared as he focused his attention inwards. Kallis and Jeta faded away. There was only Darred, filling his vision. The priest sensed the shift in his concentration, and his face contorted into a snarl.

Then the room exploded as their power collided and the release woke the dormant spell.

Too little time to think, only to react. Knowing he had but seconds to master the magic or unleash this horrifying force to wreak destruction all around, Aarin hurled himself into the heaving web, seeking the invisible signature Vianor had spoken of.

Half-glimpsed snatches of memory guided him. He had walked this path once before, when in some unknown way the Fire had insinuated its way into his being and lured him outside himself. The path of that Fire was scorched on his soul, and even as Darred's power lashed against him, a dance of twisting death, his memory marked each flicker of flame and quenched it before it could harm him. This was not a game now, not the tame, curious seeking of Fire towards its own, but pure elemental power raised to a frenzy by the hatred of its shaper.

Again, Aarin heard that eerie echo, a muffled cry of a dragon in pain, and he knew he had to end this or that dragon would die. Everything in him cried out against it. A name came to him, slipping through the barriers of time. *Eiador.* He tried to align his senses with it, to add his strength to its fight, but he was gently rebuffed. He could not take on Eiador's battle. He had his own to fight.

The momentary lapse in his concentration sent licks of flame scoring across his arms and chest, awakening him to his danger even as the door slammed shut on another's. Darred had entered the spell on his heels, finally realising how he had been tricked. Aarin could see him there on the edges of his vision, but the priest was too late. Aarin's control was far ahead of his. In a last desperate lunge, Aarin flung himself at the shuddering, breaking knot that hid the source of Darred's power, ripped himself open to it and sucked it into his being, snapping the priest's connection.

The whirlwind around him died to a whisper even as the battle inside threatened to tear him wide open. As he slumped back, he saw Darred thrown into the wall, the impact knocking him unconscious and saving him from the waking horror of the devastating recoil. But for Aarin there would be no such relief if he could not quench the fiery serpents that ate at him.

From his knees he slivered to the floor, lying flat on his back with arms outstretched, delving inwards and deep.

Kallis was by his side, his face anguished. Aarin tried to push him away.

'Don't touch me.' The words were mangled by the blood in his mouth. His plea came as much from the awakening agony as from his fear that Kallis might become entangled in the fierce, recoiling energies.

He saw Kallis hesitate, his expression uncertain.

'Stay away,' he tried to say, but the words could not come as the battle for his life consumed him. He had absorbed Darred's spell, every shred of it, but to live he would have to exert his control over it, direct its purpose and purge it from his body, or the magnitude of the power would destroy him from within.

The ceiling of his vision parted to let him through. He felt out broken bones and torn flesh, seeing from without the awful damage. He felt the pulsing of his blood as it drained from his veins inside his shattered chest. He saw crushed organs and mangled muscle, and measured the precious strength lost with each costly breath. He hesitated, caught up in wonder at the intricacies of the human body. But this time it was the pain that saved him. As he drew near to death, his concentration began to fray, and the pain came flooding back. In a final effort, he grasped hold of the runaway forces of Darred's spell and turned them back on themselves to undo the damage they had done.

His back arched in agony as shredded tissue was remade and splinters of bone began to knit. The pain of the injury had been stamped down on and locked away, but the agony of the healing could not be blocked out. He heard his own voice crying for mercy, unable to contain the shock, and then it was over, and he lay spent on the floor, finished but not yet done. Every second Darred's spell was inside him, it struggled to return to its thwarted course. If he did not cleanse every last vestige of the priest from his body, the slow agony of his dying would repeat itself on newly healed flesh. Exhausted and desperate, Aarin reached deep once more. His awareness expanded to take in every nerve, every cell that tied his body to mortal life, and he invested a tiny mote of himself in each. Those seeds of his essence burrowed cleanly and deep, disarming the invasive magics and expelling them from him, harmless and spent. He was washed clean, made pure, and the first flush of ecstatic reaction nearly sent him under.

Aarin rolled on his side, dragging his elbows under him and saw Jeta, curled in a ball and shaking with terrified weeping. He hauled himself across the floor and pulled her to him, cradling her body against his as the sobs heaved her chest. The wild elation of the storm was still on him, still flowing through him with its shocking, searing heat, and in that moment of release it poured from him into the well of her being, and for an instant they experienced a sharing of awareness as his world tumbled into Jeta's and hers into his.

He saw snatches of vision of another life, another place, of people unfamiliar to him but known so well to her that he knew them as well as she must know the faces from his past. He felt himself ripped wide open, every hidden emotion forced into view. Everything that had made him who he was was on display, and as he did not have the strength to fight it, so Jeta lacked the skill, and they lay there in utter surrender. The coil that bound them tightened its hold and tied some small part of them together with a bond that would last a lifetime.

Aarin felt the shock jolt her in his arms and clasped her tightly. 'Don't be afraid,' he whispered, stroking her hair, soothing her fear. For that moment there was no one else in the world but the two of them. The flood rose to a peak, rocking them both, then the eddying currents began to fade, leaving pinpricks of sparkling other-consciousness shivering through their souls.

Shaken and awed, she began to pull away, fighting to escape the raging heat of his skin, but her movements were slow, as though she was reluctant to relinquish the closeness. He released her with sadness, knowing the futility of clinging to those dying moments, but the feel of her remained with him, the pressure of her body fitting perfectly with his. She sat up, her fingers brushing his face, and there was desolation in her gaze.

'Are you all right?' he asked, wincing at the inadequate the words, aching to touch again what he had touched for the briefest of instants.

She shook her head numbly, staring at him as though she had never seen him before. 'I don't know. I don't know if I will ever be all right again. There is an emptiness with no end that yawns inside me, and makes me feel...' She strained for the words to describe the enormity of the sensation. She looked into his eyes. 'I feel lost.'

His hand brushed against her cheek, catching the drying tears. 'No, you're not lost, no more than I am. There is an end to that emptiness, somewhere, if we can only find it.'

Blue eyes sought his and pinned his gaze, until tear-darkened lashes swept down to shield him from their unnerving brightness. 'How do you bear it?'

'It is a part of me,' he said simply, 'and I would not wish it otherwise, even if I could.' He gripped her hand more firmly and raised them unsteadily to their feet.

She looked at him in wonder. 'I thought you were dying.'

He smiled. 'I was.'

'How?'

Before he could answer, Kallis appeared at his shoulder. 'How, indeed?' the mercenary asked softly. 'The blood...'

Aarin touched his face. He could feel the drying blood on his lips and see the torn, smoking sections of his tunic where Darred's Fire had touched him, but the skin beneath was unbroken and his body was healed. He did not have the words to describe his titanic battle with the magic, nor with himself, and so he said nothing.

Kallis turned abruptly aside, unable to hold his gaze, and a moment later Jeta also backed away. They could not understand how he stood before them, whole and undamaged, when they had seen him broken and dying, lying on the floor in his own blood. That same blood covered him still, soaking the front of his shirt and staining his arms and back where he had dragged himself through it.

He turned away from them to Darred, still unconscious, and Kallis crouching not far from his side. Understanding dawned a moment too late, and before he could cry out the mercenary was standing, the silver device nestling in his palm. Aarin felt his heart lurch, and his gaze flew back to Darred, but the priest never moved. When he looked back at Kallis, the mercenary was watching him curiously.

'What should we do with this?'

He held it out to Aarin, and the mage saw for the first time the design etched into the surface. A dragon.

He staggered as raw fury surged through him. How could something so wrong bear the image of a dragon, a creature beyond the evils of men? Its power called out to him, seductive and deadly, and he knew that, given time, he would discover the source of that power. Yet he could not bring himself to reach out and take it, for he had felt the terrible wrongness of it, and his body recalled too clearly the devastating pain it had caused.

'Leave it.'

Kallis frowned. He might not have understood what it was that he held, but he had watched them fight over it and knew it was important. 'Is that wise? He's not dead.'

'I know.'

Kallis looked from him to Jeta, seeing the legacy of Darred's mistreatment on them both. His face twisted into a snarl. 'I should kill him!'

He started towards the unconscious priest but Aarin stopped him.

'Leave him. He is no threat to us for now.'

The mercenary rounded on him furiously. 'As long as he is alive, he is a threat to you. It is foolish to let him live.'

'Foolish, maybe,' Aarin conceded. 'But we cannot kill him like this.'

It would be days before Darred woke, if he woke at all. The damage from the explosive recoil would be profound, though Aarin dared not hope it would kill him.

Kallis kicked the table, seething with frustration. 'And this?' he demanded, holding up the silver dragon. 'Should I leave this with him too?'

Aarin winced, too weary to deal with the mercenary's anger. 'Do what you want with it. Throw it away. You can't destroy it, and it would be dangerous to try.' He knew that instinctively.

'Very well,' Kallis replied, stalking to the door and hurling the thing far into the night. Aarin sensed its passage through the air and the place it came to rest, nestled between a stone and a tuft of grass. If he lived, Darred would find it. Aarin knew that, but he did not have the energy to care.

Kallis swung back to him, his expression grim. 'We should leave. Now. I want to be far away when he wakes.'

Aarin nodded, turning back to Jeta who was still staring at Darred.

'Are you ready?'

'Where will we go?' she asked him. 'Where can we go? There is nowhere far enough...' Her voice faltered, tears stinging her eyes.

'For you to outrun this?' he finished. He brushed a strand of hair from her face, his fingers lingering for a moment in the blond tangles. 'There is one place, perhaps, that is far enough for all of us,' he said, feeling Kallis's speculative eyes on him. 'We're going to Caledan.'

TWENTY-TWO

SEDAINE STOOD ON the balcony overlooking the execution ground as Nathas was escorted to the hangman's noose. He walked in silence, his head defiantly raised. He was no coward, just as he was not truly her enemy. Yet her people demanded his death for usurping her throne and her uncle demanded his death for reasons she found it hard to stomach. She felt her heart flutter as he looked up at her. His face was pinched from cold and bloody from the fists of his ungentle jailers, his hair and beard unkempt and ragged, but his eyes spoke to her with the most powerful plea of all, for his very life.

He knows he has been manoeuvred here by others. He must know I played my part in that, yet still he looks to me for mercy.

Thinking of Darred's manipulations filled her with cold anger, and thoughts of her son entangled in them brought tears prickling to her eyes. Why did she stand here preparing to execute an innocent man on his word, the word of a traitor?

'Sedaine?' Vianor was by her side, watching her with concern. 'It is time.'

Looking down on the scene in the courtyard, she saw Nathas standing by the gallows, the executioner waiting for her signal to place the noose round his neck. Rebellion surged.

'Where is my son?'

Vianor sighed. 'You must forget him, Sedaine. You gave him up long ago. Your duty awaits.'

Her stare froze him cold. 'Your highness,' she corrected him. 'I am your niece no longer, Vianor. I am your ruler. Remember that.'

'As you wish, your highness,' the magician bowed. There was fury glittering in his eyes.

'Where is my son,' she repeated.

The old man shook his head. 'I do not know, your highness.'

'Is he dead?'

'It is possible,' the magician conceded. 'But I think it more likely he is living still. Darred's plans will not easily be overset.'

'And Aarin is entangled in those plans,' she finished. 'Tell me, uncle, why should I help Darred? Why should I order this man killed when the only wrong he has done me was on your orders? Why should I yield to the wishes of a man who wants to destroy my son, who has brought my country to the edge of ruin? Tell me, or I will not do this thing.'

Vianor stepped back before her anger as though seeing her for the first time. 'I do not know what Darred wants with your son, your highness.' The admission cost him dearly, proof of how effectively he too had been duped. 'Nor why he has betrayed the Order, if indeed he has. But you must do this now for yourself and your kingdom, not for him. Whatever else he may have done, Darred has made the North yours for the taking. He has handed you Naveen, and Elvelen will follow. He promised you an empire and you have but to take it.'

'And if I no longer want that empire?' Sedaine asked softly, her gaze once more on Nathas. 'If all I want is my life to be my own, and my son to be free to find his?'

'It is too late for that, Sedaine. All that is left for you to do is reap the fruits of Darred's betrayal, take hold of your nation and guard it. For Darred spent many years planning for this moment, and he will be back to wrest it from you if you leave him the slightest opening. All any of us can do now is work to prevent that happening.'

Sedaine met his eyes in sudden anger. 'The Kas'Talani will come only because you have made it possible. I am not a fool. I know how the magicians have spent their efforts these last decades, and for whom. Your bargain with their priesthood has placed us all in danger, and all for the sake of your ambition. You are the fool if you cannot see that they will never share their power with you.'

Quivering with anger, the architect of that bargain could only stand helpless as Sedaine turned back to the execution ground. She raised her right arm and the crowd began to cheer, feet stamping out their desire for revenge on the hard-packed earth. They expected a speech, a glorious tribute to their loyalty and character, but they got no words that day. Full of shame and revulsion, Sedaine could not answer their desperate clamouring with ringing declarations. She brought her arm crashing down, and the crowd went silent. Nathas's face tipped up to her one last time and she saw a spark of understanding flare briefly in his eyes, then he was lost in the shadow of the hangman's hood as his head was placed in the noose. The crowd began chanting, baying for blood to salve their disappointment. Missiles were hurled at the platform—stones, broken pottery, kitchen slops—then the black-robed executioner released the trap door and Nathas fell sharply down. The grotesque snap of a broken neck echoed across the packed square to the drifting stench of voided bowels.

The moment it was done Sedaine turned away. Vianor stood behind her, his fists clenched in furious relief at his back.

'For that death there can be no forgiveness,' she told him savagely, as she tore the royal circlet from her head and threw it to a waiting servant. 'Nor for the hundreds more that will follow when we are called to account for this day's work.'

Across Vianor's outraged silence she ordered, 'Every Caledani priest in the North is to be found and sent south. I will have no more of their filthy work under my rule.' Receiving only his blistering silence in response, she said, 'Nathas's death is the last sacrifice I make to their schemes, and I make it only because the North must be united if it is to survive the backlash from your machinations. You are to bring your people to heel, uncle. The bargain is to be undone and all connection with the Kas'Talani rooted out and destroyed. If I decide you can be trusted, you will be permitted to remain at my court, and your efforts will go towards restoring the defences you have allowed our enemies to breach. Is that understood?'

Vianor found his voice at last. If breaking the bargain might hobble the Kas'Talani's influence in Amadorn it would also invite reprisal. 'Your courage is admirable, your highness, but open defiance will only place your people in greater danger. The Kas'Talani are far more powerful than you imagine. They cannot be stopped simply by —'

'You leave me no option. Your own actions have opened the way for their influence in our lands, therefore you *will* shoulder the risk that denouncing the bargain brings us.'

The magician's face darkened. 'You can demand nothing from us, Sedaine. We are not under sovereign obligation to obey you, and you cannot compel us.'

'Can I not?' she asked sweetly, and at her gesture five men stepped into the room to ring the magician in a circle of raised wards. 'You forget, uncle, that your people are not the only practitioners of magic in Amadorn. Luen breeds greater wisdom and strength than any that dwells in your ranks. These you see about you now all followed me to Redstone, and each one of them alone has the raw talent and innate understanding to cripple your advantage.'

She glided to him, placing a hand on his chest, her eyes raking his composure to tatters. 'Messages under my seal have already left with Brannick for Luen, explaining our peril and your role in it. They will soon know everything, and they will come to my call. We need every shred of trained talent if we are to withstand this siege, and the value they have to me is far greater than yours. Do not make me choose between you.' She smiled at his outrage. 'So, you see, my lord Vianor, you will submit to my demands, as will your people, or the confrontation you have studiously avoided all these years will come, and we both know what the outcome will be.'

Vianor was left speechless with fury, unable to move as she drifted away from him. The men around him tugged their wards tighter, until the pressure of the restraining magic began to constrict his chest. 'Wait!' he called desperately as Sedaine disappeared through the door. 'You cannot hope to find victory in an alliance with eastern hermits, and they have no love for you there. Damn you, Sedaine!' he yelled, hoarse, when there was no answer. 'If you turn your back on us now, we will expend no effort to rescue you from your folly when the Order comes to break you. No help from the east will be enough to save you!'

'Silence, old man,' a gruff voice said at his shoulder, as hands fell on his arms.

'Off!' he snapped in impotent fury, struggling to follow Sedaine. He threw off one hand, then the other, clawing at the solid bodies planted in his way, terrified anger lending strength to his efforts.

The Redstone men paid no heed to his struggles. Their orders were clear. As Vianor continued to resist, their leader focused the intent of their shared magic and sheered white-hot power through his target. The magician was brought up short by the shock, the afterburn ripping through his limbs. As the man sharpened his awareness for a second jolt, he collapsed senseless to the floor.

PART TWO
Caledan

Tesseria
The Second Age

HE DREAMED OF the hunt, of flying high above the land in pursuit of his terrified prey, watching it flee across the open country. He swooped in low, raking his claws across the horse's back. The animal screamed in pain, its long stride faltering as it fell away to one side, twisting desperately to avoid this horror of the skies. Bloody gashes marked its back and flanks. Blood dripped from his gleaming claws, ruby red and glistening in the bright sunlight.

Again and again he savaged his prey, revelling in its fear, holding back from the swift death he could bring at any time. But at last he tired of the game and lunged to take the exhausted creature's neck in his jaws, dragging it into the air and savagely shaking it, teeth ripping flesh, breaking bones, killing instantly.

He landed on the hillside, dropping his meal on the ground before him. Driven by hunger he lowered his head to eat, tearing great chunks of meat with his teeth, tasting fresh blood... then it was no longer a horse, but another dragon caught in his talons, dragon flesh that hung from his jaws. He recoiled, disgusted, yet the savage joy of the kill remained, and the bloodlust flowed through him even as he fought it. Surrendering to it, knowing as he did so what that meant, he lowered his head once more...

The dream shattered and broke apart. Aarkan jerked awake with a horrified gasp, raising a hand to his mouth that had lately been feasting on the raw, bloodied carcass. It came away clean, no blood staining his skin, but the sensation remained, the feeling of his jaws tearing into unresisting flesh. No, not his jaws. Srenegar's. And yet they had been his also. He raised his head, looking up into his dragon's amused eyes.

'Why?'

I did nothing. It was your dream, not mine.

Aarkan shook his head, withdrawing his hand from the dragon's side where it had rested throughout his sleep. He ignored the shaft of pain that ripped through him when he deliberately broke the contact. For now, just for a moment, he needed the clarity of that distance.

'No,' he insisted. 'It was not my dream. It was *our* dream.'

Maybe so, brother. Yet I did not sleep.

Aarkan shuddered, remembering the feel of his teeth shredding warm muscle. 'I no longer have control,' he murmured, his voice full of dread. 'What do we become?'

Something greater than we were. Why do you pull away from me?

'Not from you, from us.' He was trembling with the pain now, though it had been only moments since their bodies had ceased to touch. 'Do you not feel it also, my presence within you, overshadowing your own?'

I feel you, every moment. It is as we wished. Yet still I feel your distress.

'We have killed.'

We have.

'Many.'

Srenegar was silent. Yes, there had been many in the years since this war had started, human and dragons.

Aarkan stirred, pulling away still further, his fingers gouging painfully into his arms. Was this madness, he wondered, or was he only now free of the insanity?

'I cannot remember it all.' His voice shook. 'Why?'

For this, his dragon replied. *You must not fear it.*

A whimper escaped the man as he hunched over, arms cradled across his stomach, hair slick with sweat. 'How can I not fear this?' he gasped, choked with pain. 'Such power we have as I never dreamed, yet it burns me still. It burns me. Look at me!' he cried, jerking his head up. His eyes were wild and fever-glazed, glowing coals in a white sunken face. 'Look at me! How can I live like this?'

You need not, Srenegar insisted. *You need only come to me for your suffering to end. Why do you hesitate?*

'Because I fear you!' Aarkan skittered backwards, the light of madness in his eyes, so quickly now did the changes come. Srenegar's gaze followed him across the floor of the cave, impassive, silent as a stone, yet he tracked every shift in his companion's thoughts with the tenacity of a hunter.

'You seek to steal my mind!' Aarkan raged at him. 'Release me!'

The dragon's obsidian eyes met his and his dark gaze sharpened, wary. *I seek to help you. You trap yourself. Come to me, my brother, and let me ease your pain.*

'No! You would trick me.'

That is not so.

Aarkan shook his head, flinging droplets of sweat from his dark hair. As they landed on Srenegar's flanks they fizzled and disappeared in an instant, so hot was his fire, and the mage watched distrustfully. That the power of elemental Water should be so easily quenched by Fire served only to heighten his suspicion. He was not equal, he was less somehow, and even through the madness he saw this and understood.

You are mistaken. Srenegar's eyes latched onto his, drawing his gaze and holding it. *Always you were my equal, but now we are no longer two but one. Who then should you be equal to?*

'Myself,' Aarkan said slyly, his eyes filled with flawed cunning. 'My will is my own to dominate.'

The dragon felt a prickle of alarm, so alien a feeling to his vast existence. *It has always been so.*

But Aarkan's eyes were blank again. Quick as it had come, the mood had fled. 'It hurts,' he whimpered, sinking to his knees, head bowed so it touched the cold surface of the rock. 'Why are you doing this?'

I am not. It would not hurt if you would come to me.

Aarkan forced himself from his crouch, one arm still held protectively across his middle, but as he made it to his feet he gasped, staggering under the onslaught of the agony. Srenegar's alarm heightened and he sent a sliver of awareness out to his mage, probing, comforting, yet imperceptibly faint to the mind so hazed by pain.

Set your fear aside and let me heal you, the dragon urged, frightened now by the suffering their entwined state forced him to share, and he put all the sweet, seductive power of his race into his plea. *Come to me.*

Aarkan's anger vanished. 'Truly?' he asked piteously, as eager to believe as he had been to condemn.

Truly. When have I ever hurt you, little brother?

'Never.' Aarkan slinked closer, a child again, wanting comfort yet needing to be coaxed. A wistful look came into his eyes, his hand outstretched before him, reaching out across the distance. 'I remember you,' he murmured. 'I remember flying free on your wings; I remember love, a wife, a daughter. My wife, Ashlea...'

Agony flared at her name, as it always did. Fragments flashed in Srenegar's mind as his mage recalled them, memories of long ago, memories that could no longer be trusted. They were dreams, and if they had ever been real their innocence was gone past recall. The lost love that had forged their first steps on this path was lost in truth now. The dragon cared little now for any other, their pains or their joys, except for this man who had become a part of him. So, he listened as Aarkan rambled on, drawing closer with every step.

Then Aarkan stopped. Whatever memories he relived were smashed by a wave of pain that sent him sprawling to the ground. Srenegar reached out, catching his mage's mind in a silky web, shielding it as his wing curved down to shield the fragile body. This had gone far enough. He could not allow Aarkan to injure himself further, yet the damage already inflicted on his mind was like whiplash of agony through their shared being.

Aarkan lay still in his embrace, the grey mists of unconsciousness parting before the bliss of the contact. Srenegar's strength sustained and nourished him, sealing them once more into a union so strong it could no longer be undone, and the delirium of the pain subsided, replaced by the ecstasy of the magic. He let it flood him, washing him clean of the taint of madness, and felt himself filled with renewed purpose. This feeling, this power that possessed him, this was everything. And soon they would be even greater still, when the moment came that they were truly forged as one.

He drifted, content to remain motionless in the half-world as his mind reordered, and the scorching weight of his guilt fell away and was buried deep within the circle of their magic. They had done only as they had to, and his moment of weakness sickened him. Had he really thought of Riah? It seemed it was only in such moments that his thoughts turned to his daughter, when his mind was clouded by pain and he did not remember that she had betrayed him, that even now she fought against him, Lorrimer's son by her side. It angered him that his own daughter should fight with his enemy when he had offered her so much. When he had done this for her! He forgot that he had abandoned her when she needed him most, that he had left a motherless child alone to pursue the destructive course of his own grief, and he remembered only that she had rejected the gift he had tried to give her. Well, let her see for herself the power she had scorned. He would take from her what she loved so that she might see and understand the quality of his mercy. And Lorrimer... it was past time he learned that defiance always had a price. This was war. In war men died.

The rider urged on his screeching dragon, imploring the exhausted creature to one last burst of speed. His pursuers were closing rapidly, their mounts rested from the long wait lying in ambush among the rocks of the valley's slopes. The dragon swerved violently to one side, nearly unseating his rider in a desperate attempt to avoid a new enemy flying in low from the right.

'Easy, Belegast, easy.'

Looking over his shoulder to catch a glimpse of their new pursuer, Medelin drew in a sharp breath. The huge black dragon bearing down on them was unmistakable, and he finally realised with sick certainty that he had not just been unlucky in springing this ambush; he had been singled out by the enemy. In that moment he knew he would not survive.

Aarkan sat astride Srenegar with unshakeable arrogance, confident in his kill, the great dragon gliding effortlessly through the air as it sat on his tail. They would toy with him, Medelin knew, until Belegast tired and could go no further, then they would kill them both and leave their mutilated bodies on the wasted ground, an eloquent warning to those who opposed them. To his father. To Riah.

A jet of flame shot past his ear as his dragon spiralled into a dive just seconds before Medelin would have been incinerated where he sat. Clinging to Belegast's neck as they shot downwards, Medelin cursed violently, unused to such helplessness. There were no foes on Andeira to challenge the dragons, nothing that could threaten a dragon and its rider in active communion with each other. Until the outbreak of war, the pairings had roamed the skies and the world below, lords of the earth and the air. But things were changing. They had had to learn the craft of war, of death, and they had learned too of fear. Medelin knew fear now, as he found himself outplayed and outnumbered and facing death at the hands of his own kind, unless by some miracle, he could find a way out of the trap.

The landscape sped by below them and familiar territory was left behind as they were driven further and further from the outposts of Tesseria. He understood that he would be given no chance to seek aid from his own side and must find the means within himself if he was to survive. Suddenly, over the horizon and still many leagues distant, Medelin caught sight of blue water and realised that their flight had brought them near the great lake from which the Aetelea flowed on her way to the sea. The sheer grey slopes of the Athelan Mountains rose steeply on either side and he directed Belegast low through the peaks. They twisted and turned as they traversed the narrow gullies, and he saw with satisfaction that the pursuit was forced to break its formation to follow them through the treacherous passes.

Belegast saw the huge expanse of water through a break in the cloud. *I do not like what you are thinking.*

'It is as good a plan as any. They focus their energies on those powers they have newly acquired and may forget what they once knew.'

On that you would gamble our lives?

The frustration that thrummed through the link was tinged with sadness and the mage felt a surge of guilt. For he did not gamble both their lives, only Belegast's. His own was already forfeit. Only his dragon might survive, and for that end he was prepared to sacrifice himself. But even in giving him life, Medelin knew that he condemned his companion, with whom he had shared the incomparable wonder of the Joining and almost two centuries of life, to an agony of grief beyond human comprehension. No mage had ever survived the death of their dragon. They could not withstand the onslaught of grief that heightened awareness and the closeness of shared thoughts inflicted upon them in the moment the magic that bound them together was ripped apart.

'If you die, I die, old friend,' he gently reminded the tormented creature. 'Only by attempting to save you do I have any hope at all.'

Medelin looked over his shoulder in time to see Srenegar break through the cover of the cloud, sweeping in a great arc towards their position. The cold mountain air rushed through his lungs and whipped his hair into icy tangles across his frozen face. Even as the great black dragon dived towards them, he saw the shadows of the others on the mountain below and knew that they were closing for the kill. He had only moments left in which to act.

Nudging Belegast with his mind, they broke from their path of flight, veering sharply to the right and downward through a narrow cleft between the jagged peaks. A shrill scream from behind told Medelin that one at least of their pursuers had been forced to pull up to avoid crashing into the rocks as they attempted to follow. On and down they flew, Belegast navigating the route with a skill born of desperation, then suddenly they were through, and the sparkling blue of the lake rushed up to meet them.

As they levelled out over the shimmering surface, Medelin calmed his mind. He drew the power of the Water to him, sucking the energies of the lake into his being and bending them to his will. More and more he drew, filling his soul to overflowing with pure elemental power, revelling in the thrill of it as they sped onwards, and he rode with arms outstretched and head thrown back as though to capture the essence of freedom one last time. Beneath him he felt Belegast tremble, though whether it was from exhaustion or the perilous quantity of power he was drawing, he never knew. And when he had drunk in as much as he was able, almost blinded now by the singing energies, he forced the dragon to turn and hurl himself back at their pursuers.

Volatile, explosive, the pair spun around. Desperately Medelin sought to contain the power within him until he came close enough, but at the last their attackers pulled up, shrieking, sensing the flood about to engulf them. And he could wait no longer. With a shuddering gasp he loosed the magic, and a massive tidal wave of power sheeted out before him as the confined energies poured forth, and with them spilled his life energy, recklessly spent in defence of the one creature he loved above all others. Too late he realised, as the final blindness took his sight, that the greatest prize had got away, and Aarkan had not followed them out over the lake.

Yet I am glad I did not kill her father, was the last thought that ever came to him.

Belegast screamed with rage as he felt the life of his mage dwindle into nothing, sucked out of him by the force of the spell. Unable to halt his flight, he tumbled through the air, crashing against the reeling bodies of his enemies as they were whipped senseless by the ferocious attack. Then, fatally caught in the spiralling backlash as the Water's energy returned to its source, the two that had ambushed them crashed into the waiting lake, unable to free themselves as the outraged passion of their prey bound them tight beyond hope of escape.

Belegast fell with them, but Medelin's sacrifice ensured that he did not fall helpless into the icy depths of the Aetelea's great lake, and even as his perception of Water's elemental power began to dim with the passing of his mage, he found himself protected by the magic of Medelin's dying wish and the deathly cold did not touch him. As he plunged below the surface it was white-hot rage that kept him fighting. Belegast fought against the sucking depths and powered upwards, following the stream of bubbles on their way to the surface.

In a rush he broke free, water streaming from his scales, his fire temporarily stilled. Clumsily he turned in mid-air and flew back over the lake, searching, scanning the rippling water for some sign of his rider. Belegast knew that Medelin was dead, had known the exact moment when his spirit left his body, but his ravaged mind would not allow him to depart that place without him, nor let him find eternal rest in the graveyard of the enemies. The surface of the water calmed and grew still, and no bodies were returned from the chill depths. Yet still he flew back and forth, his high-pitched keening renting the skies.

Lower and lower Belegast flew, as the searing grief slowly scoured his conscious mind to madness. He knew exactly where his rider was as he sunk deeper, until Medelin fell softly as feather to rest between the body of a dragon and that of his rider. An outflung arm, no longer quite human, brushed his face, and through the disintegrating remnants of their link Belegast felt the intense wrongness of the touch, and all control shattered.

With a final scream he plunged back into the crystal water, diving straight as an arrow to the place his mage had fallen, risking the life-draining power of elemental Water stripped of the protection of the magic of the Joining. Fuelled by the madness of loss, he rescued his mage's body from the bottom of the deepest lake on Andeira and bore him away from the taint of his enemies back to his father's house. And there he lost himself in the agony of nightmares that hounded him, waking and sleeping, as he struggled to live the life Medelin had sacrificed his own to gift him.

Another watched that titanic struggle, safely hidden in the snow-covered peaks of the mountains. Srenegar had sensed his danger when Medelin drew Belegast off course towards the water, and it had been he who had screamed in fury as he was thwarted of his kill. Guided by Aarkan, they flew high above the clouds, out of range of Medelin's suicidal casting, and witnessed the sacrifice that had defeated their fellows.

As Belegast circled lower over the water, mourning his loss, his life was Aarkan's for the taking, but something held him back. It was not pity, for he no longer had any room for pity in the blackness of his soul, but something darker. It was as though Belegast's cries of grief awoke something in the two of them that had not been felt before, and as they fed on his pain they became less, and at the same time more, as they drew ever closer to their goal.

With each new evil contrived under the influence of the magics they raised, Aarkan stripped away his humanity, burned away his compassion, and gradually destroyed everything that had made him who he was. And although he no longer recognised it, as their souls grew ever closer together, his own control was draining away. The dominant will of the dragons sapped his strength and supplanted his influence with the ferocity that had marked the years of the First Age, before the Joining had tempered the wild nature of the dragons. The world of power he had glimpsed was falling by the way, but he never saw it, nor guessed the moment he had stepped from its path.

ONE

Kas'Tella, Caledan
The New Age

VASA CRUMPLED THE message in his fat hand, ignoring the bite of heavy rings in soft flesh. 'She dares defy me?' he demanded, shaking the scrap of parchment, penned in haste by a harried priest at the court of Farnor. 'She would break the bargain? Who does this woman think she is? Half my northern agents expelled to the South by a mob of half-trained eastern upstarts you assured me were all but helpless!' He rounded on a quivering page. 'You. Fetch the scribe. I will have Darred recalled to answer for this mess!'

'But Darred won't help you,' a thin voice told him as the terrified page dashed for the door. 'He has deserted your cause.'

Vasa spun around. The cowled acolyte who had spoken watched him from the shadow of his hood.

'Betrayed my cause?' the high priest repeated dangerously. 'Have you suborned him then?'

The acolyte gave a soft, hissing laugh. 'For what purpose? Are not our aims the same, Holy One?'

'Only a fool would believe that, Saal'an,' Vasa replied with a sneer, stalking back to his cushioned seat. 'If not *ours*, with whose cause has Darred aligned himself?'

A flick of his wrist brought a veiled woman gliding from the shadows, her footsteps tinkling with tiny bells.

'Your will, Holy One?' she murmured.

Vasa broke his study of Saal'an's shadowed countenance to deliver his request in terse phrases. The girl disappeared to fetch a tray bearing sweet dainties and a decanter of Karrimor's finest red. She placed the tray at Vasa's side and disappeared.

Vasa poured himself a glass of wine. Then, calmer, he turned his attention back to the provocative acolyte.

'Well?'

'I would have thought it obvious,' the robed figure remarked. 'Darred plots for his own advantage, and his revenge. Surely you know how deep his resentment runs?'

'Yet you urged me to appoint him to this task,' Vasa pointed out icily, taking a long sip of the wine. 'If you knew his loyalty was in doubt, I can only conclude you had another reason for sending him there.'

Saal'an met his gaze squarely, holding it until Vasa looked away in revulsion. 'His suspect loyalty has not been a hindrance to you, far from it. He has attacked his given task with enthusiasm, hoping to trap you by the very zeal with which he obeys your commands. But you can defang that trap because you will not do what he expects.'

'And what is that?' Vasa asked with a lazy smile. Behind the pampered, indolent façade, his senses were sharpened to a knifepoint for the verbal fencing.

Saal'an did not return the smile. He stood, long robes swishing across the marble floor as he drew closer to the high priest, sprawled in decadent abandon amid his perfumed pillows.

Vasa forced himself not to surrender to his crawling horror. 'Share your insights, Saal'an. I'm all ears.'

The robed acolyte stopped his approach mere inches from Vasa's slippered feet. It was all the high priest could do not to twitch them aside.

'Perhaps it is time to rethink your strategy,' Saal'an suggested. 'Where covert means have faltered, brute force might prevail. Your agents have achieved much in Amadorn. Most of the kingdoms have been stripped of their fighting strength, and this woman has turmoil enough in the North to contend with. Send over your armies and you would stand victorious within six months.'

Vasa maintained a thoughtful silence as he considered this. While the plan had its merits, he did not trust the source, and he dared not leave Kas'Tella bereft of the protection of her armies while the Sharhelian problem remained unresolved. The War of the Lost Houses might have ended, with him the victor, but Shrogar's Ephenori rebels stubbornly refused to accept it.

'Why?' he inquired at last, flicking a crumb from his silk robes in a semblance of dispassionate interest. 'Why now do you support an armed invasion? Always in the past you have argued against such a move. At your instigation I sent my agents into Amadorn, and now it seems they have turned against me. And so I must question your motives.'

The hooded face looked down on him with a chill stare. 'In the past you did not have the narrow advantage you now possess. Darred has done your work well, but you must strike before the seeds of his betrayal can bear fruit. Chaos will soon consume the northern continent. Let it slip too far and you could lose everything, but act now, while the kingdoms are in disarray, and you could cut the threads of his scheming in one move.'

'And divide my strength when I need it most?' Vasa protested with an edged smile. 'Surely you cannot believe that Shrogar's rebels will refrain from storming into the breach if I were to leave Kas'Tella all but undefended?'

'Then cut the head off their rebellion in the same strike. You know their lines of intelligence have a hold in the Athelan regions. Recall *that* errant priest and you disarm their greatest weapon. And settle your own score once and for all.'

Vasa's pudgy hand tightened on the stem of his glass. 'Careful, Saal'an,' he warned. 'Some things remain beyond your reach. Kinseris will fall when I decree it, not you. As will Amadorn.'

He waved a negligent hand as a knock sounded on the door. The scribe who inched across the threshold held his pens and parchment close to his chest and looked ready to run if the mood turned ugly.

'Here,' Vasa gestured sharply as Saal'an stepped back, shrinking deeper into his hood.

The scribe perched himself on the stool and laid out his board, freshly trimmed quill poised over parchment.

'Your will, Holy One?'

'You will take this down in cipher,' he instructed, his eyes on the acolyte's shrouded back. 'Address it to this man.' He thrust the offending message into the scribe's shaking hands. 'Tell him that he is to order all agents to remain at their posts and observe only. They are to take no active hand in the coming events. Make that quite clear.' Then to Saal'an he added, 'If anything can be salvaged from this idiot debacle, I will have my own on hand to secure it. Should your dire predictions prove true, I will merely withdraw and wait. Of time I have rather more than our northern cousins.'

Vasa saw Saal'an's back stiffen and knew he had touched a raw nerve. The high priest allowed himself a sly smile. Only a fool indeed would trust that creature's motives or believe he had sounded the depths of his subterfuge. So far, and to great mutual profit, their plans had gone hand in hand, but something had changed. No longer subservient, Saal'an was fighting in the open now, for a goal he must believe had come within reach, and the ruler of the Kas'Talani was no fool. Conquest of Amadorn, though close to Vasa's heart, was a far-off dream and needed no urgent action. When he said he had time he spoke the truth, for his lifespan would eclipse the next generations of the northern peoples. But Saal'an was running out of patience by the day, though he pretended otherwise. Soon now he would slip, and Vasa would pounce. If he was to extend his Order's influence across the great sea, he first had to rid himself of this nest of vipers in his midst.

'You will take down one further message,' he told the scribe, his eyes on Saal'an. 'Send copies to all our northern ports. Trade with the far continent is to be suspended. Those of our merchants who remain in Amadorn are to be recalled, and no further ships are to sail.'

Now that his Order's scheming had been uncovered, he would not risk his merchants falling into enemy hands. There was too much they could reveal about his empire. If Darred had truly turned against him, the Amadorians might already be aware of the rebellion that festered in its heart.

'It is done, Holy One,' the scribe murmured, holding out the wax for the Holy Seal. Vasa crooked his forefinger and ground the signet ring into the hot wax, transferring its imprint onto the parchment.

'You make a mistake, Chandra Vasa,' Saal'an growled, still turned away.

'Leave us!' Vasa snapped at the scribe, who fumbled over his tools in his haste to obey. That this creature should address him in such a manner in the presence of his servants! 'We shall see who has made a mistake, Saal'an,' he replied softly as the doors slammed closed. 'We shall see.'

The robed figure drew in an angry breath, swirling around in a fan of flowing black skirts. As Vasa watched him with a malicious smile, he stalked across the marble floors and followed the scribe from the room.

'So angry, Saal'an,' Vasa murmured, gesturing once more for the girl to attend him. 'What are you hiding in that black mind of yours?'

He tolerated the treacherous creature's presence only because of the undeniable benefits of keeping him on hand. Like his predecessors, he had found uses for the Arkni, but his doubts could no longer be dismissed. Priceless knowledge, powerful tools, had been placed at his Order's disposal, with barely a token demanded in return, and the unequal weight of that alliance had begun to disturb him.

Vasa touched a hand to the device hidden under his lavender silks. Its presence failed to reassure him as it once did. He was beginning to see the truth. Beneath Saal'an's black robes and chill smile lurked a power that rendered him breathless with fear. The obsession with the prophecy and Æisoul had reached unmanageable proportions, and as the pieces lined up for the final confrontation, Vasa was left with the dawning realisation that he clung to his power by the finest of threads. He would do well to treat all the man's actions as suspect and move only when he was ready.

In some matters, however, his hands were tied. There were things that demanded his immediate attention, and Saal'an's casual reference to Kinseris had come too close on the heels of the reports from his spies in Frankesh. Events there could not wait on his need to deal with the Arkni. Vasa wondered uneasily if he too had heard the disturbing news from the north. Was that why he had suggested recalling the exiled priest?

Æisoul. It all came back to that name. Æisoul would come to them from Amadorn, that much was clear from the prophecies. But what, or more importantly who Æisoul was, remained hidden from him. The uncertainty limited his ability to act and left him no alternative but to treat any Amadorian with suspicion. And the new arrivals in Frankesh had alerted suspicion in too many quarters for him to ignore. The only thing more disturbing than the reports of their activities was the absence of any action by Kinseris to curb the growing rumours. Vasa could not help but assume that the priest was making his move at last, and so, Saal'an or no Saal'an, he had taken steps to bring the traitor back under his control.

Sedaine looked up as the servant entered.

'Dispatches, my lady,' he said, holding out several rolls of parchment.

Sedaine set aside the map she had been studying and took them from him, nodding her thanks. The man bowed again and prepared to leave. Should she need a scribe to pen her responses, he told her, she had but to call.

Sedaine laid the scrolls on her desk, noting the seals. One from her uncle, another from Brannick, and two more from agents she had sent south. She opened Brannick's first, hoping for good news, and quickly scanned the contents. Those who had followed her to Redstone had followed just as willingly to Rhiannas, but those in Luen remained suspicious of her plea for aid, the more so since she had ordered Brannick to reveal in full her own part in their present peril. This latest communication from Ecyas's old friend said only that talks were continuing and that he still hoped to persuade them into an alliance.

She set the scroll aside. He had said the same for weeks now, but there seemed little to justify his faith in his people. Reluctantly she opened Vianor's message, reading carefully, as always gleaning more from what the magician did not say. She reached the end, read again, and snatched up the ciphered messages from her southern agents. Both were brief, and both confirmed Vianor's news. There was none. No indication of any retaliation from Caledan. The priests she had expelled had not left Amadorn, but they were doing nothing, not a thing. Puzzled and wary, she laid the scrolls on the desk and massaged her aching temples.

It made no sense. Darred's plotting stretched far beyond his plans for Lothane, of that there was no doubt. Her spies had confirmed that he had spent several years in the Golden Alliance, and there was evidence enough of his handiwork in the South. Depleted garrisons, festering unrest in the alliance councils. Whether it was by his hand or his colleagues', most of the southern states were caught in upheavals that would take years to settle. The continent was ripe for conquest, and yet *nothing*. Even the Caledani merchants appeared to be continuing their trade as though nothing of import had taken place between the two nations. The Kas'Talani were quiet, too quiet, as though they were waiting for something, and it made her nervous, far more nervous than overt action. At least then she would know what she faced. Of only one thing was she sure: that she could not, for any reason, relax her vigilance. For then, she was certain, they would strike.

TWO

THE ANCAI PRESSED a coin into the man's hand and sent him on his way, his thoughts turning uneasily on what he had heard. The three strangers who had haunted the dockside taverns for ten days now remained undaunted by the hostility of the townsfolk. So far their search for a guide to take them into the desert had been met with firm refusal, but eventually they would find someone foolish or desperate enough to defy the strict law of the priesthood and consent to take them.

He reviewed the details gleaned from his sources. Two men, one Caledani for certain, the other Amadorian, accompanied by a girl, also Amadorian, and one of them a wild talent. An Amadorian mage would pose problems for his lord, for Vasa's orders on that point were clear. For whatever reason, should any of the gifted peoples of Amadorn set foot on Caledani soil, they were to be handed over to Kas'Tella. What happened to them there the Ancai did not like to guess and did not much care. He knew only that Kinseris, being who he was, would wish to save them from that fate. So far, by good fortune, he had been spared that decision, but these new arrivals threatened to change that.

They had arrived on a Caledani vessel bound out of the Illeneas Archipelago, and since their arrival they had moved from one tavern to the next, asking dangerous questions. A degree of curiosity in foreigners was to be expected, but their tenacious search for answers went beyond what could be tolerated. Questions about the Kas'Talani, their prevalence and power, all made for disturbing possibilities when set alongside their desire to travel into the desert.

The Ancai watched the door of the tavern for a few minutes more before heading back to the chapter house. The choice he faced was not an easy one. Unsure how Kinseris would react to the news, he had so far kept it to himself, justifying his reticence by the fact that Amadorians were not unusual in

225

Frankesh. It was the busiest port on the northern seaboard, and the first stop on the transcontinental trading route. But neither were they common. No doubt in keeping with Kas'Tella's desire for a monopoly on trade between the two lands, as well as their invidious greed, the merchants of Caledan allowed limited knowledge of their homeland to filter into the ranks of foreign traders.

Yet that was not the cause of his concern. These were no merchants—that much he had been able to confirm. There was little to be found in the desert, just endless dunes and nomadic tribesmen. Little to be found unless it was something else they sought. Had word reached Amadorn of the rebels who lived in the heart of the Sharhelian wasteland? Was that what these strangers were seeking, an alliance with Shrogar's Ephenori? The thought made him uneasy, not least because their artless subterfuge could place those same rebels in grave danger, but also because he feared what it might mean for the man who was so hell-bent on tying himself to them that he might snatch even this dangerous chance to advance their cause.

In the end the Ancai did not have the choice of keeping the strangers' presence a secret. On his return to the chapter house, he found Kinseris pacing his chambers, already garbed for travel.

'Is it true?' Kinseris demanded. 'Are there Amadorians in my city seeking Ephenor?'

The Ancai cursed silently. Even he had not realised that thought had also occurred to the citizens of Frankesh, though he realised now that he should not have been so sanguine. If it had occurred to him, why not to others? These three were suspicious enough, with their blatant curiosity about the Order. It was but a short step to assume a connection between the two.

Still, he tried to salvage what he could from his error. 'There are Amadorians in your city, my lord. As for what they seek, I could not say. They have never said as much.'

'Do you think me a fool?' Kinseris flared. 'By now you will know the names of their ancestors, ten generations back. Your spies are mine, remember? Why did you keep this from me? Do you not realise how much danger you have placed us in?'

The Ancai endured the scathing rebuke in stiff silence. 'No danger attached to you, my lord, while you remained ignorant of their presence. It is only what you do now that places you in jeopardy. Do not judge me for wanting to steer you clear of folly.'

Kinseris's expression softened. 'Judge you? For your friendship, never. But that you think me without reason, without the means to look after my own, for that, yes. At the very least you should have trusted me to make my own judgement. I would no more endanger Shrogar for an unfounded chance than I would hand us all to Vasa's justice. Rumour this might be, but it is one that should never have started, for now I shall be forced to squash it before it reaches Kas'Tella.'

Kinseris sighed, running his fingers through his hair. 'Don't you see? I cannot simply leave these people free to foment who knows what kind of chaos, no matter how innocent they may be of any sinister intent. I must be seen to put an end to this, will be forced to in fact, for if I do not Vasa will take matters into his own hands.'

The Ancai allowed himself a glimmer of hope. 'You do not believe they are here to find Ephenor?'

'How can they be?' Kinseris asked impatiently. 'It is not possible either that my Order is so disliked in Amadorn, where they know virtually nothing about us, or that word could have spread so far of Shrogar's rebellion.' He snatched his cloak from a chair and flung it round his shoulders. 'This has gone far enough.'

'Where are you going?'

Kinseris stopped, his expression grim. The Ancai, realising his intent, shook his head, placing his solid bulk between his Vela and the door.

'No, my lord,' he said firmly. 'I cannot permit it.'

'You cannot permit it?' Kinseris repeated softly. 'You do not *permit* me anything. It is my word that rules here.'

'Even so, my lord,' his captain maintained. 'I am bound to guard your person, and I will do so. And it is also my place to shield you from the unpleasantness that must sometimes accompany your rule. If you are set on this, let me be the one to carry it out.'

Kinseris took a step back, regarding his friend with a chill stare. 'And what is it you think I go to do?' he asked dangerously. 'I said only that this must end, not how it should end. Just as I protect my own people from my brotherhood, so too will I extend that protection to those from other lands. *Is that not what we risk our lives for?*'

The Ancai's face burned at the censure but he stood his ground. If he had been concerned before, he was doubly so now. What Kinseris intended was sheer madness.

'You cannot be seen in the presence of these people,' he insisted. 'Let me arrange for them to return the way they came, if that is your wish. There is no need for your name to be tangled up in this.'

The priest laughed. 'Oh, but there is. Have I not said? I must be seen to take control, and I will. Personally.' He moved to the door, his gaze challenging his captain to back down.

The Ancai wavered. Though desperate to prevent this foolishness, he saw that he could not, and all that was left to do was abet it and hope that his counsel could temper some of the risk his lord took.

'Then I will accompany you. If you will do this, you will do it with your guard in attendance. That way there can be no mistaking on whose behalf you act.'

Kinseris nodded. 'Very well. You may attend me, and one other, no more. Someone who can be trusted. I do not wish to exacerbate the situation by giving the people cause to think the Order gives any credence to these wild rumours.'

The Ancai bowed his acknowledgement of the order and suggested a name. Receiving agreement, he hurried to organise the escort. Kinseris's mood would permit no delay.

'Now what?'

The question set Aarin's teeth on edge. He had heard it too many times over the past few days. Both Jeta and Kallis were growing impatient, unnerved by the strange city and the hostility of its people. All their efforts to find a guide to take them into the desert—where Aarin felt an overriding compulsion to search—were met with stony silence, or worse, outright suspicion. A few careless questions about the priesthood had worsened their position still further.

He glanced at Kallis, seeing the straight-backed stance, the eyes that seemed to be looking everywhere at once. The sullen atmosphere was abrading the mercenary's nerves, and Aarin could not blame him. Until now he had pretended a confidence he did not feel, rebuffing Kallis's arguments for a swift departure, but his resistance was weakening

Aarin sighed. He was tired, they both were. It had been almost six months since they had fled Redstone for the dubious safety of this land, leaving turmoil in their wake. Arriving at last in Taslor on Amadorn's southern coast, they had heard the news. Lothane hovered on the brink of war, and it was not only Elvelen but the Alliance states that were clamouring for satisfaction. On that point Jeta bore the brunt of an uneasy conscience, for it was her supposed death that had outraged her people, but the tension had risen to such a pitch from Darred's manipulations that news to the contrary would make no difference now. Sedaine had claimed the throne and executed Nathas, plunging the whole of the North into chaos, just as Darred and Vianor had planned, and Aarin dared not allow himself to believe she had not acted freely. He knew how much she wanted that crown.

But that was not the only worry eroding his peace of mind. Jeta kept intruding into his thoughts, no matter how hard he tried to keep her out. In the time they had travelled together, until disaster had befallen them in the Vale, she had begun to lower her prickly defences and they had moved towards friendship. But the moment of shared experience in Redstone had changed that. After the unbearable intimacy had subsided, she had been distant, eschewing his company when she could as though what she had seen in him repelled her. It hurt, not least because in the instant of connection she had reached for him as desperately as he had reached for her.

'Well?' Kallis demanded. 'How long are you going to make us kick our heels in this fish-rank dive? These people are not going to reward your patience, slap you on the back and offer their services. More likely they'll lose all patience and sling us to whatever counts for authority round here.'

Aarin winced. That thought worried him too. With no way of knowing for certain whether Darred was acting in concert with his Order, he had to assume that every Kas'Talani was his enemy. Vianor's suspicions about Darred's loyalty were just that, and Aarin had no way of confirming them short of handing himself over to the priesthood. Of only one thing was he sure, and that was the prophecy's existence. It was eating him from the inside out, just as Darred had said it would, as though the magic was trying to claw its way out of him back into the world. And he did not know how long he could contain it. Ever since they had stepped ashore, he had clamped down on his power, desperate not to draw any unnecessary attention to himself, but it was slowly spinning out of his control.

He needed answers, answers that none but the Kas'Talani could give him, yet he dared not go to them. If, as Kallis had told him, the people of this land believed the dragons were responsible for the destruction of the ancient world, and if the Kas'Talani shared that belief, it set them at odds. Darred had declared it his intention and that of his masters to return the dragons to Andeira. It did not seem possible that the priesthood could be those masters, not if Vianor's assertion of their fear of Æisoul was true.

Aarin sighed, rubbing a hand over his grainy eyes, when a noise caught his attention and he glanced at the door, suddenly confronted with his gnawing fear. He gave the mercenary a resigned look. 'I think they already have.'

A party of men had just arrived, and even in the gloom he could pick out the now-familiar uniforms of the two guards. The third, his clothes unmarked by rank, was a mystery.

Kallis swore savagely, tugging the hood of his cloak down over his forehead. 'Say nothing,' he advised. 'You have no idea how ugly this could get. Our only hope is to brazen it out, pretend a complete lack of common sense, and pray that they think us too stupid to bother with.'

Aarin nodded, shrinking back into the shadows, and watched the approach of the men. They spoke briefly with the landlord and the man stopped wiping glasses long enough to point in the direction of their table. Several heads turned to stare, chairs were pushed back to afford a better view, and Kallis swore again, his words mercifully muffled by his cloak.

The mage took a sip from his drink. He observed the approach of the official party through lowered lashes, thankful Jeta had become so infuriated by his persistence in trawling the dockside drinking holes that she had refused to accompany them on this latest venture.

The men reached their table. One of the guards directed a question at Kallis, the Safarsee words harsh and alien. Aarin had picked up much of the tongue from Kallis during their six-week voyage, but the mercenary's accent was softened by years in Amadorn and he always made an effort to speak slowly and clearly. This man made no allowance for unfamiliarity, and Aarin watched Kallis closely as he tried to follow the conversation.

As it happened, Kallis was not inclined to bear the brunt of the questioning alone. A few exchanges later, he turned to Aarin, translating for him.

'They want to know why we are here, and why we wish to travel into the desert. This one seems to be a captain of some sorts,' he added, jerking his head in the direction of the huge, black-skinned spokesman. 'As for the others, I suspect that the hawk-faced fellow is the authority here.'

Aarin nodded. The man's face was obscured by shadow, but even half-glimpsed he had a presence. Close to, Aarin could sense his talent, and the same mysterious depth threading his aura that Darred had possessed.

'A priest do you think?' he asked softly, then, because the captain began to display signs of impatience added, 'tell them we are seeking a guide into the desert because you wish to be reunited with your people.'

Kallis raised a sceptical eyebrow but duly translated, provoking an immediate response. For several minutes Aarin was left entirely out of the exchange, save for the intense regard of the priest that never left his face. Clearly, he was in the grip of the same recognition, of like meeting like, and Aarin realised with a sinking heart that they had little chance of talking their way out of this.

The conversation broke off and Kallis leant over. 'Apparently my people moved on from these parts some years ago. They have suggested, quite firmly I might add, that our search is therefore at an end and we should return to Amadorn. Somehow I don't think they believe us.'

Aarin hesitated. His first inclination was to tell Kallis to agree, but he also suspected that should they agree they would be accompanied every moment until they were safely aboard a northbound ship. He could not let that happen, for now he was here he was painfully sure he was where he was supposed to be. But he also feared the priesthood.

Aarin looked up, prepared to acquiesce, when he met the priest's eyes. The man had moved into a shaft of light, and Aarin could see his face clearly for the first time. The shock ran through him like a shiver on a cold day. He had seen this man before, for an instant, his bruised face haunted by unbearable grief as he held the body of a woman to his chest. He had seen him in a dream that night on the edges of the Grymwood when the ancient power of the land had magnified his magic.

'Tell them no.'

'What?' Kallis lowered his voice as the captain glared. 'What are you doing? We should fall over ourselves to agree, cut our losses here and try somewhere else. There are settlements all along this coast, most that do not have a priest in residence. Far more likely we will find help there.'

Aarin shook his head, quietly determined. The dreams that had plagued his last months in Amadorn had been filled with faces. Some from his past, others from his present, and some, he knew now, from his future. This man was one of them, and he was now certain this encounter would not end here, no matter what choice he made.

He was running out of options. Their plan had been to travel into the desert in search of the dragons, and though Kallis had warned him such a search would be perilous, the mercenary had been able to offer no alternative. The deserts of this land were vast, stretching almost coast to coast in all directions. Most of the peoples of Caledan lived in the coastal regions, for its centre was a burning wasteland. For dragons, such a place would be a paradise. Parched of water, scorched by the fire of the sun, the First Ones would thrive. But if they did, their existence was a secret, and the secrets of Caledan were kept by the Kas'Talani.

'Are you trying to get us killed?' Kallis hissed when Aarin repeated his refusal. 'Defy them and we risk losing our lives as well as our liberty.'

'Very well.' Aarin turned to the tall guard and haltingly communicated his intentions, while next to him Kallis sunk his head into his hands with an audible groan.

'What game are you playing here?' he asked, resigned, as Aarin's answer sparked a flurry of conversation between the men.

The mage kept his eyes on the priest. 'Who better to answer our questions about the priesthood than the priesthood itself?' He smiled disarmingly at Kallis, and the mercenary's disbelief gave way to despair as the guard captain rapped out a command, his gesture unequivocal.

'We're to follow,' Kallis said needlessly as he was dragged to his feet. 'They're taking us before their Vela.'

A rough hand fell on Aarin's shoulder, pressuring him to move. As he was ushered past the priest, he felt those hawk eyes boring into his back and knew that, for better or worse, he had made the only decision he could. Only with help from the Kas'Talani could he answer the questions Vianor had stirred in him.

THREE

KINSERIS WATCHED HIS prisoners through a spy hole that looked into the cell from above. The hole angled down where the wall met the floor, and it gave a good view of the cell but for the far wall.

Once left alone the men did little worth observing. The Amadorian paced fretfully near the chained door while his Caledani companion rested just out of sight against the wall, only his booted feet and knees visible to Kinseris. But it was not the Caledani he was interested in.

Back in the tavern, even in the dim light and smoky atmosphere, he had seen the Amadorian with perfect clarity, a figure limned by the bright glow of his talent, a creature apart from everyone around him. And Kinseris was intrigued, fascinated. This man, the first of his kind he had come across, had deliberately provoked his capture, refusing the simple agreement that would have seen him and his friends placed safely aboard a ship heading north. His actions made the priest doubt the confidence he had shown the Ancai. If these strangers posed no threat to him or his Order, if they were simple travellers as they claimed, they had no reason to reject the offer.

He remembered the look they had shared, full of mutual curiosity, and wondered whether there was another, equally disturbing motive.

He had ordered them brought to the chapter house because he could think of nothing else to do with them. For the moment at least he had to treat them as any other of his Order would, to allay the suspicions of those who had seen them taken. Yet now they were here, his position was no less precarious. The Ancai had stripped them of their weapons, and a poor collection it had been if they were indeed revolutionaries. Together they had searched through the few possessions the men had carried and found little. He had sent his guards to search the rooms they had rented in one of the dockside inns, but he held out little hope that they would uncover anything significant. Whoever they were and whatever they were here for, Kinseris suspected he would find nothing among their possessions that would shed light on the mystery.

And what, in the end, did he hope to find? He stood by his words to the Ancai. The War of the Lost Houses had ended decades ago, and Ephenor was all but forgotten even in his land. Nor did he believe that Shrogar would have attempted to seek aid from his estranged kinsmen in Amadorn without first informing him. His alliance with the Lord of Ephenor went beyond a mutual desire to end Vasa's tyranny. Their friendship had been forged through shared grief that had hardened them both. Besides, the priest reflected, the Ephenori had long forgotten their roots in Amadorn, so long had they been isolated in the heart of the Kas'Talani Empire.

The Caledani himself, if he truly was searching for news of his people, posed an altogether different puzzle. The merchants who plied the northern trade routes did so in close-knit family groups, spending only a few weeks of the year in Amadorn and keeping close ties with those they left behind. The nomadic tribe to which Kallis claimed he belonged was not one of those families and never would be. They were not merchants. They were poor, and they traded mostly between themselves. It was true that they had moved from the region, though Kinseris knew full well that they would return with the rains. It was something else that had stirred his memory and brought the half-truth to his lips.

Twenty years ago, when he was but newly arrived in his post, a great drought had devastated the lands north and west of the Athelan mountains, and there had been widespread unrest. Several of the tribes had been driven from the desert and into the towns for survival. There had been riots and bloodshed, and he had been forced to send his soldiers out to calm the spreading panic. They had been efficient, too efficient for his tastes, for it had been the first time Kinseris had witnessed the savagery with which his Order enforced its authority.

Overzealous soldiers had slaughtered the protestors and brought yet more to the chapter house for judgement. Sickened and appalled, it was then that the seeds of treachery had taken root. Unable to order the executions demanded of him, Kinseris had walked a more dangerous path, sorting through the captives to find those he could save, choosing families, the young and the hardy, those most likely to survive, and spiriting them away onto ships bound for Amadorn. And those few had eased his burdened conscience when the time came for him to act out the demands of his station.

Desert tribesmen had been among that number, he remembered now. Two brothers, one with his wife and child, had been caught up in the riots and taken prisoner. He had saved the family but not the brother, and it had been many weeks before he was able to forget the frantic pleas as the Ancai dragged them away, pleas to spare the life of the man left behind.

He had chosen the family for the life of the young son, no more than ten or eleven years of age, and on all but the child he had placed the enchantment that would prevent them from seeking out their homeland. In full knowledge of what he had done, allowing them to yearn for the place and the people they had lost and yet be unable to reconcile that longing with the spelled urge to remain in Amadorn, he had deliberately spared the child the measure he enacted for his own protection. The boy would grow to manhood in a foreign land, and would, he had thought, become as tightly twined to Amadorn as his parents had been to Caledan. It was unlikely he would return of his own free will.

Yet here, perhaps, he was.

Such an unlikely pair, a Caledani exile and an Amadorian mage. He had to know the reason for their presence.

Kinseris eased a crick in his back and turned his attention back to the mage. There was something strange in the way he wore his power, cloaked about him as though trying to hide either it or himself. He had made no effort to free himself and his friend, as he could surely do. Kinseris had deliberately left this wing of the compound unfettered by ward spells to tempt him into showing his hand. But when the simple enticement of an unwarded prison failed to garner a reaction, Kinseris resorted to less subtle methods.

Aware that Amadorians lacked all awareness of the Lost Elements, the priest framed his queries in those elements mankind had natural affinity with. There was not even a flicker of reaction. The effort of will required to ignore those probes, flickering like quicksilver against the edges of the mage's awareness, should not have been possible. Perhaps this man was unaware of the bright glow of power burning in him? But Kinseris did not think so. That split-second shared glance in the tavern had revealed their recognition of each other.

Frustrated now, Kinseris shifted the source of his efforts to include the Lost Elements, though without hope of success. If the mage had remained oblivious to his previous attempts, pretence or not, he could not be anything but wholly unaware of what came next.

Sending the frisson of power along the currents of Air swirling through the cell, Kinseris choked back a startled cry as grey eyes flicked up to his hiding place. He held his breath, not daring to move. The instant the weavings had touched his presence, the mage had stopped dead, a shiver running through him from head to toe. His brow furrowed as his gaze searched the ceiling, eyes flickering left and right, seeking and finding.

His companion called out a soft query, too quiet for Kinseris to hear, and he dared not expand his perceptions at this critical point. The mage tore his gaze from the concealed hole and answered him, equally quiet, his voice a gentle murmur on the spelled air. The other man disappeared from Kinseris's sight for a moment to reappear in the centre of the cell. The mage pointed upwards, directly at the hole.

'There's someone up there,' he said, his words loud enough for Kinseris to hear.

The Caledani grunted. 'I see nothing.'

'He's there,' the mage insisted. 'The man from the tavern. He's watching us.'

'He is?' The man smiled grimly. 'Then it must be a dull vigil.' He returned to his corner and drew up his knees. 'I'm going to sleep. You can keep him amused by yourself since you got us into this sorry mess.'

The Amadorian hesitated a moment before following his example, settling himself against the bars with the hole in view. Kinseris looked into his upraised face and watchful eyes and saw a mix of fear and curiosity staring back at him.

Now they were alerted to his presence, Kinseris knew he had lost his chance to overhear their plans, but he could not bring himself to leave. Those grey eyes unnerved him, gazing at him although they could not see him. The more he thought on what he had just witnessed, the more Kinseris became convinced that he was mistaken, that some noise he had made had alerted the mage to his watching presence. That it was Kinseris who watched might have been no more than an intelligent guess, but that did not explain the shock that had rippled through him.

Whichever way he looked at it, it should not have been possible. No, it was impossible. In their natural state, humans were incapable of perceiving the Lost Elements. That the Amadorian had felt even the faintest echo of Kinseris's magic defied every established precedent. And it was an area that the Kas'Talani were better versed in than most, for they alone possessed the means to expand a man's perceptions beyond natural limits.

In Caledan, when boys were tested for the priesthood, it was latent ability in the realm of humankind's priority that was initially assessed, their aptitude for mastering control of the Lost Elements considered only much later. Linked for a short time to a silver dragon held by an elder who steered them through the testing, the boys were instructed to reach out for the fickle connection that only some would ever grasp. Those who could not sense the Lost Elements when given the means to interact with them would not advance past the first rung in the Kas'Talani hierarchy, never making it to the rank of full priest or beyond. Those whose innate ability carried them through this second testing were rare and growing more so. And none, no matter how gifted, had possessed the spark of awareness to sense what could not be sensed without direct contact with the devices.

There was no way of breaching that void, that emptiness, without the enhancement of the silver dragons. Yet Kinseris had just seen it happen.

His need for answers now was urgent. The simple expedient of returning them to Amadorn could no longer suffice, and such schooled discipline as he had witnessed would be unlikely to crumble under simple questions. Kinseris was increasingly coming to suspect that whatever the explanation for their presence, it would not sit easily with his Order's rule. There was perhaps one way left to discover the truth before he resorted to the direct questions that could place them all in danger. It was not a course Kinseris would have chosen willingly, but they left him little choice.

FOUR

JETA WAS MISERABLE. Her clothes were too heavy for Caledan's oppressive heat and she was already sweating uncomfortably. She fingered the rolls of light cotton in the market longingly, but she had no money and she could understand almost nothing of what was said to her.

She was in the markets by the docks where their ship had tied up weeks ago, determined to relieve the boredom of sitting in endless common rooms where the locals treated them with suspicion if not downright hostility. She also needed to escape the unbearable tensions that had lain between her and Aarin since they had woken that first morning after fleeing Redstone, curled in each other's arms as if to recapture the closeness they had shared. But it had gone, and in its place was an awkwardness that neither had found the words to banish.

So she had snatched this chance to be alone among the crowds at the market. Every conceivable item was on display, from brightly coloured silks to gold and jewellery, earthenware, and weapons. She listened to the food sellers plying their trade in singsong voices amongst the throng of travellers and looked jealously at the outlandishly dressed men and women in their long flowing robes as they chattered in their harsh language.

Amadorn was a land of little racial variation from one end to the other, but here Jeta could see many different peoples gathered by the water's edge. While most were dark-skinned and dark-haired, they were still strikingly different, some with angular cheekbones and curving dark eyes, others with rounder faces, long beards, and thick curling hair, while still more were fairer skinned, with broad, flat features. All of them watched her with a curiosity that was not entirely friendly.

Suddenly anxious to be back among friends, she started to retrace her steps. But the twisting rows of stalls were constantly changing, as one trader packed up and another came to take their place, and she soon took a wrong turn and found herself in the marketplace proper. It dwarfed the dock area she had come from, and the array of clothing, jewellery and other goods for sale almost took her breath away. She wished again that she had the coin to buy some of the trinkets for herself, let alone some new clothes, but most of all she wished to be away from this place with its suffocating atmosphere.

It took her over an hour to clear the first part of the market, and she grew increasingly uneasy at the stares of the locals. The women were the worst, and she could feel their eyes raking her from head to foot, apparently intrigued by everything from her blond hair to the foreign cut of her dress. The men were less forthright, but she could feel their eyes on her and once or twice caught sight of a leer that was understandable in any language.

By the time she escaped the market and made it back to the tavern, the sweat was slick on her body and her mood was vile. It did not improve when she realised Aarin and Kallis were not there. She accosted the landlord, demanding to know where they were. The man shrugged, indicating he did not understand, and her gestures became more frantic.

'Perhaps I can assist you, lady,' came a voice from behind her in flawless Amadorian. She turned and saw a Caledani man lounging by one of the tavern's long trestles. As their eyes met, he got to his feet, his pale desert robe falling to his ankles.

'You have lost your friends?' he inquired, leaning against the bar with a helpful smile. She nodded, surprised by his friendliness.

He smiled and directed a stream of questions at the landlord. The man shook his head, gesturing to the door, his answer blunt and short.

The stranger looked grave. 'Two men?' he asked. 'One an Amadorian like yourself?'

Jeta nodded, biting her lip. 'We were supposed to meet some time ago. They...'

She stopped, confused, as the innkeeper placed a bottle and two small glasses on the counter.

'They are no longer here,' her new friend told her apologetically, cupping one hand under her elbow and steering her to the table, the other hand expertly juggling the bottle and glasses.

Jeta shook herself free. 'Where have they gone?'

'To the chapter house,' the man replied smoothly. 'If you'll let me, I may be able to help you free them.'

'Free them?' She looked into his dark face, taking in the aristocratic cast of his features, the hooded, predatory eyes. 'Why should they need freeing?'

An eyebrow curved upwards in amusement. 'One does not go to the chapter house for fun, my dear, especially not in the company of the Vela's own guards.' He patted the seat beside him, treating her to a brilliant smile. 'Come, sit. Perhaps together we can work out why they have attracted the Order's interest. I am not without connections in Frankesh should a word in the right ear be needed.'

Jeta sat cautiously, pulling up a bench opposite. 'And who are you?'

'Me?' The stranger leant across and filled the glasses with pale liquor. 'I am a simple merchant. But I have been lucky in my trade, I've prospered.' He winked at her, raising his glass and downing the contents in one swallow. 'And money, my dear, breeds influence.'

Jeta grinned despite herself, taking a sniff of her own glass, her nose wrinkling delicately. Her attempt to imitate his drinking style left her coughing until she was hoarse, and she did not notice him refill her half-empty glass.

'Why should you help me?' she asked when her head stopped spinning and the fire in her throat died down. 'Why risk your influence on strangers?'

The merchant shrugged, propping one negligent foot on the bench. 'What good is influence if you don't make use of it? Besides, the Kas'Talani are not well loved. I should enjoy a chance to needle them.'

Jeta considered this, studying his handsome face with unabashed curiosity. The landlord bustled over with a plate of food and a bowl of yoghurt.

The merchant tossed some coins onto the table. 'That is not reason enough?' he inquired when they were alone. 'Very well, I admit it. In you I see the chance to extend my connections in Amadorn. Since you are known to be seeking a guide into the desert, I assume you are traders yourselves?'

'We're not traders,' she said without thinking. 'It's Aarin who wants to go into the desert, not me.'

'Aarin?'

'The ma –' Jeta realised her mistake just in time, dropping her head to avoid his piercing stare.

He leant forward, adopting her cross-armed pose on the trestle. 'Come now,' he coaxed. 'One merchant to another. I have traded extensively with your Southern states, but the North is relatively unknown to me. I was hoping you could give me some advice. Some names, perhaps?' He reached out and popped a battered morsel into his mouth, smiling as he chewed.

'Well, I'm not northern,' Jeta said dismissively. The mention of Aarin had unsettled her. It felt disloyal to be sitting here, casually drinking with a stranger while he and Kallis might be in trouble. They had shared a moment of perfect intimacy, a moment in which, intentionally or not, he had opened his heart and all that he was to her, and she had answered. And since then? Since then, Jeta thought sulkily, she had been confused and lost, unable to understand the feelings he woke in her, and unable to speak of them to the one person who might have understood. But it was the fact that Aarin himself seemed untouched by the experience that angered her most.

Jeta looked back to the merchant and realised he was still waiting for her answer. She shrugged. 'As for advice, the best thing I can tell you is to stay away. The North is rather troubled at present.'

Her benefactor's interest sharpened. 'Really? And does that have anything to do with your presence here?' He paused to knock back another shot of the fiery liquor, and Jeta followed suit before she realised what she was doing. Through the pounding haze, she retained the sense to distance herself from that assumption.

'So, if not the troubles in your homeland,' the merchant pressed, his lazy smile veiling his question in harmless curiosity. 'What brings a beautiful woman like yourself to our shores?'

Jeta blushed. The drink was strong, and already the edge of her suspicion had been blunted. She reached across the table and hooked the bottle towards her, pouring them another glass. 'And why should that interest you?'

He returned her smile, raising the drink to his lips and slamming down the empty glass. She giggled, her eyes falling hungrily on the plate of food. She took a cautious bite and her mouth exploded with heat as she bit into the fire hidden inside. The merchant laughed and gestured to the dish of yoghurt.

'Quite apart from my own curiosity,' he continued, as she hastily scooped the yoghurt into her mouth, 'I thought it might explain your companions' predicament. For all their faults, the Order does not usually haul foreigners off the streets for no cause. It is not good for trade.'

'Oh.' Jeta paused, grinding her elbow into the table to arrest the spin of the room as she took a drink to calm the fire in her mouth. 'What are these?'

He laughed again. 'These are *rikiti*. It is our tradition to eat them when discussing business, to show that you will be honest. Just as the *rikita* cannot hide its nature, even when concealed, so by eating it you undertake to show your true nature.'

'And this?' she demanded suspiciously, tipping the bottle in her hands. 'Is this another symbol of your business dealings?'

The stranger took no offence. 'This,' he explained as he refilled her glass, 'is for drinking with friends.'

'So now I am your friend now as well as your business associate,' Jeta replied coolly. 'You make bold claims.'

'To a bold woman,' he returned, sitting back. 'It is a long and dangerous voyage from your homeland. Why did you come here, I wonder?'

Jeta's eyes stayed on his as he raised his glass and drained it. He looked so confident, almost as though he already knew the answer, and she longed to wipe the smug look from his face. 'I came to find a rich husband.' The declaration was accompanied by a quickly regretted toss of her curls.

The merchant steadied her. 'Here.' He nudged her glass. 'This will make you feel better. Are there no suitable men in Amadorn?'

She favoured him with an owlish stare as she slammed the empty glass back on the table. 'I've had enough of people telling me which men are suitable.'

'Your parents, perhaps?' he guessed. 'Who did they want to marry you to? Was he horribly deformed?'

Jeta giggled, resting her head in the crook of her arm. 'Probably.' Her fingers wiggled towards the glass and he filled it. 'You too.'

He smiled, obliging her. 'You never met him?'

She shook her head, cautiously this time. 'He was rich though, a lord.'

'Sounds perfect.'

This time her giggle ended in a sob. She could feel the flush rising in her cheeks. 'I didn't want to marry him. Doesn't that mean anything?' She shoved the glass back with an irritated gesture, surprised at the emotion she was too inexperienced to realise was due to alcohol. 'What do you care anyway?'

'Sometimes it helps to talk. Is that why you left?'

Jeta closed her eyes, feeling the hot sting of tears, and the words came out in a stormy rush. Her companion listened attentively, prompting her when she faltered, keeping her glass full. 'Why is love not important?' she demanded, reaching the end of her mournful recital. 'Why do women have to marry men they don't love, at the wishes of other men? You are a man. How would you feel?'

'Ah, my dear,' the merchant murmured in amusement. 'I fear I am not qualified to speak on such matters, being a man. I am not married, and I am quite confident that I will never be forced into a union I have not chosen.'

Jeta shot him a disgusted look. 'You're all the same.'

'Maybe so,' he smiled, dazzling her with this smile. 'But even so you never could renounce us forever. Did you not come here seeking a husband?'

She snorted. 'And all men are fools.'

'Ah ha!' He relaxed into his favourite pose, one foot perched on the bench, the hand holding the glass dangling from his bent knee. 'Don't tell me. The truth is far more daring and exciting?'

'Perhaps.'

'Do I have to guess?

Jeta made a show of thinking about it, unable to meet his eyes lest she collapse into laughter. 'Let us make it more interesting,' she suggested. 'One drink for every wrong guess.'

He considered. 'And if I guess right?' That lazy smile was back. 'I think we can make it more interesting still.' He gestured to the bottle. There were still two inches of clear liquid left inside. 'One guess only. If I am wrong, I will drain this dry. If I am right, you will.'

'I like a man who can raise the stakes,' Jeta replied, clinking her glass against his to seal the wager. She could not quite hide her confident smile as he screwed up his handsome forehead in thought.

He paused for dramatic effect, making a great show of pondering her mystery. Then said, 'I have it!' He leant forward in conspiratorial closeness. 'You are looking for Ephenor.'

Her confusion lasted only a moment, then bright laughter pealed out as she pushed the bottle forward in triumph. 'I don't even know what an Ephenor is. Now drink.'

The merchant shook his head, all gracious defeat, save for the slight lessening of tension around his eyes. 'You win,' he conceded. Then, taking his cue from her wistful sideways glance, dragged over the bottle and poured a clumsy slug into her glass. 'It's only fair,' he said sweetly, as she started to protest. 'After all, you are victorious.'

'Men,' she goaded, whipping the glass away. 'You can't even keep your taproom bargains.'

He picked up the bottle with a flourish. 'Can we not?' He threw back his head and poured the last of the liquor into his mouth, most of it spilling over his chin and onto his linen shirt. He choked as the liquor hit his throat. Laughing and coughing at the same time, he placed the bottle back onto the trestle with a shaky hand, his fingers gripping the edge to steady an unmanly wobble.

'You may as well tell me now,' he gasped, wiping his face. 'I'll barely remember my own name in the morning.'

The comment caught Jeta with the glass poised at her lips. She snorted with laughter, sending a spray across the table. She looked up, red-faced, and they both dissolved into fits of helpless hilarity.

Some minutes later, when they had regained breath enough to speak, Jeta tugged his head forward and whispered in his ear, still giggling. The man's eyes went wide with surprise, the hand that rested on the table stiffening to white-knuckle tension. His answering laugh was offbeat and forced, but she was far too drunk to notice. By the time she had recovered enough to sit up, he had gathered the remnants of his self-control and was able to present a passable impression of indifference.

Jeta swayed. 'Surprised?'

His arm steadied her by reflex, his smile a shade too pale.

'I think it is time to see to your friends,' he said, all warmth gone. He stood, rock steady where moments before he had been as shaky as her. As Jeta looked up, a half-formed query on her lips, a hand at her elbow lifted her protesting and squirming to her feet.

Abruptly realising she had been played, she lunged for the bottle, her boots skidding on the wet floor. The man caught her before she could fall.

'I'm not going to hurt you,' he said urgently in her ear, 'but I can't leave you to your own devices in this state, in this tavern. Do you understand? I'm taking you somewhere safe for the night to sleep it off.'

But Jeta was beyond listening. Memories of Darred, his soft voice crooning in her ear, his face as close as this man was now, all twisted his reassurance into a threat. She struggled free and stumbled a few paces before her upset balance sent her sprawling to her knees. She turned, finding a wall at her back, and he knelt beside her. His hand reached out to brush her arm, the gesture meant to soothe, but she flinched from his touch as if scalded, and closed her eyes.

She would not look at him, expecting any moment to feel that hated touch. But it did not come. Instead she heard his voice murmuring gentle phrases, calming her panic. She did not understand the words, but she understood the tone, and slowly, very slowly, it dawned on her that this man was not going to hurt her. As she stopped shaking, her sobs dying away, she felt an arm slip under her knees and another under her shoulders, and she was lifted from the cold, sticky floor and carried from the tavern. As they stepped outside into the sea air, she felt herself beginning to slip under and let the blackness take her. She did not wake as she was transferred from the merchant's arms into another's, nor did she hear the hushed conversation they carried on over her head. The knockout punch of strong spirits sent her deep into dreamless sleep.

Aarin looked up as the door to the cell creaked open. He nudged Kallis awake. A guard hustled a bedraggled Jeta inside, shoving her roughly forward.

He saw the girl wince at the sudden movement, squeezing her eyes shut, and for a moment he thought she must be sick or hurt. Kallis reached her side as she swayed, catching her arm. Then he drew away, wrinkling his nose in distaste. She reeked of cheap liquor, her sleeves were sticky with it, and the slit-eyed, pinched look was a sure sign of an almighty hangover.

The priest who had apprehended them in the tavern appeared outside the cell. Jeta twisted her head, saw the priest and gave a frightened yelp, moving to stand behind Kallis. Aarin looked from her to the priest in narrow-eyed suspicion.

'It seems you have not been entirely truthful with me,' the priest observed in fluent Amadorian, his hawk's eyes boring into Aarin. 'Shall we try again? Why are you here?'

Realising that this man had understood everything they had said in the tavern, Aarin felt a looming disquiet. He glanced at Jeta, saw the guilty flush, and immediately realised what must have happened. A surge of jealously caught him by surprise. It took an effort to keep his voice steady as he answered, gambling that Jeta had not revealed the worst of the truth.

'Our search for Kallis's people is genuine, but with the purpose of establishing trading connections that bypass your official merchants. The price they charge for Caledani goods is extortionate,' he added, reasonable. 'My masters think it is time they were made to surrender their monopoly. All in the spirit of fair trade, of course.'

'Of course,' the priest agreed. His eyes glittered, unreadable in the fickle light. 'And who might your masters be?'

'The Farnorian Merchants' Guild,' Aarin said promptly. He did not look at Jeta, could not look at her. Jealously dissolved quickly into hurt, then to anger, and he knew it would show on his face.

The priest nodded, thoughtful. His eyes drifted to Jeta, already burrowing into the blankets on the sleeping platform, then back to Aarin. 'Their official delegation arrived here only last week. I will be sure to raise the matter with them at the first opportunity. No doubt they will be anxious to talk to you themselves.'

Aarin gave him a sickly smile. 'I daresay the feeling's not mutual.'

'No, I imagine not,' the priest replied, unsmiling.

A searing sensation rippled the air around him and Aarin went rigid. It was the same sensation he had felt before, when this man had been watching them. He stifled his instinctive reaction with an effort, but one glance at the priest's intense gaze told him the shift in his awareness had been noted. It felt like a test, and he was sure he had failed when the priest cracked out an order and his huge captain entered the cell.

Aarin stepped back, twisting out of the way as the man's arm reached for him.

'You will come with me,' the priest told him. 'I would hear more of Farnor's double-dealing.'

Aarin sighed, about to move, when Kallis appeared at his shoulder. 'He doesn't believe you.' He glanced at Jeta. 'She may have told him.'

The priest gestured impatiently at his captain, who grabbed a fistful of Aarin's tunic and yanked him forward. He looked back at Kallis and shrugged. Whatever Jeta had told the man, it was too late now to wish it back. All he could do was try to discover the extent of her indiscretion and hope she had succumbed to drink before her tongue had flapped too freely.

FIVE

FLANKED BY GUARDS, Aarin accompanied the priest from the prison block across the wide courtyard and into the building at the centre of the compound. As they entered an antechamber, the guards took up station either side of the doors into the room beyond. Aarin found himself ushered into an opulent study, its walls hung with fine tapestries. In the centre stood a carved desk, ebony black.

'Sit.' The priest gestured to a chair as he took his seat at the desk. The harsh face was unsmiling but not altogether unfriendly. 'I am Kinseris, the Vela of this Chapter and the ruler of this region. For the moment, this conversation is informal. If you continue in your attempt to deceive me, I will turn you over to the less discerning justice of my Order. Now, perhaps we can dispense with this foolishness over trade routes and merchant levies. The girl has already told me why you are here.'

'She was blind drunk,' Aarin pointed out more mildly than he felt. 'Who knows what wild tales she may have concocted to keep your attention? She is not accustomed to the effects of strong drink.' There was a hint of accusation in his tone.

'My tactics were regrettable,' the priest agreed, and Aarin noted with malicious pleasure the pinched temples that suggested he also suffered the lingering effects of the afternoon's drinking. 'You should not be too hard on her. You left me little option.'

Kinseris sat back, his posture betraying a fraction of the easy grace that had charmed Jeta. 'And I think she was telling the truth. There are some things we cannot hide from one another. No matter how hard you clamp down on your talent, I still see to the core of you. So, tell me, mage, why did you come to this land seeking the dragons?'

His worst fears confirmed, Aarin had no time to indulge his shock. The priest's manner demanded an answer, and quickly, and he saw he would be given no more leeway for evasion. Jeta's indiscretion made deceit pointless.

'I have come to Caledan to find the means of returning the dragons to Andeira,' he said honestly. 'Surely one such as you does not require me to explain the need for that?'

Kinseris's smile was wintry. 'One such as me?'

'A Kas'Talani. That is what you are?'

'It is,' Kinseris agreed. 'A subject on which you have been rather too curious, or so I am told. Why?'

Aarin shrugged, fighting to maintain a semblance of calm. This man's Order believed he would destroy them, though how and why he had never discovered. Should Kinseris suspect for an instant that he was the man they hunted, his life would be forfeit. 'You consider yourselves the guardians of the magic. I too share that magic, so I wish to know: for whom do you stand as guardians?'

The hint of a smile twitched the priest's lips, but it was gone so fast Aarin was not sure it had been there at all.

'You tread on dangerous ground,' Kinseris warned, and his stern tone belied the half-glimpsed impression. 'I can only assume you are unaware of the guiding faith of this land, and of the laws that compel me to uphold it.'

He raised his hand to his throat and unclipped his desert cloak. Underneath he wore the simple linen shirt and loose trousers belted at the waist that seemed the uniform of the people here. On his left breast sat a circular silver brooch, which he unfastened and laid on the desk. He pushed it towards Aarin. 'Do you know what this is?'

The gesture was unnecessary. The moment the device was revealed, Aarin was swamped by a wave of recognition that hurled him back to his confrontation with Darred. His world lurched, almost spilling him from his seat. He closed his eyes, hands clasped over his ears as the whirlwind surged. Just as he thought he must succumb to the violence, the pressure eased. When he opened his eyes the device was hidden under the priest's hand.

Kinseris was watching him intently. 'You have come across these before, I see. Is that why you have come to Caledan, because you have seen that the powers of the dragons live on here?'

251

Rocked dizzy, Aarin could only stare at him in shock. That was the secret of Darred's power, the secret Vianor so desperately wanted for himself? But if the Kas'Talani truly possessed the power of dragons, what did that mean for the dragons?

'I...' he started, gripping the table with an unsteady hand. He looked up, grey eyes pleading. 'Dragons?' Something had gone terribly wrong, for the power in the tiny device Kinseris wore was never meant to be that way. The outraged reaction of his own magic hammered that conviction into him.

Kinseris could not hide his surprise. 'You did not know? That is not why you are here?'

'Please,' Aarin husked, his stomach roiling. The proximity of the tiny dragon made the heat in his blood flare to an unbearable pitch, and through the burning came the lament of a creature trapped and in pain. Not an echo of times past, but all too real. His hands came up to cover to ears. 'Please, take it back. Away from me.'

Kinseris did so without speaking, securing it to his shirt and covering it with the cloak once more. Returned to its keeper, the surges of the raw power died to a whisper, as though his presence itself held them captive.

Kinseris poured water into a shallow cup and pushed it across the desk. 'Your reaction puzzles me,' he said, as Aarin took the cup in trembling fingers. 'You seek to return the dragons, yet I show you their power, alive with us even now, and you recoil.'

'That thing is wrong,' Aarin said hoarsely. 'It should not be here.'

'But it is,' Kinseris countered, merciless. 'Does that change things?'

Aarin slumped back in his chair. 'You think it should?'

Kinseris shrugged. 'That depends on your viewpoint, I think. These dragons are the symbol of my Order and symbolise not only its strength but its guiding principle. From these we draw our power, and our right to claim divine rule over the people of this world.'

'Divine rule?' Aarin repeated, too off-kilter to guard his tongue. 'Your vaunted Order is no different to any other group of power-hungry fanatics. What is your justification?'

Kinseris's face betrayed none of the affront such words should have caused. 'You forget yourself,' he reproved, but without heat. 'Within the Order, by long-established decree, these devices are the Maker's gifts to her chosen successors as the guardians of this land.'

Aarin frowned, the turn of the conversation incongruous with Darred's assertions. 'Your priesthood seems to thrive on falsehood. By all means, continue this façade, but you will not goad me into unmasking your lies.'

'Really?' Kinseris's eyebrows quirked. 'But that was not my intention. Perhaps we are misunderstanding each other.' He sat back, studying Aarin through watchful eyes. 'I do not have a lifetime to impart all the tenets of a complex theology, so I will keep things simple. The Kas'Talani are collectively, through the divine channel of our High Priest, the Maker's replacements for those beings who once scourged our world to the point of destruction. When Mother Earth banished her first children for their betrayal, their gifts were passed on to us, the Kas'Talani, to maintain the balance of nature and the pure channels of elemental harmony. Far from deceiving you, I am attempting to warn you: your desire to return what is lost is worse than treason. It is heresy.'

Aarin froze as realisation hit. The Order could never have been seeking to return the dragons to Andeira. Their power derived from the dragons' absence.

Or the agency he represents.

Those were the words Vianor had used when he had taken Aarin's oath and bound him to resist Darred. It could not be for the Kas'Talani that Darred had manipulated the prophecy. Some other agency, separate to the Kas'Talani, had orchestrated his birth, and he had just placed himself in terrible danger. If, for the Kas'Talani, the return of the dragons was to be prevented at all costs, all that was left to discover was how Kinseris intended to kill him.

'It seems we are enemies then,' he said at last, forcing his voice to remain level. 'For if I succeed, your power will be toppled.'

Kinseris's eyes never left his. 'You did not know this?'

'How could I?' Aarin demanded. 'How could I know you had stolen their gifts for yourselves?'

'Stolen?' The priest's surprise was too complete to be forced. 'But we did not steal them. They were given to us.'

It was too much. 'Given to you. Why?'

'I have already told you,' Kinseris said with maddening calm. 'We are the guardians of the magic, and of Andeira.'

His mind spinning, Aarin dropped his head into his hands. 'You cannot believe that.' If the priests had truly been appointed guardians of Andeira, their magic would not be so wrong.

There was a small silence, then Kinseris said, 'I did not say that I did.'

Alert to the sudden increase in tension, Aarin looked up. 'Then what do you believe?'

And then, finally, the mask slipped a little. 'Understand this,' Kinseris said grimly. 'There is a warding on this room that only I can disarm. It will cripple anyone who attempts to enter or leave while it is active. Should harm come to me, the construct will ignite and destroy everything and everyone in this room. You cannot tamper with it, so do not try.'

Aarin sat up straighter. 'You feel the need to defend yourself against me?'

'Perhaps. The risk I am about to take makes you a danger to me, should you choose not to trust me. But more than that, it makes you a danger to many people I hold dear, and many more who have no idea I even exist. Be aware you are under judgement. React wrongly, and I *will* ignite the spell.'

'You would kill yourself?' Aarin asked in alarm. 'Then I can only hope that will encourage you to judge me fairly.'

'I will judge as I see fit. Far more than your life is at stake here.'

'You have made that clear. Tell me to what secret I am held hostage.'

Kinseris pushed back his chair and stood. 'You say the power of my Order will be toppled if you succeed. What you could not know is how close that very end is to my heart. No, let me finish. Yes, I am Kas'Talani, and all the privilege I enjoy now derives from my station, but just because I am part of the Order does not mean I cannot see its rotten core.'

He walked to the window and stood looking out over the grounds, his back to Aarin. 'You laughed at my assertion of divine rule, but your heresy is mine too, and unlike you I have seen the horrors my Order inflicts in its name. I cannot sit idle while my people are enslaved by a false religion that smothers old truths and wears the face of tyranny.'

He turned back to Aarin as he said, 'You felt a wrongness in our power; *don't think I can't feel it too*. Not so strongly, no, but it is there, lurking behind the magic, and I would see my brothers stripped of that power and destroyed for our misuse of it before I would willingly further their ambition.'

Aarin felt hope flare painfully. He saw now that he had not stumbled into the power of an enemy, but into the hands of one who could be a friend. In all Caledan he might have found the one priest who would help him rather than kill him, and the sheer improbability of it left him speechless. Then he remembered the prophecy and all thoughts of coincidence died.

He let Kinseris speak, afraid to interrupt, and desperate to hear more before he dared reveal himself.

The priest obliged him by filling the silence. Once started, he seemed almost desperate to unburden himself. 'Until this moment I had never considered the restoration of the dragons as a means to my end, though I understand that it would be an end in itself, and one that would change everything. Nor am I convinced, as you seem to be, that it is possible. You must understand that from our earliest childhood we are taught that the dragons destroyed the world and then departed from it, never to return. Whether they did in fact cease to exist is a question I have not given much thought to, for it seemed pointless to speculate.'

He turned, catching Aarin's gaze. 'Right now, I don't know whether I should simply return you to Amadorn with as little fuss as possible or keep you here and help you if I can. If you wish the latter, you must first convince me that you have any chance of success at all.'

The challenge had been thrown down, and in such terms that anything but complete truth would be a mistake, and an insult. Even so, Aarin feared to reveal what Darred had told him.

'There is a prophecy,' he said at last. 'A prophecy that foretells the return of the dragons and names the one who will bring that about. You will know the name, I think. Æisoul.'

Kinseris went rigid. 'Æisoul? Is it possible? They are one and the same?'

He stared at Aarin as he crossed to his desk, unlocking a drawer and withdrawing a sheet of parchment. 'Have you come here seeking Æisoul?'

Aarin felt a terrible urge to agree, to leave this man with the half-truth that might guarantee his freedom, and still leave him clear of the entanglement full revelation would bring. But as Kinseris had already laid bare his position, he found he could not lie. 'I am not looking for him,' he confessed in a voice barely above a whisper. 'I *am* him.'

Kinseris was silent too long, looking at the parchment in this hand. Finally, he said, 'In that case, what I hold in my hand is your death warrant.'

As the door slammed closed behind Aarin, Kallis stalked over the Jeta. 'What damn fool thing have you done this time?'.

There was a rustle of blankets and a bleary blue eye peered out at him. 'Not a fool,' she slurred, and covered her face with the rough cloth.

'You bloody well are,' the mercenary growled. 'What possessed you to get roaring drunk with a complete stranger? Did you never think he might be interested in something other than your pretty face?'

'Leave me alone,' Jeta snarled, burrowing deeper into the thin blankets.

'Don't expect me to nursemaid your sore head when the cosy bout of drinking that caused it landed us in this mess,' Kallis shot back, jerking back the blanket and rolling her onto the floor. 'Now get up and start thinking. What exactly did you tell that priest?'

Spilled on the cold stone like a rag doll, Jeta groaned. 'I don't remember.'

'Oh no you don't,' Kallis said viciously, kneeling to shake her by the shoulders. 'Something got past your careless tongue. Think. What does he want with Aarin?'

Jeta slapped him away and buried her head in her hands.

Kallis shoved up from his knees, disgusted, and Jeta crawled back onto the sleeping platform and pulled the blankets over her head as Kallis paced the small cell in restless worry. He had not liked the look on the priest's face. He knew something.

There was a muffled curse from the tangle of blankets, and Jeta shot upright. She clutched at her aching head. 'Merciful Maker! I told him!'

'*You did what?*' Kallis turned on his heel and paced back to her side, ignoring the hunched misery that begged him to be reasonable.

'Tesserion, forgive me!' she murmured. 'I told him.'

Kallis snarled his impatience. 'What did you tell him?' There were several choice details that were unlikely to be well received by the priesthood, and the facts about their encounter with Darred could be just as dangerous to them as the purpose of their journey here.

Thoroughly miserable now, Jeta avoided his eye as she related the tale. Kallis listened in forbidding silence, and when she had finished offered no word of understanding, nor even of anger.

'I didn't know who he was,' she wailed. 'How could I? He said he would help...'

'And you believed him?' Kallis sneered. 'Tell me, why should anyone here stir themselves for us? They've made their feelings quite plain.'

'And you didn't need any help,' she retorted. 'Next you're going to tell me that this is just where you want to be.'

Kallis sucked in a hissing breath, struggling with himself. Jeta had struck too near the mark for comfort. Stripped of a ready retort, he retreated, leaving her to her misery, and stalked to the bars. If this priest turned out to be another such as Darred, Aarin would realise soon enough. But would that save him? He had an uncomfortable suspicion that they had used up the last of their luck.

Kinseris looked up from the parchment. His expression was bleak. 'This is a decree from my high priest. It obliges me to hand you over to Kas'Tella. That alone is a death sentence.'

Aarin felt fear claw at his insides. 'Do you intend to execute it?' he asked cautiously. He remembered Kinseris's warning about the ward and stifled his impulse to ready his defences.

For an answer, Kinseris crumpled the paper, but his hands, so steady before, betrayed a nervous tremor. 'It is not as simple as that. Already many are suspicious of your presence here and your interest in my Order. And talk of Æisoul has been rife for years. Should any other make the connection, or even suspect it, the matter will be taken out of my hands.' He slammed a fist on the table and Aarin jumped. 'I hoped I would have more time, but I see now that I cannot count on any at all. I must think on this, and carefully, before I decide what to do.'

Aarin eyed the crumpled order nervously, afraid to break the silence. Then he felt the thrill of distant recognition that accompanied Kinseris's use of his power. For a terrified instant he thought Kinseris had decided on loyalty to his priesthood, and it took him a moment to realise the magic was not directed at him.

Kinseris saw Aarin's fear and smiled. 'The ward is released. I must return you to the cell while I consider what to do.'

SIX

WHEN JETA WOKE, Aarin was back. He was crouched in the corner with
his knees drawn up to his chest, staring at nothing. She glanced at Kallis and
saw that the mercenary was sleeping, stretched out flat on the cold stone as
though he were in a feather bed. He had pillowed his tunic under his head,
and one arm was draped across his eyes. After making sure he really was
asleep, she slipped from the blankets and padded across the cell to Aarin.

The mage looked up as she approached and offered her a distracted half-
smile. She sat down beside him and tried to find the words to explain, to
apologise. In the end all she said was, 'I'm sorry.'

Aarin glanced at her, grey eyes unreadable.

'I told him...'

'I know.'

She risked a quick peek and saw him staring at the wall once more. Irritation
flared. She had expected some sort of reaction, anything, and his lack of
response aggravated the wound that the inexplicable distance between them
had opened.

'I didn't know who he was.' It was an effort to keep from snapping. 'How
could I?'

'Of course you didn't,' Aarin agreed. A frown creased his forehead. 'Who
did you think he was?'

There was an edge to the question that put her on the defensive, and she
immediately retreated into anger. 'What should I have done?' she demanded,
feeling his silent censure. 'You were gone, I was all alone, and he said he
would help.'

Aarin's expression had not changed, but she imagined that she saw a
glimmer of the scornful disbelief Kallis had shown.

'I was trying to help you,' she insisted, furious with him and with herself.
She struck out with the only weapon she had. Twirling a curl around one

finger, she tilted her head to the side and smiled at a memory. 'Besides, he was very charming, and handsome.'

She got a reaction then. A shadow passed over Aarin's face before the shutters came down, more firmly than ever.

'Handsome,' he said flatly. 'And so, of course, you told him everything.'

This time there was no mistaking his disapproval, but despite provoking it, it only made her feel worse.

'And why do you care? You've hardly noticed I exist since we arrived here.' Far longer than that, in fact. The warmth of their shared experience had begun to evaporate long ago as they both retreated into confused silence, each unsure how to behave towards the other. She longed for the simple friendship that had been growing before everything had become complicated. 'You wouldn't notice if I were here or not.'

Aarin's expression cracked just enough for her to see a glimmer of hurt. 'That's not true,' he protested. 'And even if it was, does that give you the right to reveal my business to anyone you meet, if he's handsome enough?'

That last sneer was like touching a burning taper to tinder. 'Your business? Our business, Aarin, our secrets! We are all in this together, sharing the same danger. You don't own this, this...' She cast about, unable to find the right word. 'And you don't own me.'

His face paled. 'I know that. Jeta, I...' He stopped, swallowing hard and turning away, and she felt her heart suddenly beat faster. Then he sighed. 'And I cannot pretend that I am not glad you told him, however you did it. I should not have let you think otherwise.'

Her racing heart slowed, the disappointment crushing her. For a moment she had thought he was about to say something else. 'You're glad?' she managed to reply, her voice tight.

He smiled ruefully. 'I would never have taken the risk, though I knew the choice was there.'

But that was not what she was asking.

Jeta saw Kallis stir. His eyes were hidden by his arm, but he was awake, she guessed, and listening. His movement had been too precise. His shoulders gave a slight shiver and she realised he was trying not to laugh.

Furious, she picked up a sliver of stone and hurled it at the prone mercenary, striking him on the knee. Kallis jerked upright with an offended cry.

'Are you enjoying this?' she demanded to Aarin's look of sudden dismay.

'I was,' Kallis groused, unrepentant, dodging as she threw another missile. 'Quit throwing things at me, girl. It's not my fault your shouting woke me from a perfectly good dream. It didn't seem polite to interrupt.' He grinned as he lay back down. 'Feel free to continue. Listening to you two talking around the point is the best entertainment I've had for a long time.'

Jeta swore at him and Kallis's grin widened. 'So, you can say what you mean,' he observed. 'Why can't you do that with each other?'

She flushed and turned away, wishing very much to be alone. She heard a rustle of movement as Aarin got to his feet and moved away to stand by the bars in brooding silence. She longed to go back and start their conversation again, to try to draw out of him the feelings he had shied away from expressing. They were prisoners here, facing an uncertain future, and she might never get another chance to tell him how she felt—that for one moment, as he fumbled for words, she had felt a rush of emotion so intense it had nearly swept her away. But he had been speaking of the priest, and she felt foolish for allowing herself to believe he cared for anything except his search. For Aarin the dragons always came first, and there would never be a place for her in his life.

Choking back a sob, she wrapped her arms around her knees and sunk her head onto her laced hands. She would not let him see her misery. She was far too proud for that.

After he had escorted Aarin back the cell, Kinseris sat down heavily behind his desk and allowed his weariness to wash over him. All the strands of his plotting were coming together in this place and at this time for a final resolution, and he looked to the future with no small amount of trepidation, for he had no choice now. He had had no choice from the moment Aarin had revealed himself. All these years he had thought Æisoul nothing but a rumour, a paranoia of Vasa's, but even so he had hoped. All these years he had been waiting for this man, and now he was here all the plans he had made for this moment were unravelling. Never had he thought, never suspected, that the secret Æisoul possessed would be the power to return the dragons to his world.

His thoughts drifted to Ephenor and Shrogar. When he had sworn allegiance to Roden's son he had accepted the son's allegiance in return. And the pact they had made over Æisoul cut both ways. Ephenor was fighting a losing battle to stay alive and free in the Kas'Talani Empire. One day, as the other Lost Houses had fallen, so too would the House of Durian. No fool, Shrogar knew that as well as he did, and for that reason alone they had both agreed. Should the Kas'Talani's bane prove real, they would abandon all else but the pursuit of it.

Yet confronted with the consequences of that decision, Kinseris wavered. To involve Ephenor would be to bring the full force of Vasa's anger down on them and he knew they would never survive it. On the other hand, to abandon Aarin now meant walking away from his only chance to free his people—all his people—from the Kas'Talani yoke. Safety could be found in Ephenor, even if only for a while, and he owed the man that at least. And if Aarin was right, and the restoration of the dragons was the way to destroy the Order, he owed Shrogar the chance to help bring that about.

But the dragons? Kas'Talani taught, no matter that he had later rejected their teaching, Kinseris found the idea of the return of the dragons deeply disturbing. More than that, he did not know if he believed that their return was even possible. Yet, as he fingered the creature engraved on the device, he knew that Aarin was right. If he touched the power it held, if he allowed himself, he could feel that wrongness twisting through him like a sickness in his gut. That wrongness was the foundation of his Order, and Aarin's vision was seductive. A magic washed clean of that taint, a magic so pure it remade the world in the image of the Golden Age. The tyrannies of men like Vasa would be swept away in that cleansing, and humanity would be again as it had once been.

It was a seductive dream, but he did not know if he could afford dreams anymore. He wished this decision could be taken out of his hands before he committed himself and his allies to a prophecy he did not know and had no reason to trust. No reason, except the word of this one man and the paranoia of his superiors.

As he sat there, absorbed in his tangled thoughts, he drifted off to sleep.

It was his manservant who found him in the morning, slumped over the table well after the hour he would normally have risen. As the heavy drapes were drawn and the morning sun hit his face, Kinseris stirred. He groaned as he sat up, muscles protesting a night spent hunched over.

His manservant watched with a disapproving frown. 'I'm sorry for waking you, my lord. A personal envoy of the Holy One has arrived from Kas'Tella to see you.'

The last traces of sleep vanished. 'Vasa's messenger is here, now?'

His servant eyed him nervously. 'Yes, my lord. Shall I ask him to wait?'

Kinseris looked down at his crumpled appearance. He was still dressed in the casual garments he had worn to meet Jeta. It was unthinkable to keep the high priest's envoy waiting. It was just as unthinkable to greet one wearing merchant garb rather than his robes of office.

'Show him to the audience chamber and fetch whatever refreshment he desires. I shall be with him shortly. Please extend my sincerest apologies for the delay.'

As his manservant left the room, Kinseris took a moment to collect himself. A messenger from Kas'Tella? He had to believe that it was an unlucky coincidence. Aarin and his companions had been in Frankesh less than two weeks. Was it possible that word of their presence had reached Vasa's ear so soon? Unlikely but not impossible, given the unguarded nature of their enquiries. And now, for the first time in two decades, the gaze of the supreme ruler of the Kas'Talani had turned towards this backwater settlement.

Kinseris knew full well that his posting here was a punishment. Frankesh was important to the Order because it sat on the main trading route with Amadorn, but it was a rundown seaport where poverty abounded and the lawless thrived. The role of governor was traditionally given to those of high enough rank to be put in charge of a chapter house, but either considered beneath the old council's notice, or, as in his case, to those who had fallen out of favour. Which, until now, had suited him just fine. In Frankesh, several days journey from the centre of power in the land, he enjoyed a degree of freedom the more prestigious postings would never have allowed him. But he had also known that one day he would be called on to pay in full the price of his foolishness. But not so soon, not now.

As he stripped off yesterday's unadorned and rumpled clothes and changed into his robes of office, Kinseris forced himself to relax. He could not afford to allow his concerns to be evident to the high priest's envoy kept waiting in the rooms beyond. It was too soon. That was all he could think. He needed more time. He had wished for the decision to be taken out of his hands, but not like this. Straightening his tunic and his face, Kinseris left his rooms and proceeded to the audience chamber.

SEVEN

WHEN THE ANCAI came for him this time, Aarin accompanied him without protest. Whatever Kinseris had decided, he would rather know now than wait in nerve-wracking uncertainty. Kallis watched him leave in unhappy silence, kept in the dark by Aarin's refusal to discuss what had passed between him and the priest in anything but the vaguest of terms. Jeta ignored him completely. He knew he had offended her somehow, and it didn't help that Kallis seemed to find his attempts to speak to her vastly amusing.

Kinseris was waiting behind his desk, his fingers drumming an impatient rhythm on the exotic wood. He gestured Aarin to a chair, dismissing the Ancai with a wave of his hand. Aarin sensed the big man's reluctance to leave them and could not decide whether to be worried or reassured. It had not escaped his notice that the Ancai seemed always at the priest's side and had concluded that between these two there existed a degree of trust that transcended other loyalties. That Kinseris's most trusted companion was so unhappy about the decision his lord had reached made him more than a little uneasy.

He noticed Kinseris relax a fraction once they were alone, as though he too had been made uncomfortable by his friend's silent censure.

'He counsels caution,' he said wryly, 'but the time for caution has passed, I fear.'

Aarin waited for an explanation but none was forthcoming. Instead, Kinseris walked to his bookshelf and began combing through the volumes it contained.

'You should know some of the history of this land and its people if you are to survive here, and I may not have another chance to teach you.' He withdrew a tattered scroll from behind the leather volumes. Sweeping aside the papers on his desk, he unrolled an old map. The colours were still vivid despite its age, and delicate penned lines demarked the states of Amadorn, the Illeneas Archipelago, and the scattered islands beyond, and finally, the huge, sprawling mass that was Caledan.

Aarin reached out to turn the map around, eager to study the land he had newly arrived in, and as he did so the priest outlined the political disposition of the continent. He pointed to a small settlement on the north coast. 'This is Frankesh, the port where you made landfall. We are here, slightly inland, at the chapter house. This,' he indicated a great swathe of land stretching outwards to the south and west, 'is under the control of the Kas'Talani. The rest,' Kinseris pointed to several smaller territories to the east and far south, 'is disputed land. Or at least, that is how we see it. The people there have other ideas. Some we have allowed varying degrees of autonomy in the interests of trade, but others are more determined in their resistance to priestly rule.'

His finger travelled down the western coast. 'This is the Holy City, called Kas'Tella. The high priest of our order resides there. It is a great city, and ancient.' A tired smile lit up his face for a moment. 'It is not what it was, but it is still magnificent. Its foundations were laid in an age long forgotten, and there is no sight to equal the sunrise over the citadel.'

Aarin heard the fondness in his voice and guessed Kas'Tella was more to him than the centre of his faith.

'It was my home once,' Kinseris confirmed. 'Even before I was taken in by the Order. My parents were of the merchant class, and my father travelled often to your land. My grasp of your tongue is a gift of his passion for languages.' He smiled, the faraway smile of someone looking back on loved faces long gone. 'He has been dead sixty years or more now, and the house I knew has passed out of our family.'

'You must have been very young when he died.'

'Young?' Kinseris looked surprised. 'Not by your terms, I think. I was nearing fifty when my father passed away.'

'Fifty?' Aarin repeated in astonishment. The priest looked to be not much older than Kallis, a man in the prime of his life, not someone well past one hundred.

An impish grin transformed Kinseris's face. 'Did you not guess? Prolonged use of the dragons' gifts has extended our life spans. Vasa has ruled here for more than three centuries.'

Aarin could hardly believe it. Three centuries. Three hundred years of life—the legacy of the dragons gifted to the new guardians of Andeira, or something much more sinister?

'Why are you telling me this?' It seemed improbable that Kinseris had brought him here merely for a history lesson.

Kinseris sighed. 'Because I may no longer have the chance to explain later. Events have moved out of my control. I am recalled to Kas"Tella.'

Aarin realised he was afraid. It could not be a coincidence. Nothing about this was happening by chance. 'What will you do?'

Kinseris glanced up, surprised. 'I will go. I have no choice. When my high priest commands, I must obey. To do anything else would be an admission of treason.'

But he did not want to. Aarin could see what clearly, and he watched in silence as Kinseris paced restlessly behind his desk.

'I have not had time to arrange your removal from this place,' he said at last, 'and I cannot take you with me. So, I must leave you here, and hope that this summons has no bearing on your presence.'

'But you don't believe that?'

Kinseris half smiled. 'Vasa and I have had our differences in the past, and it may be that this sudden interest in my affairs is related to that indiscretion. But he has spies everywhere, and you, my friend, have caused no little stir in this corner of his empire. If I had not been so preoccupied, if I had known sooner...' He shook his head. 'There is nothing to be gained by dwelling on what might have been. I must accept the possibility that I have been betrayed, and if that is so my ability to help you will soon come to an end. The Ancai has instructions, and you can trust him to carry them out. When I am gone, he will get you away from here if he can, into the desert. You will be safe there until I can join you, or I am punished for my crimes. If that happens, you will have to decide how to proceed alone. The Ancai will take you to Ephenor, and if you truly are an enemy of Vasa you will find allies there. But their help will be limited, for they have no knowledge of the end you seek.'

'What about you?' Aarin asked. 'If you are right and you go to Kas'Tella, your actions here may well be discovered. If you help me now, you lose whatever chance you have of returning to your old life.'

Kinseris shrugged. 'And if I do not help you, what then? No, the time has come to act, and I can keep up this charade no longer. My own duplicity has come to sicken me. I speak truly when I say that I will relish the chance to act in accordance with my conscience.'

Aarin felt a twist of guilt. He could not allow Kinseris to go to Kas'Tella in ignorance of Darred's plotting—plotting that his high priest might also be entangled in—that had changed the stakes of the game. If there were others in Kas'Tella who worked for the same end, he was in more danger than he knew. Aarin had already tasted the power and determination that lay behind Darred's bid to use him. That power would devour Kinseris, or worse, seek to turn him against himself. Either way, everything he had worked for, all the hopes he harboured for his people, would be betrayed. If he went to Kas'Tella, he would die there.

'There is something you should know. The reason I journeyed here...' Aarin stopped as the priest's hawk eyes sharpened on him.

'Yes,' Kinseris prompted, his voice suddenly glacial. 'I thought I'd already had the truth.'

'You have,' Aarin assured him. 'Just not all of it.'

'By all means, tell me the rest. I would know what I am walking into.'

Aarin winced. 'Forgive my reticence, but it was one of your own from whom I am running, who told me of the prophecy and tried to force my part in it. And yet he was also the one who made me realise that this is where I had to come.'

'A Kas'Talani?' Kinseris's forehead creased in consternation. 'You learned of the prophecy from one of the Order? That is not possible. We do not wish the return of the dragons.'

Aarin shrugged. 'Your Order may not, but there are those who do. Darred is not one of you anymore.'

Kinseris stiffened, his hands clamped on the desk to brace his sudden unsteadiness. 'What did you say?'

Aarin stared, unnerved by his reaction. 'I —'

'No.' The priest shook his head. 'The name. What was the name?'

'His name? Darred.'

Kinseris let out a long breath, his shoulders slumping. 'Then he has finally made his choice.'

Hearing the regret in those words, Aarin guessed, 'You know him?'

The priest laughed bitterly. 'I did once. We were friends once, close friends I thought, but perhaps I was wrong.' He sighed. 'Are you sure?'

Aarin nodded. 'Beyond any doubt. My land is on the brink of destroying itself because of his meddling, though in that at least I believe he acted in accordance with your Order's interests. But he also works for another, or others, who have a very different end in mind. He knows of the prophecy and he intends to use it for that very purpose.'

He related the details of his meetings with Darred, and the plots that had plunged the northern kingdoms into chaos.

'So, the oppressed becomes the oppressor,' Kinseris murmured as he finished. 'It has happened before. He was always ambitious, convinced he was treated differently because of his race. It should come as no surprise to hear what he has become, but I find it is a bitter one.'

'I don't understand.'

The priest sighed. 'It is complicated, like so much else. Caledan is a complex place and our history has been bloody. There are four races here, four separate peoples who have suffered under the rule of one tyrant or another for centuries beyond count, and this uneasy co-existence you see around you now will not last. It can't. My people, the Safarsee, have been the ruling class since the high priest before Vasa murdered the chieftains of the Renalla clans and purged them from our Order. The guards who brought you here, they are Renallan, and they are reduced now to servitude to my people.'

'But Darred is not Renallan,' Aarin said, puzzled. 'Neither does he look like you. He is —'

'More like your people,' Kinseris finished with a sad smile. 'Yes, he belongs to neither class, neither Safarsee nor Renalla. He is from the southern islands, and his people are more marginalised even than the Renalla. That my Order took him in at all is testament to his strength, not their compassion. He knew that and resented it. Once, I think, he believed he could rise above the prejudice, prove his worth. But they wanted only to keep him close to ensure he could be no danger to them. His strength they needed, for power such as his is dying out in this land, but they will risk no threat to their rule.'

A faraway look came into his eyes. 'We met in Kas'Tella many, many years ago and became friends. But where I was destined for great honours, he was little more than a servant for the council members. There was great bitterness in him even then, but a lightness also. Together we pulled many foolish pranks on our fellow novices, sometimes even on our superiors. And even many years after leaving our novitiate behind, I allowed him to draw me into his small acts of revenge. It was one such, badly misjudged, that caused our disgrace. We were sent here as punishment, and if I lost the career I should have had, he lost far more, for only in Kas'Tella did he have any hope of advancement.'

'But he did not stay here,' Aarin prompted. 'He has been in Amadorn many years, I think.'

Kinseris nodded. 'He did not. Little more than a year after we arrived, he was recalled to Kas'Tella, and there given a new posting, to Amadorn.' He sighed. 'Something changed in him from that moment. He was elated, and he was angry. I never knew why, but I think now that part of him was afraid— afraid to be involved in whatever it is he is a part of. I have seen him only once since then, when he briefly returned some years ago, and by then he had changed so completely I no longer knew him at all. But this?' He shuddered. 'Whether Darred acted alone or at the orders of Vasa, the facts speak plainly enough. Neither he nor any other of my brothers can be trusted.'

Aarin let him digest that in silence. Though he had distanced himself from their beliefs, the Order had been Kinseris's home for many years. At length, when the priest showed no sign of shaking himself from his thoughts, Aarin attempted to steer the conversation to less painful topics. 'The last race?'

Kinseris looked at him blankly.

'The fourth race,' Aarin repeated. 'You have told me of the Safarsee, the Renalla and...'

'Ah.' Kinseris picked up the lost thread of his explanations. 'They are a puzzle, even to me, and I know them well. They bow to no one and most are dead now, save a few who hang on in lands that grow wilder every year. The Lost Houses came long ago from across the sea. They were great once, or so history tells us. They settled the lands to the south and east, across the Ranger Desert, but the desert is creeping up on them and soon they will be swallowed. It is to Ephenor, the last of the Lost Houses, that the Ancai will take you.'

Aarin nodded, taking that in. 'What will you do?'

Kinseris shrugged. 'Now that I know of Darred's role in this? What can I do? My high priest has commanded my presence, and he is a threat much closer than Darred. I will go to Kas'Tella as I planned, and you must go to Ephenor. It is the only place you will be safe. I will join you there if I can.'

'And if you can't?' Aarin pressed. 'Go to Kas'Tella and you place yourself in great danger, from more than just your Order. If Darred has allies anywhere, they will be there.'

The priest stalked to the window. 'I know that. But what choice do I have? If I disobey Vasa now, he will move sooner. You need time to get away, and this is the only way I can give it to you.'

Humbled by the enormity of this sacrifice, there was nothing Aarin could say. Once again he was caught up in an avalanche of events, and he could not fight it. And as before, he would leave behind him a life in ruins, the life of someone who had tried to help him, as he had done in Amadorn. As he felt certain he would do again before this was over. The prophecy was merciless. The fire in his blood and Vianor's oath hounded him, forcing him to snatch at every chance that came his way. He had warned Kinseris what he faced. He could not face it with him.

'You owe me nothing,' he said simply. 'Don't do this for me.'

'Not just for you, Aarin,' Kinseris replied. 'For myself also. How long can I continue to live like this, waiting for the day my actions are discovered? This way at least I cannot be taken by surprise.'

'And your allies?' he pressed. 'You endanger them as well.'

Kinseris looked anguished. 'Shrogar knows as well as I that this peace cannot last. His family has been at war for generations, and it is one they cannot hope to win. They are fighting to survive, not for victory. My help has given them time, but it was only ever temporary. They had to go on without me one day.'

Through his words, Aarin glimpsed for a moment a beleaguered people and a hopeless cause. He remembered, in a flash of vision, the army encamped around a desert fortress, and hoped it would not come to that.

'I wish I could have known you longer,' he said sadly, words alone unable to express the extent of his regret that a friendship glimpsed would never be realised.

'I also,' Kinseris replied, and Aarin knew he had heard and understood the things he had not said. He held out his hand and Aarin took it.

As their hands met, the priest gave him a startled look but said nothing. Aarin knew what he felt, the fire that seeped through his skin, for it burned in him stronger than ever now.

Kinseris withdrew his hand. Some of the doubt seemed to have vanished from his manner, almost as though the touch had reassured him. He glanced regretfully towards the door. 'I must return you to the cells. There is much I must do before I leave. Do not be alarmed if the Ancai does not free you at once. He will do so only when he judges it safe.'

Aarin nodded. 'I understand.'

He stood, and Kinseris called for the captain. He rolled up the map and replaced it on the shelf.

'Take him away, Kestel,' he ordered as the Ancai entered the study. 'Then summon the Vice-Vela. I must see to the transfer of the wards.'

EIGHT

AARIN WAS SUBDUED when he returned to them. Kallis managed to refrain from questions for almost an hour before his patience gave way. Whatever had passed between the mage and the priest, they kept their secrets close. But the mercenary was past caring what those secrets were. It was their continued confinement that worried him. If Kinseris was not an enemy, his treatment of them fell short of friendly and his hospitality was beginning to grate.

When his questions received no straight answer, Kallis gave up. He took comfort from the fact that Aarin's reticence irritated Jeta as much as it did him, and even the mage himself seemed uncomfortable. When pressed he had said only that Kinseris had left for the capital and they must wait. His eyes drifted to the spyhole and Kallis understood the unspoken warning.

So, he settled down to wait.

The light from the small window was enough, barely, for them to know night from day. As the hours dragged on, all attempts at conversation ceased and even the fetid stink of their cell began to fade into the background. As the sun moved over the chapter house and their prison darkened, a guard came in with a torch and hung it on the wall. A while later he returned, bringing three rough bowls filled with greasy, unappetising soup, and a bucket of water. All three ignored the food and instead converged on the water, quenching their thirst through dripping hands before using the rest to clean some of the filth from their skin. Then, the last distraction over for the day, they separated to their respective corners and settled down to sleep.

Kallis's dreams were restless. He waded through old battles, drank with lost comrades, and chased lizards in the desert sun. He dreamed of strange men in midnight robes, and Aarin earnestly explaining his magic. The mage grew fretful, grabbing a fistful of dirt and thrusting it out before him.

Don't you see? he seemed to be saying. *This is why we must find the dragons.*

But the men were unimpressed. He could not see their faces, for their hoods were pulled down over their eyes. Others appeared and more followed, until Aarin stood alone amidst a sea of black, but he never stopped trying to convince them. Kallis tried to reach him, but the men crowded in close and he could not get through. The blackness of their robes seemed to spread outwards, edging out the light, and the image faded.

The noise of the cell door swinging open woke Kallis from his sleep. It took him a moment to realise where he was. His head felt sluggish and dull. He groped behind him, bracing an arm against the wall and heaving himself into a crouch, cradling his aching head on his knees.

'What now?' he muttered, imagining that the guards were returning to take Aarin before Kinseris once more. Then he remembered that the priest had left for Kas'Tella and opened to his eyes to see the huge captain standing over him.

'Where is your companion?' the man demanded, and Kallis glanced around, catching sight of Jeta crawling out of her nest of blankets.

He looked for Aarin, saw the girl doing the same, but the cell held only the three of them.

'You tell me,' he replied, climbing to his feet. He refused to give in to worry yet, for he had heard nothing to disturb him as he slept, and years of soldiering ensured he slept lightly. 'Perhaps your master wished to speak with him again.' Aarin had been cagey about his interviews with the priest, but Kallis understood that the mage did not see him as an enemy. Not an enemy perhaps, but no friend either as far as the mercenary was concerned.

The captain's look could have cracked rocks. 'The Lord Vela has left for Kas'Tella. As you know well. So, I ask again, where is your companion?'

Kallis's angry retort was cut short by Jeta's hand on his arm. 'What is he saying? Where's Aarin?'

'I'm trying to find out,' Kallis growled. He turned back to the huge guard captain. 'He's not here, as you can see. If your lord has not taken him, then someone else has. It is your men who guard this cell. Why don't you ask them?'

A flicker of uncertainty crossed the impassive black face and Kallis felt the first stirrings of unease. He took a step closer, his muscles already tensing. Something had happened, something bad. And Aarin, as usual, was in the middle of it.

The Ancai appraised his aggressive stance before meeting his eyes. 'I have tried,' he confessed. 'But they are gone.'

'Gone?' Kallis demanded menacingly, closing the space between them. Jeta called his name. He ignored her. She called again, more urgent now, and he saw the guard's eyes slide past him and widen. He glanced back and saw the girl holding up Aarin's cloak, her face creased with worry. The wool was torn and filthy.

He turned back to the captain with a growl of rage, launching himself at the bigger man. As the Ancai stepped back from the charge, Kallis reached out and whipped the knife from his belt and had the big captain pinned up against the wall before he could blink, the sharp blade gouging his neck.

'You will tell me what has happened to my friend.' He pricked the knife into the skin of the man's neck. 'Where is he?'

The Ancai stared at him without a flicker of fear. 'This is foolish,' he accused huskily. 'Let me go or I will be forced to hurt you.'

'Go ahead,' Kallis growled. 'Kill me like you killed my friend.'

'You want me to talk, then give me the knife. Or don't and I *will* kill you and search for your friend without your help.'

Kallis glared at him as he weighed his options. Then with a final shove he stepped back, withdrawing the blade in one smooth motion. The captain massaged his throat.

'Talk then.' Kallis nursed the knife with one hand, a spark of violence in his dark eyes. 'Satisfy me you had no part in this and I will let you live.'

The soldier regarded him from under hooded eyelids. 'Whoever did this penetrated the compound without alerting the patrols or tripping the wards. I only became aware that something was wrong a short time ago.'

Kallis looked at him squarely. 'Who are you?'

'I am Kestel, Ancai of Frankesh. You may call me Ancai.'

'That's your name?'

'Ancai is not a name. It is a rank. You may call me Ancai. I serve the

Vela'Frankesh, at this time the Lord Kinseris, as the head of his personal guard, and as such the security of this complex is my duty. That is why I am here.'

Kallis gave him a nasty smile. 'Well, Ancai, it seems you have failed in that duty.'

'Insults will not bring your friend back,' the soldier replied mildly. 'My Lord Kinseris is also gone, called to Kas'Tella by order of his high priest, and his absence provides the only opportunity for such a thing to occur. One thing you should understand: Kas'Tella never has important business with Frankesh. This place is of little political importance and it is many days journey from the capital. My lord's appointment here was no promotion. If he is called to the Holy City, no good awaits him there.'

Kallis eyed him with mounting unease as Jeta appeared at his shoulder, Aarin's cloak in her hands. 'What are you saying?'

'I have known this Vela'Frankesh many years. I left my family in Kas'Tella and came here at his request.' The Ancai kept his eyes on Kallis, ensuring the mercenary understood what he was saying. 'I know that he is involved in something that could get him killed, and I know also that he would willingly die for it. And now, because of your presence here, he might have to do just that. Do you understand?'

Kallis did, painfully so. He wished more than ever that Aarin had not been so reticent. He was out of his depth here, caught between two men and their powerful dreams, and his ignorance was dangerous. If Kinseris had betrayed his Order and entangled Aarin in his schemes, then he and Jeta faced a bleak future. Some lessons from his childhood in Caledan had not left him. The Kas'Talani brooked no dissent.

Sensing the change in his manner, the Ancai held out his hand and Kallis placed the knife in it. The guard nodded his thanks and sheathed it at his waist.

'There is more. No messenger could have ridden to Kas'Tella, informed the high priest of your arrest, and returned with instructions in the time that you have been here. And yet it is too much of a coincidence that my lord is called to the Holy City and the very same night your friend is taken.'

'You think there are agents here who suspect your lord?'

The Ancai nodded. 'I know so. Many times I have warned him to desist, to give up this madness, but he will not. His last instructions to me were to remove you to safety, all of you. In that I have failed.'

Kallis felt a rush of fellow feeling for the massive man. 'If there is any blame, then I must share it, for I was here and I did nothing.'

The Ancai shook his head. 'Only Kas'Talani adepts could have done this, of a rank at least as high as my lord's. Their power is different then. Only they would be able to penetrate the wards around the compound, but if my lord had been here, he would have felt the intrusion because he holds the keys to all the wards. On his departure they were transferred to his Vice-Vela.' He paused and Kallis waited for it. 'Immediately I knew there had been an intrusion, I went to the Vice-Vela's quarters. He is gone.'

'Dead?'

'Murdered. Which means there are traitors among my guards as well the adepts. The man who stood the duty at his door last night has disappeared. Two adepts at least have also vanished, maybe more, though it will take time to establish all their whereabouts. It is not for me or my men to question their movements, and it was the Vice-Vela who supervised the placement of his acolytes. Neither is it politic for me to be seen to investigate this too closely. My first loyalty is to Kinseris, the Vela'Frankesh, and if he is under suspicion, I may be also. If this is the will of Kas'Tella, I must appear to accept it.'

'I would say the manner of this operation proves that those you serve in Kas'Tella are already half convinced of your guilt,' Kallis pointed out. 'Why else spirit Aarin away in the middle of the night when they could simply demand you hand him over? How long will they be content to leave things be before they act against you?'

The Ancai looked thoughtful. 'I cannot be sure. To remove me from my office they would have to do so first to Kinseris. It may be that in going to Kas'Tella he goes to his death, but to refuse would be to declare his duplicity and invite a show of force. This way at least he has a chance to save himself, although I doubt he would willingly abandon your friend.'

'You think they are together?'

'I think they have both gone to Kas'Tella. We must take hope from that.'

'We aren't going after them?'

The Ancai laughed bitterly. 'Go after them? All we would do is waste our lives and possibly theirs too. No, we wait.'

'Wait?' Kallis launched himself off the wall. Inactivity in the face of threat did not come naturally to him. 'Wait for what? Get us out of here, as Kinseris ordered, and we will go after Aarin ourselves.'

Jeta grabbed his arm. 'What has happened?' she demanded, her patience at an end. 'Where's Aarin?'

'He's gone,' Kallis snapped, shaking her off. Then, catching sight of her face as it fell, he felt a rush of remorse. He at least knew how they felt about each other, even if they refused to acknowledge it. 'But he's alive,' he assured her more gently. He gestured at the Ancai. 'He believes Aarin has been taken to Kas'Tella.'

She looked from one to the other. 'We're going after them, aren't we?'

Kallis sighed. 'Apparently not.' There was nothing he could do if the Ancai refused to release them. Aarin might have been able to open the locked door and free them, but if so their only chance of escape had vanished with him.

'Let us go,' he pleaded again. 'If your master has been betrayed, there is no point in continuing this charade.'

But if he hoped to convince the Ancai, he failed.

'For now, we wait,' Kinseris's captain repeated with quiet determination. 'The Vela'Frankesh, I hope, is still free, and we must assume your friend is still alive. We must trust them to take care of themselves. There are those in the Holy City itself whose loyalty is to my master rather than his, and they will aid him if they can. And his instructions to me were clear. When we leave here, we are to go into the desert, not to Kas'Tella. When it is safe, that is what we will do.'

NINE

JETA HAD PROTESTED further when Kallis translated the end of the conversation, but despite her threats and her tears, the huge soldier refused to back down. Kallis watched silently as Jeta pleaded with him, and knew that though he pretended otherwise, he understood her words. He could not fail to understand her tone.

Kallis winced as she abandoned entreaty and started demanding. He had forgotten just how sharp her tongue could be. He could not understand what Aarin saw in her. He was fond of the girl, and she was certainly pretty, but she needed to learn some manners. What was more astonishing was that she appeared to return his affections, despite the way they continued to needle each other. At least if Aarin had still been with them he would have had some entertainment. Much longer cooped up together in this cell and one or other of them would have exploded.

The Ancai had retreated as quickly as he could, taking his leave with his ears smarting and Kallis's heartfelt sympathy. Alone once more, Jeta shot him a scalding look and stalked away. They traded looks of mutual disgust, but for once she seemed to have run out of words. Kallis was grateful. He needed time to think, to work out what was happening. He could not sit idly waiting for a rescue that might not come. He understood that the Ancai was in a perilous position, and so were they while they relied on his help. And that was what bothered him. The longer they stayed in Frankesh, the more their chances diminished. Whatever plot the priest was involved in had been blown wide open. There was no sense that Kallis could see in pretending otherwise, unless the Ancai himself was under siege. And if that was the case, it seemed doubtful that the situation could do anything but deteriorate.

The day passed slowly. Jeta slept fitfully, and when she was awake her eyes were red-rimmed and misty. Awkward in the face of her worry, too busy battling his own, Kallis pretended he had not noticed. And that night, as he lay awake staring at the handful of stars visible through the window, he heard her muffled sobs and wished he knew how to ease them. She was a long way from home, they all were, and he was not much of a companion.

Kallis did not sleep that night. He counted the hours until dawn, jumping at every sound. At any minute he expected someone to come for them, whether it was the Ancai and freedom or another less desirable fate. Either way, he just wanted it over.

It was mid-morning when someone finally came. Kallis lifted his head from his knees wearily as footsteps sounded beyond the bars. His gaze travelled up from elegantly booted feet to the familiar face above and he sucked in an angry breath. If this man was here when he should have been far away, they had certainly been tricked. And the mystery of Aarin's disappearance became no mystery at all.

Jeta hissed a curse as she recognised the new arrival, her shoulders stiffening under his gaze. This was someone she must have hoped she would never see again, and Kallis shared the sentiment. His hand went instinctively to his missing sword and he wished fervently that the Ancai had left him the knife. He was itching to use it.

He pushed himself to his feet, reaching out to help Jeta up. The girl was holding herself together, but he could feel her trembling. Her eyes were a sea of conflicting emotions—anger, fear, but most of all revulsion. He positioned himself between her and the man at the bars and forced himself to remain calm. He would not let that happen again.

'You again,' he said bluntly. 'We'd rather hoped you were dead.'

'Indeed,' Darred replied smoothly. 'I was rather surprised to find that I was not. Are you really such a fool, or was that a misplaced show of honour?'

Kallis showed his teeth. 'Not on my part. I wanted to slit your throat.'

'A pity for you in that case. I am not so merciful.'

'Really?' The mercenary's eyebrows rose skywards in mock surprise. 'Tell me, did you come here to gloat or to bore us to death?'

Darred shook his head, amused by the insult, but his smile was vicious. 'I came to say my farewells. The preparations for your execution are already underway. It won't be long until you are reunited with your friend.'

Kallis grabbed hold of the bars, his knuckles white. 'What have you done with him?' He wanted to wipe the smile off that smug face, wanted it so much his muscles burned.

'You have more important things to worry about,' Darred replied, cocking his head to the narrow window high above. 'Can you not hear it? They are building the gallows.'

The unmistakable sounds of men at work filtered down to them on the breeze and Kallis felt an icy coldness sink into him that seemed to sap his limbs of strength. As a soldier he had expected to die violently in battle, not jerking on the end of a rope like a criminal.

'Tell me,' Darred said with a malicious smile. 'How do you plan to escape this time? There really is no one to help you now.'

'Kinseris gave his promise we were not to be harmed,' Kallis spat. 'Is this how you keep the word of a fellow priest?'

'Kinseris?' Darred laughed. 'The man whose dungeons you are rotting in? Surely you did not think Kinseris was any friend of yours?'

When they did not answer, he shook his head, the smile hovering on his lips. 'Then you have been misled. Kinseris is wedded to his Order as tightly as I am independent from it. If Aarin had only listened to me in Redstone, I could have spared you this. For Kas'Tella will certainly execute him.'

'Spare us your lies instead. You have no wish to help Aarin.'

'Maybe not,' Darred conceded. 'But I have no wish to see him dead either, not yet at least. I too desire the return of the dragons, but my brothers do not share that wish. The Kas'Talani fear the return above all else, and they will do whatever they must to prevent it.'

Kallis felt a grim sense of triumph. Aarin in Kas'Tella's hands was as much a blow to Darred's plans as it was to theirs. The mage might die there, but at least he would die free of this man's influence, something Kallis knew he feared more than anything.

'On the contrary,' Darred countered smoothly, reading his thoughts. 'He is, in fact, just where I want him.' His eyes settled on Jeta. 'But you, my dear, you are not where I would have you. I could take you away from here if you wish. Say the word and I will spare your life.'

Silence answered him. Kallis held his breath. He did not doubt it was a trick, and a clever one. Jeta had claimed the dangers of Aarin's search as her own, but she had not truly known the extent of those dangers. Confronted now with the possibility of her own death, he did not know which way she would choose.

Interpreting her silence as indecision, Darred pressed his case. 'The gallows are not a pretty way to die, my dear, and I would hate to see your lovely face disfigured by such a death.'

She moved then, standing clear of Kallis so she could look into her tormentor's eyes. The mercenary tensed. It was her choice, and he would not stop her. Jeta glanced at him, then walked to the bars, putting her hand on the door. Darred smiled, already stepping back to release the locks.

She stopped him with a hand on his arm. 'Then you had best not watch, my lord. For I would rather die on the gallows than spend another minute in your company.'

Kallis almost laughed aloud at the surprise on Darred's face. He recovered quickly. 'I regret that I will not have that honour, my dear.'

'You won't stay for the final act?' Kallis sneered. 'No doubt you have urgent business to attend to.'

'I think he does,' Jeta replied, casting a sly glance at the priest. 'When we told your colleagues of all you have done, they seemed most upset. I hear your high priest himself is extremely anxious to speak with you.'

Darred looked as though he had swallowed something vile. 'That fate is reserved for Aarin,' he assured them in a voice clipped with anger. 'And it will be a most unpleasant one. As will yours.'

'Perhaps,' Jeta allowed. 'But I think your own will be worse. If you are traitor to all, who will stand as your friend at the end? Better, I think, to know what you are dying for, and for whom.'

Kallis grinned, silently taking back every uncharitable thought, and wished Aarin could enjoy this moment as he did.

For once Darred seemed at a loss for words. 'I am fortunate indeed that you refused me,' he replied after a pause. 'I see now I would have tired quickly of such disagreeable companionship.'

She smiled sweetly. 'Not nearly as quickly as I, my lord.'

Kallis's grin widened. It felt good, for once, not to be on the receiving end of her scalding disdain.

Darred retreated with the mercenary's reluctant sympathy. 'Then I will leave you. I expect you have much to contemplate in your final hours.'

'One last question,' Kallis called after him as he left. 'Brannick. Was he also a part of your plot?' It was the question that had bothered him since Redstone. The old man's appearance had been too convenient, and the help he had given them had nearly killed them all. It would be a long time before he forgot the scene he had burst in on, Aarin's blood sheeting the ground and Jeta's terrified, half-dressed state. He would never forgive.

Darred turned and smiled. 'Let us just say I have long known where Brannick's sympathies lie, perhaps better than he did. I merely chose not to interfere when he decided to resurrect that allegiance.'

As the door slammed shut behind Darred, Jeta felt her legs begin to tremble. She reached out to Kallis and the mercenary held her steady as fear overwhelmed her at last. She had been scared before, locked in this prison not knowing when, or if, they would be allowed to leave, but she had never honestly thought they would die here.

She looked up at Kallis. 'Are we going to die?'

He shook his head, forcing a smile. 'Of course not.'

But his grim manner stole the comfort from his words. 'You're a terrible liar.'

The mercenary made a choking sound. 'And you, my dear, are a wonderful one.' He released her, his shoulders shaking. 'Remind me never to cross you again. You are altogether too vengeful.'

Jeta dried her tears with her sleeve. 'I can't stand men who need to gloat.'

'I can see that.' He steered her to the sleeping platform and sat down beside her.

She leaned into him, resting her head on his shoulder. There was nothing like approaching death, she thought wearily, to bring people together. 'What do we do now?'

If Darred was here, there seemed little chance that the Ancai would be able to free them. His presence was likely why he had not done so already. Yet she found it hard to believe that Kinseris's captain would give up so easily.

Kallis did not answer; he did not seem to have heard. She sat upright, glancing at him curiously, and saw him staring up at the window, listening.

'Kallis?'

He looked down, frowning.

'What are we going to do?'

The mercenary shrugged. 'Now we wait.'

'That's it?' she said in astonishment. 'We just wait?'

'The Ancai will help us or he won't,' Kallis explained patiently. 'Either way, there's nothing we can do right now. We cannot get out of this cell until someone lets us out, so there is no sense wasting our effort trying. If he doesn't come...If he doesn't come, then we do it the old-fashioned way.'

'And what's that?'

He jerked his head in the direction of freedom. 'Run like hell as soon as we're through that door.'

So, they waited. The sun passed over the chapter house and the light in the cell dimmed as the afternoon deepened. At some point Jeta fell asleep. It was something she had not expected to do at such a time, but there is only so much contemplation of imminent death the mind can endure. Not that her sleep was restful, but at least in dreams she was spared the nail-biting wait for the guards to come for them.

When she woke Kallis was still beside her, his arm draped protectively around her shoulders.

'They've stopped,' he told her quietly.

Jeta nodded, a lump in her throat. If they had stopped the gallows must be ready. It felt wrong to sit there, patiently waiting for the end. She did not want to die. She wanted to scream, to lash out at something, even to pace the few short feet of their cell. Instead she smiled at the mercenary to show him she was ready.

Kallis's answering smile was bittersweet, and she could see the same damned-up outburst in his eyes. Perhaps there were tears there too, more for her, she realised, than himself, and she looked away because she could not bear it. He could not break for her.

Footsteps sounded behind the door. She took a deep breath and felt a surge of awful panic. This was it. It was over. She shook her head. 'I was to marry a king.' How long ago that seemed.

'And I was going to retire,' Kallis replied. 'But neither of us are dead yet.'

The door opened and a guard stepped through. He was a slight, wiry youth they had not seen before, and behind him two adepts waited. They stood, and Jeta slipped her hand into Kallis's calloused one.

'I never told him,' she whispered in dismay. 'I never had a chance.'

Kallis squeezed her hand. 'He knows.'

Then the guard was unlocking their cell and they had no more time. He held the door wide and gestured curtly for them to move. Kallis gave her hand a last squeeze and stepped calmly out of the cell. As he passed the guard, Jeta saw a flash of steel pass between them. She froze, catching the boy's eye as he looked up. He winked, the ghost of a grin flitting across his thin features. Kallis turned to her, hand outstretched, his face expressionless. She took his hand, taking her cue from him and keeping her eyes downcast.

Together they walked past the young guard. He fell in behind them without a word. The adepts acknowledged them with a brief glance, turning to escort them from the cells. Jeta could feel her heart thumping, nervous excitement overcoming her fear. She had seen the boy pass Kallis a knife, and she had not mistaken the look he had given her. It reminded her that not everyone here was an enemy.

They were led through a long corridor, past many doors that hid other cells, and out into the main complex. Her excitement began to pale. Beyond the main building was the courtyard where the gallows waited, and every step was taking them closer. Beside her Kallis was rigid with tension but he made no move to further their escape. She felt her fear in earnest then, turning her feet to lead and her heart to ice.

Then, suddenly, the procession stopped, and she saw the Ancai walking towards them. Kallis grabbed her arm, his fingers biting into her flesh, and she readied herself for flight. But the moment did not come. The huge captain stopped, addressing the priests without even a glance in their direction. The adepts answered and he nodded, stepping aside to let them pass. The boy prodded her forward and she stumbled, feeling the crushing weight of disappointment as she realised the Ancai was not going to save them. She threw him a bitter glance, hating him for betraying her hopes.

And then he was moving, gliding in behind one robed adept and slipping an arm around his neck. Before the man could react, the Ancai thrust a knife into his spine and he dropped to the floor like a stone. Kallis was already despatching the second by the time she realised what was happening. She felt a hand on her arm and turned to see the boy gesturing frantically at her.

'We must move quickly,' the Ancai said as he sheathed his knife. 'You must do as I say. No questions.'

He bent and grasped a priest by the shoulders as Kallis did the same with the other. The boy held open a door and they dragged the bodies inside. Jeta followed, shocked to silence by the suddenness of death.

'Strip them,' the Ancai ordered. 'Then give me your clothes.'

Kallis was already on his knees, tugging the loose robes over the priest's head. Their dark colour hid the blood. Once free he tossed them to her, already turning to the next body. Jeta wasted no time in peeling off her own filthy dress, urgency overcoming any qualms about modesty. The robes felt strange against her skin, the fabric sticky with the warmth of their previous owner. She shuddered, fingering the tiny tear at the back where the Ancai's blade had slipped between the priest's ribs.

The Ancai handed her a cloak, then bent to sweep her dress from the floor. As she unfurled the cloak across her shoulders, Jeta noticed for the first time the packs lined up against the wall. She was about to take one when the boy stopped her. 'Not yet.'

Before she could ask what he meant, Kallis appeared beside her, the hood of his cloak drawn up over his head. He held out a bundle of leathers to the Ancai. 'What now?'

'You will wait here,' the captain replied. 'I will return shortly.' He called out to the boy who nodded, grabbing the packs and moving to the door.

'Priests do not fetch and carry. Trad will take your possessions.'

The boy grinned at them as they left, and Jeta found his enjoyment infectious. She did not even wonder where the Ancai was going with their clothes. All that mattered was that they were escaping. She looked at Kallis, expecting to see the same elation, but instead he looked pensive and grim.

They waited. The silence dragged on and she could feel the mercenary's tension rising. She began to fidget, made nervous by Kallis, when the Ancai returned and wordlessly gestured towards to hallway. As she passed, he caught her hood and drew it up over her face, the pressure of his hand bending her head toward the floor. Kallis followed, and she could almost feel the effort his silence cost him.

Their route took them out of the buildings and into the courtyard. The sun was beginning to set, the last heat of the day giving way to the chill of evening, and she was glad of the thick robes that hid her shiver. A crowd was gathered around the gallows. Even with her head lowered she could see the ranks of soldiers lined up before the executioner's platform, the priests they served clustered in groups in the few remaining patches of sun. Suddenly the reality of it was hammered home to her. The gates to freedom lay on the other side of that gathering, and it was a long, exposed walk to reach them. They were not free yet.

The Ancai led them in a wide arc around the ranks of liveried guardsmen. There they stopped, delayed for a moment by a crowd of common folk pushing excitedly towards the gallows. As the crowd seethed around her, Jeta wanted to stamp her feet with impatience. Every moment they wasted meant more time for their enemies to discover their deception. Already she could hear the hammering of drums as the soldiers beat out the rhythm that called the condemned to their fate. She half-turned, craning her neck to see what was happening, but Kallis grabbed her roughly by the shoulder and spun her around.

'Don't,' he whispered urgently, earning a look of sharp reproof from the Ancai. She guessed that the priests did not manhandle each other quite so roughly.

Irritated, she shrugged off his hand, determined now to see what it was he tried to keep from her. And then she wished fervently that she had not. The drums kept up their ominous beat, and they had called the prisoners. Cold with shock she saw herself walking beside Kallis, a black hood pulled low over her head, hiding her blond curls. The mercenary was a step behind her in his tattered leathers, hooded as she was, and the crowd cheered as they reached the platform.

People surged around her, struggling for a better view, and she was buffeted aside, separated from the others. From the corner of her eye she saw Kallis trying to reach her, but she could not tear her eyes from the figure dressed in her clothes. They climbed the steps, their movements in time with the remorseless drums, and then the executioner was beside them. He lowered her head, slipping the noose around her neck, and Jeta felt the rough touch of that rope as though it was around her own throat.

She couldn't move, couldn't breathe. She saw her double's hand clutching towards the man, but the executioner slapped it down. Tears sprang into her eyes and ragged breaths closed her throat. She heard a frightened wail, a sound of such pure terror that her heart stood still. At the last moment the man lunged towards the woman, then their bodies dropped down, twisting and jerking as the life was choked from them.

Jeta's legs gave way, but Kallis was beside her, holding her up. He caught a hand under her elbow and forced her to walk. The Ancai was waiting for them beyond the crowd, his face tight with worry. Kallis dropped his hand as they reached him, his eyes as haunted as her own.

'Quickly,' the Ancai said tersely. 'We should not have waited.'

Jeta nodded numbly, matching his pace as best as she could. The gate seemed an impossible distance away. She did not know if she could make it. Behind them the drums had stopped. They had beaten the way to death, and now they were silent. She caught back a sob. A stranger had died for her.

They reached the gate and the guards waved them through, bored now the excitement was over, and they barely glanced at two priests and their captain. A palm-lined avenue stretched out ahead of them, but the Ancai turned to his left, leading them instead along the path that wound round the walls. She followed in silence, concentrating on putting one foot in front of the other.

Kallis hovered at her side. He had guessed, she realised, remembering his grim tension as they waited for the Ancai to return. He had known, and he had not told her.

At last they stopped. Jeta looked around, surprised to find herself at the edges of the town. The Ancai had led them to a deserted street not far to the chapter house, and she could see Trad's face peering anxiously from a window in one of the warehouses.

The Ancai pushed open a door. 'In here, hurry.'

Kallis gave her a gentle shove and ducked through the low doorway into a dusty room. Trad came running down the steps, grinning. It had all been a game to him, she realised with a flash of anger. Didn't he realised people had died?

The Ancai must have sensed her shift in mood. 'It was the only way,' he told her in perfect Amadorian. 'They would have died anyway. Our customs officials caught them attempting to leave on one of the merchant ships.'

'And that is a crime?' she demanded, feeling the dam of her emotions break. 'What kind of place is this?'

'A harsh one,' he replied shortly. 'When Darred returned, he ordered your immediate execution. I had no time to arrange an escape any other way.'

'Darred is a traitor!'

The Ancai shrugged. 'So is my lord. I cannot denounce a priest of his rank. He is the high priest's own envoy to your land. To confront him would have been suicide.'

'You could have tried!' she insisted, her voice rising as tears streamed down her face. 'If you had maybe they wouldn't have died! You didn't even try!'

She was still shouting when Kallis caught hold of her, pulling her into his arms. She struggled, her hand coming up to hammer at his chest. He caught it, held it tight.

'We understand,' he assured the Ancai. 'We thank you for all you have done for us. I'm only sorry we made it necessary.'

The Ancai shook his head. 'It is not yet time for thanks. Until we are in the desert, we will not be safe. They will realise what has happened and send soldiers after us.'

'Then we should leave,' Kallis urged. 'The sooner the better.'

'It is dusk now,' the captain replied. 'We will wait an hour and leave with nightfall. There is enough time for you to eat and change. Trad has some clothes in your packs, and a veil for the girl. From now on you must forget that you are strangers here. Until we reach Ephenor, speaking your own language around others will only bring you trouble.'

'Ephenor?' Jeta pulled away from Kallis. 'What is Ephenor?'

The Ancai sighed. 'Kinseris's hopes rest in Ephenor. Now we will see whether those hopes are justified.'

He turned to Trad, and the boy handed him the clothes he had taken from the packs. 'Change,' he urged, 'and rest while you can. Ephenor lies in the great wasteland between the Northern and the Ranger Deserts. It is a long journey, and hard, and we will have little time for rest once we begin.' He glanced at Kallis. 'In two days, if all goes well, we should make it to the Aetelea. If we follow the river to the mountains the distance through the desert is greatly reduced, but it is also the more dangerous route. Reserves for the Second Army patrol the river. Yet I think in speed lies our greatest chance. Your people survive in the harshness of the desert because they are accustomed to it. We are not.'

It was dark when the small party of fugitives left the warehouse. Banks of cloud obscured the moon and the darkness pressed in close on all sides. Jeta shivered, cold despite the warmth of the night. She stayed close to Kallis, taking comfort in his presence, and missed Aarin with an intensity that made her heart ache. In all her life she had never felt so alone, and for the first time since she had abandoned her life and her family in Amadorn, she longed for the familiarity of the draughty, soulless hallways of her father's house.

Her home had been a prison all the days she lived there, desperate for her father's approval and her mother's affection, but she had been safe, secure. She had had status, the daughter of Ferlan Elorna, one of the wealthiest merchants of the Golden Alliance, and he had loved her in his way. But she had always known that her true value was as an asset to advance his ambitions. It was only when she had met Aarin and Kallis that she had felt what it was like to belong. And now that was gone. Aarin was lost and she might never see him again, and all the agony of being near him and unable to be with him paled in comparison to the pain of knowing she had lost him.

Beside her Kallis walked in brooding silence. She had left him talking to the Ancai while Trad helped her change. He had shown her how to wrap her hair in the veil to hide its brightness and conceal her pale skin, and she had watched from a distance as the two soldiers huddled together. She did not want to know the dangers that awaited them on this journey. She knew what it was like to be hunted, to wake each morning wondering whether that day would be the one that their pursuers eventually caught them, and this time it was not a doomed marriage that stalked her but death.

Only Trad seemed unaffected by their danger. He walked with them, a pace behind the Ancai as he led them through the dark, twisting streets. She watched his easy gait, even laden with provisions, and wondered who he was and how he came to be here, seemingly without a care in the world when all the armed strength of Frankesh might be behind them.

Lost in her thoughts, Jeta did not notice that the Ancai had stopped until Kallis grabbed her and hauled her off the street into a doorway.

'What –?'

Kallis put a finger to his lips. He pointed down the street where she could see a party of soldiers gathered at the mouth of an alleyway. Jeta held her breath, willing them to leave, but instead she saw them turn towards and make their slow, cautious way down the street.

Jeta glanced to the side and saw the Ancai and Trad sheltering in another shadowed recess. She risked a glance down the street and before Kallis yanked her back she saw the soldiers no more than a hundred yards away and knew their time was almost up. Already she could hear the soft thuds of their footfalls and the gentle murmur of hushed conversation.

From the corner of her eye, Jeta saw the Ancai's gesture. Beside her, Kallis whispered, 'Stay here and stay hidden. If this goes wrong, just go, run.'

'No,' she returned in a fierce whisper. 'I'm not leaving you.'

'Don't be a fool,' Kallis growled. 'If this goes wrong, I'll be dead, and you'll have no other choice.'

Then there was no more time to talk. Trad stumbled out into the street, one arm cradled around his ribs as he staggered into the path of the advancing soldiers. She saw them stop and call out and heard Trad's piteous cry as he reeled into them. Then Kallis was pushing her back into the shadows and drawing his sword.

The street exploded into violence as the men erupted from their hiding places. She heard the ring of metal and a grunt of pain, and then she was sinking to the floor, crouching in her doorway with her hands clasped over her ears.

There was a rush of movement by her hiding place and she bit back a cry. Even in her dark cloak, she knew they would see her, but she could not move, and Aarin was not there to hide her with his magic. They would find her and drag her back to those gallows and she would die as that poor woman had died. Once more she felt the noose fit itself around her neck, felt the scratch of the rope as it bit into her throat...

Silence fell. Footsteps. She pressed herself into the wall as a hand rested on her shoulder.

'Jeta?'

Kallis.

Weak with relief, Jeta flung herself into his arms, clinging to him as the tears began to flow. The mercenary held her, but she could feel his muscles quivering with tension and knew she needed to master herself. Slowly, cautiously, she disentangled herself and stepped back.

'It's over,' he told her gently. He was bleeding from a cut on one cheek. 'Come on.'

He pulled her to her feet and Jeta braced her shaking legs against his steady frame.

Behind him, Trad and the Ancai were stripping the dead guards of their weapons and hauling their bodies off the street. Trad was bleeding from a cut on his left arm, but he seemed oblivious to the injury until the Ancai touched a hand to the cut. The boy winced, looking down in surprise.

'You should bind that,' Kallis said, and Jeta knew he was thinking of the unwelcome attention the injury might bring them.

'There's no time,' the Ancai insisted. 'Others will have heard the fight. We have to go now.'

Then they were moving again, following the Ancai as he padded silently down the street. They were nearing the edges of the town now, closer to safety, closer to danger. Before they left the warehouse, the Ancai had explained Frankesh's defences. Jeta knew that soldiers would be guarding the outskirts of the town, and more would be patrolling the roads that led into the surrounding country and the desert beyond. The Aetelea, the great river that rose in the Athelan Mountains, could take them part of their journey if only they could evade the priesthood's guards and find passage on one of the barges that plied the trade from the mountains to the sea.

It sounded simple but she knew it was not. The Kas'Talani kept tight control over their empire's trade routes, even internal ones, and there were checkpoints all along the banks of the river. To reach it they would have to cross the fringes of the wasteland that bordered the Northern Desert. Leaving Frankesh was not the hard part.

In the end, they left the town behind them without her even noticing. Frankesh was not walled like the cities of her homeland, instead its close-packed buildings slowly dwindled until they merged into the outlying villages. They slipped like ghosts between the scattered houses, watching always for signs of pursuit. As the night stretched on, she began to hope that the priesthood had not realised their deception, and that the guards they had killed were just a routine patrol. One look at the Ancai's grim face convinced her otherwise.

'We should stop soon,' he advised as they paused once more in the shadows of an outhouse. 'They may be ahead of us and we risk running into an ambush.'

Kallis nodded tensely. Neither of them appeared to take comfort from the apparent absence of pursuit.

'If they know of my lord's treason, as they must, they know the only place we can go is Ephenor or Amadorn. They will guess that we will go by river whichever we choose, and they will be waiting for us.'

'Then let us go another way,' Jeta implored.

The Ancai shook his head. 'We cannot. By foot, across both the Northern Desert and the Ranger, is a journey few men could survive. And it would take months. No, we go by the Aetelea.'

'And the ambush?'

Kallis grinned. 'We spring it.'

TEN

THE RHYTHMIC SOUND of sword practise woke Jeta from her exhausted sleep. She rolled onto her side, stretching cramped and aching muscles, and peered out of the half-open door to see Kallis and Trad circling each other with makeshift swords fashioned from wooden stakes. The Ancai was watching from one side, occasionally calling instructions to Trad. As she watched, Kallis lowered his wooden weapon and adjusted the boy's grip on his crude sword.

Jeta smiled as she saw the sullen set of Trad's shoulders, and their swords on the ground by the Ancai. Clearly the boy felt insulted that this practise was taking place with mock weapons. He would be even more insulted, she thought with a grin, if he knew that Kallis was in fact left-handed.

She sat up, looking around the place they had chosen to shelter by daylight. The abandoned barn was several miles from the main highway out of Frankesh. The Ancai had deliberately led them away from the river for the last part of their journey, out of the way of any patrols that might be searching for them. She wished they could stay away from it forever.

As she fumbled with the veil, tying it back into place, Trad appeared in the doorway, his face flushed and dripping with sweat. She smiled companionably as he joined her, flopping in an exhausted heap on the floor. There was a painful welt across his right forearm just above the neatly bandaged cut from the night before. He studied it morosely.

'He beat you?'

'He cheated.'

Jeta raised an eyebrow and the boy grunted, tugging down his sleeve to cover the injury.

'There's no such thing as a fair fight,' Kallis remarked from the door before walking over to join the Ancai.

Jeta kept one eye on the men as she fixed the square of linen in place. Every now and then their eyes slid back to her, and she had an uncomfortable suspicion that whatever they were planning she was not going to like it. 'He's being nice. You must be good,' Jeta told the sulking youth.

'I am,' Trad agreed without a trace of pride. 'I had good teachers. They said I was born with a sword in my hand.'

There was a touch of regret in his voice that made her look at him more closely. He might have had good teachers, but he had abandoned them seemingly without a second thought.

'Why are you helping us?' she asked. 'You have placed yourself in great danger.'

Trad shrugged, embarrassed. 'Kestel says you are friends of Kinseris, and if you are his friends then I am helping him.'

Jeta frowned. 'Kestel?'

Trad nodded at the Ancai, standing with Kallis at the door of the barn. 'Kestel is Kinseris's Ancai, my captain.'

Jeta followed his gaze, watching the huge man who had bought their escape at such a bitter price. He had risked everything to see them safe, following his master's orders even though it meant defying the laws of his people. She sensed he would have done the same to carry out any order from Kinseris, and guessed that she and Kallis were otherwise unimportant to him. She looked back at Trad. He too had risked danger for Kinseris's sake.

'You are very loyal,' she said carefully. 'Kinseris is considered a traitor, is he not?'

Trad's face hardened, and she knew at once she had made a mistake. 'My lord is no traitor,' he hissed. 'Not to anything or anyone who does not deserve betrayal! Is it treason to want to protect your people from a tyrant?'

'The tyrant might think so. I meant no offence. I am just trying to understand –'

Trad shot to his feet. 'You cannot understand these things. You're an outlander!'

Jeta saw the vengeful eyes in his young face and wondered at the hate he had inside him. 'You think Amadorn is free from suffering?' she asked evenly. 'Why do you think I am here?'

But Trad stalked away from her and pushed roughly between the men by the door. As he passed the Ancai turned, his dark eyes watching her speculatively. She shrugged helplessly and clambered to her feet. It was time to find out what they were planning.

'What did you say?' Kallis asked.

She pulled a face at him. 'I did nothing.'

The Ancai sighed heavily. 'The Order killed his family. You could not have known.'

Jeta frowned, her eyes on Trad's retreating back. 'What happened?'

'Years ago there was a terrible drought. The people began to starve. There were riots. It was not long after we had come to Frankesh, and my lord was forced to send out his soldiers to keep control. They did it too well. Many died, and more were executed later. Kinseris saved those he could, but it was not many. Trad's father was one he could not save, but he brought the boy to the chapter house and enrolled him in the guard when he came of age. He meant one day to send him to Ephenor. Trad was too young to remember it, little more than a baby, but he hates the men who killed his father.'

So that was the tragic root of Trad's loyalty. Jeta glanced at Kallis and saw his face was frozen.

'How long?' he demanded, his voice husky. 'How long ago did this happen?'

The Ancai gave him an odd look. 'Twenty years, perhaps. Why?'

The mercenary did not reply, his face suddenly hard.

'Kallis?' Jeta prompted hesitantly. 'Why?'

'I remember it. I was there.' He laughed bitterly. 'It has been staring me in the face since the moment I arrived here.'

'You were there?' the Ancai asked, surprised. 'How is that possible?'

But Kallis shook his head and did not answer. Instead, he turned and walked away, and Jeta was no closer to finding out what they were up to.

They watched the river for several days, marking the routine of the patrols, counting soldiers, planning. The Aetelea was a great river, widening to almost a mile in places, with deep channels that even the sea-going vessels could navigate for several leagues inland. Her banks were steep gorges at times, shallow lapping shores at others, and the small wharfs of trading settlements jutted into her swift flowing current at regular intervals.

Each wharf had customs officials and a troop of regular soldiers. From Frankesh to the coast and upriver to the edges of the plains, their numbers were bolstered by the search parties. The few sections of the river where boats could dock between the wharfs were heavily guarded. Without a vessel of their own, they had little hope of reaching the barges that negotiated the shallower passages. Downstream and on the far bank, the Ancai assured them, a boat waited that could take them to Kouresh, the farthest settlement of any size before the plains began, and the place they needed to reach to begin their journey across the desert. But first they needed a boat.

'There.'

Kallis followed the direction of the Ancai's outstretched arm and watched as a shadowy figure walked the length of the short pier.

'And there.'

He pointed in the direction of the man's companion leaning nonchalantly against the wall of the port master's cabin.

'Only two,' Kallis grunted. 'Where are the rest?'

'They're here,' the Ancai assured him grimly. 'My men are no fools. They will keep out of sight until we make our move.'

The mercenary spat out a mouthful of river dust. 'Which is where Jeta comes in.'

'My men are no fools, but all men are fools for a pretty girl.'

'Aren't they at that,' Kallis agreed, thinking of Aarin. Only his pretty girl had fallen for him just as hard, which made him twice the fool. 'Are you sure this will work?' Aarin would never forgive him if he let any harm come to Jeta, and he was beginning to realise he might take it badly himself.

The Ancai hesitated. 'It's not without risk. But she has the courage.'

Kallis grimaced. 'Not sure how well she can swim though.'

'You want me to do what?'

Kallis winced, stepping to one side to avoid Jeta's outraged advance.

'This is your grand plan? You want me to play the half-naked maiden in distress, then turn temptress and seduce a room full of soldiers?'

'I wouldn't put it exactly like that,' he muttered, reddening.

'Oh?' she replied acidly. 'And how would you put it?'

He scratched his head, looking anywhere but at her. 'A diversion?'

'A diversion. I see. And you don't think there's a chance they might realise I'm the one they're after?' she asked scathingly. 'I know that men can miss a lot when confronted by a half-naked woman, but these are trained soldiers!'

'Indeed,' the Ancai agreed, safe on the side lines. 'I trained them myself.'

'Soldiers are the worst of the lot,' Kallis cut in, trying not to laugh. 'Especially those who guard a monastery full of priests. Not much by way of female companionship there.'

She fixed him with a cold glare. 'Just keep on reassuring me, Kallis.'

He sighed. 'You won't be alone for more than a minute, I promise. All you have to do is distract them so that *we* can do the ambushing.'

'No.'

He studied her face, seeing beneath the anger to the very real fear that stemmed not so much from what he asked her to do, but her encounter with Darred. He had known this would stir those memories, but they had been able to think of no other way to get the soldiers from their hiding place. Any one of them could have played the drowning victim, but she was the only one not likely to be killed on sight once they hauled her in.

'I won't let them hurt you,' he said quietly. 'You know that.'

'You can't promise that.'

'I'm promising it now,' Kallis replied. 'Trust me, Jeta. If you need me, I'll be there.'

She glared at him a moment, then reached up roughly to unfasten the cloak at her throat. 'You'd better be,' she muttered darkly as her tunic followed the cloak until she was dressed only in the thin shirt and loose trousers. Pale as they were, once wet, she thought bitterly, she might as well be naked.

'This has to be the oldest trick there is,' Jeta protested as she followed Kallis to the river's edge. 'How can you think they'll fall for it?'

They were on a deserted stretch of bank. The water was too shallow for the boats to dock, and the slippery mud made the going treacherous. She had hidden shivering in the shadows as Kallis dealt swiftly and silently with the guard who stood his solitary vigil by the riverside, and now there was only her part to play. She did not want to do this, but they needed a boat and they needed it soon because they were running out of time to make their rendezvous.

The Ancai had explained his plan, and he had made it sound simple. There were only two places they could go that offered any safety: Ephenor and Amadorn. Many of the barges that traded along the river met the sea-going vessels at the mouth of the Aetelea, transferring their cargo onto the ships that would take it to Amadorn. The Ancai planned to let the priesthood believe they intended to flee back to her homeland, and so they had to get aboard the boat tied up at the wharf. Once aboard, however, they would slip away on the dingy tied to its stern and lose themselves in the dark channels of the Aetelea at night. But to reach the boat, they needed a distraction.

'Because it's the best,' Kallis replied. 'Besides, it has to be tried on you for you to recognise it, and most soldiers don't get that lucky twice.'

She stopped, looking at him curiously. 'And have you?'

'Have I what?'

'Been that lucky?'

Kallis grinned at her in the darkness. 'Oh yes.'

Jeta snorted, then her feet skidded on the mud and she almost fell. Kallis caught her, his strong hand on her arm steadying her steps.

The Aetelea was almost at her widest here, and though Jeta could not see the far bank she could see the twinkling of lanterns on the barges that plied their trade down the central waterways. The pier stood a hundred feet out into the dark water far to their left, the port master's cabin at its end and a scattering of customs buildings on either side. Their ambushers waited in one of those, and she would find out which when she drew them out, providing the distraction the Ancai and Kallis hoped would be enough to give them the advantage. After all, for their plan to work, they had to be *seen* making their escape down river.

Kallis was unlooping the length of sturdy rope he carried. As he had done months ago when they forded the Istelan, he tied one end around her waist, but this time he did not fasten it securely, keeping the knot loose so that she could untie it before she was 'rescued'. Until then, however, he was taking no chances that she might be swept away by the current.

'Keep one hand on the knot,' he reminded her. 'Make sure it doesn't come loose before it should, and whatever you do, don't lose sight of the bank.'

She nodded and he gave her an assessing look. 'Once you near the pier, swim closer to the shore. Start yelling as soon as your feet touch the bottom. They will have to come out to investigate. Soon as you see them, work the rope loose, but not before you can touch the bottom, and *don't* let go of it until they have almost reached you.'

She nodded again, shivering as the cold water lapped around her ankles. Kallis smiled encouragingly, turning to stare out towards the wharf, assessing the activity on the vessel tied at its end. Satisfied, he turned back, and caught sight of her pale face.

'Don't worry,' he reassured her, his hands on her shoulders. 'I won't let you go. And if anything goes wrong, I'll reel you back in.'

She glanced at the end of the rope tied around his own waist. The length had been cut so that she could not drift further than the far side of the jetty. But it was not the drifting that frightened her. It was what would come after. She trusted Kallis, but no matter what promises he made, he could not guarantee her safety. Yet safety was a fragile thing, and she had precious little of it at that moment, so little that this gamble became less of a risk, more of a necessity. And she could never forget why she was taking it. If she wanted to see Aarin again, she had to get to Ephenor.

'They're almost done,' he told her, watching the sea-bound barge. 'It's time to go.'

Jeta summoned a weak smile. 'I'm ready.'

Kallis took her by the hand and led her into the shallows. She gasped as the cold water reached her thighs, then her waist, the gentle current near the shoreline swirling her clothes around her. Her bare feet sank into the soft mud, squelching between her toes, and she shuddered. They swam together to the lone, rotted pillar rising out of the dark water, all that remained of an older pier. She lowered her feet cautiously, relieved when they touched bottom, and watched as Kallis transferred the knot around himself to the pillar, tugging hard to make sure it would hold. Once she was safely in the shallows by the pier, he would return to the shore to join the others.

'This is where you leave me,' Kallis said as she shivered, the water at her neck now and splashing into her hair, still tied under the veil. She patted the back of her head, feeling the comforting shape of the tiny knife she had hidden in the knot of her curls. If things went wrong, she had no intention of waiting for the men to save her.

Kallis gave her a gentle push and the bottom dropped away from under her. She gave a strangled cry, splashing her arms to keep her head afloat. Away from the lights of the buildings it was almost pitch black, and down at water level all she could see was the vastness of the river. And she was all alone in it. She turned desperately back to Kallis, terrified of leaving the safety of his presence, and the mercenary stretched out to haul her back.

'I can go instead,' he offered, seeing her panic.

But she shook her head, her teeth chattering so hard she thought they must crack. Kallis could go in her place, but the soldiers would be far more suspicious of a man apparently drowning in the shallow water near their hiding place. It was also possible some might recognise him. Since they had already been 'executed', the soldiers would take no prisoners. Jeta knew the unspoken reason why she had been chosen instead. The priesthood's guards would recognise her also, but a pretty girl was much less of a threat. They might also want to have their fun with her before they killed her, she thought darkly, recompense for the tedious duty of hunting fugitives.

'We don't have much time,' Kallis reminded her when she showed no sign of leaving him. 'We can't let that boat leave without us.'

Jeta nodded, taking a deep breath. She kicked away from the mercenary and felt him feed out the rope. The current took her and she began to drift. For an instant she floundered in panic, her head slipping below the surface, and she swallowed a mouthful of rank river water. Then a sharp tug on the rope snagged her sideways and her head bobbed up again. She could not see

Kallis anymore, and her hand reached for the rope and latched around the knot. The tug had loosened it and she was afraid to take her hand away in case it unravelled.

Jeta kept herself afloat with her other arm, kicking out with her legs. The pier rushed towards her, the wooden piles rising like ghostly columns from the dark water. She turned to the shore and the slivers of candlelight from the half-closed shutters of the cabin. She tried to swim towards it, but the current was too strong, pulling her on under the blackness of the pier. Rusted nails scored across her arms and legs, and she cried out in fear and sudden pain, grabbing at the wood, but her fingers could find no purchase on the slippery sides and she was dragged on. An instant later she was out the other side and the rope jerked her up short with a lurch. She yelled as the pressure squeezed the air from her lungs, and she grappled desperately at the slipping knot. With both arms fumbling at her waist, her head submerged once more. She stretched her arms up, breaking the surface spluttering and gasping for air, and the knot came free. She grabbed for the rope as it slithered away, missed, and was dragged under again as the current caught up with her.

Jeta tumbled under the water, unable to see the surface. Water sloshed into her nose, she choked, and it poured into her mouth. A pressure settled around her chest like a vice, squeezing her lungs until she felt they would burst, then suddenly she was on the surface again, retching up water and dragging in huge gasps of air.

She screamed then, knowing she was going to drown, and splashed her arms wildly. The shutters of the cabin were thrown open and torches were carried outside. The soldiers gathered at the water's edge, calling out to each other. She screamed again, pleading with them to see her, as the current pulled her further and further from their help.

Then, above the commotion she heard the pounding of running feet, and a great splash came from her right. She called out again, thinking that one of them had seen her, and saw Kallis's head break the surface twenty feet away. He must have felt the knot come free and realised what had happened. The shouts from the shore escalated, and she watched in panic as they pointed to her, having seen her at last. Three shadows broke away from the group, running to a shallow craft drawn half-way up the bank in front of the cabin. Two more joined them as they cut the moorings and began to push the boat into the river. Behind her she heard shouts of alarm from the end of the pier and knew that the captain was preparing to make a hasty departure. Soon there would be nowhere for them to escape to.

Despair washed through her and she was sinking again, her limbs like lead and unable to keep her afloat. She felt a hand under her shoulder and she was dragged upwards. Her head broke the surface to see Kallis's dripping face next to hers, his breath coming in explosive gasps.

'What did I tell you about keeping hold of that rope?'

Jeta could not answer. She did not have the breath, and the soldiers were coming closer, their small craft arrowing towards them. They would be recognised for certain now and the guardsmen would waste no time completing their task. They would kill Kallis and have their fun with her, and the Ancai and Trad would be killed if they tried to save her.

'We're not dead yet,' Kallis grunted as though he could read her thoughts. The mercenary gritted his teeth, straining to reach the shore. They had no choice. The boat reached them, the soldiers shipping their oars and reaching willing hands down to take her from Kallis. They hauled her over the side and she hit the bottom with a thud, curling into a ball on the damp boards, gasping like a fish out of water. They ignored her as they reached for Kallis. The veil was miraculously still on her head, and the night was black enough that her wet skin seemed almost as dark as theirs.

As Kallis was pulled over the side, Jeta saw the gleam of steel strapped to his wrist. A guard knelt beside her and rattled off a string of questions Jeta could not understand. On his hands and knees, head bowed as he caught his breath, Kallis muttered an answer, gesturing behind them with his hand.

The soldier looked the way he had pointed, and it was the last thing he did. Kallis buried his knife in the guardsman's throat, yanking it violently back so that his body toppled over the side. One of his fellows gave a startled shout, and as he leant over the side, Kallis crashed into him, sending him after his friend. Then all hell broke loose.

Jeta reached into her hair, relieved to find the tiny blade still there. She staggered to her feet, the little blade in her hand, just as Kallis put two fingers in his mouth and gave a piercing whistle. The lead soldier growled and danced forward, and the rocking of the boat sent her sprawling once more. She heard the clash of weapons as Kallis met his attack and snatched her legs from under their feet. As she dragged her head above the side, she saw two dark figures run out from the shadows at the far end of the customs buildings, falling on the soldiers who remained on the bank, then her attention was forced away from them as Kallis fell heavily on top of her, cracking his head hard on the prow.

One soldier lay across his legs, blood pooling under him from a wound high on his chest. Another sprawled limply, legs twitching, across the bottom of the boat, and the third stood squarely over him, eyeing them with a vengeful gleam.

Jeta shook Kallis desperately but he was a dead weight in her arms. She tried to wriggle out from under him, praying that he was unconscious and not dead, and the soldier watched her struggles with predatory eyes.

Jeta swore at him as she shoved the mercenary from her, making it to her knees. She had dropped the knife when she fell, and her hands explored the dripping boards, her eyes never leaving her enemy. As her fingers found the hilt, he moved, leaping over Kallis's limp body and seizing her by the hair. The veil came loose and he hurled it aside, lacing his fingers through her tangled curls. She cried out as he yanked her towards him and lashed out with her knife. The blade scored a shallow cut across his abdomen and he roared in pain, his fist colliding with the side of her head.

Jeta fell heavily onto the body of a dying soldier and felt his blood soak her back. Bright specks of light sliced her vision, darkness rushed in and out like the tide, leaving her shaking from head to toe. She had lost the knife again.

Her adversary glared down, breathing heavily, one hand stained with his blood. He reached down and picked up her blade, throwing it over the side. The boat rocked violently. She gasped, drawing up her knees, and the Ancai rose out of the water behind the soldier, his hand darting in one swift motion to slice at the back of the man's neck. His blade went deep, severing the spinal cord, and the guardsmen never made a sound as he dropped onto his face.

Terrified reaction flooded her and her breath came in panting gasps. Trad slipped over the side, picking his ways through the bodies to her side. The Ancai followed him, hauling himself out of the deep water with barely an effort. As the boy knelt, silently examining the bruise at her temple, the Ancai moved to Kallis, lifting his head and probing gently with his fingers.

'Is he alive?' she asked breathlessly, swatting Trad's solicitous hand aside and crawling to join them. She took one of Kallis's hands in hers and looked at the Ancai.

'He's alive,' the captain assured her. 'Though his head has taken a knock that will keep him under for a while, I think.' He looked over his shoulder. 'We must be going.'

Jeta followed his gaze and saw another boat being launched, this one bigger and no doubt faster if their current luck held. The Ancai was already on his feet, helping Trad to heave the bodies over the side. Then they settled themselves at the oars, talking quietly as they turned the craft towards the centre of the river. The Ancai grunted, straining to drag the oars through the strong current.

Jeta placed her arms under Kallis's shoulders to pull him upright. She leaned him against the side, bracing his head on her shoulder. Then she turned into the night and stared out at the river, wondering where the Ancai could take them. The boat they had chosen to carry them downriver was long gone, and without it they had little hope of reaching the rendezvous with the craft that would carry them back the way they had come and on to the mountains.

She looked at Kallis, worried by his eerie stillness. He was a man who vibrated with life, even at rest, and to see him so quiet and unmoving disturbed her. She touched the back of his head as she had seen the Ancai do, and her fingers came away stained with blood. Alarmed, she hooked her torn veil with her foot and dragged it towards her, pressing it against the cut and holding it there. She hoped he would wake soon.

Jeta did not realise she had fallen asleep until she was woken by sunlight. Her shoulder was jammed uncomfortably against the prow and her head was tilted awkwardly to one side. Her clothes were dry, a fact she was grateful for as she caught sight of the men milling about not far from where she lay. They were not Kas'Talani guardsmen. They were ragged rivermen, dressed in coarse tunics and breeches hacked off at the knee, barefoot to a man.

She looked around for the others, but the boat was empty.

'Kallis?' she called quietly, close to panic again. 'Kallis!'

'Here,' came a disgruntled reply from her right. 'And please don't shout.'

She looked in the direction of his voice and saw him propped groggily against a tree. The boat was beached high up the bank and she leapt over the side, landing on her knees in the drying mud.

He grimaced, rubbing the back of his neck with his hand. 'No sudden movements either.'

'Sorry,' she murmured, kneeling beside him and trying to move his head to see the wound.

He shrugged her off and cursed fluidly and at length. His face seemed drained of all colour. She backed off contritely, kneeling in front of him.

'How did we get here?'

Kallis groaned. 'You're asking me? When I came to we were already here, and our friends over there,'—he waved an arm weakly in the direction of the men—'were busy hauling us up. As I understand it, our resourceful protector hitched a ride on one of the barges and managed to make our rendezvous. Which apparently this is.'

Jeta looked around her. The Ancai had not told them the details of this part of his plan, only that, given luck, they would meet up with friends who would take them up the river. She looked for him now and found him standing to one side talking to a dangerous looking man who was stripped to the waist in the baking sun. His skin was tanned a deep brown, and a crisscross of scars snaked across his torso. A curved sword hung at his side, a dagger was tucked into the strip of linen about his waist and another blade was strapped to his upper arm. As her gaze travelled upward, she saw a hard profile, half hidden by a fall of black hair. A dangerous man indeed.

She turned the other way and saw what must be his boat, shallow bottomed like the barges but slimmer and longer. It had a feel of silent, predatory speed in its sweeping lines, and she could see what looked like a giant crossbow mounted in its bow. A dangerous boat for a dangerous man.

That dangerous man was approaching them now, the Ancai and Trad with him. He walked with a deadly kind of grace that she felt an honest man would not have possessed. He grinned at her as he caught her watching, and his dark eyes danced above jutting features. It was a face that was as hard as it was handsome, but there was no menace in it. At least, not yet.

She rose as they reached her, shaking drying mud from her clothes. He eyed her appraisingly and sketched a brief bow.

'This is Captain Iraius,' the Ancai explained. 'He has agreed to give us passage to Kouresh.'

'Think of it more as repayment of an old debt,' Iraius amended. 'I don't usually carry passengers, but I'm happy to make an exception for you, princess.'

Jeta stared at him, frozen by the words coming out of his mouth. 'You're Amadorian,' she accused, shocked.

'That I am,' he agreed. 'Situran to be precise. And half my crew at least is from back home.'

'But why?' she stammered stupidly. 'Why are you here?'

Iraius shrugged, amused by the question. 'Rich pickings hereabouts. There's a fair number of us now. It's a good living, the trade up and down this old river. 'Course, we have to share with the locals, but that ain't much of a hardship, is it boys?'

The last question was flung over his shoulder at his wickedly armed crew, hanging over the gunwales of the lethal looking craft. Instead of raucous agreement, the ragged men stayed frighteningly quiet, but their eyes glinted with merriment.

'They're good lads,' their captain told her. 'This ain't like avoiding Alliance patrols on the Istelan. These cursed priests are a few lengths sharper than the South's holiday soldiers.'

'Who are you?' she asked suspiciously.

'Free traders, princess,' Iraius replied promptly. 'This is my crew, and this is my boat.'

'River pirates,' Kallis supplied from his position on the ground. He did not seem inclined to attempt to rise.

She looked back at the captain and saw a grin spread across his face.

'Pirates?' she squeaked to the Ancai. 'You've brought us to pirates?'

'Aye, princess,' the captain said with a leer. 'And none so feared as the crew of this little lady.' He looked at his boat fondly. 'She'll see you safe to the mountains, don't you worry. The priesthood's soldiers won't bother us.'

Jeta shot him a withering look. 'Strangely it's no longer the soldiers I'm worried about.'

Iraius took a step back, a hurt expression on his face. 'These here are gentlemen, princess. Ain't none of them that will lay a hand on you without asking first.'

Kallis snorted. 'Believe me, they'll only try that once.'

When she rounded on him, he raised his hands. 'Yes, I'll knock out any one of them that gives it a try. Now give me a hand, girl, and help me up.'

She ignored him, leaving the Ancai to support his wobbly legs as he made it to his feet. Iraius walked beside her and there was a proud, possessive look on his face as he watched his vessel made ready. And she was beautiful, for all her deadly lines, or perhaps because of them.

'What is she called?'

The pirate treated her to a dazzling smile. '*Situran Dawn.*'

Seeing her pleased smile, he laughed. 'That's right, she's a highborn southern lady, just like yourself, and a fugitive one at that. You like her?'

'Very much,' Jeta agreed.

'Well then, princess, I think she'll keep your secrets.'

He waved an arm at his crew and walked towards his boat. 'Hurry yourselves,' he called over his shoulder. 'The quicker we're gone, the quicker we get you where you're going.'

The *Situran Dawn* floated in deep water by a steep overhang. The pirates had slung planks across from her deck to the bank and Iraius darted across them now, dropping lightly over the side. He waved to them, then disappeared, his voice calling out orders. Jeta heard Kallis groan as he saw the planks. She stifled a smile. This was going to be fun.

ELEVEN

THE FIRST DAWN rays to hit the spires of the city of Kas'Tella turned their stonework to burnished gold, and the unearthly glow that lit the grounds of the citadel inspired its citizens to renewed reverence for the priesthood within.

The Holy City, seat of power of the religious class that ruled in Caledan, was truly an awe-inspiring sight, a fitting testament to the forgotten skills of the craftsmen who had combined their talents of masonry and spellcraft to reshape raw stone into glorious, graceful feats of architecture. Around the heart of the city, the ancient citadel now inhabited by the Kas'Talani, thousands of dwellings had sprung up in the millennia since the city's birth, and Kas'Tella had become a great sprawling mass that covered the land around for many leagues.

Kinseris had entered through the postern gate just before dusk the previous evening and made his way through the crowds to the citadel with as little fuss as possible. Had he been dressed in his robes of office, the crowds would have parted at his whim, but he had preferred the anonymity of his travel-stained riding clothes. They allowed him to pass the guards at the gates without fanfare or ceremony and take his own time on the final leg of his journey.

Kas'Tella was the city of his birth and the playground of his childhood. It had changed much in the years of Vasa's reign, but his love for its bustling, exuberant atmosphere remained, and he welcomed the opportunity to savour the sight of familiar places. United under Kas'Talani rule but little else, the city was a stew of different races, from Karrimor merchants to southern islanders to the swarthy pearl traders from the northern seaboard, and each of them had brought their own vibrant cultures to the pot.

And nostalgia aside, there were things he needed to do and people he needed to meet free from the watching eyes of the Order.

This morning, however, as he presented himself at Vasa's chambers for interview, not even the sight of much-loved and long-missed friends could stir him from his brooding intensity. He halted a moment before entering the inner sanctum of the Caledan priesthood, all too aware that these could be his last few moments of freedom.

'In your own time, Kinseris.'

The voice that mocked him came from behind the closed doors. Jolted from his reverie by the unpleasant reminder of what lay beyond, Kinseris took a deep breath and entered the holy chamber.

The room where generations of high priests had conducted their affairs was heavy with atmosphere. Gilded brackets on the walls and hanging from the domed ceiling held crystal bowls filled with scented candles, and thick clouds of incense wafted from bronze burners on the ornate altars in each of the five corners. Heavy curtains shrouded the effigy of spirit, concealing Vasa's private quarters, symbolic of his position as Sephaiir'telis, the Maker's representative on Andeira.

One long dead high priest's flamboyant taste had seen the entire chamber re-laid with the finest slabs of polished granite from the quarries in northern Karrimor, glittering a myriad of colours in the candlelight. And in the centre of the room, arranged like a fat spider on a bed of silk cushions, sat the man in whose pudgy hands the reins of power currently resided.

'Holy One,' Kinseris murmured, sweeping into a low bow. 'As is your will, so I have come.'

Chandra Vasa, High Priest of the Kas'Talani, had none of the nobility of stature possessed by his predecessors, men whose portraits adorned the walls of the chamber. Instead he clothed his portly frame in rich fabrics loaded with jewels and imposed his authority through fear and brute force. He had ruled in Caledan for over three hundred years—an unnaturally long lifespan even within the priesthood—and if rumours were to be believed, had risen to prominence through the murder of not one, but two former high priests. In that at least he was following tradition.

As a man, Kinseris despised him. Vasa's dissolute lifestyle was an affront to the moral strictures espoused by his Order, and the man's shameless lack of self-discipline and petty jealousies were the talk of the Holy City. But as a ruler he feared him, not merely for his wanton cruelty and insatiable appetite for riches, though they were reason enough. Vasa's rule had seen sinister changes creeping into the priesthood, the old ways slowly stripped away as the power was gathered ever more firmly into the hands of this one man. Gone was the council that had tempered the power of the high priest in centuries past, and the core of their belief that was reverence for the Maker and her gifts was being twisted into desire for power and conquest, for the greater glory of the Kas'Talani, not Tesserion.

But at that moment what he feared most was the reason he had been summoned with such urgency. He had been careful, but the man had spies in every corner.

'Wine?' His superior asked languidly, breaking his train of thought. 'Or is it too early for you?'

Kinseris nodded his assent, his anxiety not eased by Vasa's convivial manner. He watched as a fleshy arm was raised ever so slightly, the movement noticeable only by the flash of light across the gems on his fingers. Immediately a silhouette stirred in the shadows, sending a cloud of perfume into the air. Amid the rustle of silken robes, the figure of a woman emerged to stand by the side of the cleric.

The sight of her catapulted Kinseris back to his past, and his throat constricted painfully. Still beautiful even after the passage of more than twenty years, she stood before him now as she had done so many times in the past, so close and yet so far out of his reach. He knew that Vasa was watching him, waiting for a reaction. It was no coincidence that Shakumi was in attendance. He had expected it, even hoped for it, but even so... Even so, he could not quite hide the tangle of emotion she stirred in him.

'Lady,' Kinseris bowed again, unable to stop himself.

Shakumi ignored him. She could do nothing else.

Vasa raised a hand and Shakumi moved silently to fetch a tray of refreshments. Kinseris watched her progress from the corner of his eye, his gaze trained on his feet. Shakumi was the favourite concubine of the high priest, plucked from her home and forced into service for her extraordinary beauty. She was also the only woman he had ever loved. Dressed head to toe in embroidered silks, her eyes the only visible feature in a face concealed by a veil, she was still the loveliest creature he had ever seen.

Kinseris knew only too well just how jealous Vasa was of this woman. Guards had been flogged merely for snatching covetous glances, and a man executed who had attempted to gain her favour. As Kas'Talani, Kinseris had been spared execution, for the Order would not so publicly discipline its own. Yet Vasa did not forget. From the moment he had accepted exile, Kinseris had known that the day would come when his indiscretions would be paid for. But even that bleak thought made his heart feel a little lighter. If that day had come at last, perhaps he need not fear the revelation of his other sins.

Vasa allowed the silence to draw out as he sprawled in graceless abandon amidst his pile of scented cushions. With an expansive gesture he indicated for Kinseris to be seated.

Shakumi returned with wine and Vasa took a long drink. 'A fine vintage, don't you agree?'

Kinseris nodded his appreciation, though he had barely touched the wine, a potent and highly prized variety from the lands to the south where the climate was not so hot. For this encounter he preferred a head unfuddled by the effects of strong drink.

Vasa looked at his full glass with a heavy sigh. 'You were never much of a drinker, were you, Kinseris? Far too austere. You should relax, enjoy earthly pleasures. A man can dry up quickly who spends all his life praying.' Vasa winked lewdly in the direction of Shakumi. 'Take this wine. A gift from a southern warlord.'

Kinseris raised an eyebrow in polite query.

Vasa laughed. 'The fool man thought he could resist the might of the Holy Army on its properties alone. His whole war band had drunk themselves into a stupor. I had my men relieve him of the remains of his cellar to avoid further such delusions.' Left unsaid was the fate of the unfortunate man, who had almost certainly been relieved of his life.

Vasa sank back into the cushions, his expression of contentment at odds with the sharpness of his next question. 'I believe you have had some interesting visitors, Kinseris. From Amadorn. Is this true?'

As the first unpleasant shock receded, Kinseris watched the delicate stem of the wineglass as it was twirled between fingers like sausages and weighed his words with care. He knew what he faced now.

'Holy One, you are well informed. Had I known your interest I would have brought the foreigners with me.'

'Ah, of course,' Vasa murmured. 'You always were so dutiful.'

Kinseris made no reply. There was nothing to say.

Vasa grew tired of the silence, signalling Shakumi to refill his glass. Kinseris's own was virtually untouched. 'What can you tell me of them?'

Kinseris gave a casual shrug. If Vasa was an expert in this game, he was no stranger to it. 'They came to establish trading connections with the desert nomads,' he said, repeating the easy lie. 'Apparently Amadorn's merchants have pretensions to break your monopolies. A nuisance certainly, but hardly a threat to your trade routes.'

Vasa nodded, giving the appearance of careful thought. 'Merchants?' he asked at last. 'And you believe them?'

'There is no reason not to,' Kinseris replied. 'I questioned them myself, and my men searched their possessions. We found nothing to indicate they are not what they say they are.'

'Really?' The high priest leant forward, so close that Kinseris could smell the cloying sweetness of his breath. 'And yet you say they were seeking trading connections with the people of the deserts. An odd choice if it is trade they are after. Why go to the desert nomads?'

Kinseris kept his face expressionless. 'Ignorance, Holy One? Who can say? They displayed a dangerous lack of knowledge of your empire.'

'Strange,' Vasa mused. 'I had heard one was Caledani.'

Kinseris could feel the trap closing. Only the truth, or as close to it as he dared, would get him out of this. 'Once again you have heard correctly, Holy One, but the man left these lands as a child. He has barely retained his grasp of the language.' Which was unfair to Kallis, who spoke Safarsee like a native, but he thought the mercenary would forgive the harmless lie.

The ghost of a smile flitted across Vasa's face. 'But he himself is of the desert tribes, is he not? The merchants' council has never granted foreign trade rights to a nomadic family.'

'Such things are not unheard of, Holy One,' Kinseris replied, his throat dry. 'It is impossible to guard all your borders against those determined to leave. Perhaps he was taken in service to a merchant family.'

Vasa's smile never wavered. 'Not unheard of, indeed. In fact, I have been hearing many rumours of Caledani in Amadorn over the years with no connection to the trading families.'

'As I said, Holy One, it is impossible –'

'Of course,' the high priest replied, dismissing Kinseris's excuses with a wave of his hand. 'I expect too much of you. Just as you say, it is impossible for one man to guard an entire border. But the mage. Surely you don't mean to tell me that he too is interested in trading monopolies?'

If Kinseris's mouth had been dry before, it was a desert now. The discussion of Kallis's origins had been a distraction. 'Holy One?'

'Oh, come now, Kinseris. I could believe that you were taken in by mere travellers, but not even you could fail to recognise a fellow talent.'

Kinseris took a deep breath, swallowing to ease his tight throat. There was only one strategy left to him now. 'Holy One, I had hoped to handle this without involving you,' he confessed, keeping his eyes downcast. 'There are rumours, as you know, concerning a certain legend...'

He risked a sideways glance and saw the fat hand gripping the glass almost tight enough to shatter it. 'Personally, I give these rumours little credence, but I understand how such things can become bigger than they are. Dangerous, even.' He paused suggestively as he teetered on the edge of a precipice. Vasa's paranoia was legendary. Draw it out too strongly and he risked igniting repercussions that could destroy them all. Stir it just enough and the distraction might gain him the time he needed to find a way out of his high priest's trap.

'What are you saying?' Vasa demanded, rising to the bait. 'Is he –?'

'No,' Kinseris replied quickly. 'I do not believe so. This man is no figurehead out of legend. Surely that one would be more powerful, more impressive.'

'More powerful?' Vasa's tension had not ebbed. 'So, he has some skill? You think he could be dangerous? Perhaps a spy sent by those fools at Luen?'

'Powerful?' Kinseris shook his head, his face carefully blank. 'No, Holy One. If he was sent by Luen, which I doubt, he is a sorry indication of how diminished they have become. I must confess myself somewhat disappointed. I had expected more of a contest...' He let that last thought hang between them unfinished, letting Vasa draw his own conclusions.

His superior eyed him with suspicion, some of the tension draining out of him. 'You tested him?' But before Kinseris could reply, the jaws of the trapped slammed shut. 'Is that why you felt the need to seal both yourself and this man behind lethal wards?'

For a stunned second Kinseris could not speak. Use of such wards was outlawed for any except the high council, and since their demise to all but Vasa himself. His paranoia would allow no such secretive measures to shroud the doings of his subjects. It had been a necessary risk, and now it had damned him. He had been betrayed. Why and by whom he did not know, but no matter what excuse he offered now, there was no escaping the fact that Vasa already knew he had lied.

His high priest's patience was wearing thin. 'Well?'

Kinseris cleared his throat. 'I did not know what to expect,' he hedged. 'I wished to protect those under my charge, and yourself, if I was wrong.' It sounded lame, even to his ears.

Vasa barked a laugh. 'Protect me?' he gasped. 'How admirable, Kinseris. Such loyalty from you I would not have expected. So, you intended the wards to kill you both should he prove beyond your means to master? Did you never consider that should he defeat you, the wards would be well within his ability to unravel?'

It had occurred to him; he had hoped it would not occur to Vasa.

'Perhaps it is as you say,' his high priest allowed, though his tone and expression said otherwise. 'Perhaps this man is not Æisoul. But I will meet him to test him myself.'

Kinseris blessed the sense that had made him leave Aarin safe under guard at Frankesh. He smiled apologetically at his enemy, for enemy he was in truth now if he had not been before. 'I am afraid that will be impossible, Holy One. I left orders with my Ancai that will have seen him dealt with by now.'

He dropped his gaze, unwilling to let Vasa see his face. The man might have cultivated an image of pampered softness, but he would never have risen to his current position, or held it so long, if the façade he presented plumbed the true depths of his character. And a meeting with Aarin would expose all Kinseris's lies and evasions for what they were. It would not change his fate, but if he wished to preserve Aarin's life and freedom, he could not allow him to come face to face with Vasa.

Shakumi was dismissed with a flick of Vasa's wrist, and one glance told Kinseris his superior was far from satisfied.

'That is unfortunate,' Vasa observed, his eyes sharp and watchful. 'I must confess that I am truly anxious to meet this man. My sources tell me he searches for the dragons.'

Both men touched a hand to the devices hidden under their robes. Kinseris could feel his own trembling and he forced it steady as he reached for his wine. He knew now he had never had a chance. Vasa knew everything. All that remained to be seen was what he would do with his knowledge.

Vasa's voice was now deadly quiet. 'By law, you are obliged to report all matters that touch upon that ancient race to Kas'Tella immediately. You did not. By law, you are obliged to hand Æisoul over to me. You did not.'

Kinseris met Vasa's eyes. He did not bother to deny it. They had passed that point twenty years ago. 'No, Holy One.'

Vasa waved his hand as though brushing aside a minor transgression and rearranged himself on the pillows. 'No need to concern yourself. I sent my men to fetch the man as soon as I realised you had left without him. You will present the Amadorian to me after the morning chapter. If he intends harm to our interests he will be dealt with. And his allies. For now, you may leave. My servants will show you to your quarters.'

Kinseris could not remember standing. Numbly, he bowed his devotion and kissed the outstretched hand, utterly dazed.

Vasa's smile was beatific, his parting shot a killing blow. 'Find Shakumi for me, Kinseris. Tell her I will not need her tonight. She is free to please herself.'

TWELVE

VASA WATCHED KINSERIS leave, taking some small satisfaction from his anger and fear. But he was given little time to savour this first part of this revenge as a panel in the wall swung open.

Vasa did not turn. The Arkni's presence always made him acutely conscious of his dignity. 'So, you were listening. This was a matter of the Order and none of your concern. I thought I had made my wishes clear on this point. The internal affairs of my people are my business!'

There was a sweep of velvet behind him, too close. 'You presume too far, priest.'

Vasa felt the chill of real fear. He stood and turned to face the intruder, preparing himself for the possibility of a final betrayal. Never before had the creature dared address him with such open contempt. If the Arkni's impatience had finally peaked into outright rebellion, he would be ready.

He watched as Saal'an glided across the floor. He came to a halt mere inches from the high priest, closer than any of his Order would presume to come uninvited. Vasa steeled himself, drawing on all his long years of training to anchor his skittering thoughts into a semblance of composure.

'This matter touches on *our* business, Chandra Vasa, or had you forgotten our bargain? Anyone searching for the dragons is of interest to us both. Be warned, priest. Betray us and our vengeance will cross the ages and bridge the divide between this life and the next.'

Vasa made a strangled noise deep in his throat. He could not believe he had allowed it to come to this. That a creature he considered a servant should challenge him in his own chambers—should openly threaten him—made him sick with rage.

'And you presume too far, Arkni,' he said coldly. 'This is a matter of discipline within my Order. A priest forgetting his place is my province to judge. I would have informed you had this mage turned out to be of interest

318

to our cause, but you heard Kinseris. He is sorely lacking in both power and discipline. I cannot think he will be our man.'

Saal'an laughed. It was a horrible sound. 'That will be for me to decide. Or have you forgotten whose knowledge imparted the secret of the Illeneas Prophecies to your miserable Order?'

Vasa flushed with rage. 'Prophecies that damn you as they do me,' he grated. 'That's why we made this bargain. Or have *you* forgotten?'

'I forget nothing,' Saal'an assured him. 'There are memories in me that stretch back through millennia to a time when power such as yours was wielded by children. Do not overestimate your importance, priest. Set against such vast stretches of time, your kind lives and dies in the blink of an eye.'

Vasa felt his insides turn to ice. 'You need me yet,' he reminded the Arkni. 'You need the power of my people.'

'As you need me,' Saal'an returned. 'And because you do, you will not keep me from this audience. Do not pretend you have been taken in by this Frankesh renegade. We both know what he has been doing all these years. Your time would be better spent trying to discover what new trouble he is plotting before it interferes with our plans.'

Seething with frustration, Vasa groped for his glass. He gestured for Shakumi and then remembered he had dismissed her and why. Returned to a degree of equilibrium, he was inclined to be generous in this current dilemma. Seating himself once more on his cushions, he gestured for the Arkni to join him. The robed figure remained where he was.

Vasa sighed. 'You really should relax more, Saal'an. Come, have some wine. It's an extraordinary vintage.' He paused, eyeing his adversary intently. 'But I forget. You already know. You were listening. As to the audience with the Amadorian, I think it is best if I conduct it alone. If he is the man we seek, do you not think he would be able to sense your presence? After all, the texts point to a man whose awareness is more finely aligned to the great dragons than any other for centuries, and as you correctly pointed out, no one should be more aware of this than you.'

He realised at once he had made a mistake. Saal'an had not moved, but Vasa could feel the fury and hatred pouring from him. 'I am, of course, happy for you to watch, as you watched just now,' he offered, backtracking.

'I do not care what pleases you,' Saal'an hissed. 'Nor whether this man can sense my presence. If he is who I think he is, he will already be trapped.' And with the slippery grace of a serpent, he turned and was gone.

Vasa spun around faster than his bulk would suggest he could move, in time to see the black robes disappear through the hidden door. Emboldened by the retreating back, he called, 'What have you done, Saal'an? You will answer me! This is my palace, you snivelling scion of perversion! I am not your puppet!'

The answer came back through the walls, a sibilant whisper that echoed around the chamber. 'As long as my threads bind you to this life, Chandra Vasa, that is exactly what you are.'

It did not take Kinseris long to discover where Aarin was being held. His captivity was no secret, and the soldiers who guarded the cells let him through without comment. The thought nagged at him that he was playing straight into Vasa's hands. But try as he might, he could find no other option.

As the heavy door of the outer jail slammed home behind him, Kinseris stood for a moment in the darkness, letting his eyes adjust. The air was dank and stale and the walls pressed in close on either side. A tingle of raw power, flushing across his skin, warned him that the wards were active, as they must be for a prisoner like Aarin. The suspicion played on his mind that maybe, this time, they were also meant to ward against his interference.

Kinseris struck a spark onto the torch he carried, waiting until the flame took. Holding the light aloft, he began his cautious descent. The passage he found himself in was long, the stone mildewed and damp, and as he progressed further the rank odour of confined humanity assaulted his senses. Pressing a cuff of his robe across his face, he shone the light into the first cell. It seemed empty. A pile of rags in the corner sprang to life and launched itself at the bars. The creature snarled, teeth clacking together in an inhuman chatter. Yet it was human, or had been, Kinseris realised in dismay.

'That's Ivor.' The voice came from the darkness to his right. 'He doesn't like you.'

One hand still holding his sleeve against his nose and mouth, Kinseris lifted his torch and shone the flickering light in the direction of the voice.

'What about you?' he asked.

Two cells further along, leaning against the wall by the bars, Aarin shrugged, his expression shuttered. The dancing, fickle shadows played across his face, highlighting the hollows around his eyes and sunken cheeks. He was dressed only in a linen shirt and leather leggings, and yet even in the unnatural chill of the spell-sealed dungeons he showed no visible signs of cold, evidence that he was still master of his mental reflexes.

Silent, Kinseris raised the torch to study his face and Aarin blinked as the light hit his eyes, turning his face from the priest's scrutiny.

Moving closer, Kinseris could see what the torch-thrown shadows had disguised, the marks his captors had made. Ugly bruising marred the side of his head and the wrists that hung loose by his sides were chaffed raw and angry by past fetters. Seeing the direction of his gaze, Aarin obligingly raised his wrists to the light.

'So much for your protection,' he remarked. Whatever measure of trust had been gained in Frankesh was buried now under anger and suspicion. 'I can only hope my companions fared better.'

And in that, the only sign of weakness, was the half-asked question that begged for reassurance.

Gnawed by shame and worry, Kinseris realised with an inward sigh that he had not thought to inquire after the others. He had no word of comfort to offer. Instead he addressed himself to that which required more immediate attention. 'How badly are you hurt?' He was careful not to let his voice reveal his worry, concerned that the mage might be blocking his physical pain as he was shielding his body from the chill.

'As you see.'

Aarin pushed himself off the wall to stand full in the light, the motion still fluid and easy, whatever hurt he had taken evidently not serious enough to stiffen and impede his movement. Or he was taking great care not to show it, for he had clearly been handled roughly. Before Aarin moved back out of the circle of light, Kinseris saw his clothes and exposed skin were filthy and bloodstained. Looking around the cramped space, the priest could see no sign of his tunic or cloak, nor any blankets left by the guards to ward off the cold. One-handed, he unfastened his cloak and held it out through the bars. When Aarin made no move to take it, he dropped it on the floor inside the cell.

'Freeze if you will,' he snapped, wearied beyond patience. 'Whatever you may believe, I come as a friend.'

'So you say,' Aarin replied. 'I trusted you once, and here I am. There seems little reason to do so again.'

'Then you should look a little harder.' Kinseris struggled to keep his own anger under control. He berated himself for risking this meeting. 'I am here to warn you, and I advise you to put aside your distrust and hear me.'

'Your concern is touching,' Aarin mocked. 'You have lied to me before with just such sincerity.'

Kinseris ignored his sarcasm. The ravaging chill of the prison's wards added to his own mounting fear and he wanted to be away from this place. 'Tomorrow you will meet with the head of the Kas'Talani. Do not make the mistake other men have made and dismiss him for the fool he appears. He is a dangerous man and his intentions towards you can be in no doubt if you do not guard your tongue with him as at first you did with me.'

He gripped the bars with his free hand, his knuckles white. 'The outcome we both hope for is placed in great jeopardy by this meeting. The truth of your presence is enough to see us both dead. Do you understand?'

Hidden in the shadows, Aarin's expression was unreadable. 'I understand that you are playing a dangerous game, Kinseris. But I am not inclined to be a pawn for your political manoeuvring.'

Then he too was at the bars and Kinseris winced at the sight of the crusted bruise above his left eye. Grey eyes unaccustomed to brightness blinked, the sweep of the lashes in the torchlight casting long shadows across too-prominent cheekbones. Up close, despite his defiance, he looked young and vulnerable, and more than a little afraid. 'I will keep your secret tomorrow. But I will do so for my own reasons.'

Kinseris smiled grimly. 'I don't care what your reasons are. And my secrets are secrets no longer.' He paused, then said, 'If I can, I will find out what has happened to your friends. If I can prevent them coming to harm, I will.'

When Kinseris left, he took the torch with him and the cell was plunged back into darkness. Aarin shivered. Remembering the cloak discarded on the ground, he groped in the darkness until his fingers touched velvet. Scooping the garment up, he wrapped it round his shoulders. It had taken all his self-control to conceal the tremors in front of the priest as the powerful ward spells whipped the air into icy waves that no mere mental trick could banish. The touch of warmth broke the last of his self-discipline and he collapsed in a huddle on the floor, the pain of fresh bruises ensuring that even physical comfort eluded him.

He had no idea how long he had been in the cells, his senses confused by perpetual darkness and his innate awareness stifled by the powerful wards. No matter how he tried to extend his consciousness, his efforts came up against an invisible barrier. He could not even discern the weaves that bound him. At first he had fought against the restraint, every artifice trained at the block, until he had collapsed, exhausted beyond words. Now he tried to endure as best he could. If he wore himself out fighting the spell, he would be in no state to withstand the interrogations he knew were coming.

And then Kinseris had come. Aarin no longer knew whether he was friend or foe. He had trusted him in Frankesh—he wanted to trust him now—but he no longer trusted his own judgement. The priests who had taken him from the chapter house cells had claimed to act in Kinseris's name. He had not believed them at first, but he knew from Kinseris's own lips just how much the man was risking by helping him. Who could blame him if he decided to save his life by sacrificing Aarin's? But if he had not, if Kinseris truly stood firm in his choice, then Kallis and Jeta might already be dead, and their only hope if they were not was the promise of a man whose influence was melting away like frost at the first touch of spring. Assuming all Kinseris had told him in Frankesh was true, then here and now the priest would face his reckoning for his treachery. And Aarin knew he would likely die with him.

THIRTEEN

DISMISSED AT LAST, it was all Shakumi could do not to run back to the safety of Vasa's quarters. In Kinseris's distraught expression she had seen the mirror of her own confused emotions, and she had had an advantage, for she had known he would be here today. Yet, even so, the shock of seeing him again had rocked her in a way she had not imagined. He had not changed, though she knew he must be old now, older than her father when he died. The lines of care on his face were etched a little deeper, but he was still the man she had dreamed about for years.

Had he dreamed of her? No matter how hard she wished, she was no longer the girl she had been. The years had aged her as they had not aged him, and her beauty was sullied by two decades of service.

It had not been love. She had realised that as she grew older, looking back. A childish infatuation, maybe, at least on her part. He had not been young, even then. Exciting, exhilarating, but not love. He had been so much older, so worldly, so handsome, and his passion for her had been too enticing to resist. Remembering their covert messages still gave her a small thrill, and their stolen moments together were memories so achingly precious. Yet for all that, they had been moments only, minutes of whispered conversations, snatched kisses and promises of a love that could never be. No more. Over the years her heartbreak at his exile had been replaced by a recognition of their affair for what it was, but still he held a place in her heart, a place that she kept secret and safe, locked away from the cruelties of her world.

But now, now that she had seen him again, all the passion of that childish infatuation had come flooding back, tempered this time with the knowledge that, fond though she was of him, this time he was a lifeline. Not for her, but for her child.

When she felt calmer, Shakumi peered through the gap in the curtains. Kinseris was still speaking with Vasa, his face grave and serious and his words spoken too softly for her to hear. So grim he had become in the years that had separated them. She watched him defer to his high priest with all the proper courtesies and wondered whether he realised the distaste on his face shouted his treachery to the world.

In that moment, Shakumi made her decision. She could not rely on any lingering affection he might have for her after two decades and more, nor could she expect him to be moved by the plight of her child. But there was one other weapon she might use to sway him, one secret she had learned through her years of bitter service dreadful enough to make him break once and for all from the Order he so clearly despised.

It was some hours later when she presented herself at the door of his chambers. She had gone over and over what she would say to him, every argument prepared and ready, but as soon as he looked at her she knew she would never need them. If she had not truly loved him before, the agony of confused compassion and regret that filled his eyes won her over in an instant. She knew at once that he had never stopped loving her, and if the years had been hard for her, they had been harder for him.

The words she had ready were meaningless now. As he pulled her inside, his hand locked around her arm, she felt a flutter deep in her belly. Then the memory of the task she had been sent to perform brought her back to the present, and determination replaced the torrent of emotion.

It was not until Shakumi found him that Kinseris remembered his high priest's charge to inform her of her night's freedom. The knock at his chambers caught him unprepared. Expecting a servant bringing linen, he flung open the door impatiently, barely glancing at the woman who waited there.

'You were sent to find me,' a lilting voice called, arresting his attention. 'Am I so easily forgotten?'

Kinseris snapped around to face her as if slapped. The draft from the open doorway wafted her intoxicating scent into the room.

'Shakumi.' He stopped, words failing him. With a thrill of alarm he realised that the high priest's most jealously guarded concubine, the woman known to be the reason for his fall from grace, was standing in the entrance to his chambers, oblivious to the stares of the palace staff. Acting on instinct he grabbed her by the elbow, drawing her through the doorway, and slammed the bolt home behind her.

Raking agitated fingers through his hair, Kinseris regarded the silk-clad apparition with mounting anxiety. He had recognised Vasa's parting instructions as one more trap and he had been determined to spare them both. But now she was here, alone with him, and if the trap had been sprung, he could not find it in himself to care.

Shakumi waited calmly for him to regain command of himself. He could not speak, so he just gazed at her, drinking in the beauty and mystery of her eyes, and imagining the face hidden by silks. More than twenty years it had been and still she was beautiful, yet the changes of the years were on her, and more than just years. He saw Darred's taunts of children were true. Her body was no longer the lithe and slender figure of a girl but the soft, round curves of a woman who has given birth to new life. And her eyes held a sorrow that went deeper than any man could ever know.

Shakumi stepped forward, brushing her fingertips across his arm. 'When you did not come to me, I had to come to you.'

The sound of her voice startled him. He drew his eyes back to her face, seeing in hers the glimmer of a smile. He realised for the first time how little he really knew her.

When he still did not reply, she slid delicate fingers under the folds of her veil to unfasten the skein of silk. Revealed at last, possessed of a beauty to arrest thought, her dark eyes locked on his, stripping him defenceless in an instant.

Embarrassed, Kinseris tore his gaze away, aware his regard skirted the edges of decency, and found his voice at last. 'Shakumi, lady, why are you here?'

She smiled. If he had thought her beautiful before, the light that came into her eyes showed him how little he knew of beauty. 'Do you wish me gone?'

'No,' he replied, a shade too quickly. Though it might be wise, that was the last thing he wanted. He longed to give into this vision, this dream, to forget

Vasa and his scheming, and believe that she was here for him. But he knew better than that. And suddenly he was overcome with shame, for he had left her here, and if she had turned against him, he could not blame her.

'Shakumi, I —' What could he say? How could he explain that he had chosen his career, his life, over her?

'Hush,' she whispered, placing a finger on his lips. 'You owe me no apologies, Kinseris. We both knew what we did, and what the consequences would be. If you are guilty, so am I. More so than you know.' A spasm of pain crossed her face, and he knew she was thinking of her children, of the little ones who had suffered for her transgression. No apology would ever be enough for them.

'I should have done something,' he murmured, anguished. 'I should have stopped him —'

She smiled then, some of the pain leaving her face. 'There is still time.'

He caught the hand that reached to his face, pushing it gently aside. If he let her touch him again, he would be lost. 'Time for what?'

A shadow passed over her eyes at his rebuff, and she let her hand fall to her side. 'My master requires a service of me, one that I am loathe to fulfil.' she replied formally. 'Since his instructions touch on your life, I have brought my quandary to you.'

Kinseris froze. 'My life?' No need to belabour the obvious, that if she thought to entangle him in further disobedience to her master, both their lives were already forfeit. From the fingers that gripped too tightly in the folds of her gown to the stiffened poise of her carriage, she was the very image of beleaguered desperation.

Silently, she withdrew her hand from its death grip in her silks and held it open before him, a dipped knife nestling on her palm. Kinseris needed no explanation. The blade was poisoned, and it could have only one purpose.

His face a bloodless mask, he took a step back. He could not blame her. He had left her here. But the pain of this final and most tragic of betrayals stole the last of his strength. Groping fingers latched onto a chair and he collapsed with relief. He could not blame her.

'From you?' he asked quietly. 'Or from him?'

327

There was a sheen of tears in her eyes. 'Do you really need to ask?'

Scooting his chair back in sudden fury, Kinseris lurched away. He had left her here, but he had never stopped loving her. She knew that, and she had used it against him. 'I ask again, Shakumi, why are you here? You come seeking my help, yet you are armed with the means to end my life. Whatever your orders, as they touch on my life or my death, I have no choice but to resist. You must know that.'

She raised to him a face stripped of all pretence. 'I was a child when I fell in love with you, and as a woman I thought I had outgrown childish things. But I have not. As I love you, I could never take your life, no matter the cost. I come to you now for help, but I offer you mine also.'

Abruptly her rigid control seemed to crumble. Kinseris caught her as her legs gave way and supported her weight as she folded into the seat he had vacated. As he loved her, if Shakumi turned her hand against him, he could not harm her to save himself.

Gently taking her hand in his, he swept back a stray tangle of hair, tucking it behind an ear that sparkled with the light of tiny jewels. 'Lady,' he said solemnly, 'whatever my past actions towards you, if Vasa has called for my death, why should you risk your life to bring me warning?'

Lifting her chin, he caught his breath once more. He trailed a finger in light caress from her brow to her chin, savouring the feel of her skin. As a gesture of his regard it fell short, but the implicit compassion eased her incessant trembling. 'Tell me, what is it you fear that is worth such a risk?'

Shakumi did not speak. Instead she took his hand and guided it under the flowing silks so he could feel her gently swollen belly.

'He does not know yet,' she told him, as understanding dawned at last. 'But I think he suspects. He has not asked for me in his bed for several weeks. He does not like to be around me when I am carrying his child. But soon he will call for me and my body will reveal the truth of his suspicions. I cannot watch another child of mine die, Kinseris,' she whispered, pleading. 'He will not let me drink the loosening draught he gives the other women. He is still punishing me for –' She stopped, unable to finish that thought.

'For me?'

'For you, yes,' she answered, 'for more than you know. The first child was born not nine months after you were banished. She was a girl.'

Kinseris felt a chill squirm through him. He could hear Darred's voice, taunting him. *The first. Your daughter.*

'Vasa has never fathered a girl child,' Shakumi said sadly. 'Not with me, nor with any of his other women. He was convinced that she was yours, though I pleaded with him that it was not so, and he killed her. As he has killed all my children. Only this one can be saved.'

Kinseris closed his eyes. 'I should never have left you here.'

'What could you have done except die with her?'

'Then maybe I should have,' he shot back, angry at himself for all the things he had not done, at her for her calm acceptance, but most of all at Vasa. The blood of so many innocent lives was on his hands.

Shakumi shook her head. 'No, my love. You had to live.'

'Why?'

She smiled. 'So you could be here now, when we both have a chance.'

He turned away. Their love was as doomed now as it had ever been. If she sought to save that she was chasing an impossible dream. Yet she was not alone in harbouring impossible dreams. Every day for twenty years he had dreamed of Vasa's defeat, of his revenge against the man who had stolen her from him. She might have shared that dream, with far greater cause. He looked back. 'What do you know?'

'Enough. He thinks we have no ears, and that he does not need to guard his tongue when we are near. We fear him, so he need have no fear of us. What can we do?' She smiled bitterly. 'He knows he has Æisoul in his dungeons, just as he knows that you also know. Your hatred of him is no secret, Kinseris, neither is your alliance with the Golden Eagle. He toys with you. He toys with us all.'

Kinseris was glad he was already on his knees. Through a wave of dizziness he thought of the Ancai in Frankesh, and Aarin's companions he had promised to protect. If Vasa indeed knew everything, it was far too late for them.

'How?' he demanded. 'How can he know? And why has he not acted?'

Shakumi's face twisted with distaste. 'Because they counselled him otherwise.'

Kinseris felt a shiver run down his spine. Behind her disgust there was real, bone-deep fear. 'They?'

'I do not know who they are, or where they came from, but you must believe me. They are here.'

Kinseris gripped her arm. 'Shakumi, who are they?'

'Enemies.' She shrugged. 'My master believes they serve him, but he is a fool. They serve no one and they have him wrapped up so tight in their schemes that he no longer remembers his own.'

Kinseris felt the blood drain from his face. 'Do they know Aarin is here?'

'Of course they know. Kinseris, when will you understand? They know *everything*. They always did. Your treachery was never a secret you had a hope of keeping.'

He realised how foolish he had been. *He toys with you,* she had said, and he was filled with such rage and despair that he did not realise he was hurting her until she cried out. Then she was weeping, and he took her in his arms, forgetful of the knife hidden in her skirts. But the heat of her body pressed against his stirred his longing so strongly he almost pushed her away.

Warm questing lips, salty with tears, locked on his. He responded without thought, his own desire aroused too deeply to deny. He buried his face in her soft hair, her sweet scent filling his senses. His hand slipped beneath her silks and he felt her respond with breathless urgency. As desire finally eclipsed all reason, he swept her up in his arms and carried her to his bed.

FOURTEEN

HOURS LATER, THEIR passion spent, they lay in each other's arms. Throughout the night they had talked, and the time had nearly come for them to part. As he held her close, Kinseris turned over and over in his mind the secrets Shakumi had whispered to him before they slept and knew that a deadly game had become deadlier still.

Savouring these final moments, he watched the fall of moonlight caress her bare skin, then regretfully kissed her shoulder to bring her back to wakefulness. As she stirred, sighing contentedly in the first sweet moments of consciousness, he ran his fingers through the loosed fan of her hair.

'Kinseris?'

'I'm here,' he answered, a smile on his lips.

Her skin was flushed pink where her cheek had pressed against the pillow. 'Is it time?'

He nodded, drawing her into a last embrace, his lips lingering on hers. Then he let her go, pushing back the sheet and rising to his feet. Silently, he picked up her discarded silks and shook out the creases before helping her into them and fastening the hooks of her veil. As she smoothed the fabric over her hips, she smiled up at him.

'You look beautiful,' he said. 'Do you remember what you have to do?'

'Perfectly. You repeated it at least a dozen times.'

Kinseris laughed despite his fear. 'Your courage is dazzling, lady. I hope I can make you as proud.'

Shakumi stretched upwards and kissed him full on the lips. 'I know you will,' she whispered, her lips brushing his ear. 'Now I must go. Be careful, Kinseris. Vasa wants you dead.'

'How could I forget,' he answered, 'he sent such a beautiful assassin.'

She blushed, eyes averted. 'Expect the next to be more deadly. Whatever you do, wherever you go, he will never stop searching.' He could not tell whether she was speaking of him or of herself. For her, Vasa's vengeance would have no limits.

He gazed at her hungrily, wanting to imprint this vision of her in his mind forever. If his plan went awry, and he did not manage to meet her and take her to safety, he wanted this moment to be the one he remembered her by, standing tall in courageous, breath-taking loveliness. Then, as tears threatened, Kinseris shut his eyes tight. When he opened them again, she was gone.

'May Tesserion guard your steps in mercy, lady,' he whispered in ancient blessing. It was a cruel twist of fate that had shown him the prize he might have possessed only to take it from him in the same moment.

A sparkle of light on the bed caught his eye, one of Shakumi's tiny earrings entangled in the fine weave of the sheet. He fastened the stud in the cuff of his robes, then he forced Shakumi from his mind. There were still a few hours of darkness left, and he had plans of his own to make.

When Kinseris left his chambers some hours later, resplendent in his robes of office and sweating in the sweltering heat, the atmosphere in the palace seemed unnaturally calm set against his own fearful doubts. There was little point in subterfuge now that Vasa had moved against him so openly, yet his pretence at loyalty had to be maintained a while longer. Vasa would discover soon enough that Shakumi had either failed in her task or betrayed him, setting her at terrible risk. His only chance to buy her time was to brazen it out and sow as much confusion as possible over the events of the night.

And then there was Aarin.

No matter the cost, Kinseris knew he could not allow Vasa to discover the secrets he had been made party to by Shakumi, yet Aarin, for his own survival, needed to know the dangers that awaited him when he entered the Holy Chamber. Every instinct screamed that this meeting must not take place, but hemmed in on either side by Vasa's schemes and his own obligations to Shakumi, he could not act to free them from the swiftly closing net.

Shakumi. He wondered whether she had managed to slip out of the palace unrecognised, as she claimed she had done in the past. The address he had given her was a tavern in a poorer district of Kas'Tella and a safe haven for

Shrogar's messengers when they came to the city. The innkeeper and his wife would gladly take her in and see her safely out of the city if he did not manage to meet her there. If Vasa's spies did not find her first. He was taking a terrible risk to see her safe, and not only for himself. The chance could not be ignored that Shakumi might be the link that exposed Shrogar's network and strangled the fledgling resistance he had worked so hard to foster.

Before leaving his rooms, Kinseris had penned messages under his personal seal and despatched runners in haste to see them delivered. He had sent three copies, each one by a different route, the loyalty of the men who carried them beyond with question. He no longer doubted the truth Aarin had tried to tell him. Darred's involvement had already weighted the scales, but it was Shakumi who had offered up the final piece of the puzzle. Now fear made him play his hand, and so he sent to Shrogar a message he never thought he would send. And he prayed that now, as all the years of meticulous planning and carefully fostered loyalties came due, the trusts he had built through the decades of uneasy peace would hold during the trials ahead.

Abruptly he stopped. Ahead of him were the cells where Aarin was being held, but he already knew he was too late. He had hoped for a few minutes alone with the mage to deliver his warning, but it seemed that Vasa had moved up the audience. The bells were only now sounding for the start of the morning chapter and the pair of his high priest's personal guards waiting by the entrance were clearly part of an escort.

As he paused, frozen with indecision, one of the guards looked up and nudged his companion, and Kinseris knew it was too late to withdraw. He could only go on and attempt to bluff his way through the next few minutes. His freedom had only ever been temporary. Whatever happened here, Vasa would not let him leave Kas'Tella alive.

The guards parted silently to let Kinseris through, though their sideways glances belied their deference. Once inside he heard voices in the cells below and hurried down the steps as a gruff voice ordered Aarin to move.

'What's this?' asked another voice. Kinseris sighed in frustration as he heard the swish of heavy fabric. He had hoped to collect his cloak himself. Not that it mattered now, he thought ruefully.

'Where did you get this, boy?' growled the first voice. A silence followed, then the sickening sound of a fist hitting soft flesh.

'Answer the captain!'

Furious, Kinseris strode into the light of the guards' torches. 'The cloak is mine.'

His sudden appearance froze the scene into stillness. A huge, brute-ugly man released his grip on Aarin's shoulder, and the mage collapsed to the floor. Kinseris glanced at him briefly, his gaze scornful, before rounding on the captain. 'On whose orders do you presume to mistreat a prisoner of the high priest?'

But they had recognised him now and their fear had fled. In the face of their sneering contempt, Kinseris played the only card he had left. If they expected him to be dead, his presence here alive either pointed to a dramatic change of heart on Vasa's part, or the unthinkable failure of well-laid plans. Either way, they would be wise to obey his orders until the truth was discovered.

'You!' He pointed to man who had held Aarin. 'Clean him up. I will not have any man presented to the Holy One in such a state.'

When the guard did not move, Kinseris snapped. 'Now! You will do as I say, when I say, or I will see you flogged and dismissed from your rank!' With a confidence borne of decades of unquestioning obedience to his every command, he lowered his voice to a threatening whisper. 'If you believe you have reason to doubt my authority, you are a fool. As a member of this Order, never forget I have the power of life and death over your miserable head.'

A flicker of doubt crossed the guard's face and Kinseris gave him no time to think. 'Now,' he snapped again, before turning to the guard captain. He snatched his cloak from the man's grasp and swept it round his shoulders. 'The rest of you, wait outside. I need a moment with the prisoner.'

Aarin was on his feet now, staring at him in astonishment.

'Why are you still here?' Kinseris demanded of the guards.

The captain nodded at his two companions and they left. When Kinseris turned on him, the captain held his ground. 'My orders are to stay with the prisoner until we reach the Holy Chamber.'

'He's not going anywhere, you fool,' Kinseris growled, but his gambit had failed. The soldier knew the wards protected them. And given the nature of their prisoner, the guards would not return without reinforcements.

He risked a glance at Aarin, saw the mage leaning wearily against the wall. He was filthy and exhausted and in no kind of state to face what was coming. But there was no more Kinseris could do.

He gestured to the captain. 'Very well, take him.' But when he turned to leave, he found the two guards had not left at all. He glared at the captain. 'Tell your men to move aside.'

The man crossed his arms and did nothing. Kinseris turned to the men blocking his way. 'Move aside,' he repeated, his voice like ice.

Someone shouted down the stairs and suddenly the captain was at his elbow. 'I think you had better come with us, my lord,' he said mildly. He flicked his head in Aarin's direction and the two guards slipped past them to the mage as Kinseris found himself pressed to climb the stairs. He stifled the instinct to resist. Physical force would avail him nothing, and more soldiers waited above. As he allowed himself to be hustled up the stairs, they moved back to let him through before closing ranks again around the prisoner.

As he stepped through the ward spells, Kinseris instinctively started to draw power. Then he saw the four adepts waiting silently at the entrance to the watch room and let it dissipate. Behind him, he felt Aarin do the same, his magic flickering for an instant then dying away. Against four, acting together, they had no chance. And he felt the weariness of utter despair crash down on him then. Unable even to warn Aarin of his danger, his own freedom now surrendered, Kinseris realised all his plans had been in vain.

A flicker of power touched his mind. In startled fury, Kinseris instinctively sought to focus his defences against what he assumed was the summary execution of his high priest's will. Then another finger of raised power, feather-light, calmed his outraged senses. A voice shattered through his honed barriers and left him reeling.

I hear your warning.

Kinseris stumbled, his sudden movement bringing their startled escort to an abrupt halt.

'How…?' he began, his eyes searching for the owner of the voice. One of the priests reached out to restrain him, his gaze sharpening with suspicion. Then Kinseris's eyes met Aarin's and he knew without doubt who had spoken. Snatching himself away from the cleric's grasping hand, Kinseris soothed his ruffled composure and signalled that he was ready to continue. But the priests assigned to their escort were alerted to the focused energies, and he realised they had but seconds before their captors isolated the source and engaged their combined talents to stamp out the threat.

Without knowledge or training to guide him, Kinseris concentrated the full force of his will to frame his intent. *Can you hear me?*

I can.

The diamond-sharp clarity of the words cut through the confusion in his head, the discipline that framed them staggering in its potential.

How?

Such a thing should not have been possible. No, it was impossible.

Kinseris felt Aarin's silent amusement. *You should not be so surprised. You possess the magic of the dragons. Why should you not also be able to access their talents?*

On either side the adepts were becoming more and more agitated as they sought to identify the faint threads of power they could feel. Between them the two prisoners walked as though contained within a sphere of harmonious calm.

Kinseris grappled with the implications. *But you do not,* he pressed in anxious haste, aware that their time was running out. Before Aarin had time to reply, a ward spell snapped down and the connection died. Staggering to a halt, Kinseris felt a tingling backlash as the severed energies recoiled. Beside him Aarin's head whipped back as he suffered the exact same sensation.

One of the adepts swept back his hood and regarded them with pallid, cold eyes. He blinked slowly, his unnaturally thin eyelids reminding Kinseris unpleasantly of the *menetas* that basked in the sun in the grounds of the Frankesh chapter. The mage returned his stare, the corners of his mouth twitching in an insolent grin. Kinseris felt rather saw the flash of fury from the adept as he raised his hood and shrouded his face once more.

They walked on in silence, the only sound the swish of heavy robes on the marble floor. The invasive influence of the ward spell kept the prisoners in a permanent state of unease, and they were unable to sense the sudden shift in energies as they entered the hallway that marked the beginning of the high priest's personal domain. The combined efforts of the escorting adepts kept their trained awareness locked down between walls of impenetrable static.

As they entered the antechamber, Kinseris almost smiled as he observed Aarin's reaction to the huge doors to Vasa's sanctum. Just as he had, as a novice on the day of his ordination, Aarin stood before this grand entrance, struck dumb by the soaring majesty of the masterpiece of ebony and ivory. The effect was a stark, hypnotic beauty that ensnared a man's gaze until the act of tearing one's eyes away brought almost physical pain. Kinseris suspected that spells had been laced into the wood during the carving of the doors, and guessed they were the work of the same craftsmen who had raised the great citadel into being.

A sharp jab in his back wrested him from his musings. As he stumbled forward, he saw Aarin shrug off the steadying hand of the guards and draw himself stiffly erect, his face determined. Although familiar with the evil that resided behind such mesmerising beauty, Kinseris could not shake the terror that took hold as the doors swept open to reveal the Holy Chamber set up for formal audience.

The cushions were gone. On the central dais, flanked by black saplings in terracotta urns, the symbols of a high priest's powers of judgement, sat a plain, ebony throne. Generations of rulers had sat here dispensing justice, the seat of unadorned wood giving swift access to the powers of earth, the traditional wellspring of punitive forces. He knew then that he had been expected all along and his mouth went dry. If Vasa had anticipated his presence here, what did that mean for Shakumi?

And he understood at last what she had meant. *They know everything.*

FIFTEEN

AS SOON AS Aarin set foot in the inner chamber he felt the malevolence of the place seeping into him. It was as though the sun had disappeared behind thick clouds and plunged the room into semi-darkness, yet there were no windows here. The sanctum was hidden away in the heart of the palace complex. The guards did not pass through the great doors, and the black robed adepts melted into the shadows in the corners of the room, their watchful eyes never leaving their charges.

Kinseris had gone white. Aarin followed his gaze and saw a panel of wood behind the throne swing open. Two figures emerged. Heads bowed and dressed head to toe in black, the two men crossed the floor to stand at either side of the throne, the dark branches of the saplings disappearing against the midnight of their robes. A strange wailing rose on the air and Aarin looked around in alarm. They were singing, a low, strangled chant from the back of the throat, hypnotic and terrifying.

Aarin beat down a surge of panic, forcing himself to take calm, measured breaths. The adepts who had accompanied them from the cells joined in the chant, their voices overlaying the awful tone with a lament that jarred the senses and grated on the nerves.

'What is this?' he gasped, resisting the urge to cover his ears.

Kinseris fared no better, pale beneath his tan. 'It is the Traitor's Song.'

A new figure had entered the room and was standing behind the ebony throne, a smile on his face as thought the obscene song was pleasing to him. In no apparent haste, he crossed the marble floor and seated himself in the waiting chair. The singing stopped, the last notes dying away in a reluctant wail.

This had to be Vasa, Aarin reasoned, remembering Kinseris's warning not to be fooled by his appearance. He studied the high priest, not liking what he saw. Like Kinseris, his hair and skin were a dusky brown, but there the similarities ended. Vasa's bloated form was clothed in robes of deep purple, embroidered with gold and pearls about the cuffs and the hem. His fingers were weighed down by rings, and heavy chains of silver and gold hung about his neck. His eyes were small and suspicious and full lips twitched beneath a thin moustache. But his eyes had a spark in their black depths that told Aarin Kinseris's warning was justified. The very innoxiousness of his façade spoke to the depths of his subterfuge.

An invasive force reached out, probing at him, and Aarin reacted on instinct—and was stopped dead by the adepts. A wave of power whipped into him, ice cold, seeming to bore into his very bones. Gasping at the chill, he attempted to gauge the nature of the attack, but the adepts held him under tight rein.

As quickly as it had come, the feeling was gone. He could feel remnants within him still, as though someone had somehow woven a spell into his very being, but for what purpose he could not guess. Kinseris was staring at him, a question in his eyes. Clearly, he had not been subjected to the same force.

Aarin returned his gaze to the dais and found Vasa was also watching him. He found himself caught, pinned by the intensity of the man's regard.

'So,' Vasa drawled, speaking as Kinseris had done in heavily accented Amadorian, 'we meet at last, mage. What an uproar your arrival has created in some quarters. So much excitement! You must understand, therefore, what a great disappointment it is to find you are already involved with certain traitorous factions.' He glanced meaningfully at Kinseris. 'And I had such hopes for us.' He sighed, shaking his head in mock distress.

Aarin said nothing.

'Of course,' he suggested silkily, 'you may have been deceived. You may not have full understanding of what you are entangled in. Your companion here is clever, a master criminal, and a traitor to his people. I have been watching him for several years now, allowing him to believe he operated in secret. Just this morning the last piece of evidence was delivered to me by a faithful servant.'

Vasa's eyes travelled to Kinseris. 'Did you think I would be surprised to see you, Vela'Frankesh?' he mocked, his voice honey-sweet. 'Surely you did not believe that Shakumi would betray me, not again? Did you think she loved you, that she would risk her life for you? Ah, but so many men have fallen for her charms, incapable of reason when confronted with her beauty. You are not the first, nor shall you be the last, to be delivered to me this way.'

Kinseris's face contorted with rage and Aarin prayed that the priest could maintain his composure, sure that Vasa's needling was designed to provoke an outburst he would be compelled to punish.

'She told me everything, Kinseris,' the fat man taunted. 'All the secrets you whispered to her in the darkness of the night while you grunted and groaned all over her.'

Something inside his victim seemed to snap in that moment. For a second Aarin thought the priest would launch himself at his tormentor, but Kinseris did not move. 'Bring her out,' he grated. 'If you have Shakumi, let her speak for herself!'

'So you can face you accuser?' Vasa asked, amused. 'I think not. As your guilt is proven, what need is there for us to trudge through the evidence?'

The two men glared at each other, facing off like two dogs poised to attack, and for the moment Aarin was forgotten. The antagonism between the pair was deeply personal, one that had no intended place in this interview, and the woman, Shakumi, was at the heart of it.

The hostile silence dragged on. 'For what are we on trial?' Aarin asked loudly, his voice slicing through the tension.

'This is no trial,' growled Kinseris, his eyes fixed on his superior. 'There will be no hearing here today. He prepares to pass sentence and do not think anything you can say can affect the outcome. Always has this man acted as he wished with no regard for law or justice.'

'And you, I suppose, are the paragon of a law-abiding citizen?' Vasa sneered. 'You have been scheming in secret against your brothers, your own people, for decades. What regard have you for the laws of this land?'

Kinseris laughed bitterly. 'If the laws were just, Holy One, and your rule truly had divine sanction, I would never have acted as I have. But your regime is oppressive, and your justification non-existent. If I do not stand up for the people of this land, who will defend them from your evil?'

Aarin recalled the words spoken in hope long days ago in Frankesh. *The time has come to act, and I can keep up this charade no longer. I speak truly when I say I will relish the chance to act in accordance with my conscience.*

And now it seemed he had his wish. But at what price, Aarin thought bitterly as he stood helplessly by, for it seemed impossible that Vasa would allow his prize to leave this place alive. The depth of his hatred was clear for all to see, blazing from his eyes as he looked upon his traitor.

'So you would condemn our people to a resurgence of the madness?' he demanded now. 'Bring back those creatures of darkness who nearly destroyed our world and accord to them the allegiance you owe to me?'

Kinseris shook his head. 'You know as well as I that our Order is founded on false grounds,' he accused wearily. 'Why do you still hide behind the repetition of fictitious doctrine? Can you not admit your own deception even in your moment of victory?'

But Vasa chose not to answer him, turning his attention to Aarin.

'Do you deny that you are seeking to return the dragons to their ancient power, and overthrow the rule of the Kas'Talani?'

Unnerved by the sudden switch, Aarin said nothing. Kinseris's warning had been clear. And the desperate turmoil Aarin had sensed outside the jail had been specific enough, in its way. Though he could see little to be gained by his silence now.

'You will not speak?' The cleric leaned back in his chair, one black eyebrow sardonically raised. 'Perhaps you think I am stupid, and if you do not confess to your crime, I will simply release you? Or maybe you think only to leave the conversation to your elders, and perhaps you should. An untrained child such as yourself should not be meddling in the affairs of men.'

Aarin recognised the taunt for what it was but even so could not quite suppress a flash of anger.

'You do not like being called a child?'

The smirk that spread across the fat, dissolute face was cruelly offensive. A pulse of energy shot outwards from the throne. It caught Aarin full force and flung him into the wall like a rag doll. He crumpled to the floor, winded, shocked by an attack he could not feel.

Vasa stood, a squat, ungainly figure on the grand platform. He looked down at Aarin as he staggered to his feet. 'Only a child among us could be taken in by such a trick,' he sneered.

Aarin stared stonily back, his chest heaving as he sucked great gulps of air into his starved lungs. Kinseris looked on in disquiet.

'Perhaps we should try again,' Vasa suggested. 'I should give you another chance to prove yourself.'

And Aarin once more found himself flung against the wall, and this time he was pinned there, dangling six feet above the ground, his face forced into the cold stone. It was only then that he realised that the power of the adepts no longer bound him. But the energies Vasa directed at him were like those Kinseris had employed to guard his study in Frankesh, and they slipped through his grasp even as he reached for them.

'What do you want from me?' he demanded helplessly as Vasa advanced across the room.

As Aarin was hurled the second time against the stone, Kinseris reacted instinctively, but at once he felt the presence of Vasa's shrouded acolytes close in behind him, prepared to intervene if he attempted to interfere.

He could scarcely believe what he was seeing. Vasa was testing Aarin, and in a manner that had been outlawed for centuries. Instead of the ordered, controlled linking with an elder of the priesthood, children had once been exposed to the raw power of the elements turned against them. To survive they had to find some resource within themselves to harness that power before it destroyed them. But these were the Lost Elements Vasa used now, and where the children at least had had a chance, Aarin had none.

Vasa descended the steps, enjoying the scene immensely. 'So, you can speak?' he taunted. 'But still you won't try.'

He glanced thoughtfully at Kinseris. Then he smiled, as though taken by a pleasing thought. A flick of a fat hand twisted the mage's head so he could see straight in front of him.

'You do not look like much,' he remarked. 'But I have this gift. I can sense the danger in a man. There is a threat in you, a hidden strength. One you do not yet know is there. Maybe you simply need encouragement. Perhaps if we were to threaten harm to one you cared about…?'

Aarin looked at Kinseris with alarm, but the priest shook his head.

'I see,' Vasa pondered, following the exchange. 'Not our good friend Kinseris then. Well, I have other plans for him anyway.' He smiled wickedly. 'What about the girl? The pretty one, with those enchanting curls? I forget her name. She did tell me.'

Aarin's face twisted with rage and Vasa laughed. 'Yes, I think so.' He turned to one of his attendants and clapped his hands. 'Fetch the girl. Quickly. And clean her up. When we are finished here, I have another use for her.'

'Aarin! No!' Kinseris took one look at Aarin and surged forward, heedless of the guard at his back. Instantly, he was restrained. 'He's lying!'

But it was too late. Enraged beyond reason by the threat to Jeta, the mage smashed through the barrier and lashed out at Vasa with lethal force, turning his own magic against him. The shockwave spread outwards, knocking Kinseris and his guards to the floor, and the pulse of white-hot energy shot towards Vasa.

Then everything seemed to happen at once. As Aarin fell to the ground, released by the force that imprisoned him, a bolt of light exploded from above and caught him in its path. Even as the spell he had cast should have disintegrated Vasa where he stood, its energies dissipated harmlessly, and the high priest stood untouched in the path of destruction.

From the floor where he had fallen, Kinseris watched in disbelief as Aarin, trapped and suspended in the beam of light, threw his head back and screamed. Even Vasa's mouth hung slackly open, as though he too could not believe what had happened.

Kinseris scrambled to his feet. 'Release him! You have had your fun. Let him go before you kill him!'

Then he became aware of another he had not noticed before, who stood silent and unmoving behind the ebony throne. A frown rippled across Vasa's brow as he too became aware of the new presence in the room.

'I had not yet called for you, Saal'an,' the high priest complained, his eyes still trained on the scene in front of him.

The black clad man made no response. He seemed to glide across the room to stand at Vasa's elbow. Pushing back his hood to reveal pale eyes in a wasted face, he trained his hungry gaze on the mage imprisoned in the bolt of shimmering energy.

Kinseris paled, appalled at what he was seeing. Nightmare made flesh. The abhorrence that assailed him in this creature's presence, for he was certain this was no man who stood before him, was like nothing he had ever experienced. And he knew, without doubt, that before him stood a thing from legend, as Shakumi had warned him.

Saal'an raised his hand towards Aarin, and the mage's head came down as though dragged by a heavy weight until his gaze rested on the wielder of the force that compelled him. His face was still twisted in pain, but he did not cry out, instead his eyes creased in horror and he tried to turn his head away, to close his eyes and block out the sight. Something that he could see that Kinseris could not induced in him a terror so great that a kind of madness came upon him and he trembled in the grip of the magic.

'He sees me.' The cloaked figure seemed pleased by his response. He let his hand fall, the light vanished, and Aarin crashed to the floor, his body limp and still. Kinseris crawled to him, frantically searching for a sign of life. Aarin's eyes were open and staring, and when Kinseris laid his hand on his face and felt cold skin, devoid of the feverish burning, he nearly panicked. Then he felt the slow rise and fall of the mage's chest and as gently as he could he closed the tortured eyes.

'Who are you?' he demanded, turning to the creature next to Vasa. 'What have you done?'

Saal'an ignored him, staring at Aarin. Kinseris sprang forward, determined to be answered.

The creature turned. 'You,' he spat, pointing at Kinseris. 'You will speak no more today.'

And Kinseris stopped short, caught in mid-step, and found he could not speak. He stood helpless as Saal'an turned to Vasa.

'You have done well, Chandra Vasa. This is the one I seek. It is good that you did not try to claim him for yourself. Take them away.' He ordered the silent adepts, as Vasa's face purpled in outrage. 'I will come for him later.'

'Stop!' The adepts looked uncertainly at Saal'an as the high priest rounded on him in fury. 'I rule here, Saal'an,' he growled. 'These are prisoners of my Order, and I decide what is to be done with them. Not you!'

'This one is mine,' the creature repeated. 'That is the bargain we made. As for the other, I care not for him. You may do as you wish. I know you have a score you would like to settle.' His voice was thick with sarcasm. 'Do not try to cross me, Chandra Vasa, I have warned you before. The consequences will not be to your liking.'

The words were heavy with threat and Kinseris saw Vasa pale. He managed to hold the creature's stare for a moment more before backing down.

At Vasa's surrender, the creature turned back to the hovering priests. He nodded briefly, and they lifted Aarin from the ground. The threads of energy holding Kinseris fell away, and he stumbled forward to fall at Vasa's feet. The hated face was as pale and fearful as his own.

'What have you done?' he whispered sorrowfully as he stood.

Vasa met his eyes for an instant. 'I don't know,' he replied and walked away, leaving Kinseris to stare after him. A hand brushed his arm and he turned, surrendering himself to the waiting guards. Whatever fate awaited them now he could not fight it with force. The enemy, as Shakumi had warned him, was far more powerful than he had ever imagined, and far more terrible than his worst nightmares.

The chamber was deep beneath the citadel. Like all the important rooms of the Kas'Talani it had five corners. In each burned a candle, but the tiny flames were not sufficient to shed light on the centre of the stone floor.

Aarin lay in almost total darkness, secured to the floor by chain manacles. The room was cold, very cold, and the flagstones beneath him were damp and chilled. But he noticed none of this, still trapped in the trance he had fallen into in Vasa's chambers, his eyes staring at nothing.

Saal'an watched him with hungry eyes. He drifted closer, savouring the moment, until he stood by the mage's head. Not even the slightest movement indicated that his presence was detected. Aarin's unfocused gaze was directed at the ceiling, a trace of fear in his unblinking eyes.

'I have been waiting a long time for you, Æisoul,' he whispered. 'My people have been waiting a long time for you to free us.' One hand reached out to touch Aarin's face in an obscene caress. 'Our time has come, and yours will never see the light of day. How will it feel when you discover your own treachery? The tracer spell is already within you, and soon I will be also, to master your thoughts, your actions. You will lead us to the dragons, reopen the well of our power, and return to us the world as it should be.'

There was no reaction from Aarin. He could neither see nor hear his tormentor as Saal'an walked around him.

'You are blind yet, Æisoul. Oh, I saw your display for Vasa. Very impressive for an *untrained child*. But you do not know how you did it, do you? No one else could have triggered my spell yet still you remain blind. I need you to see more clearly. I do not have time for you to find your own way, and I cannot risk that you might die before you get there.'

Saal'an's face twisted into a sneer. 'So weak, so frail, your lives are nothing when set against ours. The might of the ancients disappeared from your race generations ago, and with it the only hope you ever had of restoring the old ways. Your kind are weak, Æisoul. They chose long ago not to accept what must be, and now their feeble plan will fail, just as they failed when they tried to fight us. We survived, Æisoul,' he crooned, triumphant. 'They tried to destroy us, but we survived. Maybe not as our true selves, but we survived. Survived and grew stronger, biding our time, waiting for you.'

He crouched down and took Aarin's head in his clawed hands, sending his awareness slithering into the mage's unprotected mind. 'Now experience the flowering of your power as you have never known it. Taste the glory of the magic you will never know as your own. When the time comes you must be ready, for we cannot wait much longer.'

But in the moment of his triumph, and almost too late to stave off disaster, Saal'an encountered something he had not expected. Something that fought against his efforts to impose his will. Pulling desperately back, he explored the anomaly, finding the threads of another's poorly woven conjury that overlaid and augmented the mage's own desires. Biting back a scream of frustration, Saal'an probed deeper still, finding the resonance of the bound oath given to Vianor months ago that tied Æisoul to death rather than allow his purpose to be turned against the calling of prophecy.

The Arkni rocked back on his heels, stunned by the galling realisation that an oath enacted by an Amadorian magician concerned only with his own survival *did* hold the power to subvert his plans and steal Æisoul's life if Saal'an attempted to bind him to his will. He could not disturb that binding without peril to himself or his victim, any effort to undo what had been freely pledged setting his own schemes into irrevocable jeopardy. It left him with no option but to let Æisoul go to answer the prophecy's desperate summons, then reel him in on the strings of his own free choice and try to snatch victory in the moment he brought the prophecy to fruition.

Saal'an restrained his first impulse to punish, biting back his seething frustration. Once more, he entered the mind held captive before him, picking his way with care around the magician's spell. There was still a chance he could turn this to his advantage. Æisoul's razor-sharp awareness of Andeira's plight made him vulnerable, for it spurred him to ignore all prudent limits in his pursuit of his dream. The Arkni's meddling had already opened the path to his dormant elemental mastery. He need only breathe life into those channels to add unbearable pressure to the man's natural impulse.

Saal'an felt the dragon-fire flare up in answer to his skilled touch. The heat would soon begin to devour the mage from within, blinding him to all else. He twisted the threads of an already well-honed desperation and set his instrument firmly on a path he would be unable to back away from. And the Arkni would be carried along in his wake to their long-awaited triumph.

SIXTEEN

IN THE DARKNESS of another cell Aarin finally stirred. Kinseris was by his side, watching him anxiously.

'Are you hurt?'

Aarin pushed himself upright cautiously. He patted himself up and down and found no hurt more serious than a bruise, and of those he had plenty.

'Should I be?'

Kinseris cocked an eyebrow and even in the dim light Aarin could make out his puzzled expression.

'You've been gone for hours. You don't remember?'

He shook his head. 'What happened?'

The priest sighed. 'I was hoping you could tell me. You truly don't remember?'

'Perhaps if you told me what happened, I might remember,' Aarin suggested testily. A headache was forming behind his eyes and he was painfully aware that Kinseris's presence in the cells was a disaster for both of them. 'The last thing I remember was the two of you arguing like children, but nothing further. Apart from that awful noise.' He shuddered involuntarily at the memory.

Kinseris cursed under his breath and Aarin sensed his rising panic. He seemed to realise how he sounded. 'It's this place. I can't settle. These wards, they're... something, I don't know, malignant, merciless.' He drew his knees up to his chest. 'I don't know how you lasted in here. Already I can feel my mind rebelling.'

The mage studied his face. The confidence he had worn like a mask was stripped away, and the man before him was almost unrecognisable in his exposed vulnerability.

'Who is she?' he asked.

Kinseris's head jerked up. For a moment Aarin saw an anger so intense it frightened him. Then the priest looked away, keeping the pain to himself.

'Shakumi is Vasa's concubine,' he replied quietly. 'I... When I said I was banished to Frankesh for a foolish prank I was not quite truthful. Foolish yes, but it was no prank. I fell in love with her, and I tried –' He broke off. What use were those memories here?

Aarin winced. He could guess the rest. What surprised him was that Vasa should choose exile over execution. It led to an uncomfortable thought. 'Do you believe she betrayed you?'

Kinseris shrugged. 'I don't know. Certainly, I wronged her enough. I abandoned her, left her to him. And he punished her, over and over, for what I did. If she has betrayed me, how can I blame her?' He sighed. 'But I don't want to believe it. She has too much to lose.'

Aarin nodded. There was nothing he could say, and it made no difference why they were here. He watched Kinseris from the corner of his eye, his shoulders hunched in private sorrow, and imagined how he would feel if Jeta was in Vasa's power. Broken, like Kinseris seemed now. And just as angry.

It was not until Kinseris shivered, cold without his official robes, that he realised the invasive, chilling magic that had so disturbed his last period of imprisonment had faded to a background irritation. The discovery caused him no little unease, as the same could not be said of the priest who slumped in the corner, his arms clasped protectively about his chest. It could not be a change in the wards then. It had to be a difference within him, and only him. Something had occurred between the time they had arrived at the high priest's chamber and finding himself back here that had caused a dramatic shift in his grasp of his powers. Not knowing what it could be, he feared that the magic bothered him less because his own was somehow diminished.

He moved beside Kinseris, resting his back against the wall and closing his eyes. At least now he knew he could sleep if he wished and was sorely tempted to let go and drift off.

'You cannot fight it,' he said quietly. 'I tried, and I suffered for it. The more you resist, the harder it pushes back.'

Breathing deeply, Kinseris nodded. 'I know, but it is an awful feeling. I have never felt so helpless.'

Aarin snorted with laughter. 'I can't remember the last time I felt in control.'

The priest's answering smile was tight. 'It's not about to get any better. I can guess what it was you saw today, but I had hoped you would remember so you could tell me it is not true.' He paused. 'Yesterday Shakumi came to me with a warning, and I cannot disregard it. I have now seen for myself the truth of her words.'

Aarin remembered the desperate warning he had felt outside the cells and guessed he was about to hear its source.

Kinseris was clearly reluctant to speak of it, whatever it was, and it was some time before he said, 'There are many legends about the origins of the Kas'Talani. They are useful, of course, especially those that speak of the foundation of the Order and its power. Those legends name a man called Kasandar as our founder. He is said to have preached against the evil of the dragons, and it is taught that long ago an attempt was made to manipulate the magic between the races and turn it from its true purpose. Kasandar held the dragons responsible, though it seems to me, as I have studied mankind's history since the Lost Years, that something such as this would be well within our scope.'

Kinseris fell silent and Aarin waited patiently for him to continue. As a boy he had been taught that a Great Betrayal had led to the loss of the link, but the knowledge of the old men of Luen went no further. The legends of the Kas'Talani might yield the answers he had been seeking all his life, but they would be answers he did not know if he could trust. Luen laid the catastrophe at the feet of mankind, whereas Aarin was beginning to realise that the learned in Caledan always held the dragons responsible.

'Not all legends come from the Kas'Talani,' Kinseris said eventually. 'There are some myths that the people know, stories told to frighten children, that speak of a new race born from the failed attempt. A race of creatures that somehow survived the ending of the magic. Nothing good is said of them.'

The priest hugged his knees to his chest. 'I had always believed them to be no more than children's tales but now I have seen with my own eyes that they are real.'

The words woke an ugly memory. 'Today? In Vasa's chambers?'

Half-recalled snatches of memory started to come together. Feeling suddenly sick, Aarin turned away. He remembered Vasa's threats and Kinseris's shouted denial. He remembered lashing out in fury, freeing himself from Vasa's magic, and then… Then he remembered his world exploding in pain as he was trapped by another's will, by a power so vast and terrifying that he was helpless before it. After that there was nothing, a blankness that was utterly complete but for the fact that he had returned here in some way *different*.

Aarin focused his whole attention inward and found he could access the deep core of his talent when before, in this place, it had been closed to him. Pushing aside that puzzle for the moment, he examined the veins of power that ran through his being, searching for the key that would unlock his memory.

The ward spells were forgotten as barrier after barrier fell before his persistent probing. Where before the lack of the link had made the channels of the Lost Elements inaccessible to him, now he could pick his way effortlessly. He wasted no time on shocked exclamation. Instead, he plunged straight into the mystery, revelling in the knowledge that unrealised perfection still existed within him, and relieved beyond measure that if the dragons were ever found, mankind retained the means to Join with them. The channels were dry, like parched and cracked riverbeds, but they were there, and they were intact, and he could see them as he had never been able to see them before. The recognition brought tears to his eyes even as his understanding of the cause profoundly disturbed him. It was a gift greater than anything in the world, but it was the gift of a creature who intended his death.

For as he pressed, the memories came tumbling free. He ran the sequence over and over, a part of his mind watching in detached analysis as the forgotten scenes played out, and the mystery of his mastery became no mystery at all. He felt again as Saal'an tore apart the veils in his mind, those veils that protected him from the knowledge he was not yet ready for, and revealed the innate understanding of the magic that all his kind had at one time possessed. He could feel the touch of a creature so wrong, so full of hate, that even as he rejoiced, he quailed.

Aarin withdrew reluctantly. Much as he longed to explore his new-found talent, the source of that same talent sickened and terrified him—the gift of a giver who would always be an enemy. An image of Darred filled his mind, reciting the prophecy that had trapped him in this path. These were the creatures to whom the renegade priest had given his allegiance, and he had done so willingly, knowingly. And yet... 'He has given me a key,' he murmured, still unable to believe it.

Kinseris looked troubled. 'That creature helped you?'

Aarin shook his head. 'He is not helping me, he is helping himself, but he is greedy and impatient, they all are.'

'They?'

'His kind. You were right.' He spoke slowly, letting his thoughts find their own way. 'I don't know what they are, how they are, but somehow they are remnants from the old time, from *before*. And they are wrong, so wrong.' He shuddered at the touch of memory. 'Somehow, we are working towards the same end, only they won't stop there. It is hard to put into words, but they want what they were becoming before the end came.'

'What they were becoming?'

Aarin shook his head, frustrated, the snatched impressions of the creature's mind sketching vague ideas but little substance. He stared into the distance, trying to recall the feelings, the images, he had experienced. 'I cannot tell you what they are, only what they want. And what they have given me. It makes no sense. I have the knowledge, but not the means. Without your help, without –'

A flash of silver caught his eye and he stopped, staring at the priest, wide-eyed with surprise.

Kinseris watched him, alarmed. 'What?'

For an answer, Aarin leant forward and flicked back his tunic, revealing the silver dragon device still pinned there. 'They left you that,' he asked incredulously, 'but they took your robes?'

Kinseris smiled wryly. 'Arrogance and tradition, the two greatest strengths and failings of my Order. I have been stripped of my robes of office to signify that I have been condemned as a traitor, but this,' he closed his hand over the tiny dragon, 'this is not removed until the day of my execution. It is meant to be symbolic. The passing of my powers precedes the passing of my life. It is also arrogance. Vasa does not believe that even with this in my possession I can escape from this place. And he is right.'

'He is wrong,' Aarin said firmly, 'and he has made a stupid mistake. With this you and I can channel the necessary elemental variations to undo these wards.'

'We can?'

Aarin nodded, already working on the problem. 'It will take time,' he murmured, 'perhaps even days.'

Kinseris leant back, left far behind. 'Should we be taking this chance?' he asked, cautious of what he could not understand. 'Should we risk doing exactly what our enemy wants?'

Eyes closed as he navigated the complex ward spells, Aarin said, 'We don't have a choice. We may not get another chance and this whole thing could come to an end on the executioner's platform. That is not a risk I am prepared to take.'

'I have sent messages to Ephenor, to Shrogar. If he can, he will come.'

'With the strength to penetrate the city walls and snatch us from these cells? He must be a powerful ally indeed.'

The priest sighed. 'No, probably not. But he will try. We are not yet hopeless.'

'But we are not free,' Aarin pointed out. 'And to accomplish our task we must be free. Better that we free ourselves than risk other lives in such an effort. And things are never hopeless, not while we still live.'

Kinseris looked unconvinced. 'I sent word to Frankesh. If your friends are still alive, my men will have taken them to Ephenor. I think they will come for you anyway, whether you want them to or not.'

Aarin could not hide his relief. 'Thank you.' Knowing Kallis and Jeta had a chance eased the burden he had carried ever since their separation in Frankesh.

He eased his back against the wall, overcome with exhaustion. Suddenly the lure of sleep was impossible to resist, and his eyelids drooped.

Kinseris gaped at him. 'What are you doing?'

'Sleeping,' Aarin murmured. 'Do you know how long it is since I last did that?'

'You can't sleep,' the priest insisted desperately.

But Aarin could not summon the energy to reply and before Kinseris could protest again, he was asleep.

'They will be allowed to escape.'

'They will not!' Vasa rose from his chair in anger. Saal'an stood before him in his private chambers, uninvited, and the high priest was feeling the cracks in his authority very keenly.

'They will be allowed to escape,' Saal'an repeated as though he had not spoken.

Vasa curled his fists in impotent fury. If he had been forced to admit that he had lost the mage, he was not going to give up the traitor. His anger at Kinseris had festered inside him like a sore, until desire for revenge burned hot enough to eclipse even his frustration over Saa'lan's interference. Let him have the mage for now. He would die either way. But the traitor was his.

'They will not,' he said coldly. 'No one escapes. No one. And especially not these two. Keep the mage if you want him so badly, but keep him here, and do not presume to tell me what to do with my prisoner.'

'Do not deceive yourself,' the Arkni hissed. 'I am not asking you. In two days they will be presented with an opportunity to escape and they will take it, even if they suspect my hand pulling the strings.'

Vasa's eyes narrowed at the creature's insolence. 'You are very sure you know what they will do. What if they refuse to co-operate?'

'They will go,' Saal'an replied. 'They have no choice. Neither do you.'

Vasa heard and understood the unsubtle threat and knew real fear. Decades ago, when the Arkni had first made themselves known to him, they had come as shadows, half-men, in grovelling supplication to a greater power. His power. It had been easy to strike the bargain that had seemed so heavily weighted in his favour, and based, he had thought, on their mutual survival. The man prophesised to reunite the races must not be allowed to succeed to his destiny or both the Kas'Talani and the Arkni would be destroyed.

But Vasa was beginning to suspect he had been duped all those years ago. In exchange for the power of the Arkni bolstering his authority and extending his life, Vasa had allowed them onto his council and into his confidence. Together, in the years that followed, they had begun their careful plan to conquer the northern continent from which they believed Æisoul would come. Together they had searched for this man, seeking the threads of the ancient bloodlines that would lead them to him. And in all that time, Vasa had believed, their efforts had been met with failure.

He knew now that was not so. In the years before Æisoul's arrival, Saal'an had become more and more difficult to control, and Vasa had often found himself forced to capitulate to the demands of creatures he considered his servants. He had wondered at their growing restlessness, their desperation, and he realised now that the Arkni had found what they were looking for long before the man arrived in Caledan. That it had been kept from him no longer surprised him, for he finally understood that Saal'an's actions had always been his own. But the Arkni had let Æisoul live, and he could see only one reason—they intended to use Æisoul to bring down his priesthood and rule in its stead.

Only now did Vasa see the jaws of the trap springing shut around him, with no weapon to fight back but his wits. His dependence on the Arkni for his very survival was the payoff for his extended life. Saal'an held his life in his hands, the ultimate bargaining chip against a man like Vasa whose sole motivation was gaining power for himself and for whom death was the greatest and most feared enemy.

Long ago he had greedily accepted the germ of his own downfall when he had permitted the creatures to intertwine the threads of their magic with his own to stave off the spectre of death long after his natural time. But he had realised it too late. It was time, Vasa accepted, to beat a cautious retreat. He would yield to Saal'an's request, but he would not surrender. It was time for a new bargain, and one better suited to his interests.

'Why wait two days?' Before he could move against the Arkni he needed to marshal his resources, and the most valuable weapon he could possess was knowledge.

Saal'an inclined his head, a hint of amusement in his manner, and Vasa knew a moment of horrid doubt. Were his own thoughts even secret? He felt like a rabbit cowering before a hawk.

'Two days and they will be exhausted and desperate,' the creature told him. 'I must give them a lead, but not so much of a lead that they have time to act before we are ready.'

Vasa heard the 'we' but was no longer sure whether Saal'an referred to him or to the rest of his foul kind.

'I have provided the mage with the means to break down the wards on their prison, but it will not be easy,' Saal'an told him now. 'I give nothing for free.'

Vasa felt his anger rising again. He had worked the spells on the cells himself, and he had believed them inviolate in their complexity. It alarmed him to realise that all this time the Arkni could have unravelled them at will. And, by inference, those he had set around himself.

His adversary was aware of the cause of his displeasure. His voice was mocking as he added his final insult. 'Do not think I have forgotten you, Holy One, for do we not help each other? Your woman, Shakumi. She left the palace at the dawn call. She was followed to a rebel safehouse in the Kitani quarter. It is to there that they will run, to her. It is fitting that you decide what they will find. I can have someone guide you if you wish.'

After delivering this parting shot, Saal'an left, leaving Vasa gaping in astonishment. In just a few sentences the creature had revealed his complete authority, brutally taking the reins of power into his crabbed hands.

Furious and frightened, Vasa was still rational enough to admit his own folly, and through that admission saw the whole of his reign recoloured as the stunted impulses of a puppet ruler. The two things he most desired were casually handed to him like treats to a cooperative child. How long had they known the location of the rebels in his own city and kept it from him? How many of his secrets had they betrayed for their own ends? He knew a moment of the bitterest recrimination for the fool he had been.

But he would have his revenge. Saal'an had said they would go to the safehouse. Well, so would he, and not merely to recapture his lost property. This was far from over.

SEVENTEEN

AARIN RAISED HIS head painfully from the cold floor and looked at Kinseris. The priest's face was swollen and bloody, a vivid purple bruise across his jaw, legacy of the blow that had knocked him out. The guards had been thorough. Aarin could feel a stab of agony in his chest where the sergeant's boot had connected with his ribs, and his head ached dreadfully. Kinseris lay near him, unconscious. He had taken the full brunt of the savage attack, already weakened by the cell's magic, and Aarin feared for him.

Aarin reached with his hand and explored his eye. Blood was crusted on the eyelid, sealing it closed. He wet his hand and tried to clean the mess away. Pain sliced through his head as he moved. He sagged against the wall and took shallow breaths, trying not to retch.

The soldiers had burst into their cell several hours before, catching Aarin working on the wards and Kinseris resting as well as he could. They had wasted no energy on words, launching straight into the assault. He guessed they had been sent on Vasa's orders. Their unthinking savagery reminded him of the high priest. The beating had gone on for hours, or so it had seemed. Likely it had been no more than minutes. When they passed out, the men revived them with buckets of filthy water, water that now chilled them as it soaked through their thin garments. They stopped only when it was clear their victims could take no more.

Aarin took a hold of himself with an effort and crawled to Kinseris. He rested his fingers on the priest's throat, feeling for a pulse, and found it faint but steady. He sighed with relief and regretted it instantly as bruised ribs protested.

Kinseris groaned, weakly pushing his hand away, trying to open his eyes.

'Don't move,' Aarin warned. 'You've been hurt, badly. Lie still and I will try to help you.'

'Aarin?'

'It's me, don't try to move.'

Kinseris screwed up his eyes, squinting into the mage's face. 'You?'

'Battered,' he admitted. 'But I'll survive.'

'You look bad.'

'You should see yourself,' Aarin answered, smiling painfully. 'They were not gentle.'

He finished his cursory examination. He did not think any bones were broken, but he was no expert. Apart from the bruising on his face, the priest's back was black and blue with boot prints and would certainly be painful, but he thought that nothing had been damaged inside. Only Kinseris could tell him that for sure.

He sat back, his own body afire with agony. Kinseris has drifted back under and Aarin decided against bringing him round. Consciousness would only bring pain, and pain in this place was intolerable. Instead he eased himself back against the wall, closing his eyes under the protests of his abused flesh. They could not risk another such beating. He had to get them out and there was only one way to do that, but he hurt badly enough that attempting it seemed beyond him.

At first discomfort defeated Aarin's efforts in slip into a trance, but in the end trained discipline stepped in and took him away to another place. He hung suspended between layers of magic, lines he could see and some he could only feel. Without Kinseris's aid he would never be able to see them, but the priest was beyond helping him for now. Carefully he sharpened his awareness and tried to sense the path of the unseen elements as they ran through the weave. The patterns had changed since his last attempt, but he was too weary to be surprised. Vasa. He felt his signature presence. The oily viciousness of the high priest had left its mark on the new spells, and with a sigh Aarin realised he would have to start at the beginning again.

Sometime later when Kinseris struggled back to full consciousness and opened his eyes he saw Aarin slumped against the wall behind him. He tried to sit, but a wave of pain kept him on his back. As he waited for it to pass, he looked again at the mage and saw his face was bloody but serene. Whatever pain he should be suffering was absent for the moment.

Kinseris gave up the struggle to move. 'I wonder how you do it.'

The mage opened one eye irritably. 'Easily, if you don't interrupt me.'

Kinseris started. 'I didn't think you could hear me.'

'Anything that happens in this space is hard to ignore when I am part of it. Are you able to help?'

'What do you need?'

'Your sight,' Aarin replied. 'I am inside the wards, but I can't see them clearly. If you can use your device, I will draw you in after me. Then perhaps we can find our way together.'

Kinseris edged his hand towards the little silver dragon. Every movement hurt. 'I have it, but I can't use it.'

'Try,' Aarin insisted. 'Use the pain, focus on it until it fills your mind and you start to drift. I will find you and bring you to me.'

But Kinseris was too hurt, too beaten, for disciplined concentration. He let the pain wash over him, but instead of releasing his consciousness it drove him under again, and Aarin was alone.

The guards returned that night. Aarin crawled to Kinseris's side, preparing to shield the unconscious priest as best he could. But they had not come this time to give pain. Instead they threw a leather water bottle and hard bread through the bars and left without a word.

Aarin scrambled forward, snatching up the precious offerings. The water was stale and filthy, but it was water. Careful not to waste a single drop, he poured a trickle of the precious liquid into Kinseris's mouth.

As water splashed on his lips, the priest opened bleary eyes. His gaze flicked over Aarin's face and the walls of their cell. A look of resignation settled on his face.

'Still here then,' he muttered, turning his head away.

Aarin's lips twitched. 'Where else would we be?'

'I had hoped I was dreaming.' He looked at the water in Aarin's hand. 'It's probably poisoned.'

'I don't think so.' He handed Kinseris a chunk of the stale bread and chewed mechanically at his.

They sat in silence for several minutes, steeling themselves to face the next hour, and the one after that. Thus was their world reduced to bearable units of time, as defiance began to crumble under the onslaught of the warding magic. As the silence stretched on it became harder and harder to break it, more and more difficult to raise the energy needed to communicate even the most basic thoughts.

This is how he will break us, Aarin thought bleakly, staring unseeing at the wall. It had been many hours since he had last attempted to enter the wards. There seemed little point any longer. Kinseris would never be able to use the dragon that sat so innocuously on his breast. Without it, Aarin would never be able to unravel the wards. They had reached a bridge they could not cross, and he had been so sure, so convinced it was possible.

At last, more from crushing boredom than any kind of hope, he prepared his mind for trance. If nothing else, playing with extinction within the ward spells was more interesting than staring at a wall. In seconds he had slipped beyond the limits of normal awareness, drifting in limbo until he directed his consciousness inside the magic. At once he was faced with the familiar problem of layers of interlaced power, some visible and some not, creating a minefield of dangers for the unwary—or a final means of escape for the despairing soul. The thought shocked him as it crossed the edges of his mind. That such thoughts were being thrust on them he had no doubt, and the realisation spurred him to renewed effort, sharpening senses deadened by tedium and allowing him to throw off the deadly apathy of the past hours.

Somewhere far below he could see Kinseris. The priest was staring upwards behind his closed eyes and for a moment Aarin thought he was looking straight at him. Then he realised that he was the one who was staring—staring through a hole in the pattern, a hole that was free of the invisible energies. It was tiny. He had ignored the existence of such holes until now, but suddenly an idea began to take shape. He imagined a fishing net, its close-meshed web similar in structure to the construct around him, imagined creating a tear in the net without actually breaking it, allowing the fish to escape. If he could just widen the holes that were already present, it might be possible for them to slip through the gap before anyone noticed it was there.

Aarin set about exploring the possibility, working on a small scale at first, then moving outwards, expanding the hole he had created until it was large enough for his purposes. For so long he had been trying to undo the spells when all he needed to do was part them, to create a door through which they could escape, provided he was able to keep it open long enough.

Then came the dangerous part, combining strands of his own magic with the complex web, reinforcing the boundaries he had made so he could keep the door open when he withdrew from the wards.

The final preparations took him hours. He worked doggedly on, ignoring Kinseris's listless queries and the weariness that willed him to rest. Each spell was laid down with the utmost precision, the weaves touching none of the original strands, yet laced over, under, and through them. Above all he had to avoid alerting Vasa to his endeavours, for at the slightest touch of his awareness against the tightly strung cords, the magic would sing out in warning and the door would be slammed shut so fast he would barely have time to pull himself free.

At last he was ready. If they were quick, and he could maintain the integrity of the complex web, Kinseris should be able to release them from the cell— he himself had no more effort to spare. Satisfied, Aarin withdrew from the wards but kept a part of himself in steady vigil.

His eyes snapped open. Kinseris, who had been watching him curiously for some time, flinched at the sudden movement. Aarin flashed him a bright smile, pausing a moment to ground his spinning senses, then pushed himself upright and stretched out his hand to raise the priest unsteadily to his feet.

'Are we going somewhere?'

He nodded, limping to the bars. 'I've created a window, a hole in the wards. If we are quick, we can slip out before it is noticed, but you must get us out of here.' He put his hands on the bars and pulled, testing their strength. With the spells in abeyance, it was just another prison. 'Can you do it?'

Kinseris joined him at the bars, his face a mask of concentration. 'I can feel the tear. How did you do it?'

'There's no time for that now. The only question that matters is how long I can keep it open.'

'Of course.' The priest reached for the tiny silver dragon, a dependency on touch he had not needed since the earliest days of his novitiate. He placed his other hand on the ugly iron lock, feeling the chill of the metal. 'This should be easy...simple earth through the core...there, done,' he finished with a smile as the door swung open. 'After you.'

Aarin walked past him and felt the first jangling dissent from the spells guarding their prison. He flinched, losing his stride for a moment, then strengthened his defences and continued on.

They were alone. There were no guards in the narrow corridor that ran along the row of cells. The unlucky few who drew this thankless duty preferred to remain in the warm guardroom at the top of the steps. They might not be many, but they would be difficult to pass, and until they had crossed through that room he would not be able to let go of the massive spells he had cast, spells that were growing heavier and more volatile with every passing moment.

Aarin halted at the foot of the stairs. 'I don't want to have to kill them. But we cannot risk allowing them to carry warning of our escape.'

'We will do what we have to,' Kinseris replied, his face grim.

They started up the stairs, ears pricked for the slightest noise from the guardroom. They reached the landing and heard the soldiers talking and laughing beyond the locked door. Kinseris released the lock and the mechanism sprang open audible click. The voices fell silent.

They pressed back against the wall. The talking resumed, quieter now, and they heard someone walk up to the door. It opened cautiously outward and they saw the point of a sword edge onto the landing. The rest of the guard followed, looking about him apprehensively. When it was clear no others were following Kinseris gave the door a shove and it slammed closed. At the same moment Aarin lashed out with his foot and the guard stumbled to his knees, dropping his sword. Aarin picked it up as Kinseris locked the door. The guard stared at them in shocked silence as his fellows called out frantic questions from the other side of the door.

Aarin raised the sword and gestured down the stairs. 'Down,' he snapped when the man did not move.

The soldier turned, unwilling to argue with a sword held against his spine, and back down they went.

'How many?' Kinseris asked as he held open the cell door. The man stared at him in sullen defiance. 'How many?' he repeated dangerously.

Aarin watched the exchange, the sword clasped loosely in one hand. His time with Kallis had taught him at least a basic proficiency with the weapon. And he found himself itching to use it. Something about the way this man held himself was sickeningly familiar.

Some of what was going through his mind must have been obvious on his face as the guard paled visibly. 'Four,' he offered at last, adding with brash defiance, 'more than enough to put you back where you belong.'

'Four?' Aarin advanced into the cell. 'Are you sure? Sounded more like six, maybe seven, to me.' He brought the sword up so its point nicked the soldier's chest. His eyes were cold. 'Tell me again and tell me the truth.'

'Or what?'

He shrugged. 'Or I kill you and ask someone else.' He half-meant it, a blood rage boiling up inside him. The magic he had to maintain was pressing down on him, clouding his judgement.

'It doesn't matter,' the soldier sneered. 'You'll never get out of here.'

'Wrong, you'll never get out of here. How many?'

'Six, only six, I swear.'

Aarin smiled grimly. 'That's better.' He lowered the sword, walked out of the cell and slammed the door. Kinseris gave him an odd look.

Aarin ignored him, his nerves strung taut and fraying under the pressure of the spells. 'There are at least five more guards outside. The question is how do we swap places with them? We cannot fight them all.'

Kinseris looked at the sword in Aarin's hand. 'Unless we want to bring the whole citadel down, only the more conventional methods are open to us.'

The mage bit back a savage curse but he knew Kinseris was right. It would do them no good to escape the cells only to find an army of adepts waiting in the palace beyond. They might be able to take down six guards with magic, but they could not fight the combined forces of the citadel's priests. 'And I thought the wards were the hard part.'

He stalked back to the cell without waiting for a reply. Rapping the hilt against the bars, he demanded the soldier's attention.

'What are you doing?'

'Something,' Aarin snapped, the strain cracking through his voice. 'If we don't get out of here soon it won't matter how many men are out there. Call them.' He commanded the guard as behind him Kinseris let go of the spell that was holding the guardroom door closed and melted into the shadows.

'Call them,' he repeated when there was no response. The man gave a half-hearted shout and Aarin prodded him through the bars. 'Not like that. Mean it. Or I will give you a reason to.'

He heard the door finally swing open and the soldiers calling cautiously down the stairs. He looked back at his prisoner, one eyebrow arched in question. The man stayed defiantly silent. The first cut of the sword across his arm drew a pained yelp, the second a full-throated roar.

There were sounds of a scuffle and footsteps on the stairs. Aarin moved to Kinseris, who was hidden from view by the overhang of the stone steps.

'This is your plan?'

'It's a plan,' Aarin allowed. Not the best plan maybe, but he was running out of time.

'Forgive me if I haven't quite grasped the finer points yet,' Kinseris retorted, listening to the argument racing back and forth among the remaining guards as they made their cautious way down the stairs. One grabbed a torch, and they shrank deeper into the shadows

'When they are down here,' Aarin explained with forced patience, 'we go up there.'

'Ah, of course,' his companion murmured in despair.

The first guard made it to the bottom of the stairs. He looked at his colleague standing moodily inside the locked cell and walked over to him.

'What are you doing in there, you daft bugger?' he asked as he fumbled with the keys at his belt. The trapped soldier shot a look in the direction of the shadows and opened his mouth to speak. His eyes met Aarin's and the mage shook his head. In the second's pause that followed, Kinseris snuffed out the torch, plunging the cells into complete darkness. Catching him by the wrist, Aarin dragged the priest up the stairs, brushing past the startled guardsmen on the way.

An enraged voice yelled that the prisoners had escaped, to shut the door and lock them in, but the prisoners were faster, running through the open door and slamming it shut behind them.

EIGHTEEN

'WELL, WELL, WHAT do we have here?' A bulky figure stood in the shadows of the guardroom, utterly unconcerned by their sudden appearance. The captain walked a few paces towards them and stopped, his face split into a satisfied grin. A mace hung from one hand, a short sword in the other.

'Now we will see who holds the power of life or death over the other, my lord,' he sneered at Kinseris. 'I don't know how you got past the wards, but you will not get past me.'

'You think you are still protected?' Kinseris asked menacingly as he eyed the man with all the contempt of his former station. 'After the wards on this place, the ones shielding you are nothing. You would be wise to put down your weapons and save yourself from discovering just how vengeful I can be. I have not forgotten either your insolence or your brutality.'

A flicker of hesitation crossed the man's face, and Kinseris started to walk past him. At the last moment, the sword came up and barred his way.

'I've listened to your lies before. Not again,' the captain replied as Kinseris glared at him with patrician disdain along the length of bared steel.

'Not wise,' Aarin remarked coolly, leaning against the locked door, all his effort going into concealing his fractured stress. They did not have time for this. He sent a trickle of energy, all he could spare, crackling along the length of the sword that hung loose in his grasp and saw the captain's eyes widen in sudden uncertainty. Pressing the advantage, he raised the ghostly blade and shrugged himself upright. 'You still wish to test us?'

The captain wavered for a second, then he threw his head back and laughed. 'Ah, boy, that's a pretty trick, but harmless, I think. Do you even know how to use it?' With his own sword he forced Kinseris back, still chuckling. 'Since you so generously offered me my life, I'll offer you yours. Kill me and you're free to go, both of you.'

'I think that about sums it up,' Kinseris interrupted with biting sarcasm.

'I've had enough of this. Stand aside or face the consequences.'

'Not so fast, my lord.' The captain ignored the empty threat, his sword still held at the priest's throat. 'I have business with this one here.' He lowered his short blade, stepping backwards, careful to keep himself between them and freedom. His eyes were locked on Aarin's and they gleamed with anticipation. 'Well, will you take me up on my offer?'

Aarin paused, a shudder running through him he could not quite hide. The soldier saw it and smiled, smelling fear, and closing eagerly.

The mage watched his sword hand warily as he tried to steady himself. Beaten and wearied and buffeted by gigantic waves of power, he knew the contest was hopeless. His opponent could kill them both without breaking a sweat. He glanced at Kinseris. The priest's restraint was pointless now and he must know it.

In that moment of distraction, the captain made his move.

Forced to parry the sudden blow, Aarin's command splintered and broke. A thunderous discharge marked the release of the magic as the spells were ripped from his control, over-stressed nerves unable to maintain their grasp on the complex net. The unleashed energies whipped through the small room like a hurricane, throwing Aarin across the floor. He lay there, half-stunned, staring dumbly as the lifeless form of the captain toppled to the floor. Kinseris was crouched in the corner, a silvery shimmer fading from around him, the remains of a shield instinctively raised. The silence was deafening.

Aarin stared at Kinseris in horror, waiting for the inevitable, but the priest reacted faster. In the split second before the ward spells crashed back down, Kinseris crossed the space between them, grabbed Aarin by the collar and hauled him through the open door. An instant later the bane-spells crackled to life and a wall of static once again marked the boundaries of the jail.

'They have left the cells!'

Vasa whirled around in fury as the adept who attended him took a fearful step back. 'Insolent boy! Does he think to stun me with my own magic, to throw the herald of his success in my face? Damn Saal'an and his meddling. Call out the palace guards and the city garrison. I want them found!'

'Holy One,' the adept answered, bowing and backing out of the room.

'And send ten elders to me!'

'At once, Holy One,' came the prompt reply as the doors opened.

'I have not dismissed you yet!' Vasa screamed in fury, stopping the retreating adept in his tracks. The man clenched his hands in front of him to stop them shaking.

'Forgive me, Holy One, I did not –'

'Silence!' Vasa hissed. He paced to his cushions, dropping into them with a sigh. 'I want an escort picked and waiting at the gates for my instructions. The prisoners are not to leave the city. If they are found, they are to be brought to me at once.' He leant forwards, his black eyes blazing with anger. 'And they are to be brought to me *alive*. If they die, I will execute those responsible. Now go!'

The young adept fell over himself making his hurried obeisance and ran for the door. Vasa watched him go. He imagined the boy's terror as he ran down the corridors. The elders would arrive in a flurry of confused haste within minutes of the summons. Ten called for a show of strength rarely required by any high priest and would give him the power to match the Arkni play for play—or so he hoped.

Vasa smiled in satisfaction. Kinseris would get only as far as he allowed him.

Aarin shook his head to clear the daze. The awful pressure on his mind was gone, but their advantage had been lost. He had planned to carefully release his spells once they were clear of the cells, allowing the original wards to spring back into place without alerting anyone to his tampering, but the stunning force with which his weavings had been torn had surely rebounded off the consciousness of every adept in the palace, maybe even those in the city beyond. The pursuit would be on them in minutes.

He pushed himself to his feet, stumbling into a run. He could not, would not, go back to those cells.

'Which way?' he asked Kinseris breathlessly.

The priest stumbled to a halt, looking around as he worked out exactly where they were. Then he doubled back and led Aarin in a torturous game of hide and seek through the corridors of the palace compound.

They were in a narrow hallway winding through the southernmost wall when Darred stepped out to block their way. Shuddering to a halt, struck speechless by shock, Aarin thought his mind was playing tricks on him. Darred could not be here, not in Kas'Tella. He would never risk it.

But he had.

For several seconds no one moved, no one spoke, then Kinseris took a step forward. 'Don't try to stop me,' he warned his old friend. Aarin felt the tingling rush of sensation as Kinseris connected with his dragon device. 'I know what you are now.'

Darred's dark eyes glittered with amusement. 'I'm not here to stop you,' he replied as their eyes locked on each other. 'I'm here to warn you.'

'Of what?' Aarin demanded, but their attention was fixed on each other. Just as in Vasa's chambers, he was a spectator to a confrontation that had been long in coming.

Darred barely even glanced at him. 'My words are not for you,' he sneered. 'Once you made your choice there was never any help for you. I am here because we are friends,' he continued, speaking to Kinseris. 'And you have no idea what you are involved in. This boy is not one of your wronged peasants to be rescued. If you help him, he will destroy you.'

'I know who he is,' Kinseris replied coldly. 'And I know what he will do. There was a time when I hoped I would be able to count on your help when this moment came, but I see now I was wrong. The corruption in your heart was always there, I just did not want to see it. Now it has gone so deep you have blinded yourself to what they are, and what they have done to you.'

'It is not too late to join me,' Darred said, as though he had not heard. 'Vasa will soon be consumed, his reign ended. There will be nothing to stop us.'

Kinseris shook his head. 'This is madness, old friend. What makes you think you are a match for them? That you will not be consumed as Vasa has been?'

Darred smiled, his eyes glittering. 'Ah, but who can say what will happen when Æisoul returns the dragons to power? When the magic flows back into the world, it will be ours for the taking. Think, Kinseris! Once the Lost Elements are restored, imagine what we could do together! The Arkni think to rule us, but why should we let them? They are cruel and deadly, and they will destroy where we could govern, kill where we could let live.'

'You will govern nothing!' Aarin spat. 'Your intent is not to save but to destroy, just as theirs is. I will not let you do that.'

'But you will be dead,' Darred returned mildly, looking at him at last. 'Your life will be spent in fulfilment of your dream, just as I promised you. A flawed prophecy cannot protect you, because you are not who you are meant to be, and your role in this has been dictated by others since the moment of your birth. You are but a tool.'

'I live still,' Aarin reminded him savagely. 'And the magic has yet to be unleashed. In that moment, who indeed can say what will happen? But I can tell you this: you will never gain any part of it. You sold yourself to your masters and you will share their fate.'

'So I hope,' Darred replied, his dark eyes flickering with amusement. 'So truly I hope. Last chance, Kinseris. Join me, or we part here as enemies.'

Kinseris sighed. 'We have been enemies a long time.'

A snarl flashed across Darred's face. Aarin felt a gathering of power and feared the renegade priest would lash out, then his expression eased and he bowed his head.

'Then go, Æisoul, old friend, and live the last days of your lives.' He stepped aside, ushering them past with that same mocking smile, that insufferable confidence. Behind him the hallway opened onto a courtyard and Aarin could see the city beyond. They were so close, but first they had to pass Darred. He enjoyed their hesitation.

'I'm not here to stop you,' he said again. 'Why should I? All our roads lead to the same end.'

'No,' Aarin corrected him as they drew level. 'Only your end.'

'And yours, Æisoul,' Darred replied as they passed. 'And yours.'

Vasa stalked across the great courtyard, scattering attendants and guards from him in reeling, chaotic obedience. A litter waited at the main gates to carry him to the Kitani Quarter and he smiled as he climbed inside. It was time for his revenge to play out and he was determined to enjoy it. His hand snaked out between the silk curtains and waved the escort into the city. Soldiers would search for the fugitives, but they would not find them, and that suited him just fine. He wanted Kinseris exhausted and vulnerable. And he wanted his companion dead before he had a chance to bring the prophecies to fulfilment and his rule to an end.

NINETEEN

AARIN CURSED SILENTLY as his toe connected with something hard and sharp. He was exhausted. Their journey across the city had been torturous, a constant battle against enemies both real and imagined as they dodged Vasa's soldiers and jumped at every shadow. Soldiers were searching door to door and Kinseris had led them down dark alleys and winding back streets. Twice they had almost been caught, and both times Aarin had spun simple illusions across their trail to distract the pursuit. It seemed to him that they had been running for days, not mere hours, but finally they had arrived, though where they were he could not have said.

Aarin looked around him, unable to suppress a shiver, his over-wrought imagination sending pinpricks of unease down his spine. There was something wrong, he could feel it. This place did not feel safe. It was almost pitch black, yet his far-flung awareness told him the cellar was not big, a small underground storeroom. He could hear people talking and moving around in the inn above, but the muffled sounds brought him no comfort. Something was wrong.

He watched the dim shadow as Kinseris felt his way through the obstacle course of barrels and crates to the far side of the cellar. He trailed his finger across the walls, feeling for the door. The mage sighed. They had nowhere else to go.

As Aarin reached him, Kinseris turned back to the door, knocking out a code on the old wood. He stopped, listening, then repeated it twice more. Footsteps sounded on the far side and they heard another series of taps, three identical sequences. Kinseris sighed with relief and gave the required acknowledgement. The door was flung open and a plump, middle-aged woman grabbed the priest in her arms and hugged him tight.

'Hallah, stop,' he laughed, struggling backwards. 'Ah, it does me good to see your beautiful face again.'

'It is good to see you too, boy,' she said with affection, studying him critically in the half-light. Then she hesitated, hovering nervously before she invited them in, and Aarin resisted the urge to look over his shoulder.

'Let us not stand around in the dark,' she said quickly, seeing his look. 'Come in and be welcome.' She bolted the door firmly behind them.

'Has there been any trouble?' the priest asked as he followed the woman up the stairs and through the kitchens.

Hallah sniffed. 'That depends on what you mean by trouble,' she replied tartly. 'Your poor girl arrived here two days ago. Two days ago,' she repeated as if to make sure they understood. 'In a terrible state, she was. Wouldn't tell us anything except you were to meet her here and take her away. When you did not come, I thought –' She turned around and eyed him sternly. 'I wouldn't like to think such things of you, but you are a man. I just hope you haven't gotten the girl into trouble.'

Kinseris's expression morphed from relief to embarrassment in a split second and Aarin almost laughed. Then his smiled faded as he saw the change in Hallah. The reproval fled before a glistening of tears and she spun away, but not so quickly that the priest did not see them. Kinseris clutched her by the arm and swung her around, panic making him thoughtless.

'What is it?' he demanded. 'Tell me.'

'Forgive me,' she whispered. 'I had no choice.'

'No.' Kinseris shook her, brushing off Aarin's hand. 'I must know.'

'Kinseris,' Aarin warned, looking past the priest.

'Leave me be. Hallah, tell me.'

'Kinseris,' Aarin said again.

The priest whirled to face him. Aarin jerked his head towards the room in front of them. Kinseris turned slowly and saw the soldiers. And behind them, his hand on the shoulder of a stooped old man, was the fat, gloating face of Chandra Vasa.

'Nothing to say, Kinseris?'

Vasa was watching his prisoners with undisguised glee. He was flanked by a group of ten Kas'Talani, hoods drawn low over their features.

Aarin and Kinseris stood side by side, soldiers with drawn weapons at their backs, adepts with raised spells at their front. Hallah and her husband, released from the threat of Vasa's magic, stood before them surrounded by their own guards. The old man's head was bowed, his shoulders slumped in fear and shame. Hallah sobbed quietly by his side.

'You didn't really think I would let you escape, did you?' Vasa asked. 'Shakumi was kind enough to show me the way to this pathetic tavern in time for our little rendezvous, but I wished you to lead me here yourselves, so you could witness the punishment I mete out to treacherous subjects.'

A spasm of pain crossed Kinseris's face at the mention of Shakumi.

'Ah, I see you still hoped she was loyal to you,' Vasa observed. 'Well, you shall see her in due course and may confront her yourself.'

He turned to the innkeeper and his wife, taking her chin in his hands. 'If you were younger, my dear, I might have considered you for my personal service. But those days are behind you now. I'm very sorry.'

He sounded genuinely regretful, and Hallah stared fearful and bewildered over his shoulder at Kinseris. Her eyes held a message Aarin could not read. Vasa seemed to understand, and he slapped her hard.

'Enough.' Vasa clapped his hands and a guard grabbed the diminutive woman by her hair. Another kept his weapon trained on her husband, but the old man never moved. He had no fight left.

As Hallah struggled, Aarin turned desperately to Kinseris. He knew with sick certainty that they were going to kill her, but Kinseris caught his eye and shook his head.

'Really, Kinseris?' Vasa asked, watching the exchange. 'No threats, no fight? You won't try to save her?'

Aarin struggled against the ropes round his wrists. He could not stand by and do nothing.

The soldier behind him clouted him with the butt of his spear and Aarin staggered to his knees. He looked up into Vasa's grinning face and Kinseris's angry one and did not understand. Then all thoughts were driven from his head.

Quick as a snake, the guard holding the woman drew his knife and sliced across her soft belly. Hallah screamed, clutching at the wound, and would have fallen if the soldier's hand in her hair had not held her upright.

Aarin yelled out in protest as the flow of bright blood drenched the front of her apron. With a quick look at Vasa, the guard made another vicious cut, this time across her breasts.

Hallah did not scream this time as she sagged, her hold on consciousness faltering. The soldiers kicked her roughly away from him, her body spinning as he twisted his grip in her hair. For an instant, she managed to raise her head to look at Aarin, and it seemed to him that even her eyes ran with blood. There was a plea in them, but not understanding what she asked of him he struggled harder.

'*Stop!*' Kinseris commanded in an urgent whisper. 'You protest the sentence of death, so she must be tried this way, until the charge is met or she bleeds to death. Her charge can never be met, don't you understand? Do nothing and he may kill her quickly!'

Aarin looked at him in horror and managed to hold his tongue. He could not bring himself to look at the woman, but Kinseris nudged him with his elbow. 'Look,' he demanded, merciless. 'Look and do nothing. Condemn her with your silence. It is the only way. It is what she begs you do to.'

Vasa watched them in amusement. 'You've changed your mind?' he asked Aarin. 'You believe now that she has earned her death?'

Aarin glared at him, pure spitting hatred in his eyes, and did not speak. Vasa gave a casual wave and once more the soldier sliced into his victim, driving the knife upwards from her torn navel to her breastbone, cutting her open like a piece of meat. Then he dropped her to the floor to lie gurgling in the frothy pool of her own blood.

'Too late,' he quipped. 'Too late. But she will die soon. Never fear that her suffering will be long.'

Aarin sank to his knees. He squeezed his eyes shut. His fault! All his fault. He gagged as the smell of blood seared his nostrils and clung to his throat, and beside him he heard Kinseris's wretched anguish.

At length he felt rough hands reach down and haul him to his feet. His limbs seemed to have no strength, and he staggered against his captors who held him upright against the protests of his body. When he could open his eyes, the woman was dead. He looked at her husband, but he was lost already. Only blankness stared out of hollow eyes at the bundle of bloody rags that had been his wife. He showed no reaction as a guard grabbed him and forced him forward, his dead eyes riveted on the mess on the floor.

Vasa raised a questioning eyebrow. They neither moved nor spoke. A minute passed, then another, and still he held their gaze. At last, bored with the game, he turned away, calling to the soldier, 'Kill him.'

The guard drew his blade across the old man's throat and dropped him dying to the floor. He reached clawing hands to the open gash, recalled to himself in the final seconds of his life, but he breathed his last bubbling breath within seconds of the knife thrust. His executioner kicked him next to his wife and their blood mingled together in a spreading pool on the floor.

They were dead. Kinseris stared numbly at the broken bodies. So many years, such loyal friendship, gone, shattered, lives needlessly lost because of the unremitting viciousness of one man. He turned to Aarin, seeing the shock in his glassy eyes. He would blame himself for the savagery he had just witnessed, but Kinseris knew better—Vasa had exploited the mage's ignorance to indulge in his favourite brand of cruelty.

Kinseris forced himself to look at Hallah, seeing not the bloodied corpse on the floor, but her face, alive and scared, staring at him over Vasa's shoulder, sending him a message. Then it struck him like a punch in the gut. Vasa was lying. He heard again Hallah's words as they had climbed the steps from the cellar. *Your poor girl arrived here two days ago.*

'Bring her out!' he demanded. 'Let me see Shakumi!'

Vasa tore his fascinated gaze from the bodies and faced Kinseris. 'So you can revenge yourself on her? I don't think so. I rather like her as she is.'

'Liar!' Kinseris roared. 'What have you done with her?'

Vasa's face hardened. 'Nothing more than the whore-bitch deserved,' he snarled, and the rare loss of composure revealed at last which of them she had betrayed.

He went cold. 'What have you done?'

'You shall see. Did I not promise you that?'

Vasa clapped his hands and a girl appeared from the doorway to the taproom. She curtsied before him and he whispered in her ear, then she disappeared back the way she had come.

'I wish you to pay close attention,' he told Aarin. 'For this is the fate that awaits your woman also.'

Kinseris felt his bowels turn to ice. Aarin shot him a horrified look but he could not respond, for behind Vasa in the shadows of the doorway he saw Shakumi. She dangled between two guards, hanging limp in their grasp, and as they dragged her closer, he saw her lips were blackened with poison. Veil gone and eyes closed, her beautiful face was marble white, her hair loose and falling in tangles to her waist. Her clothes had been stripped away leaving her nothing but a thin shift that barely concealed her nakedness. She looked already dead.

The guards stopped by Vasa. He walked in front of the dying woman and raised her head, turning her face into the light. 'She lives,' he pronounced dispassionately. 'I am surprised. I thought she would have succumbed by now, but no matter. You get to watch her die.' He nodded at the two soldiers holding his concubine. They threw her to the floor at Kinseris's feet.

'I could taste the betrayal on her,' Vasa taunted as Kinseris dropped to his knees beside the woman he loved.

He gathered her to him, enfolding her in his arms, and as he rocked her gently, he felt Aarin stand between him and her killer. He called her name, his voice cracked with grief, but he could feel the life bleeding out of her even as he held her, and he could not bear to let her go.

He called her name and saw her eyes open. 'Shakumi, lady of my heart.'

Her head was pillowed in his embrace. She looked up at him and tried to smile. Something broke inside him. Tears fell unheeded down his face, falling on her skin, as he kissed her a last time on her lips, so parched and cracked from the poison that was killing her.

'I failed you.'

She tried to reach a hand to his face, and he caught it and held it.

'No. You have saved me.'

'How? *I should have spared you this!*'

'This is a better death… than the other. You saved me from that.'

'Your courage dazzles me, lady,' Kinseris whispered. She did not know he had been taken, that he had failed in everything. He could not tell her. Let her die thinking he was still free. 'I have everything I love right here in my arms.'

She smiled up at him. 'The pain eases, my love.'

His fingers tightened in her hair. 'Soon it will pass. Soon everything will be better.'

'Truly?' She was fading fast.

'Truly,' he promised, but she was gone. His breath caught in his throat, tears stung his eyes, and the cry in his heart drowned out the world. He could not let her go, could not give up his hold on her precious form, so beautiful still, even after the passage of such a death.

Sense and memory returned piece by piece as the sounds of his captors intruded, and another emotion replaced the grief. As gently as he could, arms and hands shaking with explosive rage, he laid her out on the floor, composing her limbs and closing her eyes, giving her only a fraction of the dignity owed to her. He rose slowly, and as he looked up into Vasa's eyes, his enemy was no longer composed.

Vasa's eyes flickered with fear in the face of his hatred, a sheen of sweat glistening on his dark skin. The head of the Kas'Talani Order took a step backward, raising a hand in front of him. His acolytes closed around him, the rustle of their robes melting into the rising tide of static energy.

Aarin heard Vasa speak, heard the note of caution in his voice, but his eyes were locked on Kinseris, reliving a moment of dream-sight from long ago. He watched in dread fascination as the woman's death and the priest's savage grief threw off the shackles the assembled clerics had bound around his talent. Whether Kinseris knew it or not, his rage was drawing a vast, cresting wave of power through the silver dragon he gripped in one hand, and the raised magic was quickly crackling out of the control of Vasa and his fellow priests.

Still, Aarin saw, it would not be enough. Even as Kinseris seemed to realise what he had done, they were rallying, combining their focus as they had done before, and soon the strength of ten would overcome the anger of one, however powerful.

As Shakumi's body was consumed in a flash of bright flame, the priest raised haunted eyes to his bitter foe, but Vasa's smile had returned. In another instant, Aarin knew, he would snap down the wards, and the backlash from severing such immense force would immolate Kinseris where he stood. Without knowing why, acting purely on instinct, he stepped up to the priest, laying his right hand atop Kinseris's. His last sight before their magics joined was of Vasa backing out through the open doorway. Then his fingers touched silver and his awareness of the world dropped away.

The sudden jolt almost knocked Aarin from his feet but he held on, gritting his teeth against sheets of agony as he was subjected to the raw power of the dragon device without the protecting shield of an acknowledged identity. Then the pain eased, giving way before the iron will of its wielder, and the channel of energy connecting him to Kinseris began to flow the other way, his own resources funnelled through the link in a desperate, headlong rush. The irony did not escape him that without the clarity of understanding bestowed by the Arkni, his flesh would have been seared from his bones by the sheer heat of the fire that engulfed him.

Their eyes met over clasped hands. The world faded and they were upended in a sweeping current of pure force. Blinding light splintered their vision as sight was torn away in a tidal wave of power, but they stood untouched in the midst of the storm, and the sorcery they unleashed rocked the building to its foundations, ripping apart bricks and mortar, shattering glass, and bursting the wooden planks of the floors.

The shockwave spread out from its vortex, crushing everything before it, and the screams of the dying were lost in the savagery of the attack. Sparks of elemental Fire flashed outward, gouts of flame ate at the tinder-dry boards, and hot torrents of air fanned the rippling fire. Within moments the supporting structure of the building had been burned away. The ground around them disappeared and the old foundations subsided into the cellars with a dull screech as the proud inn finally died.

They released their hands and the maelstrom dropped away. The raised energies fizzled, coiling, twisting, unwilling to die. Then at last there was quiet, and the silence echoed loud in their deafened ears as the darkness lifted from their sight, replaced by bright sunlight. They stood unscathed in the centre of a flattened ring of devastation; not one brick of the old inn remained standing.

Aarin blinked and stepped back. As the dust settled and the spilled blood pooled in the cracks of the floor, he felt an unearthly pressure lift as the last threads of their conjury were washed away. He kept his eyes on Kinseris, unable to look at the carnage they had wrought, incapable of reconciling the bloodshed he could see with the euphoric afterglow he could feel. Sound and movement told him that some still lived in the wreckage, but it was beyond his ability at that moment to help them, even had he wished to. Kinseris was a wraith, a layer of dust obscuring his features. His eyes were red-rimmed and hazy with shock. He looked about him like a man in a dream, his eyes rinsed clear of all emotion.

Aarin laid a hand on his arm and the dead eyes swivelled to face him. He could not answer the dreadful loss in them, so he did not try. 'We should leave,' he urged, taking the priest by the arm, and tugging him towards the street. 'Soon this place will be crawling with soldiers.'

Kinseris followed him, unresponsive. But as they passed the crumpled bodies of the slave girl and a guard he stumbled to a halt.

'Merciful Maker! What have we done?'

The mage glanced at him, saw a glimmer of returning awareness and tried to keep him moving. That was a question best confronted later.

'He's still alive.'

Aarin sighed. 'I know, but so are we, which is more than we deserve, I think. We must leave, *now*.'

Already a crowd of terrified citizens was gathering around them, and many were starting to point to the two figures left standing in the middle of the devastation. When Kinseris still did not move, Aarin hit him hard across the face.

'Listen to me! Shakumi died to give you this chance. If we are taken now her death will have been for nothing. Could you live with that?'

The priest was staring at him, one hand raised to the red stain on his cheek. Anger was blazing in his eyes and Aarin knew he was back.

'Don't ever strike me again,' he warned, his voice hoarse.

'Gladly never. Now move!'

Aarin helped Kinseris through the wreckage and out onto the street. When he had the leisure, he would examine his own feelings on what they had done, but just now all he felt was relief. The blameless had already been dead. Hallah, mutilated and murdered for his ignorance and pride. Her face was imprinted on his memory, and he knew he would never be free of the sight.

TWENTY

'THIS IS THE last place I would expect to find an ally of yours,' Aarin observed as he helped Kinseris climb the steps to the gates of the mansion. The words were more for his own comfort. He no longer expected a reply. Kinseris clung to his arm, almost blinded by pain. Whatever strength of will had taken him this far was draining away and Aarin had found himself supporting more than just his flagging body as they had made their way through the twisting streets.

The city was in uproar. Soldiers fought angry citizens in the street as simmering unrest turned to open resistance. Women leaned out of windows and hurled insults at the soldiers and townsmen alike, and they had only narrowly avoided a soaking as one outraged matron emptied a bucket of slops over the men abusing her neighbour.

Aarin guessed the disturbance in the Kitani quarter was at least partly responsible for the savage mood. A beggar had stumbled into them minutes after leaving the scene, whispering quickly and urgently in Kinseris's ear. The priest gave him a coin and sent him on his way, then changed their direction and led Aarin back towards the centre of the city.

Twice more they had been approached by nervous individuals who offered information and warnings. Aarin did not know where they came from, nor how they knew Kinseris. It was enough to know they had friends when he had thought them utterly friendless. Every warning was the same: Vasa's soldiers were searching for them door to door. They had to leave. But even had they been able to find a way through the guards that ringed Kas'Tella's walls, Kinseris needed rest, his injuries needed attention, and Aarin himself could barely walk another step. So, he had cajoled the priest, then bullied him, conscious all the time of the pursuit they could never quite shake, demanding that he come out of his stupor long enough to help them.

But Kinseris was long past the point of coherent thought, and the girl they followed now filled Aarin with disquiet for so many reasons. She had found them as they were hiding from a patrol, calmly walking into the place they were hidden as though she had known they would be there. She had offered them shelter in the name of her master. Who that master was, and why he wished to help, she had not said. Kinseris had been so far sunk in exhausted misery that Aarin was not even sure he was aware of the girl's arrival.

Bereft of the priest's knowledge to guide him, Aarin had had no choice. He had accepted her offer, though everything about her made him uneasy. Had she been a man, Aarin would have said she was Kas'Talani trained. There was something in this child-woman that reminded him irresistibly of Kinseris when they had first met, but the Order admitted no women into its ranks, and he could sense no magic in her.

They had followed her to a large mansion, sitting in palatial splendour on a wide avenue in a wealthy district. The military presence was almost non-existent here. When he asked who lived in such a place, she gave him a strange look and did not reply. He was not sure whether she thought him a fool because he did not know, or a fool for asking at all.

The guards had opened the gates for her without a word, though they spared a curious glance for the ragged men following in her wake. Aarin heard the gates slam shut behind them with ill-concealed worry. Leaving that way would be difficult if whoever lived here was indeed an enemy.

Inside, the mansion was dark and musty, as if the building were deserted. A once-magnificent staircase dominated the empty entrance hall, and the girl was already halfway to the top. She paused on the landing, waiting for them to catch up. Then they were in another hallway where four bored guards in the unmistakable livery of the Kas'Talani stood outside a pair of double doors carved with scenes of banquets and merriment. He felt a surge of outraged betrayal, but it was too late.

One of the guards greeted their guide with a lewd wink and pinched her bottom. She smiled and swatted his hand away, the fey manner she had displayed at their meeting utterly changed, and Aarin forced his rapidly beating heart to slow.

'Is my lord awake?'

The guard grinned. 'He is, though we were not told to expect visitors today.' He looked doubtfully at Aarin and Kinseris.

'He will want to see them,' the girl assured him, treating him to a smile full of unspoken promise. 'He asked me specially to bring them.'

'Did he now?' The man leered at her. 'Well, he always did have strange tastes. Mind you are telling the truth, girl. I don't want to have to put you over my knee again.' His tone said he very much wanted to do just that. She ignored him and walked through the door the others had opened for her.

Lacking any other option, Aarin followed, tugging the unresponsive priest with him. If this was a trap, then the guards at least seemed to have no knowledge of it, and they were the known enemy. It was the unknown that frightened him now.

The room they entered was long and narrow and would have afforded a view of the whole front section of the grounds if every window had not been shuttered and barred. The only light came from a candle on a bronze stand to the right of the doors. The walls were hung with drapes, faded and rotting in places, and the room had the same musty smell as the rest of the house.

Aarin peered at the scenes on the tapestries and shivered. 'I do not think we will find friends here,' he said to no one in particular.

Someone cackled. 'So, sweet Kayte, what have you found for me? Revolutionaries, well, well.'

The cracked old voice came from the shadows. As his eyes adjusted to the gloom, Aarin could just make out a hunched figure sitting in an armchair by a shuttered window.

'Well, answer me, girl. Who are these men?'

Aarin felt his alarm flare up anew as the girl dropped into a deep curtsy. Gone was the flirtatious manner she had shown to the guards and the cool composure she had shown to Aarin. There was in her now a reverence that went beyond simple respect, perhaps even love. But there was fear there too, as though she knew she had dared much.

'My lord, they are enemies of Vasa and they require sanctuary. I thought they might find shelter here.'

The old man leant forward. 'You thought? Since when did I pay you to think, Kayte dear? I pay you for your willing body between my sheets when it suits me, not for you involve me in your childish games.'

Aarin saw through the lie. There was more between these two than that, as unlikely as it seemed, but he was too tired to sort through the puzzle. Utterly at sea, he could only stand there and wait.

'Yes, my lord Seledar, but I thought...'

Aarin felt Kinseris stiffen, and the dormant threads of power at last registered on his exhausted mind. He had thought her Kas'Talani trained, and so she was. The signature of their presence was all over this place, rooted in the ancient in the shadows, and whatever was going on here it was far from simple. Nor was there any clue to be found in their words. They barely touched the surface of the truth.

'There you go thinking again, Kayte. Haven't I warned you about that? Did you really think I would betray my Order to satisfy my personal slights?'

He was silent for a moment, contemplating the girl's bent head, then his eyes flicked over the two men behind her, leaning against each other for support. Aarin sensed his manner soften a fraction.

'Kayte, Kayte,' he murmured sadly. 'You are too young to understand what you have done.' She looked up and he beckoned her closer, and Aarin saw her face brighten as she crossed the floor and knelt by the old man. He rested a hand on her head, gently stroking her dark hair. Yes, there was love between these two, but it was not of the sort Seledar might pretend.

They were too far away for him to hear what the old man said to the girl, but her shoulders started to shake and Aarin could tell she was weeping. After a long moment she rose to her feet, her young hands clasped around his old ones, then she ran to the doors, slipping through them without a word.

As the doors closed behind her, Seledar finally turned his attention to Aarin and Kinseris. Still hidden by the fickle shadows, he seemed little more than a ghost, but Kinseris's tense, watching stillness warned Aarin that was very far from the truth.

None of them moved or spoke. The silence was unnerving. Aarin felt himself studied by eyes he could not see and did not know whether to hope or fear. Then, at last, the old man stirred, stretching cramped muscles with a sigh.

'The girl has placed me in an awkward position,' he said aloud, though Aarin thought he was speaking more for himself. 'One I would have avoided. But perhaps that was cowardice. Well, she has done what she has done, and we will both have to pay for it.'

'Do not punish her,' Aarin found himself saying. 'I do not believe she intended any wrong.'

'Is that so?' Seledar got to his feet, old bones creaking as he flexed limbs too long cramped in his chair. 'The girl is well looked after, not that it is any of your concern. But she has a rather romanticised image of me, I'm afraid. I took her in, you see, when she had no one. She thinks of me as her grandfather, though there are far more generations between us than that.'

As he walked towards them, Aarin felt the sudden, urgent need to back away, to put as much distance between himself and this man as he could. He could feel the power that resided in him, power that did not just come from the silver dragon pinned to his cloak. He felt Kinseris pull himself fully upright and the priest's tired courage kept him where he was.

'So, the girl brings me Vasa's traitor,' the old man murmured, looking them up and down with an expression of wry amusement. 'And I rather suspect she thought she was helping me. I will never understand youth. It has been so long.'

Utterly confused, Aarin looked at Kinseris.

'The Lord Seledar is an outcast,' Kinseris explained, speaking for the first time in hours, and his voice was raw and strained. Like his eyes, which were fixed on the stooped, ancient Kas'Talani. 'Vasa has wished him dead these seventy years and more.'

'Aye, he has, back when your star was still in ascendance, Kinseris. But I am not dead, am I? And how things have changed. I'd swear he hates you more than me now.' The old priest laughed, shaking his head. 'Oh well, you have to love the young. Even I would never have tried to steal his woman.'

'His slave,' Kinseris shot back. 'Shakumi was a slave.'

'Slave, free-woman—what does it matter?' Seledar retorted nastily. 'Although slave implies a degree of ownership far greater than lover, don't you think? What gave you the right to take his slave? And don't tell me *love*,' he sneered. 'I have no wish to be bored by romantic notions at my age. I know enough about love to know it is a foolish nonsense that gets men killed more often than it brings them happiness. How did it work out for you, Kinseris?'

When Kinseris paled, Seledar laughed. 'I thought so. Well, Vasa always was a cruel and petty man, one of the reasons I couldn't abide him, that and the company he keeps these days. Oh yes, the girl knows my feelings about Vasa. But to think that I would aid you in destroying my Order, now where did she get that idea?'

'I'd say she made a foolish mistake,' Aarin said coldly, 'to trust a bitter old man who hides in the shadows and lets darkness take his people.'

'You need light to see, boy?' the old man snapped. 'You think nothing but evil resides in darkness?' He stepped into the light, a wizened, hunched figure little more than wrinkles and bones covered in a threadbare robe. 'Have you never thought that perhaps I am very old and bright light hurts my eyes? And as for darkness, that was none of my doing.'

'He's lying,' Kinseris said abruptly. 'Ask him why he's still alive when so many others have died for far less provocation.'

Aarin looked at him with concern, arm outstretched to offer support, but the priest pushed it away in irritation. 'Go on, ask him. If what he says is true, and he is no part of this, why is it that Vasa tolerates his presence in his own city when his hatred runs so deep?'

'What is it, Kinseris?' Seledar asked. 'You think I am a liar?'

'I know you are a liar, and a traitor. But to whom? That is the question that concerns me.'

Seledar spat. 'Vasa might surround himself with powerful tricks, but he is not yet strong enough to threaten me. I live here because it pleases me to do so, and you know how the old like to indulge their fancies. I will not be chased from my home by any man.'

'Very impressive,' Kinseris replied. 'But a lie just the same.'

As they glared at each other, Aarin knew Kinseris was right. Seledar lied. Why he could not guess, but he knew Vasa would never willingly leave a rival alive and free within his own city. His eyes were drawn to the dragon pinned to Seledar's robes.

Following his gaze, the old man touched a hand to silver device. 'Does this scare you, boy?'

'Yes,' Aarin said honestly, too tired to pretend. He knew only too well what the thing could do. 'But what scares me more is why you still have it.'

A laugh lurked in those old eyes. 'I still have it because I'm still Kas'Talani boy, unlike your friend here who is nothing. I may be out of favour, which is not the same thing at all. By rights I should confiscate the one I know he has still hidden on his person. But I won't, because anything Vasa wants, I want more.'

When Aarin did not reply, he stepped closer, a skeletal hand snaking out and circling his wrist. As he jerked back, Seledar's fingers tightened.

'Easy, boy, I'm not going to hurt you.' As Aarin stilled, the fingers relaxed their grip, probing the heated skin. Seledar cocked his head, looked into his eyes, and all the mocking laughter fled. 'Dragon-fire,' he murmured. 'To think, after all these years, I would see this day.'

There was such a hunger on his face that Aarin pulled away. He had seen that look before, from Vasa and… the other.

Seledar frowned. 'Do not fear me, Æisoul. I am not your enemy.'

The use of that name sent a shock through Aarin, piercing his weary haze. The fire in his blood reacted, surging hotter still. He staggered, catching himself on Kinseris who staggered in his turn. Suddenly it was as though all the weariness, all the hurt was rushing in on them all at once, and he knew something was wrong. It was Seledar who steadied them, Seledar who was watching them with concern.

'What did you do, children?' he asked them, searching their faces. 'Why is there so much magic clinging to you?'

Aarin did not have the strength to reply, and as Kinseris slumped against him he felt his knees give way.

'No,' Seledar murmured, urgent now, reaching out an arm to hold him upright. 'Not yet, boy. You must tell me what you have done.'

But he could not. Kinseris already lay sprawled at his feet, and Seledar's feeble strength was not nearly enough to keep him from the same state. He did not understand, he could not remember…

When Aarin awoke it was to find himself on a cot in a narrow, darkened room, Seledar at his side.

'Did I wake you?'

Aarin rubbed a hand over his eyes. They were full of grit and dry as the desert. He recognised the aftereffects of spellcraft and looked at Seledar accusingly. 'What did you do to us?'

'Saved your lives, and I am ten times a fool for it. Do you have any idea what you have done?'

One arm draped across his face, Aarin was too exhausted for games. 'No doubt you will tell me.'

'But will I?' Seledar replied cryptically. 'Tell me something, boy. Kinseris should have died attempting to handle so much power at once. So, indeed, should you. So how is it that you both survived?'

Aarin opened one eye and peered at him from the sheltering shadow of his arm. 'I think you know that already.'

'Perhaps,' Seledar allowed. 'But perhaps I also wish to know how you know. That knowledge was never yours.'

Aarin studied him, seeing the lines of suffering cut deep around his old eyes. Seledar was right. His ability to handle the power Kinseris had drawn to him had likely kept them both alive, and that skill had been unveiled by Saal'an. He glanced over at Kinseris, saw him still sprawled in unconscious abandon, the area around his eyes burnt and angry where his own magic had marked him. Aarin himself remained untouched.

'It was mine,' Aarin replied honestly. 'But it took another's intervention to let me see that.'

Seledar murmured a name, and he nodded. Those memories disturbed him still.

Seledar's expression softened. 'I apologise for the way I greeted you. I did not foresee that Kayte would be so foolish as to bring you to me. If I delayed you from the help you needed, well, I am not immune to fear after all.'

Aarin propped himself up on one elbow. 'What did you have to fear from us?'

'Ah, boy,' Seledar replied. 'You are too innocent for your own good. All is rarely as it seems in this place. Those guards outside are both my protectors and my jailers. I delayed you only as long as I had to until I could be sure that Kayte had distracted them. She is a good girl, that one. Even so I feared that they would report to Vasa.' He shrugged, grimacing as the gesture tugged painfully at old muscles.

'You feared? Then you do not fear it now?'

The old man shook his head. 'No, I no longer fear they will go to the tyrant. They could not even if they wished to. He is dying, and a new power now sits on the black throne.'

Aarin stared at him, shocked. 'How do you know?'

'Because I can feel it.' He closed his eyes, his head bowed to his chest, and it struck Aarin suddenly how old he was. The vigour that characterised the man he had first met was gone, and without it he was simply ancient.

When Seledar raised his head once more he caught Aarin's look and gave him a wry half-smile, as if he knew his secret had been discovered. 'Chandra Vasa is over three hundred years old. How do you think he has lived so long? A robust constitution?' He snorted. 'He steals it. Steals the life-force from those around him. He made a bargain, a filthy bargain in blood with those black-souled creatures that call themselves the Arkni. I will not bore you with the terms, but simply put, in exchange for an extended time on this earth he sold not only his people but the life of one man: *your* life.'

Aarin sat very still, a chill spreading through him.

'In those days I was as zealous as the next of my brothers in upholding our faith. I honestly believed we were doing right, boy, can you imagine that? It does not excuse the things I did, but I am old enough now to look back on the past without wasting energy in self-recrimination. But then, oh yes, I believed.

'I was part of Vasa's inner cabal, the ruling council as it existed before he dissolved it. There were seven of us, all young, ambitious, and clever, but he outsmarted us all. Unknown to us he had already received overtures from the Arkni, and they offered him so many things. But what he did not know, what he still cannot accept, is that they were always here, among us from the beginning. The Kas'Talani exist because the Arkni created us.'

'Created you?' Aarin repeated, astonished. 'Why?'

Seledar touched a hand to the dragon on his breast. 'Because of these.'

Aarin shook his head, his mind reeling. 'How can you know?'

'Because I have spent a lifetime with nothing to do but ponder that question. Shut up here, alone and all but forgotten, I brooded long on my misfortune. And then, at last, my hatred gave way to the boredom of my existence, and when I had let it go, I could see more clearly.'

He sighed, fingering the lines etched into the polished silver. 'What these are, and how they came to be, is something only the ancients can tell us. But what they have done—that is written in the blood of our history. One day perhaps, when you have time, ask your friend to tell you the legends of our founder, Kasandar, the man the stories tell us was chosen by the Maker to build the world anew. To him was given the power to act in the dragons' stead, but it was not the Maker that gave him that power, it was the Arkni.'

It made a horrible kind of sense, Aarin realised with dismay. Somehow the Kas'Talani had gained the power of the dragons, but it was a magic so wrong and twisted that it could never have been meant to be. As wrong and twisted as the priesthood had become, as the Arkni were.

'But why share that power?' he asked with a glance at Kinseris. He did not want it to be true. 'If the Arkni possessed these things, why give them away? Why not use them themselves?'

Seledar shrugged. 'I do not have all the answers. But think on this. In the Kas'Talani they have created an Order utterly subjugated to their will. We are a religion, and who do you think we worship if not the Arkni, or what they represent? In them, all that made the ancients what they were is turned on its head. Perhaps it was the Arkni themselves who brought the old world to destruction. And this is what Vasa cannot see. He believes the legends, the myths handed down through generations as the Arkni wished them to be. He believes he follows in the footsteps of Kasandar, charged to keep this world safe from the scourge of the dragons, or at least he did once.'

Regret weighed heavily on Seledar's thin shoulders. 'He is not a fool, boy, oh no. But he is greedy, and once his greed overcame good sense and he let them in, they had him. He never had a chance.'

Seledar's fierce gaze sought Aarin's and the mage hardly dared breathe lest he interrupt the flow. 'He used the magic they offered and used it to great effect. In order to extend his life he had to augment his own energy with that which was stolen from others, and he took it from us, his friends, his council, the men who had put him where he was. The men who believed in him. He was not always this way,' the old man said sadly. 'Once I believed he would be a great leader, one who would carry our cause to all the corners of this continent and beyond, maybe even to your land. But he had a weakness in him, and they exploited that weakness, and so in the end he became the tyrant you know today.

'By the time we discovered what was happening it was too late. We were too weak to fight back. One by one the others died and were not replaced, until there was only me. But I bit back!' A fire returned to Seledar's eyes. 'I discovered his treachery and I turned the tables. I reversed his working, took some of his life force for my own, and in doing so stole back a little of my dignity and strength. It was not enough to truly hinder him, nor enough to restore my health, but it had other unexpected benefits.'

Eyes that had twinkled with something close to laughter became again dull as black stones as he reached out to close the fingers of one shrivelled hand around Aarin's wrist, enclosing it in a grip that was startlingly strong.

'I know Vasa is dying, boy, because I am too, because that's what I did. When I tried to take back what was mine all I did was somehow link the two of us together. I should have died many years ago, even with this'—he touched a hand to the dragon—'to support my life. But instead I am still here, growing ever older, weaker. What I took was only a tiniest bit of the vast pool of energy Vasa had helped himself too, but it was enough. As long as Vasa lives, I live also. If he dies, so will I. And by that same token he cannot raise a hand against me for anything he inflicts on me is reflected in himself. So, he has kept me here, near at hand and closely guarded, and though he might wish me dead, he dares not touch me, nor let another do so.'

Aarin stared at him in speechless astonishment. If the old man lied, he did so for a purpose beyond his understanding. And, if everything Seledar said was true, it explained the rift between the high priest and the Arkni. If the creatures achieved their goal, the Kas'Talani would be destroyed, something that Vasa would fear above all else. For the head of the priesthood, Aarin's death was not just desirable but essential; for the Arkni, the preservation of his life was critical until the moment when he was of no more use to them.

The unravelling of the puzzle that had begun in Redstone played itself out with shattering force. Amadorn's magicians hated the dragons, and he knew now that belief originated here, in the heartland of Kas'Talani power. And just as the Kas'Talani ruled the magicians, so the Arkni ruled the Kas'Talani. And just as Vasa now attempted to free himself from his binding obligation to the creatures that had enslaved him, the magicians fought against Kas'Talani domination. The pledge he had made to Vianor took on new dimensions as he realised the extent of the might the magician had sought to curb through that act.

'Do you believe me?' Seledar asked.

He nodded. 'I believe you.'

'He comes here sometimes,' Seledar said softly into the silence that followed. 'Even after all these years he still comes. He sits there on his cushions, young and healthy, and makes me stand before him until my old joints ache and my legs cannot hold me. He comes to gloat, to show me the difference between us, to punish me for what I have done. But I think it is more than that. I think he needs me still, needs someone who understands. He is also a prisoner and though I hate him now, once I was his friend, and so it is to me he comes.

'It would have been better,' the old man told him ruefully, 'if Vasa had continued in power, at least for a while. With him gone, they are free to do as they wish, and no one can stand in their way.' He shook his head, leaning back on his stool. 'It would have been better,' he mumbled to himself, lost in some private, tragic recollection. 'But for better or worse, you have killed him.'

Aarin's gaze sharpened, seeing the slumping shoulders, the lines of pain etched ever deeper in the wrinkled face, and knew he was watching the cruel, inexorable approach of death. 'I'm sorry,' he said, not knowing what else to say.

Seledar looked up. 'For me? Don't be, boy. It is long past my time and I do not fear this. No, you have done me a kindness. It is you who must live with the consequences.'

The consequences. Aarin saw now just how far they would reach. For, as Darred had told him, he was not who he was meant to be, and he did not know if he could fulfil the promise of the prophecy without it being twisted at the last to give the Arkni what they wanted. By destroying Vasa he had allowed them to act without restraint, and the consequences were indeed something to be feared.

Seledar was watching him and Aarin could not bear that too-bright gaze. Despair crashed down on him even as the fire in his veins hounded him always to look onwards. The effort it took to restrain even a fraction of that urging sent running tremors through his limbs, and Seledar laid a stick-thin hand on his arm.

'Do not fight it,' the old priest said gently. 'If you try it will tear you apart. Trust in the prophecy, Æisoul. It will not fail you.'

A wail rose in his throat at the awful truth Seledar could not know, the human meddling in that same prophecy that might yet doom it to tragic failure. 'Whatever you think I am, you're wrong,' he said savagely. 'If you have been waiting for a saviour out of prophecy to redeem you and the rest of mankind, you have waited in vain. He does not exist and never will. There is only me.'

'There was only ever just you. Why should that not be enough?'

'*Because the prophecy was forced!*' The fears Darred had woken in him spread their poison. 'The Arkni manipulated the prophecy. They created me.'

'And as well they did,' Seledar retorted. 'A prophecy is just words. Those words frame a need and demand an accounting, but they cannot bring about your birth. It is, and always was, the role of others to make that happen, and so often it is the very thing we strive so hard to prevent that is the result of that effort. The Arkni feared Æisoul so they set out to subvert the prophecy and create instead someone they could control. Has it never occurred to you that their doing so was the only way the words of the prophecy could ever be fulfilled?'

Still Aarin did not speak, and Seledar's sympathy gave way to impatience. 'If you are indeed a man out of his own time as you seem determined to believe, then so am I, and so is Vasa, and Kinseris. Even the Arkni. And yet our actions are still our own, just as yours are. Stop running from yourself, boy, and start facing this.'

'I'm not running,' Aarin said coldly.

Seledar cackled. 'How perfectly human, this habit we have of deluding ourselves.' He snatched Aarin's arm, his fingers probing the fever-hot skin. 'The Fire consumes you even now, and it will be your death if you deny it. Banish these doubts or you will be caught in a trap of their making, and yours. The world cannot wait for your tortured conscience to realise that all that you are in this moment is all that you need to be. And I will not offer sanctuary while you do so. You will embrace your destiny and do what is necessary or I will hand you to your enemies myself. If you are determined to die, what does it matter when that death claims you?'

Gently, careful not to cause pain, Aarin pried Seledar's hand from his arm. The challenge had been laid down, but he had no intention of picking up the gauntlet until he had all the facts. His hand holding Seledar captive, he forced the old man to look at him.

'And my enemies,' he asked coldly. 'Tell me what they are.'

TWENTY-ONE

WHEN KINSERIS WOKE, Aarin was waiting, warned by Seledar and the evidence of his own eyes that the priest had suffered a cruel reaction to the day's exertions. It was clear from the moment he opened his eyes that he did not know where he was, or how he had come to be there. Aarin bowed his head before his desperate questions and turned his face away so he should not see the realisation hit home, nor the devastation that followed.

Later, when Kinseris had slept some more and recovered at least some of his composure, Aarin related the gist of his conversation with Seledar. The old man had remained for some hours, talking as though he relished the company, filling him in on the situation outside the cocoon of the mansion's walls. Where he was now Aarin did not know, engaged somewhere in his own brand of intrigue, and he was surprised to find he felt a measure of concern for the ancient priest.

'The soldiers have been raiding houses since yesterday,' he told Kinseris as he dipped a cloth into the bowl of water he had been using to bathe the priest's raw, inflamed eyes. 'According to Seledar, they have arrested at least two hundred people on suspicion of plotting against the Kas'Talani, and many more were killed in the fighting. They were looking for us and they knew where to look.'

He paused, unwilling to repeat the names he had been given, then hurried on before his courage deserted him. 'He also bade me tell you that Ander, Li, and Cas are dead. They were killed as they attempted to escape from the palace compound this morning. I'm sorry.'

The names meant nothing to him but the white face and clenched fists of the man on the bed told him they were not unknown to Kinseris. And what was also plain was that his grief was for friends, not merely fellow conspirators. Again, Aarin found he could not bear to watch.

'One day I'll kill him.'

Aarin looked back, rocked by the vehemence in the words, and saw naked hatred blazing from Kinseris's face.

'Vasa will pay for this, I swear it.'

'He already has.' And he related what he had learned from Seledar. 'He is certain the wounds are mortal, and that Vasa cannot live much longer. So, you see, you have already had your revenge.'

'It is not enough,' Kinseris snarled. 'He should die one death for each of theirs. Any one of them was a better man than he could ever be.'

'Nevertheless, he is dying, and beyond our reach now. And if he has little time, we have none. We must be gone before we are found. Do you think you can travel? Seledar believes it will not be long before the soldiers come here, and we cannot go back to that place.'

'You really trust him?'

Aarin smiled bleakly. 'Yes. But, in any case, we have no choice. It is not safe here and the longer we remain, the more time we lose.'

Kinseris pushed himself upright. 'I can travel,' he asserted with false confidence. 'But we need supplies and water, as much water as we can carry. Ephenor is many days east of here and there is the Ranger Desert between us. It will not be an easy journey.'

'We have supplies, but no mounts. He has none to give us.'

'No matter. Horses can make the crossing only if we have water for them, and we will not have enough to spare. We walk and hope Shrogar is looking for us. He is our only hope now.'

They took their leave of Seledar that night. He stood in the doorway of his grand prison, stooped and unsteady with pain, and Aarin felt his heart wrench at the thought of leaving him alone to die. But though the old man brushed off his concerns, his voice had a tremble in it that may or may not have been fear at the last.

'My old enemy and I will go to our deaths together and perhaps at the end we can once more be friends. I find the forgiveness I have wrestled with in life comes easier now the end approaches. We have needed each other all these years and we need each other now. I wait only for him to come to me one last time.'

And so they left him there, alone with his memories. They left him waiting for his enemy to return to him for the final time, the enemy to whom he was inextricably bound in life and in death. As Aarin walked away he felt the tears rolling down his cheeks and did not brush them away.

Trapped in a hell of his own devising, Chandra Vasa fought against the black mire of pain and confusion that tried to suck him back down even as he struggled to find his way back to the waking world. At last he awoke, screaming, choking, clawing at his face, trying to rip away the darkness that obscured his sight.

The sound of his voice startled him back to himself. He blinked, twisting his head from side to side, picking out the faint glow of candles in the shadows, and realised he was not blind, but was housed somewhere deep underground where the light did not reach. The air was stale, and the candles burned low and steady. He opened his mouth to call for Shakumi, his servants, anyone, then closed it again, remembering that Shakumi was dead, and that if any of his servants remained loyal, they had certainly been killed. For he was a prisoner in truth now.

The silence was terrifying. He could hear his heart begin to pound faster and faster, and his blood roared in his ears. And then the pain hit. As he tried to move, a wave of nauseating agony flared from his groin to his chest. The room tilted sickeningly. Dark spots danced in front of his eyes. A gurgling moan tore from his lips as blackness consumed him once more, dragging him down to the quagmire of shifting nightmares so recently banished.

TWENTY-TWO

VIANOR RETURNED TO Rhiannas in the last days of summer and was shown to the queen's private audience chamber, where he waited, restless and impatient, for Sedaine to see him. Her servant offered him wine and refreshments and he refused both, though he was gratified that his niece had seen fit to extend him the courtesy. He had spent several days in the city before making his presence known, observing the mood of the place, and had breakfasted well before presenting himself at the palace. Since he did not know whether this would be the beginning of another spell in his queen's dungeons, it had seemed a wise precaution.

As the wait stretched onwards, Vianor looked longingly at the chair behind Sedaine's desk. He was old and his joints protested prolonged standing, but judging by the absence of any other seat it seemed his present discomfort was intended.

Not for the first time since coming into their company, Vianor envied the ease with which the Luen-trained mages were able to distance themselves from physical sensation. Having travelled in their company for months, he had suffered all the miseries of the old and less hardy surrounded by the energy and vitality of youth. Yet, no matter how closely he had observed, nor how hard he had attempted to imitate the methods of their self-awareness, he had been unable to bring his own arts in line with their subtlety. The constant reminder of his failings had driven him to the point of sour hatred, almost to betrayal of the charge he had undertaken, however reluctantly, in the name of his new queen. Yet fear had tempered that hatred, fear of the consequences her demands would bring on them all. And so, hating himself as much as his tormentors, he had clung to his mission in the knowledge that alliance with Sedaine presented his only chance of survival. And slowly, almost without realising it, his hatred had turned to grudging respect and Sedaine's purpose had become his.

His hunt for Darred's associates had been long and frustrating. Those priests he knew of in Amadorn were few, for Darred, in his arrogance and possible treachery, had preferred to work in relative independence. Three they had found, and those three were gone now, expelled beyond the Istelan, though not without cost. Even the Luen mages were no match for the power of the Kas'Talani, and though he knew the secret of their power, he had neither the strength nor skill to use that to his advantage. They had lost some—too many—but it was done. Men and women from Redstone guarded their southern border, seeking to prevent the Kas'Talani's return to the North, but he dared not hope that measure would be enough.

The doors to the chamber opened and Sedaine entered. She was alone. The royal circlet was on her brow, but she wore no other badges of rank. Her clothes were the plain tunic and leggings she had worn from choice in Redstone, and he imagined that the court had become accustomed to this scandalous eccentricity in their new ruler. In fact, the city seemed to have settled into peaceful complacency in the months since he had left, apparently oblivious to the threat of war. Of the Kas'Talani peril they were blessedly ignorant, but they had to know that violence was looming with their immediate neighbours.

Sedaine, on the other hand, appeared all too aware of the dangers to her new nation. She was thinner, Vianor noted dispassionately, and older. Where before her hair had been untouched by grey, silver threads were now visible amid the thick tresses, worn unbound as had always been her preference. The lines around her eyes were etched deeper, and fine creases were creeping across her forehead.

Sedaine was not unaware of his scrutiny. 'You were right in one thing, uncle,' she greeted him. 'The business of state is taxing. I am surprised my father lived so long.'

'Kaefal saw the benefits of delegating, your highness,' Vianor replied, just as blandly. 'You take too much on your own shoulders.'

The smile faded, replaced by a frown. 'But what choice do I have? There are few I can trust these days. Needs must that I take things on myself that in more peaceful times could be left to others.'

Hearing the hint of accusation, Vianor offered his belated bow. 'You can trust me, Sedaine. My loyalty is yours, to spend as you wish.'

As his head came up, he saw her studying him intently.

'I could wish that you offer that freely. Can I indeed trust this change of heart, or is it merely the case that our interests run side by side for a time?'

The magician refused to show affront. In the months of travel he had come to this choice out of necessity, but it had grown to fit him well. The loyalty he gave her now stemmed as much from his own free will as it did from self-preservation.

'You are right to question,' he admitted. 'And my answer is this: my loyalty is yours, Sedaine, as my blood and as my queen. For now, until my death, your will is my command.'

She considered him a moment longer. 'I am meeting with a delegation from Lord Delgar this afternoon. You may attend me. I would welcome your observations when we are done.'

'He is willing to talk?' the magician asked, surprised.

Sedaine shrugged. 'Elvelen must know their position is hopeless if we go to war. But it has taken careful negotiation to persuade Delgar to agree to this meeting.'

Vianor frowned. 'I expected that you would have acted before now on this matter. Why wait so long? You cannot think to squander this chance to take control of all the North?'

She flashed a smile. 'Ah, but I do not, uncle. I will take the North, but I will do it my way, not Darred's. He wants chaos and enmity, he wants us divided and destroying ourselves, but I will give him peace and unity that will stick in his throat and choke him.'

The meeting took place in a private chamber. Sedaine's servants had decked out the room with all the richness and elegance Rhiannas had to offer. It was designed to impress, to demonstrate the power of that great nation, and it did so. Lord Delgar's envoy checked himself as he entered, his eyes drawn to the gilded furnishings and vibrant tapestries before settling on the woman whose presence they honoured.

He was a slight man, his face thin and unremarkable save for the sneer that curled his lips as he took in her lack of personal adornment. In such a grand setting, Sedaine's plain attire seemed a studied insult, and he allowed himself to be fooled into believing that he dealt with someone unpractised in the ways of state. Rumours of Sedaine's sudden return after years spent in obscurity had reached Elvelen. Like his master, Lord Olivan assumed that absence had rendered her unfit for royal rule. Relieved to be shown evidence of that, he clearly imagined that the coming talks would be completed swiftly, to his own and his people's satisfaction.

With a flick of her wrist Sedaine dismissed her attendants, all save Vianor who stood silent and unobtrusive by the door. When they were alone, she turned her attention to Olivan, dark eyes regarding him in silence, waiting.

'Lady Sedaine.' He greeted her with a bow too brief for titled royalty.

Sedaine raised an eyebrow at the insult, holding out her hand for his kiss. The envoy ignored it. Behind him Vianor bristled with anger.

'Elvelen does not recognise my sovereignty?' Lothane's queen asked icily as she withdrew her hand and waved him to a chair. 'This is not the spirit in which I had hoped to begin our meeting.'

The envoy sat, arranging his courtly robes that contrasted starkly with her simple garb. Conscious of the difference, and misunderstanding it, the man answered smoothly. 'Elvelen recognises that you currently sit on Lothane's throne. It is the legitimacy of that we question.'

'Which brings us to the purpose of this meeting,' Sedaine replied just as smoothly. 'The execution of the usurper Nathas.'

The envoy's eyes narrowed. 'Your choice of language speaks very clearly your position, my lady. Yet Nathas was sanctioned for rule by Lothane's own high council. We do not deny that you are who you say you are, but if you had wished to make your claim you should have done so before Nathas's coronation.' He leant back, coolly confident. 'You took your country from the hands of its rightful king, and his murder at your hands has yet to be answered for.'

Vianor took a step forwards before a gesture from Sedaine brought him to a halt. She turned a brilliant smile on the smug Elvelian nobleman. 'His execution,' she corrected, 'was a legitimate act of state. You say you do not deny that I am Kaefal's daughter and his chosen successor. My claim did not need to be made, for it is a fact of my birth. You are the one in error, Lord Olivan.'

The envoy stiffened and began to rise. 'I see that there is little point in prolonging this meeting. It was my belief that I came here to negotiate reparations for the murder of Lord Delgar's kinsman. I see now that I was mistaken.'

'Sit down,' Sedaine said sharply. 'Do not be the fool who plunges your country into war. For I assure you, should it come to that, you will soon be disputing my right to yet another throne.'

Olivan paused, finally realising all was not as he had assumed. He looked from Sedaine to Vianor, his confidence visibly shaken.

Sedaine waited until he was seated then gestured to Vianor to bring them wine. As the magician placed an ornate table by her elbow and poured the wine, she continued to watch her opponent until he turned a sickly green and took refuge in the proffered wine with pathetic gratitude.

'My terms,' she said at last. 'Elvelen stands down, forgets all talk of war, and offers fealty to me as High Queen of the North. In return I will allow your own king to remain in power as my sworn vassal, and remove the levies raised on goods passing between both our countries.'

Olivan choked, spluttering wine all over his fancy robes. 'High Queen of the North? My lady, this is madness! Why in the Maker's name should we agree to your sovereignty over us?'

'Because if you do not, I will simply take it,' Sedaine replied with a smile that was all sharp edges and little warmth. 'Let me make myself clear, my lord. I intend to bring Elvelen under my rule, just as my father did with Naveen, and I would rather not waste lives to do so. We will be needing them soon enough.'

The envoy shook his head in astonished disbelief. 'You intend? My lady, we care not for your pretensions, or your threats. You cannot simply decide to take what you please and expect us to capitulate. Your claim to Elvelen will never be upheld in the South. They would cease all trade, cut off your supplies, as they would any other usurper. Even if you could take my country, you could never hold it.'

Sedaine met and held his gaze. 'The South is unimportant. It is already lost. No, my lord. The southern states no longer signify. Only the North can be saved, and I will do all that is in my power to ensure that it does. United we may give ourselves a chance of survival but divided and warring we will be crushed just as surely as the South will be.'

Olivan set down his glass with nerveless fingers to hide his sudden lurch from composure. 'I do not understand you, my lady. What is this threat that demands such action? What enemy is powerful enough to swallow the South and threaten us?'

Sedaine nodded to Vianor and the magician related in brief phrases the imminent attempt at conquest from Caledan. He spared none of his people's involvement with the Kas'Talani priesthood, for Sedaine had been quite clear on that point. There would be no more deception. Elvelen was to be allowed to choose freely, and they were to have all the dirty, unpleasant details.

When he had finished, Lord Olivan was ashen. He turned on Sedaine. 'You? You abetted this?'

She inclined her head, unapologetic. 'Not knowingly, not willingly, but yes, I played my part. We were all used, Nathas most of all. Perhaps now you can understand that, regrettable as it was, his death was necessary.'

'Necessary?' the envoy squeaked. 'I see that it was necessary for their plans, not yours, if you truly wish to undo the harm these foreigners have done.'

'And I should have let him live?' Sedaine demanded, her patience beginning to wear thin. 'Tell me, my lord, I should have allowed a wrongly-sanctioned and crowned king alive to contest my rightful claim? I should have let him live and return to Elvelen, to incite rebellion against this land? If our only hope lies in unity, *I should have allowed a living symbol of disharmony free to threaten that?*

Olivan was silent. He realised for the first time the distaste with which she herself regarded the expedient of Nathas's death, and caught a glimmer of the desperation underpinning her current stance. Half an hour earlier he would have seized on this, tried to turn it to his advantage, but now it merely made him quake with fear. That this woman, who already held the largest and the richest of the northern kingdoms in her power, was desperate in the face of the threat the magician had outlined, convinced him of the danger.

He stood, hiding his unsteadiness behind the adjustment of snarled robes. 'You have given me much to consider, my lady,' he told her, forcing himself to meet her piercing gaze. 'And much that I must report to my own king. I beg leave to return to Elvelen and put these matters before his majesty's council. You will have an answer, I promise you that, though what it will be I cannot say. I fear that the king and his lords will be unwilling to surrender their autonomy, no matter the stakes.'

'Then you must convince them,' Sedaine replied, as she also rose. 'I will not shy from war should it come to that.'

Olivan bowed. 'That I understand most clearly, my lady.'

She nodded, and when she held out her hand this time, he hesitated barely a moment before offering her due courtesy.

'I will expect your answer before the winter solstice,' she told him. 'We do not have time to waste in pointless bargaining. My position will stand unaltered for you to accept or refuse, as you choose, in full understanding of the consequences of either choice.'

'My lady, you will have an answer before then,' Olivan assured her. 'I will see to that.'

'Well?' Sedaine asked as the doors closed behind the sweating, obsequious envoy. 'Can we trust him to convince them?'

'Here, in your presence, I would say yes,' Vianor replied, easing himself into the chair recently vacated by Olivan. 'But once he has returned to his own court and is surrounded by his peers and their guards and garrisons?' He shrugged. 'I think he is convinced of the danger, but he is one man. His voice alone will carry little weight in their council.'

'You think they will resist? We must achieve this peacefully.'

The magician shrugged. 'You must prepare yourself to do otherwise, my queen.'

Sedaine slammed her hand down on the arm of her chair. 'To do otherwise is to throw ourselves wide open to conquest! You know this. We must convince Elvelen of the same.'

'Had you acted sooner –'

'No!' She stood, pacing to the window. 'Had I acted sooner hundreds would already be dead. I had to take this chance, and it is too late for discussions of what might have been. I need your wisdom, uncle, and I need your support. What else can I do?'

'Sedaine, you underestimate yourself. I offer you a bleak assessment so you can plan for every contingency. Yes, there is a chance Olivan will fail to convince his betters of the necessity of the price you ask, but there is also a chance he will succeed. My advice to you in the meantime is to begin recruiting. Expand your armies, train them, and have them standing ready for whatever comes, be it war with Elvelen, the South, or the Kas'Talani. Let them see the strength you can bring to bear, and perhaps you will hasten their decision.'

'Or they may suspect treachery,' she countered. 'A show of force now could ruin everything.'

'Then strike elsewhere while their attention is on Rhiannas,' he suggested, and saw the sudden stillness of her listening concentration. 'We both know that Delgar is the true power in Elvelen, the presence of his envoy rather than the king's only confirms this. Send overtures to him in secret. Let him think you will reward his help by removing King Elian and setting him up in his place. A vassal-king in name, but with your promise of virtual autonomy.'

'And when he gives me his assistance in expectation of his reward?'

'You have two choices. Elian dies, or Delgar does. Elian is little more than a boy, while Delgar is a man in the prime of his life. He is strong, but he lacks subtlety. Of the two he would be easier to control, but Elian gives you the greatest chance of stability in Elvelen.'

She turned, looking at him with both admiration and distaste. 'Your mind is more devious than I suspected, uncle. Your plan has merits, but I cannot be party to the murder of a child, nor a man whose only true fault lies in an ambitious nature and a lack of common sense.'

'Delgar is more than that, as you know well. Neither is Elian an innocent child. You know the unpleasant practices that have been resurrected under his brief rule. Slavery for condemned criminals, torture for his enemies. In all this Delgar has supported him.'

Sedaine sighed. 'So, they are not perfect. No one is. Yet it is not my place to judge them for it.'

'No yet,' Vianor replied. 'But once you are high queen over Elvelen they become your subjects, and if you were to discover some of their more unpleasant secrets, which you would of course make public, who would blame you for acting to remove such cankers from your land?'

This time she laughed. 'More devious still. I am glad indeed that you are on my side, my lord.'

And, fool though he knew himself to be, Vianor basked in the compliment. 'Shall I call the scribe?' he asked. 'If you send your message by courier this very day, it will reach Delgar before Olivan does. The better for you to have the Valan Lakes in your pocket before the council meets to discuss your terms.'

PART THREE
Ephenor

Tesseria

The Second Age

MY SON IS DEAD. The words were hollow, meaningless. They could not encompass the enormity of his loss, but neither could he move beyond them to confront the gaping hole of Medelin's death.

Another thought kept intruding.

He killed my son.

Aarkan was his enemy and they were at war. But for hundreds of years before that they had been friends.

He had stood as guardian to Medelin at his naming.

He had loved the boy as his own.

He had hunted him down and killed him.

He killed my son.

My son is dead.

Lorrimer knew now there was no way to win the war. There was no outcome they could hope for that would undo the damage already done. They could not win, and Aarkan had already lost.

The doors were flung open and someone entered his sanctuary. He turned slowly, unwilling to let another intrude on this instant of raw pain, and saw Riah. For a moment she stood poised as she searched for him, her body taut with anger, her own pain held numb under tight rein, and his heart mourned anew for the necessity that had forced his people to become warriors. To become killers.

He stepped out of the shadows and she spun towards him. Hair deep red like the autumn leaves framed a face hardened by trials no one should have had to bear. For she was the daughter of Aarkan, and the son Lorrimer had lost had been her lover.

She dropped to her knees, head bowed in acknowledgment of their shared loss. Lorrimer took her hand to raise her to her feet and he saw in her face what he most feared to see. And again the thought came to him. *He killed my son. We cannot win this war.*

'Daughter,' he murmured, breaching her unspoken thoughts. 'Grieve for Medelin as you will, but do not seek vengeance for his death, I beg you.'

Riah jerked back from his touch, grey eyes blazing. 'He was your son!'

'For that he died. Medelin was killed for the power his death would have over me. My love can cause no more of my people to die.'

He held out a hand to her as he spoke, but Riah would not even look at him. Her fury singed the air around them into crackling waves of power. Elemental Fire flowed through her, fanning her rage.

'Coranu stands ready,' she told him coldly. 'If you are not prepared to act, we will. I will fight to avenge the man I loved, as you would if you truly loved him!'

The words hurt as she intended them to. He had loved her as a daughter, raised her as his own after her father abandoned her, and he could not bear her grief on top of his.

He felt so old, the weight of the world resting on his shoulders. As he watched Riah struggle against the peaceful tenants of her upbringing to embrace a violence that was never in her nature, he knew the danger posed by the madness of Aarkan was too great. Even though they fought now to preserve the purity of the world's elemental harmony, his people could not help but become corrupted by the conflict. Riah's desire for vengeance against the father who had wronged her was but a natural expression of the hatred nurtured on slow burn to deflect a people's grief too unbearable to shoulder.

'He is my father,' Riah broke in, her words falling like an axe on the splinters of his hopes. '*It is my right!*'

She turned to leave, her intent set in her mind. Spurred to action by the unthinkable consequences of her choice, Lorrimer reached out and touched her mind to stillness. His contact was deft and gentle, and she gave way before him with only the barest flicker of resistance. He had hoarded his secrets too long.

He did not disturb Riah's active link with Coranu. The dragon was wise beyond human comprehension and she would help steady her rider through the revelations to come. As he slipped into the swift-flowing stream of her consciousness he spun for her the possible futures of the world in harrowing detail…

…The war raged on. Fire-blackened, barren landscapes stretched out before them, and a dry, cracked riverbed threaded a scar across the land, wending its way towards a shrinking sea. A fortress appeared, its outline blurred to the eyes by magic twisted to malevolence. The foreground was littered with bleached bones, and from within mindless creatures gave voice to their agony. In the skies above flew horrors to send a man witless—neither human nor dragon, but a soulless embodiment of every selfish impulse in those two races. The human traits that had tempered the wild nature of the dragons were lost, burned away by the terrible course of their merging. Sentient awareness was buried past recall and primal instincts scoured the land as magic grown powerfully strong was engaged without conscious restraint.

Yet for all their seeming omnipotence, these creatures were not alone in the world. Small pockets of life existed in resistance, but as her vision surveyed their outposts and scouts, Riah recognised that those who still fought had lost their understanding of their cause. She saw in them the ruthlessness and desperation of men and women forced to fight every day to survive, and the magic they raised was kinked and snarled, corrupted by their fear and hatred. And she understood that they no longer fought for the survival of the world, for what they had become was no more than a reflection of the evil they opposed.

Her senses spiralled onwards as the scene changed. As her vision steadied and grew still, she saw that now Andeira was not merely ravaged but cold and dead. No life had survived whatever searing catastrophe had torn the thread of elemental harmony. Riah realised with mounting horror that her awareness no longer picked up the pure, interlinked energies that underpinned the existence of all living things. She cried out in despair as realisation dawned that the chance had slipped by for the races to repent and reclaim their place in the earth's order. What she saw now was the irrevocable destruction of the creation she had believed herself to be safeguarding.

She felt strong hands hold her steady, the same hands that were guiding this augury. Gentle reassurance followed—it was not too late. But before she could recover, the vista shifted to reveal another strand of possibility.

Riah saw sprawling cities, great deserts, and green woodlands. Men covered the land like ants, nations came and went, dynasties rose and fell, as time rolled inexorably onwards.

But familiarity and relief had left her temporarily blinded. Prompted to look closer, she saw that even here the harmony of the earth was damaged. Lack of purity in the elements had caused imbalances in nature: seas had swelled; great fissures deep in the earth had torn the land apart and new continents had formed; forests flourished in the lowlands, but green life was dying out the mountains and high places; and great deserts were creeping their slow death across the world. And worst of all, she saw no dragons. The magic she sensed in the gifted men and women of this time was incomplete, and the elements they lacked were those the link had bestowed. A grief too great to contain welled up inside her at the possibility that they should ever be faced with such a future.

And yet, amidst the wreckage of her dreams, she divined a thread of hope that flickered through the ages. As events became legend then faded out of memory, and knowledge was irretrievably lost through the passage of years, still the promise remained that someday the old ways could be restored. But there was no certainty. Too many possibilities existed that could cut the single thread of continuity that might lead humanity to redemption and bring back the ancient dragons from wherever they had been forced to hide. As she strained to discern more, the image began to blur…

…Weeping, Riah raised her hand to wipe away the tears. Lorrimer watched her, his too-bright eyes filled with unbearable compassion.

'Aarkan's life is no longer yours to take,' he told her when she had gathered herself. 'Killing him will not end this; only we can do that.'

Riah stared at him wordlessly, her mind still snared by the devastating revelations. At last she asked, 'There is no other way?'

Lorrimer shook his head. 'I wanted to think so, and I let that hope blind me for too long. But after, after…' He stopped, unable to finish that thought. 'I have searched, again and again. What I have shown you is both the best and the worst that could happen.'

'The best? You condemn us to a future without hope! Better that we perish than be forced to live so maimed.'

The old man shook his head. 'No hope? Daughter, I thought you saw more clearly. There is always hope. But the world we have known and loved is already gone, we just refuse to accept it. We no longer stand on the precipice—we have fallen. To undo what Aarkan has done, we must cut him off from the source of his power. Then we must erase the memory of this conflict from the world so that future generations can restore Andeira's elemental harmony free of his taint.'

Riah paled, appalled. 'But what of Andeira if your plans fail? If they succeed? You will shatter that harmony to save it—what if you're wrong?'

'Would you truly rather I allowed events to follow their present course?' Lorrimer asked. 'You've seen with your own eyes the devastation that *will* result from the continuation of this war. If your father and his followers are allowed to advance unchecked, their powers will soon be beyond our ability to counter, and the madness that already afflicts their minds will grow to ravage and destroy all conscious control. If that happens it will be too late for all of us.'

He reached out and grasped her hands. 'We must act, Riah, before our choices are taken from us. Surely you see that? How awful to know we could have stopped this and yet we stood by and did nothing!'

Her tears were falling freely now. 'But what you are asking… such a sacrifice as this? I thought I could face anything, but my heart quails at the thought. What if we are not strong enough?'

But the terror she felt, he shared also. To give up the beauty, the wonder, the power of the Joining was to cut the heart living from the body. All that they were, and all they would become, was shaped by the wisdom and gifts endowed in the moment of Joining. To deny that experience to future generations was not only to damn them to a paler existence. The loss of elemental harmony would condemn the world to a gradual deterioration.

What if I am wrong?

He killed my son.

We cannot win this war.

Lorrimer looked into the tormented eyes of Aarkan's daughter and smiled sadly. 'Child, you are stronger than you know. And if you, who has suffered so much and lost so many dear to you, can embrace an even greater sacrifice for your people's future, there is hope indeed.'

She swallowed and looked away. 'When?'

'Soon.' It had to be soon. There was so little time. 'The council meets three nights hence.'

'And if they don't agree?'

It was Lorrimer's turn to look away. 'They must,' he said at last. 'This must be our choice. If we are to survive it, we must embrace it. Will you stand with me?'

Riah was silent so long he thought she would refuse him. Then she placed her hand on his old one, her touch light and gentle. 'I will.'

Her dragon was sleeping, but Riah's call woke her from her slumber. Coranu was with her instantly, sending her love through their link to bolster her flagging spirit, a surge of emotion that was both vital and tender.

Riah hurried through the passageways, seeking the rock stalls where the dragons sometimes slept, seeking her companion. She needed no light to find her way to Coranu, laying her hand on the creature's scaled flank. She needed no light to see the yellow-gold sheen of her hide, nor to trace the long pale scar that arched over her haunch and into her belly. The lance thrust had nearly ended them, and Riah had sat up through the long nights as Coranu languished in wound sickness, ravaged by the same fever that afflicted her dragon. The link was strong. If Coranu had succumbed, Riah would have died also, her body unable to support the loss of her partner. So now, when she felt her heart could not bear the death of her lover and the terrible knowledge of what was to come, she sought out her dragon to provide her with the strength to survive.

She buried her face in the dragon's side and let her tears seep into the fiery body in affirmation of the power of their bond. Coranu bore the sacrifice and the gift and extended herself in return, her magic cradling her mage. At last Riah exhausted her tears and slid down the dragon's flank, curling up within the protective shelter of her folded wings.

'I miss him.'

As do I. But your heart will heal, little sister, and by your memories you will keep him alive within you. You will keep your love alive.

A wave of hopelessness flooded her. Her love had died with Medelin. It had died when her father had taken him from her. And now, because of him, she would lose the only other creature she truly loved, and she felt her heart breaking all over again for a loss she did not know how to survive.

Coranu's head came down to rest against her. *Not so, little sister. I have never known you to give up. I know you will not now. Never think that your love has died, or we will all be the lesser for it.*

So too had Lorrimer said before she left. He had taken her hand in his and his eyes had implored her to listen. She could hear his voice in her mind, telling her not to give up. Finally, he had said to her, 'Daughter, listen to the wisdom of an old man who has known much sorrow. It is not our strength in magic, or in battle, but our capacity for love that will save us.'

'I have no more love,' she had told him. 'I have only hatred.'

'Then you must find it within yourself and embrace it, as we must embrace those who oppose us, for if you do not, and our people do not, then there truly is no hope for us. Future generations must be built on true foundations or we will never again be ready to undo what must be done. That would be the greatest tragedy of all.'

'Why me?' she had asked him, her voice cracking with strain. 'Let others survive and lead our people forward. I cannot.'

Lorrimer shook his head. 'The others are not you,' he told her. 'It is you they will need. So, I beg you to survive—to live!—and preserve our traditions for those who will come after, who will never know what we have known. One day, one of them will be ready.'

Such a burden. She did not want it, and it would be so much easier to give up caring and gamble her life away without thought for others. Tonight, if she wished, she could fly with the patrol, risking both their lives as she had done many times before, and there was the seduction of freedom and abandonment in that choice. Or she could bow to Lorrimer's entreaty and remove herself from the last days of the war so that the knowledge she possessed could benefit her descendants.

Riah said a silent prayer to Tesserion, Maker, Spirit of Andeira. *Give me the strength to choose life. Guide me, protect me, and show me the way I must choose. If I follow my heart, I betray my people. Tesserion, guide me.*

But in the end the choice was hers alone, and she knew what she had to do. So she remained where she was, sheltered by the warmth of her dragon in the cold stall, and that night she slept while others fought and died in the conflagration that was engulfing her world. And her dreams were soothing and free from pain, a gift from Coranu through the channel of the link, given to ease her through the first bitter ravages of grief.

ONE

Ephenor

The New Age

'MY LORD, A messenger comes.'

Shrogar turned from the window. 'I have seen him. Send him to me when he arrives.' He had been watching the rider's progress since he had first appeared as a dark speck on the horizon. Months had passed with little to mark the passing of the days and his instincts sensed trouble. Things were too quiet, too calm, and the waiting was a strain on his nerves.

Six nights ago, the first warning had come, a shadow full of menace, invading his dreams and clouding his mind. Ever had his talent come to him thus, in fits and starts, offering glimpses of things he could never quite catch. But this was different—darker, more real—and he woke to a sense of cold dread.

Frustrated, Shrogar rested his head on his raised arm. He had neither the training nor the knowledge to decipher the meaning of the dreams. His natural talent remained unschooled and ungovernable. A strong, proud man, assured of his skills in leadership and battle, he found it disconcerting to be so unsure of his ground. Not for the first time he wished for the counsel of Kinseris, but no word had come from the priest for a long time.

Before long he heard the messenger mounting the staircase to his study, his hesitant, uneven footsteps heralding the exhaustion of too many days in the saddle. Shrogar sprung to open the door, holding it wide in welcome as the weary man reached the top of the stairs, regretful that he had not thought to spare him this last part of the journey by descending to the meeting hall. Then, as the messenger raised his face, Shrogar cried aloud with joy, sweeping the dusty figure into a bear hug, arms enveloping the smaller man and lifting him off his feet.

A muffled laugh erupted from the new arrival. 'Put me down, brother!' he gasped. 'Is this the way you greet all your guests?'

Shrogar laughed and let him go, holding him out before him and taking in every detail of his face. The difference between the two was startling. The Lord of Ephenor was a huge man, tall and powerfully built, and possessed of a charisma that saw men follow wherever he led. His brother was slightly built, though just as fair of hair and eye, and his features favoured the more delicate cast of their mother rather than the bluff, rugged countenance Shrogar had inherited from their father.

'Iarwin. It has been too long, little brother. I had almost given you up. Come, relax. I will attend you.' Shrogar ushered his brother inside and sat him down on the only chair, kneeling to remove his travel-stained boots.

Iarwin eased himself into the chair and allowed his brother to see to his needs. 'You have not lost all your manners, I see.'

The Lord of Ephenor glowered, but a twinkle of amusement flickered in his dark eyes. Then he stopped as a hiss warned him of some concealed hurt. Looking up he saw Iarwin's face had paled, lines of pain etched deep around his eyes.

'You are injured. Should I send for Callan?' He surveyed his brother's face with concern. 'What has happened? What news do you bring?'

With an effort the weary man steadied his breathing and held up a hand to stop the flow of questions. 'Slowly, brother,' he pleaded. 'The hurt is slight. I was pursued from Kas'Tella but managed to lose them in the Sharhelm Pass. I fell from my horse onto some rocks. My leg is bruised and cut, but not more seriously damaged.'

Shrogar unlaced the high boots and carefully removed the left to reveal the damaged flesh beneath. With skilled fingers he probed the wounds then opened the door to call for hot water and bandages. Then he returned to his brother's side and pulled up the footstool and gestured for him to continue his tale.

'The message I bring is from Kinseris —'

Shrogar looked up sharply, and Iarwin raised a questioning eyebrow. 'You feared for him? If so your fears were well founded. Kinseris hoped to come here himself, but word reached me two days out of Kas'Tella that he had fallen out of favour with his high priest once more and is now a prisoner. I do not know the details, but I fear our secrets remain hidden no longer.'

'He would not betray us,' Shrogar said firmly. Kinseris's loyalty was beyond question, but he also knew that for a long time now they had been surviving on borrowed time. For years Vasa had been seeking them, ferreting out their agents, destroying whatever refuge he could find. If Kinseris had been taken, it might be the spark that ended the uneasy deadlock. Their enemy must know more than they had thought.

Looking up, he saw his brother's sympathy clear on his face.

'These are rumours only,' Iarwin assured him. 'He was alive and well when he gave me this message. Three of us were sent, each bearing the same missive. We parted on the Redfern Plains just before the pursuit came upon us. Of the others I know nothing, but I fear the worst. If they are not here already it can only mean they have been captured or killed as I took the longest route. It has been seven days since I left Kas'Tella and I would have been here sooner had it not been necessary to ensure no one followed.'

'Seven days?' Shrogar whispered. 'Six nights ago I felt a darkness settle in my dreams, a threat that has grown with every day.' He tensed as an unwelcome thought occurred to him. 'The message? If the others have been caught as you fear, your news may already be known to Vasa.'

Iarwin reached under his cloak and removed a black cylinder. He rested it in his palm a long moment before placing it on the chair between them.

'This must be news indeed, for he has risked much to get it to you. It is keyed to you. If anyone else tries to break this seal the message will be destroyed. I would have destroyed it myself if –'

He broke off as the door opened and a servant entered, carrying water and bandages. 'Fetch my brother some refreshment and send the Lady Dianeth to us,' Shrogar called as he left. 'Then tell Ieshwen to assemble my officers at sundown.'

Ignoring the cylinder, Shrogar washed the injured limb. Two jagged cuts sliced through the flesh of the calf and the area was badly bruised. Despite Iarwin's protests to the contrary, the wounds were deep and inflamed.

'You fell, you say?' Shrogar asked, studying the cuts.

Iarwin shrugged carelessly. 'The rocks were sharp.'

Shrogar decided not to press. He could imagine the dangers of the journey through these inhospitable lands with Kas'Tella's soldiers in pursuit.

Iarwin sat silently as his brother cleaned the wounds, his knuckles white as he gripped the sides of the chair. Shrogar hastened to finish his work, deftly winding the bandage. He had just finished when there was a knock at the door.

Shrogar called out his permission to enter without looking up, and only when Iarwin tensed and tried to stand did he realise it was not his manservant returning. He stood, placing a firm hand on his brother's shoulder to keep him seated.

'Indeed, there is no need for you to rise, dearest brother,' agreed the lady who entered. 'There is no need for formalities among family.'

Smiling, Shrogar slipped his arm around his wife's waist and drew her close. She was a slight woman, silvery blond hair framing pleasant, kindly features. No great beauty, perhaps, but possessed of a quiet dignity that complemented her husband's vibrant presence.

'My young brother,' Shrogar said proudly. 'Gone for years, and just look at the state of him when he returns. I always said he needed his family to take care of him.'

Iarwin took no offence. He grinned at them, pleased by the warmth of their welcome. 'Lady Dianeth, it is always a pleasure. I do believe you become more beautiful with every passing year.'

'Indeed, she does,' agreed her husband warmly, and his hand came to rest over her stomach. Seeing the secret happiness that passed between them, Iarwin was quick to offer his congratulations.

'We only knew for certain this last month,' Dianeth replied, her pale face alight with a warm glow. 'Your brother hopes for a son to be his heir. For myself I think your family needs more women.'

She smiled at her husband as she spoke, then her gaze fell on the bandages and she became instantly concerned. 'You are hurt.'

Shrogar laughed as his brother brushed aside her concerns. 'He fell from his horse. His horsemanship has always been poor.'

Dianeth smiled as Iarwin protested, but the banter could not disguise the air of anticipation, and her eyes were drawn to the message cylinder still resting on the chair.

'Kinseris sends news at last?'

Cued by his wife, Shrogar picked up the cylinder and broke the seal. Long moments passed as he read and reread the message. Then he looked at Iarwin with a frown. 'You saw Kinseris? He was well?'

Iarwin nodded. 'He seemed so. What does he say?'

Shrogar looked down at the scrap of parchment, turning it over in his hand as if looking for more. Growing concerned, Iarwin reached out and took the message from his brother's slack grasp.

'What is this nonsense?' he demanded. 'Why does he speak of trade and the price of silk?' He snorted, tossing the paper aside.

Shrogar leant down and picked it up. 'He does not,' he said heavily. 'It is but one of many codes we devised.' He shook his head, unsure how to feel, how to react to the tersely phrased message. 'I never thought we would have need of it.'

Dianeth laid a hand on his arm. 'Tell us.'

Shrogar's hand covered hers for a moment, then he gently pried it loose and moved to stand by the window. 'Long ago Kinseris told me of a legend of his Order. It was late. We had been drinking, and...'

He paused, his voice suddenly choked. Kinseris had come to Ephenor only once that he remembered, during the dark days after his father died. Ephenori scouts had found his father's body in the deep desert, two days from the edge of the Redfern plains where the Kas'Talani had left it for them to find. Roden had been dead for weeks, his body ravaged by the elements and desert scavengers, but the priests had left tokens enough on the body to ensure his identity would be known. Tokens, but not his sword, the sword of his house that Shrogar now wore at his waist.

He touched a hand to it now. Kinseris had returned it to him, Kinseris who had known his father since before Shrogar was born. An alliance forged out of necessity had become something more, deepened by friendship and mutual respect. Kinseris was the man who had kept Ephenor fighting, the man who had kept their resistance alive, and he alone understood what had driven his father. They had dreamed together, shared their secrets and their fears, and through his memories the priest had been able to give Shrogar back a small part of the father he had lost so young. He had also drawn the young ruler into his confidence, transferring to the son the loyalty he had given to the father, and receiving the son's in return. While Kinseris lived, the link with his father, so precious to him, would remain, but the contents of the priest's message threatened to sever it forever.

'We spoke of many things,' Shrogar continued finally, pushing back the memories of a grief that was still too raw, even after so many years. 'One of those things was Æisoul.' He heard Iarwin make an impatient noise. 'I do not speak of barroom gossip,' he snapped, 'but of Kas'Talani lore. This legend comes from the priests themselves and if they think there is truth in it, then I will not dismiss it lightly.'

'And what did Kinseris say of Æisoul?' Iarwin asked scornfully. 'What is this thing the priests fear so much?'

'Æisoul is a man. The man the Kas'Talani believe will destroy them.'

'Destroy them?' Iarwin sneered, but his face had paled. 'Who could the priests possibly fear?'

'I do not know,' Shrogar admitted. 'Kinseris could not tell me, and I did not think, at the time, that he believed the tale to be true.' He set the paper to the flame burning in the lamp on his desk, watching as the corners curled and the message blackened and burned, crumbling to ash on the table.

'At the time?' Dianeth prompted.

Shrogar gave her a reassuring smile. 'If he did not believe it then, he does now. Kinseris sends word that he has found Æisoul, and that he is a captive of Vasa. They both are. He asks for my help.'

'Your help?' Iarwin repeated. 'What help can you give them? If they are prisoners of Kas'Tella, nothing can save them.'

Shrogar sucked in a deep breath, forcing himself to show the restraint his brother lacked. Iarwin himself had only narrowly escaped that same fate, and he had spent many years in Kas'Tella. He had served the Order. Iarwin knew far better than any of them the horrors they were capable of.

'There is more,' he continued, ignoring Iarwin's hostility. 'The man had companions who might be on their way to us even now. He asks that we give them shelter.'

'Of course,' Dianeth murmured. 'Friends of Kinseris are always welcome here. We will offer them what help we can.'

Shrogar squeezed her hand. 'I know you will.'

Dianeth lowered her eyes, and Shrogar knew that she would guess his intentions and fear for him. He understood her fears and was torn. What Kinseris asked for—the risk he asked Ephenor to take—might take him from her and their unborn child forever, and love for her made him waver as no amount of reasoned argument ever could. Taking a deep breath, he steeled rebellious nerves and tightened his grip on Dianeth's hand. 'The council meets at sundown,' he told them steadily. 'I wish you both to be present. Kinseris has asked for our help, but he asks a lot and we must consider this carefully.'

'No!' Iarwin surged to his feet, careless of his injury. 'To do what he asks is suicide! If Ephenor had the power to challenge Kas'Tella we would not have fought all these years in secret. We cannot do this!'

Shrogar regarded his younger brother calmly, seeing the creeping exhaustion that had abraded already fraught nerves. His thin face was creased with pain, but his pallor had given way to bright spots of passion on too-prominent cheekbones.

'Kinseris would not ask such a thing unless there was no other way. And he does not ask it for himself, but for another.'

'We cannot do this,' Iarwin repeated. '*I will not go back there!*'

Shrogar's head came up sharply. 'You would not have to accompany us. Indeed, I would not expect it. You should remain here and give yourself time to heal.' Iarwin's physical injury would not prevent him riding if he had need, but Shrogar recognised that there were other raw scars in him that would take much longer to fade.

Stung by his brother's tone, Iarwin turned away from them. 'I am not afraid,' he insisted. 'But it is too great a risk. We should not risk our people for the sake of a legend that has nothing to do with us.'

Dianeth glanced at her husband, unsure whether she should stay. Shrogar nodded and she gave him a small smile, a wisp of golden hair escaping her combs as she turned to leave.

As the door closed behind her, the Lord of Ephenor studied the brother who had not even acknowledged her departure. 'What is it that you know?' he asked gently, placing a hand on Iarwin's shoulder. 'Tell me. If I am to make this decision, I need to know everything.'

Iarwin winced at his touch. When Shrogar did not remove his hand, Iarwin stepped away from him. He turned slowly, his face white with strain, and a muscle twitched in his clenched jaw.

Shrogar watched him with concern. His brother had been away a long time, but he could not have changed so much. He was so rigidly controlled that he seemed almost on the edge of hysteria.

'Tell me,' he urged.

Iarwin shook his head.

'What is it you fear?'

'I am not afraid!'

'Then why is it that you look so terrified?'

Iarwin glared at him, a savage light in his eyes that sent Shrogar reeling back a pace. Something in Iarwin seemed to crumble at the shock on his face and his shoulders slumped in defeated exhaustion.

'I am sorry. I am merely tired, so tired.' He scrubbed a weary hand across his face and eased himself back into the chair.

'It is more than that.'

Iarwin sighed, looking away from him towards the room's sole window. 'There is nothing,' he insisted. 'I swear I have told you everything.'

Shrogar seated himself on the stool once more, close to his brother should he be needed.

'Do you believe in this legend?' Iarwin asked at length. 'Do you really believe that any man can end the tyrant's rule?'

'I do not know, but legends have power, even if men don't. If the priests believe this Æisoul can destroy them, that belief might be their undoing.'

Iarwin laughed bitterly. 'And your idealistic dreams might be our undoing. I do not think it wise to place our faith in a legend, even less one the priests have created.'

Shrogar studied his taut profile. 'If I do not dream, I accept defeat.'

'Be careful,' Iarwin warned. 'Kinseris may not be the man you knew if he escapes Kas'Tella. There are... things... there that could turn even him against you, against himself.'

Shrogar felt a flicker of fear, a sliver of nightmare come to life. 'What are you saying? That he might have betrayed us? That this is trick?'

Iarwin paled. 'Not willingly. Maybe not even knowingly. But even if he has not betrayed us, he is still Kas'Talani. I have lived in that place for many years and I know our enemy as you cannot. They are dangerous, and they are secretive. They shroud themselves in their mysteries, and they never reveal their purpose to anyone. Kinseris might be your friend and our ally, but he is Kas'Talani before everything. In this he is no different from the rest.'

Shrogar listened in stony silence as Iarwin fretted with his cloak. 'Who can say if Kinseris has truly found this Æisoul, whether he even exists or ever will? And who knows what his purpose truly is? How can you really know that we should trust him?'

'He has earned my trust,' Shrogar replied simply. 'And until I have proof that I should do otherwise, I will honour the years of loyalty between us.'

He stood, pacing restlessly to the window. 'You say we cannot know his purpose, and perhaps you are right. Æisoul is but a name to me, not a man, not a hope of victory. Yet I will welcome an end to Vasa's rule however it comes about. If Æisoul can make that happen, how can I stand aside and let Vasa destroy him?'

'And if you do not stand aside and you die in Kas'Tella's dungeons along with him?' Iarwin countered. 'You would leave Ephenor defenceless and Vasa will destroy our people too. Please, Shrogar. If this is indeed a trick, and you ride to Kas'Tella, your people could lose more than their lord. They could lose everything.'

'Iarwin, I know!' Shrogar drove his fist into the wall, swearing as the impact left his knuckles bruised and bloody. 'Do you think I do not understand what is at stake? Do you think I have given no thought to our people?' He cradled his damaged hand to his chest, focusing on the pain to dull the edge of his anger. 'That is why I ask—*if* I go—that you remain here. Should I perish, it will fall to you to continue our struggle. The people will need you. They will look to you to give them courage, and I would have no one else care for my wife if I cannot.'

'You think there will be any struggle to continue if you are gone?' his brother shot back. 'Shrogar, my lord! Should you fall into Vasa's hands, no matter your courage, he will get the answers he wishes from you in the end. If he should come to Ephenor, we cannot stand.'

Shrogar whirled around. 'You can, and you will! And I will stand beside you.' He crossed to his brother, kneeling before him to take his shoulders in both hands. 'Vasa will come,' he told him more gently. 'Do you not yet understand? He was always going to come eventually. And if this is the end, Iarwin, then we cannot escape it no matter what we do. We can remain here and nurture our strength, or we can look outwards for our salvation. Perhaps in Kinseris and Æisoul we have been given the means to survive.'

He held Iarwin's gaze, searching his eyes for a sign of understanding, but his brother lowered his lashes and looked away.

Shrogar sighed, releasing his grip. When Iarwin still refused to meet his eyes, he walked to the door and flung it open. 'Go, rest,' he urged. 'You are tired and hurt, and I have kept you talking too long. Nothing will be decided while you sleep. Your apartments are as you left them, and you will not be disturbed.'

Iarwin rose to his feet. 'I did not mean to offend.'

'I know,' Shrogar replied. 'And you did not. We will talk later, when you have rested. There are matters I must see to that cannot wait.'

TWO

ALONE IN THE darkness with only pain as his final companion, Vasa's mind wandered in delirium, switching from the present to the past to things only dreamed of without conscious awareness of his drifts. At times he called out for servants, to friends long dead, but most often he called for Shakumi. He could not understand why she did not come, only that she did not, and the tears rolled silently down his face for this cruellest of betrayals.

In some moments, as he crossed from dark dream to darker reality, he knew snatches of lucidity. He remembered the sight of her body, blood and poison crusted round her beautiful lips, bursting into flame on a thought. He cried out his confused grief, and cruel sanity prevailed that did not allow him to retreat into the comforting arms of oblivion.

'Shakumi, forgive me,' he whispered into the blackness, and he heard a rustling of movement answer him.

'It is too late for that, old friend,' a brittle voice told him. 'She is dead and her forgiveness will never be yours. Absolution rests with the Maker now.'

Vasa moved his head towards the voice, too weak to do more. 'Seledar?' he called softly, 'have you come for me at last?'

'It is I.'

Vasa settled back with a sigh. 'I knew you would come, at the end.'

'And I did,' the old man answered, arriving at his side. The knowledge of his approaching death was etched starkly in the lines of his face, and each movement was burdened with the exhausted pain of great age. 'I waited for you these last nights,' he said in a voice that rustled like the wind among dry leaves. 'And when you did not come to me, I came to you. Long ago, old friend, I warned you that it would come to this, but you would not listen.'

'Can you not leave off the sermons even now?' his high priest pleaded. 'I find I have no stomach for them, quite literally. All I ever wanted was to protect our Order, can you not understand that?'

'Maybe at the beginning that was all you wanted,' Seledar replied, folding his scarecrow limbs as comfortably as he could on the stone floor. One hand stretched out to find another, limp and cold, and grasped it tight. 'But did you never stop to think whether it deserved protection? Such power corrupts as it always must, and there was never a time you did not long for power.'

'You were not innocent. In those days your hatred was for what you had lost, for the youth and vigour I had taken from you, and the glittering career you saw ahead of you. You were not so sanctimonious then.'

'I was not,' Seledar agreed, 'but I have had long years of old age with nothing to do but think on the past. That was your gift to me that was meant to be my punishment. Many things became clearer to me once I could no longer influence them. You might say I have had an unfair advantage.'

Vasa laughed, his breath coming in wheezing gasps. 'That was not quite how you represented it to me when I visited you. You, ah –' He stopped, his fingers tightening around the hand in his grasp as pain hit him. 'You told me... I... I had consigned you living into the lowest of Andeira's hells, and I believed you... For me it would have been so. It should have been you,' he admitted, each word an effort now. 'The black throne should have been yours. I knew it, and so I could never forgive you.'

Seledar did not reply, waiting out the spasm of raw pain. But Vasa had not yet said all he wished to say and tried to force the words past the agony in his chest as tears of frustration poured down his sunken cheeks.

'Don't speak,' Seledar soothed. 'No more words are needed between us.'

'Not for us,' Vasa gasped, sweat beading on his brow despite his trembling cold. 'But for her. I did not mean –'

His words faded but the old man at his side understood. 'Why?' he asked in gentle reproof, 'why could you not give her up, let the young ones have their time? He would have loved her well, better than you ever could.'

'Because I loved her!' He was weeping now. 'I couldn't let her go. She was mine and I loved her, but she never loved me. She wanted him, my enemy, my traitor, and I couldn't stand it.'

'So, you killed her and destroyed him, as you hadn't been able to destroy me.'

'Tesserion forgive me, yes.' Vasa turned to his friend, his enemy, mere shadows of suggested form in the blackness of his prison. 'One I had allowed to escape me, this one I never could. He would have destroyed me.'

Seledar breathed softly in the darkness. 'He still can. He has.'

'No,' Vasa said, calmer now. 'I have destroyed myself. My only regret is that I could not take Saal'an with me. In that I wish them both luck.' He squeezed the fragile bones in his hand and felt an answering pressure so slight he almost missed it. 'Lie down with me here,' he urged. 'Rest your head a while if you grow weary. We have not long to wait.'

'No, we have not,' Seledar agreed. 'Not long at all.' He leant forwards gratefully, his head cushioned on the shoulder of his old enemy as tense muscles unwound with unfettered finality. 'Yet I am not without fear of the unknown though I have longed for this moment for so many years.'

'We are neither of us innocent souls who can look ahead with untroubled hearts,' Vasa answered in raw self-honesty. 'But at least we are spared the horror of facing it alone. We never could be rid of each other.'

'As to that,' Seledar murmured, 'maybe we never truly wished it.'

They lapsed into silence, cold stiffness closing vocal cords and stilling limbs. And so they were found the next dawn, the bloated, ruined body of the high priest cradling the remains of an old man, no more than a bundle of bird bones and silver hair but clothed in the pristine black of the priesthood. No one knew who he was or how he had come to be there, but that they had died together no one doubted, their hands entwined and locked as one in death.

As they could not be prised apart, their bodies were removed together and burned on the same pyre. As the priesthood mourned its high priest, a girl wept in a dusty room in an abandoned mansion, and a man stood alone on a tower in Kas'Tella and rejoiced.

Vasa was dead. The flames of his funeral pyre had barely begun to die before Darred made his move. The palace was in turmoil. The riots in the city had been brutally quashed and the Arkni had assembled the army. It would leave with the dawn to begin the long trek to Ephenor, the march arranged with a speed that revealed their meticulous preparation for this day. The Kas'Talani were confused, leaderless, for the Arkni were abandoning them, so confident were they in their victory, and Darred would exploit that confidence.

He watched the soldiers lining up from the top of the centre tower, the sunlight glistening on burnished helms and polished armour. Far below him, at the front of the formations, Fadar Wedh paced. The general who led the First Army of Kas'Tella was the Arkni's creature, as he was, but the soldier lacked the skills that allowed Darred to retain his self-mastery, that allowed him to enact this betrayal of his forced obedience. Already he had gathered many of the elders to him in secret, those he knew to be ambitious enough to accept the choice he offered them. Risk everything to gain everything. Caledan was his for the taking, and Amadorn was waiting.

THREE

KALLIS STUDIED THE fortress that rose steadily before him. The desert had begun to recede over the last day of their journey, but his soldier's eye could see that a settlement built in such a place would benefit from the difficult and treacherous location. He regarded it with no little trepidation. Despite the Ancai's repeated assurances, he was not yet convinced that the people here were friends. Once they were inside those imposing stone walls, escape would be impossible if they found themselves in enemy hands.

Their journey across the desert had been harsh, erasing the memory of restful days aboard Iraius's little pirate vessel. He sighed wistfully. There had been a certain attraction to the pirate's existence, one that reminded him of everything that had drawn him to a mercenary's life. He had spent many evenings with the pirate captain, drinking Amadorian brandy and reminiscing about home. For Amadorn was his home, he knew that now, not this dusty, barren land where he had been born. Whatever pull Caledan had once had, it had faded the moment he stepped ashore and discovered the corruption at its heart.

Iraius had told him of his adventures in Caledan in colourful style, and Kallis had believed less than one word in ten. He had been sceptical that the slender craft, even with its wicked crossbow, had achieved the feats her captain attributed to her, but when they had been met a day upriver by its twin he had understood. The Aetelean pirates hunted in packs, just as Amadorn's clans did. When Iraius had offered him a place on his crew, he had refused with regret. He had obligations to fulfil, but once they were done, perhaps he would return to taste that freedom once again for a time.

Kallis knew Iraius sometimes ferried supplies, and even people, from Frankesh to the edge of the desert for Kinseris, and he knew those supplies were headed to Ephenor, the fortress standing proudly amidst this stark landscape. But he could not shake his sense of foreboding as they drew closer. He had never been comfortable within a city's walls, legacy of a childhood spent among nomads.

When the small party reached the gates at last, ragged, dirty, and tired, the heavily armed guards on the wall did little to reassure him. They waited while the Ancai talked quietly to the men at the gates, then followed him through the stone archway and another beyond it into a large courtyard. As he helped Jeta dismount, Kallis watched a tall, rugged man striding purposefully towards them.

The Ancai stepped forward as the man approached, bowing stiffly in greeting.

'Lord Shrogar, I am the Ancai of Frankesh, servant of the Vela'Frankesh, the Lord Kinseris.' He spoke in Amadorian, and Kallis realised with a jolt that the people around him had more in common with those of the northern continent than any of the peoples of Caledan.

He was still digesting this fact and its implications as the Ancai introduced them to Shrogar, who studied them with equal curiosity.

'We have come on Kinseris's orders,' the Ancai continued. 'He was to meet us here if he could.' The formal tone hid an unspoken question. Despite the big captain's outward calm, Kallis knew he was as desperate for news as they were.

Shrogar clasped his hand warmly. 'You are welcome here, my friend. Kinseris has spoken often of your courage and loyalty.' Then his face grew shadowed, the smile fading. 'He is not here. Word reached me this morning that he is a prisoner in Kas'Tella.'

Kallis saw the Ancai's shoulders slump, but he said nothing, merely nodded. Then Shrogar turned to him, and Kallis knew what he was about to say. Wherever Kinseris was, that's where Aarin would be too. 'If you are friends of the companion he spoke of, I must tell you that he is also held captive in the tyrant's city.'

Painfully aware of Jeta's distraught face, Kallis spoke quickly. 'My lord, that is no less than we feared. We would like to accompany you when you ride.'

The Lord of Ephenor quirked an eyebrow. 'When we ride?'

'To Kas'Tella,' Kallis replied smoothly, holding his gaze.

Shrogar matched him stare for stare. 'We shall see,' he said at last. 'That decision has not yet been made. I have called a council to discuss these matters and I wish you to attend. But first you must come inside and partake of our hospitality.'

Kallis nodded, satisfied. 'We will, my lord, but we have news that cannot wait.'

'What news?' Shrogar asked, turning as another man appeared at his shoulder. 'Iarwin, these are the friends that Kinseris has sent to us from Frankesh.' He looked back at the three road-weary travellers. 'This is my brother Iarwin who brought word of your coming from Kas'Tella. He arrived only hours ago.'

'Really?' Kallis remarked in surprise. 'Then you must already know the news we bring. These last two days we have sighted scouts and a great dust trail far to the west. An army is on the move, my lord, and we believe it is headed here.'

Iarwin's face darkened. 'If that were so, I would have seen them.'

'Then you must have missed them,' Kallis replied evenly, 'because they are coming.'

'It is true, my lord,' the Ancai confirmed.

Iarwin spun round in sudden fury. 'I was not followed! They cannot be coming here.'

Kallis looked at him curiously, surprised by his reaction. Shrogar seemed not to have noticed the undercurrents of the exchange. He was staring thoughtfully at them, his gaze seeing not what was in front of him but a huge army out in the desert. 'You are sure of this?' he asked finally.

'Quite sure.'

'They must be mistaken,' Iarwin repeated, calmer now. 'Perhaps you are not used to the desert sun,' he suggested to Kallis. 'It can play tricks on the eyes. This must be what you saw.'

Kallis bit back a retort as Shrogar laid a hand on his brother's arm, at last awakened to the simmering tension.

'I would not blame you if you missed the signs, brother,' he soothed. 'You were injured and fleeing pursuit. You have done enough just by delivering your message.' To the others he said, 'My brother means no offence. He is exhausted, as you must be. Please, let us continue our discussions at the council. As for your news, I will send out scouts of my own. If there is an army heading for Ephenor, they will find it.'

Jeta stood still for a long moment after the door closed behind Dianeth. Shrogar's wife had shown each of them to a room in the citadel, promising to return when it was time for the council. Food had been laid out for them, a simple meal of bread and dried fruit with a flagon of fresh water. She drank the water greedily but ignored the food. She was not hungry. She looked around the small, neat chamber with its steaming tub and felt a rush of exhausted gratitude.

The days aboard *Situran Dawn* had been both restful and hard, and a dearth of privacy meant she had been unable to wash her clothes—or herself, as often as not. Iraius had been a charming and accommodating host—his own words—and he had set them to work almost as soon as they stepped aboard. But he had been as good as his word, and no Kas'Talani presence had threatened them for their journey upriver. In fact, she had found herself growing rather fond of the pirate, despite the way he leered at her when he thought she was not looking. Neither he nor his crew had bothered her with more than looks, a fact that had pleased Kallis. The crack he had taken to his head had kept him down for several days, and he had been in no condition to thump any man for wandering hands.

They had been fun days, but they had been followed by a gruelling ride into the Northern Desert that had rubbed her thighs raw, burnt her hands and face, and left her mouth and throat parched and dry. All that to get here, and now she had arrived she seemed unable to summon any emotion at all.

At last Jeta shook herself and walked to the bed, picking through the garments that had been laid out for her. The dresses were beautiful, she noticed vaguely, coloured silks embroidered with exotic patterns and beaded with tiny pearls. They reminded her of the dresses she had lost when her caravan had been attacked in Lothane. So long ago that seemed. She looked from her travel-stained desert robes to the borrowed dresses with sudden longing, running her fingers over the silk. Amidst the strangeness of this place, they brought a glimmer of familiarity back into her life.

Sudden revulsion made Jeta rip off her filthy clothes, and she slipped into the warm tub, savouring the feel of the clean water against her skin. A cake of soap sat on the edge of the tub and she cleaned away the grime of the journey, soaping her tangled curls. Drying off, she stood before the mirror that hung on the wall. Her hair hung limp to her waist, straggling in long tresses that seemed to bury her under their weight. On impulse she picked up her knife and sheered them off until the curls clung close to her head. She stared at her reflection and saw a stranger looking back, a stranger who had endured things Jeta Elorna could never have survived.

She turned away, unsettled by the image. It made her want to clothe herself in pretty things, to pretend she was safe. She ran her hand through the dresses, discarding them without thought. Then she found a pale silk gown, light enough to sit comfortably even in the heat of the day. A row of pearls ran around the neckline and the cuffs, and silver stitching wove a pattern on the silk. The skirt panels were lined with black silk that flashed when she moved, a reminder that even surrounded by beautiful things, danger remained.

She turned as the door opened and saw Shrogar's wife watching her. She flushed, realising whose dresses she had cast into heaps. Dianeth followed her guilty gaze and smiled, but it was a smile that did not reach her eyes.

Jeta frowned, surprised she had returned so soon. 'Is it time for the council?'

Dianeth shook her head, closing the door firmly behind her. 'The men will not meet until sundown. It is better that we settle this matter between us first, to save them hours of fruitless argument.'

Jeta arched a delicate eyebrow as she perched herself on the edge of the bed. 'My lady, I do not understand you.'

The flicker of amusement crossed Dianeth's face. 'Let us not pretend with one another,' she said. 'And let us dispense with titles that belong as much to you as they do to me, if I have not missed my guess. I am here because I wish to assure myself that you mean my husband and my people no harm.'

Jeta's answering smile was brittle. She understood this game, the hidden play of politics that swirled just beneath the surface. 'Did your husband send you?'

Dianeth smoothed a crease in her skirts, her composure icy cool. 'Let me speak plainly. My husband will decide the outcome of this council, and he will rely on my judgement when he makes his decision. If you wish to convince him that your cause is worthy of the risk you ask of him, you must first convince me.'

'And if I fail?'

Dianeth held her steady gaze without flinching. 'Then there will be no rescue.'

'And Kinseris?'

'I bear Kinseris no ill will, nor do I wish him harm,' Shrogar's wife admitted. 'But should it come to a choice, I will protect my own first.'

'As will I,' Jeta replied coldly.

Dianeth nodded. 'Then I take it we understand each other.'

'Only too well.'

If Dianeth heard the anger in her words she gave no sign. Instead she settled herself in the chair, watching Jeta from a face that was deceptively gentle. There was steel beneath that pale composure, but it was a weapon in which Jeta had also been trained. She had been the daughter of a powerful man, and she knew the subtle power that a woman could bring to bear. Should Dianeth decide against her, Shrogar would likely go along with her choice never realising that it was not his own. Persuade Dianeth, and she would have found a valuable ally.

'Very well,' she agreed at last. 'What do you wish to know?'

Dianeth smiled. 'What power does Æisoul possess that can destroy the Kas'Talani?'

FOUR

THE COUNCIL OF Ephenor met at sundown. The setting sun streamed through the high windows, illuminating Shrogar's troubled face. Jeta watched him, hiding the hammering of her heart behind outward calm. It had seemed so simple when she had talked with Dianeth. Surrounded by these grim-faced men, she knew it would not be so.

She looked back at Shrogar, studying him intently as she replayed Dianeth's words. *I owe Kinseris my life and my happiness. But I must be certain that this message has truly come from him, for I will not allow my husband to be taken in by an enemy in the guise of a friend. His loyalty to the priest will urge him to go, and if the risk were to himself alone, he would go to Kas'Tella to save both his friend and yours with never a thought that this might be a trap.*

She began to see just how much was being asked of these people, and she understood Dianeth's need to protect her husband from his own nature. She also knew that Shrogar was not the one she had to fear here, for as she watched him she saw that he was not a man who did not know his own mind, but one who sought desperately for a means to bring others to his side.

My husband need not have the agreement of the council, Dianeth had explained, *but he will want it. He knows he cannot hope that all will agree, but should the council be split he will feel justified in ordering their obedience.*

She glanced at Shrogar's wife, but Dianeth did not acknowledge her look. She had gained her ally when she had revealed Aarin's secret, but Dianeth could offer her no overt help here, and would not. She had accepted Jeta's explanation, but she had been as stunned by her revelations as these men would be. Jeta had been made to understand that returning the dragons to Andeira was something no man or woman in this land would embrace, not even in Ephenor, if not for the possibility of freedom it offered. She had to make them see past their fear or there was little chance they would endorse Shrogar's wish to ride to Kas'Tella. Tempted to keep uncomfortable truths to herself, Dianeth had made her understand that without the chance to destroy the Kas'Talani, the Ephenori would feel they had no choice but to leave a friend and ally to his fate. The risk was too great.

Jeta wondered whether Shrogar knew this as she waited impatiently for him to speak. There were ten seats and ten people in attendance. Three she knew, three who had their own reasons for supporting Shrogar, but it was not their voices that would count tonight. She turned to the others, identifying them from Dianeth's descriptions. At Shrogar's right sat Iarwin, a taut-strung bundle of nerves even to her eyes. She disliked him on instinct, but he was well loved here, and his words would carry weight. On his left was Dianeth, showing no sign of the nerves that afflicted Jeta. Beside Dianeth sat Ieshwen, oldest and most trusted of Shrogar's captains, and beside him Callan, soldier and healer, another friend who was valued and trusted. Finally, there was the other half of that pair. Callan's twin brother Lysan was seated next to Iarwin, smiling Lysan who seemed as sunny as his brother was grave.

At last Shrogar moved. 'It is already late,' he told them as he took his place at the table, 'so let us get straight to it. I have called you here for two reasons: the first, to discuss the news brought by Iarwin from Kas'Tella, and the second, the arrival of our guests and the word that they have brought us. Gentlemen, an army marches on Ephenor.'

Silence greeted his announcement. Scouts had been sent out hours ago, seeking signs of that same army. Shrogar's captains waited patiently for him to continue. Jeta held her breath, willing him the courage to speak the whole truth. Once again, she heard Dianeth's hurried instructions.

I know my husband, and he will not wish to raise the subject of Æisoul with these men, for he knows they will not understand, but neither will he wish to lie to them. Should he skirt the issue, you must bring it to the fore.

'Kinseris sends us dire news,' Shrogar continued almost as though he had read her thoughts. 'He is a prisoner in Kas'Tella, awaiting execution, and there is another held captive with him, one for whom he has risked both life and freedom. He is an enemy of the tyrant Vasa, but he is more than that. Kinseris names this man Æisoul, the downfall of the Kas'Talani, and because it is Kinseris who makes this claim, I believe it.'

Jeta sat upright as a muttering broke out around the table. Shrogar ignored it. He drew his sword and laid it on the council table, and Jeta knew a moment of sweet relief. Dianeth had told her how Kinseris had returned the sword to them when they had thought it lost, and she realised that Shrogar drew it now to remind his men of the debt they owed the priest. It seemed he was prepared to fight this openly, but even she could see the magnitude of the task he set himself.

She sat in silence as Shrogar revealed the things he had kept from them, of the legend Kinseris had told him when he had returned his father's sword. It was the first time she had heard the tale, and she listened eagerly, for it touched on Aarin and she was starved of contact with him. The news of his captivity had hit her hard, though she had prepared herself for it. Back in Frankesh she had known that the priesthood had taken him, but the Ancai's quiet confidence in Kinseris had allowed her to hope. Now, confronted by a reality she could no longer ignore, she steeled herself to fight for him.

'Æisoul in Vasa's hands will be executed,' Shrogar told them as he finished, sending a flutter of panic through her once more. 'It is for this reason that Kinseris asks our help, as he has given us his times beyond count. If Vasa is allowed to destroy this man, he removes the only true threat to his reign, and our only true hope of victory. Yes, an army marches on Ephenor, but an army is a cumbersome beast, and it will take many days for it to find us here, many more days than it would take for a small party to ride to Kas'Tella and return in time to fight. This is what I propose: that we set out tomorrow at dawn and strike while the main force of Vasa's troops is absent. I ask for your thoughts.'

No one spoke for a moment, and from the stunned expressions on their faces Jeta could see just how shocked they were.

'Brother, I have one,' Iarwin murmured into the pause. 'This is madness. You cannot leave Ephenor undefended at such a time, no matter whose life is at stake. Your duty is here.'

'I agree, my lord,' Ieshwen replied, clearly unnerved. 'It is true that a small party could cross the desert at speed, especially knowing the fastest, safest routes, but if Vasa has finally moved against us, we need our strength here, where it will do most good. I beg you to abandon this plan.'

Jeta listened with narrowed eyes. So far it had progressed much as Dianeth had predicted.

Your main opposition will come from Iarwin and Ieshwen. Ieshwen because he is a soldier first and will see that the odds are against us. My husband will not look to him for support, but he will listen to and value his advice. Iarwin is the real danger. He has been gone too long and he can no longer see clearly where Kas'Tella is concerned. His reaction will not be rational, and you must force him to reveal that if you wish to lessen his influence.

Jeta studied Iarwin, seeking the hook that would unmask him. His emotions were already close to the surface. It should not be hard to bring those out of him. She looked back to Shrogar, saw him nod thoughtfully as he turned to the others.

'I say go,' Lysan offered. 'Kinseris has proved his worth to us time and again. I know nothing of Æisoul, but we should not abandon Kinseris. If the main army has truly departed Kas'Tella, what better time to attempt such a thing?'

Callan leant forward, his fingers steepled together. As soon as Lysan had spoken Jeta had been waiting for his brother to speak.

Callan and Lysan are another matter altogether. If you win them you split the council and free my lord to follow his heart, but it will not be easy. The brothers are tied to Iarwin by deep friendship and his influence will be strong. But it is to them that my husband will look for support. Lysan is a gambler, an adventurer at heart, and he is the most likely to advocate such a reckless venture. His brother would have us believe he is none of those things, but do not be fooled by their bickering. When they move, they will do so as one, and it is Callan who will make the final decision. It is Callan most of all you need on your side.

It was one thing to know that and quite another to achieve it, Jeta decided as she watched the man. Dianeth had been able to give her little advice on how to win him round.

Callan is as complex a man as I have met, and I have known him since he was a child. He is a soldier, but he is also a healer, and nothing has been broken yet that he did not wish to mend. He will recognise the damage in Iarwin far quicker than my lord will, but I cannot be certain which way that will sway him.

'I agree with your sentiment, brother,' Callan said gravely, 'but they may already be dead. And even if they are not, I cannot believe that one man alone can bring down the priesthood. This feels like a lure, a trick to draw out our forces and attack Ephenor while we are at our weakest.'

Jeta felt a lurch of disappointment.

'I do not believe it is a trick.'

Shrogar turned to Dianeth, but her eyes were fixed on Jeta. 'Vasa is too arrogant to believe you would ever attack Kas'Tella itself. The city cannot be taken except by magic or trickery. He controls the magic and he does not count us clever or brave enough to defeat him with trickery. Nor do I believe they are already dead. Vasa is as cruel as he is arrogant. He will want Kinseris to witness the end of his rebellion and the death of his friends. He will wait until he has taken Ephenor before he takes their lives.'

'You cannot know that,' Ieshwen broke in. 'My apologies, lady, but we do not have the luxury of acting on theories we cannot prove. The situation is this: we know that Ephenor is threatened, and we can only speculate as to whether Kinseris and this other are still alive. Our duty is clear. We must stay and face the known threat. To do otherwise is folly.'

'To do nothing is folly.'

All heads turned to Jeta. For all Shrogar's courage and honesty, his men stubbornly refused to look beyond plain facts. They focused on the army alone and ignored the deeper truth. This was so much bigger than them.

'You can stay holed up here in your precious castle, but you will be leaving your only real hope of survival rotting in a cell. Don't you understand? This is not about your squabbles with Vasa. This is about all of Andeira.'

They stared back at her and she saw not a flicker of understanding. 'Did the desert always reach almost to your gates?'

That brought Callan up short, his eyes latching onto hers speculatively. *Nothing has been broken yet that he did not wish to mend.*

She held his gaze, imploring him to listen. 'The Kas'Talani are your enemy, but they are not the scourge of your land. What is killing Andeira is far greater than they are, and there is only one person that can reverse it. Aarin, Æisoul, is a prisoner because of who he is, because of what he will do that is so much more important than any of you. If you truly wish to destroy the Kas'Talani, you would not throw away this chance.'

'Fine words, girl,' Iarwin sneered at her. 'But you will not have to shoulder the risks of this foolish endeavour. Perhaps you should speak only about the things you can participate in, like the bandaging of the wounds that will surely come later.'

'I will share those risks,' Jeta corrected him coldly. 'Who are you to tell me what I can and cannot do? Was I not called to this meeting just as you were? You know nothing of me or what I have gone through to be here. It is you who speaks of things you do not understand.'

Iarwin surged to his feet. 'And you know nothing of us or the issues at stake! You were invited only out of courtesy. Your thoughts were neither asked for nor welcome!'

Jeta regarded him with the cool, disdainful stare she had used so often to rile Kallis. *You unmask yourself, my friend,* she thought silently. 'I understand much more than you. I have seen what your Order's plotting has done to my land, and it has all been for Aarin. Even if you cannot understand what he is, you must understand that. If your enemies want him so badly, how can you countenance leaving him to die at their hand?'

'Because he is nothing to us,' Iarwin replied harshly. 'And we have no room for legends here.'

'Enough! This serves no one.' All eyes turned to Shrogar as Iarwin fell quiet, resuming his seat in sullen silence. 'This error is mine,' he admitted. 'I should not have asked you to make this choice with so little knowledge. I see now that this is not something I can –'

'My lord, I know something of this legend.'

The words were spoken urgently. Jeta turned to Callan and saw the others do the same.

It is Callan most of all that you need on your side, for he is the only one of us who treasures the diminishing power in our people. But you must understand that we have fought too long against one enemy that far outmatches us that the prospect of returning an even greater power to this world will not sit easily, even with Callan. If you wish his support, you must force him to accept that the danger, and the hope, are real.

444

'I do not pretend to understand much,' he said quietly, 'but I do know that if this man exists, he is not here to destroy the Kas'Talani. That they fear him there is no doubt, but that fear stems from a far deeper one: that he will, in fact, topple the very foundations of their rule. My lord, this is not a legend of men.'

'If not men, then what?' Ieshwen demanded. The oldest of the gathering, and a soldier to his toenails, he would not be entranced by myths. 'Let us put riddles aside, Callan. Speak plainly. What do you know?'

It was Kallis, in the end, who laid the truth out in the open. 'It is a legend of the dragons, is it not?'

Callan nodded, looking torn.

'And more than that,' Kallis said, 'it is one that the priesthood has long been seeking to control. Will you give them that chance?'

Ieshwen glared at him. 'Do you know what you ask of us? To endanger our whole people for the sake of a child's tale that promises us only greater enemies and a return to the devastation of the Lost Years?'

Callan flinched, his eyes fixed on his hands, and Jeta understood that though Ephenor might not hold to the Kas'Talani faith, the roots of the priesthood had nonetheless sunk deep.

'I had not thought you shared the beliefs of your enemies,' Kallis replied, finding the chink in their armour. 'For that one is theirs, not yours.'

'What do you know of either?' Ieshwen demanded.

The mercenary shrugged. 'All I know of you is from Kinseris, who led us to expect we would come among friends. Not a people so used to hiding they no longer have the courage to venture out even to save themselves.'

Ieshwen's face contorted with fury. 'We have the courage to do what is necessary,' he snarled. 'And this is not. You forget your place when you call us cowards. You are guests at this table. It is not for you to judge us.'

'And as a guest he has the right to speak,' Shrogar reminded his captain. 'More than that, it is to our guests that we owe warning of the army that marches on us.'

Rebuked, Ieshwen subsided with an angry muttering, and Shrogar turned his attention to Kallis. 'Forgive our lack of understanding. We know little of such matters, it is true, but as a companion to Æisoul I ask you to tell us what you know, that we might understand a little better.'

Kallis sighed. 'I am not the one to explain these things to you. And Æisoul is not a name I know. My friend is called Aarin, and it is from him or Kinseris that you need to hear. What I can tell you, what you need to understand is this: twice now we have come up against the Kas'Talani, once in Amadorn, once in Frankesh, and both times they have tried to take Aarin against his will, to use him for their own ends. And now they have him. If there is nothing in this legend, why would they fear him?'

He paused, struggling to find the words to continue. 'Of what passed between Aarin and Kinseris in Frankesh I can tell you little, for he told me little, but I do know they reached an alliance of some kind. And as I know Aarin I can guess what it was—to find and restore the dragons to Andeira.'

Shrogar silenced the murmuring with a wave of his hand, though Jeta could see his tremulous excitement. Until now he had known of Æisoul only what Kinseris had told him, and the priest himself had not known the truth behind the legend. Now, just as Dianeth had, he was beginning to understand. Disturbing as the thought no doubt was, it would also make powerful sense. Restoring the dragons to Andeira would bring the priesthood to its knees.

Turning to the Ancai, Shrogar invited Kinseris's closest confidante to speak. If he wanted to know of Kinseris's intentions, there was no one else who might know. The Ancai nodded, sharing a meaningful glance with Jeta. It seemed that her actions were rather more transparent than she had thought, at least to those who knew her.

'My lords, Kinseris would not ask you to take this risk if he did not believe it necessary. His loyalty to you would never permit it. From the outset he intended to bring this man to you, to seek your friendship and your assistance, but he was betrayed. It is my belief that Vasa has known of his treachery for a long time, and I think I now understand why he did not act before. It is no coincidence that the very moment this man appeared, Kas'Tella moved against us. Within the priesthood itself the orders were sealed long ago. Any Amadorian mage that comes to our shores must be handed over to Kas'Tella. It was merely this fate that Kinseris tried to avoid when he took these people into his custody. But that changed. Like Kallis I cannot tell you what they said to one another, for my lord sealed the room behind lethal wards, but his orders to me thereafter were clear. When he was recalled to Kas'Tella, he entrusted me to safeguard this man's life and his freedom with my own and bring him here to you.

'The priesthood left me no time to act. That very night they took their prize, and now they have my lord also. If Kinseris is correct, and this man has the power to destroy the Kas'Talani, then I will go to Kas'Tella and do what he has asked of me. If we lose this chance, we will never get another.'

Iarwin lurched to his feet. 'Brother, you cannot bring this man here!'

Shrogar turned to him. 'Why not?'

Iarwin swayed, caught himself on the chair. A grimace of pain flashed across his face and Shrogar reached out to steady him. But Iarwin shrugged him off, visibly trying to master himself.

'If this man is who you think he is, then Ephenor must have nothing to do with him. Kas'Tella has paid us little heed for years. They think us all but broken, but this! If you do this thing, if you take this man from them, they will ignore us no longer. Brother,' he implored, 'if we ally ourselves with this man, we give them the reason they need to destroy us.'

Shrogar met this impassioned plea in stunned silence, seemingly torn between concern and confusion. Jeta watched, fascinated, as Iarwin's emotions rolled unchecked across his face, and felt an unexpected flash of sympathy. Dianeth was right. He was damaged somehow, and she was not the only one to see it.

'And if we do not, Iarwin, what then?' Callan asked, the same concern in his eyes.

Iarwin shot the man an anguished look. 'Then we go on as before.'

But Callan shook his head. 'We cannot. If Kinseris is right, we will never have another chance. To let this one go is to admit our eventual defeat.'

'It is not!' Ieshwen protested. 'My lord, forgive me,' he said to Shrogar, 'but this is rank folly. You cannot mean to go through with this.'

Shrogar turned to his oldest, most experienced captain, and his expression told Ieshwen all he needed to know. Iarwin spun away, his grip on the chair tightening until his knuckles shone white through his skin.

'I'm sorry, Ieshwen. For friendship alone I would have gone to Kas'Tella. For friendship and the chance to bring an end to Vasa's tyranny, I must go. Besides,' he added wearily, 'their army is already on its way.'

Jeta felt a rush of relief that made her unsteady. In the end, he had not needed much convincing, and she loved him for it.

Ieshwen scrubbed a hand over his face and sat back, defeated. 'Very well. If that is what you wish, that is what we will do.'

Shrogar nodded his thanks, catching Jeta's eye as he did so. Perhaps he was not as unaware of his wife's interference as she had believed. 'Iarwin?'

His brother shrugged, refusing to meet his eye. 'You lead these people, my lord, not I.'

'You will lead them until I return,' Shrogar pointed out. 'You will assume command –'

Iarwin shook his head. 'No. If you go, I go.'

'My lord, that is not wise,' Ieshwen objected. He did not agree with this decision, but now it was made he had put those disagreements behind him like the soldier he was. And as such, it was his place to weigh the risks. 'Should the worst happen, we would lose both of you.'

'He is right, Iarwin,' Shrogar said mildly, plainly concerned for his brother. 'You should remain here.'

But Iarwin shook his head stubbornly. 'I have ridden those routes more recently than any of you. I know which paths the Kas'Talani have found, and I know where they station their patrols. You need me.'

Shrogar wavered. 'I need you here. You can provide us with –'

'Do not try to protect me,' Iarwin snapped. 'And do not pretend that should this fail there will be any hope of continuing on. If you sanction this mad gamble, you stake everything on it. Leave me behind, and if you are taken, I will outlive you only by days.'

Shrogar could not deny that. Shooting his brother a frosty glare, he turned to Ieshwen. 'It seems I leave you in command, old friend. I know you will not fail me. Callan, I leave it to you to make the arrangements. Pick out the men you think best equipped for the march. Choose no more than thirty –'

'We will go with you,' Kallis cut in. 'I know how much is being asked of you. Do not think we take it lightly. Your captains have offered you sound advice and were it not for what I have seen, I would urge you to take it. Since you have not, the least I can do is see that you do not face this danger alone. And I speak for all of us when I say we have come too far together to turn back now.'

Shrogar nodded. 'Very well, you may accompany us and welcome.' He turned to Jeta. 'However, I ask that you, at least, remain here. I do not doubt your courage, my lady, but my wife has asked for your companionship and I would count it a kindness if you would stay with her.'

Jeta's face flushed and she turned away, feeling his knowing regard and suddenly shamed by it. Dianeth smiled at her across the table. 'There is work that must be done here to prepare for war,' she said with a wink, 'and not all of it is men's work. We must find safe places for those who cannot fight, stock up on food and water, and do what we can to deny that to the enemy. The people must be organised to help themselves when we cannot help them, and there is much more. The men forget these things sometimes in their eagerness for battle. It is as much our work to see that our city is safe.'

That settled, Shrogar dismissed the council. 'Let us retire for the night and allow those of us who must leave tomorrow to get some sleep. We leave at dawn.'

FIVE

IT WAS THE steady vibration of hoof beats pounding on the sand that finally penetrated Aarin's muddled mind and brought him back to consciousness. Kinseris still sprawled on the ground where he had fallen, the side of his face not buried in the sand scorched red and blistered by the ferocious sun.

Aarin forced himself to his knees, shaking his head. The sudden movement was a mistake, and it was long moments before his head stopped spinning. When his vision finally cleared, he crawled to the prostrate priest, shaking him by the shoulder. His head ached and his mouth was parched, unable to form the words of warning as he willed the other man to wake. Their carefully rationed water had run out a day ago, and not a drop could he wring from the atmosphere in this driest of places. It had been days since they had fled Kas'Tella. The desert was brutal.

Kinseris stirred and groaned, weakly trying to push Aarin's hand away, refusing to open his eyes. The mage shook harder and was rewarded by one half-opened eye peering at him without recognition.

'Horses,' he croaked. 'Must move.'

His words had the desired effect and the priest came fully awake, alarm and confusion on his sunburnt face. Aarin eased himself to his feet, stretching out a hand to help his companion, and the two men half ran, half stumbled across the sand. Aarin did not even bother trying to conceal their presence with a glamour. Illusion was water magic, and here there was none. A cluster of rocks they had not seen in the dark offered meagre protection from prying eyes, but it was all they had, and they sprawled to the ground, unable to go further.

Kinseris sat with his back to a rock, his breathing laboured. His hand shot out to grab Aarin's arm with surprising force. The mage looked from the hand to the priest's face and saw a resignation that frightened him.

'They must not take you,' Kinseris rasped. 'I will distract them if I can... give you time... to escape. Go!' he ordered, releasing his grip and pointing to the east. 'We are not far now. The scouts will find you. You must finish what you have started, Aarin, I beg you.'

Aarin shook his head. 'I will not leave you. Even if I had the strength to do what you ask.' For in fact he could not have taken another step. The desert had won. 'But we are not taken yet.'

The priest's face twisted in anguish, but further argument was beyond him. His head fell back and his eyes closed. Alarmed, Aarin sought for a pulse, sitting back in relief on finding one. The pounding of the horses drew ever nearer, and he inched himself backwards, dragging the comatose priest with him, deeper into the shelter of the rocks. Then he too collapsed to the ground and allowed his eyes to slide closed, listening to the rhythmic beat pulsating through the sun-baked earth.

He lay still, measuring the strides of the horses as they approached, then suddenly his eyes flew open. Remembering Kinseris's outflung arm, pointing towards their distant haven, he realised that the horses came from the east, not the west, not the direction of their enemy. He tried to get his feet under him but could make it no further than his knees. Blackness swamped his vision in a sickening rush and the world tilted, spilling him back onto the sand. Desperate now, Aarin dragged himself onto his elbows and inched his way clear of the edge of the rocks and their precious shelter, shading his eyes against the glare even as his sight began to fade. And there, halted on the top of a dune, he saw riders.

Riders who did not wear the insignia of the Kas'Talani.

A great banner hung limp in the still air, but the occasional breath of wind flicked it to life, and the last thing he saw before he passed out was the golden eagle of Ephenor blazing in the sun.

'If we do not find them on the way, what then?' Kallis rode at the head of the column with Shrogar, the Ancai and Trad at his shoulder. They had camped last night in the open desert, breaking early to spare the horses, and all three had fretted at the delay.

Shrogar did not answer at once. He had been preoccupied since leaving Ephenor, and Kallis guessed that his mind was worrying the same problem. If Kinseris and Aarin were still prisoners in Kas'Tella, what could thirty men do?

Finally, Shrogar turned to him, his expression grim. 'We are not strong enough to mount any kind of assault on the citadel, even with the main army absent. And even with ten times our number I would not attempt it. We cannot fight their magic and their swords. But,' he paused, looking back at the horizon, 'it may be that Kinseris still has friends in the city—that we still have friends there—who can help us.'

Kallis raised an eyebrow. 'He *may* still have friends?'

Shrogar glanced at Iarwin, riding further down the column with Callan and Lysan. 'My brother was in Kas'Tella for many years, in service to the priesthood. He is but one of many of our people living and working among our enemies. And Kinseris has a network that extends across this continent. If we can make contact with that network, and if there are secret ways into the citadel, they may be able to help us.'

Kallis looked from Shrogar to the small column of men. 'If we are too few for an assault, we are still too many for secrecy.'

Shrogar grunted. 'There are too many *ifs*. I cannot forget that Kinseris has been taken. His network may have been compromised and our agents betrayed. I can make no assumptions. I must leave myself options.'

'You think he might give you up?' Kallis asked, surprised.

'I think he might not have to,' Shrogar replied. 'If the Ancai is right, our secrets are no secrets at all—that is what worries me.'

As he studied the Lord of Ephenor's grim profile, Kallis could not help but admire the man's resolve even as he realised just how high the odds were stacked against them. 'What will you do?'

Shrogar hauled on his reins, pulling his horse across the column to bring it to a halt as they crested the top of a great dune. 'Wait and see,' he replied as he gestured for his men to spread out along the ridge. 'From here you can see almost to the Redfern Plains, which surround Kas'Tella on three sides. I sent scouts to Kas'Tella to contact our allies as soon as Iarwin brought word of Kinseris's capture. We will wait here till morning and maybe by then we will have a better idea of what awaits us in Kas'Tella. And if, by some miracle, they have escaped, we may be able to locate them without committing ourselves to a march on the city.'

Kallis followed the Ephenori as they strung out along the ridge, scanning the barren landscape for signs of life, but the desert was empty. Endless dunes rippled outwards as far as he could see, the afternoon sun turning the swirls of golden sand a deep red. Nothing moved. The only break in the undulating dunes was a scattering of distant rocks that cast long shadows across the desert floor as the sun dropped towards the horizon.

Shrogar was right. The great dune offered an unrivalled vantage point as the desert sloped gently towards the start of the plains, but as Kallis's eyes strained in the direction of Kas'Tella he felt a surge of hopelessness. In Ephenor, the choice had seemed an easy one. But now, confronted by the vast expanse of barren, lifeless desert, and the impossible obstacle of the city beyond, he realised just how badly he had let friendship cloud his judgement. And he was not the only one.

Shrogar sat atop his horse staring at the horizon as intently as Kallis had been, and the mercenary knew the same thoughts must be running through his head as the desert before them stayed stubbornly empty. The fan of horsemen on the ridge were slowly regrouping around their commander and Kallis could feel the weight of their disappointment and resignation. Every man here knew the risks if they had to go to Kas'Tella itself, and each one of them must have harboured the irrational hope—as he had—that the men they were seeking had managed the impossible and made their escape.

Kallis waited with Trad and the Ancai as Shrogar spoke to his men. He knew that the Lord of Ephenor intended to follow the ridge of the dune to the north as it descended gradually to the desert floor, where they would camp for the night. It would take them away from the direct route to the city but would conceal their camp from a distance. It was a sensible decision, but it still felt like giving up.

'They might still be out there,' the Ancai rumbled, his eyes fixed on the hazy horizon.

Kallis grunted, hauling his horse around to follow the Ephenori as they began to file along the edge of the dune. Then he saw something that made him stop still and stare.

A little apart from Shrogar, Iarwin stood as though rooted to the spot, his face wracked with strain. As Kallis watched, he tried to turn towards his brother but seemed instead to stumble, landing on his hands and knees facing the opposite direction with a cry like a scream of fury.

At Iarwin's shout, Shrogar's head snapped round. Reaching his brother's side, he dismounted and crouched beside him. Kallis joined them a moment later, thinking Iarwin overcome by his injuries, but the look the man gave him was one of such hatred that he backed up a step. Then Iarwin pointed past him, towards Kas'Tella.

Shrogar took his brother by the hand and hauled him to his feet, turning to follow his outstretched arm. 'Iarwin, what —'

'There!' Iarwin snarled, his eyes still locked on Kallis.

Kallis turned slowly, unwilling to turn his back on such enmity, and like Shrogar looked in the direction Iarwin pointed. 'I see nothing.'

Angry now, Iarwin shook off Shrogar's hand. 'The rocks. Movement.' Then he turned on his heel and stalked away.

Kallis and Shrogar exchanged a glance, then Kallis was running for his horse, Shrogar shouting after him. He swung himself into the saddle and urged the mare down the steep slope, heedless of the danger, Trad and the Ancai at his heels. He could hear a commotion behind him as the Ephenori reacted, and more riders pitched their horses down the dune, then the sand levelled out and he was galloping towards the outcrop.

Kallis threw himself off the mare as it skidded to a halt. At first he thought Iarwin must have been mistaken, then he saw the body huddled around the curve of the furthest rock and felt a surge of blind panic. As he reached Aarin's side, he squatted down in the sand, gently turning his head to check he was breathing. The mage's face was sunburnt and peeling, his skin hot and dry to the touch, his eyes sunken in dark pits and skin patterned by bruises. A few paces behind him, Kinseris lay propped against a weathered stone, and a quick glance told him the priest had fared no better. But they were alive, unbelievably and against the odds, and he rocked back on his heels with a sigh of exhausted relief. They were alive.

Trad ran up, panting for breath. He took in the sight of the two men and his face paled. 'We're too late!'

Kallis grinned. 'They're alive. But we need to get them out of the sun, and quickly.'

Willing arms reached down to lift the mage and carry him out of the blazing sun to the temporary shelter of the shade. Kallis stepped back as Callan pushed through the growing ring of soldiers to kneel at Aarin's side and found himself face to face with Shrogar and his brother. Shrogar's eyes were suspiciously bright.

'I did not think we would find them,' he admitted, smiling. 'I have never been so glad to be proved wrong.'

Iarwin stood beside him, tense and angry, his whole body twitching and trembling as if he was in the grip of a fever. 'We must leave here at once,' he insisted, his voice skirting the edges of hysteria. 'The pursuit will not be far behind. We should march through the night and put as much distance between us as we can.'

Shrogar laid a calming hand on his brother's arm. 'Iarwin is right,' he told Kallis, as he started to protest. 'Now that we have them, we must return to Ephenor as swiftly as possible.'

'We can care for them better in Ephenor than out in the desert,' Callan said quietly, appearing at his shoulder, his eyes on Iarwin. Shrogar's brother looked away, his expression agonised, and Kallis saw the flash of concern on Callan's face. 'They are lucky. We found them in time. Another day...' He shrugged, his gaze drawn once more to Iarwin's retreating back.

Kallis nodded tightly, glancing behind him to see that both men had been safely stowed in the covered litters they had brought for the purpose. The Ephenori had slung the poles between the horses and were already saddling up. The whole thing had taken a matter of minutes.

Shrogar followed his gaze and clapped a hand on his captain's shoulder, calling out to his men to move. 'The litters will slow us down, but if we leave now and don't stop, we will be back in Ephenor tomorrow afternoon.'

Callan was already moving away, following Iarwin, and Kallis watched as his approach was angrily rebuffed. Clearly, he was not the only one who found Iarwin's behaviour disturbing. Then he collected himself and nodded at Shrogar. 'Let's go.'

SIX

CONSCIOUSNESS RETURNED SLOWLY. Aarin lay a long while caught between sleeping and waking, unwilling to open his eyes and confront the harsh sands of the desert. The soft murmur of voices hovered on the edges of his awareness, tugging him towards wakefulness, and he resisted, burrowing deep into the soothing darkness of sleep. But sleep was slipping away. The voices persisted, like the buzzing of insects, and as he drew closer to the surface the aches and pains of his body began to reassert themselves with renewed vigour.

Aarin opened his eyes reluctantly to find himself on a narrow cot in yet another unfamiliar room. He suppressed a sudden surge of panic as he rolled onto his side and looked around. This was not Kas'Tella. He remembered the line of riders cresting the dune. *Ephenor.*

He lay still, letting his eyes adjust as he assessed his physical state. His skin felt burned and tender, the painful consequence of days spent in the desert, and the bruises from his captivity in Kas'Tella were still painful. Even so, he felt better than he had in days.

There was a jug of water on the floor. His thirst returned with a vengeance, and he lifted it to his lips and drank deeply, the water pouring over his chin in his rush. As he wiped away the trails of water, he saw the loose linen shirt and trousers someone had dressed him in. He fingered the coarse fabric, vague snatches of memory returning. Hands lifting him. A quiet voice talking calmly, helping him drink. Kallis's face hovering in the background. But he recalled little else, nothing but the banner that had flown above the troop of horsemen, the golden eagle that had hung limp in the windless air.

Ephenor. He had not believed they would really make it, that last day in the desert.

He looked around. There was little to see. The room was small and draughty, the rough walls unadorned by tapestries. Yet there was a simple

457

majesty to this humble room, with its soaring, high ceiling and massive, ancient stones. He felt welcomed, safe, as if he knew somehow that those stones would never be slaves to the evil he was running from. But safety was only an illusion. He would never be safe, not while the Arkni existed and he was their only way to the power they craved.

At the thought of the Arkni his head began to ache, a deep thumping in his skull, and he rested his back against the cool wall and closed his eyes. The water he had drunk now churned uneasily in his stomach, chilling him from the inside out. He began to revise his assessment. He felt wretched.

The voices grew louder, rising and falling in an increasingly heated discussion. He opened his eyes and noticed for the first time the door that stood ajar in the far wall. Beyond it was the source of the murmured conversation, and he thought he recognised Kallis's distinctive voice—the accent that was at times Amadorian mercenary, at others Caledani tribesman. He smiled to himself. If there was one thing Kallis could be relied on to do in any situation, it was find someone to argue with.

Aarin swung his legs cautiously over the edge of the cot, swaying as the world tilted around him. He sat there a moment, giving himself time to ground his reeling senses, before pushing upright. Steadying himself against the wall, he gauged the distance to the door, wondering if he could make it without falling flat on his face. Standing up had increased the pounding in his head and dry thirst made swallowing difficult. He looked longingly at the empty water jar even as his stomach revolted at the prospect of more liquid so soon. It was an evil combination, he decided, the coupling of such thirst with churning nausea, and he would have laughed if it had not threatened unpleasant consequences.

At length, his legs warned him that he would have to move or collapse, so he relinquished the support of the wall and shuffled to the door. Holding the doorframe with both hands, he peered inside to see three men sitting round a table, their heads bent close in conversation. As he stepped inside one of the men looked up, smiled, and touched Kallis on the shoulder.

'He's awake,' he announced with a certain amount of satisfaction, and directed the mercenary's attention to the candle on the centre of the table.

Notches had been carved down its length to mark the hours, and the man counted them triumphantly. Kallis sighed and tossed a handful of coins onto the table. Then he got to his feet, grinning when he caught Aarin's eye.

Aarin took a step forward and nearly fell.

'Easy,' Kallis said as he caught his arm and guided him to a chair.

Aarin sat, resting his elbows on the table, and studied his companions. They smiled in welcome, identical smiles on identical faces. Untidy light brown hair framed two fine-boned faces, brown eyes set wide beneath expressive brows. Aarin rubbed a hand across his eyes. He blinked and looked back to see the same apparition.

Kallis laughed. 'You're not seeing things. Meet Callan and Lysan L'Faer, captains of Ephenor.'

'Twins?'

Callan nodded, and Aarin noticed a small scar above his left eyebrow that marked him apart from his brother.

'Welcome to Ephenor,' Callan said. 'We have heard much about you.'

Aarin winced, wondering just what Kallis might have told them. 'Then you have me at a disadvantage.'

Lysan laughed. 'Kallis does not know you as well as he thinks. He thought you would wake long since.'

Aarin looked at Kallis's irritated frown and realised they had been betting on him. Kallis slouched back in his chair and scowled at Lysan. 'I said he would make it in here on his own. You said he would not be out of bed for another day.'

Lysan shook his head, clearly enjoying himself. 'The bet was on when he would wake,' he reminded Kallis, cupping his hand protectively around the pile of coins. 'Not whether he would be foolish enough to get up. Besides, he does not look like he will be up for long.'

'Forgive my brother,' Callan murmured, and his resigned manner suggested it was a phrase he used often. 'He does not always think before he speaks. How do you feel?'

'Well enough,' Aarin lied, his eyes straying to the jug of water by Callan's elbow. The irritating thirst had not gone away.

Callan followed his gaze and pushed a cup towards him. 'Drink,' he advised. 'But not too much. Your body lost a lot of water in the desert, but if you replace it too quickly you will make yourself ill.'

He spoke as one well versed in the ways of the desert and Aarin nodded, forcing himself to take only measured sips when he wanted to drain the cup dry. He caught Kallis's eye and the mercenary understood the question he wanted but feared to ask.

He grinned. 'She's here, she's fine.'

Aarin felt a knot of tension release inside him at those words and it felt like he could breathe easily for the first time since Frankesh. 'Kinseris?' he asked at last.

'He is resting,' Callan told him. 'He suffers from the desert sickness, as you do.'

'Desert sickness?'

'The heat,' Lysan explained. 'No one can survive long in the desert sun without water. If we had not found you when we did...' He shrugged, letting that thought trail away unspoken.

If they had not been found, they would have died. The desert was merciless, and Aarin had learnt that the hard way. He had no words to adequately express his thanks, and they brushed aside his clumsy attempts.

'Anyone who escapes from Kas'Tella's dungeons is worthy of our help, and anyone who has been in those dungeons in the first place is a friend,' Callan told him, but his simple words hid a decision that could not have been easy to make. 'And any friend of Kinseris's doubly so.'

Aarin looked up, surprised by the strength of the sentiment. Loyalties, he was beginning to realise, ran very deep among the priest's allies. 'You know him well?'

'Barely at all,' Lysan replied. 'Who can know the Kas'Talani?'

Kallis grunted his agreement, shifting in his chair to look at Aarin. 'So, what happened? How did you escape?'

Aarin did not miss the look that passed between the brothers. His time in Kas'Tella was not something he wanted to revisit, much less now when he was tired and his thoughts were all over the place, but he owed them an answer. More than that there were things they needed to know, about Vasa, the Arkni, and the army that followed. But he wanted time to speak to Kinseris privately and discuss what they should reveal. And time, he knew, was growing scarce.

Lysan seemed about to speak but Callan forestalled him. 'Stories can wait,' he said firmly. 'My Lord Shrogar will wish to hear what you have to say, and such tales should not have to be told twice.'

Lysan nodded, and he could see in their shadowed faces that they knew that he would have experienced things in Kas'Tella that would be painful to remember. Grateful for their understanding, he nevertheless sensed Kallis's impatience and knew that, for his benefit at least, he should tell them something.

But at that moment another joined them. His back to the door, Aarin could not see the new arrival but he saw the smile of welcome on Kallis's face and turned to see who came. The dark-haired boy paused in the doorway, surprise on his lively face. Aarin's grip on the cup tightened as he was rocked by the shock of unexpected recognition. His vision tilted, and he grabbed the edge of the table to steady himself as half-glimpsed snatches of vision returned in a rush. He had seen this boy before, had seen him crouching in the shadows watching the fires of a distant encampment. He knew then that Ephenor would not escape the onslaught from Kas'Tella. The battle he had seen in the vision would engulf these people, and the thought twisted his insides with sickening guilt.

Through his haze he became aware of hands holding him, lifting him to his feet. He shook his head, trying to clear the greyness from his sight, and focused on Callan's concerned face.

The soldier frowned. 'You should rest now,' he urged. 'When you wake you will be much recovered.'

Aarin nodded, shamed by his moment of weakness, by the knowledge of what was to come. He pulled himself free of Callan's support and turned to the boy who watched him uncertainly. He wanted desperately to be alone, to recover from this latest shock, but he could not help staring at the boy, remembering the details of his face from that instant of dream-sight.

'This is Trad,' Kallis offered, thinking he was awaiting an introduction. 'He came with us from Frankesh.'

The boy inclined his head in the barest of greetings. 'You're Aarin,' he said, voice and face guarded. 'Jeta has told me of you.'

Better and better, Aarin thought. If Jeta was the source of his information, he would hardly expect a friendly reception. Just thinking about her awoke all his confused feelings, and his desire to see her was almost overwhelming, as was his dread at another awkward encounter that hurt them both. The thought that she too might arrive at any minute sent a flutter of panic through him. He stumbled back, waving away Callan's attempt to help. He ignored Kallis's concerned glance and Trad's ambivalent stare and mumbled his need for air. Silently, Callan directed him to another doorway that led up onto the walls of Ephenor.

Gratefully, Aarin took his leave, heading for the escape Callan had indicated. He hauled himself up the stone steps, his feet slipping in the smooth hollows worn away over the passage of centuries. The cool night air beckoned, blowing a gentle breeze across his burnt skin, and high above he could see the moon. It was several nights past full, but still bright enough to illuminate the ancient, chipped blocks of the walls. He ran his hand over the pocked stones, feeling the power in them, the elemental magic that imbued them with self-awareness. Awareness that was sleeping, dormant until its creators called upon it.

He sighed, resting his forehead on the cool stone. Its creators were long gone, and no one now possessed the means to call the citadel to wakefulness. The army of Kas'Tella was marching on them, the army he had seen in his vision, and he could feel that vision falling into place around him, trapping him.

Trad. For the instant Aarin had seen through his eyes in the dream, he had felt the concentration with which the boy had studied the enemy, and the hopeless determination that lay behind it. He had sensed that this was a last desperate effort to stave off defeat and knew that he could not allow it to come to that. He would not give in to a future fate tried to force on him, nor a prophecy the Arkni could twist away from him. He would fight them all.

I will not let you use me, he swore silently, looking up at the bright, desert moon. *I will do this my way.*

Like Aarin, Kinseris found his way back to wakefulness slow and painful. Like Aarin, he awoke as one who did not expect to see the light of day again, and shied from its brightness, looking longingly back at the peaceful dark. But a sense of urgency had wakened in him as he dreamed that would not allow him to wallow in sleep. And so he fought to open his eyes.

Confused and disorientated, Kinseris tried to push himself upright, hampered by impaired vision. This was not his bedchamber in Frankesh, nor in Kas'Tella. A door opened and he edged back, wary of the approaching figure he could not bring into focus. The man stopped at the foot of the bed, a looming shadow in the darkness that clouded the priest's sight.

'Do you not know me?'

Kinseris started. 'Shrogar? My lord, is it you?'

The shadowy man knelt on the floor by his side. Now he was closer, Kinseris could indeed recognise the outline of his friend, but no matter how he blinked and rubbed his eyes, his vision remained misty. Shrogar took his hand and pushed it gently down. 'It is I.'

'I cannot see you.' He felt close to panic. 'My sight is almost gone.'

'Callan says your eyes have been damaged, perhaps by the sun, and though he thinks they will improve in time he cannot say whether your sight will ever completely heal. I am sorry.'

Kinseris sank back into the bed, a mixture of relief and despair washing over him. He remembered now. Burned by the sun perhaps, but the real damage had been done in Kas'Tella when he had looked into the fire that had consumed Shakumi. Staring straight ahead, he strained to make out the wooden rest at the end of the bed, but the effort hurt his eyes and he closed them. 'Aarin?'

He felt Shrogar rise from his knees. 'Your friend is fine. Like you, he was exhausted and weak from desert sickness, but he is young. Dianeth has seen that he is not alone, should he wake.'

At Shrogar's mention of his wife, Kinseris opened his eyes again. 'How is

463

your lady wife?' He had known Dianeth since she was a child. When Loransoft had fallen, many years ago now, some of its people had shunned the safety of Ephenor, fearing it would not be long before that ancient fortress suffered the same fate. Some had fled north to the sea, thinking to make their way to Caledan's outlying islands or even to Amadorn, Dianeth's family among them. Few had survived the perilous trek, fewer still had made their escape across the sea. Some had come to Frankesh, others to smaller settlements along the coast, but Kas'Tella's spies had marked them almost immediately. In the confusion of violence that followed, as Vasa's zealots roused a mob on the streets, Kinseris had managed to save one child, a girl, hiding her in his own chambers. One more child orphaned by the Order and fallen into his care. As soon as he was able, he had sent her to Ephenor and to Shrogar.

Shrogar could not keep the pride from his voice when he spoke of his wife. 'She is well, so very well in fact,' he laughed. 'She is carrying my heir, Kinseris, the son I have dreamed of. I could not be happier.'

'And if it is a girl?' Kinseris teased, taking refuge gratefully in happy news. He was aware of their long wait for a child.

Shrogar was not put off. 'Any girl-child of mine will be more than capable of ruling this rabble. The old blood runs strong in our veins. Haven't you always said so? And it seems I owe you my thanks once again. Once more you have returned something very dear to me.'

It took him a moment to understand Shrogar's words. 'Tarwin is safely with you then?'

At Shrogar's nod, Kinseris felt a great burden lift from his shoulders. One at least had survived. 'I knew the journey would be dangerous, but I could not risk leaving him in Kas'Tella. If I had been betrayed to Vasa as I suspected, I could not hope that those loyal to me would be spared. It would have been a slaughter. No, it *was* a slaughter,' he amended, his hand balled in a tight fist. 'So many good men are dead, and I could not save them.'

And you, Shakumi. I could not save you either.

The thought was like a dam breaking. 'He killed her.' The words were raw and full of rage and he could not see the sudden alarm on Shrogar's face. 'He

464

murdered her because she came to me. She saved my life and in return she trusted me to see her safe, but I failed her and now I will never see her face again, except in my dreams.'

Her loss had left a gaping hole in his heart, and such a sense of loneliness he had not realised he had felt until she filled it, however briefly, with the gift of her love. And then, finally, the tears came, and he wept more for what might have been, and the years that had been wasted, than for the few hours they had spent together. Those memories he would keep with him always— the sound of her laugh, the contours of her face—but it was not enough. It was not nearly enough, and the tears stung his eyes until he had exhausted himself and the pain receded.

Shrogar sat in silence, watching as a man he respected and admired beyond all others broke apart before his eyes, and felt a strange mix of white-hot anger and another man's grief. He thought of Dianeth, and how he would feel if Vasa had hurt her, and of Iarwin, so recently delivered from Kas'Tella's clutches by this same man. And there was a part of him that rejoiced that his enemy was coming to him at last.

Once Kinseris was asleep, he staggered from the room and made his way to the walls, needing the feel of the night air to soothe and unwind his taut emotions.

As he climbed the stairs and stepped out onto the roof, Shrogar was instantly aware that he was not alone. Thinking that one of his men had also sought this refuge he turned to leave, unwilling to intrude on another's solitude. But the sound of his approach had alerted the other to his presence and he turned to see who came, moving into the moonlight. It must have been a trick of the light, Shrogar thought later, but as the man stepped forward the moon shone full on him and a white light seemed to glow all around, threading silver through his hair and illuminating his skin.

Shrogar felt something stir inside him then as he looked at the stranger—a spark of recognition perhaps—that triggered the untrained well of his gift. As the man stepped through the shaft of light, he knew him not only as the man they had rescued with Kinseris, but as the foil for the darkness in his dreams. For a second he couldn't speak, then the moon moved behind a cloud and the parapet was plunged into semi darkness again.

'I believe I owe my live,' Aarin said. Even in the dim light Shrogar could see the burns and scabs on his skin, and the bloody, cracked lips. Mortal after all when the spell was broken. 'Thank you for the risk you took to reach us. We could not have lasted any longer out there. The desert is harsh.'

'But beautiful too,' Shrogar replied with a smile. 'As the Lord of Ephenor I bid you welcome and rest.'

'Kinseris? He is well?'

Shrogar flinched, shying away from the memory of the shattered man he had just left. 'He is weak still from the desert sickness, and his eyes are burned. Our healer believes they will recover in time, but he suspects there was some previous hurt.'

Aarin nodded. 'In Kas'Tella. The magic damaged them, and they have grown steadily worse. But I think your healer is right, and they will heal.' He looked away. 'I fear we have brought you only great danger in return. There is a pursuit, and they will follow us here. What will you do?'

'What we must. We know of the army that hunts you. Your companions reported their scouts before we found you, and since then our own have been shadowing them. But we have been expecting them for many years now. We will be ready.'

Aarin looked away. 'I'm sorry,' he said at length. 'I have brought this on you. I will do whatever I can to help, but it is only fair that you know this army might be after me alone and the danger to you and your city could be prevented if you cast me out.'

Shrogar studied him. 'You know this?' he asked at last

'I cannot be certain, but I believe it likely.'

The Lord of Ephenor nodded. 'I would not let you leave here unprotected even if that were a certainty. Our enemy is the same and that makes us friends. Save your suspicions, they will get no heed from me.'

Aarin shook his head. 'I don't deserve such generosity from you. I have done nothing but bring you trouble.'

'Not true,' Shrogar replied. 'You have brought me a friend I feared I had lost. For that you have my thanks. Without Kinseris, this place would have fallen to Vasa years ago with the rest of the Lost Houses. It was his conviction that persuaded my father to keep fighting, and his help that allowed us to keep our independence so long. We owe him more than we can repay, and you for restoring him to us. Kinseris believes that you will turn the tide of this conflict. If that is so, Ephenor is behind you heart and soul. Your fight is our fight. It is not trouble you bring us, it is hope.'

SEVEN

JETA FOUND HIM as he returned to his room. He heard her footsteps stop at his open door and turned to see her hovering in the doorway as though unsure of her welcome. He said nothing, he simply looked at her, taking in the shorn hair, the elegant dress, the air of forced indifference. So many feelings flooded him—relief that she was alive, terrible shame that he had put her in such danger, and, stronger by far, the overwhelming need to hold her. Yet something held him back.

'You're alive then,' she said when he did not speak. Her tone was flat and try as he might he could not read her face.

She drifted into the room, stopping a few paces from him, waiting. The coolness of her manner was making it hard to think.

'Jeta, I –'

She cocked her head to one side, watching him through guarded blue eyes. The distance between them yawned endless and deep, and he understood for the first time that he had put it there. He had pushed her away. When he had thought Vasa had her he had been forced to realise how much he cared for her, but it was too late for words to brush aside all the hurt between them. She deserved more than that, more than he could give her, so he retreated into courtesy and watched as the hurt blossomed in her eyes.

'It is good to see you.' Where he longed to take her in his arms, he settled for drinking in the sight of her.

'Good?' she echoed, a bite in her voice. 'Well, I'm glad you are pleased.'

He recognised that tone and instinctively drew back. 'I have missed you,' he said earnestly. 'You and Kallis.'

That was a mistake. She sucked in a breath and jerked away from him, preparing to leave.

'Jeta,' he called, reaching out to catch her hand and turn her round to face him. She threw off his grip, pulling away, anger darkening her eyes.

468

'What do you want me to say?' he pleaded, weariness tugging at him.

'What do I want you to say?' she repeated scornfully. 'You should not need me to tell you that.'

Aarin sighed, frustrated. His legs were beginning to protest, and he wanted very much to sit.

'Jeta, I can't –' he began helplessly. 'I don't understand –'

'No, you don't,' she broke in. 'There are many things you don't understand, but why should you have to understand this? Why can't you just accept it?'

Why indeed? How to tell her that he could not just let go and accept this, not here, not now? Ephenor was but a temporary safety. They would soon be engulfed by the army he had seen in that long-ago vision. Ephenor was about to be torn apart, lost in a blaze of blood and pain, and anything good that was born here would be destroyed in the firestorm. Somehow it did not seem right to expose something as precious as the love that could exist between them to the hell that was coming.

'I don't know,' he lied, defeated. 'I just can't.'

Her face stilled, though her eyes continued to rake him. He endured the scrutiny as well as he could, unable to help the flush of shame.

'Fine,' Jeta said at last. 'But if you can't understand, don't expect me to.' She turned away and this time he did not stop her. But as she reached the door she stopped, half-turning back. 'I promised myself I would tell you. When Darred found us, I –'

'What?' Darred's name shocked him from his exhausted daze and he instantly feared the worst. 'Did he…?'

'No!' He saw the spasm of disgust that crossed her face. 'No, he did not,' she repeated more calmly and Aarin felt himself go weak with relief. Her eyes held the shadow of an unbearable grief on her face, worrying him anew. 'He ordered us executed,' she told him. 'You were gone, and I thought I was going to die, and all I could think was that I had never told you. I promised myself if I ever had the chance that I would, I would tell you.'

'Tell me what?' Aarin asked, his throat dry.

Jeta smiled sorrowfully at him, raising a hand to brush against his face. He tried to catch it, to hold it there, but she twisted out of his grasp.

'But you don't understand,' she said sadly. 'You just don't understand.'

She stepped back, a sheen of tears in her eyes. Aarin tried to speak, to tell her to stay, but she shook her head, fighting back the tears and all but ran from the room. He stood silently, watching her leave, and an emptiness akin to his yearning for the dragons settled in his heart. He had let her go, the one true treasure in his life, and he had just let her go.

EIGHT

'ARE YOU SURE we're in the right place?' Aarin looked at the rusted door uncertainly as he pushed it open and guided Kinseris inside. The room was dark and dusty and the air smelt stale. He fumbled with a striker and lit the torch he had brought with him, fitting it in a bracket on the wall. It was not much, but it allowed him to pick his way through the jumble of shelves to the desk at the far end of the room.

He moved a pile of books from the room's only chair and offered it to Kinseris. They had come to Ephenor's library at the priest's urging, despite the exhaustion he could not hide after the many hours they had already spent with Shrogar, and Aarin had agreed. He could not pass up the chance to examine the ancient texts Kinseris had gathered over the years and sent here for safe keeping. Perhaps in here he might find some answers.

The library might have been dusty and neglected but it was still impressive. Rows of shelves groaned under the weight of books and scrolls. They were seeking maps and plans of the citadel. The place was imbued with magic, magic that thrummed through the stones of its walls, but its secrets were long lost to the Ephenori. The army that was marching even now across the desert might be stopped if they could harness the power of the citadel to defend them.

'Where should I start?' Aarin asked when all the candles were lit. The sheer number of books was overwhelming. 'Are all these yours?'

'Not all. The library has been here as long as Shrogar's people, but it fell out of use many decades ago. It was revived by Lord Roden—Shrogar's father—for his daughter Mirriel. She loved to read, and she was his only daughter. But after she went missing, he closed it up and would let no one use it. Dianeth and Callan come here sometimes, and Shrogar too when he wishes to be alone, but this place has none of Mirriel's brightness, only her father's sorrow.'

Aarin paused, running his hand down the spine of a book. He turned to Kinseris. 'What happened?'

'She was killed, by Vasa or one of his agents. She ran messages between here, Kas'Tella, and Loransoft, an ally that has long since fallen. Her father did not approve, but she insisted, and one day she was captured. They found out who she was and got a message to her father. Shrogar thinks there was a traitor at Loransoft because word came from there, and Roden set out to save her. He knew it was a trap, but she was his daughter so he went. Shrogar and Iarwin were only young but they remember the deaths of their father and sister. Their mother gave up not long afterwards.' He sighed. 'This is a family that has been honed by tragedy, and yet still they fight, and they are well loved here. Everyone at Ephenor has vengeance close to their heart.'

Aarin stared at him, horrified. 'You knew them didn't you, Roden and Mirriel?'

Kinseris nodded. 'Very well. I was sent to Loransoft as an envoy for Vasa early on in my career, some years before I was thrust out of the way in Frankesh. I met Roden then and realised that there was true strength behind the rebellion. The Houses of Durian and Wesden were the only survivors of the War of the Lost Houses and I thought their cause was lost until I met him. They are gifted you know,' he told Aarin. 'All the sons of Durian, and I believe of the other houses as well, but it is a skill that grows weaker through the generations, and they are unschooled. They can never come to my Order for training, and there are few others who could teach them who would dare associate with the Lost Houses. Even I could not help, for I was far away in Frankesh.'

Aarin heard the bitterness in his voice and wondered where it was directed. 'Both you and Shrogar have mentioned the Lost Houses. What, who are they? Wesden and Durian are Amadorian names, and Shrogar hardly looks like a native of your land.'

Kinseris smiled. 'Then you have guessed their secret. The Lost Houses were founded by Amadorians who travelled to Caledan many centuries ago, during the Lost Years. They carved out realms for themselves in the south and east of the continent, which was largely unclaimed, and for many years lived there in peace. They married mostly among themselves and spoke only the language they brought with them, at least to begin with. Safarsee is spoken here now, but Amadorian is still the dominant tongue.'

Aarin was fascinated. At last he felt he was on the way to unravelling at least some of the mysteries of this strange land.

'The Lost Houses came into conflict with Kas'Tella when the Order began its expansion across the continent,' Kinseris continued. 'Their rebellion has lasted over two hundred years, for a decade of which there was all-out war across the southern regions, called the War of the Lost Houses. Ephenor and Loransoft survived because they were farthest removed from the fighting. Now there is only Ephenor, and though they still fight against Vasa's tyranny they fight mostly for revenge.' He looked at Aarin thoughtfully as he continued. 'The old lords must have known the truth about the dragons. Who were they?'

'They were my people, or at least I think they were.' Aarin sat down on the desk. 'Many left Luen hundreds of years ago and were never heard from again, even their names were forgotten. Maybe they came here?' He shook his head. 'We have forgotten so much. The Lost Years stole too much from us.' He stared at Kinseris, ideas, questions, running through his mind. 'But why did they come here?' he wondered. 'Do you have any maps that show the borders of their lands?'

'The bookcase by the wall,' Kinseris answered, pointing to the shadows behind Aarin. 'The maps are kept on the top shelf. The one you seek has a red ribbon tied around it.'

Grabbing a candle, Aarin pulled over a dusty stool and clambered on it, holding the flickering candle high so the light fell on the piles of scrolls, pulling aside map after map, searching for a red ribbon. When he found it, he carried it back to the table.

One hand holding down a corner, Aarin placed a candlestick and a book on two others, smoothing the crumpled old parchment flat so he could read it better. The names were in the strange Safarsee scrawl with translations underneath. It took him only moments to find what he was looking for.

At his cry of triumph, Kinseris leant forwards, his eyes straining to read the tiny words. 'What is it?' he asked. 'What have you found?'

Aarin laughed with delight. 'A clue, I think.' He moved the candle so its light fell on the southern portion of Caledan. The domains of the Lost Houses were clustered together in the southeast, along the coast and stretching northwards as far as Loransoft, which had controlled the area bordering the Northern Desert and the Athelan Mountains beyond. With his hand he indicated the names. 'They are gathered together around this place, Tesseria. Do you know it?'

'I do. It is not called that anymore. It is Rybacih now, ever since Vasa conquered it during the war. The House of Haram held it for many years but after their southern allies fell, they were fighting a losing battle. What is the significance?'

Aarin tapped the map with his finger. 'There is something here, something they were guarding. That's why they came to Caledan, and that's why they fought so hard against your Order. They knew something that my people have long since forgotten and they came here to ensure it would stay safe. Tesseria,' he rolled the name off his tongue. 'Tesserion, Maker... The Maker is the heart, the spirit of Andeira. We call her Tesserion, which means Guardian of our Spirit. Tesseria means Place of our Spirit, Place of our Maker. Whatever it is, it is there, I'm sure of it.'

Kinseris stared at the hazy outline in front of him. 'I think,' he said sadly, 'that your people are not the only ones who have forgotten much. The old lords are long gone, and if once they were mages their descendants could never be counted as such, even if they were trained. And neither Roden nor Shrogar knew of any other cause for their fight than the persecutions and injustices of my brotherhood. The knowledge you seek is buried very deep.'

'As deeply as this?' Aarin asked, sweeping his arm to encompass the rows and rows of books around him. 'The old records must be here somewhere.'

'If there ever were any,' the priest corrected him gently. 'Knowing they might one day be overrun, surely they would not leave details of their duty for the enemy to find.'

But Aarin was not listening. He was already staring at the books as if hoping the answers he sought would leap out at him. There was so much history here, he could feel it, in the stones and the books. But if he wanted answers, he had to understand. 'Tell me of your people, of the Kas'Talani,' he asked, abruptly recalling Seledar's words. 'Tell me of Kasandar.'

'Kasandar?' Kinseris looked up, puzzled. 'Why do you ask?'

Aarin related what Seledar had told him of the origins of the Kas'Talani and saw Kinseris's face darken at both the name and the words. Regardless of the shelter the old man had given them, he still harboured doubts.

'Seledar cannot know what he says he knows,' he objected when Aarin finished. 'None of us can. They are legends only. The Order has existed for a thousand year. Of its origins we have tales, not histories.'

Aarin said nothing. He just waited.

At length Kinseris sighed. 'Very well, though I cannot see what good can come of storytelling. The legends tell us that at the end of the Second Age the Maker banished the dragons from this world, but she did not banish their gifts. For Andeira is built on and survives through the shared magic of the races, and without it She will die. So, She fashioned these effigies'—he touched the silver device he still wore—'and searched the world until She found a vessel for their magic, someone capable of withstanding the destructive nature of the dragons. She found Kasandar.'

'Who was he?'

Kinseris shook his head. 'Who knows? Does it matter? These are legends. To Kasandar the Maker gave the source of the dragons' magic, and he in turn gave it to others. According to the ancient texts, Kasandar went out into the world and gathered to him those who could still wield magic and formed them into an Order that took his name—the Kas'Talani, the followers of Kasandar. To these he imparted the wisdom of Andeira, which forms the central belief of the Order to this day—that the dragons brought about the end of the old ways and were banished for it. We are the new custodians of their magic, and of the world, protecting it from all who would see it harmed by the resurrection of those ways. The Maker,' he intoned softly, reciting words learned long ago, 'is all things and none. We, her children, must wield the elements of which she is made. We must be the conduit that she cannot be that brings them into the world.' He shrugged. 'Well, so we are taught.'

Aarin frowned. 'That is what your legends tell you?' If Seledar believed there was some important truth here, he could not see it.

'They are legends, Aarin,' Kinseris repeated. 'You cannot hope to find the answers to your questions in old stories.'

Aarin smiled, remembering his father's tales. 'Yet in all legends there is a grain of truth.' He shook off the memories, as painful as they were sweet, and paced the narrow space between the shelves. 'Let us suppose for a moment that Seledar was right, that the Arkni created the Kas'Talani. If they also created these legends, then might they not have done so to explain not only your existence but theirs?'

'It's possible,' Kinseris conceded, 'but I fail to see –'

'If they created the legends—if they, in fact, gave the power of the dragons into your hands—they have cast themselves in the role of the Maker. She did not give the power of the dragons to your Order, the Arkni did. And if their legends tell you the Maker bestowed that power on Kasandar because She herself could not wield it, because She needed a conduit for the elements in order to survive, then perhaps it was the Arkni themselves who couldn't use them, but who needed a channel for their power to come into the world in order to secure *their* survival. Perhaps, somehow, they need the magic to anchor their own existence. But where then does the power come from?' He stopped pacing, his face suddenly pale.

Kinseris shook his head. 'This is foolish. There is no point in such speculations, no sense in them.'

'Why?' Aarin demanded. 'Because you do not want to face it?' He reached out and snatched the silver dragon from Kinseris, curling his fist around it as the desolate cry echoed through his bones. 'Can't you feel it? Can't you feel *her?* These things do not hold merely the magic of the dragons! They hold their very lives! Somewhere, somehow, each time you use this thing you draw on the life force of the dragon whose essence is captive within it. Listen!' He thrust the device back into Kinseris's hand, closing his own over it as they had done in Kas'Tella. As their fingers met the surge poured through them. Aarin disengaged almost at once, desperate to spare the last of that dwindling, valiant strength, but it was enough.

The priest's face was white. 'It can't be true.'

'It is,' Aarin replied mercilessly, feeling the pitch of the fire in his blood rise up to match his burning anger. 'The dragons are alive, they are out there somewhere. This proves it. And you are killing them, bit by bit, each time you exert your will over theirs. No wonder the Arkni gave these into the keeping of mankind! They built a whole religion around themselves. What could be more fitting than having their devoted followers carry out the final destruction of their ancient enemies?'

'But that cannot be,' Kinseris protested, recovering his composure. 'We know that the Arkni seek to reopen the link between the races. Is that not why it was their hand that brought about the prophecy?'

'I don't know!' Frustrated, Aarin began to pace again. 'I don't know,' he repeated, suddenly weary. There were too many ifs, too many maybes. Once again Seledar had managed to leave him with more questions than answers. He knew he was right, but so was Kinseris, and he was still no closer to discovering the truth of the Arkni's existence. The question that Seledar had been unable to answer remained the crucial piece of the puzzle. The 'why' did not matter nearly as much as 'who', and 'how', the Arkni were.

He looked back at Kinseris, saw the fatigue etched deep around his ravaged eyes, and felt a flash of remorse. 'You should rest,' he said, glancing around at the shelves, sagging under the weight of hoarded knowledge. If he could not solve that riddle, he could at least focus on the more immediate problem—what to do now. He turned back to Kinseris, his smile wistful. 'We both should.'

NINE

KINSERIS SAT VERY still, his head pillowed on his arms. He had fallen asleep some time ago and Aarin was loath to disturb him. Books and scrolls were piled high on the desk around them both, and Kinseris had fallen asleep over the map of the Lost Houses. Aarin looked again at the scrap of parchment in his hand and then back at the map. Cautiously, he reached out a hand to try to slide the map free, and Kinseris jerked awake.

'I'm sorry,' he said at once.

Kinseris groaned and massaged his neck. 'Have you found something?'

Aarin sighed. 'Many things and none of them make sense.'

He handed Kinseris the parchment and then remembered that he would not be able to read it.

'It's in an ancient form of Amadorian,' he explained. 'It has taken me an hour to translate it, and now I have it still makes no sense.'

'What does it say?'

Aarin looked down at his hastily scribbled notes. 'The secrets of the Five lie within the stone that holds the truth of the ages.'

Kinseris rubbed a hand over his face. 'The five?'

'The five elements. May I?' He reached out for the map and tugged it toward him. 'The Lost Houses guarded something in Tesseria. It was the heart of their territory and linguistically it also implies heart, spirit.' He shrugged. 'The old languages are long dead, but that we call the Maker Tesserion must be significant. And that same style of language is all through these writings. Listen: *A land of cold ignorance, sundered from the heart...* '

Kinseris looked up. 'What's that?'

'Amadorn,' Aarin replied. 'It must be Amadorn, which broke away from Caledan long ago—*sundered from the heart*. These are written in Amadorian, probably in Amadorn itself. The language is similar to many of the texts in the library of Luen. Your lost lords may have brought these with them when they came. Here,' he pointed to another line. '*In the sun-drenched land.... here dwells the heart.* It all points to this place, to the heart being Tesseria. It is where they came and where we have to go. I don't know what we will find there but we must go.'

'We can't.'

Aarin stared at him without understanding. 'Can't?'

'There is an army marching on Ephenor,' Kinseris reminded him. 'They need us.'

Aarin shook his head impatiently. 'They would not need us if we were not here.'

Kinseris frowned. 'You can't be sure of that. Vasa has long wished for the destruction of this place. When he finds it, he will not leave until he has taken it apart, stone by stone.'

Aarin paused. 'Vasa is dead.'

'And that also you cannot know! You would risk the lives of everyone in this fortress on the word of a man who was once Vasa's closest friend? How do you know he is dead?'

Aarin sighed. Neither of them had mentioned the Arkni to Shrogar, reluctant to undermine the confidence of Ephenor's defenders when they would need it most. Aarin had felt uneasy at the omission, thinking to remedy it later, it never being his intention to deceive. But now he was not so sure. If, by leaving Ephenor, he could draw the Arkni after him, Shrogar's people need never know the awful truth. 'Even if you are right, what would you have us do? We know now where we must go. And knowing that, how can we risk remaining here to be trapped by a besieging army? If we stay here, we may never leave.'

'I will not leave them to face this alone.'

'Then we will all die!' Aarin flung back. 'For that is the only thing that is certain. Ephenor cannot defeat the army out there, no matter who commands it. But they may not have to. *If* I am right, where we go—where I go—they will follow, and that is the only chance Shrogar has.'

Kinseris glared at him. 'We can help them. *You* can help them.'

'What can we do?' Aarin asked, anguished. How could he say he had seen the conflagration engulf Ephenor? 'The enemy is more powerful by far than we are. And we can no longer count on the magic of the device you wear, not if what we suspect is true.'

Kinseris looked at him oddly, fingers drumming on the wooden desk. It was plain that something was troubling him.

'Would you rather wait here, and when this city is reduced to rubble and everyone is dead, then let the Arkni take us and know that everything we hope for is lost?'

'You do not know it is the Arkni,' he insisted. 'The scouts have reported seeing Vasa with the army. His banners fly in the columns, and it is his tent that is pitched each night.'

'Vasa is dead,' Aarin repeated. 'They are wrong.'

'Are they? Perhaps we are wrong. How do we know he is dead? All we have is Seledar's word and when last we saw the old man, he was very much alive. You must at least consider the possibility. Perhaps Seledar wished me to tell you the legends so you would reach exactly this conclusion. But that doesn't make it right.'

'And why would he do that?'

'Think, Aarin!' Kinseris snapped. 'What have you discovered here? That we cannot use the power in this thing for fear that by doing so we might cause harm to a dragon. The only weapon we had for this coming battle is then stripped from us, making us far more vulnerable to Vasa's army. If he is in league with Vasa, what greater service could he do his lord? How do you know it is a living creature you can sense, and not an echo of something long dead?'

Some of Aarin's certainty left him then. There was a cold, calculating logic to what the priest suggested, that he could imagine both Vasa and Seledar more than capable of. But could they take the risk? He knew what he had felt and heard when he touched the silver dragon. He could not believe it was a trick, or perhaps he just did not want to. His desperation to find the dragons made him easy to manipulate.

'I am right,' Aarin insisted but with less conviction. 'What I felt, what we felt... It must be real.'

Kinseris bit back his irritation. 'You would not be so quick to trust had you known Seledar before his fall from grace. I remember it, Aarin, I was there in Kas'Tella for the crisis that broke the council, and I still do not know what is true or false about that time. All I know is that they were like brothers for many years and even now, even knowing Vasa as I do, I find it hard to believe the violence with which that bond was broken.'

'Considering the man he is, I would not think you would be so surprised that he turned on his own,' Aarin retorted. The fire in his blood, awoken by his brief touch of the priest's magic, was burning him from the inside out. He could no longer quench it, no longer ignore it, and his agitation eroded his patience.

'Perhaps not, but back then it was a shock. It had been a year of tragedy. An epidemic spread through the city killing thousands and wiping out the ruling council. Only Vasa and Seledar survived, and they spent their time locked in the inner chambers. I was not long out of my novitiate, but I remember the day they fought. We could not hear what was said for the wards prevented eavesdroppers, but the violence was felt throughout the palace. When at last there was calm, we still could not enter the room for many hours. At last a group of elders managed to unravel the weakened wards and found them both unconscious. Seledar had come off the worst—he barely survived—but for all that his wounds were slight, it was many days before Vasa awakened.

'Not knowing what had happened, the healers kept them together so they were not forced to divide their attentions, but when they woke their hatred was a terrible thing. Vasa commanded his friend to be locked in the dungeons. We expected him to be executed, but weeks went by and the order did not come. Then one day Seledar simply vanished, and no explanation was ever given for his disappearance.

'There were rumours. That he was dead, or exiled. That he had been freed by sympathisers, or even that he had been pardoned and was living free in the city. But other more sinister rumours suggested there had been no rift at all, that it had all been a ploy by the high priest and his advisor. No one took his place, no new appointments were ever made to the ruling council, and all its functions became Vasa's alone, and as his power increased so did his paranoia. We were never the same again, the Kas'Talani. The disappearance of Seledar was like a poison that spread through our ranks. You never knew who to trust, and it was no longer safe to speak too freely. Someone was always listening—listening and reporting to Vasa. And eventually it was revealed that Seledar was alive, that he had fallen out of favour but had not been sent into exile, and we began to wonder. Someone was directing the web of spies and informers, and who better than the man who been Vasa's closest companion and whose loyalty no one had ever dared question?'

'Who better than the Arkni?' Aarin countered. 'What you have said does nothing but confirm what he told us. With their help Vasa would not need this elaborate scheme of spymasters and informers to know what was happening within his own ranks. And why should an ambitious man like Seledar consent to such ignominy in the name of another's success?'

Kinseris spread his hands. 'I do not know. Whatever the truth of it, we cannot discount the possibility that both our enemies survive and are marching together on Ephenor. We must not allow them to take it or we will leave the peoples of Caledan defenceless.'

Aarin laughed aloud. 'If we fail? If we fail it won't matter what we leave behind, it will be gone soon enough. Ephenor cannot stand against the power of full elemental mastery even if they had a hundred times their number. Their best hope is to send us on our way now, before we get hemmed and are helpless to act. Force me to stay here and you are killing them all.'

'It's so big,' Jeta observed as she walked with Dianeth through the great square at the heart of Ephenor. The city streets were laid out in a grid, with wide uncluttered avenues. There were none of the narrow twisting alleys of Rhiannas and the other northern towns. Such places would become death traps should an army breach the walls and take the fighting to the streets

'We are built for war,' Dianeth had told her sadly. 'Our soldiers need to be able to traverse the city at speed when the battle begins, and this design enables them to do that.'

It had been a sobering thought, and one that had been reinforced by their tasks that day, checking on the shelters for the children, the sick and the elderly near the evacuation points, and inspecting the granaries where the food was stored.

Dianeth went about the task with patient calm, taking time to speak with frightened families, anxious officials, and boisterous children. As they headed to the granaries, Jeta saw an old man making his way towards them through the crowd in the square. He held his cap in his hand and his fingers fidgeted nervously with the brim.

'That is Sefu,' Dianeth told her as she watched him. 'He is in charge of the grain storage. He does not look happy, and if I am not mistaken, he is about to make me very unhappy also.'

TEN

THE ARMY WAS a day away at the most. Scouts had returned in the night and spoken with Shrogar as the city waited in hushed anticipation for the announcement that would mean the culmination of years of preparation. The tyrant was coming for them at last.

Aarin entered the council chamber with some trepidation. Shrogar had called this meeting some hours ago but he had not attended, his thoughts still unsettled by the argument with Kinseris. He was ashamed of the anger he had failed to rein in, caught up in the excitement of at last having somewhere he could set his sight on. But that could not excuse his treatment of the priest whose concerns for the people who had rescued them should have been his also. And that same concern had kept him from this discussion.

Aarin could not deny that Kinseris had good cause for his suspicion of Seledar. Much as he wanted to, he could not ignore the possibility that Vasa was still alive. Indeed, he *hoped* he was. It was the only thing that might tip this conflict in their favour, and exactly because he knew that, he was loath to mention the possibility of his death. He had no wish to destroy the confidence of Ephenor's defenders when so much would rest on their shoulders in the coming days. He regretted his hasty words to Kinseris, but he stood by his reasoning.

All eyes turned to Aarin as he entered and the conversation ground to a halt. Kallis had told him of the council that had preceded his rescue and he had spoken long with Shrogar once Kinseris had woken. He knew that Ephenor looked to him to save them, to protect them from the wrath of Kas'Tella that his presence here had brought on them. Yet Ephenor's captains treated him with quiet respect, asking no questions of him, making no demands, and he guessed he had Shrogar to thank for that. The Lord of Ephenor had made his understanding clear. He knew that Aarin had not come to destroy the Kas'Talani, but he also knew that, in aiding him,

Ephenor could help bring that about. He asked only that while he was with them, he helped them in return. Now as he watched them, huddled together in council, Aarin knew he owed them far more than that.

Shrogar stood by the oval table, one hand resting over a large map, and his face held an unvoiced question. Beside him his captains also paused in their study of the diagrams, lifting their heads to see what had captured their lord's attention. With the bloody business of battle drawing perilously near, they seemed more annoyed for the disruption than curious as to his intentions.

Aarin nodded at Shrogar and went to stand by Kallis, resting his hand on Kinseris's shoulder in unspoken apology. When the Lord of Ephenor saw he would not speak he turned back to his captain.

As Shrogar outlined his plans, Aarin studied the drawings of the desert fastness. He had not been conscious for their arrival at Ephenor and so far had seen little of the citadel, barely enough to gauge its construction or defences. That it was old he was sure beyond doubt, as old at least as its sister construction in Kas'Tella. But now, as he looked at the maps laid out one atop the other on the great table, he saw for the first time the genius and significance of the sanctuary to which he had been brought.

Five sided, five corners, one for each of the elements, meant this place was ringed with protections all Shrogar's warriors together could never hope to better. It also provided military advantages. Watch towers on each of the corners gave archers good vantage over the walls that would have to be breached if the enemy hoped to gain access. The addition of a glacis, overhangs, and death holes on those same walls by later commanders made the place a formidable obstacle.

'Surely you have not forgotten the danger of mining?'

Aarin's attention shifted back to the discussion as he realised Kallis was speaking.

'Not forgotten, dismissed.' Shrogar replied. 'Ephenor is built on bedrock and cannot be undermined. Their only options are destroying the walls themselves or scaling them with ladders. For either strategy they need wood, and lots of it. The walls are over forty feet high, and that fact alone will hinder their efforts. My men have been bringing in all the people from our villages.

We are stripping the immediate area of any useful materials as we speak. What they cannot salvage they will destroy, even the settlements. If the Kas'Tellians wish to build siege engines they will have to spend many days searching for wood to do so.'

'They won't bring it with them?'

Shrogar shook his head. 'Perhaps, but it is unlikely. Moving so many men with only basic supplies and water would require an enormous number of horses and wagons. To bring enough wood for an escalade would mean yet more horses to carry the equipment, and still more with water for those, and so on. More likely they will bring only what they absolutely need, and trust to foraging when they arrive. And thus they give us a small advantage.'

'The only weak spots are the gates,' Ieshwen put in, pointing out the three breaks in Ephenor's defences. 'These two we will seal, as has always been our way. The blacksmiths are already smelting the bars and hinges and reinforcing the wood. When they are done, even we will be unable to open them without days of work. This last,' he indicated the main gate, a huge stone arch with ponderous wooden doors, 'has one portcullis here, and another here, some forty feet back. If the enemy breaches the first they will find themselves trapped by the second in the killing ground. There are death holes along the walls and placements for archers. They will be cut to pieces.'

He smiled grimly, a note of relish in his voice that made Aarin shiver. Yet for all Ieshwen's bloodthirsty reassurance, he found the information disturbing. 'You seal the other gates?' he asked. 'You would close your people in with only one means of escape that could easily be destroyed?'

Shrogar laughed. 'We are not so foolish. No, the gates will be sealed for they are our weakness, but there are many other ways out of Ephenor that the enemy cannot see. Should the need arise, our people can leave safely and secretly under the very eyes of the besieging army.'

'I would caution you against relying on those, my lord,' Kinseris warned, as the doors behind them swung open. 'Better you keep one other gate open and the castle well provisioned to withstand a long siege. Vasa is a man who seeks out secrets.'

Aarin glanced at him, frowning. It was clear Kinseris had not yet raised the possibility of Vasa's death. Perhaps the same concerns restrained him also, or maybe he truly did not believe it. But whatever his reasons, his advice was sound. Aarin watched Ephenor's commander to see how he would react.

Shrogar seemed unconcerned. His confidence was both inspiring and worrying. 'At any time we have enough supplies within the city to feed everyone for several weeks. Extra supplies have been brought in and there are enough wells inside the walls that water will not be a pressing concern. Dianeth is seeing to the placement and storage of what we have, but I can no longer risk sending further parties out to forage for food. What we have must be made to last, and it can, if we are cautious.'

'Then let us be cautious,' Kinseris urged. 'For it seems that Vasa's only hope lies in starving us out if all that you say is true.'

Aarin felt a flash of alarm and an unseen hand reached up to clench around his throat, making him dizzy. He resisted the urge to flee the room as he wished to flee the fortress itself. The thought of spending weeks pinned behind these walls with little hope of eventual victory terrified him more than the fighting to come. Every instinct screamed at him to leave while there was still time, but in his heart he knew he could not abandon these people who had taken him in, not knowing him, and now prepared to fight to protect him. By leaving he might be able to spare Ephenor, but he could not be certain, and while that certainty eluded him, leaving became no more than running away. And he could not run from this.

Dianeth watched the men. They were so absorbed in their discussion that not one of them had noticed her entrance. She would have smiled had her news been any less dire. Then, as the conversation turned to the supply situation, she could keep her peace no longer.

'That he will do very quickly, I fear.'

Shrogar's head snapped round. She could tell he had not heard her enter. She felt his sharp gaze studying her, seeing her weariness and strain, and she took his hand gratefully as he led her to a chair.

Ieshwen stirred impatiently. 'My lady, what do you mean? What will he do quickly?'

'Starve us out,' she replied, looking into her husband's worried eyes. 'I have just returned from inspecting the grain stores. They have spoiled.'

Silence fell. Then Iarwin slammed his fist into the wall, breaking the tension. Aarin and Kallis looked at each other, withdrawing into the background to allow Ephenor's officials space to deal with this new crisis.

'How?' Shrogar asked, crouching down by his wife.

She shrugged. 'Rats got into the granaries and have eaten much of the grain, and more has been ruined by damp, though we have had no rain for many weeks.'

'What do the caretakers say?' Ieshwen demanded. 'If their carelessness has doomed the city they must be punished.'

'No, Ieshwen,' Dianeth protested. 'I have spoken with Sefu and he is distraught, and as much at a loss as I am. He insists they were fine a week ago and I believe him. It is not his fault.'

'How can that be?' Ieshwen insisted, a man of action frustrated by unfamiliar helplessness. 'He has charge of the food storage, who else can be at fault? He is lying to protect himself.'

Shrogar shook his head, pushing himself to his feet. 'And what if he is? Punishing him will not bring the food back and will only cause panic once the people discover what has happened.' He turned back to his wife. 'He has told no one?'

'Only the others who work in the warehouses. He discovered the loss today and they were needed to assist him in salvaging what was left. All of them understand the need for silence, though he is frightened,' she added with a glare at Ieshwen, 'that you will punish him for failing in his duty.'

'As he should be,' Iarwin interjected. 'The man was practically a pirate before he came here, he was never to be trusted. Surely you cannot believe his story? He has likely been stealing the stuff and selling it on and now seeks to excuse himself through flimsy lies. He should be made an example of!'

'Who will that help?' Shrogar protested wearily. 'Besides, we need his continued service, and gratitude for our understanding might ensure the same mistakes are not made again. Our efforts would be better spent thinking of a solution. What has been done to save what remains?'

Dianeth sighed. 'They have moved what they can and are now checking all our stores for damage. I fear more losses will come to light by the time they are finished.'

Shrogar squeezed her hand. 'Come, let us not despair. I had no desire for a long siege and now we have even more reason to make sure it does not come to that. And if we have little food, always remember our enemy has less, and far more mouths to feed. This changes our timetable but not our chances. We just have to send the tyrant running a little sooner than anticipated.' He grinned at them. 'So, though I hate to curtail your pleasures, I must ask all of you to resist the temptation to toy with the enemy.'

Lysan laughed. 'My lord, though it pains me I will heed your counsel. A swift victory it is.'

Callan grunted, eyeing his twin with a brooding expression.

Lysan's smile widened. 'My brother does not approve of optimism. He likes to expect the worst.'

'With you around the worst is normally the best I can hope for,' Callan retorted. 'And your brand of optimism has nearly killed me more times than I can count.'

'Enough.' Shrogar held up his hand to forestall the inevitable bickering, but Dianeth was grateful for the distraction as she saw looks of amusement and irritation replace the bleak despair of moments earlier.

'*That* was not my fault,' Lysan hissed at his brother in an undertone and Shrogar sighed.

'Oh no? Who was it who moved the target in the first place?'

'Iarwin.'

'It was not,' Iarwin protested, indignant. 'That was entirely your idea. I am innocent, I assure you.'

Shrogar's patience snapped and he thundered for silence. 'That would be one of the few occasions you were innocent,' he informed his brother with an angry glare as the door was pushed open once more. 'What now?'

The servant eyed his lord nervously. 'Gwayr sends word, my lord. The army has been sighted.'

ELEVEN

VIANOR DISMISSED THE messenger in simmering disquiet. It was the third such rumour he had heard in the last month and could no longer be explained as coincidence. Three Caledani caravans had failed to arrive, three merchants whose schedules you could mark the seasons by. If this was the first sign of Kas'Talani retaliation, Sedaine had to be told. Whatever the reason the Caledani trade was faltering, they had to assume the worst.

He found Sedaine as she left the great hall after her morning audience. She looked strange and formidable, garbed for state in a severe silk dress buttoned high round her throat. It made her look older, and he knew it was deliberate. She had made it clear she had no time for her many suitors, a fact that frustrated him almost daily. He made a mental note to remind her of the need to take a husband, and soon, for her childbearing days were almost behind her and the succession had yet to be secured. The son she had, unknown to her nation, might as well be dead.

She saw him immediately and gestured for him to attend her. They walked in silence to her chambers, and he waited while her maid helped her out of the dress and into her tunic and leggings. As she laced up her tall boots Sedaine looked at her uncle. 'You have news?'

'Your highness,' he bowed, waiting while the maid gathered up the silk gown and left. 'I do not know if this signifies anything...'

She flicked him a curious look. 'Important enough to bring to me. I trust your judgement.'

Vianor acknowledged that with a slight smile. 'My news concerns the Caledani trade,' he told her, and saw her expression sharpen. 'Three of the most prominent trading families have failed to arrive for their yearly trade assemblies. Another two are overdue. I am concerned.'

'As am I,' Sedaine remarked, straightening up. 'There has been no word of the reason for their delay?'

'I fear something more permanent than delay. If the priesthood controls the trade between our two nations, as we suspect they do, then the absence of their merchants takes on an unpleasant aspect. This could be the first move in their planned conquest.'

'Or it could be a sign of troubles in Caledan that have disrupted trade or raised taxes at our southern borders. The Alliance states could be using their customs levies to punish us for their missing lady and the betrayal of their hopes of influence in the North.'

'All true,' Vianor replied, but he was doubtful. 'I suggest we send a detachment of troops to Forthtown and Carter's Ferry. If taxes have been levied to disrupt our trading connections, they can *persuade* Alliance officials of their folly. And you should send someone south, to find out whether the Caledani are still trading there. To speak with them, if possible.'

Sedaine considered this. She looked tired, Vianor noticed, and strained. The winter solstice was only days away and still no word had come from Elvelen. For new trouble to come with that one unresolved was too cruel.

'We need one of our own in Caledan itself,' she complained fretfully. 'We need facts, not rumours.'

Vianor remained silent. This was an old bone of contention between them that sprung more from her continuing heartache over Aarin than from real belief in the success of such an unlikely venture. They had no one to send and no time to send them. Rumour and gossip would have to suffice.

'Who to send, Vianor?' she asked after a time, and for an instant he thought she was talking about Caledan. 'Brannick is still in Luen, and those from Redstone are stretched thin already.'

'I will go.'

'No. I need you here. It must be someone else.'

Relieved, Vianor considered the dilemma. On the face of it, it was an innocent enough mission, one that any good ruler would act on to protect the interests of her merchants. But a merchant would not do, could not be relied on to act without one eye fixed on his profits. Besides, the Lothani merchants were still smarting from their recent fleecing at the hands of those same Caledani under Darred's tenure. However, there were some who would be far more concerned about the loss of that particular source of revenue, and they were the Lords of the North, the men who lined their pockets with riches from trade with Caledan.

He outlined his idea to Sedaine and saw her initial scepticism deepen to appreciation of the subtlety. A son from a major family, rewarded lavishly for his service, would tie that family even closer to her. A certain choice could even win back the loyalty of the most important of them all.

'Lord Morven's youngest,' she suggested thoughtfully. 'His father is still brooding over the fiasco with Nathas. If I were to give Derias a living, not a large estate but big enough for the modest needs of a minor noble, his father might be tempted from his hostile seclusion.'

'My Queen is wise. The very one I would have chosen.'

'Save your flattery, uncle,' she snapped, suddenly impatient. 'Have him summoned immediately, and then start planning for what we will do when he returns with confirmation that there is an army on our doorstep.'

The magician accepted the rebuke in stiff silence, wincing for what he had steeled himself to say next. 'There is one other thing I would discuss with you, Sedaine, before I leave.'

She looked up, her expression unreadable, though he knew she recognised his tone. 'Go on.'

There was a challenge in that blank stare, a line that Vianor knew he should not cross. This too was something that festered between them. Though she had loved him for a while, she had left Ecyas of her own free will. It was not the pain of an abandoned love that haunted her still, but shame for the devastation she had left behind her, and the death of a man who had loved her with all the passion of his great heart.

'If an estate for Morven's son will win the old lord back to your side, marriage to his heir will win you his confidence and the backing of his wealth.' He felt her go still and endured her icy regard with forced calm. 'Sedaine, you must take a husband, you must try for a child. For the sake of your people, you must secure the succession.'

Her anger was not the towering rage it had been last time he had raised the issue, but it was still hot enough to leave him scorched and smoking.

'I cannot be incapacitated by a child,' she said coldly. 'Nor can I afford to show such favour to one of my own lords when the nobility of Elvelen and Naveen are clamouring for that honour.'

Vianor could not conceal his surprise. 'They are?'

She checked. 'You know they will. And I would be wise to choose a husband not of Lothane if any child of mine hopes to hold this empire we strive for together after my death.'

'Then choose one from Elvelen,' he advised, stubborn in his refusal to drop the subject. 'Naveen has grown accustomed to your rule. It is Elvelen that wavers.'

'And will continue to do so while the council considers my terms,' she shot back, stalking away. 'No proposal of marriage to any one of those lords will sway the rest, unless you are suggesting I should marry Elian himself?'

Vianor stared, aghast. 'Never that. Elian is a spiteful child, and a marriage would leave both him and his lords with the impression that he is the true power. No, he would not be a suitable consort.'

'And another would?' she demanded. 'Any lord from Elvelen would believe the same, and I can do without the nuisance of pandering to any man's delusions of power.'

'Then take a lover,' Vianor urged desperately. 'It hardly matters who as long as you bear a child. Illegitimacy alone is no bar to inheritance, not if you name the child as your heir with the Lords of the North as witness. It has been done before.'

Sedaine trembled with cold fury. 'Leave me,' she hissed, and the magician paled at her tone.

'Your highness …'

'Leave,' she repeated, cutting across his protests. 'And do not speak of this again, do you understand? My mind is made up. From now until the North is secured against the Kas'Talani threat, I will take no husband, nor bear a child. And if we survive what is coming and it is too late for me to produce an heir, so be it. A successor will be chosen from those who survive. I will have ample opportunity to assess their metal in the days to come.'

TWELVE

DARKNESS CONCEALED THE arrival of the enemy and dawn found them surrounded. The last scouts had ridden in just hours ahead of the army, and though the defenders were prepared for what to expect, it seemed that the encampment went on forever. Much of the talk on the walls ceased as men stopped what they were doing to gaze on the great host.

For Trad, his first sight of the army arrayed against them sent a shiver of pure terror down his spine. All at once it seemed hopeless. As he looked out over the spears of the enemy, he saw only his own death, impaled on their sharp lengths. Then Kallis came up behind him, laying a strong hand on his shoulder as he joked with an unseen companion.

'Good odds you say,' the man laughed. 'I'll take that. Two days at most, that's all I give them.'

'Two days?' Kallis scoffed. 'That's generous. They'll be running in one.'

Trad turned disbelieving eyes on the mercenary who grinned at him.

'Do you doubt me?'

'Yes,' he said bluntly. 'Look at them. There are so many I gave up counting long ago.'

'Numbers don't mean a thing,' Kallis assured him. 'It's the quality of the men and their commanders that count, and Ephenor has the best of both. Do as we do and stay out of trouble and with any luck you'll live to see me proved right.'

'You reassure me,' Trad threw back, eyes straying once more to the soldiers assembling on the plains below. His fingers tightened on the bow in his hand, curling and uncurling round the grip, but the levity had washed away some of his terror and for the first time since glimpsing the enemy he was able to imagine a future past the coming battle.

The rest of the morning passed in a blur. He had been expecting an attack as soon as the sun had risen but the besieging army seemed content to mill

494

around just outside the range of the defenders' bows. He could see little activity in the great camp. Small groups came and went through the picket lines. As the sun reached its height, many of the soldiers dozed in the shade of the wagons. Insults were traded back and forth, and gradually the tension around him eased and the joking resumed.

At some point in the afternoon, long after he had been relieved of his watch, he saw Jeta and Aarin picking their way towards him across the crowded bailey. The man still made him uncomfortable, and he had not forgotten his reaction at their first meeting. Despite Aarin's repeated assurances, he knew it was his appearance that had caused him to behave so strangely.

'You should take your rest while you can,' Aarin greeted him with a tired smile. 'Let others stand this duty, you will be needed soon enough.'

Trad shook his head. 'I would not like to miss the start of the fighting.'

Aarin gazed out over the plains, but his eyes seemed not to see the army waiting there. 'There will be no battle today,' he murmured. 'Nor tomorrow. This will not be quick, Trad. You will miss nothing.'

Jeta shot the mage a frosty look and turned to Trad. 'Come.' She held out her hand, and the smile she raised for him did not encompass her companion. 'Kallis boasted to Ieshwen that he could beat him at foils left-handed, and a crowd is already gathering to lay their bets. The soldiers seem to have great faith in their captain. We could win our fortunes today.'

Trad grinned uneasily. 'Or lose the rest of our coin. Wrong-handed? He'll never do it. I've seen Ieshwen at practice and he is very skilled.'

'I wouldn't be too sure,' Aarin replied, stoically ignoring the chilly atmosphere. 'This is Kallis's favourite trick. Don't tell me you haven't noticed that he's left-handed?'

'He is?' Trad's eyes widened as Jeta dragged him away. 'But when he was instructing me –' His face fell in sudden realisation.

Aarin suppressed a smile as he watched them go. He did not need to follow them to know what the outcome of this challenge would be.

Instead he turned back to scanning the plains, searching for some clue as to who commanded this host, a glimpse of Vasa or Saal'an. But as the day crept by without any sign of the Arkni, he was forced to consider the possibility that Kinseris might be right. He knew he should be relieved. But he was not, and the tension inside him only grew.

There was no fighting that day, or the next. Shrogar had been as good as his word, and the hunt for siege materials took the foraging parties well out of their way. But slowly the huge war machine of the enemy began to get into gear. As the defenders watched, ladders were lengthened, catapults were constructed, and great cumbersome siege engines began to take shape. Trad and the other archers sent a volley of fire arrows into the work parties, but after it was established that the distance was too great, Shrogar ordered them to stop. Plentiful ammunition was more important than the tiny pockets of chaos caused as the flaming projectiles fell short of their mark. Then finally, on the morning of the third day, the fighting began.

The attack, when it came, saw the enemy hurl its strength against Ephenor's weakest point, the main gates. But Ieshwen had spoken the truth when he said the gates were well protected. Whoever gave the orders cared nothing for the lives they squandered, as more and more soldiers poured into the space between the two guard towers and were cut down by the archers waiting above. A battering ram stalled just feet from the wooden doors, left abandoned on its logs, the soldiers unable to get near it through the rain of arrows from the towers. But even so, as the morning wore on, sheer numbers began to tell against them as the besiegers managed to throw up ladders against the wall around the gate and the first of the enemy set foot on the stones of Ephenor.

Shrogar was in the thick of it, roaring orders at his men, hacking about him with his sword. The beleaguered defenders rallied to their lord, heartened by his courage, and in a few bloody minutes the first of Vasa's soldiers to cross the ramparts were cut down or thrown to their death on the glacis below. Shrogar's men picked their way among the bodies left on the walls, carrying off their wounded to the women and healers, but those among the enemy left injured received no such care. The law of the desert held sway in Ephenor, and the desert was a harsh place. A quick thrust of a knife ended cries of suffering and mercy alike, and they were thrown from the walls with the rest of the enemy dead.

The soldiers went about their grisly task as swiftly as they could, the lull only temporary. Others brought torches and fired the ladders that remained propped against their walls as archers on the towers kept away the men sent to retrieve them, pushing them off as they flamed and scattering those who braved the archers' rain.

Most ladders fell short of the overhangs and any attacker attempting to scale those great walls had to haul themselves over jutting ridges of stone that protected the fortress from just such an assault. But while the overhangs bought the defenders precious time, they were also old and pocked with handholds, so Shrogar sent men to the kitchens for barrels of specially rendered fat that was smeared onto the rock. Before long, the slickness of spilled blood would add to the slippery fat, making the overhangs treacherous indeed. And when the sheer numbers of the enemy forced Vasa's soldiers over the defences and onto the swords of the defenders, one touch of a torch to those walls would do the rest.

Kallis watched the process through narrowed eyes, observing how each man who handled the barrels stripped off his clothes and doused them and his hands in a tub of soapy water, scrubbing vigorously to remove all traces of the substance.

'I hope he knows what he's doing,' he muttered, nodding towards Ephenor's commander. 'This whole place could go up if he's not careful.'

'He knows,' Aarin replied. 'These walls won't burn.' He sat with his eyes closed, his concentration focused outside himself as assessed the damage to Ephenor's defences.

Kallis caught the inflection and bit back his retort that it was not the stones he was thinking of but the wooden structures all around them and the people they sheltered.

'Well, I'm not getting near it.'

The mage grinned and stood up. 'I hope not. Unless you're planning to dangle yourself over the edge. Listen, they're coming back.'

The sudden roar of noise from below them clashed with the distinctive twang of hundreds of bowstrings as the archers on both gate towers poured their deadly rain on the men storming the glacis. Kallis hefted his sword and gave his companion a black look.

'Whoever's giving orders out there doesn't care one whit for his men. This is nothing short of murder.'

Aarin grimaced. 'Better theirs than ours.'

'True.' Kallis held out his hand and Aarin grasped it. Then they turned their attention back to the attack as the first ladders landed with a thud on the walls and the crash of the battering ram against the gates sent a tremble through the stones beneath their feet.

They came in their thousands, hordes of faceless adversaries screaming their battle-rage, each man boosted over the parapet by those behind. Grappling hooks were thrown up, and men swarmed up ropes with unnatural speed, and all the while the attack on the gates did not cease. Great lumbering siege engines hurled boulders at the walls, hurled them over and through the ranks of their own men. And covered by an interlocking barrier of shields, another party made it to the battering ram left abandoned in the earlier attack.

This time the enemy commander did not confine his attack to the main gate, choosing to send another division of troops against the lightly defended eastern doors. Shrogar had withdrawn his main body of archers to the battle for the gates but enough remained to cause havoc among the soldiers who flung themselves with futile desperation against the reinforced doors. Few ladders or siege engines had been brought to this side of the citadel, and the fighting did not come to the walls. Yet the attack served to expose something Ephenor's commanders would have preferred remained hidden—the fact that the gates had been welded shut.

'He would not have expected that,' Kestel observed to Kinseris, watching the rout from the tower ramparts. 'He will know now that there must be other ways to leave this place.'

'He knew that already,' Kinseris replied. 'He is merely testing us. Seeing if we play along and show him where they are.'

The Ancai grunted, his face expressionless as he watched the slaughter of

Kas'Tella's soldiers. 'Then it is an expensive game he plays.'

'So it is, but he has many men, and we have few. Vasa knows he cannot wait us out, for his army will not survive a prolonged siege, and he also knows that in the end we will weary and falter and then he will have his chance. Shrogar can ill afford to spare men from the walls to rest as they must while they maintain multiple fronts, yet Vasa need use no man twice to continue the attack.'

'So, it is hopeless?'

Kinseris shook his head. 'It is our only hope.'

His friend studied him, no longer constrained by the formalities of the ranks they had both discarded. 'Why did you not leave with Aarin when he wished to go? You could have been long gone from here by now and closer to the end you wish for.'

'Because we had to face him.' Kinseris kept his gaze fixed on the bloody field below him 'This is not an enemy I would leave at my back. We are seeing the last days of an age, my friend. If we want the next to dawn on a world made whole again then we must all fight for it, every one of us. Ephenor cannot escape this war, no matter how far we run. The might of Kas'Tella is out there. If we can cripple them here, it can only be a good thing.'

When Kestel did not reply, Kinseris's uneasy conscience imagined accusation in the silence and he grew angry. 'Would you too have me desert these people, leave them to their fate? Leave them here to die when I could help them?'

'Not if that is truly what you believe.'

Kinseris rounded on him, and for a moment the man who had been his loyal captain saw all the fury of a thwarted Kas'Talani in his dark gaze. 'Do you doubt me?'

'You are no longer the Vela'Frankesh,' Kestel replied calmly. 'But you are still my sworn lord and my friend, and I am as loyal to you as I ever was. So, tell me truly, does the desire for revenge play no part in your decision to remain?'

Kinseris stood quivering with anger, then as abruptly as it had flared it was gone, and his eyes held only the misery of uncertainty as he said, 'I do not know anymore. I cannot believe that Vasa is dead. Surely I would know? I have hated him so long, even before –' He stopped then, finding that he couldn't finish that thought. Sighing, he looked away again. 'If I am seeking revenge, I do not think I will find it here. And if Aarin is right and Vasa is dead... can anything I do save these people?'

'You have done what you can for them.'

Kinseris laughed bitterly. 'All our efforts must go into countering the power that is used against us. Who knows how many of my colleagues are out there, or worse, how many of *them*? I have not done nearly enough.'

'The fact that you are here at all is more than enough, my lord.'

They had not heard Callan approach. He gave them a distracted smile. 'The men fear the power of the Kas'Talani and are happy to have one of their own.'

'I wish I could justify their faith in me,' Kinseris replied. 'What of the battle at the gates?'

A frown marred Callan's forehead. Kinseris knew Lysan commanded the archers on the northern towers and guessed that he suffered agonies of concern for his brother.

'The gates hold for now. Though if they break through, they must face the killing ground Ieshwen has prepared. They won't fight their way through to the second gate without heavy losses, if they make it at all. Yet I fear this whole game is one that will be played out and decided with time as the final factor. In the end we cannot hold them if they continue the attack.'

Kinseris looked away. Shrogar had estimated Vasa's army at fifteen thousand. Ephenor, he knew, was home to no more than five thousand, many of them women and children or those too old to fight. But although the War of the Lost Houses was over, everyone who was able had received some form of training. And the fortress itself was formidable. It was not the numbers alone that worried Shrogar's captains, it was the loss of the supplies that could have bought them a lengthy siege sure to destroy the enemy. While Ephenor might have been able to hold back the advancing tide for many days, waiting for the army to weaken and retreat, they could no longer prevent the same fate from leeching the strength from their own men.

'I always believed we were ready for anything they could throw at us,' Callan murmured as he shouldered his bow and prepared to return to his post. 'And though he does not show it, I know Shrogar is afraid. If he is afraid, what are we to do?'

'Keep fighting,' the Ancai told him calmly. 'The enemy has yet to make any advances for all their thousands of men. And there is nowhere better in all this land to stand against this threat.'

Callan smiled. 'Thank you. I will try to remember.' He raised a hand in wry salute as he began to walk away, making for the far tower closest to his brother.

'They cannot lose hope,' Kestel observed to Kinseris as he watched him go. 'It is the surest route to defeat.'

Kinseris watched Callan. 'It is Shrogar I fear for. These are his people and for every one of them who gives their life for him a part of him will die. He must believe he can save them, or that alone will destroy him.'

Aarin heard the splintering crash and the cheer that followed and knew that the enemy had broken through the first gate. On instinct he turned towards the noise and nearly missed the blade that came whistling towards his head. He jerked backwards, slipping on the blood-slicked stone, and crashed to the floor, his concentration shattered as the breath was forced out of him. As the shield he had been holding around himself broke apart, he brought his unfamiliar sword up desperately to catch the downward swing of his assailant's stroke before it would have sliced his shoulder. Forcing the man's weapon to one side, he parried desperately as the half-glimpsed opponent above him pressed his advantage.

Breathing in great gulps of air, Aarin felt his arm begin to tire with the effort of holding the heavy sword above his head, and clutched his knife tight in his left hand, looking for an opening to strike. Then, just as a space appeared around him, a heavy boot stamped down on his wrist, twisting the knife from his grasp. The sword swung down, aiming for his neck, when the hand holding the blade went slack and it fell harmlessly by his head.

He looked up, dazed, into Kallis's angry eyes as the mercenary yanked his own weapon out of the Kas'Tellian's back and reached down to haul Aarin to his feet, giving him a shove towards the tower. 'Get off the walls!'

Aarin stumbled back, massaging his wrist, as the mercenary turned back to the fighting. First Kallis and then Shrogar had begged him to stay away. His life was too precious and his skills more usefully employed, but he had stayed, determined to help where he could. Yet, in the midst of the savage fighting, he had been hard pressed to defend both himself and others, and little use to either.

The enemy were coming faster now, pouring over the ramparts with unnatural speed even as far below them the cheers turned to screams as the men above the killing ground took their revenge on the soldiers trapped by the double portcullis. But success by the gates would mean little if the enemy took the walls and Ephenor's defenders would soon be overwhelmed if he could not slow down the attack.

Aarin looked desperately for Kallis and saw him fighting right up against the ramparts, leaning over and hacking down at the men as they tried to scale the lip of the walls, screaming his fury at them. Even as he watched, Aarin saw a Kas'Tellian climb the overhang to his friend's left and come at him from behind. As he shouted his warning Kallis swung around, the movement saving him from the stroke that would have killed him. But he could not quite evade the blade, which sliced a shallow cut across his arm. The mercenary yelled his rage and pain, shifting his sword to his other hand and running his assailant through, the momentum of the stroke pushing the man back so he toppled off the wall, screaming as he fell.

Aarin saw Kallis stagger, clutching his arm, even as the man next to him disappeared under a swirl of blades. The fighting surged, hiding the mercenary from sight for a moment. Aarin clawed for the dropped threads of his talent and forced an opening through the mass of bodies, creating an instant of calm in the midst of the horror. Kallis was on the ground, trampled under the feet of attackers and defenders alike, and Aarin grabbed him and dragged him to his feet before the frantic motion of battle could overwhelm his fragile defences. All around them men were dying, and he no longer knew which side was which, just a desperate need to escape the press of bodies.

Then the flow of fighting ebbed as the centre of conflict moved away, giving them a moment's respite. Kallis was breathing heavily, one hand pressed to the cut, but he angrily shook off Aarin's steadying hand.

'It's nothing. But you need to get off the wall. *Now!*'

A massive explosion rocked the tower from the inside and out, showering broken splinters of rock down on the defenders. Aarin was thrown from his feet in the blast, crashing to the floor against the wall, blood streaming from a cut on his temple. Through a red haze he saw Kallis crawling towards him, covered in dust and streaked in blood like some kind of fearful apparition. For some reason, the sight brought a laugh bubbling to his lips, spilling over into helpless mirth at the sudden panic that crossed the mercenary's face.

Kallis knelt beside him, peering at him anxiously as Shrogar's voice called out orders to his men. 'What's so funny?'

Then the next moment he was grabbing Aarin by the shoulder and hauling him upright as several Ephenori ran past with flaming torches.

'Move!' He shoved Aarin in the back, forcing him clear of the parapet as the deadly flames started to dance. Then they were both dropping to the floor amid the exhausted defenders as the fire swept the walls clear of attackers and those few who had scaled the walls threw down their weapons.

Aarin heard Shrogar shout, 'No prisoners!' and turned his face away.

Then he heard it, the echo of his name in his ears. 'What was that?'

Kallis shook his head. 'I heard nothing.'

Aarin struggled to his feet, wiping away the blood. 'I did.'

It came again, his name shouted from somewhere inside the citadel. This time he recognised the voice. 'Kinseris.'

'What?' Kallis was beside him, eyeing him uneasily. 'Sure you're all right?'

'I'm needed. Stay here.' He ran to the tower stairs.

'Where are you going?'

Aarin stopped, looking up. 'I'll be back soon,' he promised. 'They need you here.' And then he was gone, disappearing round a twist in the spiral stairs.

THIRTEEN

JETA WATCHED THE stream of wounded as they were carried down from the walls, her eyes searching for Aarin's face as she tried to suppress her fear and horror. All around her men lay dying of hideous wounds, and the sight and sound and smell of their suffering was almost more than she could bear. The man whose hand she held rambled deliriously as blood seeped from the cauterised stump of his leg, hacked off by his friends when it became entangled in the grappling hooks of the enemy. The stink of burned flesh made her gag, but she gripped his hand harder as he cried out, helpless to ease his pain.

A hand touched her shoulder and then Dianeth was there. Gently, she uncurled Jeta's fingers from their grip on the man's hand and laid it down by his side. He had died and she had not even noticed. Numb, she wiped her bloody hands on her dress, unable to meet the other woman's eyes for fear that the sympathy she would find there would break her.

As if sensing the fragility of her control, Dianeth offered her refuge in work with a request for more bandages, and Jeta took the opportunity to escape the makeshift hospital for a few precious minutes. As she left the dying behind, she passed the less badly injured as they waited for help, and forced herself not to run, her need to escape the sight of the carnage suddenly urgent. Then, as she passed through the chamber beyond, an explosion rocked the room and her world was torn apart.

On the eastern wall Kinseris felt the thumping explosion as two magics collided, and the shock as his weavings were snapped slammed him to the ground. Blackness closed over his sight and his ears rang with an awful cry, one that came not from him but from some creature linked to the power he had used. He lay stunned for a moment, trying to force his muddled brain to make sense of the horror, and then he was running.

504

Something had gone terribly wrong, and the protections he had tried to extend to Ephenor's defenders had been turned against them. Already he could feel the agony and death beating against his mind as he ran headlong across the citadel, heedless of his exhaustion and his damaged sight. And then he was in the midst of the carnage, his feet slipping on a slick of blood, and he would have sprawled on his face if he had not crashed into a curled-up body. The man moved, sobbing, gasping great cries of misery. Kinseris pushed himself to his knees to ease his weight off the injured soldier and saw the body was covered in blood, drenched in it. It was then he realised it was not a man but a woman, her dress bloody and torn, her face buried against the wall.

Gently he turned the face towards him. With his hand he cleaned her face of the blood and tears, pushing back the short curls of her hair, her beautiful golden hair. He pulled back, frozen, horrified.

In another second he was on his feet, stepping past her to the foot of the stairs. He stumbled again, holding himself up against the wall. It too was slick with blood.

'Aarin,' he yelled as loudly as he could. 'Aarin!' He knew the mage was on the battlements, hoped he could hear him. He took another couple of steps, shouting again, his voice growing hoarse from the effort.

Footsteps pounded and Aarin came careening down the steps, bouncing off the walls in his hurry. He saw Kinseris leaning over, gasping for breath, took in his blood-soaked robes where he had fallen against the girl, and ran to his side. The priest shoved off his steadying hand and forced Aarin past him.

Aarin followed the direction of his outstretched arm and uttered an agonised cry. He stumbled forwards over the bodies and fell to his knees before the girl. She opened her arms and he gathered her to him, rocking her against his chest as she sobbed. Then the sound of her tears faded as the mage shielded them in the circle of his power.

Kinseris watched the barrier go up and feared the worst, that the girl was dying and Aarin could not bear to let her go. He turned away, unable to watch, and felt tears in his eyes. He staggered up the stairs. He could guess what must have happened and felt a terrible guilt. Threads of magic still clung around the chamber of blood, both the broken strands of his spell and the clashing, discordant residue of the enemy's attack. How they had managed it he could not tell, but that they had was clear. The spells he had laid on these defenders had been used against them, and the opposing forces had literally ripped them apart, turning this innocuous room into a charnel house and striking right into the heart of Ephenor. If they could do it once they could do it again, and Kinseris broke into a run.

As he stepped into the light, he looked up into Kallis's anxious face. When the mercenary saw Kinseris's expression, the smile of greeting died. He tried to shove past but Kinseris barred his way. He shook his head sadly. 'Leave them be. You can't help them now.'

Aarin gathered Jeta close, his heart breaking. He held her and wept because he thought she was dying. There was so much blood. Then, as she stilled, he clung to her tighter.

'They're all dead, all dead.'

She spoke so softly he almost did not hear. Then he froze, hardly daring to hope.

'What? What did you say?' He pulled back so he could see her face.

'I tried to help them,' she whispered, and the pain in her voice was for the men around her, the bodies he had barely noticed. 'They were in so much pain, I tried to help them, but they're dead, Aarin. All dead. Why?' She held out her hands to him and they were covered in blood. 'All this blood!' She was hysterical now. 'Why? Why did they all have to die?'

Aarin looked around him, saw the bodies. They were mangled beyond belief, great gaping wounds opening their insides to the world. The small landing was drenched in gore. He choked back bile. What had happened here? He turned back to Jeta. Had she seen it?

He realised like a man in a dream that the drying blood on her clothes and skin was not hers. The relief made him dizzy

'All this blood,' she repeated, quieter now. 'All this death.' She still held her hands up before his face, touching them to the bleeding cut on his temple.

506

He took them in his own, felt them tremble in his grasp.

'Jeta,' he whispered. 'I'm here now. It's over.'

The sounds of battle carried down the stairway from the battlements above, giving the lie to his words. He pushed them from his mind, shielded hers. He wrapped them both in a bubble of calm and let the madness of the world beat heedlessly against the edges of the spell. Nothing mattered now but the two of them, and he made sure nothing could intrude.

Aarin eased the door open and stepped into the room. Dianeth touched her finger to her lips. She gestured at the bed where Jeta lay sleeping and smiled in reassurance. With a final glance at the girl, she walked to the door.

'She's fine,' Dianeth told him in a gentle whisper. 'She will need you when she wakes.'

Aarin nodded. 'I will sit with her for a while. I am not needed for the moment.'

'Very well,' she agreed. 'But do not wake her.'

He shook his head. Dianeth gave him a last warning look as she went out, closing the door behind her.

Aarin watched the sleeping girl, reliving the moment he had known he had not lost her. Dianeth had helped her out of her filthy clothes and washed the blood and grime from her face and hair. She looked peaceful, but he knew it would not last. Even encased in the shelter of his protective magic it had taken a long while to calm her, and she had cried until she had no more tears to shed. It was only with a lot of coaxing that she had allowed him to carry her clear of the place of slaughter to the women's apartments. There he had given her into the care of Dianeth and her serving women, and reluctantly returned to the walls, not knowing it was already over.

Kallis, who had been frantic with worry, had been visibly relieved when he emerged unhurt from the stairwell and told him that Jeta too would be fine. Kinseris he had not seen, but guessed he had gone to lift the rest of his defensive wards. Though a part of him knew he should help, Aarin had been drawn inexorably back to Jeta.

Now, as he watched her, a small frown creasing her forehead, he wished he had not left. He pulled up a chair and sat down, taking one of her hands in his. She cried out at his touch, but his voice banished the spectre of the nightmare and she subsided into restful sleep. When he was sure she was sleeping easily, Aarin laid his own head on the edge of the bed and allowed his eyes to close. He was asleep in seconds.

Sometime later he awoke. The candles had burned right down as he slept. He had not realised he was so tired.

He saw up and saw Jeta watching him, her hand still in his. She looked at him with huge, smudged eyes, and he saw a whole dam of misery waiting to break.

He took her in his arms and held her as the dam broke. Why was it only in such painful moments that they shared this closeness? The arguments and objections he had used to armour himself against this girl now rang hollow and false. It had taken nearly losing her to see that he could not go on without her, but now he had to face a new fear, that maybe in his confusion and indecision he had held her at arm's length too long.

Aarin stroked his hand through her hair, his fingers entwining themselves in her shorn curls, combing out the tangles as he cradled her against him. Jeta lifted her head, her eyes full of questions. He knew words were needed, that he could not simply brush aside months of awkwardness and hurt and take what he wanted, but he did not know where to start. How to simply say that he had been wrong, and she had been right, when it was not simple at all?

Her eyes were very blue as she watched him. 'What are you thinking?'

Leaning forward, he kissed her forehead. 'That I love you.'

She smiled. 'I know.'

'I've been such a fool.'

'I know that too.'

'Can you forgive me,' he asked her earnestly.

She laughed. 'Kiss me.'

He hesitated and she pulled his head down with an exasperated sign. And then she was kissing him, and he forgot everything else.

FOURTEEN

KINSERIS HAD BEEN tapping the powers of the dragon device for so many years that the magic tumbled from him with barely a thought, and it was a terrible thing to accept that he could no longer draw on that well. The echo of the dragon's pain haunted him. Each time he touched its core of power, he knew he was touching a living creature, draining it, spending its strength for his own ends. The weavings that had been so simple only days ago now came sluggishly, reluctant, and he recognised the reluctance as his. He needed the power to defend Ephenor, to hold back the army, but he could no longer bring himself to call it forth. So he abandoned his magic and pushed through the mass of defenders to Shrogar's side.

The Lord of Ephenor was on the wall above the main gates, a huddle of men surrounding him as he gave hurried orders. He bled from a cut in one arm, but if the injury bothered him, he showed it not at all. He looked up as Kinseris approached, frowning at the expression on the priest's face.

'Trouble?' Shrogar asked, drawing him to one side.

'Of a kind. I have done all I can, all I know. My magic is failing,' Kinseris lied, keeping the ugly truth to himself. 'That which I can call my own is of little use in a place of stone.'

Shrogar studied him intently. 'What does that mean for us?'

Kinseris looked away. 'I have laid what spells I can into the walls. They will, for a time, help repulse those who attempt to scale them, but when they fail, I cannot replace them. I have also spelled as many weapons as I can find, bows, swords, spears. All your arrows will find their marks. But other than that, my lord, it is down to your men. I know no other way to help them.'

'You've done enough,' Shrogar reassured him. 'Together we have done all that can be done. Now we wait. We stung them just now, but they will be back. You should rest,' he advised. 'The attack will come soon enough.'

'I will stay,' Kinseris replied. 'Aarin is –'

'Here.'

They turned as the mage joined them. His clothes were filthy, the leather soaked through with blood and blackened with grime and soot. His shirt was ripped, his sunburnt face tired and smudged, and his hair hung untidily about his collar. He looked, Kinseris thought, like they all did, exhausted and worried, but not grief stricken.

Shrogar voiced the question Kinseris dared not ask. 'How is she?'

A half-smiled hovered on Aarin's lips. 'She will be fine. Your wife has shown great kindness to her, my lord. I thank you.'

Kinseris felt a weight life. 'She was unhurt? All that blood, I thought –'

'Not hers,' Aarin answered, quickly turning to more urgent matters. 'My lord, I have walked the guardroom and felt the traces. Somehow the confined space amplified the strength of the magic they used against us. We are hopelessly vulnerable to such attacks while we continue to shield our men.'

'I have removed the shields from the soldiers,' Kinseris told him. 'Save the stones themselves, all the magic I have used is ours by right. They cannot corrupt that.'

Aarin nodded, thinking. 'The walls are still a risk.'

Kinseris shook his head. 'These walls will not stand to be used in such a way by those who serve Vasa. They are far too old; their loyalty will hold. He may sound for weaknesses, may even be able to search out their secrets, but he cannot bind them to his will.'

'You're sure?'

'I am. I can touch them through this device, but they will not obey me. Ancient magic guards these walls. If we could awaken it, much of our work would be done for us. But that, I fear, is not within our scope at present. I have strengthened the old spells with my own, but I will do more.'

Aarin's grim look said he understood what had remained unspoken. 'It is time we found strength in our weakness and turn what we have to our advantage. Come with me.'

As the enemy regrouped and made ready on the plain below, harried by Shrogar's archers, barrels of fouled, muddy water were hauled out onto the ramparts. At Aarin's direction they were spaced along the line of battlements and he walked the walls with Kinseris, pouring their energy into the pliant element, giving it power rather than taking its power for their own. They took two barrels to the company of archers on the towers and instructed them to dip their shafts in the spell-turned water, enhancing their speed and strength and binding them to their owners. Shrogar's archers could not simply walk the fields of the fallen, as Vasa's could, to retrieve spent shafts. Their need to conserve their ammunition would soon become urgent.

Aarin showed Kinseris how to create buffers of air, spells that when tripped by an escalade would create barriers of great density to slow the enemy's progress and give the defenders time to repel the attack. The presence of the water provided them with the means to draw energy for their magic when all their own was spent, and to maintain the integrity of the spells against direct attack.

He paid special attention to the gates, refusing Kinseris's aid in fashioning protections in the wood. He would need to stay close to maintain them, and with the damage to his sight, it would be far too dangerous for Kinseris to be on the walls during an assault. Having seen the design of the battering rams, with their steel-capped heads, Aarin wove spells to turn metal, to blunt the force of the blows, and laced spells for strength and suppleness into the planks of the doors. If the creaky old wood, patchily repaired, could be persuaded to give a little under the hammering, it would hold a while longer. The Arkni, he knew, would send their men into battle with their own power behind them, but he hoped the influence of their more powerful magic would be tempered by the intransigence of the fortress itself. On that guess rested the hopes of a whole city.

Together they worked illusions that made sheer rock faces seem pocked with handholds, and rough, easily scaled stone appear smooth and treacherous. The numbers of the men along the walls were bolstered by illusionary soldiers so the least defended areas seemed the heaviest manned, and they anchored the magic within themselves to hold even in the face of Kas'Talani probes. It was a risk, but as he said to Jeta, there was little enough they could do that it was a risk worth taking.

Many more such tricks they wove to surround the fortress of Ephenor in a maze of spells and illusions. Not all would work, but perhaps enough would to give the defenders an advantage when they needed it most. They worked until exhaustion put an end to their efforts. When at last he had done all he could, Aarin looked about him at the soldiers waiting for the battle to resume. Some of them grinned and shouted out to him, pleased with the tricks he had given them, and he smiled back, though he knew it was not much.

Later, Kallis found him staring out at the enemy camps. Night had fallen swiftly as it did in the desert, and the twinkling of hundreds of fires was all that could be seen of the vast army. The mercenary stood beside him in silence, and Aarin found his thoughts turning back to Jeta. A smile he could not conceal lit up his face with private joy and Kallis, seeing it, guessed its source and was happy for him.

FIFTEEN

'THEY ARE COMING!' The shout came from a sentry on the eastern tower and was taken up by the men on both sides as a surging tide of the enemy swept in for a second assault. Hundreds of defenders left their posts and ran through the abandoned streets to the threatened walls, leaving behind them only skeleton forces to guard the main gates.

Aarin looked up wearily as Kallis roused from an uneasy sleep. He twisted around to peer at the oncoming wave, fearing that this time they must break through Ephenor's outer defences, and knew a moment of utter confusion when he saw what was happening. The main gates had been repaired, but the work was hurried and incomplete and even with his spells they could not hold long under a sustained attack. The enemy must know that. What they did now made no sense.

All around them captains shouted orders, soldiers gathered weapons, and groups departed for the eastern walls as quickly as they could. He watched them, disturbed.

'I don't like this,' Kallis growled. 'Wasteful they may be, but stupid? Nothing that I have seen so far would indicate that. This is a feint, it must be.'

Aarin nodded. 'I agree. They know they cannot force those gates and an escalade is too costly and uncertain. Their way in is right here. They have broken through once and they can do it again. It makes no sense to change their strategy now.'

'And all our men have gone.' Kallis slammed his fist down on the rough stone. 'What is Shrogar thinking? It's here they're needed.'

'He'll need them there too. It may be a trick, but he cannot let them take the eastern walls.' Aarin looked around and saw Trad running towards them, leaping over men and weapons in his haste. Even from a distance he could see the anger on his face.

'Where are they going?' the boy demanded, as he reached them, waving his arm at the disappearing soldiers. 'Do they wish to make a gift of this place?'

'Where's Lysan?' Kallis asked.

'On the tower, cursing,' Trad replied, moving to peer into the darkness of the plains. 'Callan too. You have never heard a pair squabble as they do. It will drive me mad!' He spun around. 'They're out there, can't you see them? They're coming for us.'

Aarin looked thoughtful. 'How do you know?'

'Look!' Trad pointed out over the walls. 'See the banks of shadow. There were fires there before, but they are gone, hidden by soldiers. I am sure of it. And we are defenceless!'

He turned as footsteps behind heralded the arrival of his captain. Dishevelled and weary, Lysan held up his hands as Trad said angrily, 'Do you still not believe me?'

'I believe you, Trad. I know what this is. My brother has sent runners to Shrogar and the western walls, but there are few men to spare. If we pull our men back from the east, they will take us from behind.' He looked at Aarin. 'I know you have done what you can. How long can the gates hold?'

'A while, not long. What are you thinking?'

The archer sighed. 'Little enough. You can cover these walls in men?'

'But I cannot make them fight.'

'Then perhaps you need some who can.'

Iarwin was making his way towards them. Behind him groups of men ran swiftly to the walls, joining the few who had remained. They came mostly from the western sides of the fortress, stationed on the walls least likely to come under attack, and many were old, or half-trained, but they were still sorely needed.

Lysan greeted Iarwin with a huge smile of relief. 'I am so glad to see you,' he confessed, grasping his arm in welcome. 'Are there more to come?'

Iarwin grimaced. 'My brother suspects a trick, but he is hard-pressed to the east. I have brought all those we have been holding in reserve and any Gwayr could spare from the west, but he will leave no wall unmanned. Until the other attack is beaten back this is all we have.'

'Then we may yet need to rely on your men,' Lysan said to Aarin.

'No.' Trad pushed his way into the small group. 'Would it not be better to make them think this wall is almost deserted? We may show them thousands of defenders and they will not stop their attack, but they might strengthen it. We cannot risk that. Let them see we have sent all but a handful of our soldiers to the east and we have the advantage of surprise. It may be the only advantage we can get.'

Iarwin looked reluctantly at Aarin. 'Could you do that? Hide the men we have from their sight?'

'I could,' he said. 'But better to take advantage of the darkness and let me concentrate on the gates. Conceal your men below the parapet and in the towers. Then they may believe you have fallen for their trap.' *Which we have*, he thought wearily.

Iarwin was already calling orders to the men. Lysan clapped him on the shoulder. 'I must return to my men. Then we should send up a volley of fire arrows to see what we face—and show them what they wish to see.' He glanced at Trad. 'Stay here and give the signal to fire to both towers. Then return to me.'

As he walked away, Iarwin called after him.

Lysan stopped, frowning. 'What is it?'

Iarwin cleared his throat. 'If something should happen to me, you and Callan must take command here. These are your men. They will respond to you best. If I should die –'

Lysan gave a choked laugh and thumped him on the back. 'Is that all? I beg leave to question your judgement where Callan is concerned. You really think my brother is capable of controlling this rabble?'

Iarwin snorted. 'Go now,' he ordered, 'and sort out your rabble or I *will* put your brother in charge.'

Lysan shot him a pained look. 'I thought I was in command.'

'*If* I die.'

Aarin heard the strain and studied Iarwin's taut profile. Was he expecting to die tonight? The tense anger he had come to associate with the man was present in every gesture. He realised for the first time that it was fear.

Trad tugged on his sleeve and pointed. 'They're moving.'

Aarin glanced at Kallis and nodded. As the mercenary slipped into the tower, he caught Iarwin's attention and indicated the advancing shadows. 'Are we ready?'

'As we'll ever be.'

Aarin gave him a curious glance. 'Good luck.'

Iarwin ignored him, his eyes hard. He walked to Trad who waited by the walls, bow in hand and arrow notched, waiting for the order to light it.

Aarin sighed, moving to where Kallis waited.

'I wouldn't mind those few thousand defenders, if you decide to change your mind,' the mercenary muttered with a glance at the pitifully few men behind him.

Then the night was torn apart by a hail of flaming arrows. Aarin watched in horror as the rain of fire lit up a huge formation of the enemy rolling towards them. 'Merciful Maker! They'll never hold.' The words came out before he could stop them, and he instantly regretted them.

'If you think that then I *am* scared,' Kallis retorted, sounding not in the least bit fearful. 'Iarwin will fire the walls again, there'll be some screaming, and it will all be over in no time.'

Aarin forced a smile. The frightened faces behind him would take no courage from his grim assessment. Both he and Kallis knew that there was little remaining of the compound Shrogar had used, but it would do no good to let the beleaguered defenders know that.

Then the bugles were calling the attack from the towers and the time for talking was past. The muted roar of the eastern battle was drowned by the thunderous cacophony of thousands of men hurling themselves against the gates and clawing their way up the walls.

At the last moment, as around them the concealed soldiers rushed out to meet the first wave, Kallis said fiercely, 'If they break through, don't hesitate. Find Jeta and get out of here. Don't wait for me.'

Kinseris watched in horrified fascination as a soldier was disembowelled before his eyes. The man screamed, clutching his hands to the wound, trying to hold in the guts spilling out in a blue sheen over his fingers. His killer kicked him in the back, sending him sprawling at the priest's feet, then reached a hand down and raised Kinseris from his knees.

'Are you hurt?' the Ancai asked.

He shook his head, forcing a smile. The soldier's blade had missed him by inches, slicing past his head as he slipped to the floor. He closed his eyes briefly, blotting out the ghastly sight. When he opened them again the Ancai had already waded back into the fight. Soldiers on both sides fell away before his advance.

Kinseris backed away towards the southern tower. In the darkness of the night his damaged sight was too much of a danger to him, just as he had been warned. There was little he could do here. Away from the bitter struggle on the walls he could better direct the latticework of spells he and Aarin had laid down hours earlier. His roving gaze sought out Shrogar and Ieshwen, fighting side by side in the centre of the conflict, and he noticed in concern that the wound on his friend's arm was bleeding freely again, the blood running down his wrist and onto the hilt of his sword. Then chaos erupted around him and they were lost from sight.

He heard a voice scream his name and his head whipped round. His hand gripped his borrowed sword with strength born of sudden terror as he recognised a man who had served under him at Frankesh, one of the many Kestel had reported vanished after his Vice-Vela had been murdered. Dressed in the livery of the high priest, Torban stood poised on the parapet, bloodied sword in hand and savage glee on his face. With a sinking heart, Kinseris knew he had brought this enemy on himself. It was Torban's brother who had been in the wrong place at the wrong time all those years ago, the brother he had killed to protect the exiles and his own position. *My lady, forgive me,* he whispered. *I need you now.*

Screaming his blood-rage, Torban leapt over the heads of the defenders and landed light-footed before him, unaffected by the barrier Kinseris instinctively erected between them. Behind him came the rest of the missing Frankesh guards and Kinseris knew they had come for one purpose only— to kill him. He did not like to guess how his position had been pinpointed with such accuracy. He backed away, gauging the distance remaining between him and the safety of the tower steps, and raised a shield. To his horror, the threads of his magic sheered away as soon as they touched the soldiers sent to kill him.

'Traitor,' his enemy hissed, advancing on him with sword raised. 'Murderer. I have waited a long time for this day.' He swung his blade in a lazy arc, and the point whistled close to the priest's head.

'Traitor? Me?' Kinseris goaded, as he tried once again to shield himself. He was not a soldier, not trained to fight. Against Torban alone he had no chance. Against them all he may as well just turn the sword on himself. 'It was your brother who was the traitor!'

'Liar!' The sword came hissing down and Kinseris, shield in tatters, managed a clumsy parry, retreating until his back came up against the inner wall. Terrified but defiant, he glared at the men who threatened him as he fashioned a different kind of defence.

'You murdered my brother, betrayer,' Torban accused. 'You killed him because his presence was *inconvenient* for you.'

The Frankesh guards flanked him on either side, trapping Kinseris in place, their faces devoid of emotion.

'I did it for him,' Torban sneered. 'I informed Kas'Tella of your actions, for years I reported to Vasa, and now I will execute you for your crimes.'

'Vasa is the traitor,' Kinseris flung back, as Torban lunged, the tip of his sword catching in the fold of his cloak, pinning him to the wall. 'He is the one responsible for your brother's death. He has sold his people into slavery to an evil that will destroy us all. He has betrayed this whole land.'

As he spoke, Kinseris unleashed the spell, sending its tendrils to snake around Torban's mind. 'I acted only to prevent this tragedy. You must believe me.'

But his opponent laughed, and the priest felt the threads of his conjury rebound on him once more, shaken off with ease. 'Do you think I don't know this, betrayer? They have rewarded me well for my service. They have given you to me.' He yanked his blade free and brought it up to Kinseris's throat, leaning against the hilt. 'Your tricks won't work on me. You cannot escape.

Is this how you killed my brother? Did you look him in the eye as you took his life?'

But Kinseris could not speak. He could not even swallow. He stared helplessly into the wild eyes of his executioner and saw instead a flicker of movement in the shadows behind him. As the guards on either side spun away to face the threat, Torban tired of his game and drew back his sword for the killing stroke. Over his shoulder Kinseris looked up into Shrogar's furious face and hurled himself to one side as a jet of blood vomited from the man's mouth, but he was not quite quick enough. The cold metal bit into the muscle at the base of his neck and warm blood flowed over his shoulders and down his chest as he collapsed against the stone. He felt someone kneel beside him and press a hand to the wound, and the last thing he heard was a voice he recognised telling him to hold on.

SIXTEEN

AARIN WAS EXHAUSTED. It felt like hours since the attack had begun, hours in which they had fought alone with no reinforcements from the east, but he knew it could not be nearly so long. He had stayed with the archers, away from the fighting on the walls. But even so he had not escaped the fighting. Several Kas'Tellians had sought him out, ploughing towards him through the mass of men with such determination that he knew he must have been marked somehow.

Minutes earlier, the Ancai had come charging out of the tower stairway beside him, his expression blackly furious. Assassins had been sent to kill Kinseris. With that man by his side, Aarin doubted they had been successful. But the fact that the priest was nowhere in sight worried him. He glanced over to where Kestel was talking with a harried looking Lysan and wondered what was happening. Then the Ancai disappeared back down the spiral stairs and Lysan came toward him.

'The attack to the east is falling back, but at a cost,' he told Aarin. 'Kinseris has been hurt and Shrogar is also injured, though how badly I do not know. As soon as they can, they will send men to us here, and we need them.' He looked down onto the walls. 'We cannot hold much longer.'

Aarin followed his gaze, his eyes seeking out Kallis. The walls below him seemed to heave with men, yet the spells he had laid had been more effective than he'd dared hope, and the tide of the enemy was slowed as they fought against the heaviness of the ascent. Many ladders had been cut down before the soldiers could scale them, and many more men had been slaughtered as they hauled their leaden limbs over the parapet. But the sheer weight of numbers was beginning to tell against them.

A new wave of attacking energy collided with the protections on the gates and Aarin reeled, too tired to absorb the recoil of the wards without punishment. The Arkni, or the priests, had been battering at his defences as soon as they realised what he had done. Lysan caught him as he stumbled, easing him to his knees.

'Rest a while,' he advised. 'We need you.'

Aarin shook his head. 'I must guard the spells. They try to undo them.'

'They?'

He waved his hand towards the enemy encampment, and Lysan followed the direction of his arm in understanding. 'Can you hold on?'

'I must,' Aarin replied, leaning his head against the wall and closing his eyes, his mind slipping inside the spells and repairing the damage.

When he opened his eyes again Lysan was gone and Trad stood beside him, guarding his rest. He took the proffered hand and allowed Trad to haul to his feet, glancing over the tower to the wall. In the minutes he had been apart from it, the struggle had not changed, the tide flowing one way then the other, and in the centre of the madness was a sight more insane still.

Iarwin's sword flashed white in the moonlight. His enemies lay dead all around him, but no matter how many he killed, the anger boiled inside him. He stood on the battlements themselves, balancing his weight on nimble feet, defending his home from any who dared try to cross into Ephenor within reach of his arm. That Ephenor might fall to Kas'Tella was a lance of agony in his heart, and he was determined that he would not live to see it.

His men cried a warning, and he twisted so fast he almost fell. Grabbing an outstretched hand to steady himself, he leapt across the ramparts to reach the latest group that had dared to trespass on his stretch of wall. The stone beneath his feet was wet and slippery with blood but he did not stumble, thrusting himself into the knot of Kas'Tellians.

Two he sent sprawling to their deaths as they overbalanced on the treacherous surface. A third fell onto the waiting swords of the Ephenori behind him. But the last two did not prove so easy, pressing him together so he was forced to defend. One blade nicked his ribs, another drew a line of blood along his cheekbone. Then a lucky blow tripped him, spilling him onto his knees. Iarwin heard a cry of rage that sounded like his own as he raised his sword above his head. The impact of the blow jarred his arm and upset his precarious balance. On his back now, one leg trapped under him and sword clattering to the ground, he looked up into the eyes of his killer and smiled. If this was to be how the torment ended, he would accept it gladly.

But the blow did not fall, or rather it did, but so slowly that he could watch the play of emotions on his opponent's face as he struggled with a weapon that resisted his efforts. He heard someone calling his name and saw Aarin shouting for him to move. He looked back at the soldier, still suspended in slow motion, and knew the mage had somehow interfered with the combat. He could not refuse to take the reprieve, not like this, but it was with reluctance that he tore himself away and rolled off the wall. Aarin reached him at the same moment, ducking under the weapons of the defenders and helping him to his feet. Iarwin brushed his hand away, unable to mask his quivering anger.

'You may come to regret that,' he hissed as he retrieved his sword and turned away. Then Aarin was forgotten as a fresh wave of Kas'Tellians poured over the overhangs and into the deadly dance of his sword. One chance had been snatched from him, but the mage could not protect him forever and the enemy was not finished with them yet.

SEVENTEEN

THE MINUTES AFTER Aarin left were the most terrifying of Trad's life. A wave of attackers had appeared over the lip of the tower, invading one of the few stretches of walls as yet untouched by hand-to-hand fighting. He saw Lysan jerk back, a knife in his shoulder. Releasing his last arrow into the throat of the man who had injured his captain, he ran to Lysan's side, reaching him at the same moment as his brother.

Surrendering him into Callan's frantic care, Trad drew his long knife and launched himself into the mass of soldiers crossing the parapet before he could think about what he did. All around him the archers were throwing down their bows and scattering before the oncoming wave. He screamed at them to hold. If the towers went, the wall would follow, and it would all be over. He rallied them with desperate courage, his slender blade moving with all the deadly, instinctive skill his teachers had praised.

Behind him, through a daze, he could hear Callan shouting, and risked a glance over his shoulder. Lysan was on his feet, sword in hand, and Callan was screaming at his archers to hold and at his brother to leave.

Trade struck out at the man who had tried to flank him as Callan fought his way to his side. Lysan stood by the tower stairs, turning his men back to the fight with the sharp edge of his tongue and the blunt edge of his sword. The chaotic rout stalled and began to reverse. As Trad discarded his knife to collect a sword from the ground, he noted with grim satisfaction that most of the company of archers had now returned to the fight, forming a knot around Callan.

'We must push them back to the wall!' he yelled at Callan and saw the older man nod his understanding. They had to take the fight to the parapet and stop the tide of soldiers from crossing over into the small space.

Callan shouted orders to his men over the deafening clash of metal, roaring at them to be ready to push forward as one. And as they surged forward,

Trad saw a Kas'Tellian engage Lysan by the stairway, trying to force an entry into the castle itself and watched, horrified, as they fell together.

Callan screamed with rage, thrusting forwards with a fury that scattered the men before him like leaves in the wind. Trad sliced his sword against his opponent's side, shoving him aside as he forced his way to the walls. Hacking around him, tiring now, he saw that enough of the archers had followed their captain, and those that remained behind picked off the few Kas'Tellians who had escaped their charge.

Then, at last, the wave of soldiers crossing the parapet slowed to a trickle, and those who made it over moved with exaggerated heaviness, and Trad knew Aarin had returned. As he despatched the last of the enemy, he looked for the mage and saw him kneeling by Lysan, a bloodied knife falling from one hand. He held the archer in his arms, braced against his knees as he pressed down on his injured shoulder with both hands. Lysan's face was white but he was conscious, smiling even. Callan skidded to a halt by his brother and took his face in his hands. Ignored by all, the broken body of the man who had attacked the archer, Lysan's sword in his chest.

Stumbling in his weariness, Trad tripped over a tangle of weaponry on the ground and saw scores of precious bows strewn across the tower floor. Gathering those nearest to him, he called to the men to collect their weapons, realising with a sinking heart that many had been trampled in the panicked struggle. Arrows lay scattered by their quivers, bowstrings twisted around the searchers' feet as they dragged them out from under bodies, and swords lay abandoned amid pools of blood.

'Get the bodies over the edge,' he told a passing soldier and it was only after the man obeyed him without question that he wondered at his own audacity. He was not only a stranger to them—and little more than a boy in their eyes—he also had held no rank here. But the men had seen him fight beside their captain, the first to engage the enemy as they crossed into the tower, and they were glad to have someone take charge of the chaos. Callan nodded his approval before turning his anxious gaze back to his brother.

At length, when Trad had done all he could, setting the surviving archers back to their posts, he joined the small group by the stairs. Lysan was sitting up on his own now, but his face was pinched with strain. Callan was talking urgently to him as he bound the wound in his brother's shoulder, but Trad was relieved to see more amusement than concern on Aarin's face when the mage looked up at him. The wound could not be too serious.

Trad crouched down beside them, reporting to Callan.

Callan tied off the bandage and rocked back on his heels. 'I must go to the far tower,' he decided at last. 'They have escaped direct attack so far, but I think that will not last.' He glanced at Lysan. 'My brother is in no condition to be here any longer,' he said firmly as Lysan protested. 'You will go to the healers, brother, if I have to order the men to carry you. Trad, you will take over the command in his absence. Indeed, it seems you have already.'

Callan ignored the flush of pride Trad could not hide. He looked at Aarin. 'You slowed the attack here. Can you do the same for other tower if it comes to it?'

Trad saw Aarin wince and Callan's gaze sharpened on him. 'Can you do that without endangering the spells you have on the walls?'

Aarin shrugged. 'I can try.'

'Good.' Callan stood, helping his brother to his feet. He called over another injured archer and instructed him to take Lysan to the healers. Then he laid his hand on Trad's shoulder. 'They will follow you; you've earned it. If Kestel was right, you should have reinforcements coming soon. Use them as you see fit.' He nodded at Aarin. 'Let's go, and hope we are not too late.'

After what felt like hours since the bugles had first signalled the attack, Kallis dropped his sword, collapsing in a heap on the flagstones. Blood dripped from cuts on his arms and chest, but none was a serious wound. It was exhaustion that stole his legs from under him, though many others were not so lucky. The dead and dying from both sides lay all around, the sounds of battle replaced by the cries of the injured.

Reinforcements had arrived just as it seemed the battle would be lost. The gates had been smashed through in the final minutes, Aarin's spell snapping with a suddenness that made him worry for the mage, but the majority of the enemy were already falling back and there had been no new wave to replace the soldiers who died in Ieshwen's killing ground. The left tower had escaped assault, but only just. The first ropes had been hurled up her height just as the reinforcements arrived, and the few who made it to the top had been swiftly despatched, lacking the surprise that had taken their comrades almost to the corridors of the fortress. Iarwin was alive, by what miracle Kallis could not guess, and though he disliked the man he was forced to a grudging respect for his courage. There was no engagement he had backed away from, no matter how outnumbered he had been, and Kallis had not missed the strange by-play when Aarin had saved him from certain death.

Kallis pushed himself to his feet, eyes searching the throng of men working through the carnage. His heart hitched in worry when he did not see Aarin, aware that the tower he had been on had fallen under heavy attack. Pushing his way to the steps, he saw Trad coming down and grabbed him, demanding to know Aarin's whereabouts. Trad grinned at his concern, pointing behind him. Callan and Aarin were picking their way towards him, each leaning heavily on the other, their faces reflecting their total exhaustion.

'Blessed Maker.' He caught Aarin and held him steady as he swayed. 'What have you done to him?' he asked Callan.

The captain looked startled for an instant, then his face relaxed. 'I've been putting him to good use.' He turned to Trad. 'Lysan did not come back?'

The boy grinned 'He did not.'

'Good, because I need him now. My Lord Shrogar is waiting for a report on the action here.' He grimaced, looking at the carnage about him. 'I hate to ask anymore of you, Trad, but someone must remain here to oversee this.' He struggled to find the words, and Trad nodded, saving him the trouble.

'Thank you,' Callan said sincerely. 'For all you did today.'

Kallis glanced at the boy, whose face had flushed with pleasure. Clearly something had transpired tonight he knew nothing of, and it must have been significant for Callan to place Trad in temporary command of the wall.

'I'll tell you later,' Aarin mumbled into his shoulder, and Kallis shook his head in exasperation.

'You don't need him for now, do you?' he asked Callan.

Callan smiled tiredly. 'Would it make a difference if I did? I think he would sleep through anything else tonight. You will see him to his rest?'

'I will. Then I will return here if you need me?'

Trad nodded, as tired as any of them. 'You will be most welcome.'

Callan took his leave, issuing final instructions as he did so. Finding Aarin already asleep on his feet, Kallis sighed. Draping the mage's arm over his shoulder, he half-carried him down the stairs and off the walls for a few hours of sleep before it started all over again.

'Our magic is failing,' Aarin told Kallis wearily, slumped against the wall of the chamber that had been set aside for them, a cup of water in his hand. 'That which is contained within the device Kinseris holds is draining away, and it cannot be replenished. We dare not drain it further.' The thought of the death that waited at the bottom of that well was too painful, too sorrowful to speak of. They could no longer risk the life that sourced Kinseris's magic. He sighed. 'My own is pitiful against theirs. How can I counter magic I cannot see, cannot feel? How can I protect men from that?'

'You're asking me?' Kallis asked, looking up the sword he was cleaning.

The mage sighed. He was silent a long time, his gaze turned inward, back to his childhood and his father's hearth. There they had dreamed together of elemental mastery in all its mystery, and the endless possibilities stretching out before them. How bitter it was that he should live to see the powers of the dragons wielded by men, and those men were trying to kill him.

'You have done more than you think,' Kallis told him now, examining his blade in the candlelight. 'Both of you. You cannot ask more of yourself than you can give.'

'But it is not enough. They have elemental mastery, and we have a poor reflection. Our options are limited, theirs are endless.'

'Endless?' Kallis asked idly. 'But a stick would still be a stick, isn't that what you told me?'

'I did not mean...' Aarin froze, his fingers clenched in a death grip on the glass. He remembered the stick he had changed to a knife in Kallis's hand. But it was just illusion. *I cannot change the true nature of a thing*, he had said. *To do that would be to bring something into this world that was never meant to be here.*

Like the Arkni.

Oh, Merciful Maker, could that be the answer?

The Arkni were unnatural, utterly wrong. He knew instinctively that they were never meant to be. But they *were*, somehow.

The endless possibilities of full elemental mastery were not endless at all. Creation, as he had told Kallis, was the one gift that was the Maker's alone. True, unlimited creation was too powerful, too deadly a force to be entrusted to any living creature.

But the Arkni could not have been born; they must have been *made*.

'Aarin?'

Kallis was watching him with mild concern. 'What are you thinking? Talk to me.'

But his thoughts were in too much disarray to put into words. How had they been made, why? And how was it that the power of all five elements resided in them when they were not two, but one?

The magic was the Maker, her essence, her nature. Yet She was Five in their totality, their separate natures surrendered to the whole. Not Five melded into One, but One that was also Five. Was it possible, he wondered, hardly daring to breathe, that Five could become One? Could a union between human and dragon be that flawless? No, it was not possible. They were two separate creatures, mirror images and utter opposites, two living, breathing creatures. They could not become that One. Unless, unless...

He jerked upright, the force of his grip breaking the cup into pieces that cut into his palm.

'Aarin!'

Kallis leaned forwards, trying to pry open his hand, but Aarin was barely aware of him.

It was not possible unless they had sought that place, that dark, terrible, beautiful place at the heart of the nothingness. The place he had glimpsed for an instant that night in the Vale when the fury of the elements had raged through him; that place he had seen, almost touched, that had called to him. If the ancients too had glimpsed that place, he realised with sick certainty, they would have stopped at nothing to reach it. But Men alone could not have done this thing. It would have taken two together, one from each race, and those two would have become—what?

'You bloody fool,' Kallis cursed him. 'That's your sword hand!'

Aarin looked down and saw his hand in Kallis's grip, the red of his blood in stark contrast to his pale palm. As he watched, a drop of blood dripped between his fingers and splashed on the floor.

'What?' Kallis demanded, seeing his stricken look. 'Say something.'

Aarin shook his head. He could not tear his mind away from the dawning realisation.

What would they become? Not a man in a dragon's body, nor a dragon in a man's, but some unspeakable combination of the two. For that dark beauty was also treacherous. Seeking the power and desiring it would not be enough, it would be the end.

The pain in his hand flared with sudden intensity as Kallis wound a strip of linen around the injury. An image of Saal'an flashed into his mind, the feel of his clawed hands, the heat of his skin... Oh, Merciful Maker! He could not breathe, he was choking, gasping for air, and yet he never moved. He knew with absolute certainty that they had once tried to find that place, and the true nature of his enemy crashed down on him. *Oh Tesserion, Blessed Mother, how can we fight such creatures?* They would never win free of this place, and if they did, where could they go? Call back the dragons now and unbar the means through which the Arkni could continue their path to utter destruction. And they would take everything with them.

EIGHTEEN

AARIN WAS DREAMING. He stood alone on the tower, watching the dawn rise over a desert of blood-stained sand, ushering in a new day, the last day. Far below, he saw the enemy's host arrayed before the walls of Ephenor, sunlight glinting on weapons raised to attack. Shrouded in an eerie silence, the ranks extended as far as he could see in all directions. Even the wind was stilled. It was an army of the dead. He could feel the death, smell it on the air even in his dream, and it sickened him. But he knew it was not their death he saw, but his own.

There was nowhere he could go they would not follow.

As Aarin watched, the front rank parted and a horseman rode out to stand at the head of the army, hooded and cloaked in the black mantle of the priesthood. Fear and outrage surged through his mind as he saw Vasa alive, and himself caught in a tangle of lies and betrayal that could only end in his death.

Anger surged through him. 'Why are you doing this?' he heard himself shout. 'This land was never yours. What right have you to claim it for your own?'

Only silence answered him. The unseen gaze of his enemy never wavered, and as the utter stillness stretched on, he felt fear tighten his throat. Then at last the man moved, raising an arm to push back his hood, and as the dark cloak fell away fear turned to terror.

Saal'an gazed back at him from the ravages of his deformed humanity.

'But I come for you, Æisoul. It is only you that I want.'

Only you that I want... Hypnotic, terrifying, the refrain echoed over and over as dark magic twined its coils through his mind. At last he saw his enemy through his enemy's eyes. The whole of his vision was filled with the awful presence, huge and powerful as a dragon, tall and slender as a man, yet lacking true physical form still, as shadowy as the night with eyes like flame. As that

530

terrible gaze settled upon him, he was confronted with the full force of Saal'an's hatred and contempt.

A horror fell upon Aarin then that paralysed his will and froze his mind. Even as he strove to resist he felt himself slipping, succumbing to a will greater than his own, that had taken Darred and Vasa before him and was even now marching across Caledan bringing war to the last of the rebel lands. In an instant he was caught, tossed before the tempest, and the shrieking of a great wind filled his ears until he was aware of nothing else. Night fell across his sight. Bereft of his own senses to guide him, he was adrift in a place of another's choosing, and he did not know which way to turn.

A strange calm descended. Soft whispers licked against the edges of his mind, sweet promises of rest, of freedom, of a life unfettered by the demands of destiny. All this if he would but surrender his autonomy, betray his heart and his friends, and yield his magic to his enemy who would use him to do what he feared he could not do alone. So seductive were the whispers that for a moment it seemed only a small thing to ask in exchange for offering up his dreams. But that part of his will that was not entirely his own, that was bound by an oath sworn in blood in Amadorn, gave him a strength he should not have had. The dragons would be returned only to be subsumed. Knowing that, he could never yield.

The laughter swelled, a breaking tide of hatred washing over him, but it did not pull him under. Instead of falling back, he advanced, challenging his enemy to confront the very core of his being where defiance still burned. Throwing caution aside, Aarin surrendered to the truth he had feared, and embraced the burden laid upon him through prophecy thousands of years before his birth. In desperation he shielded himself with his birthright, an armour bright enough to repulse even this darkness. And in the instant he finally accepted all that he was, he was free.

Aarin hurled his refusal at the creature that assailed him, shattering the webs that held his awareness in thrall. As he plunged back into the dream, he felt Saal'an's fury as a backlash ripping through his limbs.

'So be it, Silver Mage,' the creature hissed as he wheeled his horse around. 'Know that you have doomed them.'

And with a blinding flash the army came to life and the hordes of the dead raised their weapons in grim salute. The walls crumbled before them as if they were no more than dust, and the soldiers of the enemy rolled ever onward. Death marched with them and before them and the screams of the Ephenori filled the dawn.

Aarin fell to his knees. He clasped his hands tight over his ears, but he could not shut out the sounds of the dying. Then he too began to scream...

Aarin sat up, the cry dying on his lips as returning consciousness banished the dream. His hands trembled as he brought them to his face and ran tense fingers through sweat-drenched hair. The door swung back on its hinges as Kallis rushed in with his sword drawn, his eyes quartering the room before coming to rest on the huddled figure on the floor.

Aarin struggled to calm his ragged breathing. It was just a dream, a nightmare. It had not happened—yet. He reached up his hand and Kallis hauled him to his feet.

'I thought you were being murdered.'

Aarin managed a faint smile as he splashed water on his face, shaking the drops out of his hair as he tried to shake off the cobwebs of the nightmare. He took a deep breath, then another. He knew what he had to do. He made for the door. 'Come on.'

'Where to?'

'To find Kinseris,' Aarin answered, grim-faced. 'We've made a terrible mistake.'

Shrogar sat with his head in his hands. A bloody bandage covered the wounds on his upper arm, but he had ignored the advice of his wife and Callan who both begged him to rest. Instead, he was closeted with his captains and Kinseris as they discussed the course of the conflict. The priest studied the weary men around him. All of them bore injuries, but Shrogar had been lucky and none of his key commanders had been lost, though all were reaching the end of their endurance.

The despair in Shrogar's posture was mirrored in all the faces in the room, and Kinseris realised with a sinking heart what no one wanted to say.

It was Ieshwen, in the end, who said what everyone was thinking. 'My lord, I do not believe we can hold. Their numbers grow every day, and this is but the first army of Kas'Tella. They have reserves in their thousands, and nearly half our number are already wounded. We have lost two hundred dead and as many again will probably die from their wounds.' He looked around the room, seeking support. 'The gates can be repaired, but they will not hold for long. My lord, it is time to order the evacuation.'

Kinseris stirred restlessly and Shrogar raised his head.

'You don't agree.'

The priest shook his head carefully. The thick bandage round his neck made the movement painful though the wound had been messy but not too serious. 'You cannot order the evacuation. It would be a mistake.'

'We have nothing left to throw at them!' Ieshwen broke in, furious. 'Good men will die if we continue this madness. They have us beaten, can't you see that?'

Shrogar waved them both to silence. To Kinseris he asked, 'If you have other advice you would give, let me hear it, but unless you are offering me a miracle, I do not see what else I can do.'

Kinseris hesitated. He was little better than a stranger to most here, but Shrogar valued his advice and he prayed that he could make the man listen when, as the commander of these men, his heart was telling him it was already hopeless.

'My lords,' he warned, 'if you order your men to leave now you will be sending them to their deaths. I know this man, and I tell you that Vasa is not interested in conquest, not this time. Your defiance has come to torment him like nothing else. All he desires is to wipe out the Ephenori to the last man, woman, and child, and scour the last remnants of revolt from his land. If you run, Vasa will follow, and outside these walls you have no defence against him. He will waste his men to see you destroyed. He will throw them against these walls again and again, for he knows he must break you quickly, and he will trust in his superior numbers, not strategy. But you must stand and fight. It is your only hope.'

'His superior numbers may well be enough,' Shrogar pointed out. 'If not tomorrow, it will be soon. Vasa has the resources of an empire to draw on. We have nothing but what you see. Tell me, how can we hold?'

'Consider his situation,' Kinseris implored. 'If nothing else he is disadvantaged by the terrain and the distance from Kas'Tella. His supply lines run straight through the Ranger Desert and his army is neither small nor easily provisioned. If you can hold him long enough, they *will* begin to starve, and when that happens the army will fall apart. Their water will run out first and all the wells outside these walls are spoiled. Dying men cannot take Ephenor, my lord.'

Shrogar shook his head wearily. 'We cannot wait for them to starve when we ourselves are so ill-equipped for a siege.' So bitter now the thought of the supplies lost to careless storage that might have seen them through.

'Ephenor is defensible, my lord,' Kinseris insisted. 'Smaller numbers have beaten greater odds than these in worse places. It can be done again.'

Shrogar rubbed a hand over his face. 'I know it can be done. But I do not know any longer that *we* can do it.'

Kinseris did not reply. There was no answer to that.

Shrogar sighed. 'I cannot do it. I have a duty to my people, and I cannot ask any more of them than they have already given.'

Kinseris saw the cost of his decision and was determined to use it to keep him fighting. 'They will give their lives if you order the evacuation.' It was brutal but true. 'When the first wave of refugees emerges from your secret tunnels, they will be cut down by Vasa's troops. None will be spared, not even the smallest child. He will have men stationed at each and every one of them by now, waiting for you to send your people through. They won't stand a chance.'

'You cannot know that!' Ieshwen protested. 'My lord –'

Kinseris cut him off harshly. 'Can't I? He will have had adepts searching for your hidden tunnels since the moment he arrived. It is his way. The citadel of Kas'Tella is riddled with them and Ephenor is the sister of that place. He will discover your secrets as easily as if he were in his own palace. The magic may prevent him from entering Ephenor that way, but it will also trap your people with no means of escape.'

'Kinseris is right.'

Shrogar turned as Aarin and Kallis walked in. 'Why?'

Kinseris frowned, alert to the signs of stress on Aarin's face. 'I thought you were resting.'

'I was dreaming,' the mage replied bitterly. 'But it is time now to face the truth.'

He turned his attention to Shrogar. 'Evacuation would be a mistake, even if it were Vasa out there. But it is not. It is something else, and I fear that all strategies are worthless now.'

Kinseris looked at him sharply. Aarin nodded in bleak confirmation.

Shrogar sat down heavily, looking from one to the other. 'How do you know?'

'It doesn't matter,' Aarin replied. 'Only that I know it. It is not Vasa who commands the army out there, and the rules of the game are no longer the same.'

'You have remarkably good intelligence of the enemy,' Iarwin sneered, and the accusation was plain. 'I think my brother deserves an answer. How do you know?'

Kallis rounded on him, the colour rising in his face, but Aarin ignored Iarwin's jibe, addressing himself to Shrogar.

'Kinseris is right. You must make your stand here. To do otherwise is certain death. The commander out there, the *thing* whose orders this army follows, is not interested in you or your people. It's me he wants.'

'So, we fight and die to save your precious skin,' Iarwin spat.

Aarin ignored him, one hand reaching out to grab Kallis by the wrist as the mercenary bristled with rage.

'I do not ask that of you,' he told Shrogar. 'If I leave, Ephenor will be safe. But I need time, for I cannot abandon the task I have set myself. Give me a day, my lord, one day to get clear, and then you may give me up, tell them I have gone. If you can hold on one more day, I promise you Ephenor will not fall.'

Shrogar regarded him thoughtfully. 'You told me once before you could not be certain the threat would leave with you. That has changed?'

'It has.'

'I will go with you,' Kinseris said quietly.

Iarwin threw his hands in the air. 'Like rats leaving a sinking ship! And this story of yours is just as full of holes. If you let them go, brother, they will go straight to the enemy.'

Kallis snapped. His fist slammed into Iarwin's head, and as the stunned man stumbled, Kallis grasped a fistful of his tunic and thrust him against the wall, his hand around his throat.

'Say that again,' he threatened, 'and it will be the last thing you say.'

Iarwin looked at him with sneering contempt, a trickle of blood starting at his temple.

'So, you can silence the suspicions?' he taunted. 'Kill me and you seal your guilt. You'll both die before you can leave this room.'

Shrogar shoved past Aarin. 'Let him go,' he told Kallis, his voice harsh. 'I'll deal with this.'

Kallis did not seem to have heard, then he gave Iarwin a final shove and stepped back, breathing hard. Aarin had gone white and he was staring at Iarwin with something close to horror on his face.

Shrogar stood between them. 'This is not the time. No one doubts you, either of you,' he assured Kallis with a dangerous look at his brother. 'Please. We have enemies enough as it is.'

Kinseris watched, deeply disturbed, as the look of hatred on Iarwin's face sent his brother reeling back a step. Then he moved away to stand between Callan and Lysan, who silently closed ranks around him, their expressions carefully blank.

Shrogar turned back to Aarin, and Kinseris could see his exhausted struggle to concentrate. 'You say Ephenor will be safe if you leave. How can you be sure?'

Aarin tore his eyes from Iarwin. 'This is not an attempt to squash your rebellion,' he told Shrogar. 'Nor even at conquest. The creatures out there are not interested in land. They could have provided Vasa with the means to finish you long ago if that was their wish, but I suspect it suited them that you kept Vasa's attentions directed elsewhere. Think, my lord! Why are we not dead yet? Without a doubt they possess the power to take this place apart if they wished. With each attack they have been on the verge of victory and then, when it seems they must overwhelm us, they retreat. I do not underestimate your men, but these creatures are a power apart from the world of men and they could have taken Ephenor long since. They have not done so because they cannot risk a sack of the city. They need me alive.'

Shrogar looked unconvinced. 'Then if you leave there will be nothing to stop them from destroying this place. It seems to me that the longer you stay, the safer we will be.'

Aarin shook his head impatiently. 'For how long? Already they have endured thousands of years of waiting. If I do not leave soon, they will come for me, and we will see their full might wielded against Ephenor. They might keep me alive, but they will show your people no such mercy. All they care about is the magic, and if they get their hands on it then none of this will matter anymore. The only way for them to achieve what they seek is through me, or I would never have been allowed to reach here alive. My lord, they are getting desperate, and so are we.'

Kinseris watched the impact of his words on the faces around him. These were good men, brave men, and they did not deserve the burden of the truth. Until now, Aarin had deliberately held back his suspicions, but whatever had happened, he was keeping his secrets no longer.

'We cannot wait on the resolution of this war to reunite the races,' he told Shrogar now. 'This would not even be happening if it were not for me. If I leave, they *will* abandon this army and follow.'

'You cannot do it,' Kinseris protested. 'You would play right into their hands.'

Aarin shrugged. 'One way or another the prophecy will be fulfilled. I *must* do this. No one has to come with me. Despite appearances, you would be safer here.'

Kinseris sighed. 'I will come with you. How can I not?'

Aarin smiled. He looked at Kallis, who raised a surprised eyebrow.

'Do you really need to ask?'

NINETEEN

SHROGAR WATCHED AS Aarin and Kinseris chose the course that would take them from Ephenor, robbing him of their assistance when he needed it most. Yet, even so, he could not share his brother's suspicions. He had known and trusted Kinseris too long.

He glanced at Iarwin, standing stiffly in the corner. Shrogar recalled the hatred in his brother's eyes when he had pulled Kallis from his throat. He worried that he had done wrong somehow, though he could not guess how. Iarwin's behaviour disturbed him. It was so out of character that Shrogar had to admit that he did not know him as well as he had thought. Either that, or his time in Kas'Tella had changed him more than he had realised. Something was amiss, and he meant to find out what.

Shrogar felt a prickle of envy as he turned to the others. He hated the siege and ached to have the freedom to fight on his own terms, but he was wise enough to realise that the true battle would be fought by these men, on a level he could not understand. He clung to Aarin's promise like a drowning man. He would give them their day, if he had to do it through a river of blood. He would give them the chance they needed to save his home, for it was a concept beyond his comprehension that the whole world was at stake. He had no effort to spare for the world outside Ephenor.

'The evacuation is delayed for one more day,' Shrogar told his captains. 'Any man who can hold a weapon should report to his company at first light. I will join you on the north wall at dawn. If they come before, send word at once, though I do not think sleep will find me this night.'

He studied his men. They might not understand what had gone on here, they might not want to, but they were his unquestioningly, and they would fight for him as long as they drew breath. For that he said a thousand thanks. 'Go now and see we are prepared to face whatever tomorrow may bring.'

They went, Iarwin wearing his injured silence like a cloak.

'We need to talk,' Shrogar said quietly as his brother brushed past. 'Will you come to me?'

Iarwin's gaze shifted from his face to the restraining hand on his arm. His face twisted in derision. 'Don't I always, brother?'

'Yes, you do,' Shrogar sighed, wondering that he knew this man so little. 'Give me one hour, back here.' He released his grip and Iarwin walked out without another word.

As Kinseris moved towards the door, Shrogar caught his eyes and the priest stopped. 'You want to talk to me?'

'All of you.' Shrogar nodded at Aarin and Kallis. 'Please.'

He sat down heavily behind his desk and rested his elbows on the solid wood. He was skirting the edges of total exhaustion and the wound on his arm ached with a vengeance. It felt tight and hot.

'I apologise for Iarwin,' he said hoarsely. 'He is tired and angry, we all are. I do not think he means what he is saying.'

'He means it.'

Shrogar glanced at Kallis. 'Perhaps. I do not know anymore. We have been parted for so long, and I fear the boy I once knew is gone forever.' The pain of that loss was sharp.

He saw their awkward sympathy and could not bear it. 'When and how do you plan to leave?'

'As soon as we can,' replied Aarin. 'Before dawn if we can, at first light if we cannot.'

Shrogar cast an assessing glance over the men before him. They were all exhausted, all of them hurt. They had been in the thick of the fighting for two days, snatching what rest they could between assaults, and they were calmly proposing to leave without sleep to restore either body or mind. They were mad, he decided, and desperate.

'Very well. I can't offer much help. Take what you need from Ephenor's stores. Only one other thing can I offer you, and that is a way out.'

Iarwin stood in the shadows and watched the men file past him. He had remained outside Shrogar's study as they talked, standing as far from the door as he could and straining desperately after the muffled sounds on the walls to shut out their voices. He had no desire to hear their plans, nor their opinions, especially as they touched on him. No, far better to remain ignorant and save what was left to be saved. For so much it was already too late, and no amount of regret could change that now.

Iarwin was a child of the rebellion, born and bred to fight Kas'Tella in any and all its manifestations. For years he had served in the city, playing a role he despised but one that gave him access to information that could be used to protect his people. He was proud of what he had achieved, proud that he had been chosen by Kinseris to bear his last message to Ephenor, but he was not proud of what he was becoming. He had seen the way his brother looked at him. It shamed him and made him angry. Shrogar did not understand, he *could not* understand. This could never have happened to him. And no matter how hard Iarwin tried to fight it, it would never be enough. He had tried to stop them, tried to distract them, but he had failed.

Only when the last footsteps had died away did Iarwin enter his brother's study.

Shrogar looked ill, worse than he had seemed only an hour ago. He sat slumped in his chair, and at first Iarwin thought he was asleep, but as the door swung closed, Shrogar raised his head and smiled a pale greeting.

'We can talk tomorrow,' Iarwin suggested, concerned. 'You should rest now.'

'No, this cannot wait.'

He shrugged. 'As you wish.'

'No, I do not wish this,' Shrogar exploded. 'What is wrong with you? Those men are our friends, our allies. They will not betray us. If there is something you have not told me, I need to hear it. Now. Otherwise, as your commander and your brother, I am ordering you to stop this.'

Iarwin laughed bitterly. Oh, he had information, but it was not the sort he could share.

'Well?' Shrogar demanded, his voice cracking. 'Answer me, Iarwin, reassure me! Tell me you will leave this alone.'

The appeal in his brother's voice was almost more than he could bear, and

Iarwin strained against the impulse to break down, to beg forgiveness and be welcomed back into the fold of his brother's love. But he could not, so he remained silent, staring straight ahead. This was the only way, the way it had to be. He owed it to all of them. He owed it to himself.

'Why are you doing this?' Shrogar asked, devastated. 'Talk to me.' It was a plea.

'What do you want me to say? Do you want me to tell you I don't like them? That I am jealous because you listen to them more attentively than you listen to me, your own brother? I have fought for you my whole life, yet you discard my advice in an instant when it clashes with theirs.'

Shrogar's face paled. 'Is that what you think? That I have more care for them than I have for you?'

'That is not what I said. That is what you chose to hear. Is it true?'

'No!' Shrogar protested. 'You are my brother. I love you, whatever you think, whatever you do. We are blood. Nothing can come between us.'

'Nothing?' Iarwin sneered. 'You might come to think differently soon.'

His brother froze. 'What does that mean?'

Iarwin sighed, his anger disappearing as quickly as it had flared. 'Nothing, it means nothing.'

'That is not nearly good enough, not this time. You seem to bring me only more questions, my brother, not answers. What happened to you, what changed? Before you left for Kas'Tella you were never like this.'

'Before I went to Kas'Tella I was not fighting for my life every day.' Iarwin looked at his brother sadly, tired of deceit. He groped for a chair and sank into it. 'I am scared, so scared I can't sleep at night, so scared I can barely hold my sword without shaking. I wake slick with sweat, with a sickness in my mouth that does not fade with the nightmares. They caught me,' he admitted finally, eyes on the floor. 'I did not escape the pursuit on my way here, the pursuit caught me. That's why I took so long to reach you.'

'Merciful Maker!' Shrogar fell to his knees beside the chair, one hand on his brother's chin as he wrenched his face into the light. 'And you didn't think to tell me? Your wounds... did they hurt you? What did they want? The message, did they get the message?'

'They didn't get the message. They weren't interested in the message. Don't you understand yet?' Iarwin asked incredulously. 'Kinseris escaped because they let him, just as they let me. They already know everything. The priest and the mage have no secrets from them. Aarin is right. Vasa is gone. They are in command, and they are evil.' He shuddered, unpleasant recollections crowding his mind.

Shrogar stared at him. 'They? Who are these creatures? And why scorn the Amadorians when they tried to tell us the truth?'

'Does it matter who is out there?' Iarwin countered. 'We will be just as dead when they kill us as we would be impaled on Vasa's swords.'

'Then what would you have me do?' Shrogar demanded. 'Are you telling me this battle is over, that you agree with the others? Should I order the evacuation?' He forced Iarwin to meet his eyes. 'If you tell me so, I will do it.'

Iarwin froze, caught on the horns of an impossible dilemma. But he could not do it. 'We are trapped here. We were always going to be trapped here. There is nowhere else we could have gone, given one day or one year to get there, that is as defensible as this place. You had to make your stand here and you did. Did you also need to know from the start that you would lose? Let our people hope while there is hope. There will be time enough for despair before this is done.'

'You have given up,' Shrogar murmured. 'I would never have believed it. What did they do to you?' He paused, shaking his head. 'One day. One day is all he has asked for, and he has promised me my city shall stand.'

'On that you gamble everything?' Iarwin asked. 'This is one man, a stranger, one life. Ask yourself, my brother, what are you really doing this for?'

Shrogar glared at him. 'One life, ten thousand lives, it makes no difference. This was always about more than just one life. But I talk now not of principles but of reality, Iarwin. And the reality is that I just do not know how long we can go on, all desires and promises aside. We are only men.'

Iarwin saw his brother's exhaustion, his strength spent for the sake of a stranger, and it touched a part of him he had kept cold and numb since the encounter that had forever altered him.

'If this was for me,' he began, the words torn from him before he could call them back. 'If it was for me that all the hordes of Kas'Tella had come, how long would you go on?'

He saw Shrogar's eyes widen, his breath hitch in his throat, and the words of reassurance he craved did not come. The moment stretched on and Iarwin felt the hurt strike so hard and so deep that he almost cried out, then his brother seemed to wake from his shock and a smile touched his lips. 'For you, I would never stop fighting.'

Into the charged silence that followed, Iarwin smiled, a bitter smile the mirror of his brother's and filled with regret. 'Then you have your answer.'

'Then will you help me?' Shrogar asked quietly. 'Will you help me find one day?'

The lie, the easy untruth that would salve his brother's hurt, rose in Iarwin's throat. One word from him was all it would take to heal the rift between them. Yet if he gave Shrogar the answer he wanted there would be nothing left he had not betrayed. So he smothered the lie and remained silent.

'What more do I have to give you?' Shrogar whispered brokenly. 'What more can you ask of me?'

'Nothing. Not from you.'

'Then what?' his brother asked, his voice rising sharply to anger once more. 'From Aarin? Do you wish him to give himself up? He –'

'No! Don't tell me their plans. What they do is not my concern.'

'I will tell you because it is important,' Shrogar shot back. 'Because you need to understand.'

'No, I don't want to know.' Iarwin could not keep the desperation from his voice and Shrogar's head snapped up.

'You'll listen because I need you to. They need time, we need time …'

'Time you don't have,' Iarwin said harshly, rising to his feet. 'No one of us has any time left. This is the end.'

Shrogar stared at him. 'You don't care.'

'Oh, I care,' Iarwin said. 'I care more than anything.'

'Then help me, damn you! Help me or get out!'

Iarwin froze in the act of opening the door and turned around. They glared at each other in outraged silence. But at the end Iarwin found he could not leave it like this, with such resentment at his back. He craved the solace of friendship too much. If they were going to die, what did it matter anyway? If he could not save his brother, then the least he could do was ease his heartache before death put an end to both their struggles.

With a sigh, he returned to his seat. Shrogar gave him a tired smile and the relief in his eyes cut through Iarwin's heart more surely than the thrust of a knife. Then his brother began to talk and he forgot everything else.

TWENTY

JETA STRUGGLED OUT of the dream, the smell of blood still clinging to her, and opened her eyes to the welcoming darkness of her bedchamber in Ephenor. The bodies were gone, the blood was gone, and only her memories refused to leave her. She lay still for several minutes, eyes open and staring at the ceiling as her sight adjusted to the darkness. Then she sat up, intending to dress and head out to the wall. She needed the feel of fresh breeze on her skin to cleanse her mind.

As she was flinging back the sheets she stopped, aware of another presence in the room. A shadow stood in the doorway, leaning against the heavy stone arch, and though she could not see his eyes, Jeta knew he was watching her. Checking her alarm, she slid the rest of the way out of the bed, reaching for a robe to cover herself against the desert chill.

'Are you lurking in doorways now?' she asked. 'You are welcome to come in if you wish.'

Aarin laughed. 'I am not lurking, my lady. I've been here only moments.'

Now she knew whose presence had pulled her free of the nightmare.

Aarin crossed the room towards her. 'I have come to speak with you.'

'In the middle of the night? Are you sure it's talking you're after?'

His stride faltered and she knew that she had hurt him somehow. When she could at last see his face, there was a sadness there that filled her with disquiet. She stared at him, caught by a sudden fear, and though she wished to reach out to him she did not. Beneath the fear there was anger.

'You're leaving.'

When Aarin nodded she felt something inside her break. She wanted to scream at him and beg him to stay. She wanted to cry like the child she had been not so long ago, but instead she said only, 'Why?'

'Because I must.'

'Why?'

He teased his fingers through her sleep-tasselled hair. 'I have no choice. To do what I set out to do, to do what I *have* to do, I must leave. But I don't want to leave, not when that means leaving you too.' Aarin looked at her earnestly. 'There is nothing more I can do here except die. If I go maybe there will be no more killing.'

She was not satisfied, far from it. 'You don't know that.'

'I don't,' he admitted. 'I don't know anything anymore. But it makes no difference. I have to go. Better to go now while I still have a chance, while Shrogar still has a chance, than to wait until this place is destroyed and running is the only option any of us have if we are still alive.'

Jeta understood he would not be persuaded. 'I will come with you.'

He shook his head, wiping the tears from her face, the traitor tears that leaked out despite her resolve. 'No, you must stay here. It is safer.'

Jeta tore herself away. 'I don't want to be safe! I don't want to be left behind. If I am going to die, I want to die with you, not trapped inside these walls.'

Aarin looked heart-torn. 'I can't take you with me. If anything happened to you because of me –'

'Everything that has happened to me has been because of you,' Jeta reminded him mercilessly. 'And I would not have it any other way. Let me come with you. Let me see this through at your side.'

When she realised he would refuse, she added harshly, 'I thought you were done with hurting me. Have you changed your mind that you would do this to me now?'

Aarin's head whipped up, his cheeks burning as if she had slapped him. 'That's unfair,' he whispered. 'I'm doing this because I love you, because I want to keep you safe, and I want that enough to ask you to stay when I know you won't want to, when I know it will anger you. Don't come with me, Jeta. Stay here where you are needed, where you will be safe. I'll come back for you, I promise.'

'You don't need me?' she asked, her tone dangerous.

'I didn't say that.'

'But you meant it.' She shook her head. 'Don't make me empty promises.

I know the truth as well as you do. You will come back only if you don't get killed first. You say you love me, but you would abandon me in the middle of a siege we cannot win. I think I would rather take my chances with you and Kallis. He would not let you go alone because it might be dangerous. Why should I?'

Aarin held her gaze, unflinching. 'Because I am asking you. Because you are everything to me.'

'No, I'm not,' she told him sadly. 'I'm just a distraction.'

He protested and she smiled sadly. 'You love me, I know. But I am not enough, and I never will be, otherwise you would not be doing this.' She raised determined eyes to his. 'I won't stay here without you, Aarin. That is not up to you. I can make my own decisions, and I'm prepared to live or die by the choices I make.'

Saal'an could feel the man's torment as he delved into his mind, making no effort to conceal his intrusion. He wanted him to feel this, he wanted him to suffer all the poisonous guilt of his betrayal, knowing that it could have been averted if only he had been stronger.

Slowly, the Arkni unhitched the thread of memory and drew it into him, each tug jerking through the man's mind like a needle pulling stitches through his flesh. Saal'an let his victim watch as his own forced permission allowed the sequence of images to pass from his memory to the Arkni's own, as the voices and faces of his immediate past were swallowed up in the black gloom of that twisted creature's soul.

Greedily, Saal'an lapped up the knowledge he craved as he tracked the movements of his prey through the other's eyes, and he gorged on the man's pathetic attempts to free himself by his recklessness. A brother's love would not entertain the possibility of betrayal even when such defiance in another man would have alerted him long since. And Saal'an knew he had chosen well, for he had broken a good man, a brave man, but not quite brave enough to take his own life outright and perhaps save those he loved from the evil he would bring on them.

He showed him Ephenor destroyed, a smoking, blackened ruin, its people reduced to withered corpses, mummified by the heat of the desert sun. He showed him a future where the army did not abandon the siege but renewed their attack, bursting through the weakening defences and sacking the city, firing the buildings, raping the women, killing the children. Those who escaped through the secret tunnels were massacred as they emerged onto the southern plains. Kas'Tella's ambush parties stacked their bodies in huge piles that buzzed with flies and were circled by vultures who pecked out the eyes of the corpses while four legged scavengers ripped at exposed entrails. He showed him hell come to Ephenor and a sky drenched in the blood of its people. A sky that would never turn back to blue as the whole world fell to the same madness.

Iarwin woke soaked and screaming and knew his betrayal was complete. He finally understood the scope of what he had done, but the Arkni's control over him was too strong now and he could not resist. His chance for redemption had passed, his only consolation the fact that his life was running swiftly to its end. Even dishonourable death was better than the torment of living with what he had done. And what he was about to do.

'Brother, forgive me,' he whispered as he quickly dressed, watching the sky for the approaching dawn. He left his family tunic on the bed. For the work he had yet to do he would not wear the colours of his house. As he slipped through the darkened doorway onto the stairs, he paused a final moment, searching his childhood room for some sign of the boy he had been. But there was nothing left of that time now except the cold stone. At the last moment he paused, removing the silver pin he wore at his throat and placing it atop the discarded garment. Perhaps only Callan and Lysan would understand what that meant, and he took some comfort from that. Then, at the behest of the insistent prodding in his mind, he walked away. He did not have much time, and he had plans of his own to make.

PART FOUR
Exile

Tesseria

The Second Age

IT WAS ALMOST dawn when the final council ended. Even deep within
the mountain Lorrimer could sense the hours of the day as they passed. And
now, finally alone, he faced the empty cavern as he faced the emptiness in his
soul. It would all end soon. His one comfort, his one strength, was flying to
meet him. He could feel the rush of air as the dragon entered the great tunnel,
and could sense the same turmoil, the same emptiness in Silverwing. And the
same resolve. It had to be this way. The path he was about to tread might kill
them both, but the war that had brought them to this point would surely
destroy them all.

Lorrimer looked once more about the proud hall. Its walls were harsh,
unforgiving stone. The silence of the empty chamber weighed heavily on him.
The echoes of past convocations seemed to haunt it, the whispers of men
and women, past, present, and future hanging in the air like ghosts.

A beating on the air heralded the arrival of his dragon, the silver scales that
gave him his name dulled in the dim light. Leaving the speaker's platform,
Lorrimer walked toward him. The weight of his advanced years had never
seemed such a burden. It was almost as if his body knew the magic that
supported his extended life was coming to an end.

'We are all agreed. The Joining must be severed. They have gone to prepare
themselves and their families. We perform the Severing at midnight.'

He spoke with great calm, but from Silverwing he could never hide his pain.
It was shared.

It is the only way.

'I know, my friend, but I am sorry from the bottom of my heart for the
pain this will cause you.'

The dragon bowed his head, unspoken between them the knowledge that
Lorrimer could not survive the severing of the bond that joined them.
Silverwing would survive him, *must* survive him. It would be his task, and

those of his kind who survived, to ensure no man was able to undo the magic performed this night.

Lorrimer felt and understood his dragon's grief, and his fear of the loneliness that stretched ahead. For a moment he allowed himself to imagine the unimaginable, the ecstasy of the perfect union Aarkan sought. For a moment only he surrendered himself to the memories of long ago, of a time when he and Silverwing had discovered the possibilities of taking their union beyond the wonder they already shared. But he had been young then, and filled to overflowing with the exhilaration of his newly tapped power, and Silverwing had been swept away by the novelty of his first partnership.

They had seen their danger. Aarkan, driven mad by the death of his wife and his dragon's memories of loss, had seen not danger, but opportunity, then temptation, once he glimpsed the power that lay at the heart of life. And if it had snared him, it would take others. He and his followers had to be stopped before they went any further, but to stop them they had to destroy something so precious. The Joining was life, to men, to dragons and every living thing on Andeira. As Lorrimer faced the possibility that Silverwing and all his kind might never know that joy again, he knew it was a better fate by far than the one that now confronted them all.

You will remain here until midnight?

Lorrimer nodded. 'My daughter and I have said our goodbyes. She is with her children.'

He did not want to think about Alisa, not now. He needed no more reasons to turn from this path. His sons were all dead, killed in the war. Alisa was his only surviving child, though not the only child of his heart. His heart ached for her and for Riah, Aarkan's daughter, who he had raised as his own. If they survived, their lives would be desolate. That they might not survive was a fear he dared not voice.

'We must prepare ourselves, Silverwing. We can afford no mistakes.'

Nor will there be any. I know you have been preparing for this day since Aarkan first brought his proposal to the council. And I know my role well enough. Never think I will falter.

'I do not think that,' Lorrimer replied, his voice shaking with emotion. 'You are my strength, without whom I would be less than nothing. But I do not think I can last the hours in inactivity, and my time in their world is done.' He smiled. 'I am an old man, Silverwing. Indulge me.'

Then let me take you on a final ride. See the world one last time from the back of a dragon. Enter my dreams and we will soar together over mountains and oceans and green fields. What has long been forbidden to protect the weak of mind is safe with you.

Lorrimer found himself unable to speak. The dreams of dragons were the stuff of legends, long lost to men. They were a gateway to another time, when men were mere shadows in the half-light of their dawn. Centuries past, when the two races had first come together, the mages had invaded these dreams on the slipstream of the link, and many had been seduced by that heightened existence. A few had tried to remain, and in their ignorance they had caused the first great crisis. That Silverwing offered this now was as true a sign of his trust as he could possibly bestow.

Unable to speak, Lorrimer closed his eyes and let Silverwing take him far away.

To those who lived through the final hours it seemed that the earth itself sensed the impending disaster. All through the day, dark and forbidding storm clouds had obscured the sun. Men, women, and children swarmed like ants through the passageways and halls of their subterranean home. The atmosphere was as bleak as the sky. Many wept openly, uncaring who saw them. Others stood silent, staring at nothing, grieving already for the pain that was coming. Those who had raged against their fate had long since become reconciled to what they could not change. The council had decreed that they were free to leave, but few did. No amount of distance would protect them from the Severing when it came.

In the sky above swarmed the dragons, silent and graceful, ready to defend the two who prepared to cause the breaking of everything they knew. They were an awesome, deadly sight as they swooped below the clouds, but for all their seeming calm they could not escape the turmoil afflicting their human counterparts. Having given themselves to the Joining long ago, theirs also had been the choice that had brought the races to this pass, and clear, far-sighted wisdom, born of longevity, gave the dragons a greater understanding of the nature of the conflict.

This crisis threatened the very survival of Andeira. The elemental harmony of the Joining succoured and supported the natural world. Severing that link would be fatal over time. With memories that spanned millennia, the dragons understood as few humans could the burden of doubt Lorrimer had carried when he had urged his people to accept a course of action that might only spare them for a slower, more painful death in the generations to come.

And it was the dragons, through Silverwing, who would devise the counter spell, a remedy created partly of the fabric of the magic of severance and partly in the shrouded events of the unwritten future. Through the language of prophecy and hope they would create the seed of the world's cure, but the responsibility of enacting the cure would be left to the progeny of those who survived this cataclysm. In the ages to come, the enmity and ambition that had caused the war must have faded out of memory before it would be safe to renew the ancient covenant. Only their chosen instrument would be able to unravel the mystery of the link and recall the dragons from their voluntary exile.

Now, as time grew short, Riah ran through the deserted tunnels near the dragon stalls. Evil was coming, she could feel it, and she called out to Coranu as she ran. The dragon wheeled and screeched, flying high above the mountains. Like so many others, their link was active still despite the danger, neither willing to give up their partnership until the very end. She knew, as they all did, that should she be caught in communion at midnight, the shock of the Severing would surely kill her, but several hours remained and she meant to hold on to the last.

Premonition of approaching danger licked at her mind and she framed her query in her dragon's mind. 'What do you see?'

Dark clouds, little sister. I cannot see through them, and I fear.

'As do I,' Riah replied, running faster still. 'I fear my father is coming at last.'

Then you must flee. Take your people and leave this place.

'No! I will not leave you!'

Coranu felt the fear of loss take hold in her rider's mind. *You must, little sister, as you promised Lorrimer. Do not fear for me, I will be well. My brethren and I will defend this place and the two within, but all will be for nothing if you do not save your people.*

Riah slowed to a walk but the ache in her chest had nothing to do with exertion. 'I cannot bear for this to be the end between us. I had thought…' she stopped, her heart lurching as a tear slid down her cheek. 'I thought it would be different somehow, though I do not know why. I thought at least to see you once more, to touch you and be one with you one last time.'

You touch me now. I feel your presence as though you were standing before me. But I need you to live, little sister, please. I need to know you will go on, or I fear my heart will break.

The dragon paused in her flight, wings beating a harsh rhythm as she hovered in place, black eyes straining towards the place she knew her mage stood weeping.

I never thought I would have to beg you for anything, but I find I was wrong, and that dragons are as weak in this as humans. Go now, daughter of Ashlea. Do what you must and please survive it. We may not be destined to meet again but know that I will bear your memory with me into the unknown places and you shall never be forgotten.

Abruptly the link went dark as Coranu withdrew from Riah's mind. A final flash of agony rushed through the fading pattern of the magic and she fell to her knees in a reflection of her dragon's pain.

'Oh, please do not leave me,' she pleaded, pushing herself back to her feet. But no answer came. She knew in her heart that Coranu would not refuse to answer if she pressed, but she understood that her dragon had done what she had done to protect them both, and she could show no less courage.

'Nor will I forget you, Coranu, though the days of my life fall forevermore into darkness. You will ever be loved.'

And then she was running again. There was so little time.

Deep within the mountain, Silverwing slumbered on, carrying Lorrimer on his final journey through the dragon dream. While his brothers and sisters readied themselves for the last battle, they flew together through blue skies untroubled by conflict and soared over the dramatic landscape of the First

Age. None dared disturb their moment of peace, not even to bring warning. There was nothing they could do to influence the tide of the battle that was coming. They had a fight of their own to win.

ONE

Amadorn

The New Age

BRANNICK'S RETURN TO his queen occurred with even less fanfare than Vianor's. His arrival came just two days before the winter solstice, and the day after the envoy arrived from King Elian, formally accepting Sedaine's terms on behalf of his kingdom.

The old man had rarely seen Sedaine as jubilant as when he was ushered into her presence, with barely a moment given to refresh himself after his long journey. She was alone but for Vianor's silent presence, and he was grateful for that, for the news he brought concerned the magician also.

'Brannick,' she greeted him, striding across the room to embrace him with every appearance of delight. She felt thin under his hands, lean muscles burned away to sharp bones, but as she released him he saw the vitality in her that allayed his concerns.

'Your tidings are good?'

'Your highness,' he murmured, casting a suspicious glance at Vianor. The magician gave him a thin smile, acknowledging his rival for her affection and her confidence.

Sedaine looked between them and laughed. 'Your suspicions are wasted, Brannick. The Lord Vianor has had a change of heart.'

'As you say, your highness.' But Brannick's eyes did not leave Vianor. His ingrained distrust of the magicians ran too deep.

'We are alone, Brannick,' Sedaine said fondly. 'There is no room for such formalities between friends. Come, sit. I can see you are weary, and I have allowed you little time to rest. Your journey has been hard, I can see that. Will you not relax, take the burden from your feet, and tell us your news when you feel ready?'

Brannick stared. The urgency of his mission had allowed him no pause to consider his own considerable discomforts, yet now he had returned—with the news she had hoped for— Sedaine seemed almost careless of the effort he had gone to on her behalf.

'Has something happened?' he asked, more curtly than he intended, and she laughed, a bright peal of sheer joy.

'Oh, my friend,' she murmured. 'You arrive at a most auspicious time. Elvelen has chosen the prudent course and we have the chance we need to survive this.'

Vianor stirred from his brooding silence. 'At what price?' he demanded coldly. 'It was rash, my Queen, to promise yourself to this man when you know what he is. If you had consulted me –'

'What is this, Vianor?' she asked playfully. 'Was it not you badgering me for weeks about the need to take a husband? And now I have chosen one you object.'

'A husband?' Brannick interjected, surprised and not a little jealous. Though he knew she did not return the affections he cherished in secret, though he would not act on them, he had never considered that she might remarry. That she seemed so happy at the prospect galled him. 'Who?'

'Lord Delgar,' Vianor informed him sourly. 'For his help she has promised to reward him with marriage and status.' He rounded on Sedaine again. 'You yourself argued against marriage to a man who would claim any portion of your power, and yet you have chosen the one man who will never settle for anything less than total supremacy.'

Sedaine laughed again. 'Am I married yet, uncle?'

The magician stiffened. 'So, this is a ruse? That is a dangerous game, Sedaine, for you are committed now. Until he is dealt with, Delgar will be a thorn in your side. Should he make public your acceptance of his proposal you cannot simply have him killed. The suspicions might eventually destroy you.'

'He will tell no one,' she replied, a trifle coldly. 'Nor will he live to be a nuisance to me. While his wife lives, should he reveal that he has made such a proposal he will be condemned by his own people, and should he do so after she dies, he marks himself for her murder. No, it is from me the announcement must come, after the ratification of my claim in Korva, as we agreed. I am not such a fool, uncle, and I have had a good teacher. Delgar will be dealt with. Did you not show me how?'

Vianor subsided, though his mouth thinned in an angry line. Brannick watched with undisguised distaste. The talk of subterfuge, of murder, disturbed him, and he saw Vianor's hand in this change.

Sedaine caught a glimmer of his feelings from his expression. 'Believe me, I dislike this as much as you, but I must fight my enemies with their weapons. I *need* the North secure, Brannick, and I will not baulk from any tactic that gives me that. It is best if you understand that now, for this is only the beginning.'

'Your highness,' the old man answered stiffly. 'I do not judge.'

Sedaine snorted. 'Yes, you do, just as Ecyas did. I was never good enough for him and I will not endure the same from you. I act as I must, in things that are beyond your experience, so berate me now if it makes you feel better, then say no word more, for I will not have you standing as my conscience.' She fixed him with dark, tormented eyes. 'I could not bear it.'

Brannick returned her gaze and felt his heart lurch in sympathy. 'Every ruler needs a conscience, Sedaine. If you let another stand for you, you do not have to bear the burden alone.'

When she remained silent, he sighed. 'I am not Ecyas, to judge all others by impossible standards. Nor am I as Lord Vianor, steeped in the intrigues of court, to advise and guide you. But I am your friend, and you cannot ask me to keep silent if I see you suffer for what you feel you must do.'

Her eyes glittered as she regarded him in silence. 'As you will then. Far be it from me to deny the support of your friendship.' She nodded to a couch. 'And now, let us hear your news.'

Relieved, Brannick settled his weary frame into the soft comfort of the couch. 'I bring word from the elders of Luen. They will come to your aid, should you call them, but they do not recognise your sovereignty over them or their lands. They will come as your allies, not your subjects.'

'That is their right,' Sedaine allowed. 'The eastern lands have always been outside the rule of any nation, and I will respect their autonomy. Let them cling to a dying land. I lose nothing by it.'

Brannick bowed his head. 'Of this I have already assured them. But that is not the extent of their terms.'

Her eyes narrowed. 'By all means, tell me the rest. What else do they demand?'

The old man took a deep breath, unsure how she would react to Luen's final and most important condition. He knew Sedaine's beliefs were influenced by her upbringing in Rhiannas and the teachings of her uncle, but she had lived many years with Ecyas, and she had borne a son who was as final a repudiation of those beliefs as anything could be. He knew also that she had absorbed the wisdom of Ecyas's people as no magician ever could. Surely now she could not object to the realisation of all that implied. Vianor, however, was another matter.

'The elders desire from you a proclamation, an acceptance, of the five powers in their entirety. The false premise on which Redstone is founded is to be torn down. Our people and yours are to be reunited in understanding of the magic we practise.'

He risked a glance at Vianor, saw the magician's watching stillness where he had expected outright rejection, and dared to say, 'And yours, my lord.'

The magician could not hide his startled reaction, and mistaking it for anger, Brannick hurried on. 'If this threat you have called on them to defend against is real, Luen offers an exchange of knowledge. My lord, forgive me. They see your ignorance as the foothold for the Kas'Talani's influence in these lands and wish to close that door forever.'

He held his breath, hardly daring to disturb the silence. The magicians were notoriously proud, and they had hated and envied their eastern cousins for so long. It was doubtful they would willingly submit to the position of pupils to their old enemies, but Vianor could command it. His supremacy in the North was undisputed, and if he could be swayed, the others might follow. If only Vianor could be convinced, they could build an army of mages of staggering power. He *had* to see the wisdom of it.

Sedaine watched them both, taking in Vianor's scowl and Brannick's anxious frown. 'I cannot do this alone,' she said bluntly. 'They have to know that.'

Brannick did not reply and Sedaine growled in frustration. 'Redstone's foundations were laid by others,' she protested. 'Long before I ever led them there. It was Darred who engineered this split, not me.'

'Darred is gone, lady,' Brannick reminded her gently. 'It is for you to heal the breach.'

'And what of those who followed me to Redstone?' she demanded. 'Do I abandon them now, after all their faithful service? Do I denounce their pledges and their faith?'

Brannick shook his head. 'Long before they were of Redstone, they were of Luen. It will be a return for them, not abandonment. They followed *you*, Sedaine, and the hope you gave them. They will follow you again.'

'And if I do not accept it?'

'But you do,' Brannick insisted. 'You must. Aarin is your son, and it is for him that you stand here now. If you had not seen what he is, would you have forced an end to the bargain and plunged this land into peril?'

'It was already in danger enough,' she snapped, disliking his methods. 'Kas'Talani conquest, however it comes, will exact a brutal price.'

'You must do this, Sedaine,' Vianor interrupted, startling them both.

She turned to stare at him, clearly believing him touched by a fit of madness. '*You* support this? Well, you astonish me, uncle. From you I expected a furious denial at the very least.'

The magician's frown deepened. 'Do not mock me. Nor assume that I am too stubborn to have seen the errors in our ways after months surrounded by those whose understanding is so far beyond ours. These times have turned the world on its head. Old convictions cannot hold in the face of what threatens us. Though it galls me to agree with Brannick, if you consent to this exchange between our peoples, you could win the strength to make even Darred think twice.'

Vianor turned to Brannick. 'And it would be an exchange, though you do not think so now. There are things we can do that you cannot, that you dismiss as mere tricks. Years in the company of Darred and his colleagues have taught us secrets you would give much to learn. Secrets, perhaps, that you can unravel as we have been unable to do.'

Brannick acknowledged this. 'Do not think us unmindful of the power your people possess. At heart we are all one, and it is time we realised that.' He turned back to Sedaine. 'It is your choice. Luen will only come to you on these terms.'

She glanced between them, seeing them fixed into an alliance she would never have believed possible. She shook her head, a small smile on her face. 'Very well. If you can bring your people to the table, uncle, I will make this proclamation. We may as well die united.'

TWO

IT WAS ALMOST dawn when Shrogar led them down into the depths of the citadel, past the heavy doors that barred the entrance to the lower levels. He lit a torch, illuminating the passageways that wended further downward still, until they were some considerable depth beneath the earth. The corridors were high and still, paved with smooth flagstones. The air grew chill and they clutched their cloaks more tightly around them as they walked.

'These are the tunnels that lead out under the plains,' he told them as they passed several dark openings. He ignored Kinseris's worried glance. He knew he looked bad. The throbbing wound in his arm and his gnawing worry over Iarwin had kept him awake too long.

As the entered a circular chamber, Shrogar hung the torch on the wall and walked to the centre of the room. With a quick glance at Kinseris, he reached inside his shirt and withdrew a pendant on a slim gold chain. A golden eagle flashed in the torchlight.

Crouching down, his hand hovering over a tiny depression in the paved floor, Shrogar looked up. 'Stand back. I have only done this once, and I cannot remember quite where it is.'

As they obediently moved back, he placed the eagle face down in the depression and stepped smartly to one side. Ripples swept across the floor and an opening appeared in the once-solid ground, slender and shadowed. Steps led down into the darkness and disappeared from view.

Aarin's eyes widened.

Shrogar cut off his questions. 'There is no time. It will not stay open long. The tunnel leads into the land now called Rybacih, far from here. Even if their spies have found our escape routes, this one will remain hidden.'

Aarin turned to Kinseris, a question in his eyes.

'Yes,' the priest agreed. 'It is where we wish to go.'

Shrogar was surprised. 'There is nothing there, not anymore. Vasa laid waste to it during the war. Once this tunnel led to our allies, but they are gone now too.' He stopped, watching the entrance and saw the shadows begin to flicker. 'Quickly, go now while you still can.'

Kallis went first, gripping his hand and nodding his thanks as he slipped down the stone steps. Shrogar beckoned to Jeta next, handing her down to the mercenary before turning back to the others.

Kinseris hesitated when it was his turn, clearly struggling with conflicting emotions. 'I feel like I am abandoning you,' he said eventually. 'I am sorry.'

Shrogar pulled him impulsively into an embrace. 'Not so. May we meet again in happier times.'

'Happy times or sad,' Kinseris replied as he returned the embrace. 'Let us just meet again.'

Then he disappeared down the steps, leaving Shrogar alone with Aarin.

'I'm sorry for what this has cost you,' the mage told him as they faced each other over the doorway Ephenor's lord had opened in solid rock. 'You have given more than anyone had a right to ask.'

'It was not for you,' Shrogar answered honestly and saw that he understood. 'May the powers of Earth and Sky, Ocean and Fire, go with you as you leave this place, and may the mother spirit protect you and guide your steps in mercy,' he said in ancient blessing. 'Not all is forgotten, Aarin, not here. Trust in that and know we will not fail you.'

Shrogar stood in silence for long minutes after the mage's departure, watching the darkened shadow of the entranceway slowly dim. At last he lifted his weary head, taking a deep breath as he prepared to face what was still to come. Fingers gone stiff with cold curled around the outline of the pendant through his shirt, feeling the heat of it, the heat of the fever that was slowly spreading through him. Hot tears were in his eyes—for his friend, for his people, for the heart that was breaking in his chest. Without turning he asked sadly, 'What are you doing here?'

'What I must,' came the reply from the shadows as the silent watcher stepped out into the room.

'Please, Iarwin, don't do this.'

His brother chose not to answer, crossing the space between them with swift strides, and dropping down into the fading stairway, holding it open with his presence.

'Please don't leave me, not now,' Shrogar begged him, ashamed of the weakness he had no more strength to hide. 'I need you here.'

At the last moment Iarwin paused, looking up into the forlorn face of the man who was both kin and liege lord. If he felt any regret for this parting it did not show on his face.

'I am needed elsewhere, and you have a battle to fight. One that has no easy end. Farewell, brother. We will not meet again.'

Then he was gone, swallowed by the darkness as the tunnel finally vanished, sealing him below the rock fortress with no way out except to go on.

Shrogar sank to his knees, his head cradled in his hands. 'Why?' he demanded of the silence. 'Why, Iarwin?' But the only one who could tell him was gone, and he grieved for the brother he would never see again, the brother who, in the end, he had not known at all. Who had abandoned him when he had needed him the most. His lips moved in silent blessing, repeating the prayer he had whispered for the others, and adding another of his own, asking the Maker's protection for his wayward brother through whatever dangers lay ahead. And for Ephenor, which would soon face its greatest challenge just as a new dawn was about to brighten the cold earth.

Callan paced the north wall with long restless strides, snapping at Ieshwen when the older man asked him to stop. Lysan grinned at his brother's agitation and the grizzled captain's affront, but Trad was beginning to see through the man's unruffled façade. Beneath the ever-present smile, was the same tension that affected them all. They waited for Shrogar and Iarwin, and the sun was already well into the sky with no sign of either.

Finally, Callan's patience ran out, and he sent messengers to their chambers just as Shrogar appeared at the tower door.

Ieshwen frowned. 'My lord, are you well?'

Shrogar looked up. 'Who among us is that, old friend? You need not worry for me. I am merely tired.'

Ieshwen eyed him doubtfully but did not argue, turning his attention to the gathering of the enemy out on the plains. 'They begin to draw up their attack. They will come at us from three sides, I think, against the gates and the walls to the east and west of us here. We must split our forces for it will be no good if we hold the gates but lose the walls.'

Shrogar sighed, nodding his assent, and looked out at the formations his captain indicated. 'Callan and Lysan, you will take command of the east. Ieshwen, you go west with Gwayr. I will remain here. Trad, Kestel. You will hold the northern towers.'

The Ancai nodded his silent acceptance of Shrogar's orders and Trad could see he was still brooding about Kinseris's refusal to allow him to accompany him. Kestel been protecting Kinseris for so long, it had become second nature. To allow the priest to walk into danger without him would be hard to accept. It was clear to Trad that Kinseris did not expect to survive, that he somehow believed he did not deserve to. And if he could see that, Kestel would know it too. But Kinseris had been adamant. Shrogar needed them. They had to stay.

Trad turned his turned to Shrogar as he spoke quietly with Ieshwen. He looked terrible, and he tried to hide it as he observed lightly, 'Their numbers seem less. Let us hope it is because they are expecting little resistance.'

Lysan exchanged a look with his brother. Callan was watching Shrogar unhappily.

'My lord, what of Iarwin?'

Shrogar's head snapped round. 'My brother keeps his own counsel these days. He is where he is needed, he tells me. As you should be, all of you. Now go, they will be here soon, and we will not be caught unprepared indulging in idle chatter. Go!' he shouted when no one moved.

They scrambled to obey. Callan offered his arm to his brother but Lysan shrugged him off irritably. Ieshwen hovered a moment longer, but the glare Shrogar shot him sent him scurrying to the west wall, Gwayr at his heels. Trad and the Ancai separated, each heading to take up command of the archers on the north towers.

As he left, Trad glanced over his shoulder at Shrogar, and saw the Lord of

Ephenor slump against the wall as he rested his head in his hands. All was not well with him, anyone could see that, and he wondered where Iarwin really was, and why he was not at his brother's side where he belonged.

THREE

THE ENEMY DID not advance on all sides at once as Ieshwen had predicted, but came first to the west, then the east, their attacks short and sharp, testing the defences and the fight left in the defenders. But brief though they were, every assault did damage, killing men, destroying weapons, wearing them down inch by cruel inch, and though many of the enemy were lost, thousands more remained. And worst of all was the word carried to Shrogar of the death of Ieshwen, cut down even as the enemy began their retreat. But he was given little time to mourn before the next attack came, aiming straight for the gates.

On the tower, Trad watched as the battering rams were rolled up to the gates and screamed at his archers to kill the men who operated them. But for all the soldiers their arrows cut down, more came forward to take their places, and he could only look on in horror as the huge steel-capped logs smashed through the weakened timber and into the courtyard. This time the wrought metal of the inner gate did not close behind them and the Kas'Tellians flooded into the killing ground. Fewer defenders now manned the parapets above and the wave rolled on, up to the second portcullis, where soldiers were boosted aloft by their fellows to scale the inner gates.

Trad ordered thirty of his archers to follow him down onto the wall, leading his men to the aid of the defenders above the courtyard. Across the open space, he saw Kestel do the same, pulling his men back to protect the second gate. Well-trained, the archers spaced themselves along the battlements and directed their fire at the soldiers attempting to break into Ephenor, stepping round the men who hurled their missiles through the holes at the base of the walls, smashing gaps in the mass of the enemy below.

Another group of soldiers tried to take the stairs, and Trad spun away from his archers, grabbing the nearest man with a sword in hand, and ran to intercept them. Suddenly Shrogar was beside him, shouting himself hoarse, and his men were drawn to him. Together they charged the rag-tag party of Kas'Tellians that made it to the top of the steps, driving them backwards and sending them sprawling onto their companions below. His men screamed insults, waving their bloodied swords at the enemy.

And then, at last, the first portcullis began to fall, halting the tide of attackers flowing into the courtyard and trapping those who had made it inside. Flaming arrows rained down now, setting fire to the battering ram caught between the gates, and men screamed as they scrambled out of the way of the flames. Soldiers climbed over the living and the dead in their attempt to free themselves, forcing those in front up and over the inner gate and onto the defenders' swords. For a few minutes, madness reigned as fear and desperation gave strength to the enemy's attack, but without reinforcements the men in the killing ground were doomed.

Trad braced himself wearily on the hilt of his sword, breathing deeply to steady the wild thumping of his heart. They had come within a whisker of losing the outer walls and the relief made him giddy. He glanced at Shrogar, a grin forming on his lips, but his smile faded. The Lord of Ephenor was chalk-white, an uncontrolled stagger to his steps as he reached to steady himself. Trad called his name, shouldering his way through the men to get to him, and Shrogar turned pain-hazed eyes on him as he collapsed.

Shouting a desperate denial, Trad reached his side, lifting his head from the stones and cradling it in his lap. Looking up he saw panic in the faces of the men and snapped at them to fetch Iarwin. Wherever Shrogar's brother was he would have to be told. He sent runners to the east and west, sure that he must be somewhere. He had seen the man fight and knew he was no coward. He would be wherever the fighting was at its thickest. With the gates in such a perilous position, the north was where his skills would be of most use, and the men needed him to take charge.

Looking down at Shrogar's face, he saw the man had slipped into a faint, and his eyes were drawn to the soaked bandage round his arm. Shaking fingers probed the injury, feeling the unnatural heat radiating from it as a shadow appeared above him. It was not Iarwin.

'How is he?' the soldier asked, one he recognised but could not name.

'Not good,' Trad answered. 'We must get him off the walls.'

The man nodded, beckoning men to carry their lord to the healers.

As he surrendered Shrogar into their care, Trad looked about again. 'Where is Iarwin?' he asked again.

'He has gone.'

The words were so quiet it took a moment for Trad to realise they were addressed to him. Then he saw Callan holding Lysan upright in his arms. The brothers looked terrible, their faces pale and streaked with blood. Lysan's head lolled against his brother's shoulder despite his efforts to stay alert. Trad thought he saw tear tracks smearing the dirt on his cheeks.

'Gone? Gone where?'

Callan held out his free hand and opened clenched fingers. A silver pin lay in his filthy palm. 'This was found in his room. Along with the emblems of his House.'

Trad looked from the small thing to Callan's haunted face without understanding. Then the man touched a hand to an identical pin at his own throat.

'The three of us made a promise long ago and had these made to remind us of it always. We were children, but we promised...' He looked away. 'We promised that we three would stand together to the last against Kas'Tella. If he has left this behind it can only mean one thing.'

'Iarwin would not betray us,' Lysan insisted, but his protest lacked strength. It was clearly already an old argument.

Trad hung his head in despair. If Iarwin was a traitor and he had abandoned the fortress there was only one place he would go, and that was wherever Aarin had gone.

Callan staggered as Lysan's weight shifted in his arms and he lowered his brother to the ground. 'Shrogar?' he asked.

'His wound is poisoned. Badly, I think. He will not be returning to the walls.'

Callan nodded bleakly, reaching a hand to shake his brother who had slumped over, eyes closed. When there was no response he cursed in frustrated worry. 'Of all the times to pass out on me. Ieshwen?'

'Dead.'

Callan's head jerked up. 'Dead? Blessed Maker, how much more will you punish us?' He passed his hand over his eyes to hide his grief. 'Well then, Ephenor is mine until my lord recovers.' He did not sound pleased and Trad could not blame him. He was taking command of a dying city.

Callan straightened wearily, shooting a sidelong glance at his brother. 'We must get these bodies moved.' He looked down into the courtyard. 'See what can be done for the gates, then have the bodies piled up before them. If they want to come through again, they will have to wade through their own dead. Gather up any weapons and see that every man who can fight has the means to do so. Get the archers back to the towers. We must be ready.'

Trad nodded, his mind worrying the problems and thinking of solutions even as he listened. Men scattered to obey as he relayed the orders, two leaning down to take Lysan in their arms. He cried out and his brother winced.

'I must go to Gwayr,' he told Trad, 'and see what can be done for the west.' He looked at the sun, already past its height. 'With any luck they will not come back today. But tonight?' he shrugged. 'Tonight will decide this.'

And with that he was gone, jogging down the steps to the courtyard, every inch the commander his men needed to see. Trad watched him go, humbled by the strength of will it must have cost him. He looked around him at the living who moved among the dead and dying on the walls, never questioning, never giving up, and wished that courage was all that was needed, for then Ephenor would never fall. Then his gaze turned to the enemy arrayed below and knew that courage alone would never be enough.

FOUR

AS THE DAY drew to its close, they gathered again, those who were left. Shrogar remained unconscious, the infection rampaging through his weakened body, and Dianeth wondered whether he even wished to waken and face the griefs the last few days had placed upon his heart. She tore herself from his side long enough to offer what counsel and support she could to his captains who carried on the struggle in all their names. With Ieshwen dead and Iarwin gone, there were few of them left.

Lysan and Callan were there, and they clung to each other now with affection stripped of all pretence. Iarwin's defection had shattered them, and only Dianeth, who had known and loved them since all three were little more than children, could guess the true extent of that wound. Lysan's fingers were still curled around the silver pin Iarwin had left behind, and her heart wept for the childhood promise broken when it had been removed. Gwayr was in attendance also, a sturdy, reassuring presence, and along with Trad and the Ancai, the six of them were the core. Four whose home it was and two strangers, their hopes resting on those who had left them for their own battle a world apart from Ephenor.

'Our losses have become critical,' Callan informed them. He stood behind his brother. Lysan sat with his head rested on his crossed arms, too exhausted for speech. 'One day they asked for and one day we have given them. We can do no more. There are but two choices left to us, for I do not intend to give them up. Surrender, or fight on knowing it will be to the death. Though I fear it will be death whichever we choose. If we order the evacuation now, they will be free to take their own chances, if that is what they choose. We owe them that at least.'

'Kinseris warned my husband of the tunnels,' Dianeth reminded him. 'Do you intend to disregard his counsel?'

'No, my lady,' Callan replied. 'But we no longer have the luxury of choice.

The army has not departed as we hoped it would, and should they attack again, Ephenor *will* fall. I have made my decision. I will not leave and there are many, I think, who will remain with me, but we cannot and should not prevent those who wish to leave from taking the only chance they may have. All will be made aware of the priest's warning, to heed or ignore as they will. But we must give them the choice.'

Lost in thought, Trad looked up at this. 'What if there was a way?'

'To do what?'

'To save the city.'

Callan shook his head. 'What more can we do? We cannot replace the men who have died while their numbers continue to grow, not lessen as we had hoped.'

'But there are things they cannot replace, not easily anyway.' Trad stood up, crossing to the table, and even Lysan lifted his head to watch him. 'With Aarin gone, what is the weakest part of our defence and their surest way into the city?'

'The gates,' Gwayr supplied. 'We have repaired them, but we cannot continue to do so forever. Without the mage to protect them, they will break as soon as the first siege engine is brought bear.'

'Exactly. The gates are our most vulnerable point, but they are still a formidable obstacle to men alone. One battering ram might take them out, but it will take many men much longer to hack them down on their own.'

Lysan gave him an irritated look. 'What's your point?'

Trad grinned. 'Suppose they had no siege engines? No rams, no catapults, no towers, no ladders. What if they had to rely on men alone, would we be able to hold them?'

'Perhaps,' Callan allowed cautiously. 'We have enough archers to cause serious casualties among a party before the gates—more if they have no ladders to send men up onto the walls—but siege machines they have aplenty and we cannot hope that they will not use them.'

'They cannot use them if we destroy them.' Trad lifted the map he had been studying and smoothed it out on the table. 'The main army is camped between these points, here and here.' He indicated the stretch of land between the north and eastern walls. 'Their siege engines are concentrated here, where they have focused their attack. And this here,' he drew his finger along a line stretching from within the citadel out into the encampment, 'is one of your evacuation routes. The tunnel comes out no more than a hundred yards from the pickets nearest the siege equipment.'

'Trad is correct,' the Ancai observed, immediately understanding his intention. 'A raiding party could exit the tunnels under cover of darkness and destroy the weapons with little fear of detection.'

Callan looked from one to the other, and Dianeth saw a glimmer of excitement in his steady gaze. 'Surprise might take them to the camp,' he agreed. 'But their chances of making it back again would be slight. Those who went would not be returning.'

'Not necessarily.' Trad glanced at Dianeth. 'The tunnels only allow passage one way, is that correct?' When she nodded, he turned back to Callan. 'Since we could not return the way we came in any case, there is another more obvious escape route available, the army itself. Find me some men native to Caledan who will not stand out, dress us up in Kas'Tellian uniforms—there's no shortage of those—and we could disappear with ease into the ranks of the enemy in the confusion. Then we need only make our way back to Ephenor as the opportunity arises. Let down ropes and haul us in. You would not even have to open the gates.'

Lysan sat up, tiredness forgotten. 'It is a good plan. I volunteer.'

'No, you don't,' Callan retorted. 'You can barely stand.'

'I suppose you think you're going without me?' Lysan protested, but Dianeth silenced the argument before it could begin.

'Neither of you will go. With my lord injured command of Ephenor falls to you, Callan, and then you, Lysan, and so you must remain here. Now is not the time to leave us leaderless, besides,' she added to Callan, 'Lysan clearly cannot go, and I am not inclined to endure his temper waiting for your safe return. Trad will lead the raiding party. It is his plan and there is no chance of his being recognised as Ephenori.'

The Ancai nodded his approval, but it was Gwayr who decided things. 'My lady is correct. You cannot be risked, Callan. And you, Lysan, though you may think yourself invincible, could not fight off a small child, let alone an army. None of us may go, for we will all be recognised for who we are.'

'I will not,' Kestel said. 'And I will accompany him. Safarsee is my mother tongue and that is not the case for most here, even those who are not of the old blood.'

Gwayr nodded and Callan sighed. 'Very well. But you will need someone to lead you to the tunnels and I will take you that far. We must move quickly for night is already on us. When do you wish to go?'

'A few hours before dawn,' Trad replied, 'if you can find me enough volunteers.'

Callan came to wake Trad several hours after midnight, leading him down under the citadel along the same passages Shrogar had taken Aarin and Kinseris the day before.

He had seen little of his commander in the intervening hours. Lysan had collapsed not long after the council had ended, and though he hid it well, Trad could tell Callan feared for him. Even in the dim light his face was strained with worry, and Trad hoped fiercely that it would not come to that. They were all so close to breaking, one step from the despair that would destroy them, and Lysan's death would break his brother.

The Ancai was waiting for him with the group hand-picked to accompany them. They were twenty. Any more, he had argued, and they would run a greater risk of discovery, but any fewer and they would have little chance of fighting their way through to their target should they be exposed.

In addition to their weapons, each man carried jars of the remaining fire compound and flint strikers. Once the siege machines were alight, it would be impossible for anyone to get close enough to put out the flames, and they would keep burning until they were consumed. Though other methods might accomplish the destruction with a chance of secrecy, Trad was confident that the inferno they planned to start would create enough confusion to allow his men to escape.

Callan led them in silence to the beginning of the passage that would take them into enemy territory. He stopped at the threshold, unable to progress further without being caught in the spells that guarded the tunnels.

'I would go with you,' he said softly, as he placed a hand on Trad's shoulder. 'But I am needed here. We are too close to the end.'

Trad watched his men file through the darkened doorway. 'If we are successful tonight, who knows what changes tomorrow may bring.'

Callan's smile was tired. 'I hope you're right. Just make sure you make it back. If your actions save my city, I want to be able to thank you in person, understood?'

'Yes, sir,' Trad saluted, before turning to the Ancai and following the last of the raiders. 'Look for us at dawn,' he called as he disappeared into the darkness.

Trad called a halt just as a shaft of pale moonlight told him the end of the tunnel was approaching. They would have to separate once their mission had been accomplished, so he had divided his men into pairs, knowing two stood a better chance of survival than one. Callan had chosen the best for this mission. He was sure they all understood the roles they had to play, and now, as they were about to break from the cover of the tunnel, he ran through the plan one last time, hoping there would be no mistakes.

He gestured to Kestel and the huge man padded silently to end of the passageway and disappeared. Trad led his group after him, stopping just at the edge of the overhang that masked the entrance from prying eyes. There was no sound to be heard over the noises of the desert at night, no cries or thuds, but within minutes Kestel emerged from the shadows with the limp form of a soldier in his arms. He dumped the man inside the tunnel and disappeared again, returning moments later with the body of the second sentry. Kinseris had been right that the commanders of this army would seek out the Ephenori's means of escape, but Trad was relieved all the same. There had only been two.

'Their lines are about two hundred yards due east,' the Ancai whispered. 'There is one guard roughly every twenty yards, but they do not appear very alert. If we approach a little to the south, we will be covered by the rocks of this outcrop.'

Trad nodded, risking a few steps into the night and peering in the direction indicated. He saw at once the wisdom of the Ancai's choice. The rock formation that hid the tunnel extended southeast towards the encampment, only a little further down the lines than the area where the siege engines were kept. If they managed to reach the lines unseen, they would be able to slip into the camp in ones and twos with no one any the wiser.

He ducked back into the cave and motioned for the men to gather round as he outlined their strategy. Then he drew his sword and moved to the entrance, turning back to give them their final instructions. 'Once you are through the lines, there is a row of tents near the siege machines. Make for the tents but keep out of sight. We will meet you there. Make no move to destroy the equipment before I get to you, understood?'

They nodded and grinned at him. Then he was out into the night and running to the nearest rock, Kestel at his heels. Once there he twisted back, waving to the first pair, sending them on behind the great boulders towards the lines. Soon they were all past him, and as he darted to join them, he saw Kestel step out from the safety of the shadows. For such a massive man he could move with remarkable stealth. Even with the moon and stars all shining brightly, casting an eerie silver glow over the whole army, the guard had no chance. The Ancai slipped one hand over his mouth and drove a knife between his ribs with the other, and he never made a sound.

Hauling the body back behind the rocks, he motioned for another of the men to come forward and take his place. The man sauntered into position and ran a casual eye over the immediate area, checking to see if the exchange had been noticed.

Receiving the all clear, Trad turned to the first pair and sent them forward into the heart of the enemy camp. They slipped across the lines, walking slowly and steadily towards the tents, stopping by a dying fire to talk quietly. At least he hoped they were talking quietly. A moment later they moved off and disappeared from his view. He turned to the next pair and they were off before he had a chance to speak. These also crossed without incident, as did the next, and the pair after that. Then the guard at the lines showed them a clenched fist, and the waiting began again.

When it was safe, Trad sent the men faster, knowing that the longer he left those few alone inside the camp, the greater their risk of discovery. As the last pair disappeared from his view, he glanced at the Ancai and they made their way toward the lines. Their guard grinned as they passed him, turning to check on his partner. They would stay there until the chaos of the fires gave them the cover they needed to return to Ephenor.

As Trad forced himself to walk across the open space to the tents, his spine prickled as though a hundred eyes were trained on his back, and he wanted to jump at every shadow. Sensing his nerves, Kestel laid a hand on his shoulder behind his neck, the pressure enough to remind him to look straight ahead. Though he might be in nominal command of this raid, he was under no illusions about who held the ultimate authority. Long years of obedience to his captain went deep.

As they too turned aside by the tents, soldiers slipped out of the shadows to surround them and it took an instant of raw panic for him to realise they were his own men. Breathing deeply, and hoping none had noticed his sudden horror, he crept forward to get a better view of the compound.

Inside a roped-off area were the battering rams, ladders, catapults, and siege towers that had been used to such effect against Ephenor's walls. Around the perimeter, milling together in small groups, were the guards. A quick count revealed that their numbers were fairly evenly matched, but even with the advantage of surprise, Trad knew his men could not take on so many and fire the engines, not without causing a scene that would attract the attention of every soldier within hearing. The flames would do that too, of course, but by then it would be too late.

Trad unslung a leather flask from his shoulder and handed it to Kestel, who had one of his own already in his hand. The Ancai walked out into the open, calling a greeting to the nearest group of guards. Trad held his breath. He hoped they would take the wine from a stranger. He hoped the drug was strong enough to knock them out fast, and for that he had only Lysan's word. The archer had assured him the concoction was potent enough for his needs, claiming he and his brother had made use of it many times in their younger years. He had not liked to enquire too closely into why. Callan had looked doubtful, but he was beginning to think he would be more worried if they were ever actually in agreement.

When the Ancai raised the flask there were muted cheers. Men converged on him, thumping him on the shoulder, and he realised that for these men this was the eve of their victory. The Ancai pretended to drink before handing the flask on, walking to stand at the farthest edge of the compound, taking his new friends with him.

Not all the soldiers followed. Three stood by the largest battering ram and Trad's heart clenched as he saw them whisper amongst themselves. One walked towards Kestel's group, calling out a challenge, while the others slipped off towards the main army. Trad and two others peeled off and followed as a noisy argument started. They came up on the men from behind, silencing them with brutal efficiency, and dragging their bodies into the deepest shadows.

Trad turned back to the compound and watched in horrified fascination as a fight broke out between the Ancai and the man who had challenged him. The others gathered round, passing the flask between them, calling out encouragements and insults in increasingly loud voices. Trad blessed the distraction and cursed the noise as he waved his men forward. It was now or never.

They darted from the shadows and ducked under the ropes. Discovery was only minutes away now, whatever happened, and they set to work with a will, causing damage where they could, slicing through ropes and knots and smearing wood with the fat they had brought. As the first man emptied his jar and put flame to the tainted wood, the night exploded into action. Trad heard the frantic cries and saw the guards running towards them. Some were weaving on their feet, but others had not partaken of the drugged wine, and they rushed forward, calling out to their comrades. His eyes sought out Kestel, still caught up in the fight. As he watched, the huge man crashed his fist into his assailant's temple and the man crumpled to the floor. Then he was running towards the fire, and Trad ducked under a burning beam to join him, seeking out the safety of his captain's side.

A Kas'Tellian appeared before him out of nowhere, lunging with his sword, and Trad leapt to one side a split second before a blade in his chest would have ended his life. Bringing his own sword up in a desperate parry he twisted round, letting the man's momentum rush him past, and brought his weapon down to slice across the soldier's back. The man stumbled to his knees and Trad kept running. All around him his men were engaged in struggles of their own as they edged towards safety. He could see one of them down, his head split apart where he had fallen against the steel-capped end of the battering ram. Tongues of flames were licking at his tunic, their fierce heat turning the leather to crisped rags as the fire swept over him. Another, in his rush, had smeared some of the compound on himself and the flames leapt onto him as he ran towards the ropes. A sickening burning choked the air, the flames crackling and spitting as they melted flesh from bones, and still the inferno grew until it seemed the darkness itself would be beaten back by the fury of the fire.

Shouting filled the night. Dark shapes ran from the shadows and converged on the chaos, the soldiers trying desperately to put out the fire. But the flames leapt hungrily from wood to men, and screams drowned out the shouts as human torches reeled through the conflict, scattering men as they staggered back and forth, their cries descending into inhuman gurgles as they were consumed by the fire.

Overwhelmed by the horror of it, Trad found himself rooted to the spot, staring at the carnage. A man crashed into him from behind, shouting at him in Safarsee and pointing towards the fighting. He nodded, pretending to follow the officer as he charged into the fray. Then another hand grabbed his collar and his heart froze with dread.

A voice he recognised urged him to move and he dragged himself from his daze, stumbling after the Ancai. They ran as fast as they could away from the confusion. He no longer had any idea in which direction Ephenor lay. Hearing shouting close behind, Trad glanced over his shoulder to see a group of soldiers running away from them. Then he turned a corner and collided with a man as he stepped out of his tent, half-dressed and sword in hand. Trad barely had time to note the bars of rank on the unbuttoned jacket before the man turned on him.

Trad did not hesitate. He drove his sword deep into the officer's belly, the momentum throwing them both to the ground. As he rolled off the dying man, Trad felt the Ancai's huge hands pull him away and lift him to his feet. His captain knelt beside the body of the Kas'Tellian, and there was a coldness in his eyes that chilled him down to the bone.

'General Wedh?' Kestel asked. 'Do you recognise me?'

The man's eyelids fluttered open and he blinked, trying to focus on the face that hovered above him.

'Kestel?'

'Yes, General,' the black man agreed. There was not even a flicker of emotion in his voice. 'Do you remember what I promised you?'

The man's eyes grew wide and he raised his hands in a feeble attempt to push his assailant away.

'I see that you do.' The Ancai clasped both hands round the hilt of Trad's sword. Placing his foot on the man's chest, he yanked out the blade and brought it down in one smooth motion across the general's throat.

Trad stared at him. 'What was that for?'

Kestel shook his head slowly, staring down into the face of the man he had killed. 'That is not my story. Old debts have been paid this night. His death will be a blow for this army.'

He reached down to rip the insignia off the jacket and stopped, his head snapping up. Quick as a flash he grabbed Trad in one hand, the bloody sword in the other, and began to march the boy forward. 'Do not speak,' he ordered in a whisper. 'You are my prisoner.'

Trad squirmed in sudden fear, for a horrible second thinking he had been betrayed, then he saw another figure walking swiftly towards them and realised their killing of the general had been witnessed. He held his tongue, wondering how the Ancai planned to get them out of this mess, and tried to look scared. It was not hard.

FIVE

'GENERAL GALYDON,' KESTEL called, holding Trad out before him. 'I have caught the man responsible for the death of General Wedh.'

The man stopped, his eyes narrowing as he took in the pair before him. He was tall and lean, his dark hair turning silver at the temples and his face lined by years of campaigning. His black eyes flashed over Trad and the body behind him and back to the Ancai's face. 'Do I know you?'

'No, sir,' Kestel replied without breaking stride. 'The prisoner, General? Should I take him to your tent?'

'What?' Irritation and suspicion bloomed in the general's gaze. 'My tent?'

'So we can decide what is to be done, sir, now that Wedh is dead.' Reaching the general, Kestel steered him back the way he had come. 'Kinseris sends you greetings,' he said, staring straight ahead. 'From Ephenor.'

The man's eyes widened but he gave no other indication he had heard the words. 'Yes, take the prisoner to my tent,' he agreed distantly, walking on ahead and holding open the canvas door for the Ancai. Kestel pushed Trad before him, sword still in hand, and Galydon followed, tying the flaps together behind him.

The tent was sparsely furnished. A low cot on one side was covered with maps of Ephenor and its hinterland. A small desk took up the centre of the space and a candle burned low in a brass stand. It appeared the general had been working late and had not yet retired though dawn was not far off. It was to this desk he now walked, sitting behind it and studying them with suspicion.

'Who are you to bring me word from Kinseris,' he demanded. 'And why should you think I would listen? What are you to him?'

'My name is Kestel, formerly the Ancai of Frankesh,' the soldier replied. 'This is Trad, also once in the service of Kinseris in Frankesh.'

The general leant forward, his gaze sharp and wary. 'He is not your

582

prisoner? Explain yourselves quickly, or I will have my guards drag the truth from you.'

'I was the Ancai of Frankesh,' Kestel repeated. 'Of Kinseris. I am here in his service.'

'And where is your lord? In Ephenor? So, he is the traitor that rumour has named him.'

'To whom?' the Ancai asked. 'To Vasa? Where is *he*, general?'

Galydon sat back, his eyes flicking over them appraisingly. 'Vasa is dead,' he said at last. 'He has been dead these last weeks, but that is a secret known only to a few. You cannot be one of them.'

'And yet am I,' the Ancai replied. 'And that is just one of the many things we know that you may not.' He did not elaborate, feared to. This man was known to be honourable and fair, though rigid in his loyalty once given. Vasa's death had freed him from that allegiance, and one that had likely become uncomfortable, but discovering that those who now sought his aid were responsible for that act would put him in an impossible position. Instead he pressed, 'If Vasa is dead, why are you here? Whose orders brought this army to Ephenor?'

Galydon's eyes glittered with sudden anger. 'I am asking the questions. By your own admission you are both traitors to Kas'Tella, and more than likely the men responsible for the recent disturbance in my camp. If you wish to spare yourselves the attentions of my soldiers, you had better give me a reason, and quickly.'

'Two swords to one,' Trad offered, breaking his silence. 'If you raise the alarm, we will kill you.'

The general laughed. 'Not that kind of reason, boy. A *real* reason.'

Sensing his interest, the Ancai did not hesitate. 'My lord Kinseris approached you once, many years ago. I know because he told me. He watched you for months, spoke to those of your friends and men in your command he could reach without alerting you, until he was sure you would listen to what he had to say.'

'He did,' the general nodded. 'And I refused him.'

'But you did not give him up.'

Galydon paused. 'I did not, though I wrestled long and hard over that decision. For many years I wondered whether I had made the right choice, whether I should inform the Kas'Talani of his activities. Do you know why I did not? Because in the end he was not conspiring to destroy his Order, merely to help his people, and whether I agreed with his methods or not, I could not disagree with the sentiment. My loyalty was sworn to Kas'Tella and I could not break it, not on his word alone. But I had not seen then what I have seen now.'

'The Arkni?' Kestel queried sharply and at the general's startled look he added, 'The men who took command from Vasa.'

'Men? You call them men?' Galydon asked in disgust. 'I call them monsters.'

'Where are they now?'

'They are gone. They left at dawn yesterday.'

At Trad's sharp intake of breath, Kestel sighed. 'It is as we hoped. Aarin knew they would follow him.' Turning back to the curious general, he asked, 'Who is in command now?'

'Wedh.' Galydon spat out his distaste. 'Or he was, until you killed him. He was their creature; he had been for years. But now he is dead overall command of the First Army falls to me.'

'Then call off this siege, general,' the Ancai implored. 'These people are not your enemy.'

Galydon looked at him intently. 'Are they not? Many thousands of my men lie dead on this field at their hands.'

'You brought this war to them,' Kestel reminded him, a hand latching tight around Trad's arm to silence his half-formed retort. 'Your men need not have died if they had remained in Kas'Tella. By your own admission, it was no Kas'Talani order that brought you here. Your loyalty to the priesthood stands threatened only as long as you continue this siege.'

The general's face hardened. 'Do not take me for a fool,' he warned. 'Your master never did. Vasa himself desired to destroy these people.'

The Ancai met his gaze steadily, said softly, 'But Vasa is dead.'

Fierce anger boiled in Galydon's eyes for an instant, then he scrubbed a hand over his face and for the first time they could see the extent of his exhaustion.

'That I know,' he agreed at last. 'But it is not that easy.'

'Then make it that easy,' Trad insisted. 'You command the army. They must do as you say.'

The general looked amused. 'Must they? Not everyone will think as I do, and never forget that your people have killed many of mine. Some will want revenge, not peace, and payment from the city that has bloodied them.'

'Your men have killed many of ours also,' Trad responded angrily before Kestel could stop him. 'Your army has laid siege to their home! If Ephenor is prepared to set those deaths aside and accept peace, you can do no less.'

Galydon laughed mirthlessly. 'But Ephenor must have peace, for it is about to fall. Why should we surrender on the eve of victory?'

'You need not surrender, general,' the Ancai jumped in before Trad could worsen an already perilous situation. 'And you might find that victory is not as swift as you believe now so many of your siege engines have been destroyed.'

'So that was you. Your idea?'

'It was mine,' Trad growled. 'And every time you rebuild them, we will return and destroy them.'

'Peace, young man,' Galydon said tolerantly. 'In your anger at the how you have been wronged, never forget that others have also suffered, that others have also been used.' He nodded at Kestel. 'I can promise you nothing. A peace will not come cheap, and there are many men I must find and speak with.'

He collected his sword belt from the desk and strapped it on with an air of resignation. If his assessment of the mood of his troops was accurate, this course would not be without its dangers. 'You must remain here. It will not be safe for you out there, though I hope I will have need of you later. There are so many things about this war I do not understand.'

'We are to trust you?' Trad demanded, clearly disinclined to trust an enemy, any enemy. 'And wait here for you to send your soldiers?'

Galydon's tolerance snapped. 'Do not test my patience,' he warned, a hand on the hilt of his sword. 'I have told you I will attempt what you ask, and my word when given should be enough for you. If I wished to hand you over, I could have done so long since, despite what you believe about your weapons at my throat.'

The Ancai rested his hand on Trad's neck, the pressure of his hand insistent. The boy stilled. 'Forgive my friend,' he said to Galydon. 'He has been given little reason to trust those who serve Kas'Tella. We await your return, General, and wish you luck. Many lives depend on you now.'

'That I also know,' Galydon replied. 'It remains to be seen whether I can convince my colleagues of it.'

'Six,' Callan muttered. 'Only six and neither Trad nor Kestel among them. I only hope this was worth the price we paid for it.'

'You saw the flames,' Lysan replied, 'and you can see the destruction they caused. More than their war machines were destroyed last night. Do not despair of them yet, I have not.'

'And when will you despair, brother? When you see the bodies?'

Lysan looked thoughtful. 'Perhaps, though I might suspect a trick.'

Callan made a strangled noise halfway between a laugh and a sob and turned away again, staring out at the enemy camp as he had been doing for hours, ever since there had been sufficient light to see. Lysan had joined him minutes ago, staggering bleary-eyed up the stairs from the ruined courtyard, spitting curses at his brother for allowing him to sleep through the night.

'Sleep?' Callan had retorted. 'Do you often fall asleep standing up?'

Lysan glared at him. 'When was the last time you slept? If you don't rest soon, you'll find out for yourself how easy it is to drop off whilst on your feet.'

Callan sighed. That the raid had been successful he could see for himself. The area of the camp around the site of the flames had been devastated and the chaos of the night had not yet abated. He could see officers directing groups of soldiers in salvage operations, more still were scurrying between the command tents. But there was still no sign of Trad or Kestel and he was losing hope. Dawn had come and gone, and they would no longer have the cover of darkness to make their way back to the walls. It had occurred to him that they might try to skirt the fortress and return by the western walls, but no word had come from the soldiers there, and his mood grew bleaker.

'What's this?' Lysan asked, drawing his attention back to the field.

Following the direction of his brother's gaze, Callan saw a flurry of activity at the centre of the encampment. Horses were being led round to the command tents and officers were emerging. A party was being mounted, and an escort organised.

'I wonder,' he murmured, sprinting up the steps to stand on the walls, shielding his eyes from the sun as he stared at the distant movement.

'More steps,' Lysan cursed softly, hauling his tired body up next to his brother. 'What are they doing?'

'I don't know.'

'Are they coming here?'

'I don't know,' Callan snapped as he looked at his brother. 'Here,' he offered in concern, seeing the unsteady stagger Lysan tried to hide. 'Lean on me. It's a long way down.'

'So it is,' Lysan observed, peering over the edge with a total lack of concern. 'They are coming here. And if I'm not mistaken that's a flag of truce.'

Callan spun around, almost losing his footing. Lysan was right. The small group was mounted now and moving towards them, a phalanx of guards on foot surrounding the two riders. 'Well this is better than we hoped. Maybe Aarin was right after all.'

'Or maybe Trad's plan was more effective than we thought.'

'Well, I'll take a truce any way I can get it,' Callan replied, as they watched the party draw closer. 'Though I am surprised they would offer one so close to victory. Who comes to our gates?' he shouted in challenge minutes later as the riders stopped short of the walls, their horses shying from the corpses littering the ground.

The lead horsemen looked up, his reins held in one hand as his horse picked its way delicately forward. 'I come under a flag of truce. I would speak with your commander.'

'You're speaking to him.'

The Kas'Tellian appeared surprised, twisting in his saddle to confer with a person behind him. Then he nudged his horse to one side as the figure stepped out of his shadow.

'Let them in, Callan,' Trad called. 'They've come to offer peace.'

'Well, look who we have here,' Lysan whooped in delight. 'You call this dawn, laggard? We were about to send out a search party!'

Trad grinned.

Callan ordered the portcullis raised and the party rode into the courtyard as the brothers jogged down the steps to greet them.

'Kestel is with you?' he asked Trad, looking around.

'Here,' the Ancai answered. Callan smiled with relief, taking his hand and shaking it. 'It is good to see you both.'

'Even late as you are,' Lysan drawled, his face split in a wide grin.

'Callan, this is General Galydon, commander of the First Army of Kas'Tella,' Trad interrupted. He spoke in Amadorian, a language Galydon had assured him he was familiar with. 'And this is his captain, Timeke. General, Captain, this is Callan L'faer, commander of Ephenor, and his brother Lysan.'

As he spoke the tall man stepped forward, the sun glittering off the braid on his formal uniform and the crest of Kas'Tella emblazoned on his chest. 'I would never have guessed,' he murmured as he bowed his greeting. The little captain bobbed his head and smiled, though it was clear he did not understand what was being said.

The general looked from Trad to Callan. 'It was my understanding that House Durian ruled in Ephenor.'

'That is so, general,' Callan replied stiffly, his hand still resting on the hilt of his sword. 'Lord Shrogar was wounded in the fighting. You may have confidence that I speak in his name.'

'Ah, I meant no offence,' Galydon soothed. 'Your friends have spoken highly of you both, and I would be honoured to deal with you.'

Callan led the Kas'Tellians to Shrogar's council chamber, sending servants to fetch wine for their guests and bowls of scented water so they could refresh themselves. As the last was leaving he called him over, instructing him to inform Dianeth of the discussions in progress.

At the mention of her name, the Ancai looked over at General Galydon, a question in his eyes. When the general returned a look of bland disinterest, he stopped the servant by the door. 'Please also inform the Lady Dianeth that Fader Wedh is dead.'

Callan's head snapped round. 'Dead?'

'Very.'

Lysan laughed delightedly. 'Now that is reason to celebrate. Did you kill him?'

The Ancai turned to Trad who blushed, confused. 'It was a joint effort,' he allowed at last.

'Well, whoever did the deed it is news to brighten the coldest of mornings. And Dianeth will have another reason to bless this dawn.'

'Shrogar has awakened?' Kestel asked.

Callan nodded. 'He regained consciousness a few hours ago. The fever has broken.'

'Should we wake him?'

Callan hesitated. 'That depends on what comes from this meeting,' he began, eyes drifting to Galydon who had sat silent through the exchange about his erstwhile commanding officer. 'You wish for a truce?'

'Not just a truce,' Galydon replied firmly. 'I wish for peace.'

Callan's eyes narrowed. That an enemy in such a commanding position should wish to parley at all made him suspicious. That he should come to the table and state his aims so plainly made him downright nervous. 'Why should you wish for peace? Why not pursue this war to its conclusion? I find it hard to believe you don't expect to win.'

'Would I win?' the general asked mildly. 'Your friends were adamant that there is no easy victory for me here.'

'We said nothing about easy,' Lysan interjected. 'Nor victory, except in your expectations. Ephenor has plenty of fight in her yet.'

Galydon gave them a wry smile. 'Of that I have no doubt if last night is any indication. But that is not why I am here. Your companions have urged me call off this siege, and they have also rid me of the last impediment in doing so—General Wedh. Let us speak honestly with each other, Callan, for we both wish for the same thing. Vasa is dead and has been for many days. I know you know this, and moreover that you are aware of the creatures commanding in his stead. They are gone now, and it is no longer their will that dominates us. The high priest who commanded my loyalty, for better or worse, is dead, and I find myself reluctant to align myself with those who have replaced him. And from the little I have been told, though I must confess I understood even less, the sole reason that my army was brought here was to trap one man who is no longer within these walls. Since I can see little threat to my people from this man, he concerns neither me nor my army. So why then should we continue this waste of life?'

'The Lost Houses, of which Ephenor is the last, have long been at war with Kas'Tella. That does not concern you?'

The general shook his head. 'Your fight was with Vasa and he is dead. The Kas'Talani are in disarray. They have no successor, no leadership, nor much of an army since we are here. I think you have won that war, my lords.'

'I've seen victors in better shape,' Lysan commented ruefully.

'The offer is genuine, Callan,' Trad assured him.

Callan nodded absently, drumming his fingers on the table. He was so tired. Lysan was right, he had not slept in days.

'You offer me peace today,' he said at length. 'But what is to stop you marching on Ephenor once more when order is restored in Kas'Tella?'

Galydon shuddered. 'Believe me, I will not be returning here,' he said with feeling. 'But you are right. I cannot speak for the Kas'Talani, though I very much doubt they will have attention to spare for you in the near future. They have their Order to rebuild and I am sure there are many who will be sympathetic to Kinseris now that Vasa is dead. If he wished, Kinseris could walk into Kas'Tella tomorrow and take the black throne for himself. It is my hope that he will do so, and it is to him that I will offer my sword and my allegiance.'

Callan glanced at Lysan. 'Kinseris is no longer here. It is his party these creatures pursue, and it is doubtful any of them will return.' He turned back to the general in time to see the spasm of disappointment that crossed face. 'If he does, I doubt he will willingly return to the Order he has forsaken.'

Galydon frowned. 'Then he must be persuaded otherwise. Understand this, all of you. There are elements in Kas'Tella who will desire to continue in Vasa's footsteps. His way brought them power and they will be reluctant to give that up. If we are to salvage anything from this mess, we must install on that throne someone who will give this land the peace it sorely needs. If you truly desire to save Ephenor, you will wish the same, for Ephenor is a part of Caledan no matter how much you might wish otherwise. We are all in this together. Let Kinseris walk away from his duty, and you allow your enemies to set up another tyrant in Vasa's place, and it will not be long before you feel the noose begin to tighten once more.'

'Understand this, general,' Callan replied harshly, leaning forwards. 'We do not bow to threats, no matter what is at stake, and I will not force any man to walk a path he does not choose for himself. But,' he continued more quietly, 'that does not mean that my heart does not wish to do otherwise.'

Galydon nodded his head, satisfied. 'Then we agree on something.'

Lysan elbowed his brother as Callan hesitated. 'We agree on one more thing,' he said. 'That this land needs peace.'

He held up his hand as Galydon would have spoken. 'I agree to peace on your promise that you will never lead an army back through the desert, nor furnish any other with information about this place and its defences. And that you will march your men away as soon as is reasonably possible. In return, we promise to cease hostilities towards Kas'Tella until such time as a new high priest is appointed and his policies towards our people are made known. Should it be Kinseris I will rejoice with you, but if it is not I give no assurance that we will not act to defend ourselves as we have always done should we again be subject to persecution or attempts at conquest by the priesthood.'

'Agreed.' Galydon held out his hand and Callan hesitated only a moment before taking it, his face breaking into a smile for the first time since the talks had begun.

Trad and Kestel sighed with relief and Timeke beamed at everyone, understanding the gesture of friendship, while Lysan looked on with a small smile.

'With one small change.'

Callan's smile froze and he jerked his hand away, suspicion flaring anew in his blood-shot eyes.

'Ah you misjudge me, my friend,' the general laughed. 'I do not seek to alter the essence of our agreement.'

'Then what?' Callan demanded. 'Speak quickly or I must withdraw our terms.'

Galydon leant forward, hands clasped before him on the table and a twinkle of merriment in his dark eyes. 'What would you say to an alliance?'

SIX

THE TUNNEL THAT led to the ancient land of Tesseria was long and narrow, winding deep below the earth. Kinseris had estimated that it would take them at least two days to reach the other side, possibly three, and the thought of spending that long so far underground was not pleasant. The pressure of the darkness was compounded by the restrictive way they travelled, forced to walk in single file and burdened with the knowledge that they were unable to turn back. If, by some chance, any part of the passage had become impassable, they would be trapped. The magic that guarded the last escape for the lords of Ephenor would not allow them to retrace their steps and return to the city. That did not mean they could not turn around and walk back the way they had come, only that doing so would never lead them back to Ephenor. They could wander in the dark forever without gaining even a step on their destination.

They stopped every few hours to rest, catching brief periods of sleep, unwilling to delay their journey by pausing for longer. When they moved on the order was always the same: Kinseris leading, then Jeta, followed by Aarin with Kallis at the rear.

In one of their rest periods Aarin heard Kallis take out his knife and begin to sharpen it.

'What are you doing?'

'Someone is following us.'

Aarin sighed. 'I know.'

Kallis ran the whetstone down his blade in an aggressive gesture. 'You go on. I'll wait for him here.'

'No. It's too dangerous. You don't know who is behind us.'

'I have a good idea.'

'Kallis —'

'Just go, Aarin. Take the others and get out of here. I'll catch up.'

'See that you do,' the mage replied. Then he got to his feet and crouched down beside Jeta. She came awake with a start, blinking against the darkness. 'Is it time to go?'

'Yes.'

She squeezed his hand in the darkness then knelt beside Kinseris, waking the priest from his uneasy sleep, and they were on their way again.

It was several hours later when the first glimmer of light could be seen in the distance. Though they were tired, no one suggested stopping now they were within reach of their destination. It was not long before they could see the tunnel mouth itself, a golden glow promising release from the confining dark. At length, the passage opened into a large cave, the ceiling above them rising sharply and fresh air streaming in through the wide opening. A fine layer of sand blown in from the desert covered the rock floor and strange paintings swirled across the rough-hewn walls.

Jeta twirled around in delight, sending ripples across the dusting of sand. She smiled at Aarin, then the smile froze on her face as Kallis failed to emerge behind him.

'Someone was following us,' Aarin told her. 'He stayed behind.'

Kinseris looked round. 'Someone was following? Who?'

Aarin shrugged. 'I don't know.' It was only half a lie. He knew who Kallis thought it was—and he could think of no one else who might have gained access to the hidden door—but he was not going to voice that suspicion.

'They cannot go back,' the priest warned. 'What will we do?'

'It will be dark soon. We will spend the night here. It's the best shelter we're likely to find.'

Kinseris looked unconvinced. 'We should leave with nightfall. That way we are not forced to travel in the heat of the day and the darkness will hide our movements.'

'We're waiting here,' Aarin repeated, a bite in his tone. 'If we leave without Kallis he will not be able to find us, and I will not abandon him in this desert.' Not until he had to, at least.

Kinseris raised his hands in surrender and walked to the cave mouth. Jeta watched him, biting her lip. 'He's right, isn't he? We should go on.'

'Perhaps.' Aarin shrugged. 'But I'm not leaving without Kallis.'

She slipped her hand into his. 'He will be angry with you for waiting.'

He laughed. 'When is he not?'

Kinseris joined them. 'We should see what we can gather for a fire. It will get cold come nightfall.'

Jeta went with him and Aarin cautioned them not to stray too far from the cave. No fire was preferable to alerting the enemy to their position.

When they had gone, he drew out the map he had brought with him from Ephenor and sat studying it in a patch of dying sunlight. Kinseris had never been to this land, and all they knew about the tunnel was that it led somewhere inside the ancient province of Tesseria. Marked on the map was the abandoned fortress of the Haram, but it was no ancient citadel like Ephenor. He doubted it would hold the answers they sought, nor was he drawn to it. The fire in his veins, ever more intense since he had arrived in Ephenor, was driving him forward as it had done in Amadorn, and he let it guide him. Somewhere to the south of them, to the west of the ruined settlements, was the place they were seeking. The stone that held the secrets promised in the prophecy. He had never seen the thing he sought, but he would know it when he found it.

Kinseris and Jeta returned as Aarin was still pondering the puzzle. They had found little more than the spiny sticks of desert plants, but the dead brush was tinder dry and burned merrily. As the sun sank behind the far horizon, they wrapped themselves in their cloaks, and shared a quick meal from the supplies they had brought. Jeta curled up by Aarin's side, drifting off to sleep while he and Kinseris organised the watches.

To avoid an argument, Aarin agreed to wake the priest midway through the night, but even as he made the promise, he knew he would not sleep. He rested his back against the wall and prepared to keep his lonely vigil.

Come on, Kallis, he urged silently. *Don't leave me now.* For he knew, come the dawn, that they must leave, whether Kallis had returned or not.

The heat of the desert faded rapidly with the setting of the sun, and Aarin was soon glad of the small fire. The flickering flames played out a swirling, violent dance of shadow-characters on the rock walls, acting out their own legend. He imagined his enemy in those shadows, growing deeper as the fire died down. Unsettled, he reached for the tinder and saw a pair of red eyes watching him from the darkness at the cave's mouth.

His start of fright made Jeta stir and he stilled at once, not wanting to wake her. The eyes continued to watch him, unblinking. Slowly, calmly, he laid the kindling on the fire, and as the flames leapt up, he saw the creature that watched him. Almost four feet long, scaled and heavily muscled, the lizard was motionless but for the tongue that flicked and darted, tasting the air.

Menetas. Kallis had told him of these creatures. His people believed their presence heralded the coming of death. With its patient, eerie stillness, it was easy to understand the tribesmen's fear of the eyes that haunted them from the darkness outside the firelight. But it seemed to Aarin that the lizard was more interested in the fire than him, its watchfulness only the wariness of all wild creatures confronted with something unfamiliar. He stoked the fire again and saw it blink at last. When he made no further move, the creature crept closer, drawn in by the warmth.

'Little dragon,' he murmured, remembering Kallis's words. Then a soft scraping made him look up, and he saw a line of red dots break the darkness behind the first. Almost as though they knew he would not chase them away, the lizards emerged cautious and silent from the shadows until he was all but surrounded.

'Share my fire, little brothers,' he invited softly, strangely comforted by their presence. He kept the fire burning as long as he could, feeding it with his magic as he had done as a child, as he had never dared to do since. They did not come within reach, never made a sound, but their eyes never left him. Until, as dawn approached and he let the fire die down, they began to disappear as silently as they had come, the only sign of their presence the tracks in the sand. By the time Jeta and Kinseris awoke the last had gone.

Aarin watched the dawn rise with regret. Kallis had not appeared and he began to worry that the suspicions about the *meneta* might be justified. Kinseris repeated his assertion that they should leave, and Aarin swallowed an angry retort just as the wards around the tunnel came to life.

He scrambled to his feet and gestured for silence, throwing sand over the remains of the small fire as they gathered their possessions and slipped out of sight. There was no way to be sure whether those coming were friends or enemies, and they had already delayed too long.

The minutes stretched on and there was still no sound or movement. If not for the singing of the wards, Aarin would not have believed anyone approached. Finally, he heard a faint muffled footfall, then another. The sounds grew louder, and he smiled as he heard a rough voice raised in anger. He would recognise that tone anywhere.

It was several minutes more before they were in sight, but long before he saw them Aarin knew who their shadow would be. He felt a profound sense of regret. Kallis stalked out of the shadows and into the cave, one hand gripped around the forearm of Iarwin Durian. His pained eyes sought Aarin's and held them, sharing the same nameless sorrow, then with a rough shove he sent Shrogar's brother sprawling in the dust at his feet.

'He says he wishes to help us,' Kallis told them angrily. 'I say he is lying.'

Iarwin lifted his face from the ground and glared at his captor with unconcealed loathing. His eyes were red-rimmed and swollen and an ugly bruise marred one cheekbone. He began to push himself to his knees, his movements hampered by hands bound tight before him, but Kallis's foot in the small of his back forced him back down.

Kinseris took a step forward, shocked. 'Iarwin?' He stopped short as Shrogar's brother shifted to face him, then turned his horrified gaze on Kallis. 'What is this?' he asked dangerously. 'What have you done to him?'

'A better question would be what he has done to you,' Kallis retorted. 'To all of us.' He grabbed a handful of hair, yanking Iarwin's head up. 'Well? Tell them what you've done, what they paid you to betray us.'

Iarwin spat a mouthful of blood and sand and stayed defiantly silent. Kinseris started forward, trembling with outrage, but Aarin's hand on his arm brought him to an abrupt halt.

'Let him up, Kallis,' he said quietly.

Kallis jerked back, removing his weight from Iarwin's back. 'He has betrayed you.'

'I know. But I want to know why.'

Kinseris dropped to his knees beside Iarwin and helped him rise to his feet, his face a mask of anger. 'You'd better have a good reason for mistreating a son of his house in such a way. Shrogar will not forgive this.'

Kallis glared back at him. 'I think he will when he realises his beloved brother has betrayed Ephenor to its ruin. Tell him what you told me,' he insisted as Iarwin winced at the mention of his home. 'Tell him why Ephenor will fall because of what you have done.'

At this Iarwin's sullen silence broke. 'What *I* have done? Ephenor would not even face this foe if it were not for you. It is your troubles that have brought this peril to our gates. What I did, I did for my people. *I did not know you then!*'

Kinseris flinched, hearing the truth at last. His face drained of colour, his fingers tightening on Iarwin's arm.

'Why?' he whispered. 'Why will Ephenor fall? What have you done?'

Iarwin looked away, unable to meet the priest's eyes. 'I did not wish this, I meant for none of this to happen.' His words were a plea for understanding. 'When they took me, I knew nothing of any of this beyond our fight against the tyrant, and even then I would not give them what they wanted, though it was nothing to me.'

Aarin went cold. Iarwin had mentioned no names, but he did not need to. He felt a pang of sharp sympathy. Shrogar's brother was a wretched sight, dusty and bruised, burdened by shame, but the choice had been his, and he alone had taken this path.

Iarwin drew in a ragged breath. 'They would not stop, always they were there. When they did not have their claws in my flesh, I could hear their voices in my head, over and over. What they wanted was so small, and I did not know you,' he repeated in pathetic appeal. His eyes met Aarin's. 'They were not interested in us or our rebellion. They wanted you, someone I had never met, someone I had never even heard of! And all they asked of me was a simple permission, to use my eyes and ears to follow you. I did not want to give in to them, but in the end I could not think through the pain. All I wanted was for the nightmare to end.'

'So you gave in,' Kallis taunted.

'Stop it, Kallis,' Aarin warned.

Shrogar's brother grabbed a handful of his shirt in his cuffed hands and clumsily pulled the fabric over his head. Across his back, snaking over his shoulders and onto his chest, were deep, ugly lacerations, and suddenly his mention of claws took on a sinister new meaning.

'I wanted you to find me,' he insisted, his voice choked with anger. 'I wanted you to hear me and take me. There was no other way for me to warn you! They are coming. They know where you are going, and they are following.'

Kinseris stared in horror. Shaking fingers traced the line of a mottled red scar down the length of his spine. 'These have never been cared for,' he reproved gently, steadfastly ignoring the implications of the marks. 'Why did you not seek healing?'

'How could I?' Iarwin asked brokenly. 'How could I let my brother see this, knowing the ruin of my flesh was nothing compared to the ruin of my soul? How would he believe I endured it without breaking?' A single tear leaked out and snaked its way down his filthy cheek. 'There are more, elsewhere. They were thorough. But this is the worst of it. And yes, I was weak, I should not have given in, but I did not understand. You never told me any of this.'

Kinseris looked away in his turn, accepting the accusation for what it was. 'I could not risk it, Iarwin, you have to understand that. It was never a question of trust, but of survival. No one could know.'

'My brother did.'

The priest shook his head sorrowfully. 'No, he didn't, not everything. I used him too, in a way, but I never meant for any of you to come to harm.'

'Well, we did!' Iarwin flung back, shrugging free of Kinseris's support to stand unaided in brittle defiance. 'Ephenor may be finished because of what I have done, but you are just as guilty!'

Aarin drew Kinseris away. 'You are not at fault here. I insisted we leave them defenceless. I believed our absence would guarantee their safety. And that may still be true.'

'It is not,' Iarwin said wearily. 'They know your plans, all of them, and they will leave nothing you love standing. I tried to stop you, to distract you, but you paid me no mind, even my own brother ignored me. Both you and then Shrogar spoke your thoughts in my presence, *and I could not stop them from hearing everything!* They will follow you, but they will destroy Ephenor and everyone in it, for each bit of pain they cause you is joy to them. They have forced you to betray you allies as they forced me to betray my family, and in the end you will betray yourself and they will have won!'

Aarin reeled before his sudden devastating understanding. His eyes locked onto Iarwin's and he saw there the same sickening knowledge that stared from his own. He had abandoned Ephenor to its destruction. Shrogar and his people would all die, all those who had sheltered them and fought for them, and they would die because his enemy wished to spite him and no more reason than that.

He understood now why Iarwin had hated them so. Not simply the product of his thwarted loyalty, it had been the only way he knew to avoid the knowledge of their plans from falling into the hands of the Arkni. But Shrogar had trusted him, refusing to give up on the brother he loved no matter how inexplicably he behaved. Only Kallis had suspected the truth, or near enough to make no difference.

You may come to regret that, Iarwin had told him when he had saved his life on the battlements. Iarwin had been inviting death in those moments of reckless, desperate fighting, inviting an end to his torment. But Aarin had saved him, and what a joke that must have seemed. Only Iarwin's death could help him, and Shrogar's brother knew that—knew it and had tried to bring it about. Aarin owed him a death, and now, Tesserion forgive him, he would see that he got it.

Almost as if he could read the thoughts in Aarin's mind, Iarwin reeled and would have fallen if Kallis had not eased him to his knees.

Aarin knelt. Leaning in close he asked, 'Where is Saal'an now?'

Iarwin's head snapped up, his eyes suddenly wild.

Of course, it would have been that one. He would not have missed a chance to inflict such pain.

'You have met him?'

Aarin nodded and saw a flicker of empathy cross Iarwin's face, the first sign of acceptance the man had extended to him. That it should come at such a time, and at such a price, was almost more than he could bear.

'I cannot tell. I can feel him always, but I have no skill to track him, or resist. Just as I cannot free myself.'

'Try,' Aarin urged. 'You are gifted, Kinseris told me. Somewhere in you there is a spark. Find it, use it.'

Iarwin shook his head. 'Do you think I have not tried? I can do nothing against him. But he will follow me and whatever you do he will know as long as you are with me.'

The mage searched his face, wondering. Tightening his grip, he allowed his awareness to seep into the other man, seeking a glimpse of the magic the Arkni had used to snare him. Like the wards in Kas'Tella, he could sense the dark threads entwined through Iarwin's being without truly seeing them, and something in the patterning struck a chord deep in his memory. It was possible the Arkni had used Iarwin's own passive talent to somehow link with his mind in a manner similar to the pairings of old, but the forced limitations of their existence meant they could achieve little more than a connection allowing them to manipulate an unprotected mind. No more, but more than enough.

He withdrew and sat back on his heels, his hands still clasped around Iarwin's shoulders, keeping him from slumping to the floor. In that brief moment of contact he had understood what Iarwin wanted but could not ask him to do. It made him sick.

'You know they will kill me.'

He nodded.

'What will you do?'

Iarwin did not want to live with the evil he had caused, but he could not turn his hand against himself. Aarin dropped his hands and stood, looking down at the man who could have been a friend had fate not intervened.

Iarwin read his answer in the silence. A grim smile twisted his mouth. 'I didn't think you were ruthless enough to do what you must, but I see I was wrong.'

Aarin held his gaze. There was fear behind Iarwin's weary acceptance. 'I'm sorry.'

'You would be.'

Kallis came up behind him, looking between the two of them uneasily. 'What's going on?'

Aarin turned away. 'Tie him securely, hands and feet. We're leaving.'

'What? We won't get far if we have to carry him. Let him walk.'

Iarwin laughed bitterly. 'He doesn't get it does he?'.

'Aarin?' Kallis pressed.

'He's not coming with us.'

The mercenary's expression darkened. 'You can't leave him here. If they find him, they will kill him! And if they don't, the desert will.'

'I believe that's the point,' Iarwin told him, holding out his wrists where the makeshift bindings had come loose. 'You heard him. Tie me tightly.'

'You be quiet!' Kallis hissed, turning back to Aarin. 'What are you doing? If you leave him like this, you may as well just kill him yourself. Take him with us. I'll make sure he doesn't do any harm.'

Aarin shook his head. 'You can't.'

'I can try!' Kallis exploded. 'You can't do this! At least free his hands so he can fight!'

'Or so he can untie himself and follow us?'

Kallis stared at him as though he did not know him. 'You can't do this,' he repeated.

'What would you have me do?' Aarin demanded, angry now. 'Kill him? Or will you do it for me?'

'Yes, if that is the only alternative. It would be the merciful thing to do.'

Forgotten for a moment, Iarwin murmured, 'You're too kind. But please, don't do me any favours.'

Kallis rounded on him, enraged. 'What is wrong with you? Don't you care that he is planning to leave you here to die? I'm trying to help you!'

'You can't help me,' Iarwin said bluntly. 'Listen to your friend. Bind me well and leave while you have the chance, for as long as I am free and have life in my body *I will follow you*, and as long as I am with you everything you do is known to them. You have two choices: kill me or leave me to take my chances. Who knows, maybe they won't find me?'

'You know they will.' Aarin knelt beside him and began to retie the rope round his wrists, then more around his ankles. 'He will know of your betrayal even now and he will have his revenge.'

Iarwin shrugged. 'Tell me you don't think I deserve it.'

'You don't.' They both looked up as Kinseris dropped to his knees. 'Please Iarwin, it doesn't have to be this way. What will I tell Shrogar?'

At this, suppressed emotions finally flared. 'Nothing. Nothing of this! Though he may suspect, he knows only that I chose to leave him alone to face this enemy. If he survives, my brother does not need to know that I betrayed him. I beg you, please, do not tell Shrogar what I have done.'

Kinseris nodded.

'Promise me,' Iarwin insisted, the mention of all he had left behind smashing his fragile control. 'Promise me. It will break his heart to learn of my death, but the truth would destroy him. I do not deserve such consideration, but for the love you bear my brother, spare him this.'

Kinseris reached out to grasp his bound hands. 'You could not have stood against them, you would only have died. This is not your fault.'

'And neither is it yours.' Iarwin withdrew his hands and made a show of testing the strength of the knots Aarin had tied around his feet. 'These will hold,' he said, under control once more. 'And you should go. Time is running out for all of us.'

SEVEN

IT TOOK TWO days to travel across the wasteland of Rybacih. They saw no more *menetas*, and Aarin tried to tell himself that it was because they could risk no more fires, not because the death the creatures had sensed had come. But as he sat in the darkness at night with the fever burning in his blood, he was not so sure. He would lie awake, his eyes straining towards the distant mountains, refusing to think of what lay behind.

On the second night after they left Iarwin, Kallis sat beside him in hostile silence, his attention focused on the broken strap of his belt. But his quiet was not the companionable silence of old. Kallis might have hated Iarwin, but he hated the manner of his death even more, and he could not accept when Aarin had done. And Aarin did not bother to explain. It would have made no difference. After all, Kallis was right.

Jeta was asleep by his side, huddled deep in her cloak for warmth. She had not questioned his decision, but it was hard on her, even so. She had disliked Iarwin, but now he would die to protect them, and so she grieved for him. Kinseris had taken it the hardest, as Aarin knew he would, and no words could ever ease the pain the priest felt for allowing a friend to fall into such danger on his behalf. But he, of all of them, placed no blame on Aarin's shoulders for this tragedy. He claimed all that for himself.

Abruptly Kallis stopped playing with the strip of leather. 'Iarwin did not deserve this, no matter what his crime. *We had no right.*'

The accusation hurt. 'Is that what you think this was? You think that I judged and condemned him and left him to die as a punishment?'

Kallis did not flinch before his outraged hurt. 'Didn't you?'

'No! Who am I to judge him? Wasn't I the one who promised Shrogar his city would stand if he let me go? Iarwin is no more to blame for Ephenor's fate than I am.'

'Then why?' Kallis demanded. 'What is he to blame for?'

Aarin looked away. 'Nothing.' The truth of that was what hurt so much. If he had not submitted, the Arkni would simply have killed him, and all to protect someone he had never met and who was nothing to him. Would he not have done the same? Wouldn't any of them?

'It is not what he did. It is what he *is*. What they made him.'

'And what is that?' The anger was still there, boiling away, tearing apart the bonds of friendship.

Aarin shrugged, desolate. 'Their threads were all through him, winding around his being, twisting it. He was their creature. They took him for their own uses, used him to watch us, to listen to us. They left him enough self-awareness to know what he did, but not enough to resist it. Letting you catch him was all he could do, and even then we had to drag it from him.'

Kallis would not be convinced. 'Then why couldn't you free him? You freed yourselves in Kas'Tella. Why could you not do the same for him?'

'Because it's not the same.'

'Why not? Because it was him?'

Too weary, too conflicted, Aarin did not have the energy to face down that accusation. 'I could not save Iarwin, Kallis, because he did not want to be saved. If I had simply torn the bindings apart, I have no idea what it would have done to him. Probably he would have died.'

'Which he will anyway,' Kallis pointed out, remorseless. 'Maybe that would have been better.'

'Could you really have done that, Kallis?' Aarin asked. 'Or are you angry because you know you could not? It is the Arkni who destroyed Iarwin, the Arkni who will destroy Ephenor. We can take on the guilt of that until it kills us, and then they will have won.'

'How very convenient for you,' Kallis retorted, pushing himself to his feet. 'I'm glad to see your conscience is clear. It's not so easy for the rest of us.'

Aarin watched him stalk away, back stiff with anger, and bitterly regretted a friendship lost.

'Let him go,' Jeta said softly. 'He needs time.'

Aarin had not realised she was awake but was suddenly glad. After Kallis's scalding hostility, he needed the understanding only she could give him. He had protested his innocence to Kallis, but he did not really believe it. He needed to be with someone who did.

As if she knew that, Jeta uncurled from her cloak and crossed to him, holding out her hand. He took it and was pulled to his feet, following in silence as she led him away from the others until they stood alone in the fall of the moonlight.

She took his face in her hands. 'Let Iarwin go, Aarin. He is what the Arkni made him, and it is the Arkni who have killed him. Not you.'

Aarin closed his eyes, drawing her to him, his fingers entwining themselves in her short curls. 'I could have given him a kinder death.'

'And taken that decision from him? Only Iarwin could make that choice, and he did not. He will die the death of his choosing. How many of us will be able to say the same?'

'That doesn't make this right.'

'Oh, Aarin,' she whispered. 'Nothing about this is right, but if you give in now you will never make it right. And I will not lose you that way.'

His breath hitched in his throat as he tightened his grip on her. 'You won't lose me,' he promised. 'No matter what happens, I will never let you from my side again, nor leave yours.'

Jeta pulled away from him. 'Don't make me promises you can't keep. I know what we are going to.'

'Then you know that should I fail, the most I promise is that we will die together.'

'And if you succeed?' she asked. 'It is not your failure I fear.'

He read her thoughts as though she had spoken them aloud and had no words to offer that would not have been a lie. She needed no one else in the world but him, but he had always belonged to another, and it was to that other they journeyed now. If he succeeded, he would never again be able to offer her his whole self.

He pulled her to him impulsively and saw his own desire reflected in her eyes. If he succeeded, everything would change, but tonight was theirs.

Jeta smiled as she stepped back out of his embrace. Her skin glowed white in the starlight as her robe slipped from her shoulders. Her eyes never left his as she unfastened the ties at her back and let the tunic fall to her bare feet. As she stepped out of it, he took her in his arms, running a hand up her back and into her hair, burying his face in her curls. Her head tipped up, her lips seeking his, and everything else was forgotten.

EIGHT

THE DESERT WAS behind them at last. Shrogar's tunnel had spilled them out at its very edge onto the huge expanse of the great plains. Cutting across these like the lash of whip were the Heth'anian Mountains. And it was to the mountains they headed now, to the first among them, the tallest and the oldest, following Aarin's lead. He needed no map to guide him now. He knew where he was going as if he had walked the route a thousand times.

This was the heartland, the first place, and it was dying. Here, in the most sacred of lands, lay the centre of the elemental imbalance that was crippling Andeira. That the waters of the world were rising he had known for many years. He had spent hours listening to the tales of sailors and rivermen about the high seas and unpredictable floods. The Istelan itself, the great river of Amadorn's northern kingdoms, had burst its banks with the thaw each spring for a hundred years and more, and the Sunken Isle off the coast of Luen had once been the Eastern Isle, before the sea claimed it for its own. But he had never imagined this.

Water was the dominant element at work in the world but in this ancient haunt of dragons there was none. Parched streambeds threaded their way through the valleys, the thunderous roar of waterfalls was silenced, and not a leaf of living green could they see. Dead and wasted trees twisted their branches towards the sinking sun, their ancient, blackened trunks casting eerie shadows on sun-baked boulders that rejected growing things in a land squeezed dry of the last drop of moisture. Each winter in Amadorn was colder than the last, but here it seemed it only grew hotter. Caledan's deserts were spreading, a slow death creeping across the land, and it all came from this place.

Tesseria. Aarin stood on the narrow mountain path and gazed out at the land around him. Dragons had once flown across this barren wilderness. If he closed his eyes, he could see them now, wheeling in flight as they had sprawled across the walls of his home. Here their essence remained, and it called to him. The dragon-fire flared until it burned through every inch of him, heating the skin that still tingled with the afterglow of Jeta's touch. The prophecy was stirring in earnest now, and it was calling him home.

When they found the tunnel mouth, he knew they had arrived. A rockfall centuries ago had hidden the entrance but he knew it was there, just as he knew what lay beyond—the ancient home of his ancestors, and the stone that held the answers to the mysteries of the ages. Memories were stirring deep inside him, memories that did not belong to him. The destiny of all mankind was bound up in the deserted places under the mountain, and it waited for him to set it back on the right path.

He slipped through the opening, ignoring Kallis's half-hearted protest. The darkness was complete, as though the tunnel rejected the light of a sun that was destroying the land. He stood alone in an emptiness that was endless and breathed the air his ancestors had breathed. Their ghosts were all around, calling him on, almost as though he could hear their voices clamouring for release. Then a torch shattered the blackness and Kallis was beside him, holding the light aloft.

'Just another bloody tunnel,' he muttered, walking forward to throw the torchlight on the soaring walls.

Just another tunnel it was not. This was the way the dragons had entered the home of their mages. At least ten times as high as a man and almost as wide, the stone was worn to a smooth polish by centuries of use. The paved floor bore the same swirling pattern that had led them from Ephenor, and it was pitted with the marks of huge talons.

The fire flared, unbearable, and he staggered, catching himself on the smooth walls. His vision tunnelled to grey as the urgency of the prophecy's call became too much to endure.

Firm hands closed on his shoulders. 'Aarin?'

It was Kallis.

He tensed, fearing another barrage of hostility, but the mercenary's touch was gentle, his tone concerned. If he had not laid aside his anger over Iarwin, he had not let it erase their friendship entirely.

Aarin gathered himself with an effort. 'We're running out of time,' he said truthfully. 'I cannot stand this much longer.'

Kallis eyed him uncertainly. It was clear he did not understand.

'Get the others,' Aarin murmured, forestalling further questions. 'We must hurry.' Even if the Arkni did not catch them, their time here was finite. If he did not do this soon, the magic would tear him apart from the inside out.

The mercenary nodded, disappearing with the torch to guide Jeta and Kinseris through the narrow opening. As he was plunged once more into darkness, Aarin allowed himself to fall into a trance, to savour this chance to let his awareness range unfettered through the home of his ancestors. They had entered a place of utter stillness, not the stillness of death but of the total absence of life. The hidden city remained as it had been the day it had fallen, the homes of men and women long dead untouched by the passage of time. And it was waiting, expectant, for its lost people to return.

As his awareness roamed through the passageways, through the empty homes, Aarin felt a deep awe for the people the ancients had been. They had carved their city out of the living rock of the mountains and yet it seemed to him that the mountain had always been this way; instead of cutting into it, they had somehow reshaped it to their needs.

He could scarcely imagine the power it must have taken to achieve such a feat, and he was given little time to marvel at it. Distant voices intruded on his trance and he reluctantly returned to himself. All three of his companions were gathered round him, watching him anxiously.

Aarin turned from their scrutiny. Their worry only added to his own. 'This way,' he said, gesturing to the tunnel. It would lead them to a vast chamber, the chamber that had once held men and dragons, united in harmony.

He took another torch from Kinseris, lighting it from the one Kallis held. It never crossed his mind to try to conjure light. The air contained not a drop of moisture he could coax to spread the light of the torch around them.

As the second torch flared, Kinseris sucked in a breath. 'Blessed Maker,' he murmured. 'What is this place?'

Aarin shook his head, walking after Kallis as he disappeared down the passage. He had no words to explain all this place was.

The air grew cooler and musty as they drew further from the entrance, and as the walls fell away and the shadows deepened, he realised they had entered the cavern. Jeta slowed her step so she walked at his side, looking about her with trepidation, unsettled by the darkness that seemed to have no end.

A light flickered in the gloom ahead of them. 'Kallis?' he called, unable to see the mercenary.

The torch stopped and began moving back towards them. 'We should stay together,' he cautioned. 'We could lose each other too easily in this place.'

'There's something up ahead,' Kallis called, waiting for them to reach him. 'A stone of some sort.'

Aarin felt his heart begin to pound. He had found what he was seeking.

Kallis held the light high, letting the dancing shadows play across the smooth lines of the stone plinth. 'Aarin, look at this.'

The mage arrived at his shoulder, peering at the design carved into the face of the stone. 'Am'ien. The rune of opening.' His fingers stretched out to trace its fine lines. *'The stone that holds the truth of the Ages.'*

Kinseris shot him a questioning look but Aarin ignored him. He was filled with a tingling anticipation that had nothing to do with what he was about to do and everything to do with what he *knew* was coming. In his own mind he had already taken the next step, and the burning in his blood urged him onwards in a storm of heated compulsion.

'Be careful,' Kallis warned, but his words came from far, far away.

Aarin settled his hand into the groves on the stone, and felt the magic sing out in response. It reached out to him, snaking itself around him and drawing him in, then suddenly he was snatched from its grasp.

Kinseris held his wrist firmly, breaking the contact. 'Do you know what you are doing?'

Aarin reeled from the shock of the separation and vainly tried to pull his hand free. Speech was beyond him. All he knew was the desire to surrender to the magic of the stone.

'Aarin,' the priest demanded, insistent.

Then Kallis was pulling Kinseris away. He looked deep into Aarin's blurred gaze. 'You cannot stop him. He's dying anyway.'

So, he had understood. Darred's long-ago words swam in his mind. The prophecy demanded its fulfilment. If he failed, he *would* be consumed. But it would not be the prophecy that consumed him. It would be the Arkni, and after him they would go on to consume every living thing on Andeira until his world was a dying husk. The Arkni's victory would be his death.

It was that truth Kallis had seen in his eyes. With an effort he looked beyond the mercenary and saw Jeta watching him. The smile she gave him was shadowed by sadness, but the memory of their night together was etched in her blue gaze. Though she lost him now, a part of him she had forever, and with that smile she silently released him.

His gaze clouding with tears, Aarin turned back to the pedestal. He laid his hand over the carved sigil, feeling the lines with every nerve in his palm. 'Ami'en.'

And a new world opened to him and welcomed him home.

To those watching nothing seemed to happen. Aarin stood there, still as the rock he touched, and there was nothing in the cavern but silence. Then a burst of light exploded from the stone to light the vast cavern in an eerie glow. With a small sigh, Aarin crumpled to the floor.

For a moment no one moved, then Kallis pushed his way forward and knelt by his side. He eased the mage's head from its awkward slant on the cold stone and rested a hand against his throat. Aarin's pulse was slow and steady, his breathing even, and the mercenary rocked back on his heels, confused. At length he looked up at Kinseris who was hovering just paces behind him. 'What's happened to him?'

The priest shook his head, crouching beside Kallis. He studied Aarin's face, and the limbs that hung loose and easy, and frowned. 'This is no trance. He seems to be sleeping, but I doubt we could wake him, nor do I think we should try. Whatever magic this is we should not interfere.'

The men turned as a shadow fell across them. Jeta stood above them looking down, her expression grim. Thinking to reassure her, Kallis climbed to his feet and saw what she had seen when the light poured forth from the stone.

'Well, that's just perfect,' Kallis muttered as he positioned his body between Aarin and the entrance to the hall. He felt Kinseris stand beside him, both of them shielding the mage from the shadows that had begun to creep in through the tunnel, spreading out around the edges of the rock chamber. Their forms were indistinct, but their menace was not.

'What do we do?'

'Nothing,' said Kinseris wearily. 'We have no power to match theirs.'

'They won't take us without a fight,' Kallis growled, flexing his fingers around the hilt of his sword. 'If steel bites them, we still have a chance.'

Kinseris dug his fingers into his arm. 'Make no move,' he insisted. 'Do not provoke a fight we cannot win. We must protect Aarin. Only he has any chance against these creatures, and he is helpless for the moment. Remember, their ambitions can only be achieved through him; they will wait until he has acted before they do the same.'

'Stalemate,' Jeta said grimly.

'For now,' Kinseris agreed. 'All we can do is wait.'

NINE

AS AARIN'S VOICE activated the rune, a sensation of warmth spread
through his hand and into his body. A blinding light seared through his head,
distorting his vision and upending his senses. He felt his body falling to the
floor, but the anticipated impact never came. Instead he was lifted up,
supported by a cradle of magic that defied the total sum of his knowledge.
Threads of power insinuated their way into him, wrapping themselves round
the core of his being and unlocking the deepest secrets of his race.

In an instant, his mind was enabled to handle a flow of power previously
unimaginable. He was merely the vessel, the means by which the long-
prophesised counter spell was spilled into the world, and yet he was given no
chance to assimilate the fact that, had he not been who he was, the magic
would have faltered and failed. And he would be dead, for the magnitude of
the raw energies would have immolated any other mortal creature that
stumbled upon them unprepared.

He was floating. All around there was an emptiness that both terrified and
excited him for he knew it would soon be filled. The burst of creation that
exploded into the scene was no less magnificent for the fact it was anticipated.
The vision unfolding at lightning speed before his mind's eye was the creation
of Andeira, and he was overcome with wonder as he watched the birth of the
first dragon. Thord. The name rang out in his head, and with the name came
knowledge. This, the oldest and wisest of the dragons, the first of their kind,
was the one who had brought the races together in the Joining. This great
creature of blistering fire and dazzling scales had brought elemental harmony
to creation and ensured a future for his kind. But he had not done it alone.

Aarin watched as mankind was born, and cried and laughed, loved and
hated with them as they evolved to fill their place in the world. It was a long
road, but eventually one among them had the wisdom and insight to step
away from her fellows. Sorlanna. Another name, another pattern of

knowledge. This time a young woman had the clarity of thought to rise above the fears that had held her people in thrall and envision a brighter future, a future in which her people no longer had to stand alone against the world. And she found a mate for her desires. She found Thord, old now but wise beyond measure, and together they enacted the magic that lay dormant within them all. The magic of the Joining.

Aarin watched them, feeling like his heart would break. He saw the unparalleled perfection that resulted from their selfless act. He rejoiced in the companionship, the complete understanding between them and the others that followed. Just as the First Age had passed into the Second in the space of a heartbeat, he was thrust headlong into the fever pitch living of the Golden Age. The thread of peace was marred by infrequent conflict, but nothing could prepare him for the explosion of violence that broke that utopian existence. He was picked up by it and flung forwards on the wave of its dark power, and though he tried to steady himself there was nothing to cling to that could save him, that could save any of them. They were doomed. And he would have screamed with them if he had known how.

Yet as he watched, Aarin realised this was not a wholly objective viewing. Someone, something, controlled the scenes, sorting through the combined memories of the races, and in doing so shared part of themselves with him. Occasionally, fleetingly, he felt that he caught a sight of his guide, but always the glimpses were ephemeral, and half-felt impressions turned to dust before his scrutiny. Yet for all that, Aarin knew him. He could not help but know the heart of the creature that rode this sequence with him, just as his guide must know him. He felt naked, stripped to his soul as he, in turn, stripped the other. And in this other he found something unexpected, something that crystallised the half-spun thoughts he had been harbouring, something he was sure he was never meant to know, and almost wished he never had.

The images slowed. With vivid clarity he saw himself in this same hall, thousands of years ago, surrounded by men and women long dead and forgotten, who met to decide the fate of the world. He was with them and he was apart from them, a splinter out of time that nonetheless belonged. The council meeting unfolded as he watched, and he learned the dark secret of his people, the Great Ambition that would and had destroyed them. The sequence spun onwards. He watched Lorrimer reveal the futures of the world to Riah, felt her reach the decision that saved her people, without which he would never have been born, without which she would have left that dark night and died with the rest of the patrol in the firestorm.

Then the vision slipped into real time and he was no longer caught in flashback. He had been spun out into the actual events themselves, forced to watch as the old man and his dragon sliced through the bindings of magic that linked their beings to one another. He felt his feet touch something solid and stumbled to his knees. The rock under his hand was rough and cold and the harsh surface cut his palms, drawing blood. He stared at the lacerations, stunned and amazed, and raised his head.

The old mage stood within a five-sided figure drawn across the whole space of the floor, with his eyes closed tight. Inside the markings was a dragon. It was enormous, its long, sinuous body visible for a moment before the great wings curved down. Its scales shone silver and reflected the light from the candles in a blinding, dazzling array of colours. Awesome, mysterious, heartbreaking, and known to him on so many different levels.

Aarin could not move. He could only stare as the great dragon turned its head and met his gaze. Huge liquid eyes shone with recognition and welcome. If the old man was aware of him, he did not show it.

Watch, Æisoul, a voice spoke inside his head. *Learn now the price of our ambition that you may never again yearn to violate the Elemental Law for the forbidden graces.*

Then the dragon turned its head away and he was no longer a part of the scene, merely an observer.

Lorrimer opened his eyes as he felt Silverwing move. Tears misted his vision and he neither saw nor felt the presence that invaded the moment, and Silverwing did not tell him. His role would end here; the future was no longer his concern. The dragons had been bequeathed the task of ensuring the survival of the races. Now Silverwing had seen the man they would shape their spells to call. That those spells had yet to be made did not signify, for dragons understood the vagaries of time better than any.

He felt Lorrimer's eyes on him, and turned his attention to his mage, so old and frail now that the end of his life was upon him. Shielding the intruder from his mind, Silverwing stretched himself out to the old man and experienced a strange sense of divided loyalties. If all went well, the one who watched from the shadows would be his next rider, and Silverwing yearned to reach out and know him. But it was not time yet, and more than just years stood between them.

A tremor ran through the rock as distant thunder beat against them, even here. Outside this sanctuary a battle raged, and Silverwing's questing awareness tagged his brothers and sisters as they flew to meet the minions of Aarkan, come at last to the stronghold of their enemy.

A flicker of air, stiffened at will, caught Lorrimer as he stumbled. He laid his hands on his dragon's head and surrendered to the sorrow that lay just beneath the surface. Silverwing's heart cried out in answer and the other was forgotten. For now until his death, this man was his, and his care for him could not be put aside so easily.

'It is so hard, dear friend,' the old man mumbled, unable to ignore the conflict beyond the walls of the chamber, or the surge of panic that had gripped his people. 'To inflict such devastation, and all so another generation can live free. How can I do this to them?'

Because you have no other choice. Silverwing knew that his words were not as important as the understanding he offered. Lorrimer was well aware of the necessity of what he did, but he needed an outlet for the guilt that was killing him. *And they chose with you, never forget that.*

'In the council yes, but later Kasandar came to me. He came to plead with me not to do it. After the council had voted, after *he* had voted. Do you know what he said to me?'

His tone was that of an old man outraged by fickle youth, and Silverwing felt a moment of great fondness. He knew what Kasandar had said; he had heard every word. It had been many days since they had let go of their link, even for a second. Time was too precious, and their enemy was closing in.

'He told me I was punishing my own race for the crimes of another. He blames you, Silverwing. He blames the dragons, and says we could not have conceived of such an ambition as this without you. Has he no eyes? Can't he see the ambition that burns in each of us? I tell you, if not this then something else would have eventually come between us. We are not worthy of your wisdom, First Born, we cannot match it.'

Silverwing heard the shame in his mage's words, and he felt it too when his thoughts turned to those of his kind who had turned away from the true path. Both races had those who were worthy and those who were not, and Lorrimer had guessed only part of the truth. They could never risk a return to the way things were that had led to this day. Neither human nor dragon would ever again be indiscriminately offered the chance to Join together. That time was passing and would never return. The future would be different. The future would be lonely.

What had Kasandar to offer instead?

The old man laughed. 'It is ridiculous. We have no time for that now.'

We have time for laughter. You and I will never laugh together again. Do not deny us this last opportunity.

Lorrimer stopped and stared. 'You have a point, but you make it in such a way that I no longer feel like laughing.' He shook his head, smiling fondly. 'Very well, Kasandar suggested that we hold back some of your power, steal it, before it is too late. Too late! He wants to transfer the powers of your race into an effigy that can be tapped at will, as though anything we might make could contain the grandeur of your spirit. He says that he wishes this only for the benefit of Andeira, but I know him better. He wishes it only for himself, and he has the audacity to tell me the dragons are at fault for the Great Ambition. And no, I will not tell you what I said, for I know you heard that, and such words spoken once in a day are once too often.'

And you would tell me that men are not worthy of us. The world will be the poorer for your passing. My world will be the poorer.

A single tear slid down Lorrimer's face and dropped onto Silverwing's scales. He wiped the wetness away, fingers lingering on the silver hide. 'How long before you can bear that again, old friend?' he wondered sadly, his tears not for himself but for his dragon. 'How long will you have to wait for another to hold your heart in his as I have?'

Too long, and not long enough. Though my being will yearn for union, my heart will always call to you before any other. It is both a gift and a burden that you give me when you set me free for the future. I will not fail you, for in doing this I honour you, and hope that one day a part of you returns to me.

Lorrimer understood and was comforted. 'No more farewells. I cannot bear them. Midnight is almost on us, and we must begin.'

And outside, where magic flared like lightning in the storm, the dragons' valiant defiance was running swiftly to its end. If they did not act now, Aarkan and his followers might yet destroy them all.

Silverwing bowed his great head, pushing all other thoughts from his mind. He felt Lorrimer do the same, calming the tremors of dissent that he could never quite banish, and stamping down on his instinct for self-preservation. But his mage did not hesitate. Silverwing felt him go straight for the knot of power that held them together, and for a frantic second opposition pulsed unbidden in his heart. It flared once, then was gone. They were committed now.

In his mind, Silverwing saw Lorrimer turn and look at him, a small figure disappearing on a journey from which he would not return. The old mage gazed at him fondly then faced the path once more and began to walk the long road to the Severing. Silverwing watched his spirit go, sent his awareness roving after him, and saw Lorrimer stop by the glowing construct, the spinning elemental orb that was the embodiment of the Joining. For a long moment he stood there, studying the twists and turns of power that so perfectly matched the two together. Inside each of them such a net existed, but here was the master spell, the one from which all the others had come, the knot of Thord and Sorlanna, hidden just beyond the veils of spirit.

Lorrimer acted, plunging his hand into the centre of the pulsing spell, his back arching in agony as the power swept through him. Silverwing felt his heart falter and recover as the pain shocked him, but the old man held onto his life with a discipline that was staggering and closed his hand around the central cord.

Silverwing felt each movement of Lorrimer's like a great tear deep inside. The pain ripped him again and again and still it did not stop, and then the outer barrier fell away as the whole construct collapsed in on itself. Lorrimer sought out his gaze one last time, but as his eyes strained to see they misted and darkened, and his soul departed. Silverwing howled in agony, his mind scrambling to hold onto the image, but with the passing of the mage who controlled the sequence, the vision faded, and he was once more in his own body in the council chamber.

Lorrimer lay on the floor, no more than a collection of bones in white rags, the companion of his heart and mind for eight hundred years. Life and spirit were gone, the link was broken, and not just in him. The Joining had been severed, the last traces of it draining out of him with his strength, and all around him he could feel the vibration of horror that ran through the earth, the debilitating backlash that swept through the substance of Andeira and her children, striking them down in swathes. The world seemed to dim. Before his senses spiralled into darkness, Silverwing heard a voice screaming in shared agony, crying out in horrified disbelief.

'Mercy! We did it to ourselves!'

And then the prophecy found him and sprang into being.

TEN

AARIN WAS ON his hands and knees, shaking, retching. *Mercy! We did it to ourselves!*

He had not understood. He had watched the images come and go, he had seen the evil that threatened his people, and he had seen as they planned their course, but the reality of what they planned was too final, too awful for him to comprehend, until he saw Lorrimer begin his spirit walk. He had followed, tagging along on the reflection of the dragon's presence, and he had recognised the glowing spell. What he had thought of as illusion was revealed for what it truly was, and he knew now why he had suffered so harshly in the Vale. When he saw it, he understood, but he was not a part of this time and he could not interfere.

The bodies in front of him were already fading. The spell was moving him on, tearing him away from that haunting place, and he let it take him. Time once again became meaningless as the ages spun onwards. Images flashed before him, but he was too numb to take them in, and they made no more than brief impressions on his mind. Then they stopped.

Once more he was in the great cavern, the Hall of the Five. He knew it now—the place of the Severing.

Slowly he became aware that he was not alone. He was standing before the stone pedestal. On either side stood Kallis and Kinseris, and Jeta was behind him. He knew she was there without turning his head. He tried to speak to them, but they did not answer, did not move. They could not hear him. He was with them and he was not, separated by the magic from their sphere of existence. He studied their faces. Their attention was fixed on something behind him, and he turned to see what it was.

His heart turned to ice. The edges of the cavern were hidden in black shadows, only they weren't shadows, they were figures. Dark twisted figures shrouded in midnight black that faded into nothingness in the dim light of the chamber. They were the Arkni and they had come for him. They had come for the power only he could give them, and they would take it and use it to destroy the world.

Aarin turned back to the stone, his fingers cramped in a death grip on the pedestal, trying to keep himself upright. *Help me!*

His knees gave way, forcing him to the floor, his arms embracing cold granite. He laid his head on the stone. *Help me!*

Desperate hands sought the surface of the tablet and the rune carved there. He placed his right hand flat on the engraved surface. *Help me!*

A presence brushed against him and the darkness retreated. The cavern had gone, vanished as though it had never been, and in its place was bright sunlight shining on green, rolling lands. And before him, perched on the mountainside, was the great silver dragon from his visions, older now, his scales less burnished, his aura less scintillating, yet still magnificent.

The dragon lowered his gaze so that his eyes looked into Aarin's. A glimmer of triumph flashed through them for an instant, lighting them with a fire that was bright and desperate. The recognition was immediate and endless.

'I know you,' Aarin whispered. 'You were there.' Three thousand years had passed, hundreds of generations of men had lived and died, and yet he knew him. Before the dragon's awesome, timeless majesty, his life was little more than a heartbeat.

The dragon bowed his great head in greeting. *I am Silverwing. And you are Æisoul, the man who rode the Severing by my side.*

Aarin could not speak. The moment was still too close, and the sorrow of it shone from the dragon's liquid eyes, drenching him in memories so achingly bitter.

'Where have you been?' he asked, the words torn from him as he felt all those long years of separation march across his soul. 'We needed you.'

Silverwing looked at him sadly. *We have been dreaming, Æisoul. You stand now in the dreams of dragons, in an age that has never known the footsteps of man.*

Aarin looked around him at a landscape unchanged since the dawn of time and knew the dragon spoke the truth. This world in which he stood was

Andeira as she had been in the First Age, as she had been before mankind came into existence and changed her forever. Before the union between the races had perfected and completed her and made her both weaker and stronger for it.

This is still your world, but the time is mine, as this dream is mine. While the magic remains broken, I cannot enter your time, nor you mine. We are in the Long Dream, but it is no longer the haven it once was.

The dragon raised his head, looking beyond Aarin, and as the mage turned, he saw through the glimmers of time to the place he had left behind, the place where the Arkni waited.

You have brought your shadows with you.

'Forgive me,' Aarin murmured. 'I did not know what else to do.'

Silverwing's molten eyes were boring into him. Aarin stood there, raked by the dragon's gaze, and felt his inner self rise up in answer. For a moment that seemed to last a lifetime, they silently measured each other, and found an understanding that went deep into their very souls.

You have called, and I have come, the dragon replied simply. *Three thousand years is a long time to be alone, and your call I could never refuse. You did only as you had to do. As I have. We also have our shadows, Æisoul.*

And Aarin saw the snaking, twisting slivers of darkness that writhed just beyond the dragon's silver glow.

Fear tightened his chest. 'What are they?'

That part of our enemy that remained with us when they should have died. The other halves of the followers of Aarkan and Srenegar, the pairing that birthed the ambition that broke the Second Age.

'They are dragons?'

He saw a flash of anger in Silverwing's calm gaze. *Are the Arkni men? No, Æisoul, they are not dragons. They are beings without life.*

But even as the dragon looked at them, his manner softened, turning from anger to pity. *They are with us and apart from us, and we cannot reach them, though we have tried. What the Joining gave, the Severing stole, and the terrible magic they raised has already begun the decay. They are pitiful, and though they do not bother us they are the nightmare that disturbs our dream.*

Aarin stared transfixed by the writhing shadows. These half-things were what the Arkni were seeking. They had looked within that secret well and seen the power that resided at the heart of the Maker, and they had hurled themselves at it, opened themselves to its dark promise, and his ancestors had destroyed the magic to stop them. And now he must stand in the breach and hold them back. While the magic remained broken, they could not return to what they were, to what they were becoming, but the demands of the prophecy could not be reasoned with. He was here for one reason only—to reopen that door.

'What went wrong?' he asked miserably. 'Why did the Severing not destroy them?'

Silverwing's gaze strayed to the Arkni and back again. *Because there is something in your world that should never have been there, something that bridged the gap between our races when all connections should have ended. This we did not foresee, that some small part of ourselves would cross over in the moment of the Severing and save our enemies from destruction. Such a loss as we asked of our people could not be borne by all, we knew that, but we did not expect such subtle resistance. Some of our number tried to give to each other a part of themselves that would endure after the end, but the legacy of that gift was our enemies' survival and the enslavement of many souls.*

Aarin followed his gaze and once more saw a glimpse of the time he had left behind, a glimpse that showed him the friends whose love and loyalty had brought them here, with him, for this climax. He saw Kinseris standing by the pedestal, unmoving, frozen in a moment of time, and the flash of silver on his breast sent a shaft of sharp pain through him.

Yes, the priest bears one such gift, his people the others, and the dragons from whom they were given are now chained to them, a resource to be tapped at will by men who have no understanding of what they do.

A memory ripped through Aarin's awareness, the sound of a creature's agony, caught in the tendrils of Darred's spell. 'Eiador.'

The dragon's dark eyes glittered. *He is one, close to his end now. I have watched his body writhe in the grip of nightmares that keep him apart from us, even here. He too is trapped in the half-place between our worlds, but he is tied to the one who holds his essence captive. Unless he is freed, he will linger long in his dying.*

'The Arkni gave those devices to the priesthood,' Aarin said in defence of Kinseris who had not known the terrible harm he had caused. 'They gave them the power they could not wield so that they could survive. But why?' He looked up. 'Why could they not wield it?'

Silverwing glanced behind as the slivers of darkness danced closer. *Our enemies could not use these things, Æisoul, for they are already bound in union and their dragon selves still live. To make use of the powers stored within the devices, the Arkni had to give them into human hands and feed off their use of the magic. That is why we failed. What the Severing should have destroyed, our own people allowed to survive. Through their ignorance and their desperation, they created a channel through which the spirits of our enemies could seep back into your world. While access to all the elements of creation remained in one place, the Arkni could cling to life and wait for the fulfilment of the prophecy that would one day bring our two races together again.*

A shudder ran through the dragon, his great folded wings trembling for an instant, and Aarin sensed the revulsion that filled him.

Even in their shadows something has been stirring these last years. When the prophecy came alive in you, our worlds began to draw closer, and they are drawing some power, some life, from that closeness. With your birth the magic began to trickle back into the world, as it had to if you were ever to find us. Never believe that you are not as you are meant to be, Æisoul, Silverwing said gently, and as Aarin looked up he saw understanding that made him want to weep. *The prophecy was framed around a living man, though your birth was thousands of years in the future, and it was into that image of a living man that some of me bled. The fire that has always been within you is my fire, and three times you have come so close to touching me that I thought you must already be here. And three times I looked behind me at the shadows at my back and saw them drawing closer. There was never a way to escape this day, Æisoul, and though I have long dreaded it, I welcome it now.*

And Aarin felt the full weight of the loneliness the dragon had endured, so many thousands of years alone, waiting for the day the man he had glimpsed would return to him and make him whole once more. It was a tragedy he could barely comprehend that the price should be so bitter.

'Forgive me,' he said again.

For what do you ask forgiveness? You could not stop this.

Aarin drew in a shuddering breath. He forced himself to look into the dragon's eyes. 'I know no other way. I have come to do as they have done.'

The silence yawned deep. This was the desperate plan he had made in the darkness of the night when Saal'an's forces had surrounded Ephenor, when he had known there was no escape. They had reached the crisis with an enemy at their back. If he healed the world now it would be to let the Arkni destroy it.

Slowly, so slowly, the dragon shook his head, as Aarin had known he would.

You do not know what you ask, Æisoul.

Silverwing had lived through the Great Ambition. He had seen what it had done to his kind. To follow in those dark footsteps was something the dragon would never willingly do. And yet he hesitated, as if he knew the finality of that choice made a certainty of their failure.

I know what you are thinking, but it cannot be done this way. Even if we survived, we would be unable to undo what we had done. Their evil would be replaced with our own.

But Aarin was committed now. No matter how much he might wish an alternative, how desperately he might search for one, the sheer power of his enemy demanded that they do this. 'I know I am asking the only one who knows how this can be done. I know you, for you have shown yourself to me. They were your memories locked inside the stone, your knowledge. You know the way, I have seen it.'

I have never done this.

'But you know it can be done.'

He looked deep into Silverwing's eyes and knew he was not mistaken. But he also saw the horrors of the war that had destroyed the dragons' world and understood Silverwing's reluctance. How could he not?

We knew, Silverwing confessed at last. *But that knowledge was never meant to be shared, much less used. It is not meant for us, and for those who would try, it would end only as with Aarkan.*

Silverwing turned his head away, staring back into the past. *When Lorrimer came into my keeping we were both so young. The Joining was the only thing that existed for us and we followed where it went. But we were foolish and what we did was dangerous. For to follow that power to its source is to become one with Andeira once more, to return our energies to the Mother. The half-way place the Arkni seek does not exist. We cannot simply divert that power from its path and take for ourselves only as much as we desire. The Arkni go to their own destruction, just as we would. But before we get there, we will suffer the madness of all mortal creatures as what makes us separate and distinct is stripped away in the slow mingling of life as it returns to the Maker.*

We realised what was happening before it was too late. Aarkan did not. Should we go down that road now, there will come a point when we can no longer turn aside, and we will become as they are, drifting in madness towards our deaths.

Aarin listened and understood the truth in Silverwing's words. That place he had sensed inside himself as he hung between life and death in Redstone— that was what the dragon spoke of. That treacherous beauty, that seductive power, was the core of Andeira that burned in every living thing, and it was the place Aarkan had glimpsed. He remembered his own near passage to that place, and he heard and understood Silverwing's warning. The river of power led only to death. But what were their deaths when set against a world? What were their deaths if they meant the Arkni's also?

'Even so,' he said slowly, 'we have to try.' He would force this choice if he had to, for he *was* the prophecy, and this was his time. But he knew also that only complete acceptance could carry them far enough to do what they had to do. 'When we remake the Joining, the magic will flow back into the world, back into *them*. Even Joined as we will be, we will not have the power to face them and win. Only by doing as they did, by taking their power for our own, can we hope to defeat them.'

You have seen what we were driven to, Silverwing reminded him. *You were present at the Severing. We gave up everything to stop them once. And now you would have us do the very thing that so many of our peoples died to prevent. How can we succeed where all others have failed?*

How indeed? It was the question he had asked himself, over and over, since the moment he had realised what they had done, since the moment he had realised that the only way to fight such power was to become it and then destroy it. If they did this thing, if they became that which their enemy aspired to be, they would, for the briefest of instants, have power over creation itself. That power would devour them, just as Silverwing predicted, only if, in the moment they acquired it, they forgot the reason they sought it. Seeking that power and desiring it would never be enough; the river of power would wash them away. And so the Arkni were ever doomed to fail. But if they could hang on to their purpose, if they could ride that wave and stay afloat, they could use the power of creation to dam the river just long enough to let the Arkni break themselves apart against it.

But in the end, they would do it because they had to, because there truly was no other choice. To simply heal the Joining would be to hand Andeira over to their enemies and they could never allow that. Better to risk it all to win it all than just give it up.

And Silverwing, for all he feared this choice, understood that.

You ask something of me, Æisoul, that I fear and long for beyond anything. I have tasted a fraction of the power they wish to take, and I gave it up once. I do not know if I can do it again.

'But you will,' Aarin replied with a smile. 'Because you have also seen what lies at the end of that road. And you love this world too much.'

And you, Æisoul? Do you love Andeira enough? Could you do as Lorrimer did if this proves to be a mistake? Could you end it forever if we succumb to the darkness inside us?

Aarin understood the choice the dragon offered him: swear to end the magic once and for all if they did not succeed, or walk away now, before they even had a chance to heal the broken pieces of the spell. If he did not swear to sacrifice both of them if they failed, the dragon would never give him the chance to try, and he had to have that chance. But could he do what Lorrimer had done? Could anyone abandon that much power?

'I love this world too much not to try,' he said at last. 'And if we fail, I think the end will come whether we wish it or not.'

Silverwing's silver scales flashed as he bowed his head. *Then you do what Lorrimer could not, and I will do it with you, because I chose you, and if this is your choice, it is mine also.*

ELEVEN

A FIGURE STEPPED from the blackness of the shadows. The creature threw back his hood, red eyes blazing hungrily at them, and Kinseris shuddered, engulfed by a deep, formless fear. The thing that stood before him had no weight, no substance. Beneath the robes that gave it a semblance of human form there was only shadow.

Saal'an raised his arms, holding them out before him in grasping need. 'Give him to me.'

The words reverberated around the cavern and for a long moment they could not speak, then Kallis pushed his way forward, his bow in his hands, the arrow pointed straight at Saal'an's breast.

'If you want him, you will have to take him.'

The Arkni laughed. 'You think your weapons can hurt me?' As he spoke the arrow burst into flames that crackled along its length and fired the bow in Kallis's hands. He dropped it with a cry of pain, nursing burnt fingers. But he did not back down, reaching for his sword.

'We will never give him to you. If you try to take him, you will die.'

'Brave words,' Saal'an sneered. 'Your weapons are useless against us. Arrows cannot hurt us, steel cannot touch us.'

'Then why do you hesitate?' Kinseris demanded. 'What are you waiting for?'

'Not for fear of you, *priest*. We have dealt with the rest of your kind. Kas'Tella and Ephenor are destroyed. You are all that is left.' Saal'an held out a hand, beckoning, mocking him. 'You are the last,' he repeated. 'Do you wish the chance to die as they did?'

As Kinseris started forward, Kallis grabbed him by the arm. 'He will kill you.'

But Kinseris threw off his arm. 'I have to do this. He has destroyed my people, killed my friends. I owe them this.'

'You don't owe them your death!'

The priest stared at him bleakly. 'What else do I have left?' And he walked forward in answer to the creature's challenge.

Kallis turned to glance at Aarin and swore softly. The mage was gone.

They stood on the mountainside looking out at the world together. The shimmering mists of Silverwing's dream parted to let the words through, and Aarin felt the tug of that other-time, and the people who waited for him.

'They are coming,' he told the dragon.

They were always coming.

'What must I do?'

The dragon lowered his wings so they sloped gently down. *Fly with me.*

Aarin laid his hand on silver hide, running his fingers across burnished scales until they caught on the first ridge of the wing. He curled his fingers around it, reaching for the next, and swung himself up onto Silverwing's back, finding his seat easily in the hollow at the base of the dragon's neck. Then, with a thrust of those great wings, they left the ground far behind.

They flew higher, soaring into the endless blue, and the First Age disappeared below them. The dragons had hidden themselves in a time when the Joining did not exist to shield themselves from the pain of its loss, and now Silverwing let his dream take them onwards. As the Golden Age exploded into being around them, Aarin saw the world far below him change, and felt himself come alive with sensation.

Then they were no longer flying. They were in a time that had never been, and they were all alone, surrounded by the empty night, waiting for a dawn. He slipped from Silverwing's back and found no ground below him, and yet he did not fall.

The dragon turned to him. 'Three thousand years ago I hid the Joining where no one would ever find it. I hid it in you. Bring the magic back into the world, Æisoul.'

Aarin looked around, gazing into nothing, and knew where he was. He met Silverwing's ancient gaze and smiled. And the prophecy burst inside him.

The Fire consumed him. He opened himself to it and gave way before it.

The magic poured out of him, filling every corner of creation with its blistering light. It lifted him up, carried him away, and reshaped the world through him. The master spell reformed itself inside him. Andeira's elemental channels flowed pure and strong as they rushed towards their core, and the turn of the earth was righted on its new axis. As Earth, Air, Fire and Water became once more as they were meant to be, the soft glow of Spirit bled outwards from the centre, enveloping them in its silver light. And the sun rose on a new dawn.

In the citadel of Kas'Tella, surrounded by a small army of scribes, Darred got jerkily to his feet. His eyes glazed over, and he took a stumbling step as all around him Kas'Talani adepts stopped what they were doing and looked up. Then he was running, and all through the city and the lands beyond men and women ran to see the sky as the bright burst of magic touched them. He pushed his way through crowded corridors, running up the spiral steps to the high priest's tower, and threw himself through the door into the dawn. The silvery glow of the new age bathed the world in its light, and he gazed up at the heavens as his knees gave way and spilled him to the floor. The magic had been healed, and his eyes searched the skies above for the wings of his masters even as his heart rejoiced at the pure joy of reunion.

The crowd that packed the audience hall in Rhiannas's royal palace fell suddenly silent. Tears poured down the face of their queen as she sat there, hands gripping the arms of the throne. The magician always at her side stood as though carved from stone, and her eastern advisors were on their knees as silver light streamed through the high windows and lit the room with ribbons of bright flame. Then she stood, and the mages followed her, walking in silence between the packed ranks of petitioners out into the palace grounds. They felt the healing run through them, felt the elements come alive, and their eyes searched the skies above for the wings of dragons.

In the silver dawn, Aarin faced Silverwing across the landscape of a world made whole. The dragon's eyes blazed with fire and his scales shone bright in the new sun. He reached out, stretching through the free-flowing magic. *Come to me, Æisoul. It is time for us to Join.*

Aarin let himself go. Instantly, he was caught and borne away by the flood. He let the power burst over him, let it fill him with euphoric energy, floated on it, waiting. He felt Silverwing's presence beside him caught in a similar flood, but the dragon knew this, and Aarin felt his flawless control. Their minds met and embraced. There was none of the clashing rejection he had known before and feared. They met and melded as effortlessly as if they had always been one. The knot was formed, its interlaced glowing strands of energy sinking into their beings and binding them tight. In wonderment he felt the link form between them, felt the wild two-way flow of energy that pulsed along the connection.

They were Joined. It was done.

It was done and it was not finished. It was not enough. An enemy waited for them. And so they went further, further than was safe and further than their lives could support, and they looked on the place the Arkni had seen. They took the magic that Joined them and they used it to open the way to the river of power that would take them there. They did it because they had to, because only then would it be enough.

The earth trembled. Kinseris was shaken from his feet by the tremor that ran through the rock and stayed there on his hands and knees. Before him Saal'an was thrown back, but the Arkni did not fall. Rising up on a tide of energy, the creature crowed, a shout of triumph that stopped Kallis's heart.

The creatures were in a frenzy, feeding off the energy that crackled all around them, and they were growing, changing.

Kallis held Jeta tightly to him, her head pressed against his shoulder. If this was the end, he was determined that she would not see it, to spare her that at least, but as he watched the Arkni shimmered and changed, and in the place of their cloaked and shadowed forms he saw men and women emerging. Suspended on the magic, they threw back their hoods, revealing faces as human as his own gazing upwards in rapture. He stared in astonished fear as they came to settle once more on the ground, their forms taking on the substance they had lacked, but his eyes could not quite fix on them, his gaze always sliding past, their outlines blurred to his sight.

Slowly, his arms trembling, Kallis let go of Jeta. As she pulled away from him, the man that had been Saal'an took a step forward, a smile of triumph on his dark face. There was not a thread of grey in his black hair, nor a line on his skin, but he knew that this man, this thing, was ancient beyond his understanding.

'What are you?' he whispered, and he did not care that they would hear his fear. That these creatures, their enemies, should suddenly appear as mortal as they were made the horror of it worse.

Saal'an's arm waved in a wide arc, taking in the ranks arrayed behind him. 'We are the heirs,' he answered. 'And this is the moment we come into our inheritance.'

Kallis tore his eyes from the face that never quite came into focus and let his gaze slide over the others. There was a ghostly stillness to them, yet at Saal'an's words he had seen the hungry fire that lit their eyes. Shuddering, he felt Jeta grip his hand so hard he was sure his bones would crack, but he did not let go. He needed the comfort of touch as much as she did.

'You do not exist!' From his hands and knees, Kinseris staggered to his feet. The priest was shaking, his hands clenched tight at his sides to still their trembling. 'You cannot exist!' There was a desperate denial in his words.

'Oh, but we do,' Saal'an replied, a flicker of amusement in his dark eyes. 'We always have. It was you who kept us alive. It was your Order that nourished us and gave us the means to survive.' His eyes were like shards of ice. 'Kasandar died when the world was broken,' he told Kinseris, each word a hammer blow. 'I was the one who gave the magic into your hands.'

Kallis felt a cold dread creep over him. He needed neither priest nor mage to tell him that this being, disguised as a man, held within him more power that any living thing. Kinseris staggered back, his hands reaching for the device pinned to his tunic. He tore the tiny dragon from its clasp and threw it away as if the touch of it burned him. Then he was backing away, his feet tripping over the stone steps, and as Kallis reached out to him, the fear a living thing that leapt between them.

Saal'an's gaze followed the flash of silver as it fell. 'We have no more need of those,' he sneered. 'For the Severing is healed, and Æisoul will make the world whole once more.'

The men and women at his back moved, breaking their close-packed ranks to spread themselves out. Kallis watched, unable to move, as they ringed the pedestal.

'And he will give it to us.'

'He will give you nothing,' Kallis retorted. His words were barely more than a whisper.

'Oh, I think he will, because if he does not,'—the smile that crossed Saal'an's face seemed to suck all the warmth from the world—'you will simply die.'

And the circle closed around them.

TWELVE

CAUGHT IN THE current of his change, Aarin saw the Arkni take his friends. He felt their fear thunder against him and knew an instant of rage so powerful it almost undid him. Silverwing was in his head, a coiled bud of awareness that was one with his own, and the dragon shared his fury, awakened to kinship with the people he loved through the fiery course of their Joining.

No words were needed. As one they awoke, shrugging off the dragons' dream to break free of the half-time and re-enter the world that awaited them. The sound of their entrance was a crack to splinter rock itself, the power of their presence the light that threw back the shadows, as a dragon set foot on Andeira for the first time in three thousand years.

Their enemy stood in a knot around the Speaking Stone, their captives hemmed in between them. As Aarin slipped from Silverwing's back, one man broke the formation and came to their fore, and Aarin knew him. He knew them all.

Everything else seemed to melt away, everything but the two of them, until they were all alone, an island amidst the flood. Their arena was the most ancient of magic places, the place where it had all begun. The place where it would end. Saal'an stood before him. His hood was thrown back but his face was no longer the ravaged, inhuman features of the thing that had challenged his dreams before the walls of Ephenor, no longer the shadowy presence of a creature tied to a half-life by the limitations of the world. Here, before him now, was the man he had seen in Silverwing's visions, the man who had conceived the Great Ambition. He stood face to face with Aarkan himself.

And he knew in that moment the *menetas* had not come for Iarwin, they had come for him.

Aarkan watched him with the same hungry gaze Aarin remembered, when all else about him had changed. As he stood there, in the moment of his triumph, Aarin glimpsed the man he had been before the ambition had taken hold of his soul, and remembered his own kinship with him. Black hair framed a dark face that might once have been handsome had cruelty not sharpened its lines to a cutting edge, and his eyes were as hard and cold as night. Yet he was, and would always remain, damaged past the magic's ability to heal. The purity of the elements had given him back his life; it could not also give him back his humanity.

'So, it has come to this, Æisoul,' Aarkan said at last. 'Just as Lorrimer before you, you stand between me and my prize. But it is my blood that flows in your veins alongside his. Will you do as he did? Will you sacrifice your people on the altar of your pride, or does my blood yet sing to you? Can you look beyond the weakness of the ancients and embrace the true future of our people?'

'There will be no sacrifice,' Aarin told him grimly, awash with the magic. 'Your future will claim no more lives.'

'You reject what you do not know,' Aarkan replied, unperturbed. 'Let me show you, Æisoul. Let me show you my future. Our future.'

And the man who was no longer a man held out his hand, beckoning, and the world fell away. Aarin felt himself wrenched from his own time into another's. They stood once more atop the mountain, the world arrayed below them in all its untarnished splendour. He faced Aarkan across the landscape of an age lost to living memory.

'My world, Æisoul,' Aarkan proclaimed, and the pride in his voice was a dreadful thing. 'Yours too, should you choose it.'

Aarin shook his head. This was not real. It was illusion. 'This is not my world. This world is gone. You destroyed it.'

'I?' Aarkan quirked a dark eyebrow. 'No, it was Lorrimer who destroyed this world. But I will remake it. You and I together. We can take back what the Severing stole from us.'

'You cannot take back what is gone,' Aarin said with the wisdom of the dragon that had become a part of him. 'And though you seek creation, there is nothing of the Maker in you. You cannot rebuild, you can only destroy.'

Aarkan's smile was condescending, indulgent. 'Ah, I hear the echoes of

Lorrimer in you, Æisoul. I can never say he did not choose well. But in this, as in so much else, he was mistaken, for he did not have the courage to go where we went.' He took a step back, his eyes raking Aarin, seeing him from the inside out, seeing what he had done. 'But you have that courage, you have that strength. You have already followed in our footsteps as I knew you would, as I made you to do. *Brother.*'

There was savage joy on his face, even a terrible kind of love in the kinship he sensed. 'We have been here before, you and I,' Aarkan murmured. 'Do you remember?'

Aarin looked into eyes glazed by the glow of magic on a scale he could barely comprehend. 'I remember,' he replied, just as softly. It had been Lorrimer, not him, standing here so long ago with Aarkan. Lorrimer who had stood between Aarkan and his dream and denied him the right to take it. But the magic was blurring the lines between the past and the present, between his memories and those of a man long dead. He remembered the night they had stood here, looking out on the last days of the old world together, the night that had set the seal on their enmity. He remembered the sadness he had felt, that Lorrimer had felt, and he felt it now, as Aarkan turned to him, and Aarin knew his eyes were seeing the old man not the young one.

'You told me I did not understand what I was seeking, and you were right. I did not understand then, but I do now.'

'What do you understand?'

Aarkan's smile was slow, the rapture of delusion. 'This life I am reaching for, it is more than that.'

'And less.'

A mirthless laugh answered him. 'You have not changed, have you? Still you would have me believe that only death lies at the heart of life.' He shook his head, the smile slipping away as his face hardened. 'At the heart of life there is no death.'

At the heart of life there is no death. The words echoed through him, a parody of Lorrimer's warning so long ago.

No death. Immortality. But that was madness. Aarin could feel it, in Aarkan and in himself, a swirling pool where time had no meaning, where his memories were supplanted by another's, and it was with another's voice he spoke now, in denial of his enemy's dream. 'No, old friend. You were wrong then, and you are wrong now. At the heart of life there is only death.'

And gently, so gently, he sliced through the fading threads of Aarkan's vision, leaving the past behind, where it belonged. The future was what mattered now. Not one moment longer could he stay in that creature's dreams, gazed upon as a master looks upon his creation. Not a moment more could he allow that illusion to hold, as he lost himself in the memories of a man who had died millenia before his birth.

He was not Lorrimer, he was Aarin.

'You have something of mine, Aarkan.' If he forgot himself, he forgot the people who mattered to him, and he could not let that happen.

For a moment Aarkan did not respond, unfocused eyes seeing past him, through him, but it was a moment only and then it was gone. As the cobwebs of the past fell away, Lorrimer's ghost went with them, exposing them both to who and what they had become. The mocking half-smile returned. 'And you have something of mine. Shall we trade?'

'There will be no trade. There will be no bargaining, no more sacrifice. You will return them to me or I will take them from you.'

Anger flashed across Aarkan's face. 'You would fight one who is now your brother?' He threw his hands wide. 'For the sake of three lives you would deny us our inheritance? Can you not feel the power that is in you? Surrender to it, join us. We could rule the world together.'

Aarin's laugh was bitter. 'You will rule nothing. You will only destroy.'

But he could feel the power. He was aware of almost nothing else as they rushed towards the core of the magic. Everything Aarkan would become, that he was becoming, swamped his mind in its dreadful promise. Silverwing's coiled form was behind him, his silver flank within touching distance, and the vibrations of the immense wave of power rocked them both.

Aarkan moved closer and Aarin watched his every movement through narrowed eyes.

'Think, Æisoul,' he urged, throwing the well of his memory wide open once more and inviting Aarin to drown in it. Aarin, not Lorrimer. 'Before you attempt to banish this magic from the world, think what it will be like if you are forced to live without it. How can you go back to what you were when you have felt this? Look at this world, Æisoul. Look at it as it is now! This is what you will die for. Is it worth it?'

Aarin saw again the cliffs of his home, the winter sea pounding against their crumbling height, the tide sucking the rocks deep into the green depths. He saw the barren deserts of the southern lands, the blazing sun that robbed the earth of moisture and turned it to dust, their frontiers creeping outwards to swallow towns and cities. He saw a sky empty of dragons. It was a world in which he no longer had a place.

Then pure sweetness flooded him, carrying him away on a wave of sensation that left him breathless. Light burst over his vision, showing him a world alive with the Maker's power, a world Aarkan believed it was his right to claim, a world he believed would still exist after he had claimed it. 'Andeira as she could be, Æisoul. Why should this not be ours? There is no power on this earth greater than ours. Who else is worthy of such a prize?'

The temptation swamped him, the river of power swept through him and past him, and he longed to give himself to it, as he had almost given himself to it once before, to be swept away on its dark current to the glories it would yield to him. But there was still enough of the man he had been in him, enough for him to realise this vision could never be.

'I am not like you,' he replied grimly, each word forced out through gritted teeth. He closed his mind to that glorious, swelling tide, to the lie that would seduce him. 'I will never become what you are.'

He met Aarkan's eyes, expecting anger, and saw a chill, knowing smile light the man's face.

'Then what are you, Silver Mage? You have the body of a man and the soul of a dragon. What does that make you? Certainly not the man you were meant to be. You broke faith with the ancients when you willingly became the very thing they gave up everything to destroy. You chose our path and you can never go back. If we are abominations, what does that make you, or your dragon?'

'We are only one.'

Aarkan laughed, an edge to it that skirted hysteria. He was close now, so very close. 'You begin to understand. Only one can survive, and that one will inherit the powers of two. One must die for the other to live, for one soul cannot survive in two bodies. Will it be you? Will you go meekly to your death to save your dragon, or will you destroy him and take what is yours?'

'You lie.' But the pain of separation tore through him, and he reached out to touch the dragon before that separation could cripple him.

'Do I? Can you not feel the truth even now? If you do not fight, the dragon will overwhelm you. That is what they are.'

'No, that is what you made them.'

'And you think you will be different?'

'I am different.'

Aarkan shook his head and stepped aside as the ranks behind him parted. 'No, Æisoul. You are the same.' From the midst of the Arkni, first Kallis, then Jeta and Kinseris walked forward to stand beside Aarkan. The chains Aarkan had set about them had no substance, but they appeared as shimmering bands of light to Aarin's eyes, tying them to his enemy. He saw Kallis struggle against the restraints he could not see, saw the wild fear in the soldier's eyes, confronted with an enemy he could not fight. Kinseris did not look at him, his face bent towards the floor, his shoulders slumped as though burdened by the weight of his guilt. If he had not believed before, Aarin saw in him now the understanding of what his people had so blindly done. He saw the hole torn on his tunic where the dragon of his Order had been ripped from its fastenings.

Between them stood Jeta, and on her face alone he saw quiet calm, and her trust in him shone from her blue gaze. And over them all Aarkan held the threads of his murderous magic.

'Do you not yet grow tired of death, Æisoul?' Aarkan asked silkily, 'for whom so many have already died? You need only open the way to save their lives. Recall the dragons and I will give them up to you. Or will you let more die for you to deny us our rightful place, as you left an innocent man to die in the sands of the desert?'

640

Aarin closed his eyes as a shudder seemed to rock him where he stood. He held tight to the vision of the silent plea in Iarwin's eyes that, if it could not give him absolution, at least offered understanding of that harsh choice. He kept his fury from his face. He held it bottled inside him, a storm of rage to bring down the mountain. 'Innocent he may have been, but he was still your tool, your spy. You used him to hunt us, to destroy his own people, and it destroyed *him*. After what you did to him, what I gave him was peace.'

Aarkan laughed. 'Then how is it we are here? No, Æisoul, we never needed him. It was you who led us here. The tracer spell was in you, not him.' He watched the horror rise on Aarin's face and his mouth twisted in sick delight. 'Did you think we would have let him reach you if we had not desired it? He was our messenger to you, and the message, for his people have fallen with him. We used him only because we could, not because we needed to, in case you found the spell we laid in your bones in Vasa's chambers, but you never looked. You never thought that you would betray yourself. Your arrogance was your downfall, my brother, and now a man is dead who did not need to die. His death is on your head.'

He did not see the snarl that contorted Kallis's face, nor hear Jeta's anguished, pleading cry. The guilt rushed in, doubly potent for the strength of the magic thundering through him. He knew Aarkan's words for truth and they shredded his heart. *Mercy, Iarwin, forgive me! Shrogar, forgive me! What have I done?*

'You have killed a man for your own ambition.' Aarkan answered his thoughts. 'And he is not the only one. The Ephenori also paid the price for their loyalty to you, who gave them nothing but war.'

Visions came to him then, swamping his mind in the blood of that valiant people. Just as Iarwin had, he saw Ephenor laid to ruin, her walls crumbled into dust and her people destroyed. He saw the faces of the brave men he had known, frozen forever in the stillness of death. He felt the terrible weight of Aarkan's magic, forcing the images on him, and he heard the inhuman voice as it dragged him deeper.

'Oh yes, Æisoul, you betrayed them to their deaths, but the trail of your dead is even longer still.'

Grey eyes looked up from under lashes black with tears. His purpose was slipping from his grasp, driven back by the burden of guilt Aarkan laid on his soul. A pressure settled in his chest, suffocating him, driving a wedge between him and Silverwing, trying to break them apart. He knew what was coming and he could not help himself, though he heard Silverwing cry out in warning. His tortured conscience could not share responsibility with the dragon, but there was no room for such individuality in what they were becoming, and huge cracks were forming in the Joining as it splintered under the weight of a guilt he could not share.

Aarkan's eyes glimmered with secret triumph as he watched the magic that bound his enemy into one begin to disintegrate. 'What of your homeland? What of Amadorn? Even now Darred prepares his fleet for conquest. He knows Vasa is dead and he thinks to rule in his place. His empire will be vast.' He took a step forward, and Aarin swayed. 'Amadorn is his prize,' he crooned. 'Your mother will resist him, but she will fail. Just as you have. And all the lands of this world will be ripe for our dominion.'

Once again Aarin felt Aarkan's magic pounding him, brushing aside his feeble attempts to shield his mind. From the ruins of Ephenor, his sight hurtled across the sea to his homeland. He saw the vast fleet that landed on its shores, the army of priests and soldiers arrayed in Kas'Talani livery, and he watched their advance across the rich southern lands to the Istelan. The earth was left black and scorched in their wake, as though their very passing was enough to bring death to the land. He saw the man who led the army and the last of his resistance crumbled. Aarkan spoke the truth. Darred had always coveted Amadorn, and there would be no one left to stop him. The pain of it swelled inside him, pouring ice on the fire in his veins. The part of him that was Silverwing screamed in denial, flaying his grief with hot anger. He staggered as the earth tilted, spilling him to the floor. At the last his vision was drawn to Rhiannas, and his mother's face filled his mind, the tears she had shed for him marking silver tracks down her blood-stained skin

'She tried to protect you,' Aarkan said, merciless. 'For that you abandoned her.'

From far away he heard the voices of his friends calling to him. They told him not to listen, not to believe, but he knew the words were meaningless. Blackness swam in front of his eyes, spots of light danced in the shadows. Something was ripping, tearing inside him. Darkness closed over him and he floated free. Oblivion waited to comfort him, to soothe the coil of his guilt and lull away the pain of their deaths. He felt himself give up the struggle for the magic, felt it slip through his fingers and swirl away from him, and even in the darkness that cloaked him he could sense Aarkan reach out to take hold of the power he abandoned.

He slipped from his knees onto his back, leached of all strength by cruel despair. Yet even in surrender he could not give up. Deep inside him a magician's meddling had stoked the fire of his resistance, had bound him never to abet this man's triumph, and even as he fell, drifting into the darkness, he reached out to the only thing that could save him.

Silverwing.

As he latched onto their bond, Aarin threw off the last shreds of the individual he had been, let go of his hold on a separate self. The final barriers holding them apart fell away, and where Aarkan and all those that followed him had failed, unable to conceive the utter surrender of self demanded by the magic, they succeeded, transcending the limitations of the mortal bodies they inhabited. By pushing him to the brink, Aarkan had done what Aarin and Silverwing could never have done alone. He had made their union perfect, and he had given them the power they needed.

Kallis's cry was drowned by Jeta's as Aarin fell, and he struggled harder, frantic now, as Aarkan used his words like weapons, bleeding the life from his victim. He was within arm's reach of Aarin, and Jeta was on her knees, calling his name, pleading with him.

Aarkan ignored them all. 'She tried to protect you,' he told the slumped figure. 'For that you abandoned her.'

And something in Aarin seemed to break.

Kallis looked desperately at Kinseris, begging the priest to free them, but Kinseris's magic was as useless as his sword. Neither of them could be reached. Sheer terror made him fight, terror for Aarin and for them all if he should die, but the harder he fought the tighter his invisible bonds became, and his shout of rage turned into a cry of pain as they bit into his flesh.

And then he was blind. Just as it seemed the darkness would win, a burst of light drove it back, and Aarkan's triumphant cry echoed through his ears. It burnt his eyes, stung them closed, and when he opened them again everything had changed. Aarkan stood with his back to him, one hand raised to shield his eyes from the brightness that came from above. Aarin and the dragon were no longer crumpled on the floor, they flew high in the great cavern, and they were utterly changed.

The skies had opened. A great chasm yawned in the night, and the cavern was bathed in scalding sunlight. A ripple passed through the massed ranks of the enemy as they beheld the fulfilment of their ambition, then they were cast once more into blackness as the shadow of great wings fanned them from above.

On Silverwing's back, Aarin flung his arms wide. 'I give you what you want, Aarkan!' he called. 'Now return to me what is mine.'

The dragons had come at last.

Hundreds, thousands of dragons filled every inch of the sky, and behind them, returned to their ancient forms, were the dragons of the enemy.

Aarin turned his eyes from the awesome gathering and looked down at Aarkan. He knew what he had done. He had summoned the dragons to his aid, and he had shown his enemy the way into their existence.

Aarkan's shadowed face betrayed his terrible joy. His people gathered close at his back, straining to reach past him. Their dragons called out to them, trapped behind the ranks of those who had come to Aarin's call, and their need swept all caution aside. He had opened the way, and it had brought the madness on them. They forgot the prisoners still bound behind them. They forgot everything.

'Here is what you want, Aarkan!' Aarin called again, high above them. 'Take it if you can.'

He had reopened the door to their river of power and invited them in, and they could not help but follow him. They wanted the power they had glimpsed, and he would give it to them, give them so much they would choke on it. And they would take it. They had watched as he had become all that they yearned to be, and they could not conceive that he could give it up. They never could.

Aarin and Silverwing looked down at them through a shared gaze. They saw as their enemy abandoned caution, as they prepared to take back the power they believed was their inheritance. And in the moment the Arkni acted they did the only thing they could.

They stood aside.

The Arkni swarmed past them, clawing their way into that chasm, into the arms of their one-time comrades, into the world where their dragons waited. Aarin sat astride Silverwing in the centre of a storm and endured the buffeting of their furious passage as magic splintered the air around him like lightning. All around him his dragons gathered their strength, for their enemy had returned to them and they would fight.

When the last had crossed the divide, Aarin looked down once more. Three friends still waited below him, still bound and helpless. They could not stay here, could not be a part of what was to come. He had left them so far behind he barely knew them anymore. He cut through the magic that bound them, freeing them from Aarkan's abandoned spell. For an instant he hesitated, something half-recalled crying out to him, but he forced it down and prepared to leave them. He was no longer a part of their world.

Then he heard Jeta's cry and he faltered. His head jerked round, drawn by the sound of her voice, and he saw Kallis holding onto her as she tried to run to him, crying his name. The mercenary had his arm around her waist, half-lifting her as he attempted to drag her away, but she fought against him, stretching out her arms to Aarin.

She knew what was coming and still she would not leave him.

He remembered her then, remembered that this was a woman he had once loved, and remembered the promise he had made her; a promise he would now break. And he wavered.

She cannot stay with us.

The words were Silverwing's, but they came from deep within him, and he knew them for truth. He swung the dragon around and heard the hurt of his betrayal in Jeta's desperate cry.

Fly, he ordered, tears streaming down his face. And they flew, deep into the heart of the dragon's world, and left the other far behind. Aarin did not look down. He could not. But a splinter of his awareness followed his companions as they staggered across the great cavern to the safety of the tunnel. Then there was no more time for them.

The echoes of that cataclysmic conflict rocked Andeira to her core. As the two halves of her existence came together and clashed, it felt as though the world would shake itself apart. The yawning chasm in the sky boiled with violence as the Arkni flowed across the bridge Aarin and Silverwing had forged, and the dragons were ready for them. They reached out to Aarin, each of them straining to share in their union, and he gave himself to them all. A thousand consciousnesses washed through him, a thousand yearnings broke him in pieces and remade him in the raptures of their welcome.

Great wings whipped the air into a gale, and Aarin held tight as Silverwing flew through the darkening skies. They flew high into the other world, at the centre of a flight of dragons from the Golden Age of Andeira. Their majesty awed him, their grace and beauty dazzled him, and their hatred flowed through him. For these creatures that lived for millennia, the battles of the final days of that age were only heartbeats ago. The war that had shattered their existence was ingrained in their souls, and the memories of past battles merged with the present in Aarin's mind. He saw through their eyes the last moments of the fight to defend Lorrimer and Silverwing, just seconds before the Severing. Then, as now, they fought without their riders, against an enemy whose resources outmatched theirs. Then, as now, they refused to falter. Far below, through the great chasm, was the battleground the New Age had become, the prize they all fought for, and they would not give it up.

Through a thousand eyes Aarin watched as the Arkni were reunited with their dragons. He saw the madness rinsed from their eyes as they were brought back into their deadly union. Aarkan and Srenegar flew at their head, and as the huge black dragon screeched his challenge it was as though the ages dropped away and all that had passed in between was gone. They were as they had once been, and this was once more the last battle of the Second Age. No Severing could stop them now.

But this time there would be no battle, for their enemy no longer sought to keep them from their prize. This time their enemy was one of them, an enemy no more.

Silverwing flew side by side with Srenegar, and Aarkan dipped his head in salute.

'Was it not worth it, Æisoul?' he cried, caught in an instant of purest life that was but a footfall from death. 'Is this not worth any price?'

Beside him Aarin smiled. 'Any price at all. Come, brother, follow me. Let us go together to claim our prize.'

And he took control of the vast well of the magic of creation. For the briefest of moments, they stood in the place of the Maker herself, and they used that power to throw the river wide open. The Arkni followed them, for even at the precipice itself they still believed in Aarkan's vision. But they were wrong. Aarin saw Aarkan and Srenegar caught in the torrent, heads thrown back as they cried out their ecstasy, and he closed the trap around them all. He dammed the flood.

The waters of their river closed over them, the magic they had sought began to drown them. Triumph turned to fear, then to rage. Trapped with nowhere to go but the source itself, Aarkan finally realised that he had only ever been rushing towards his death.

'What have you done?' he screamed, as Srenegar began to fall.

The wave crested and smashed itself out of existence against the dam held in place by his very life. And the Arkni were falling, sucked down deep by the returning tide.

Aarin watched their fall, watched as his enemies hurtled towards their Maker, the place they had seen inside them, the heart of the magic, the source and the end of all life. This was no slow drift into death; this was the final shattering undoing of all that they were.

'The half-way place does not exist,' he murmured, as his own dragon began to falter. And then they too were falling, spiralling out of the skies as the magic began its inevitable backlash. The trap they had set for the Arkni closed on them also, seeking out the same fault-line that snaked through their nature, the pressure poised to shatter them.

Consciousness hanging by a thread, Aarin lay sprawled on Silverwing's back, gazing upwards. As the darkness robbed him of his sight, he saw the last fading of the Arkni, unstrung by their own natures in the moment they achieved all they desired. For in the end, all life is just the energies of the world given flesh, and in death those energies return to their source. There was no way for the Arkni to save themselves, for he had dammed their river and there was no going back. They were sucked deep into the swirling haze of the forbidden magic as it laid claim to them. As it laid claim to them all.

They watched the Arkni die and then, at the last moment, something in them cried out for survival and they tried to save themselves. A memory woke in them of what they had been, two where now there was one. One thing alone had Aarkan understood. For one soul split between two mortal forms there could be no survival. But if one could die, the other might live. And in that final instant of awareness each tried to pull away from the other, each seeking to sacrifice their own life to give life to the other. But the tide swept them onwards. The dam held.

A blinding explosion rocked Andeira, engulfing them in a burst of flame as the great cavern destroyed itself, closing the chasm between the worlds. The mountain shuddered, the living stone crying out its agony, and then there was nothing at all.

THIRTEEN

IN THE PALE dawn Kallis and Jeta picked their way through the wreckage of the ancient city, the city that had survived for millennia only to crumble into ruin as its creators' prophecy came to its devastating fulfilment. Kinseris had not come with them, and so he did not see the great cavern that was now open to the sky, a scar blasted into the rock of the mountain. They clambered down the rumble of the roof that had collapsed in on itself. All night long they had waited, scanning the darkened skies for a flash of silver. They had watched as the mountain imploded, and they no longer expected to find Aarin alive. They searched for his body, and that of his dragon, and neither spoke as they set about their grim task.

But they found nothing. When the sides of the cavern had collapsed, they had buried everything within the chamber. There were no bodies, friend and enemies alike hidden from sight.

Tears filled Jeta's eyes. She sank down, utterly numb, her mind filled with the devastation all around that had stolen Aarin from her. She felt a hand on her shoulder but could not look up. She could not look into Kallis's eyes and confirm the knowledge that they had lost him, after everything they had been through.

The pressure on her shoulder vanished as Kallis knelt beside her. He reached out and tipped her face towards him, forcing her to look at him. She turned her eyes away, blinking back the tears that blurred her vision.

'Jeta.'

She shook her head, a sob escaping her.

'Jeta,' he said again, and there was a gentleness in his voice that broke through her daze.

'Don't,' she whispered, pleading. 'Let me hope.'

She felt his flinch, heard the hitched intake of breath. He wanted to hope as much as she did, but he was wiser than her, and he was already letting that hope flow from him to make way for the grieving that would follow. She knew she had to do the same, that if she did not this wound would never heal, but she could not.

'He's gone,' Kallis said gently and she heard a sadness that almost matched her own. Only then did she look at him, only then did she understand the depth of the bond that had existed between the mercenary and the mage. Awareness of his pain brought the full weight of her own crashing down on her. As the storm broke, she rested her head on his shoulder and let the tears come. She felt his hand cradle her head, rocking her gently, and felt the wetness of his tears as they fell on her hair.

He was gone.

I am Aarin.

The words echoed through the endless night, and they stirred a memory, a memory of a man.

I am Aarin.

And the man awoke.

Aarin looked down on the world from somewhere far above, in the half-light on the edges of existence. They had died and yet they were alive. They had touched the very core, become one with it, but they were alive. For in travelling that river of power, that great circle of life, they had passed into death and out into life once more, and they were remade as they had been, two souls, two bodies.

A gift, perhaps, for their sacrifice, but a gift that came with a price.

The magic of the Joining was healed, and through them it would flow back into the world, but neither he nor the dragons were yet free to return to it. The taint of Aarkan's ambition remained and there would be no return to the Golden Age. So few dragons remained, so many still endangered, their magic trapped in human hands. And it was the dragons to whom his life had been given, because it was the dragons who needed him the most.

Yet as Aarin prepared to relinquish his world for the Long Dream, everything he would leave behind was arrayed below him. He saw the army caught mid-step in its march across the wastelands, the priest who watched their approach perched on a rock on the broken mountainside. He saw the two small figures on the rockslide, frozen in a scene of utter stillness in their grief, and he thought his heart would break.

She is young yet, Silverwing said quietly, following his stricken gaze. *But we are joined now. Your life will be long, and you will still be as you are now while she grows old and dies. You cannot go back to what you were. Would you make her endure the pain of such a life with you?*

'No,' Aarin sighed. 'And still I can't let go.'

He tore his eyes from Jeta to look at the dragon and saw another life stretching out before him. It was a long, lonely road. No, not lonely, for he would always have Silverwing, but there would be no others of his kind to share this new life with him, only the ghosts of those lost in the Severing, whose memories endured in the hearts of the dragons they had left behind. He could feel Lorrimer's memory nestling in his dragon's mind and knew that if he wished he could take those memories for his own and let Silverwing's recollections of youth and happiness augment his own vision of Lorrimer at the end of his life, but he was not ready to embrace that yet. His own losses were too close.

My kind needs you, Æisoul, they need us. Do not forget my brethren who yet linger in the prison their gift has become. Someone must wake them from their drift into death.

He looked up at Silverwing. Through the dragon he felt the pain of those trapped spirits. Only the magic of the Joining, the magic that existed solely in them, could wake them from their nightmare, and until the very last had awoken, the dragons could not return to Andeira.

So many lives depended on him. Even now the prophecy was done, he was still not free. He had discovered something he wanted just as much but he could not take it. He felt the crack that ran through him, cleaving him in half. Because he could not walk away, he could not abandon the dragons to follow his heart, but a part of him would always remain here, in this moment, when the choice still remained to him.

'There are so many dangers before them.'

Darred and his fleet filled his mind. They would burn their way across the southern states of his homeland to the Istelan, and from there they would threaten the newly united North.

There will always be dangers.

'I could help them.'

His presence would be a foil to the magic of Darred's priests, for they would not relinquish the devices that gave them control of their army. But there he could only counter the magic. In the Long Dream, with Silverwing, he could wake the dragons from which they drew their power. With Silverwing he could, in time, break the connections that linked them.

You have helped them, Æisoul. Now they must go on without you.

The mage turned to him. 'I am Aarin.'

Silverwing met his angry gaze steadily. *You always were. Yet long before you were Aarin, you were Æisoul as the dragons named you. You cannot now be both.*

Aarin choked back a bitter laugh. 'I have no choice, have I?'

There is always a choice. But the link between us cannot be dissolved this side of death, and that is not a decision you have a right to make.

'Then what choice is there? I cannot foreswear the Joining, nor abandon your kind, but neither can I go back.'

You cannot change what you have done but you may remain here if you wish. The Joining has been made whole and the world will be renewed, but if you do not embrace the gift and perpetuate the cycle there will be no new generation. Eventually we will die and there will be no others to come after. The moment will have passed.

'That is no choice at all.'

The dragon bowed his great head, the light shimmering on his silver scales. *Yet that is the choice you must make.*

Again, Aarin turned away, again he looked down at the world. Below him lay his old life, and the people he loved. The desire to go with them was strong, to forget, to live as they did, but he knew he could not. Behind him was everything he had ever wanted.

Silverwing waited, his patience endless. He would not push, or persuade, but his very presence was enough. Reluctantly Aarin turned back.

Through the open channel of the magic that bound them together, the dragon sensed the moment of his resolve. If he had been a man, he would have held his breath, afraid to speak, but he was not, and he did not fear to speak for he knew that Aarin could not yet do so for himself. So, he asked, *Will you come with me?*

It was Kallis who felt the change first, a chill shiver running down his spine as he felt eyes on him. He stiffened, raising his head to look past Jeta, and he saw them. Where before there had been only rubble, the great silver dragon now rested, and by his side, sheltered by his wing, stood Aarin. Aarin, bruised and tired and covered with dust, but alive.

Kallis's fingers tightened in Jeta's hair, and it felt as though he stopped breathing. He did not understand, and he dared not believe. Neither dragon nor mage moved, but Aarin's eyes were locked on his and beneath their silvery glaze he saw his friend. Ever so slowly he began to rise, taking Jeta with him yet keeping her head turned from the strange vision. But as they stood, she pulled away, her eyes searching his face. What she saw there made her frown, and before he could stop her, she was turning.

Jeta froze. For a moment she felt nothing. Just like Kallis, she could not believe the evidence of her eyes. Moments before she had been grieving him and now here he stood, silently watching her, and she felt nothing. She wanted to touch him, to confirm that he was really there, but something held her back. He was too still, too silent, and she could not cross the distance between them. Even as the joy flushed through her, she sensed the shadow of another parting and it threatened to tear her heart in two all over again.

She watched him, eyes huge in her pale face. He was standing by the flank of the silver dragon, staring back at her, his clothes torn and smouldering, streaked with blood. She let her gaze travel up to his face, taking in every bruise, every graze that marked familiar features, trying to match this image with the man she loved who was now so changed, who had died and was now returned. He had not moved, nor had he spoken, and she saw the sheen in his silver-bright eyes. There was such sadness in them. A heavy weight settled in her chest.

She could not bring herself to speak as the awful realisation yawned empty and deep. He was leaving. More than union with the dragon now stood between them. She had thought to share him, to give up that part of him that belonged wholly and utterly to another and be content with the part of his love he could still give to her. She had not realised he would truly leave. The realisation that this parting was forever almost brought her to her knees.

Motionless, Aarin held her entire attention, his eyes begging her to understand. She looked up into the black depths of the dragon's obsidian gaze, seeing there the reflection of Aarin's grief, and knew that he had found his future and there was no place in it for her. She had lost him to this majestic creature, just as she had always feared she would.

There were so many things she wanted to say, so many things she wanted him to know, but the most important he knew already.

At last she forced her leaden limbs to move, taking a step forward, then another. As she moved, she saw a tremor run through him. His hand came up, reaching out to her, and then she was running. Her feet flew over the jagged rocks, scattering splinters of stone, and as her fingers touched his and he reeled her in she felt the dragon fire burst around her. Unleashed at last, his magic lifted her up and embraced her, and this time he opened himself willingly. As her spirit tumbled into his she felt him soaring to meet her, sharing himself completely. But it was not just himself he shared.

As Jeta fell headlong into the link that flowed between Aarin and his dragon she knew he had given her the only gift he could. For an instant he allowed her to join him where she could never go, in the heady euphoria of the Joining. She felt the raw elements as they flowed into him and through him, passing out into the world to breathe life into it as rain renews the drying river. She saw him as he now was, sitting at the juncture of the living elements, bathed in the silver light of the new dawn of creation, and she understood that he was the one thing that tied this newborn world together. Through him the balance would reassert itself, and she understood why he had to go.

Return to me one day, she whispered, and felt him answer with his whole being. Love flowered all around her, enveloping her in its warm embrace until she thought she might lose herself in it. The forging of the bond that had started that night in Amadorn was completed in an instant of perfect union. Then, ever so gently, she felt him release her. The arms that were wrapped around her let go, and she felt him withdraw. She let him go, saddened but triumphant, and felt the coldness of his absence seep into her. When she opened her eyes, he was gone.

EPILOGUE

A DARK SPECK flew high over the desert, scanning the sands below. Two pairs of eyes watched the progress of three tiny figures as they made their weary way over the dunes to the rag-tag army that marched to meet them. Wings thundered, too far distant to hear, as the banners came into sight— the Golden Eagle of Ephenor flying beside the Black Trees of Kas'Tella. And beyond them, far in the distance, the great citadel of Ephenor stood proud, its spires soaring towards the sun, an island of hope in a barren land.

As Silverwing bore his rider through the dawning skies of the new age, Aarin borrowed his eyes. Through the wise gaze of the ancient dragon he watched that bitter reunion—the army come too late to fight a battle far beyond its strength, and the survivors of that almighty conflict. He saw Shrogar slide from his horse and walk the final yards with halting, hesitant steps. He saw Kinseris come to meet him and did not need to hear the words that passed between them. The Lord of Ephenor staggered, clutching the priest's shoulder for support, and his cry of grief crossed the vast distance and echoed through Aarin's heart.

Then the others reached them, gathering around in a tight knot. For a moment he lost sight of his friends, then the crowd parted to let another through. Dressed in the livery of their enemy, he addressed Kinseris. The priest shook his head, but the soldier was insistent. As Kinseris began to turn away, Shrogar stopped him. For a long moment those two friends stared into each other's eyes, no words spoken or needed. Then, still silent, Kinseris turned back. The soldier dropped down on one knee, holding out his sword hilt first, and Aarin willed the priest to take it. The banner of the twin trees dipped, and as Kinseris took the sword, a great cheer rose from the ranks of Kas'Tella's weary soldiers.

Sedaine was on the balcony overlooking the parade ground when Vianor found her. She came here when she could, to remind herself of the reason she had chosen this path. And she came here also to gaze into the empty skies, searching for a sign that the new world they lived in had not abandoned them, for she already knew the message that Vianor had come to deliver. She had known it for days, deep in her bones. They were coming.

'How long?' she asked the magician without turning. If she concentrated hard enough she could see Nathas's face upturned towards her in the final moments before the hangman had taken his life. Before she had taken his life. That was why they were here. Because Darred had forced it on them.

'No more than weeks, your highness,' Vianor replied, moving to stand beside her, his eyes also straying to the skies. They could not help themselves, those brief yearning glances, searching for a sign of what they knew to be true but could not see. 'The ships landed on the southern coast three weeks ago. By now they will have taken Farnor and it will not be long before the rest of the South follows.'

Weeks. What could be done in that short time that had not already been done?

'Send word to Elvelen and Naveen,' she ordered. 'And to our allies in the East. I want our borders held open as long as possible. Anyone who escapes from the South is to be given sanctuary here. We will need them.'

'And when they reach our borders?'

She looked at her uncle, her gaze steady and hard. When they reached the Istelan there would be no escape. 'Then we pull back. Rhiannas must hold the line. If they take the city, they control the gateway to all the North. We make our stand here.'

Vianor bowed his head. 'As you say, my Queen. It will be done.'

'Will it?' She felt the absurd desire to laugh. How could they hope to hold off this armada? All they could hope for was time, though time for what she did not know. For the dragons to come? For her son? A fool's hope, and she knew it, and yet it persisted.

'See that it is, my lord. They are coming.'

THE END

An excerpt from

SILVER DAWN

The Long Dream Book Two

Caledan

THE PRIEST WAS dead when they found him. He had died in his sleep and it had not been a peaceful death. His body was contorted amid unwashed sheets and his face frozen in an expression of horrified shock, as though he could not believe death could come for him this way.

The villagers met this calamity with weary resignation. The man was disliked. He was corrupt, but then so many were, and his greed had caused many families great hardship. But none of that mattered. Nor did it matter how he had died. He was dead and they would be punished for it.

Everyone had heard the rumours of Vasa's death. There was a new high priest in Kas'Tella now. Even here, far away from the capital, that news had reached them. But it made little difference to their lives who sat on the black throne. Nothing ever changed, and the priesthood would not overlook the death of one of its own.

So, they took the body from the hut when it was dark and buried it in the hills. With it they buried all the priest's possessions they could find, among them a dull, metallic disc they found clutched in one hand. Then the women stripped the bedding and burned it. And when, a month later, the men from the Order arrived, they told them the priest had left to return to Kas'Tella. And to their surprise, the huge Kas'Tellian captain accepted this unlikely explanation without comment as he stood looking around the priest's empty hut. To their relief, he refused their offer of hospitality, and the soldiers returned the way they had come.

Trad slipped into his place by Kestel's side as the soldiers joined the dirt track leading from the village.

'Well?'

Trad shrugged. 'He's definitely dead, but I don't think they killed him.'

Kestel glanced at him, taking in the dirt under his fingernails and the stains on his clothes. 'Why?'

The boy grinned. 'They didn't do a very good job of disguising the grave. I found this.' And he held out his hand.

Kestel looked at the silver brooch. It had acquired a patina that spoke of age and neglect and its face was utterly blank. He sighed. 'Another one. They were warned.'

Trad tossed him the device, harmless now, and he put it in a pouch at his waist where it clinked against others, equally blank. Not all their former owners were dead. Some had handed over the devices willingly, before the dragons they bore had erased themselves, but too many had ignored their high priest's command, and his warning. And some had simply vanished.

'At least we know what happened to this one,' Trad observed, reading his thoughts.

Kestel grunted. There was truth in that, if an uncomfortable one. Better dead than an enemy. But Kinseris would not see it that way, and the mystery of the disappearances gnawed at him. 'We need to know where they are going.'

Trad kicked a stone. 'We already know.'

The Ancai stopped. 'No, we don't. We're guessing. And we've found no bodies.' Not one of the missing priests had turned up dead. So far. Was that just chance? Had they simply left Caledan? Or had they found some way of keeping both the devices and their lives? He took out the brooch they had just collected, turning it over in his hands, ignoring Trad's questioning look and the soldiers milling uncertainly at his back. Every instinct warned him that this was important. 'We're missing something.'

Trad's expression was resigned. 'What do you want to do?'

Kestel looked up, squinting against the sun. 'Frankesh,' he said at last. It was the main port on the Amadorn trading route and, so far from the capital, it had always been difficult to assert Kas'Tella's control over the region as firmly as a high priest might wish. As he had cause to know. More, Darred would take perverse pleasure in using the escape routes established by Kinseris to smuggle his allies out of Caledan. 'If they are going to Amadorn, they are leaving from Frankesh.'

'Frankesh,' Trad agreed. 'And Kinseris?'

The Ancai suppressed a sigh. He knew what Trad was really asking. Detouring to Frankesh would add weeks to their journey, weeks he was reluctant to spend away from Kas'Tella. He had not wanted to leave at all, no matter how important the task, but Kinseris had insisted. *I need someone I can trust completely. I have no one else.* The truth of that was why he had not wanted to leave his lord's side, but someone had to enforce the high priest's edict in the remoter provinces and no matter their oaths, no matter how willingly they might have surrendered their power, no priest could be entrusted with the task. No priest could be trusted to take from another the thing they all craved. Trust. They had so little of it and needed it so badly.

'Escarion is no fool,' he said at last, wishing, not for the first time, that Kinseris had kept Galydon by his side. 'And if Darred is gathering renegades to him, we need to know.'

If Darred was gathering renegades with their power intact, they were facing a crisis that his presence in Kas'Tella could do little to avert. So, they would go to Frankesh and they would see what they could find. And then they would return to Kinseris and lay before him all they knew of Darred's schemes. And perhaps then they could persuade him to recall Galydon and look first to the defences of Caledan. Because a storm was coming, he could feel it.

Printed in Great Britain
by Amazon

25189360R00381